Quarter
to
Midnight

BY KAREN ROSE

KAREN
ROSE
Quarter to Midnight

HEADLINE

First published in Great Britain in 2022 by
HEADLINE PUBLISHING GROUP

1

Cataloguing in Publication Data is available from the British Library

Hardback ISBN 978 1 4722 8291 0
Trade Paperback ISBN 978 1 4722 8292 7

Offset in 11.59/17.51pt Carre Noir Std by Jouve (UK), Milton Keynes

Printed and bound in Great Britain by Clays Ltd, Elcograf S.p.A.

HEADLINE PUBLISHING GROUP
An Hachette UK Company
Carmelite House
50 Victoria Embankment
London EC4Y 0DZ

www.headline.co.uk
www.hachette.co.uk

To my darling Sarah. I am so very proud of you.

And, as always, to Martin.
For forty years you've been my very best friend.

PROLOGUE

Lafourche Parish, Louisiana
SUNDAY, JUNE 12, 10:15 P.M.

"OH NO. NO, no, no." Rocky Hebert smelled death, the stench hitting him hard as he approached the doctor's kitchen door. He was no stranger to the smell of a decaying body, having encountered it multiple times during his career. But this was different.

This was . . . not more important, because all of the dead were important. *Well, not all of them,* he allowed. Many of the dead deserved their fate. But the doctor wasn't one of them.

He'd needed the doctor alive and well.

And able to tell him things. Important things.

Maybe the dead guy isn't the doctor, he thought. But it was a fool's hope, he knew. The doctor lived alone, and nobody came out this far into the sticks without good reason.

Maybe he'd died of natural causes. Maybe it wasn't anything nefarious. Maybe they were both simply unlucky, he and the doctor.

Rocky eyed the doorknob with a growing sense of dread. The lock was scratched up, like someone had broken in. He withdrew a disposable glove from his pocket and twisted the doorknob, unsurprised when the door opened easily.

It's a trap. Turn around and leave. But he didn't. He couldn't. He was so close. He needed to know if this was the doctor or—

He released the breath he'd been holding, reflexively sucking in another when the stench hit him full force. *Fucking hell.* His eyes stung, his stomach rebelling. *Fuck, fuck, fuck.*

It was the doctor, all right. Or it had been. The man's throat had been slit and—

He swallowed hard, taking a step back, away from the grisly sight.

The man's throat had been slit, his gut eviscerated. There was blood and intestines and—

Spinning around, Rocky vomited into the doctor's rosebushes. *Goddammit.* He was too late.

Too late by at least a day, if the flies covering the man's open wounds were any indication.

He hovered over the rosebush, frozen in place, hands on his knees as his body continued to shudder. *I should call the police. But not here. And definitely not from my own phone.*

Luckily, he had a burner—the same one he'd been using to communicate with the doctor for the past two weeks as he'd nagged and encouraged and begged the man to meet with him.

He'd stop on his way home and make the call. The guy deserved better than to be left to rot on his own kitchen floor.

He spat again, wishing for a strong drink. Wishing he hadn't finally gotten sober.

Wishing he'd done so many things differently.

He straightened with a muted groan, looking around to be sure he wasn't about to meet the same end as the poor doctor. There was no one around, the only sound the croaking of frogs in the small marshy canal behind the doctor's house.

There was more than frogs in that water. Gators were more than likely, this close to the bayou.

Rocky wondered why the man's killer hadn't simply dragged him to the water's edge and tossed him in. And then he froze again because he knew why.

I was supposed to find him. They knew I was coming.

Except he didn't know who "they" were. He'd been searching for "them" for more than fifteen years.

I was so damn close.

Or was I?

At this point, "they" were probably just playing with him. Cats taunting a mouse.

Rocky drew his gun from his holster. "I ain't no damn mouse," he muttered, making his way to the shed in the doctor's backyard with unsteady steps. He half expected to be gunned down before he reached the rusted-out shed. Half expected to be attacked from behind, to feel the bite of a knife against his throat.

But nothing happened and he opened the shed door without incident, peering inside and feeling a small wave of relief when he found what he'd been hoping for.

Bleach, the jug about half full. He took the jug and dumped its contents over the rosebush, rendering any DNA in his vomit useless.

Then he walked to his old Ford truck, tossed the jug in the bed, closed the tailgate, and slid behind the wheel. He'd seen no one lurking in the shadows. Didn't mean there was nobody there, but he had a feeling that if someone had been there, he wouldn't be alive to be wondering about them.

He drove for a half hour, pulling over when he reached a point halfway to his own home. Taking the burner from the truck's glove compartment, he dialed 911, reported the man's death, and hung up, refusing to give his name.

Driving another five minutes, he slowed the truck on a bridge, rolled the window down, and tossed the burner into the river. Nobody would find it. More than thirty-five years of being a cop had taught him all the best tricks.

He hesitated, thinking of Gabriel. His son would be working, doing what he loved best. Rocky was glad he'd seen him the weekend before, glad he'd hugged him hard when they'd parted. Glad he'd told Gabe that he loved him. Because he had the awful feeling that it would be the last time he did so.

As much as he didn't want to be the mouse, the cat was powerful, its reach long, its claws sharp. At least they wouldn't go after Gabe. He'd at least done that part right.

Gabe knew nothing of any of this. He never had. His boy would tell him, "Call the police, Dad!" Because Gabe still thought the cops were the good guys.

Maybe I should have told him the truth. Maybe I should have warned him.

Maybe I should warn him now.

No. He'd done the right thing, keeping Gabe in the dark.

Rocky continued to drive, his thoughts in turmoil. He was half tempted to bypass his own house, the home into which he'd carried Lili over the threshold when they'd been young and carefree newlyweds, the home in which they'd raised their son to be a good man. He was tempted to keep on going, tempted to run.

But to where? There wasn't anywhere he'd be able to hide.

And what kind of life was that anyway?

But Gabriel . . .

Rocky's chest ached at the thought of never seeing his son again. Of not finishing what he'd begun.

Of not getting justice for the real victim of this nightmare.

In the end, he decided to face the inevitable, because running away was not who he was.

Metairie, Louisiana
SUNDAY, JUNE 12, 11:45 P.M.

Pulling into his driveway, Rocky sat looking at his house, thinking about the doctor lying dead on his own kitchen floor.

Don't let Gabe find me that way. Please.

Hands trembling, he reached for his cell phone, tapping his camera roll and staring at the last photo. Him and Gabe last weekend, standing shoulder to shoulder for the photo. Both smiling.

He traced a fingertip over his son's face. Everyone said that Gabe resembled him, but all he could see was Lili's eyes smiling at him. She'd be proud of their boy. So proud. And, should the worst happen, he'd see her again.

The thought made his heart trip. He'd missed her so much, and he was so damn tired. He'd never understood what hell she'd gone through with the chemo, not until he'd started treatment himself.

Damn cancer. Knowing that his time was running out had made him take risks that he never would have taken otherwise. Made him pressure the doctor to meet him, and now the doc was dead.

It's my fault. Logically he knew that the true fault lay on the killer's shoulders—or killers' shoulders. There were probably multiple heads on that hydra. But he'd pressed the issue, threatening to expose the poor doctor. Giving him no choice. He should have been more careful.

He should have done a lot of things that he hadn't done.

And if "they" came after him? The joke was on them. The doctor had been his last hope. He'd never figure out who "they" were now. He didn't have the time.

But he'd fight a little longer. For Gabe.

He closed his camera roll and opened a text window. To Gabe.

Just in case.

Hope you're having a good night, mon ange, he typed. *Love you, son.*

If the worst happened, Gabe would figure it out. His son was smart. *Hopefully smarter than me.*

Rocky dug into his pocket for the small leather pouch that he'd started carrying with him everywhere. He poured the contents into his cupped palm—a paper clip and an unused SIM card. Willing his hands to steady, he popped the SIM card from his phone and did a factory reset, wiping everything stored on the phone's internal memory.

Then he inserted the new SIM card into his phone and slipped the old one beneath the floor mat at his feet.

Just in case. If he lived to see the morning, he'd fetch the card and put it back, then restore his phone's memory from the cloud. If he didn't live to see the morning, he wasn't making it any easier on them. Whoever "they" were.

Dragging himself from his truck, he forced one foot in front of the other until he was at his own front door. He turned the key in the lock, stepped inside, and had a single moment to register the lack of a barking dog before cold metal pressed against his temple.

Shoulda run. But there was nowhere he could hide, and he found that he didn't want to.

His only regret was that Gabe would find him.

Gabe would mourn him.

But Gabe would pick himself up and go on, because his son was strong.

"Where is my dog?" Rocky asked quietly. If they'd harmed one hair on his dog's body . . .

The thug gave him a shove, remaining silent.

Rocky stumbled forward. "To where?"

"I'm in the kitchen," another voice called. "Bring him to me."

Rocky felt a laugh bubbling up from his gut. It came out sounding hysterical. Which was understandable, he supposed. The kitchen was where they'd killed the doctor. "Of course." It was darkly poetic, in its own way.

He moved stiffly, narrowly missing the rocking chair that Lili had loved so much. He brushed a hand over the smooth wood. *Soon,* mon petit chou. *Soon.*

His eyes had adjusted by the time he reached the kitchen and he abruptly stopped at the sight of the man sitting in Lili's chair at the opposite end of the table from his own place.

Fury bubbled up, replacing the hysterical laughter. Because he recognized the man. He'd never met him in person, but he recognized him all the same.

"Get out of her chair," Rocky growled, surprising himself with the words. There were so many others that he could have said. That he should have said.

The man simply lifted his brows, black threaded with silver. He looked expensive. He looked like a movie star.

He looked . . . bored.

Rocky wanted to tear the bastard's heart out for all that he'd done. For the lives he'd ruined.

For desecrating Lili's kitchen chair.

"Why are you here?" Rocky demanded.

"Because we've come to the end of our dance," the man drawled. "And I needed to be sure this was done right. Finally. You should have listened, Rocky. You should have backed away years ago."

"I did."

"And then you didn't." The man studied his nails, then lifted his gaze to Rocky's. "Sit."

The thug behind him shoved the gun into his temple when he didn't immediately obey. "You heard him, Hebert. Sit the fuck down."

That he recognized the gunman's voice should have been a surprise, but it wasn't. He lifted his chin defiantly. He didn't want to sit. He'd die standing.

A sad sigh from behind him signaled the presence of a third man. "You should've let it go, Rocky. Please, sit down. It'll go easier for you this way."

Rocky tensed. He knew that voice, too. But it couldn't be . . . Except that it was. "No," he whispered, the weight of betrayal too heavy to bear.

He slumped into his chair, trying to remember all the good times he and Lili had shared around this table over their years together. All the birthdays, the holidays, the anniversaries. Her last meal.

Anything but this treachery.

Rocky was barely aware of his gun being removed from its holster, being laid on the table just out of his reach. The barrel of the pistol disappeared from his temple and the man gripped his nose, pinching it shut, forcing his head back.

Rocky struggled, but he was no match for the strong hand that held him immobile. He tried to resist when a glass was pressed to his lips, tried to keep his mouth closed, tried not to let a drop in. But eventually he had to breathe, and the liquid burned his mouth, his throat. All the way down.

He hadn't had a drink in three years and the fact that the taste was like an old friend shamed him.

The table began to sway, the face of the man in Lili's chair blurring.

There must be more than booze in this glass.

His last thought was that Gabe was going to think he'd broken his promise. That he'd broken his sobriety. *I'm sorry, son. I'm so damn sorry.*

1

WELL, WILL YOU look at what the cat finally dragged in an hour late," Molly Sutton drawled from where she sat perched on the edge of Joy's desk. It was an old desk, a little battered, but beautifully carved. It fit with the art deco decor in the lobby of Broussard's Private Investigations, LLC.

Her boss, Burke Broussard, liked nice things and he loved New Orleans. Their office space on the Quarter's edge was a lot more expensive than an equivalent space in the burbs, but Burke swore it was worth it for the foot traffic alone. Their full roster of well-to-do clients seeking "Highly Qualified & Discreet Private Investigators"—as their business cards said in a very dignified script—seemed to prove him right.

Scowling, Joy Thomas piloted her electric wheelchair behind the desk with practiced ease. "You shut up. I am not that late."

Molly laughed. "You're always here at eight and you know it. Besides, is that any way to talk to the person who brought you coffee?"

She held out a cup from the coffeehouse, fixed just the way Joy liked it. "I figured you'd be a little rough this morning, so I came prepared."

Joy eyed the offered cup, then took it with a reluctant nod of thanks. "Considering you're the reason I feel like death warmed over this morning, you should have brought me coffee."

Molly lifted her brows, unable to hide her smile. "I'm the reason? I don't remember holding your nose and pouring three hurricanes down your throat, Mrs. Thomas." She held up three fingers. "Three hurricanes, Joy. Three." She cocked her head. "Do you see three fingers? Or six?"

Joy flipped her the bird. "I see just one."

Molly choked on another laugh. In her midfifties, Joy looked so prim, so . . . matronly and proper. Never a hair out of place, she always dressed like a woman going to afternoon tea, a string of pearls ever present around her throat. The only thing missing was elbow-length gloves, and Molly bet that Joy had a pair of those, too.

Joy might have appeared prim and frail at first glance, but the woman was strength personified. One of the first Black women to reach detective rank in the NOPD, Joy's career had ended after she was injured in the line of duty. Reinventing herself, she'd gotten her CPA license so that she could support herself and her four kids—then teenagers, now amazing adults.

She was more than their office manager, their bookkeeper. She was like a mother, too.

Having lost her own mother, Molly accepted Joy's mothering with gratitude.

"Don't know why you're not miserable," Joy groused, but her expression softened with her first sip of the coffee. "Mm. It's still hot." She narrowed her eyes. "You brat. You were late, too."

Molly grinned, unconcerned. Burke ran a pretty loose ship and they all worked plenty of hours when they were on cases. "Guilty as charged."

Joy took another sip, closing her eyes. "This is the good stuff. None of that burned crap from that other coffee shop."

"Never," Molly said solemnly. "And I'm not miserable because I was the designated driver who got all y'all's asses home safely. You're welcome, woman."

Joy shook her head, wincing at the sudden movement. She turned on her computer and sat back in her wheelchair with a frown. "I never did figure why you were the designated driver. It was your damn birthday, after all. You should have been the one drinking three hurricanes."

Shoving her hands in the pockets of her trousers, Molly shrugged. "Chelsea's been under a lot of pressure. She needed to let loose a little. Especially since she had a babysitter. Tell Louisa thank you for staying with Harper, by the way. That was so nice of her."

Joy's daughter Louisa was a grad student who could have been out partying with her friends, but she'd agreed to sit with Molly's eight-year-old niece. Harper had been through so much trauma over the last few years. Molly and her sister Chelsea didn't trust just anyone to stay with her.

Joy smiled proudly. "She's a good one, my LouLou. She said thank you for the dinner you sent home for her. She wasn't expecting the Choux's shrimp and grits."

"It was the least I could do, seeing as how she wouldn't let me pay her." Molly had celebrated her birthday at Le Petit Choux, her favorite restaurant in the Quarter, its name a play on the French endearment. Because even though the food was amazing, the place was known for its desserts, including its choux pastry. And for its head chef, of course.

Joy aimed a sly smile across the desk. "She'd have preferred an eyeful of that chef."

Molly chuckled, her cheeks heating. "Because LouLou's not stupid."

She'd be lying if she said she hadn't kept her eyes open for the restaurant's chef and co-owner, who was also New Orleans' newest celebrity, having won a Food Network competition the year before. The win had driven droves of tourists and locals alike to the Choux, at least half of whom stood in line mainly for a chance to ogle Chef Hebert.

At around six feet tall, Gabriel Hebert—pronounced "Ay-bear" in the New Orleans way—was very handsome. His square jaw, sexy grin, and dark red hair that curled loosely in the ever-present humidity checked off *all* of her boxes. Not to mention how his shoulders filled out that chef's jacket. And—not that she'd ever admit to ogling—his butt looked very nice in the black trousers that completed his uniform.

While she wasn't looking for any relationships, she'd never pass up an opportunity to admire the Choux's head chef. He'd personally served his decadent chocolate cake last night with its single burning candle, standing at her shoulder while her sister and friends sang the birthday song before cutting the first slice for her with a flourish.

Like he'd done on every one of her birthdays for the past three years.

Like he did for everyone on their birthday.

So it wasn't special, per se, but Molly's cheeks had still burned hotter than the damn candle. A fact that hadn't escaped her sister's attention. Even rip-roaring drunk, Chelsea had an eagle eye for such things, and she'd teased her unmercifully once they were finally alone in the car after dropping everyone else off. Luckily Chelsea was a sleepy drunk and was snoring by the time Molly had parked the car in their building's ground-floor garage.

"My daughter is certainly not stupid. Hell, I like to look at that man, too," Joy said, then glanced at her screen, her eyes going wide. "Well, my goodness."

Molly leaned forward, trying to peek at Joy's screen. "Well, my goodness what?"

Joy tapped her mouse, minimizing the window. "It's labeled 'Need to know,'" she said seriously. "Besides, don't you have an appointment this morning?"

Molly respected "need to know." She wouldn't push. "I wish I had an appointment. I just have a mountain of paperwork after closing that case last week. And I don't think anyone should have to do paperwork on the Monday after her birthday."

"You also said that no one should have to do paperwork on the Friday before their birthday," a male voice said dryly. "Or the Thursday before. Or the Wednesday before, for that matter."

Molly looked up to find her boss standing in his office doorway. Burke Broussard was in his midforties and, other than a few silver hairs at his temples, hadn't changed a bit since he'd been her CO in the Marines a decade before. "Morning, Burke. I brought you coffee, too." She held up the cup.

"Thank the good Lord for that," he said fervently. "I've been here since six."

Molly shuddered in mostly mock horror. "Why?" She'd left rising with the sun behind when she'd finished her final tour with the Marine Corps. Burke, however, had a love-hate relationship with mornings. He said he hated them, but he continued coming in earlier and earlier. The man was a fool.

He was also smart as hell, driven to succeed, compassionate, and generous to a fault. But a morning fool.

"Come into my office," he said. "I have a new client you should meet."

Joy's eyes widened further, and she maneuvered her wheelchair so that she could unabashedly watch Molly walk into Burke's office.

And Molly immediately understood why.

Sitting in the chair at Burke's conference table was none other than Gabriel Hebert, Choux chef extraordinaire. He looked tired and tense and very unhappy.

She wondered if he'd been so unhappy the night before. He had looked tired, but not this unhappy. Of course, he might be one of those people who could put on the face they wished the world to see.

"Molly, this is Mr. Hebert. Gabe, this is Miss Sutton. I'm going to assign her to your case."

Molly's brows shot up. *What?*

Gabe's brows shot up as well, then crunched together in a disgruntled frown. "*What?* You're handing me off?" He came to his feet. "What the hell, Burke?"

The two men faced off, and they couldn't have appeared more physically different. Burke's skin was olive toned, his deep tan a testament to all the road biking he did in his spare time. Gabe was so lightly tanned that she might still call him pale. And, like a lot of redheads, he had a smattering of freckles across his nose.

She'd always wanted to trace those freckles with her fingertips. She'd wondered where else he had them.

Both men were tall, but Burke's body was bulky where Gabe's was lean. Molly loved to watch Gabe move. When he was cooking in his restaurant's kitchen, it was like watching a choreographed dance.

Only their accents were similar—both speaking with that smooth New Orleans drawl that sounded like hot summer nights with jazz music thick in the air. Except that Gabe's voice made her shiver, when Burke's never had.

She probably shouldn't have shivered at all, considering how angry he seemed, but her body couldn't help how it reacted. *Sue me.*

Burke waved at him to be seated. "I'm too close, Gabe. Your father . . . he was important to me, too. He was my partner. I had his back, and he had mine. Whatever else went down when I was on the force, I knew your father would stand by me, and he did. I don't know that I'd be able to keep an open mind."

Gabe did not sit down, his frown deepening to something almost dangerous. "Open to what?" he asked, each word dripping with anger and warning.

"The truth," Burke said simply. "Whatever it might be. Molly's my right hand. She will not let you down. Now, please, have a seat. If, after you've talked with her, you want someone else, we'll figure it out. Don't worry. You can depend on her discretion, no matter who you choose to work your case."

Gabe released a harsh breath. "Okay." He sat, then shifted his gaze to Molly, who still stood in the doorway, having not moved a muscle. He did a double take. "Do I know . . ." He trailed off. "Right. Last night. Happy birthday, Miss Sutton."

Burke looked between them, his expression suddenly unhappy. "You two know each other?"

"No," Gabe said.

"No," Molly said at the same time. "I've been to his restaurant a few times, that's all. The girls took me there last night for my birthday. I brought you some cake," she added lamely. "It's in the fridge in the break room."

"Thank you, Molly." Clearly relieved, Burke gestured to one of the empty chairs at the table. "Join us. As I'm sure you've figured out, this case requires extreme discretion."

Molly nodded. "I understand. Mr. Hebert, if you decide I'm not the best fit, there will be no hard feelings. But should you choose to work with me, I'll do my very best."

Gabe's shoulders slumped, his exhaustion clear to see. "I appreciate that." He swallowed hard. "I need to find out who killed my father."

Molly glanced at Burke. "Are the police involved?"

Gabe's laugh was bitter. "Most likely, yes."

Burke sighed. "What he means is, someone in law enforcement might be complicit. Or responsible."

Molly sat back, wishing she was surprised. "All right, then. Let me have it."

The Quarter, New Orleans, Louisiana
MONDAY, JULY 25, 9:25 A.M.

Molly Sutton was . . . Gabe wasn't entirely certain how he'd describe her. Serene. Unruffled. Unwrinkled and crisp despite the already-steamy air in the room. Despite wearing a jacket in late July, for heaven's sake. She'd been the same way the night before and every other time she'd walked into the Choux.

And yes, he'd noticed. Every single time. There was something about the woman that always drew his gaze. Okay, several things. She was exactly his type, golden blond with a face like Grace Kelly and a body like Marilyn Monroe. But it was more than her looks. There was something about her that settled him.

She was the only diner to whom he'd personally delivered a birthday cake last night. He'd foisted all of the other cakes onto Patty, his cousin and co-owner of the Choux. But Molly's cake he'd placed on the table with as much of a flourish as he'd been able to muster.

Patty had teased him about it when he'd returned to the kitchen, but she didn't mean any harm. She didn't know what he'd done. Didn't know why he was torn up inside. Because he'd kept it from her.

He hadn't intended on keeping it from her forever. Just until he'd had his suspicions confirmed. Otherwise, she might think him batshit paranoid and call for a family intervention.

Unfortunately, he hadn't been paranoid. He'd been right.

Now he wasn't telling Patty because he didn't want to put her in danger, because danger was coming their way. It already had, leaving at least one body in its wake.

And now he was supposed to drag Molly Sutton into this mess with him? Just telling her the truth would put her in a killer's crosshairs. His parents had raised him better than that.

"Miss Sutton," he began, trying for a kind smile. "I'm not sure you're the right person for this job."

She smiled back, but not kindly. Not meanly, either. Just . . . warily. "I may not be, but then again, I might." Her accent was Southern, but not New Orleans. Georgia, maybe. Or maybe one of the Carolinas. "Maybe share the details and we can go from there."

Gabe cast a sideways look at Burke, who was frowning. "What's your concern, Gabe?" Burke asked. "Feel free to be candid, but first let me tell you Molly's credentials. She served with me, one of the finest Marines under my command. I'd trust her with my life. Importantly, I trust her with yours."

Gabe swallowed, hating that tears burned his throat. *Dammit to hell.* "What about hers?" he asked, his voice gone raspy. "What if I don't want her involved? This will be dangerous."

Burke opened his mouth, but Molly shook her head. "No, Burke, he's got a right to whatever it is that he's feeling." She lifted her chin a fraction, meeting Gabe's gaze directly. "I've got black belts in three different martial arts, Mr. Hebert. I'm no sharpshooter, but I can hold my own." A muscle twitched in her cheek, making him realize how tight her jaw had become. "I've killed to protect, so if you're concerned that I'm not physically or mentally up for the task, or that you're in any personal danger, I can assure you that I am quite capable of protecting both of us."

Gabe shook his head, feeling sorrow for whatever she'd seen, whatever she'd done, but it didn't matter. Taking on a dirty cop wasn't the same as taking a life on the battlefield. At least he didn't think so. Fucking hell if he knew anything anymore. *I'm only a goddamn chef.* "Killing in war is different."

"I didn't kill in war," she said simply, but there was an entire story there that he found that he really wanted to hear. "Well," she added with a grimace, "I did that, too. What I mean to say is that I can take care of myself and anyone else who's placed in my care."

"Tell her about your dad, Gabe," Burke said quietly. There was compassion in his voice and his eyes. "Like I said, if you're not satisfied by the time we're done, I'll find someone else. I'll even handle it myself if that's what you still want. But give Molly a chance. Please. Your father was important to me. I want him to have the very best. And that's Molly."

Gabe sighed, too tired to argue anymore. "Okay. The truth is, I'm not really sure what the case is. All I know is that my father died six weeks ago. It appeared to be a suicide."

"But it wasn't," Molly said.

"No. At least I don't think so." He considered his words carefully. "I don't want to believe so, anyway. And if it wasn't, I want whoever killed my father to pay."

"Then that's what I want, too." She tilted her head, the light from the lead-glass window picking up the gold highlights in her blond hair. "Your father was Burke's partner, which means he was a cop?"

"Yes. His name was Robert Hebert, but everyone called him Rocky. He retired six months ago after thirty-seven years with the NOPD." His voice broke. His father had been so much more than a cop. He'd been the best father any man could ask for. "He was only fifty-seven."

She didn't say she was sorry for his loss, although he could see that she was. "Why do you think he was murdered?"

It wasn't a condescending question. She believed him already. At least she believed that he believed it, and for now, that was enough.

"My father had been behaving strangely. Startling easily. More than once I caught him looking over his shoulder or doing that cop thing where they look through a crowd, searching for one face."

"So, he was cautious. Maybe even afraid. Do you know why?"

"No." Gabe bit out the word in frustration. "I surprised him one day about two weeks before he died. He was on his laptop and when he saw me, he went ghost white and slammed the lid shut."

She nodded once, her gaze never leaving his face. Her eyes were blue-green. Which wasn't important. That they were sharply intelligent, however, was important. "Were you able to get into his laptop after his death?" she asked.

That he'd tried seemed to be a given, and he appreciated that. "Yes. And it was wiped clean. Factory new."

Her brows lifted. "Well, shit," she said, her accent drawing the expletive out to three syllables.

He snorted a surprised laugh. "Yeah, that's about right."

"Your father could have wiped it. Or whoever killed him could have done it. Have you taken it to an IT expert for analysis?"

"He brought it with him," Burke supplied. "I'm going to hand it over to Antoine as soon as he comes in today."

Antoine Holmes, Burke had explained, was their IT guru.

"That's good," she said. "If there's anything left on it, Antoine will find it. What about his cell phone?"

Gabe shook his head. "They didn't find his phone." He had to draw a deep breath because his chest seized up just thinking about his father's last text. "He texted me at a quarter to midnight the night he was killed. Said he loved me." He swallowed hard. "So I know he had his phone then."

Molly sighed, a soul-weary sound. "So, your dad was afraid, and whatever he was checking on his electronics is now gone. At least to us mere non-hacker mortals. I wonder why his killer took his phone and left his laptop? Honestly, I'm shocked that the cops didn't take his laptop into evidence."

"I'm not," Burke said grimly.

Nor was Gabe. Rage began to bubble anew in his belly. "The cops didn't do a lot of things."

"Which is why you believe they're involved," she said, her tone matter-of-fact. "What did the medical examiner say?"

The bubbling rage became a geyser, because the damn electronics were the least of the reasons that he *knew* the cops were involved. "Not much. He didn't do an autopsy. Or at least not a thorough one."

Her eyes narrowed. "Why not?"

"Because someone told the ME not to look too closely," Gabe said bitterly. "This was according to the ME's assistant, who seems like a good man. I went there to check on the progress because the cops were giving me the brush-off."

She pulled her phone from her jacket pocket and opened a note-taking app. "Name of the assistant?"

"Harry Peterson." Gabe watched her type the name into the app. "He wouldn't tell me which cop, but he said that he couldn't look himself in the mirror without letting me know that something was dirty. I'm worried about him, to be honest. He was young and he looked terrified." But resolute, and Gabe both respected and appreciated that more than he could express. "The autopsy report still hasn't been released. Every time I call the coroner's office to ask if it's been finished, they cite 'overwhelming caseloads' and say that they're behind and will get to me as soon as they can."

She glanced at Burke. "Can we keep eyes on Peterson, just in case? DeShawn's working in the coroner's office now, isn't he?"

Burke nodded. "That's who I thought of, too. I'll check into it."

Gabe looked from Molly to Burke and back. "Who's DeShawn?"

"DeShawn Holmes," Burke answered. "His brother, Antoine, is our IT specialist. D's just started his residency in the coroner's office. He's trustworthy and well trained, so if something goes down, he'll be able to help."

Gabe frowned. "Well trained how, exactly?"

"He served," Molly said, then smiled. "Army, but we don't hold that against him."

"His other brother is a cop," Burke added, "but one of the ones I trust."

Gabe scowled. "But *I* don't trust him. I don't *know* him."

Burke didn't look annoyed. "Do you trust me?"

"Yeah. Because you got out." Gabe remembered the day Burke had resigned from the NOPD. His father had been devastated because Burke was one of the few he'd trusted to have his back.

Burke shrugged. "I keep up. I know who's who in the force. Antoine and DeShawn's brother is one of my best friends. He is . . . well, let's just say he's been a useful resource since I've gone private."

"Which shouldn't leave this office," Molly murmured, her smile gone. "I'm serious, Mr. Hebert. It could cost our friend his job and maybe even his life."

Gabe swallowed hard. *Mr. Hebert* was his dad. And his dad was dead. If this cop could help Burke find his father's killer, he'd have to deal with his hatred of whoever in the NOPD had blocked the investigation into his father's murder. His father had been a good cop. A good man. He'd have to believe that there were others out there and that Burke's instincts were good.

His father had trusted Burke with his life. Now Gabe would have to trust him with his father's death, too. "I understand. I won't tell anyone about anything. And please call me Gabe. Mr. Hebert was . . . That was my dad."

Her expressive eyes flashed sympathy. "I get it, Gabe. I lost my dad, too."

Her empathy rankled. "Not to murder, though. With all due respect, ma'am, it's different."

Burke winced, and Gabe realized he'd stepped in it.

Molly's smile was tight now, and the muscle in her cheek twitched once again. "You know what they say about assumptions, Mr. Hebert."

Okay. They were back to surnames. He'd upset her, but she was keeping it professional. He needed to do the same. "I'm sorry. I'm . . . I have no excuse. I'm sorry, Miss Sutton."

She nodded once. "Thank you. Apology accepted. And you're right that every case is different, but I do understand something of what you're going through. That's all I meant to say." She squared her shoulders. "Back to business. That there was no thorough autopsy isn't good,

I'm not gonna lie. But it doesn't mean we don't have other sources for our investigation."

Gabe smiled grimly. "I didn't say there wasn't an autopsy, just that the ME didn't do jack shit."

Molly frowned, and then understanding dawned, her lips curving. "Did you get a private autopsy, Mr. Hebert?"

"I sure as hell did."

2

XAVIER MORROW SHIVERED, but he wasn't cold. It was almost ninety degrees already, for God's sake.

He was scared. And he didn't know why, which made him feel stupid. Which pissed him off.

Carlos poked his arm, hard enough to make him wince. "Yo, X." His best friend was looking around them with a puzzled expression. "Why is your head swiveling on your neck like a rotating fan?"

"I don't know." He looked around them again, seeing nothing but people eating breakfast. Just like they did every Monday when he met Carlos at their favorite diner near Rice University's campus. This place had been Xavier's home away from home while he'd been in college, and he was going to miss being part of its staff. Still, this morning felt different. "You ever feel like you're being watched?"

Carlos grinned. "Every time I walk into a bar."

"Not like that, unfortunately."

Carlos's grin became a frown. "What's going on?"

Xavier shrugged. "I don't know."

Carlos's expression became angry. "It's that guy, isn't it? The old dude who visits you sometimes."

Xavier blinked, surprised. "How . . . Never mind." How Carlos learned anything was a mystery best left unsolved. His friend was a true-crime addict and his favorite shows had caused Xavier nearly as many nightmares as the real crime he'd witnessed all those years ago. "No, not today. He, um . . . He died."

Carlos's eyes widened. "What? When? And who was he?" Wide eyes narrowed as he leaned forward over the table. "Was he threatening you?"

"No! He was not threatening me." Rocky had been more like a guardian angel. "He was a friend of someone I knew a long time ago."

Which was more or less true. Even though Rocky had never met the woman who'd brought them together. They'd both been scarred that night, just in different ways.

Carlos leaned back in his seat. "Well, I'm sorry he died. Did you go to his funeral?"

Xavier shook his head. "It was in New Orleans. I . . . Well, I don't want to go back there." *Not ever again.*

Carlos frowned again. "And? Aren't you going to tell me?"

Xavier opened his mouth, then shut it, unsure of how to answer.

Hell, no. You'd get us both killed for sure. Because Carlos couldn't keep a secret to save his life.

"It's not my story to tell," he finally said. "Please let it go."

Carlos got uncharacteristically serious. "Why are you afraid, then? You can tell me, X. I won't tell anyone, I promise." He crossed his heart, then raised his hand as if swearing in court. "Hand to God."

"I'd tell you if I knew, but I don't. It's just—" He exhaled heavily. "I thought I was being followed this morning, but every time I stopped to look, the footsteps behind me stopped."

But it was his imagination. It had to be. He'd been on edge for the past six weeks, ever since Rocky's death.

Rocky had always said that there were no coincidences.

"I'll walk with you, then," Carlos said with a sharp nod that brooked no argument.

Xavier smiled. "I'm gonna miss you, man."

It was true. Carlos had been his best friend since the first grade, two kids of color in a sea of white faces. Both brown, Xavier's skin was a dark walnut like his birth mother's had been, and Carlos's was a warm bronze. They'd bonded over nearly everything back then—video games, love of science, hatred of broccoli.

Carlos smiled sadly. "Same goes, *hermano*. But New York isn't far from Philly. I already priced the train."

Xavier was leaving soon for Philadelphia and med school at the University of Pennsylvania. Carlos was headed to NYU's graduate program in engineering. They'd never been apart, not since they were six years old.

This was going to suck.

"Every other week," Xavier said, holding out his fist to bump.

Carlos complied, then cocked his head, studying him. "How did he die? The old dude, I mean."

Xavier had to swallow hard as bile instantly gurgled up to burn his throat. "Killed himself."

Carlos flinched. "Oh shit. I'm sorry."

"Me, too," Xavier murmured. "He was . . . bigger than life, you know? And now he's gone and I'm wondering all the what-ifs. What if I'd visited him? What if I'd called more often?"

Neither of which were true possibilities. Rocky hadn't wanted Xavier to have any traceable connection. He'd been afraid and sad.

"You can't think that way," Carlos said, ever loyal. "From what I've read, people who are considering suicide in an actionable way don't let their friends and family know, because the people who love them will try to stop them. You're a good guy. If he'd wanted you to see, you would have seen."

"I hope so." God, he hoped so. He'd thought the worst when Rocky's lawyer had contacted him about the inheritance. He'd thought Rocky had been murdered.

But suicide? Xavier had never seen that coming.

"How did you find out he was dead?" Carlos asked.

Xavier hesitated, contemplating telling Carlos a lie. But they didn't lie to each other. Carlos was incapable of telling anyone a lie. Not that he might not want to. He just sucked at it.

Xavier, on the other hand, was a damn good liar, but he'd never lied to Carlos. He might have avoided the truth. *Okay, fine, I've totally avoided the truth.* But it was to keep his best friend safe.

And nightmare free.

Xavier looked around the diner again, still seeing no one paying them any attention. "His attorney contacted me," he said softly.

Carlos's eyes popped wide again. "Why? Did he leave you money?"

"Some, yes. A bit." Not as much as Rocky had already given him, but still . . . It would come in handy when he left for Penn Med and was no longer living at home. Apartments in Philly were not cheap.

The money hadn't been the important thing, though.

The important thing had been the small ceramic angel that Rocky had given him a month before he died. Couldn't have cost more than ten bucks. But Rocky had had it inscribed on the base. *Reach for the stars, mon ange.*

It was an exhortation.

It was also a memory.

Either way, Xavier was never letting it go. He'd attached it to his key ring and carried it with him everywhere.

He pushed his plate across the table, no longer hungry. "You want my bacon?"

Carlos grinned. "I'll never say no to bacon." Sobering a little, he lifted his glass of orange juice, waiting until Xavier did the same. *"Al futuro."*

"To the future," Xavier echoed and made himself smile. "We are going to change the world, *hermano*."

"You're damn right we are." Carlos demolished what was left on Xavier's plate. "So where are we going today?"

Xavier blinked at him. "I'm going to weed my mama's garden. Where are you going?"

"I'm your shadow, dude. You're not going anywhere without me." He leaned forward, dropping his voice to a whisper. "Your spidey senses have kept us on the right side of safe for too many years. If you think someone is following you, I'm not letting you walk alone."

Xavier swallowed again, incredibly touched. "And my mama's icebox pie doesn't have anything to do with it?" he teased.

Carlos's grin was back. "I'm a multitasker. I can watch your back *and* raid your fridge at the same time. I think it's my turn to pay." He pulled his wallet out and left enough cash for both meals and a sizable tip for the server. "Let's go. Icebox pie waits for no man."

The Quarter, New Orleans, Louisiana
MONDAY, JULY 25, 9:50 A.M.

Burke scowled. "Way to bury the lede, Gabe. Why didn't you start with the private autopsy?"

"I wasn't sure if I could trust Miss Sutton. I've decided that I can." Gabe drew the autopsy report from his pocket and handed it to Molly. She opened the report, silently scanning its contents before handing it over the desk to Burke, her features expressionless.

Damn, he'd never play poker with her. Because the report would shock anyone, whether they'd known his father or not.

Burke read the report and Gabriel knew exactly when he'd hit the first shock because Burke gasped, his gaze flying up, eyes wide. "He had *cancer*? Your dad had *cancer*?"

"I didn't know, either." And Gabe felt guilty, both for not knowing his dad had been so sick and for resenting that his father hadn't told him.

"Knowing your dad, he wouldn't have wanted you to worry about him. Especially after . . ." Burke fidgeted. "Y'know. Your mom."

Gabe knew. He and his father had watched his mother waste away before their eyes.

And now both of them were gone. He managed a nod at Burke, who, after a moment of wordless sympathy, began reading again.

Gabe knew when he'd reached the second shock because Burke muttered a violent curse. He shoved the report across the desk to Molly. "The presence of cocaine is bullshit," he said furiously. "I *might* be able to believe the blood alcohol of 0.25, because Rocky did have issues with alcohol, but your father was *not* a drug addict. That much I know."

"No, he wasn't." But the private pathologist had found enough coke in his father's body to have killed him from that alone. "My father was a recovering alcoholic," he said for Molly's benefit. "He'd been sober for three years. But he never did cocaine. Never."

But his father had never struggled with cancer before, either, a small voice whispered in his mind. *Maybe you didn't know him as well as you thought you did.*

The thought bounced around his head for a few seconds before he shot it down. *No.* His father would not have done illegal drugs, especially the way the cops said he had. Booze, maybe. Hard, *illegal* drugs? No way in hell.

Molly was rereading the report with a frown. "What is this? It says: Secondary source revealed the presence of flunitrazepam." She looked up. "Rohypnol. And a lot of it. Whoever killed him incapacitated him first. They probably gave it to him in whatever booze he consumed—willingly or not."

Gabe had to close his eyes against a wave of grief, rage, and loss. They'd drugged his father and then shot him.

His body jerked when a cool hand briefly touched his. "Gabe." Molly's voice was quiet and sad. "We can continue this later."

"No." He forced his eyes open and met her gaze. "I'm okay."

She shook her head, her expression incredibly kind. Her eyes, a vivid blue-green like the ocean in the Caribbean, were filled with true understanding. "No, you're really not okay. But we can keep going, if that's what you want."

His eyes and throat burned, and he had to swallow before he could speak. "That's what I want."

"All right." She returned her attention to the report. "The final coroner's report will have the cocaine," she said. "But I'm betting that it won't show the Rohypnol. That way they'll be able to say that your father was high on coke at the time of his death. The presence of alcohol will strengthen their case that he'd broken his sobriety and make the cocaine more believable. And given his cancer, they'll argue that he couldn't take the pain and just wanted it to end."

"That's—" Gabe's voice broke and he cleared his throat. "That's what I thought, too. That the cops would say that. Not that Dad did that."

"What was the 'secondary source'?" Burke asked.

"A blood sample and a urine sample. Harry Peterson, the ME's assistant, slipped them into my pocket. I didn't find them until I got home from the coroner's office. That's why I'm so worried about Harry. He went out on a limb for me. He said that he'd known my father, that Dad had been good to him. I don't want Harry to be punished for giving me those samples or for telling me that the autopsy was fixed."

"I'll see if I can get one of my people into the coroner's office," Burke said. "DeShawn's a great guy, but he won't be able to watch over Peterson all the time."

Molly set the pathologist's report aside. "The date on the report is yesterday. Sunday."

Gabe nodded. "The pathologist emailed it to me last night. I saw it when I finished my shift. She said that she normally would have waited until today, but she didn't want to make me wait any longer than I already had, especially with what she'd found. It took nearly six weeks to get the report and she was worried that I might be in danger, too."

"Which you might be," Burke said. "We'll discuss your personal security when we're finished going over the details."

Gabe exhaled carefully. He was tempted to deny that he might need personal security, but he wasn't stupid. When the cops found out that he'd done a private autopsy . . . It wasn't gonna be pretty.

"Was there a police report?" Molly asked.

Burke handed her a copy of the report that Gabe had memorized, down to the printer stripe that ran across the width of the page six inches from the bottom margin.

Molly's brow furrowed as she read the very short report. "This says that your father's body was found by his neighbor."

Gabe swallowed. "Mrs. Dobson, yes. She and my mother were best friends for as long as I can remember. She found my dad's dog in her flower bed and brought him back. Said she was already fussin' at Dad when she opened the kitchen door." Nausea rolled through his stomach, making him grateful that he hadn't eaten that morning. "She found him slumped over the kitchen table. His gun was on the floor where it appeared that he'd dropped it. There was an empty bottle of Grey Goose and an empty glass next to his head." He rubbed his hands over his face, wishing he could wipe the image from his mind. But he couldn't. Every time he closed his eyes, he could see his father. Lying there in his own blood and brains.

Gabe wished he'd never looked at the photo. Cursed the cop who'd shown it to him.

Cursed the fact that he'd been too busy to be there when his father had needed him most. Not to beg him not to kill himself, because Gabe knew that his father hadn't done so.

If I'd been there, they wouldn't have hurt him. They wouldn't have dared.

Or maybe I'd be dead, too.

"Gabe? What kind of dog?"

Gabe's gaze flew to meet Molly's, her question jerking him back from the awful place his mind had gone. She waited patiently for him to answer, and he got the feeling that she'd asked the question at least once already and that he'd been zoned out for longer than he'd thought.

"Lab mix. Some golden in there. Maybe some pit bull. A mutt, really. Goes by Shoe."

"Like your restaurant?"

"No. S-h-o-e. Like on your feet."

One corner of her mouth lifted. "Because he eats shoes?"

The tightness in his chest lessened a bit, enough for him to breathe. *Thank you, Molly.* "That, too. My dad called my mom his *petit chou*. When I was little, I asked why he called her a shoe." His eyes burned at the memory. "After she passed, Dad was so lonely. I talked him into getting a dog from the shelter. One day he came home with this half-bald mess who'd been so stressed out that he'd scratched himself raw, but that dog loved my dad already. Within five minutes of settlin' in, he stole one of the shoes I'd left there. Dad called him Shoe and it stuck."

She smiled, and it warmed him, deep inside where he'd been so numb. "Where is Shoe now?"

"At my house. Dad insisted that he'd trained Shoe not to eat shoes, but I keep mine on a high shelf, just in case." He drew a breath and let it out. "Thank you. We can keep going."

"If you're sure." At his nod, she asked, "Was Grey Goose his drink of choice before he got sober?"

"It was. Everyone knew it. Mom got him a bottle every Christmas. He wasn't a drunk, not then. He started hitting the bottle hard after she passed."

"But he got sober," she murmured.

"He did. He was so proud of himself and we were proud of him. The family. My aunts and my uncle and cousin." He closed his eyes again. "I'm going to have to tell them about this, sooner or later, and, though it makes me a coward, I'm dreading it."

"Maybe tell them later," Burke said softly. "No need to burden them just yet."

No need to make them targets, too. Gabe didn't need for Burke to say the words out loud. He'd known from the very beginning that it would come to this.

"It doesn't make you a coward." Molly waited until he opened his eyes. "You love your family, yes?"

"Yes."

"Then it's perfectly natural not to want to cause them emotional pain."

He shrugged. "Emotional or physical."

"That, too," she allowed. "The report says that your neighbor discovered your father's body the next morning, but it doesn't say whether or not she heard a shot."

"She didn't," Gabe said. "I asked. She was beside herself after she found him, second-guessing herself, asking what if she'd checked out the scratching noise that she thought she'd heard the night before, which was probably Shoe at her door. She heard the dog scratching, but not a gun firing."

"And the gun found with your father's body didn't have a suppressor." She exchanged a glance with Burke. "Did he own a suppressor?"

"Not to my knowledge," Burke said, "and I've seen his gun, the one found with his body. It's not equipped to take a suppressor."

"His killer got sloppy," Molly murmured. "A point for our team. Although the fact that the bullet that killed him didn't match his personal weapon isn't in the police report, and I doubt it ever will be. Another sign of involvement. Gabe, you clearly suspected that the cops were involved after speaking with Mr. Peterson, but did you have any indication before that?"

"Yes." Nervously, he picked at one of Shoe's hairs that clung to his slacks. "When I went to the police station to demand an investigation the day after Dad died, my father's old captain met with me. Said the officers on the scene found a quarter kilo of coke in Dad's pantry."

"Fucking bullshit," Burke muttered.

Gabe managed a weak smile. "Yep. Said he'd hidden it with the sugar and flour. Said they'd tested it and it was a match for coke stolen from the evidence locker. That my dad had signed for it shortly before he retired. They showed me the log. The signature wasn't my dad's, but it was a damn good fake."

Molly's cheeks puffed before she blew out a breath. "Well, shit. Let me guess—they said they'd keep it off his record if you didn't push."

Gabe touched his nose. "Right in one. He pretended to be all serious and sad, you know?"

Her gaze became unfocused for the briefest of moments before she nodded. "Yes, I know."

He wondered about her father, about the circumstances of his death. About how she'd coped. Because he could sure as hell use some advice. This was tearing him apart.

Burke was frowning. "I'm surprised that whoever's pulling the strings here allowed you to have a private autopsy done. They could have 'lost' your father's body or put any number of bureaucratic obstacles in your way."

"They didn't know. I didn't tell them. When I found the blood sample in my pocket, I contacted a friend at the funeral home that would have tended to . . . to my father's body. The owner of the mortuary is an old friend. We go back to high school. When the ME's office released Dad's body to him, he had it transported to the private pathologist's office and we had the memorial service like nothing had happened. We had an urn on the front table and just let people believe what they wanted to."

"And now?" Molly asked. "Where is your father's body now?"

"Still with the pathologist. She'll transport him to my friend's mortuary when I give her the go-ahead and he'll be cremated." It was what his father had wanted. "I, um . . . I still have my mother's ashes. Dad wanted me to mix their ashes and . . . Well, he wanted me to bury them at sea together."

"Hold on that go-ahead," Burke said quietly. "For now, anyway."

Gabe nodded stiffly. They might need a corroborating exam at some point. "I figured as much."

Molly met his gaze. "Is there anything else we need to know?"

"No. I don't think so."

Once again, her smile was kind. "Well, if you think of something, you know where to find us. I think we need to start with any cases he worked where there was a probability of high-profile exposure. For this level of cover-up, the stakes need to be big. Money or important people or other cops, even. Did your dad keep records that you know of?"

"I couldn't find anything." Because that had been Gabe's first thought as well. "You're welcome to search the house."

"I will, if you're agreeable to me working this case. Is that what you want?" she asked. "Again, no hard feelings if the answer is no."

He studied her for a long moment. Her eyes were sharp, and he could almost hear the gears turning in her mind. She'd be respectful of his father's memory, and that was important to him. "Yes, but I don't want you to take any unreasonable chances. If it looks dangerous, you'll bail."

"If I feel I'm unable to handle the situation, I will call for backup," she replied.

Burke raised his hand. "That's me. I'm the backup. Me and the rest of my staff. Don't worry, Gabe. I wouldn't put Molly in a situation she couldn't handle."

"Then yes. I'd be grateful for your help." Gabe turned to Burke. "I have my winnings from the Food Network competition. I can sign it over to you now to pay for the investigation."

Molly stood. "I'll leave you all to the administrative details. I'm going to start digging into your father's old cases. I'll be in my office if you need me."

Gabe had the unsettling urge to grab her arm and beg her to stay. To not leave him. But he quelled it and let her go, hoping that she could find the answers he sought. And that he wasn't putting her in the line of fire in the process.

Tulane-Gravier, New Orleans, Louisiana
MONDAY, JULY 25, 11:00 A.M.

Checking his reflection in the mirror on his office washroom door, Lamont gave himself a nod of approval. He was clean-shaven, his face just tanned enough to be healthy-looking thanks to regular appointments at the tanning salon.

The scar that had once bisected his cheek from his eye to his chin was barely visible now, thanks to a very talented plastic surgeon—the same surgeon who'd continued to nip and tuck over the years, keeping his face youthful and smooth. The scar had served its purpose, once upon a time, winning the sympathy of the woman who'd become his first wife.

He hadn't expected to get the scar, of course. After studying the incredibly rich—and unmarried—woman for weeks, he'd hired one of his former clients to mug her. He'd been on hand to "save" her. Unfortunately, the former client had gotten carried away, slicing his face.

It had been painful but had earned him the gratitude of both the woman and her old-moneyed father, so when he'd asked for her hand in marriage, it had been a done deal.

Their money had allowed him to become the man he was today. Powerful. Well-connected. Poised on the brink of greatness. His first wife would have approved were she still alive. But she wasn't, having taken her own life.

Or so the medical examiner had declared. *Just like I planned.*

Rocky Hebert's hadn't been the first suicide he'd staged.

He tilted his head, studying the face that stared back. He had a few silver hairs among the black, but not bad for a fifty-two-year-old man. He knew that people liked his face, and he made the most of it. His face, combined with the sophistication and respectability that came with his wealth, would take him wherever he wanted to go.

At this moment, he wanted to go to the mayor's office. They had a lunch meeting scheduled, and Lamont knew there'd be cameras about. A man such as himself was nearly always in the public eye.

Except when he didn't want to be, but that was necessary less frequently these days. He could afford to pay others to get their hands dirty.

Pity. He kind of missed the personal touch.

Deeming himself ready for his meeting, he walked to the window where his burner phone got better reception and dialed his second-in-command. "Did you get him?"

"I have him under surveillance," Stockman said quietly, like the narrator of a wildlife documentary. "He's been with people all morning, but I'll take care of it as soon as he's alone."

"See that you do," he snapped. "The kid is the final loose end." The kid who'd seen him kill the woman whose name he hadn't said aloud since that night during Katrina. The kid who'd seen his scar. The kid who might be able to identify him.

The kid who he hadn't even known existed until two months ago. The kid who'd been allowed to live because Rocky Hebert had protected him.

Rocky was no longer a problem, but the kid still was. Because even if the boy couldn't identify him by name, he might come forward at any time and testify about his scar. There were enough photos of him before his plastic surgery that people would make the connection. And once the accusation had been made, it wouldn't take much to link him to that damn house where he'd kept the woman. Back then, getting his mistress pregnant was the worst scandal he could think of. Now, no one would blink at that, but murder . . .

Just the whisper of that kind of scandal could tank his political aspirations before he'd even begun. Lamont couldn't take the risk.

"I know," Stockman said evenly. "I'll do my job, but these things take time."

"I've given you plenty of time, most of which you wasted. It took you long enough to find him." Because Rocky had encrypted his hard drive and it had taken Stockman weeks to unencrypt it. Lamont had considered bringing in an expert, but hadn't wanted anyone else to know that he'd located the kid. Especially not his partners in crime. They'd horned in on Rocky's murder and had made it a lot more complicated than it had needed to be, what with planting drugs in Rocky's pantry. It hadn't been necessary and now he didn't trust either of them. He only trusted Stockman. "Just finish it."

"I'll do my job," Stockman repeated, sounding offended.

He didn't care how offended Stockman was. He paid the man a helluva lot of money to do his job. Let him be a little offended if it made him do his job faster.

"See that you do," he repeated, then grimaced as a call came through on his regular cell phone. "I need to take another call." He ended the call with Stockman and composed his features before he answered the other call. This was a FaceTime call, and he couldn't grimace.

Damn, he wanted to grimace.

Instead he pasted a smile on his face. "Hello, darling. Is everything all right?"

His third wife's smile was lovely. She was lovely. To look at, anyway.

Beneath the pretty face was a whiny bitch whose voice made him want to drive spikes into his ears.

He wished he'd had her taken care of years ago. Now it would raise too many questions, so he'd learned to smile and nod and then do whatever the hell he wanted to once she'd stopped blathering.

"Just reminding you that we have reservations for seven o'clock tonight," she said. "We're meeting the Nelsons."

He hated the Nelsons, too. But Lyle Nelson was useful—or, at least, his money was—so at least there was that. "I remember. Did you get reservations at the place I wanted?"

"Yes. But I still don't see why you want to go there." Her tone held a combination of confusion and condescension. Le Petit Choux was not their normal kind of restaurant, lacking the elegance to which his wife had so quickly become accustomed. But he had his reasons for choosing the place, reasons she didn't need to know.

"I'm thinking of investing in a similar restaurant, and I need to check out the competition." It was a lie, but one she wouldn't be able to refute. She was not privy to his business dealings. He didn't trust her that much.

He didn't trust her at all.

"Oh. I guess that makes sense."

So happy to have your approval. "I'll meet you there. I need to go now. I have a lunch meeting."

Her lip poked out in a pout that she thought was charming. It had been, when she was younger. But she was no longer young, and that pout was more irritatingly ridiculous than anything else. "I was hoping you could come home for lunch."

He wondered what she wanted now, because she sure as hell wasn't excited to see him. "What do you want?" he asked, managing to keep the snarl from his tone.

Or he thought he had, because her eyes narrowed. "Don't take that tone with me, *darling.*"

He closed his eyes and reminded himself that he couldn't kill her because the husband was always the lead suspect. He couldn't even divorce her for at least a few more years. He had goals to attain first and a divorce wouldn't make them impossible, but it would make them harder. So he'd swallow his contempt and smile.

"I'm sorry, Joelle," he said, and he sounded sincere even to himself. "I've had a stressful morning and I shouldn't have taken it out on you."

"No, you shouldn't have." Her teeth were grinding, and he hated the sound. "I'll just ask you later, since you have a meeting." Her lips curved, but the smile was as fake as his own. "See you later."

She ended the call, and he gave in to the urge to roll his eyes.

But he had more important things to worry about than Joelle. He considered calling Stockman back to find out if he'd been able to get the kid alone but controlled the impulse. He'd wait for the text telling him the job was completed.

It wouldn't say that, of course. They never spoke plainly about such things in any way that could be traced, and texts were definitely traceable. The message would read, "It's a beautiful day," just like it always did.

And when he got the text, he'd be able to breathe easy for the first time since he'd learned that there was an eyewitness to his crime.

The Quarter, New Orleans, Louisiana
MONDAY, JULY 25, 12:00 P.M.

Molly looked up from her laptop when Burke entered her office. "Well?" she asked.

Burke dropped into one of the chairs on the other side of her desk. "Antoine has the laptop. He's gonna try to work his magic and hopefully find whatever was wiped."

Molly already knew that, having just come from the IT guru's office. "I meant Gabe. You know, my client?"

"He's gone to the Choux."

Her brows shot up. "Alone?"

Burke scowled. "Of course not. I sent Lucien with him until I get his actual security set up. I was surprised that Gabe allowed it, honestly. He's nearly as stubborn as his father was."

There was sadness under the scowl. Sadness and a grim affection. "His father was your friend," she said quietly. More than a partner, then. *Kind of like us.* She'd clicked with Burke within the first few weeks under his command. They'd never had a romantic kind of relationship, though. They considered themselves more like siblings than anything else. She guessed it was the same for Burke with Rocky. "Rocky was kind of like a brother?"

His scowl softened. "More like a father."

Oh. That was important because Burke's actual father had been truly awful. Her own father had seen the need in Burke, the need for someone to love him like his own father should have. And her dad had provided that, too, before his death. Damn, she missed him. "Did you know Gabe also?"

"Sure. Well, kind of. He was busy a lot, doin' all those . . ." He waved his hand. "You know. Chef things, whatever that is. Until his mama got sick. Cancer," he added when she tilted her head in question. "She was a good woman. Rocky was lost without her."

"Poor Gabe. To lose his mother and father to cancer."

"At least he got to say goodbye to his mama. Rocky . . ." He swallowed hard. "That was a shock."

"When did you know that Gabe suspected his father had been murdered?"

"This morning." And his deepening scowl showed exactly what he thought about that.

She sighed. "Well, shit."

"Yeah," he agreed, slouching down in the chair. "We were never close, Gabe and I, but I'd have thought he'd have trusted me enough to bring me in when he suspected foul play. I mean, I went to the memorial service. I hugged him. He could have told me."

"He brought you in as soon as he knew for sure. I think he trusts you more than anyone."

Burke huffed. "Yeah, maybe."

"It couldn't have been easy for him. Either way that private autopsy came out, it was going to be bad news. His dad was either murdered or he killed himself." She closed her laptop and leaned her elbow on it, propping her chin on her fist. "Any guidance? Where would you start?"

"Where you said. His old cases."

"I have some of them, but I haven't read very far yet." She patted her laptop. "Antoine downloaded Rocky's case reports for the last five years of his career. And no, nobody will know that we downloaded them. He set it up so that it would look like someone from NOPD Internal Affairs was looking. If anyone notices at all."

"Somebody's gonna notice," Burke said darkly. "When I think about Cresswell saying that Rocky stole cocaine . . ." He looked down, seeming surprised to see that he'd clenched his hands into fists. Slowly he relaxed them. "This is why I didn't want to take the case. I'm too close."

"I take it that Cresswell is Rocky's former captain?"

"One and the same."

"Tell me what you know." She opened her laptop, prepared to take notes, then saw the quirk of his lips. "What?"

"You. Taking notes like you always do."

That stung more than she'd expected it would. "That's me," she said grimly. "Predictable."

"Steady," he corrected. "Your habits are the foundation of your attention to detail, and that's one of your best qualities. Don't change."

Her irritation melted away. "Aw, shucks, boss."

He rolled his eyes. "Don't you be gettin' a big head, now."

She mimed popping a balloon. "Head shrunk. Now tell me about Cresswell."

"He's rotten to the core, but very, very smart. Nobody's gonna easily catch him."

"Well, that sucks."

He snorted. "Indeed, it does. I've suspected for years that he skims off the top, taking drugs from arrests and selling them back to the dealers he has on his payroll. Or that he's blackmailed into servitude. He's thick as thieves with a number of the New Orleans elite. Old money. Dirty money. If he's not looking the other way in exchange for payoffs, he's on their payroll. Either way, he gets rich."

"You tried to prove it while you were on the force?"

"I tried. I failed."

"Is that why you left and started the agency?"

"Let's just say that my departure was mutually agreed upon. I couldn't take the stink anymore and he wanted me gone."

She leaned back in her chair. So this would be personal, then. Another good reason for Burke to recuse himself. "I'm surprised he didn't just do away with you somehow."

Burke grimaced. "He tried. He failed."

"You mean that he just gave up? Let you go?"

"Nope. I kept a little souvenir. Nothing big enough to take him down, but enough to make him back off. He was cheating on his wife with a male prostitute. He's a closet case. I don't care, but he does, and that was enough for him to give me a wide berth."

"So you think this Cresswell person could have murdered Rocky Hebert?"

"He *could* have without blinking. But I don't think he *would* have. He's not one to get his hands dirty. He would have farmed it out. If he was involved."

"So it's possible that he really thought Rocky stole the coke?"

"Possible. I mean, that's what he does, and he'd assume other cops would do the same. So Cresswell's not a slam dunk."

"That's clear as mud," she said grumpily, and he grinned.

"That's why you get paid the big bucks."

He did pay her well, so she wasn't going to say a word of complaint. "So Cresswell's on the list of suspects as well as anyone who had access to that cocaine. I'll check it out. What about Gabe's security? You said that Lucien's only on the case until you got his 'actual' security set up."

"Gabe wants you."

Molly frowned. "I'm investigating the case. I can't be his security, too. I'd be stuck in his restaurant." And in his home. Where he lived and slept and took showers. That the thought wasn't unwelcome was . . . unwelcome.

Burke's expression became suspiciously uneasy. "Well . . ."

She crossed her arms over her chest. "What did you do, Burke Broussard?"

"He's going to investigate with you."

Molly froze. "He's what?"

Burke winced. "You heard what I said."

"I did, but it's not computing. He's going to follow me around?"

"Basically?" It came out as a rather undignified question.

"Basically? Why? If he doesn't trust me, he can hire someone else. I won't be offended." Except she would be. Gabe's distrust was troubling. And that she was thinking *I thought he liked me* was making her feel thirteen years old.

"It's not that. Well, not like you're thinking."

Molly reviewed the short meeting with Gabriel Hebert in her mind, then lurched to her feet when she remembered him worrying about her safety, the puzzle pieces falling into place. "He's *my* protection?"

Burke winced again. "He thinks he is. He's at the restaurant now, arranging for a leave of absence."

"Burke." She shook her head, slowly sinking back into her chair. "Why would you agree to such a thing?"

"I didn't really, but I didn't fight him because he's his father's son. He's protective. And if it makes you feel better, he'd do the same if it were me. He's worried that someone is going to get hurt and it's going to be his fault."

Molly rubbed her temples. "God save me from Neanderthal men."

"He's not a Neanderthal. Not any more than I am."

She glared at him. "Not helping." When he said no more, she sighed. "And if I refuse?"

He gave her puppy-dog eyes. "Please don't refuse. I'm rearranging schedules so that you can call for backup if you need to go off and check out something alone."

"Gabe's going to allow that?" she asked sardonically.

Burke shrugged. "Just say you're going to get your hair done. That's what women do often, right?"

Molly laughed in spite of herself. "Yes, Burke, that's something that women do. Some more often than others." She sobered. "But I'm not going to lie to him. If it's too dangerous, I'll call for backup to stay with him, but he won't be coming with me. That's simply ridiculous. And dangerous."

"I agree. I think he believes that your job is more exciting than it is. He said that he wants to see what investigating is like. When he sees that it's boring, he'll back off and go back to his own job."

She rubbed her temples again. She didn't believe that. "I suspect he's more interested in seeing what his father did for a living."

Burke looked stunned for a moment. "I didn't think about that. You think he wants the connection with Rocky?"

She considered it. "Maybe that, too. What I really meant is that Rocky may have been onto something that got him killed. I think that Gabe wants to walk in his father's footsteps to better understand what was so important that his father died for it."

"Oh." Burke's lips pressed together. "I guess I'd feel the same way."

"So would I," she said glumly. "Difference is, we can take care of ourselves. We were cops. He's a chef. I mean, I imagine he's good with a butcher knife, but that might not be enough to save his life."

Burke smiled beatifically. "Then I'm glad he has you."

Her lip curled in a silent snarl. "You're an asshole, Broussard."

"Many have said far worse."

"And they'd be right."

He stood up. "He's expecting you at the Choux in an hour or so. He asked if you could work there while he gets his staff ready for his absence."

"I'm not going to read these reports in public. I'll go get him and bring him back here." A thought occurred that made her smile. "Maybe he can cook for us while I research." The old building came with a small, ancient kitchen. A chef wouldn't be excited about it.

Maybe then he'll go back to the Choux with another bodyguard.

Burke's grin had spread all over his face. "I knew I liked you. We can put in a grocery delivery order once he gives us a list. That'll keep him busy while you review the police reports."

"Fine. I'll run home and pack a bag and let Chelsea know that I won't be back for a while."

"Tell her I said hey. Harper, too."

"I will." Her irritation softened. He'd been an incredible support when she, her sister, and her niece had needed somewhere safe to start over. She'd owe him forever. "You realize that me agreeing to having Gabe Hebert as a shadow shaves off a considerable amount of our debt."

"Never was any debt to shave off," he said simply. "Keep me in the loop. And do not tangle with Cresswell or any of his people without backup. Man's a fucking snake."

"I promise." She crossed her heart. "Let me know when you've rearranged the schedule and who my backup's going to be."

"Probably Val. She's between assignments." He sobered. "Thank you, Molly. I mean, really. Thank you." He saluted and left her in peace.

Well, not peace. Her mind was too jumpy for there to be any peace.

Gabriel Hebert. The two of them were going to be joined at the hip until she figured out who'd killed his father. *Be still, my stupid heart.* Because it was beating all out of rhythm.

He is a client. So be professional. No sitting too close. No sniffing his aftershave. No shenanigans of any kind.

This was going to suck.

3

I THINK THAT'LL DO it," Gabe said to his assistant manager, ignoring the withering look on his cousin Patty's face. "Did I miss anything?" he added, because his assistant manager was biting her lip.

Donna Lee Green shook her head. "Nothing, Chef. We've covered it all and there's nothing here that we can't handle in your absence. We'll be fine." She winced a little. "But are *you* okay?"

He drew an unsteady breath. Her compassion was expected, but it still rattled him. He didn't want sympathy. He didn't want pity. But this wasn't either of those things. It was concern that stemmed from genuine affection. He'd worked with Donna Lee for years, long before he'd started the Choux. He'd handpicked her, lured her away from their former employer, and she was the best assistant manager anyone could ask for.

"I'll be okay. It's just that I need a little time. To process."

Donna Lee nodded. "For what it's worth, we all thought you came back too soon after Rocky's passing." She cast a glance heavenward, crossing herself. She'd loved his dad, too.

Everyone had.

Except for the bastard who'd killed him.

Gabe found a smile. "Thank you. You have my number. Call me if you need to."

"I will." She squeezed his arm. "But I won't need to. Take care of yourself, Chef. See you soon."

The office was quiet after Donna Lee had shut the door behind her, leaving him and Patty alone. Patty was short for Patience, but his cousin didn't have much of that. Five seconds ticked by as Gabe waited for his cousin's explosion.

He wasn't disappointed.

"What the fuck, Gabe?" she hissed.

"I have vacation saved," he said mildly, knowing his leave of absence wasn't what had her so heated up. "Several weeks' worth."

"Because you work yourself to damn death." She sat on the corner of the desk closest to his chair, hugging herself. "And you know that isn't what I meant."

"I know," he said quietly. "But it is true. I need some time away."

"Why? What's wrong? And don't tell me nothing. I know you, boy. I know your tells." She leaned forward until they were nose to nose. "I know that something's happened, and I know it's bad. So tell me." She lifted her chin. "Or I'll tell Mama on you."

He narrowed his eyes. "That's low, even for you." Because his aunt Viola was a master interrogator. Gabe was never sure just how she did it, but she got results. Vi would never tell his secrets to a soul, but she wouldn't rest until he'd unburdened himself.

He always felt better afterward, but this time was different. The image of his father flashed through his mind. Not the one he wanted to remember, his dad smiling at him, chowing down on a bowl of gumbo, but the photo from the police report. The one that bastard Cresswell had "slipped" and shown him.

His father, slumped on the kitchen table, the exit wound in his skull the size of Gabe's fist. That could happen to his aunt Vi. To his uncle George. To Patty. At least his aunt Gigi on his mother's side was safe up in Montreal. But the others? They were right here, in New Orleans. They could be in danger.

They were the only close family he had left. The less they knew, the safer they'd be.

Bile rose in his throat and he cleared it roughly. "Patty."

Patty paled. "Tell me," she whispered.

He swallowed hard. "I can't. Please. I can't."

Patty's face lost more color, making the freckles across her nose and cheeks stand out in stark contrast. "You're scaring me, Gabe."

A light knock at the door interrupted the moment.

"Go away," Patty said loudly.

"Come in," Gabe said at the same time, even more loudly.

The door cracked open. "It's Molly, Gabe. Molly Sutton."

Relief washed over him. Saved by the Molly-bell. "It's okay, Molly. Please, come in."

Patty's glare said that he'd be sorry for this, but she slowly stood and faced the door. Then stared in stunned surprise. "Well, hello."

Molly smiled uncertainly. "Hi. I'm sorry. I'm clearly interrupting. I'll wait in the dining room."

"No." Gabe rose and rounded the desk, his hand outstretched. "Please. Let me introduce you to my cousin, Patty." His back to his cousin, he mouthed to Molly, "She doesn't know."

Molly tipped her head down in the slightest of nods. "Hi, Patty. It's so lovely to meet you."

Patty shook Molly's hand, her eyes narrowing as she glanced between him and Molly. "Likewise. Happy birthday."

Molly smiled as if she and Gabe were going on a date instead of embarking on a murder investigation. "Thank you. I have to say, your étouffée was amazing last night, just like always. Your restaurant is where we always come to celebrate."

"I'm glad you enjoyed it." Patty's gaze darted back to Gabe. "So . . . you two are together?"

He opened his mouth to correct her, but luckily Molly beat him to it.

Molly's smile never wavered. "We're colleagues, of a sort. He's going to teach me to make that sinful cake that my friends and I demolished last night."

Patty's lips curved, and Gabe drew an easier breath. "You'd be the first person he showed how to make that cake," she said with false casualness. "It took me years to get the recipe, and Gabe and I grew up together."

So, not such an easy breath. Patty was still suspicious. She'd have to stay that way.

"I'm ready to go whenever you are, Molly." He made a show of cleaning off his desk, even though it was already spotless.

"And how long will you be gone?" Patty asked. "*Teaching* her how to make your secret cake?"

Oh yeah. She was still suspicious. And pissed off. Bad combination.

"I don't know. After I've taught Miss Sutton how to bake *a* cake—and I never said it would be my secret-recipe chocolate cake—I plan to get away by myself for a little while. I should still be in cell range, so call if you need me." He leaned in and kissed Patty's cheek. "I'll be okay. I promise."

Patty nodded, her throat working as if she were trying not to cry. Then she turned to Molly, looking her up and down, her eyes narrowing in on the slight bulge at Molly's side, covered by her jacket.

"You're carrying," Patty said, her voice barely a whisper. "Gabe, why are you leaving with a woman carrying a gun?"

Molly looked down at herself. "Well, shit. You've got a good eye, Patty."

"You've got a good tailor," Patty replied evenly. "I might not have noticed, but it's not normal to wear a jacket in this heat." She turned to Gabe. "I'm waiting."

Molly's brows lifted, seeking guidance.

He lowered himself to the edge of the desk, letting his head fall forward. "Fucking hell, P."

Patty came into his field of vision, squatting low and looking up. "Tell me."

Gabe met Molly's gaze helplessly.

"You want me to tell her?" she mouthed silently.

He shook his head, his gaze locking onto Patty's, rising as she straightened to her full height, which was only five foot two. "I think my dad was murdered," he said softly, so that no one outside the office could overhear. "I hired Miss Sutton to investigate."

Patty's mouth fell open. Then closed. Then opened again. She remained silent, though, maybe for the first time ever.

From the corner of his eye, he watched Molly walk to the corner of the office where they kept a case of bottled water. She pulled two bottles from the case and handed one to Patty and the other to Gabe.

Patty nodded her thanks, still silent. She took several big gulps of water, then sat in one of the visitor chairs, visibly shaken. Finally, she cleared her throat. "How?"

"I don't know. That's why I hired Miss Sutton—to find out."

Patty shook her head. "That's not what I meant. How did you know? How did you even suspect?"

Gabe didn't want to have this conversation. Not ever. But especially not here and not now. "I don't want to talk about it here."

"Then let's go where you *do* want to talk about it," Patty snapped. "Because you *will* tell me. Are you in danger?" Then she blinked. "Am I in danger?" she whispered.

Gabe had intended to keep his family in the dark until he saw the fear in his cousin's eyes. He met Molly's gaze, found her as calm and compassionate as she'd been in Burke's office. "I need to tell her," he murmured. "So that she can be careful, too."

Patty went sheet-white at that. "Mother of God," she whispered.

Molly smoothed a hand over Patty's back. "Come with us. We'll sit in a secure area and have a chat."

"Where?" Patty asked mutinously. "Gabe may have hired you, but *I* don't know you."

"Let's go to our office. I work for a guy named Burke Broussard."

Some of Patty's tension dissipated at that. She looked at Gabe. "Your dad's old partner? That Burke Broussard?"

"One and the same. I trust him. And I trust Molly."

Patty nodded once. "Then let's go. I'll tell Donna Lee that I'm leaving for a while."

The Quarter, New Orleans, Louisiana
MONDAY, JULY 25, 1:45 P.M.

"Did you have a nice lunch with the mayor, sir?"

Lamont slid into the back of the town car. Black, of course. In New Orleans in damn July. Thank the good Lord for air-conditioning.

"I did, indeed," he told his driver, whose name actually was James. Telling him *Home, James* had gotten old after the first week, however, which had been at least twenty years ago. Loosening his tie, he handed a paper bag over the front seat into James's hands. "The mayor's chef made shrimp po'boys. I asked him to make one for you."

James beamed because shrimp po'boys were his favorite. "Thank you, sir." He set the bag aside and turned to face traffic. "Where to now?"

"Back to the office."

His meeting with the mayor had been very successful, but he had

actual work to complete. One of these days, lunch with important people would *be* the work, but he wasn't there yet. Soon. Very, very soon.

He shrugged out of the hot jacket and pulled his phone from a
pocket, hoping to see a message from Stockman, but there were no new
messages from his right-hand man. Which meant the Houston kid was
still breathing, dammit.

There was, however, a text message from a very familiar number.
Call me.

He swallowed his sigh. Jackson Mule was becoming a pain in his
ass. Correction: Jackson Mule had always been a pain in his ass, ever
since they'd been kids back in the old neighborhood. Some people did
not change.

Irritated, Lamont settled into his seat and hit Jackass's name in his
contacts list—labeled "Jackass" because that had been Mule's nickname for decades. "What?" Lamont snapped when the man answered.

"Monty, please. Is that any way to speak to your partner?"

Lamont ground his teeth. He hated to be called Monty, and Jackass
knew it. He supposed it was only fair that the man called him a nickname, too, but it didn't mean he had to like it. "What is it?"

An exasperated sigh was his reply. "I've got information you will
want to know, but I can always hang up and let you get back to whatever it was you were doing that's more important than talking to me."

Someday . . . Someday he'd kill the bastard. He'd make it hurt, too.
For now, he needed him. "For Christ's sake, just tell me."

"Your boy's boy has done hired himself a PI."

Lamont went still, his heart skipping a beat. *Calm. Be calm.* "Explain, please."

"Well, since you said please so nicely." A deep chuckle resonated
through the phone. "I got a call from my mole in the Choux."

"Your *what?*"

"My mole in Le Petit Choux."

"You hired a—" He broke off, his glance flicking to James, who, thankfully, was paying considerable attention to the midday traffic. "I didn't tell you to hire someone."

"Hm. I don't suppose you did. Because you are my *partner*, not my boss."

I'll be your fucking executioner, you stupid piece of shit. It was Jackass's fault that he was in this mess to begin with. His partner had kept Rocky's investigation to himself for years. Hadn't seen fit to share that there'd been a goddamn witness until the Morrow kid's name popped up again two months before. "Why did you?"

"Because I wanted to have eyes on our boy's boy. You wouldn't agree to killin' him, after all."

"You are correct about that last part." Because killing Rocky Hebert's son was too damn risky. One washed-up, drunken ex-cop killing himself was totally believable. But his up-and-coming chef son? Who had no history of depression or alcoholism or suicidal tendencies? That would never fly. Although now that the son had hired a PI, he might need to rethink that decision. "Nor did I agree to hiring someone."

The deep rumble on the other end grew cold. "Do you want to know about the PI or not?"

"I do." He gritted his teeth. "Please."

"She came into the Choux to see Rocky's boy. Left with the boy and his cousin."

"The co-owner."

"The very one. Both cousins seemed agitated and worried, but the woman PI was as cool as a cucumber."

Agitated and worried. *Dammit.* "Wait. He hired a woman?"

"He did. Pretty thing, too. Wearing a jacket in this heat."

Which meant she'd been armed. Fucking hell. He hadn't anticipated this, but knowing that Gabriel Hebert suspected something was good intel. The mole had been useful, not that he'd ever admit it. "Do you have a name?"

"My mole got a gander at her license plate as she was driving the cousins away. Registered to a Margaret Sutton. Got her PI license a few years ago."

"Her background?"

"Been here in New Orleans for three years. Before that, she was a cop in North Carolina, State Bureau of Investigation. Before that, she was a Marine."

Fuck. She'd be formidable, then. "Who's her employer? Or does she run her own business?"

"Not sure yet, but I'm gonna find out. There's one question you didn't ask, but should have."

He ground his teeth again. "Which was?"

"Why she left the North Carolina SBI."

After a pause of several seconds, he ground his teeth harder. "Why did she leave?"

Another annoying chuckle. "I thought you'd never ask, Monty. She killed her own brother-in-law."

He blinked. He hadn't expected that. "Why?"

"It was ruled self-defense, but you know how that goes. One cop coverin' for another."

"Yes," he said dryly. "I know all about that."

"I'm sure you do. I'll find out who her boss is and let you know. I suppose the question we both should be asking is, why now? What does Rocky's boy know that had him hiring a PI?"

"And who has he told?"

"Exactly. I'm on it and I'll let you know when I find out more. Then we can figure out how to handle him."

"What do you mean, you're 'on it'?" Lamont asked warily.

"I've got eyes on the woman as we speak."

"Make sure they're discreet," he snapped.

"As always." The reply was an infuriating drawl with a touch of malice.

"Fine. I'll be waiting." Lamont ended the call and, looking around, found that they'd progressed all of two blocks. Damn festivals. They gummed up the works, seemed like every damn week.

"What's going on this week, James?"

James's gaze flicked to meet his in the rearview mirror before returning to the long line of cars that stretched before them. "Satchmo, sir."

"But that doesn't start for two more days." He shook his head. "Never mind. Damn tourists."

"Yes, sir. I'm glad for their money, but not for their traffic jams."

"You and me both," he grumbled, checking his calendar. At least his personal assistant had cleared his afternoon of meetings. He tapped on her name, unsurprised when she answered on the first ring. "Ashley, I'm stuck in traffic."

"I figured you would be, sir. That's why I cleared your calendar. SummerFest traffic."

He smiled in spite of his irritation at the delay. Ashley always made him smile. She'd make a good wife number four, if she stuck around long enough for him to be rid of wife number three. "Any calls while I was out?"

"Just your wife, sir. She said she'd talk to you later."

He ground his teeth again. He had to stop doing that. His teeth would be nothing but nubs by the end of the day at this rate. "I talked to her before I went to lunch."

"I know, sir. She told me. She was . . . well, unhappy with me."

He frowned. "Did she say anything to you?"

"Not really. Accused me of lying about your whereabouts like she always does. But—" Her voice dropped to below a whisper. "I think she suspects."

Not a surprise, considering Joelle had been his personal assistant when he'd had an affair with her while married to wife number two. "Just stay out of her way. I'll deal with her later. Can you send the Nelson file to my email? I have no idea how long I'll be stuck in the car, and I'd like to have it read before I meet with him at dinner."

"Doing it now." Her voice warmed. "I'll, um, see you later."

"Yes, you certainly will." He ended the call and leaned forward. "James, did my wife call you today?"

James's wince was answer enough. "Yes. Three times while you were in with the mayor."

"I see. I'm sorry about that. She's in a mood today."

James said nothing because he was a very smart man.

Joelle would have to be dealt with soon. She needed to be calm and unruffled and proper, not some screaming fishwife. Looking out the window at the tourists, he scowled. He couldn't divorce her soon enough. And, as tempting as killing her was, having her commit suicide was too risky, seeing as how that was what ended wife number one. It was one of his favorite ways of eliminating human obstacles. Case in point, Rocky Hebert.

His son knows. Although what the chef knew was still to be determined. He could have hired a PI to investigate something entirely unrelated to his father's "suicide."

Lamont would worry about that when they knew for sure what Rocky's boy had discovered.

He reined his thoughts back to the annoyance that was Joelle. Eventually, once his political career was firmly established, he would get rid of her. But he didn't think she'd agree to a simple divorce, and he didn't want to have to create a sexual scandal like he had with wife number two, who'd expected to receive alimony.

Alas for Francesca, she'd been caught cheating with one of his best interns. Kid had unwittingly done him a real solid by fucking his wife, but the aftermath had been embarrassing.

So suicide was out. Divorce would take too long. But maybe Joelle could meet with an unfortunate accident.

That cheered him immensely. Hell, he could milk the hell out of being a grieving widower.

Should be worth a few votes when election time rolled around. Assuming he won—which he would—he could introduce legislation to decrease the danger of whatever it was that had killed her. He'd even name the bill after her. It was only right, after all.

The Quarter, New Orleans, Louisiana
MONDAY, JULY 25, 1:55 P.M.

Molly Sutton drove a big-ass, double-cab Toyota Tundra truck in fire-engine red, which had surprised Gabe. It seemed very conspicuous for a PI's vehicle, but Molly had told him that it wasn't her normal ride when he'd said as much. Normally she drove a boring sedan, but her sister had borrowed it today. After that exchange, they'd fallen quiet, Molly focused on the snarled traffic while Patty sat beside him in the back seat, her body tense, her expression frightened. Gabe knew how she felt.

He'd been foolish to think that he could keep this from her. She knew him too well.

He'd expected her to demand answers as soon as they'd closed the truck's doors, but she hadn't. He wondered if she was as afraid to ask as he was to explain.

Trying to redirect his own anxiety so that he didn't feed Patty's, Gabe sniffed, his nose detecting an earthy odor beneath the onion and garlic of Patty's chef's uniform. He sniffed again and concentrated.

Molly caught his eye in the rearview and smirked. "Horses."

"Excuse me?"

"You're smelling horses. My saddle, mainly. I usually keep it on the back seat."

Patty had been leaning against the headrest, eyes closed. But at the word "horses," she opened them. "You have a horse?"

Molly nodded. "We have two, my sister and I. We grew up on a farm and rode nearly every day. When we moved here, we brought our girls with us."

"A farm where?" Patty asked, and Gabe was grateful to Molly for the distraction. His cousin wasn't a nervous sort, but she was scared shitless right now and he couldn't blame her.

"Western North Carolina, near Hickory. My family lived there until recently." There was a slight catch in her voice, but Molly cleared her throat and went on. "My dad died three years ago, and we moved to New Orleans afterward."

Her father, who'd been murdered and maybe even framed. *Like Dad was.* There was a story there. Gabe could look it up right now for an even bigger distraction, but Patty was hanging on Molly's every word and, he could admit to himself, so was he.

It wasn't Molly's words, really. She had a soothing tone. He could imagine her using it to quiet a nervous horse.

"I'm sorry for your loss," Patty said with genuine regret. "What about your mother?"

"She died about ten years ago. I miss her every day. She was the heart of our family."

"My mother is, too. She's a huge part of my life." Patty patted Gabe's upper arm. "Of *our* lives."

Because he was alone now, his parents gone. The fear he'd felt while leaving the Choux was still present, but it was now mixed with both sadness at his loss and comfort in the knowledge that he was still part of Patty's family. He'd never truly be alone.

"It's just me and my sister now," Molly offered, as if sensing his mood. "And my niece."

"And she rides, too?" Patty asked.

Molly chuckled. "She could ride almost before she could walk. She's a natural."

Patty leaned forward. "What kind of horses?"

"Ginger is a mustang. We adopted her from the Bureau of Land Management after one of their sweeps. They auction off the horses every year. She's my sister's horse. My Shelley is a quarter horse. She's old now—nearly twenty—but we used to do barrel racing when we were both much younger."

"I've seen that on TV," Patty said enthusiastically. She talked on and on, becoming less tense with every moment.

Not so Molly. Her tension was barely detectable, and he wouldn't have noticed had he not been watching her so intently. Her hands tightened on the steering wheel, her jaw going tight. She flicked a glance in the rearview, but not to look at them. She was looking behind them, a sense of alertness charging the air around her.

Patty kept chatting, not seeming to notice, and Gabe didn't want to scare her by twisting in his seat. He slid to the left a little, peering into the side mirror on the driver's side.

All he saw was the slow-moving traffic that plagued the Quarter every week of the summer. It was festival season and this weekend was one of the big ones—the Satchmo SummerFest. There'd soon be music and crowds and busy, busy shifts at the Choux.

He'd picked a terrible time to take off. Patty should hate him.

But she wouldn't, because Patty was the most generous soul on the planet. And, clearly, still as horse crazy as she'd been as a teenage girl.

Molly was telling her about the riding lessons offered at the stable where she and her sister boarded, and Patty was making plans to go for a ride. Which she wouldn't follow through on, of course. Not that Patty wouldn't want to, but the two of them spent nearly all of their waking hours at the Choux.

Maybe that needed to change. When this was over, he'd insist on Patty taking some time—

He sucked in a breath when Molly abruptly turned into an alley.

"Sorry, folks," she said cheerfully over the cacophony of car horns pro-testing the sudden move. But she checked the rearview several times as they drove the length of the alley. "This is a shortcut out of all that traffic."

Shortcut my ass, Gabe thought, as his breath stuttered in his lungs. Someone had been following them. That was why she'd been so alert. She still was.

Patty realized it, too, her chatter ceasing. She twisted to look behind them. "Who was it?"

"I don't know," Molly said, not even trying to sugarcoat it. "Maybe no one, but I'm going to be excessively careful with you two."

"Tell me now," Patty hissed, turning to Gabe. "I really don't want to know about any of this, but I also don't want to draw it out any longer. So tell me now."

Gabe pinched the bridge of his nose. Then told her everything—the intentionally botched investigation, the cocaine that had been planted in his father's house, the threat delivered by his father's old captain, and the results of the private autopsy.

Patty was pale and shaken by the time he was finished. And Molly had been taking a most circuitous route back to her office, going around a block, then forward a few streets before going around another block—over and over again. Either she was giving them time to talk or trying to lose their tail. Or both.

"And you kept this nastiness all to yourself?" Patty demanded. "Ga-briel Hebert, how could you?"

He shrugged, shame and fear thrashing in his chest. "I didn't want to believe it, either way. Either Dad killed himself or he was murdered and framed. Neither option was one I wanted to consider. And if I told you, it would be real."

Patty sighed. "Dammit, Gabe. I wish you'd told me. I would have helped you somehow."

He appreciated the sentiment but doubted she would have been able to help no matter how much she wanted to try. "There wasn't anything you could have done."

There was a moment of silence between them, which Molly broke with a quiet question. "Did you notice anything odd about Rocky's behavior before he died, Patty?"

"He was upset," she said. "And worried about something. And talking to his attorney."

Gabe turned to her, surprised. "About what?"

"I only caught the end of one conversation. He'd come to the Choux for lunch, and I'd gone out the back door to . . . well, to take a break."

"A smoking break," Molly supplied.

Patty shot Gabe a sharp glare when he opened his mouth to chide her. "Yes, I was smoking," she snapped. "But last I looked I was a grown-up and you can't snitch to Mama." Her glare faded. "This was about two weeks before he died. Your dad was in the alley, on his cell phone, talking about a trust. When he saw me there, he ended the call. Asked me what I'd heard. I told him that I hadn't heard anything. He just harrumphed and went back inside."

Gabe was stunned. "A trust?" There hadn't been any such thing in the papers his father's lawyer had given him after the memorial service. "What kind of a trust?"

Patty closed her eyes, her lips pursing as she considered. "A trust for 'X,'" she said slowly. "That's what he said." She opened her eyes. "I don't remember any more."

"What is 'X'?" Molly asked.

"Hell if I know." Gabe's heart began to pound so hard that the sound of his own pulse filled his ears. "I need to pay a visit to Dad's lawyer."

"*We,*" Molly corrected. "You don't go anywhere without me."

Terror for his cousin's safety gained new intensity. "What about Patty? She wasn't supposed to be involved. Nobody in my family was supposed to be involved." He rubbed his temples. This was what he'd been afraid of. "But that was never going to work, was it? Whoever killed my dad won't want me investigating. Nobody I love is safe."

"This isn't your fault," Patty insisted. "And maybe we're overreacting. Maybe none of us are in danger."

Gabe just shook his head. He'd seen what his father's killer had done to him. He couldn't take the risk that the bastard would come after the family he had left. "How can I keep them safe, Molly?"

"We'll talk to Burke." Molly's voice was calm. "I'm sure he'll have a plan."

4

M OLLY GLARED AT her computer screen, the result of her search on the car that had followed them having taken far longer than it should have. *Motherfucking sonsofbitches.* It was every bit as bad as she'd feared.

"Hey," Burke said from the doorway to her office. "You okay?"

"Yeah." She glanced away from her screen to Burke. "Patty get back to the Choux okay?"

"She did," Burke said warily, sensing her fury. "She's safe."

It had been hard to listen to Gabe telling his cousin about his father's death. On their return to the office, Molly had retreated to her office to give them space to grieve and talk things out.

"Who took her back to the restaurant?" she asked.

"Val. She's going to remain on-site, just in case someone comes looking for Gabe or Patty."

That was reassuring. Of all Burke's PIs, Val Sorensen would have been Molly's first pick. The woman was nearly six feet tall and tough as nails. She had long blond hair that made her look like a Valkyrie, the source of her nickname. She was sass and swagger. But underneath all that, Val was a marshmallow. She'd be gentle with Patty, even as she watched her back.

"I've got info for her, then. We were followed on the way back."

Burke's brows shot to his hairline. "What the fuck? Why didn't you say so before?"

"Because I'd hoped to get an ID on the vehicle so I could give you something concrete."

"Did you?"

"Kind of. I circled around and got behind the car long enough to catch the plate." She had to breathe for a second to calm her anger. "It was a fucking unmarked NOPD sedan."

Burke closed his eyes briefly. "Of course it was. Someone must've been watching the Choux. Did the sedan come close enough to get your plate?"

"Probably." *Dammit.* "Which isn't good because I'm driving the truck today—the vehicle that Chelsea usually drives. If they follow her tomorrow, I've potentially put her in danger, too."

"She still working from home?"

"Yeah, but she had a job interview in an office today with on-street parking. She has a hard time parallel parking the truck, so I told her to take the car."

"Hopefully she'll get the job but won't need to start until after this case is closed. Until then, you can take your car and I'll loan her mine if she needs one, just in case anyone gets too curious about you. I've been biking to work lately. Easier to get around traffic that way."

Relief washed over her. "Thank you, Burke."

He waved her thanks away. "Least I could do. What will she do with Harper while she's at work if she gets the job?"

"Louisa is doing some summer classes online. She's coming over to work at our place so she can keep an eye on Harper." Joy's daughter had been a godsend. Harper trusted her, and that was no small feat. "I might be overreacting, but knowing a cop was following me has me rattled, to be honest."

Burke's expression didn't make her feel better. "Knowing what they're capable of, I don't think you're overreacting. I saw the photos of Rocky's body in the police report."

She swallowed. So had she. Keeping her expression neutral in front of Gabe while looking at his father slumped over his kitchen table had been difficult. The exit wound had been . . . bad.

"I'll tell Louisa to lock the doors and windows, to set the alarm, and not to let anyone in, not even delivery people." She met Burke's steady gaze. "I hate this. I hate even the notion that I've put them in danger. Harper and Chelsea are just getting better. Chelsea doesn't bust out of her skin when someone talks behind her anymore. Harper's nightmares are slowing down."

"You didn't put them in danger. Gabe didn't, either. Whoever was following Gabe did this. I don't want you to be distracted worrying about your family. I'll assign someone to watch over them."

Gratitude lessened a portion of her fear. "This case is going to cost you more than Gabe is paying you." Especially if he had to take investigators off other jobs to work bodyguard duty. Burke's firm wasn't small—he employed six full-time investigators and at least a dozen part-timers—but this was still a major diversion of resources. "You can't sustain throwing most of your staff at Gabe's case. Not for long."

Burke's jaw set. "I don't care. I want Rocky's killer to pay, and I want Gabe, you, and your families to be safe. I don't care what I have to do to make those things happen." He shrugged. "And I'm not charging Gabe a full fee, either. Rocky was my family, too, just like Chelsea and Harper are. I'll juggle priorities so that none of our other clients are shortchanged. Don't worry about it."

Burke wasn't hurting for cash, so she decided not to argue. For now. "All right. I'll let Chelsea know."

"Did you get a look at the unmarked car's driver?"

She shook her head. "Tinted windows. All I could see was that the driver wore a Saints cap."

"Like a couple thousand other people in the city," he grumbled.

"Sucks," she agreed. "Where is Gabe now?"

"Kitchen."

She chuckled at that, despite her worry. "Would've loved to have been a fly on the wall when he saw it."

"I would've given the fly earplugs. Gabe was not complimentary."

"Gabe would be right. That 'kitchen' is a disaster."

"It'll get fixed. Eventually."

It was exactly what he'd said when she'd started working for him three years before. She'd given up trying to make a nicer kitchen happen. She gestured to her laptop. "I need to go back to reading these police reports. I hadn't realized that Rocky worked homicide before he retired."

She'd read through two reports already and was experiencing minor PTSD, the crime scene photos stirring memories she'd rather have forgotten forever.

"He was Vice when I worked with him. He got transferred to Homicide after I left." He tilted his head. "He'd asked for an IA assignment, but was turned down. It was the second time that I know of."

"Who turned him down?" she asked, ears perking up. If Rocky Hebert had tried twice for a transfer to Internal Affairs and was denied both times? He might have been looking for something—or someone. And someone didn't want him poking around.

"Don't know. Had to have been higher than Cresswell. I'll ask around, see what I can find."

Mont Belvieu, Texas
MONDAY, JULY 25, 4:30 P.M.

"Xavier!" His mother stood in the kitchen doorway, shielding her eyes from the sun.

Crouching next to her tomato plants, Xavier mopped the sweat from his forehead with his bandana, then shoved it in his back pocket. "Still out in the garden, Mom," he called back and watched as she carefully picked her way across the backyard, a paper bag in one hand.

She was dressed up, wearing makeup and heels and everything. "What's going on, Mom?"

"Hey, Mrs. Morrow," Carlos chimed in. "You look really nice. You got a hot date or something?"

She laughed. "Or something. It's book club night. I'm going into Houston, and we are going to drink a *lot* of wine."

Xavier grinned up at her until he'd stood to his full height, then he grinned down at her. Cicely Morrow was a small woman, barely five feet tall. Her mahogany skin was as flawless as it had been the day she and her husband had brought him home from the social worker's office for the first time. He'd been five years old and so damn scared.

The Morrows had given him a home. A family. It hadn't been automatic—he'd been a traumatized kid who'd watched his own mother die in the Katrina waters that had flooded their tiny house. She'd boosted him to the roof with the last of her strength, her hands the last thing he'd seen. And the image that haunted so many of his nightmares.

But the Morrows had been kind and loving and patient, and within a few years he'd been calling them Mom and Dad. The loss of his father to a sudden heart attack during his sophomore year of high school had gutted him, and his mother had been so depressed that he'd feared she'd soon follow. But she'd bounced back. His mother was a strong woman.

"You want me to drive you?" he offered. "I can be your designated driver."

She smiled. "Oh no, it would be an hour and a half round trip this time of day."

"You know I don't mind, Mama."

"I know. It's very sweet of you to offer, but I'm going to drive to Willa Mae's house and we're taking an Uber. I'm staying with her tonight and we're taking vacation days tomorrow to go shopping in the city. I'll be back for dinner tomorrow night. I left you boys a casserole in the fridge for tonight and here's a snack. Ice-cold lemonade and some cookies."

"Mmmm." Carlos clutched his hands to his chest and pretended to swoon. "I want to marry a man who makes cookies like you, Mrs. M."

"Find him first, and I'll teach him," Cicely said with an easy chuckle, because Carlos's sexual orientation had never been an issue with either Carlos's or Xavier's parents. "Have a good evening, boys. And thank you. My garden looks so nice now. Carlos, when it's time to harvest, I want you to take some of the tomatoes and zucchini to your mother. She makes the best zucchini bread, and we have a lot to share."

"Will do, Mrs. M. You have a good time at that book club."

"Oh, we will," she said with a suggestive waggle of her brows. "We're reading one of the *Fifty Shades* books."

"Mama," Xavier whined, his cheeks heating. "I don't need to know that."

Cicely laughed again. "I know. And we're really reading a book about bees. I just wanted to tease you." She backed away, waving. "See you tomorrow. You staying over, Carlos?"

"Yes'm. Xavier and I are planning weekend trips to Philly and New York."

"Good." Her smile faltered just a smidge before she gamely forced it back to her face. "Lord, I'm gonna miss you two. But it's high time you get outta my house, Xavier Morrow," she added lightly. "My son, the doctor. It has a nice ring to it."

"You can always send us cookies," Carlos said hopefully.

"Every two weeks," she promised. "Bye, now."

When she was gone, Xavier turned to Carlos. "You're staying over? Why?"

Carlos gave him a *duh* look. "Because you're still freaked out. Don't tell me you're not."

He couldn't deny it, because it was true. All day he'd felt . . . odd. He'd taken a bag of yard waste to the curb a few hours before and had sworn there was a guy in a blue car on the curb, watching him. But when he'd blinked the sweat from his eyes, the car was empty. *I should have checked it out.* But part of him didn't want to know. Sometimes real estate agents came to show the house for sale next door, right? "It's just my imagination."

Carlos shook his head stubbornly. "I'll stay. No arguments."

"I won't argue. But it's gonna be boring. I was going to read a few chapters out of one of my anatomy books. I want to walk into my first class ahead of the game."

Carlos shrugged. "I have a physics book in my backpack. We can read, play some *Call of Duty*, maybe get the group online for some D&D. And then order pizza."

"Mom made a casserole."

"Which we will annihilate, because I am *starving*. After we annihilate these cookies." Carlos shook the bag. "Feels heavy. Your ma is a cookie wizard."

Xavier's lips curved. "She really is." Damn, he'd miss her. But she was so proud of him. So he'd go to Philly and ace med school and make her even prouder.

Carlos gathered up the garden tools and started for the shed in the back. "Hurry up, *hermano*. I'm starving to death here."

Chancing a look over his shoulder, Xavier froze. The blue car was back. The one with the guy who'd been watching him before. *Get in the house. Run into the house.*

He shook himself. He was being stupid. Nobody was out for his hide. Nobody was watching him. He hustled himself to the shed to help Carlos put the tools away.

He was going to chill the hell out and memorize all the bones in the hand. And eat cookies. And casserole. And pizza. And stop worrying.

He blew out a breath, knowing he'd continue worrying. "Four out of five's not bad, at least," he muttered.

The Quarter, New Orleans, Louisiana
MONDAY, JULY 25, 5:05 P.M.

Molly's attention was yanked from the police report she'd been reading by three things simultaneously: her stomach growling, the sublime aroma of the dish being placed next to her keyboard, and Gabe's gasp.

"Oh my God," he whispered, horrified.

Molly realized too late what he'd seen on her screen and closed her laptop abruptly. This was why she hadn't wanted to read Rocky Hebert's reports in public. The photo hadn't depicted a particularly gruesome crime scene—Molly had seen far worse—but the victim had been a child and that was always harder. She'd had to psych herself up to open the file. She'd been able to maintain her composure until Gabe had interrupted. Now the reality of what she'd been reading rushed in, and she felt unsteady, too.

Gabe Hebert was pale, his skin a little green. She stood and pushed him into her chair, taking another big bowl of food from his hands. Which were shaking.

"Why—" He swallowed. "Why were you looking at that?"

She placed the bowl on her desk, ignoring the rude rumble of her stomach because it smelled so damn good. But her priority at the moment was her client, who looked like he was going to pass out. "Your father investigated the homicide two years ago."

"Oh." Gabe pressed the back of his hand to his lips. "Who killed her?"

"Her father."

Gabe's gaze met hers, stricken. "Why?"

She lifted one shoulder in a helpless shrug. "Because he was a shitty, abusive bastard. If it makes you feel better, your dad made sure that he was put away for a long time. It's a solid case and your father's work was impeccable. The prosecutor's job was easy."

"Is the shitty, abusive bastard still in prison?"

"Yes, and will be for another twenty-some years before he's eligible for parole."

Another swallow, this one audible. "Then why were you reading it?"

She hesitated, then decided that he could handle the truth. If he couldn't, she was going to make Burke give him another bodyguard so that she could do her damn job without messing Gabe up even more than he already was. "Because the child's mother was not a cooperative witness. She swore her husband didn't do it and gave him an alibi, which your father easily disproved. The mother threatened to see your father in hell. Said she wouldn't rest until Rocky Hebert paid for his lies."

"Where is she?"

"That's what I have to find out." She pulled a water bottle from her bag and handed it to him. "Drink. I don't want you to pass out on my watch."

Irritation flashed in his hazel eyes, his cheeks flushing with color. He snatched the bottle and twisted off the cap angrily. "I'm not going to pass out, goddammit."

"Good to know. At least now you're no longer pale as a ghost."

He frowned. "You said that on purpose?"

"Mostly. Partly because what you saw was horrible and any normal person would be shaken. And because I really didn't want you to pass out."

He drank again, more calmly. "So you're not normal?"

She tilted her head, studying him. His breathing had slowed, and his pulse was no longer visible in the hollow of his throat. But his hand still trembled. "You mean because I don't appear to be upset by the photograph you saw?"

"Yeah," he said curtly. "*Are* you upset?"

She pulled one of the visitor chairs around her desk and grabbed the bowl he'd brought her. *Mmmm. Shrimp and grits.* Simple enough, but it smelled delicious. "The first time I investigated a child murder, I had to go to therapy for a year. And I'd seen a lot of death already." She took a bite and closed her eyes. "This is so good."

"Thank you." His tone was still abrupt, but less so than before. "Does it still affect you?"

She opened her eyes and let her inner shields drop, showing him how much the photo had upset her. On a scale of one to ten, it had been a twelve. "Of course. But I had to learn to compartmentalize, or I'd never be able to do the job."

His expression softened. "What was your job?"

"I was a cop." That seemed to surprise him. *Please don't ask me why I left. Please.*

"Why did you leave?"

Dammit. She deliberately took another bite, forcing the images from that night into the darkest recesses of her mind, where she kept all the bad shit. She debated putting him off, telling him it was a long story, letting him just look it up on Google. That was what she usually did when clients asked her that question.

But Gabriel Hebert felt different. He'd just lost his father to murder, and Molly knew how that felt. She sighed and pointed to the other bowl he'd brought. "You gonna eat that?"

He glanced at her closed laptop and shook his head. "Not now. I don't think I can."

"I hope you don't think badly of me because I can. I was a Marine. We ate when food was served or when we had a moment of downtime, no matter what was happening around us."

He motioned to her bowl. "By all means, go ahead. And you don't have to answer my question if you don't want to. I can ask Burke."

She snorted softly. "And here I thought you were being so agreeable and noninvasive." He lifted a ruddy brow, and she exhaled. "I killed my brother-in-law."

His mouth fell open. "You did what?"

"I killed my brother-in-law," she repeated slowly. "Shot him, right between the eyes." *And I'd do it again in a heartbeat.*

He rubbed the back of his neck. "Why? What did he do?"

She took another bite, taking extra time to chew while she got a hold on her emotions. "He killed my father and tried to make it look like my father had committed a crime." A dirty, disgusting crime that Molly had to shove into the dark along with all of the other images that she couldn't deal with.

"But your father hadn't done it."

"No. My father caught my brother-in-law trying to . . ." She put the bowl on her desk, grabbing a tissue to wipe her mouth. She couldn't eat now, either. "I have a niece." She could see understanding dawning in Gabe's expressive eyes. "My brother-in-law was a sick sonofabitch. My dad suspected what he was up to and waited. Caught him going into my niece's bedroom one night. Grabbed him and they fought. Jake— that was my brother-in-law—grabbed Dad's gun and shot him with it."

"Your dad had a gun?"

"He did. But he was a farmer, not a cop, and he hesitated. He'd never shot a person before. He couldn't even shoot a coyote trying to steal his chickens. He always aimed over their heads and just bought more chickens."

Gabe's smile was sad. "He sounds like he was a nice man."

"The nicest." It was her turn to swallow hard. "I miss him every day."

"Jake told everyone that your father was trying to molest your niece?"

"He did. But he underestimated my dad, who'd hidden a camera in my niece's room."

"So your niece was . . ." Gabe trailed off. "Jake was successful?"

She nodded once. This was the part she hated the most. Unfortunately, it was all covered in various news reports, so Gabe could read it for himself. None of them mentioned Harper by name, of course, but it wasn't hard to figure out. Jake and Chelsea had only had one child. Molly only had one niece.

Molly wished she could dig Jake up, bring him back to life, and kill him again. Sometimes the fantasy was the only thing that kept her going, especially when Harper cried in the night.

"So you killed him." Gabe's mouth tightened. "Good."

"Not in cold blood. It was ruled self-defense."

She almost believed that herself.

"What happened?" he asked gently.

"My sister confronted him, and he came after her. Was beating her. When he saw me, he started hitting me." Because she'd goaded him into it. Had relished the sharp pain of his fist as it had hit her eye, knowing she'd have a shiner. All the better to support a claim of self-defense.

She hadn't planned it. Hadn't known Chelsea would confront him that night. Although she should have known.

I should have known.

And maybe she had. The uncertainty behind her motivation and her preparation had kept her up a lot of nights.

Gabe simply shook his head. "I'm sorry."

She managed a smile. "Thank you. So, after the dust settled and my name was cleared, I knew we couldn't stay there. Not in that house."

"I don't guess you could have."

There was sympathy in his voice. Sympathy and a grim understanding. Which was why she'd told him herself.

"I was reinstated on the SBI—that's the North Carolina State Bureau of Investigation—but I couldn't go back. I just couldn't." She'd known there were corrupt cops, of course, but she hadn't worked with any. Not that she'd known of. But then Jake destroyed all of their lives, and she'd seen corruption up close and personal. Jake was a cop himself, and his friends had rallied around him, protecting him, painting her father as a pedophile. They'd been vile. They'd closed ranks.

But, after putting Jake down like the dog he'd been, she couldn't help but wonder if she wasn't a little corrupt, too.

"So you came here?"

"Yeah. I called Burke when my dad was killed. He'd known Dad, too, and loved him." She smiled sadly. "Kind of like he loved your dad."

"Father figures."

"Exactly. Burke was on his way to me, only half an hour out when Jake started hitting Chelsea and me. He got there after the cops did and . . . just handled everything. Got me a good lawyer. Made sure he got photos of my face. And Chelsea's. And he checked in on Harper when she went to emergency foster care."

As had her SBI boss and his wife. Steven and Jenna were good people. She missed them.

"So you went to work for Burke?"

"I did, but not right away. There was an inquiry, and I was cleared. Especially when Chelsea turned over the tape showing that Jake had killed Dad."

He was quiet for a long moment. "But it also let everyone know that her daughter had been molested. That can't have been an easy decision for her to make."

Molly stared at him, something inside her chest squeezing almost painfully. "No one else has understood that. Everyone was all, like, of course Chelsea showed the tape, but she and I fought about it. I didn't want her to because it would put Harper in the spotlight, but my lawyer was afraid I wouldn't be cleared without it."

He tilted his head, studying her, his hazel eyes filled with an understanding she hadn't seen anywhere else. Not even from Burke. "You feel guilty about that, too."

She swallowed. "I do. I mean, we got Harper out of there, but she's always going to have that over her head. That it happened, *and* that everyone knows. Therapy has helped—all of us. But . . . yeah, I feel guilty." A whole lot more over that than over shooting Jake in the head.

Molly owed her sister a debt that she'd never be able to repay. But she'd tried, taking care of them and making sure they were safe. Until today.

She hoped she was overreacting, hoped that whoever had been following them earlier would focus on her and not her family. Part of her was tempted to quit this job and go home and barricade herself in their apartment. But that would be overreacting. Burke had said that he'd put someone on protective detail, and she trusted him to do so.

"I'm sorry," Gabe said again.

She shrugged. "It's done. It's over."

"I meant that I'm sorry I made your father's death seem unimportant earlier today."

She met his gaze, finding his eyes had grown calm and warm and . . .

Nope, nope, nope. She did not find his eyes compelling. His gaze did not make her feel . . . safe. She wanted to snarl at herself, but he'd think she was crazy. So she only nodded. "Thank you. I'll do whatever I can to find out who killed your father. I hope you know that."

"I already did. Now I'm even more certain." He glanced at her closed laptop. "What else did you find in the police reports while I was cooking in that horrible thing you dared to call a kitchen?"

Her lips twitched up in a small, but real, smile. "It really is pretty awful."

"It's a hot plate, a refrigerator that was built while there was still a Berlin Wall, and a microwave that may have cooked my liver while I stood in front of it. What is Burke thinking? It's a menace."

"He's thinking that if he puts in a better kitchen, we'd all live here, and he wants us to have 'work-life balance' or some such shit."

"I hope irradiated livers are covered by his insurance."

She chuckled. "It's not that bad. The microwave makes a mean bag of popcorn."

He scoffed. "It couldn't make a kind bag of popcorn."

Feeling better, she reached for the shrimp and grits and took another bite. "You managed okay. This is delicious."

"Thank you, but anyone could make this. It's simple."

"We can't. Well, maybe Val can. She's one of our PIs. She has hidden talents we keep discovering like Easter eggs in a video game."

She went back to eating and he watched her, saying nothing until she'd scraped the last grain of grits from the bowl. Then he nodded to the laptop.

"What did you find?"

"Three cases that your father investigated where either the perpetrator or a family member vowed revenge. Of course, there are likely other cases where the angry party wasn't stupid enough to threaten a cop where he could hear it and put it in his report. But I've got something to start on. I'll do background checks on the three possibilities and see if they're still alive, for starters. Then I'll find out where they are now and . . ." She hesitated, not wanting to cause him pain. But he'd said that he wanted to be a part of the investigation. "And where they were six weeks ago."

Gabe flinched. "That makes sense."

"I'm also going to need access to your father's financial accounts."

He frowned at that, visibly bristling. "What do you expect to find?"

"I don't know. But we say 'follow the money' for a reason."

His jaw went rigid. "You think my dad was on the take?"

"Nope. But I wouldn't be doing my job if I didn't check."

"I understand," he said stiffly. "And I'll come with you when you do these checks. No more trying to shove me in a half-assed kitchen so I can make your dinner."

"Burke says you can come, so yes. I'd prefer you choose another bodyguard, but if you don't get in my way, we can make this work. But," she added as gently as she could, "I may find things that you don't want to see. That happens sometimes when someone dies suddenly."

His jaw was still square, his eyes now cold. "Did you find anything weird when your father died?"

"Well . . . We found out that he had quite a collection of porn. That was uncomfortable, to say the least. It was all pretty vanilla, and the activity was recent. Mom had died years before. She had an aneurysm and Dad missed her so much. We didn't find any lady friends. Just the . . . you know."

He grimaced. "If you find something like that, I really don't want to know."

"I don't blame you." She injected lightness into her tone. "I needed brain bleach after that."

He smiled and seemed to relax. "Thank you. I do want to accompany you. It's my responsibility. He was my father."

"I get that." She hoped his *responsibility* wouldn't get him hurt. Or worse. Which was her responsibility to prevent. "Do you have any self-defense training?"

"Some Brazilian Jiu-Jitsu."

She was impressed. One of her black belts was in BJJ. "How much is some?"

"Brown belt."

She was even more impressed. "All right, then, that's more than I was expecting. Are you proficient with any weapons?"

He made a face. "My dad was a cop. He took me to the range for the first time when I was ten years old. It was our bonding time."

"Did you hate it?"

"So freaking much." He shuddered. "But I can shoot okay. My knife skills are *very* good."

"If we get attacked by an onion, I'll hide behind you. Otherwise, you hide wherever you can. If bad shit goes down, I want you safe. He was your dad, but this is my job, therefore this investigation is my responsibility. Are we clear?"

He huffed an annoyed breath. "Yes, ma'am."

She grinned. "I like being called 'ma'am.'" She pointed to the bowl of untouched shrimp and grits. "Can you eat now?"

"I'll try."

"Good. You eat while I run background checks. I want to check out your father's house next. I don't imagine we'll find anything since you searched already, but you never know. Then we'll head for your place."

"I can make up the guest room for you."

"Actually, I'll probably just sleep on the sofa so that I'm near the front door. Do you have a security system?"

He rolled his eyes. "My dad gave one to me as a housewarming present."

"Any weapons in your house?"

"My Wüsthof knife set. And the damn dog."

She'd forgotten about the dog. "Why didn't you say something about the dog? You've been gone all day."

"I had a doggy door put in the week after Dad passed. Shoe's got access to food, water, and a half acre of grass to sniff and pee on. He'll be okay."

She lifted her brows. "You have a doggy door? There goes your security system."

He winced. "I didn't think about that."

She started packing her things. "I can do the background checks once we've secured your house. We can go to your father's house tomorrow. Grab your dinner and let's go."

5

WHO BROUGHT YOUR car home?" Molly asked as she pulled her truck into Gabe's driveway, parking behind his very old, but still reliable Honda Accord.

"Nobody. I walked to your office this morning." He shrugged. "I walk to work nearly every day."

"Makes sense. I'd walk, too, if I lived so close to the Quarter." She was eyeing his house critically, and he felt himself becoming a little defensive, because he loved his home. "How many exterior doors do you have?"

Oh. His irritation subsided. She was checking security. His father had done the same thing. "One in the front and one in the back. One on one side, two on the other. So five total. It's a common design for these old shotgun-style houses."

Supposedly named because one could shoot a gun at the front door and the bullet would exit the back without hitting anything.

She turned to smile at him. "I like it. How long have you lived here?"

He relaxed even more. He didn't think he could tolerate someone who didn't like his house. It was almost as much his baby as was the Choux. "Six years. I've owned it for seven, but it took me most of a year to make it livable. It was truly a fixer-upper."

"Katrina?"

"Yes. It wasn't bad enough to be tagged for demolition, but pretty near."

"You did it yourself?" she asked, sounding impressed.

He almost preened. "Most of the grunt work, yeah. One of Patty's cousins on her mom's side is a general contractor and he helped." He grinned. "Free gumbo at the Choux for the rest of his days."

"I've tasted the Choux's gumbo, and I think he got a great deal. Show me around?"

"Of course."

She grabbed a duffel bag from the back seat of her truck and, shouldering it, followed him up the front steps. "It's very cheerful, with the red siding and the green door. Was it this color originally?"

"As close as I can figure." He unlocked the front door, opened it, then disabled the alarm, cocking his head to listen for Shoe. Sure enough, he heard the dog's excited yelp and the scrabble of claws on the hardwood floor of the narrow hallway that ran the length of the house.

He laughed, relieved. Part of him had been worried that they'd get to the dog. And guilty because he hadn't considered the risk to Shoe when he'd left that morning.

He went down on one knee when Shoe ran at him, wagging his tail so hard it was a wonder he didn't fall right over. "You're okay," he murmured, hugging the dog's neck, feeling his eyes burn. The dog was all he had left of his father, and the thought that someone might have hurt the sweet mutt had him tearing up. He squeezed his eyes shut, surreptitiously drying them on Shoe's coat. "We have a visitor," he said more loudly.

"Oh, he's a cutie." Molly held out one hand to the dog so that he could sniff her. "Hey there, Shoe. Don't eat my shoes and we'll be friends forever."

"I keep mine on a high shelf," Gabe said. "Come on in. Make yourself at home."

She shouldered her duffel and followed him into the house, then began turning in a slow circle, her admiration clear. "Oh, wow. I love the wood flooring. And the windows. Is this how it would have originally looked?"

"I kept the details as close as I could, but I had to guess on most of it. Then an old woman knocked on my door, about five years ago now. She'd lived down the street before Katrina, but lost her home and never moved back. She was in the area visiting some friends and she saw that I'd fixed the place up." He smiled, remembering the woman's emotion. "She had tears in her eyes. Said she'd lived in what used to be the house four doors down for most of her life, but it was demolished when FEMA came through. Whoever rebuilt there didn't reproduce the old house, but mine looked exactly the same as before. Said her best friend used to live in this house."

"Did she ask for a tour?" Molly asked, biting on her lower lip as if she wanted to say something but was holding back.

He wanted to nudge her poor lip to save it from her teeth, but he kept his hands to himself. Which was a real shame, because she had very pretty lips. Which he wasn't going to notice. *Stick to the program, Hebert.* "No, but I gave her one. You're thinking that she could have robbed me."

She lifted a shoulder. "Once a cop . . . But I'm glad that you didn't think that way. She must have been so happy."

"She cried. Sobbed like a child. We took a photo together and I emailed it to her grandson, who was driving her around. She and I have exchanged Christmas cards ever since."

Molly was smiling at him now. "I think you're a very nice man, Gabriel Hebert."

His cheeks heated. "Anyone would have done the same."

"Anyone nice," she corrected. "I'm not sure I'd have been that nice. Show me the rest."

He led her through an open archway into the kitchen and basked in her gasp. He'd spent the most time and money on this room, and he was proud of it.

"It's beautiful," she whispered. "Marble and natural brick. And all this light."

He admired his handiwork fondly. "Took me years to save up to do this room right, but I'm a chef. I couldn't cook in a shitty kitchen."

She chuckled. "You did just fine in the office's shitty kitchen." She trailed her fingers over the marble island. "Gabe, it's incredible. And it's so much bigger than I expected. Are you sure it's not a TARDIS?"

He laughed. "The high ceilings give the feeling of space. But the house really is big for its style. It had four bedrooms, but I turned one into an office and one into a man cave. Left me with the master and a spare. Come on. I'll show you to your room and you can drop your bag there."

She followed him down a hall that was barely wide enough for one person, Shoe tagging along behind them. Gabe pulled the bifold door open to the spare bedroom and gestured her inside.

She gasped again, stroking his ego. "Gabe, it's amazing." Lowering her duffel, she walked to the French doors, which led to the garden. But she checked the alarm contacts first, which made him smile.

"I love this," she said. "How tropical it looks. But I don't love that there are doors in the bedroom. So many points of entry."

He sighed. "It was my favorite thing. Before now."

She turned, her expression contrite. "I'm sorry. After this is over, you can go back to loving it."

"I intend to." He showed her the office and the theater room, a.k.a. his man cave. "All the bedrooms have windows and doors to the outside, except for the man cave. I wanted a place where I could watch TV without the light. There's a veranda that runs the perimeter of the house and a deck on the back."

She checked the security of those doors as well. "The locks aren't bad, but they could be better."

"They were a compromise. I would have used a normal lock, but Dad wanted the Fort Knox model. We agreed on these. He would've had me living in a concrete bunker to keep me safe. I did get the hurricane glass he insisted on. It'll keep prowlers from breaking the glass, and also got me a discount on my homeowners insurance, so that was a win–win."

"Hurricane glass is a good security measure. Where is the doggy door?"

"In my bedroom." He led the way, very relieved that he'd picked up his dirty clothes that morning. He pointed to the flap in the wall next to the French doors. Tail wagging, Shoe disappeared through what was, now that Gabe was looking at it through Molly's eyes, a big hole in his wall. "It's magnetic," he felt compelled to point out, "so it stays put against the weather."

"But not against someone who's trying to break in."

He frowned. "It does lock." He wasn't a total fuckup. "And there's a security bar that came with it. It's in the closet somewhere."

She arched a brow.

He sighed. "Where it does no good."

"We can secure it from the inside, which means you'll have to let Shoe out periodically during the day rather than letting him have his freedom and—" She stopped abruptly when Shoe barked, the sound high-pitched and oddly aggressive. "Is that normal?"

The hairs rose on the back of Gabe's neck. "No."

He ran to the French doors, Molly directly behind him. "Me first," she insisted, pushing him aside. Opening the doors into the backyard, she ran out of the house and leapt the rail around the deck like it was a track hurdle. "Stop!" she shouted to . . . who?

Fucking hell. Gabe raced down the back stairs to his backyard in time to see her yanking at the gate in the eight-foot security fence. His heart pounding, he started to follow, but she pointed behind her. "Get your dog," she said urgently. "Somebody threw something over the fence."

Luckily his backyard wasn't too huge, and within seconds, he was yanking Shoe by the collar, dragging him away from something brown. "No, Shoe! No! Leave it!"

Meat. The something someone had thrown over his fence was meat. Steak, actually. *Cooked steak.* He inched closer, keeping Shoe behind him, out of reach of the meat. Luckily *leave it* was one of the commands that his father had taught to Shoe.

Then Gabe stared. There was white powder sprinkled over the steak. A lot of white powder.

He swallowed back the bile that rose to burn his throat.

Poison. Someone had tried to poison his dog. Dropping to his knees, he pried Shoe's mouth open, searching for any evidence that he'd consumed it.

"Did he eat any of it?" Molly asked from behind him. He glanced over his shoulder to see that she was on the phone. She tapped the screen, putting the call on speaker. "It's Burke. Burke, it's a cooked steak with some kind of white powder on it. Gabe, did Shoe eat any of the meat?"

Gabe shook his head. "I don't think so, but I want to take him to the vet to make sure."

"Okay, we'll do that. Let's take him inside now. I'll get a plastic bag, and wrap that up. We need to find out what it is."

"Are you all right, Gabe?" Burke asked through the speakerphone.

"I'm not sure. I'm not hurt, anyway." Gabe rose, his legs embarrassingly unsteady. He had to lock his knees to keep from falling on his ass. "Did you see who did it?"

She shook her head. "He was driving away by the time I got the gate open. Burke, I'll text you the vet's address. I'll take the meat with me. Can you send someone to pick it up?"

"Of course. Take care of Shoe."

Molly ended the call, then put a hand on Gabe's lower back. "I'll take the dog. You go inside. Now."

Gabe obeyed, stumbling over his own feet. He had to stop, had to suck in great gulps of breath.

Molly stayed with him, her hand on his back as she pulled Shoe along. "Breathe. Just breathe. Shoe doesn't seem like he's in any pain, but we'll make sure."

"Someone was here," he whispered hoarsely. "Someone wanted to kill my dog."

"Or make him sleep. Either way, someone wanted your best alarm system here offline." She took his arm and urged him up the stairs, dragging Shoe behind her. "Come on, boy. Let's go inside."

Once inside his bedroom, she led Gabe to the bed and gently pushed him to sit. He obeyed again, closing his eyes. Humiliation bloomed, making him feel sick again.

"Sorry," he muttered. "I freaked out."

"You had every right to do so," she said, matter-of-fact. "Someone means you harm and tried to hurt your dog to get to you. I'm just glad we were here to hear Shoe bark."

His gut roiled. "If we'd been a little later . . ."

She closed the French doors and locked them. "But we weren't." She closed the drapes, casting the room into shadow. Somehow the darkness made him feel better. "Stay here. I'm going to take care of bagging the steak, then we'll go to my truck. I'll escort you, so don't leave the house without me. The intruder drove away, but he could come back. I'm not trying to scare you unnecessarily," she added, probably because all the color had drained from his face.

He felt like he was going to pass out. "Unnecessarily."

"Exactly. But you need to be on alert. Do you understand me?"

He nodded weakly. "Yeah."

"Good. I'll be right back. Breathe. Put your head between your knees if you feel faint."

He breathed, practicing the in-hold-out pattern until his head stopped spinning and the room around him settled, all while Shoe panted happily. *At least I didn't need to shove my head between my knees. Small mercies.* He might even be able to walk without face-planting on his bedroom floor.

A warm bottle of water was pressed into his hand. "It's not cold," she apologized. "I had it in my duffel, so I know it's safe. I've got the meat and your laptop. I also checked all the locks and secured the doggy door. You can arm the alarm. If you're okay, we need to go."

Gabe pushed to his feet, shuddering once more. "I'm good." *No, I'm really not.* But he needed to get Shoe to the vet. He gestured with a hand that, thankfully, no longer trembled. "After you."

The Quarter, New Orleans, Louisiana
MONDAY, JULY 25, 6:58 P.M.

"Excuse me," Lamont said, interrupting his wife's chatter when his cell buzzed with an incoming call. "I need to take this."

Joelle pouted. "You promised."

"Business pays for dinners like this," he said mildly, when he really wanted to slap her. She always pouted when he needed to work, as if his money didn't pay for her lavish lifestyle. He stepped away from the front of Le Petit Choux and into the bustling crowd on Chartres Street. "Is it done?" he asked quietly, forgoing a greeting.

"No," Stockman said. "I've been waiting for the kid to come out, to take out the trash or something, but he's still in the house and he still has company."

"Then—" Lamont caught himself before he said *break in*. There were too many people around and one never knew who was listening. Especially if someone recognized him. "Find a way."

"I will. Sometimes these things require some delicacy. This is one of those times."

He laughed humorlessly. "You're telling me to be patient?"

"Basically. There aren't many houses here, but I don't want a neighbor calling the cops."

"Then after sundown."

"That's my plan."

"I want it done," he said, leaving no room for argument.

"I know. Have I ever let you down before?"

"No." Which was why Stockman was still alive. He was a useful fucker. "No, you have not. Don't make this the first time."

Stockman was quiet for a very long moment. Seething, no doubt. Good. He needed some shaking up. "I said that I will get it done," he said, sounding like his teeth were clenched.

"See that you do. I have to go now. My dinner companions have arrived."

Ending the call, he navigated through the crowd, pasting a smile on his face. "Nelson!" He shook the man's hand. "Good to see you. And Lorraine. You look lovely tonight."

Lorraine Nelson was a pleasantly round woman who was somewhere in her late sixties. Nelson was around seventy. And richer than God.

"I've heard good things about this place," Lorraine said, sounding genuine. "I've been wanting to try it for a long time."

Joelle's facial expression said the exact opposite. Le Petit Choux was a cozy, homey kind of place, where families went to celebrate. But it wasn't elegant. There were no white tablecloths. No sommeliers. No tuxedos. It wasn't her style.

"Lamont is planning to buy into a similar place," Joelle gushed, link-ing her arm through Lorraine's. "He's checking out the competition. I have heard wonderful things about their desserts. I may have to cheat on my diet tonight."

It was a dig at Lorraine's weight, albeit a classy one. Joelle was good at that. She put the bless into "bless your heart." Her quick wit had been among the qualities that had initially drawn him. Now, seven years later, he wanted to kill her for it. Daily.

"If it's not to your liking, we can go somewhere else," Lamont said, knowing that Nelson would say no.

"No, that's not necessary," Nelson said. "This will be fine, I'm sure."

They approached the hostess station, manned by a young beauty in a sleek, black, formfitting dress. Lamont eyed the woman appreciatively. The hostesses here all wore the same style dress and were always a visual feast. He'd been here before, but only for lunch. This was the first time he'd come for dinner.

"Welcome to Le Petit Choux," the young beauty said with a flirtatious smile. "Do you have a reservation?"

"Yes," Joelle said, giving the woman a dark stare that was both envious and warning. "Table for four at seven o'clock, under Joelle."

They were seated quickly, given menus, and promised that a server would be by soon. Lamont looked around the place, searching for Rocky Hebert's son. He popped in occasionally for lunch to check the man out. To see if he was anxious or seemed distracted—more so than would be expected from simply losing a parent. Anything that would indicate that he suspected that his father hadn't died by suicide.

Which it seemed like Gabe Hebert now suspected, since he'd hired a PI. If Rocky's son started sniffing in Lamont's direction, he'd have to reevaluate the risk in killing him. If it became necessary, he'd tell Stockman to make it look like a robbery. After suicide and accidents, robberies were his next favorite method.

Observing Hebert here was kind of a long shot, but the food was good and the desserts really were sublime, so it was worth the small effort it took to do reconnaissance. He immediately saw Rocky's niece through the wall-width window into the kitchen. She was smiling as she spoke to one of the cooks. She and Rocky's son co-owned the place, so he wasn't surprised to see her. But there was no sign of Gabriel Hebert, and he couldn't just come out and ask where the man was.

He'd be subtle. Poke a little. Enjoy the étouffée and the crème brûlée. And if he was lucky, Joelle would be so drunk by the time they got home, she'd fall asleep without asking him any questions about the restaurant he planned to buy into. Because of course there was none.

He opened his menu with a snap. "I don't know about you, but I'm starving. I haven't had a bite since lunch with the mayor. What looks good?"

He'd barely perused the night's offerings when his phone buzzed with a text message from Jackass. Keeping his expression neutral on the outside, he was more than irritated on the inside. The man needed to stop contacting him.

Both of them knew that frequent contact would lead to suspicions. *I will kill him. I swear to God.*

He peeked at his phone, ignoring Joelle's scowl.

Well, fuck. The message read: *Why are u there?!? My mole sees u. Are u insane?!?*

He glanced around the restaurant, wondering who here was Jackass's mole. Quickly, under the shield of the tablecloth, he replied: *Later.*

And later, he'd give Jackass a piece of his mind. That piece would be the only evidence of a brain in the fool's head. "I'm so sorry," he told his tablemates, who'd stopped their chatter while he'd checked his phone. He shot them a conciliatory smile. "I'm not trying to be rude, I promise. My answering service got a call for me, but it's not an emergency. I'm putting my phone on Do Not Disturb right now."

Which he wasn't going to do, of course. He was expecting a text from Stockman confirming that Xavier Morrow was no more.

Metairie, Louisiana
MONDAY, JULY 25, 9:45 P.M.

"How is the dog?" Burke asked when Molly and Gabe met him in Rocky Hebert's front yard. They'd parked at the curb because there was only room for one car in the driveway and an old Ford truck already occupied the space. It had been Rocky's vehicle.

She'd been planning to check Rocky's house the next morning, when there was daylight, but given the attempted attack on Gabe via his dog, she didn't want to waste any more time. Burke was there as backup, in case someone else tried getting to Gabe while she was searching.

"He's okay," Molly answered, because Gabe was staring up at the house with a look of dread. "The vet didn't think he'd ingested any of the poison on the meat but wanted to keep him overnight for observation." She touched Gabe's arm lightly. "You okay?" she murmured.

He nodded jerkily. "Yeah. It's just . . . I haven't been back here. Not for a while."

"I get it." And she did. She hesitated, then took his hand, giving it a squeeze. "You don't have to go in. You've already had one helluva day. Nobody'll think badly of you if you don't want to go inside. You can wait outside with Burke."

Gabe squeezed back, so hard that she had to work to hide her wince. "I need to do this."

He'd said the same while they'd sat in the waiting room at the emergency vet's office, hoping that Shoe was all right. Molly did get it. She'd done the same after her father's murder, needing answers. Needing to prove she was strong enough to look. She'd been rewarded with the discovery of the camera that her father had hidden in Harper's closet, rewarded with confirmation of what she'd already known in her heart—that her father had not touched Harper, that the girl's own father had been the guilty one. Guilty of raping his own child and guilty of killing her dad.

"Then let's go in." Still holding his hand, she walked with him to his father's front door, Burke trailing behind them.

Whoever had tossed that steak over the fence had wanted to silence the dog. Which made her wonder how they'd planned to silence the alarm system when they came back to silence Gabe. She'd mulled it over while Gabe had paced across the emergency vet's waiting room and concluded that they'd planned to shoot Gabe and make their escape so quickly that they'd be gone before the alarm brought the police.

Or that they already knew how to disarm the alarm, the code for which was Gabe's mother's birthday. Molly had wanted to roll her eyes when Gabe had admitted this. *Civilians.*

So when Gabe entered the exact same code into the keypad inside his father's front door, she gaped. "You both used your mother's birthday for the alarm code?"

Gabe shook his head. "Not exactly. That was just the code Dad set up for me. I use it for everything, so I don't forget. Dad had the master code. It was the date they met and—"

He flipped on the overhead light and gasped. Behind them, Burke cursed.

"Well, shit," Molly muttered.

The living room was in shambles—sofa cushions slashed, the foam filling all over the floor. Photos and paintings had been tossed to the floor, several holes punched into the walls and the ceiling. Several of the paintings had been slashed.

"Stop," she said, grabbing Gabe's arm when he started toward the mess.

"Don't touch anything," Burke added.

Gabe froze, a muscle twitching in his cheek, his jaw clenched hard. "Oh my God," he whispered. "What . . . ?" He turned to her, his expression full of pain. "Why?"

Molly's heart hurt for him, but she had to focus on this new viola-tion. "Someone was looking for something. I'm betting that they came back when they didn't find what they were looking for on your dad's phone."

"Safe bet," Burke growled. He gently pushed ahead, searching room to room while Molly stood with Gabe. She took his hand again, but this time he didn't squeeze. He just stared around him, shell-shocked.

She got that, too.

"I want them to pay," Gabe whispered.

"They will."

He swallowed audibly, his voice still raspy and faint. "It wasn't enough that they killed him. They came back . . . and did this."

"I know. I'm sorry, Gabe."

He nodded once. "You'll find them?"

"I will do everything in my power."

"Thank you." He looked away, but not before she saw the tear that rolled down his cheek. "My mother painted those." He laughed, but it sounded more like a sob. "She was an awful artist, but Dad loved them. I should have taken them with me."

That they'd slashed the paintings was a definite "fuck you." They hadn't needed to do that. This was cruelty, plain and simple. This was *personal*.

Whoever had come back and done this had been angry and frus-trated and full of hate. Which would hopefully be useful in tracking them down.

Whoever had come back and done this might have been the police, so calling 911 wasn't an option, just like it hadn't been when tonight's intruder had tried to poison Shoe.

At least she knew the answer to what they'd planned to do with the alarm. They'd entered Rocky's house without setting it off. Almost cer-tainly they knew the code.

Which meant that, at the very least, they knew enough to guess that it was the late Mrs. Hebert's birthday. Again, personal.

Burke reappeared, expression grim. "They tossed his office, his bedroom, and the kitchen. Papers are everywhere in the office and the kitchen is a mess. Flour and sugar and spices on the floor." His shoulders sagged. "Dirt, too. They yanked out all the herbs in the window planters. I'd been watering them once a week or so, until you decided what you wanted done with them. I thought you might want to use them for your cooking. They were fine last week, so this was done recently."

Gabe closed his eyes and drew deep breaths. His lips were tight, and the tears flowed freely. He made no move to dry his face and Molly didn't offer.

Gabe Hebert had earned his tears.

She understood that as well.

"Those were my mother's herbs. She planted them all with her own hands. Dad—" Gabe broke off, choking on a sob. "Dad tended them like they were gold."

"They were gold," Molly said quietly. She exhaled and squared her shoulders. "I'll call Antoine. He's our IT guy, but he's also a forensic investigator," she explained when Gabe looked at her blankly. "We can process the crime scene ourselves, and then call the cops. Do you think André can help us?" she asked Burke.

André Holmes was Antoine's older brother, a captain in the NOPD, and a very good man.

Burke shook his head. "Not his jurisdiction, but maybe he'll know someone we can trust. You call Antoine, I'll start taking photos. I'll call André when we're done." He looked around the devastation, then dragged an undamaged rocking chair from the corner of the room. "Gabe, have a seat. Let us take care of things."

Gabe just stared at the chair. "This was my mom's chair," he said numbly. "I can't."

"She'd want you to be okay." Molly stroked his upper arm, trying to give some comfort and feeling like she was failing completely. How could anyone give comfort in this situation? So she channeled her own father, remembering his words after her mother had died. "Sit in her chair, Gabe, and let her memory hug you."

Gabe shot her a look so full of gratitude that she had trouble holding back her own tears.

Okay, she failed at that, too. Quickly she wiped them away and pulled out her phone. She had work to do. "Antoine? Sorry to call so late. We need you here at Rocky Hebert's house."

6

W HAT'S HAPPENING TO us?" Carlos joked as he toed off his shoes. "We used to be able to stay up all night, but it's not even midnight and I'm beat."

Carlos's words barely registered because, standing at his bedroom window, Xavier's heart was galloping in his chest. The blue car was there again. Sitting under the streetlamp. And there was still someone inside.

"X?"

Xavier jumped when Carlos poked his shoulder. "You're freakin' me out, man," Carlos said, his voice having dropped to a whisper. "Why are you staring out that window?"

Xavier stepped away from his window and leaned against his bedroom wall. "There's a car out there, on the curb. It's been there off and on since we got home—before noon."

Carlos frowned. "So? Your car has been on the curb since before noon, too. Because we parked it there." Then he sucked in a startled breath. "This is what's had you jumpy all the damn day."

Xavier nodded. "There's a guy sitting behind the wheel. Big guy. He's been watching. I don't know why."

Carlos pulled the blinds aside. "He's not there now."

Xavier felt as if he'd been punched. "He was just there. A minute ago." He looked out of the window and squinted into the darkness.

The car was empty.

"Fuck. Oh, fuck fuck fuck."

Carlos grabbed his upper arm. "Let's call 911."

But Xavier knew better. "No, that'll make it worse, even if they get here in time. My mama's not here. I'm a Black man and you're Latino, and we're here in this house alone. Cops'll shoot first and ask questions later."

Carlos grimaced because he knew it to be true. "Then what—?"

A thump made them both jump.

Carlos swallowed. "That came from downstairs," he whispered.

Xavier tried to remember to breathe. He'd practiced this scenario, years ago. When Rocky had first found him. Rocky had told him what to do.

Get out of the house. Run. Call me.

But he couldn't call Rocky, could he? Because the man was dead.

Hands shaking, Xavier reached into the drawer of his nightstand, pulling out the gun he'd hidden behind all the other junk years ago. He checked to make sure it was loaded and flicked off the safety.

Carlos's eyes went wide. "What the *fuck*, man?" he hissed. "Where did that come from?"

"It was my dad's," Xavier said, so quietly that Carlos had to bend closer to hear. "I know how to use it. Mostly."

Carlos paled. "Mostly? You're gonna get us killed."

That might be true. Xavier had a moment of sharp regret that Carlos had been pulled into his mess. He'd known something was wrong. He'd known it. But he hadn't wanted to seem hysterical.

"We need to get out. That noise came from the garage door. So we can't go out the front."

Carlos closed his eyes, visibly fighting panic. "The spare room window?"

Because that was how Xavier had slipped out to meet the guys back in high school. The window in the back of the house opened next to a huge oak tree with a sturdy branch. They could climb down. They'd done it many times before.

"Yeah." Xavier pointed to Carlos's shoes. "Get your shoes and your phone and your wallet. And be quiet."

Carlos shoved his feet into his shoes and squared his shoulders. He gave Xavier a nod, then lifted a finger for him to wait. Quickly, he searched Xavier's closet. When he turned around, he held a baseball bat in one hand and a golf club in the other.

As quietly as possible, they crept to the spare room. But the window creaked when they opened it. The two of them froze, waiting for . . . Xavier wasn't sure what.

Until he heard it.

Footsteps on the stairs. *Oh fuck, oh fuck, oh fuck.*

Adrenaline spiking, Xavier punched the screen hard, popping it from the window frame. Tilting his head to the window, he mouthed, "Go."

Carlos didn't hesitate. He dropped the bat and golf club out of the window and grabbed for the branch, swinging himself to the tree trunk.

When the branch was clear, Xavier threw his leg over the windowsill.

"No," a deep voice growled. "You're not going anywhere."

Xavier grabbed the branch one-handed, as his other hand still held the gun. He was nearly clear of the window when a big white hand grabbed his shirt and yanked.

He didn't let himself think. He swung the gun toward the man and saw that he, too, was armed. Not hesitating, Xavier fired.

Then he jumped to the branch, shimmied a few feet down the trunk, then jumped to the ground where Carlos waited, the bat and the golf club in his hands.

"Are you—"

"I'm fine," Xavier gasped. He was not fine. "Run."

They took off through the garden to the back fence. Luckily it was a normal chain-link fence, only four feet high. Xavier scrambled over it, then turned to hold Carlos's weapons.

Carlos was a little slower, but soon they were both running again. Xavier's pulse pounded in his ears and his breath sawed in and out of his lungs.

He wasn't a runner. He wasn't any kind of an athlete. He was studying to be a doctor, goddammit.

And he might have just killed a man.

Don't think. Just run.

"Where are we running to?" Carlos asked, his breath coming more easily, because Carlos was a runner. Every damn day he ran, and Xavier was kicking himself for not running with him.

"I don't know. Oh God. What if I killed him?"

They'd run across the five acres of land on which Xavier had been raised and were now in their nearest neighbor's yard. They stopped behind her shed, Xavier struggling for breath.

"If you did," Carlos said, panting only a little, the bastard, "then he deserved it. He broke into your house, X. He had a gun, for fuck's sake. We can only assume he was going to try to hurt you. Did he follow us?"

Xavier peeked around the shed, afraid to look. But he forced himself to keep his eyes open and saw no one running toward them. "I might have killed him."

"Then he deserved it," Carlos repeated flatly. "Where are we going?"

"I don't know." Xavier felt a sob rising in his throat and fought it back. "I can't call my mom. She'll call the cops and . . ." He tried to control his breathing. "She can't do that."

Carlos's eyes narrowed. "Why, X? Why is this guy chasing you? Are you in some kind of trouble? Tell me. I'll help you, I promise."

That his best friend immediately offered his help made Xavier want to cry. He owed him the truth. Or as much as he dared to tell.

"I saw something. A long time ago. I didn't think they'd find me." But Rocky had. It made sense that the men Rocky feared could as well. "Maybe it was just a matter of time."

Carlos pressed his lips together, anger snapping in his eyes. "It's that guy, isn't it? That old guy that used to visit you? I knew he was no good."

"No, he *was* good. Look, let's figure out where to go. I'll tell you, but . . . not here. Not now."

Carlos put both the bat and the golf club under one arm and pulled his phone from his jeans pocket. He hit a contact and held the phone to his ear. "Manny? Yeah, it's me. I need your help. But you can't tell anyone. I'm serious, bro."

Xavier let his head fall forward, his pulse beginning to slow as he listened to Carlos's end of the conversation. Manny was Carlos's oldest brother. He and Xavier had never been close, but he was a nice guy. Too nice to be dragged into this mess, too.

Part of Xavier wanted to tell Carlos no. That they'd find another place to hide. Then again, he didn't have a better idea, so he stayed quiet.

Carlos ended the call. "Manny's on his way. He won't ask questions. He won't tell our mama or yours."

"Thank you." Xavier gave in and leaned his head on Carlos's shoulder. "I shouldn't let you do this, but I'm too scared to think right now."

Carlos rubbed the top of Xavier's head fondly. "It'll be okay, X. We'll figure it out."

"No, I'll figure it out, and then I'll get out of your hair. I'm not dragging you into this."

The set of Carlos's jaw said that they'd debate the issue later. "Manny's meeting us on the highway."

Xavier stared at his friend. "That's a mile away."

"I know. But if this guy didn't die, we don't want him to see us driving away with Manny. We'll stick to the shadows and hope we don't step on any snakes."

Xavier shuddered. "Fuck you, Carlos."

Unbelievably, Carlos chuckled. "But now you're not scared of tall, dark, and deadly back there. Come on. You got a little more running in you. I know it."

He set off at a slow jog and Xavier had no choice but to flip the safety back on the gun, shove it into his waistband, and follow. He certainly didn't want to be seen running with a gun in his hand. The cops wouldn't even hesitate before shooting him.

I don't want to die.

Twelve agonizing minutes later, they could see the highway. Just a couple minutes after that, a rusted-out Dodge Charger pulled onto the shoulder and slowed to a stop. Xavier let out a quiet sigh of relief. That was Manny's old junker. Looking both ways, Carlos made a run for it, out of the shadows and into the back seat of the old car.

Xavier followed once again, grateful that Carlos could think fast on his feet. When the door was closed, Manny carefully pulled back onto the main road again.

"I'm not supposed to ask any questions," Manny said, his voice gruff as always. He sounded like he smoked three packs a day, but Xavier didn't think he did. If he did, he'd been smoking like that for as long as Xavier had known Carlos, because he'd always sounded like that. "But what am I looking for? In case we're followed?"

"I don't know," Xavier said. It could be cops, if Rocky's suspicions were correct. "A blue Camry was watching my house. A guy broke in and tried to grab me when we were going out the upstairs window."

Manny glanced up into the rearview. "You don't know why?"

"I . . ." Xavier swallowed. "I'm not sure. I need to make a phone call.

You don't have to put yourself in danger, Manny. If you want to let me out somewhere, that's okay."

Manny made a rude noise. "Don't be stupid, X. You're Carlos's best friend. Of course I'm gonna help you."

"Thank you. My God, thank you."

"Make your call," Manny said kindly.

Xavier took out his phone and blew out a breath. Then reconsidered. "I shouldn't call from my cell phone. Maybe I shouldn't even have my cell phone."

Manny glanced into the rearview mirror again. "Ooookay. Here." He tossed a flip phone over the seat. "It's a burner."

Carlos frowned. "Why do you have a burner phone, Manny?"

"Because my hours at the store got cut, and I can't afford a plan," he said brusquely, like he was embarrassed by the admission. He, along with dozens of others, had been laid off the year before when the factory where he worked had lost a big contract. Now he was working at the gas station's convenience store, and that didn't sound like it was going well, either. Xavier hadn't realized Manny's finances were so tight. "Got that phone at Walmart and I pay as I go. Use it to make your call, Xavier, then take the SIM card out of your phone and power it down."

Xavier stared at Manny's phone for a long moment, his brain abruptly spiraling as his adrenaline began to crash. He'd shot a man. He'd *shot* a *man*.

Oh my God. What if I killed him? What if he's bleeding out in my mama's spare room right now? What if he was a cop? A white cop. Oh my God. What if I killed a white cop?

Goddammit. His hands were shaking so badly that he could barely hold his cell.

Carlos took the phone from his hands. "Name?"

Xavier cleared his throat, but his voice still came out raw. "Lott. Paul Lott."

"There's a 'PL.' No names."

"That's him." Xavier looked at his cell screen, then punched the man's number into Manny's burner phone.

"Hello?" a man answered.

Xavier stuttered, shocked that the man would answer this late. "Mr. Lott? This is Xavier Morrow. I'm—I mean, I was—friends with Rocky Hebert."

A long silence. Then a sigh. "What happened?" he asked, not unkindly.

"Um, I need to reach Gabriel Hebert." There was silence on the other end. "You know," he added nervously. "Rocky's son?"

"What happened, Xavier?" he asked again.

Xavier frowned. It was like he hadn't even asked for Rocky's son. But this was Rocky's lawyer. Rocky had trusted him. So Xavier came clean. "A man broke into my house tonight. Tried to . . . I don't know what he wanted to do, but he'd been watching me all day."

Lott sighed again. "Where are you?"

"Still in Houston. My friend was with me. We ran. We have a ride."

"Someone you trust?"

Carlos was staring at him, wide-eyed. The same expression his best friend had worn for the better part of an hour now. Slowly Carlos nodded, clearly having heard what Lott had asked.

"Yes," Xavier said.

"Hang tight. I'll come and get you."

Xavier's mouth fell open. He hadn't been expecting that. "Y-y-you don't have to do that."

"Oh, I think I do. Text me the address, but not to this number. I have another phone I use for private matters. Can you remember it?"

"Yes." Memory was a skill he worked on, especially because he was going to have to memorize all the bones in the human body for anatomy class.

If he still had a future after this.

God, please don't let that guy have been a cop. Please.

Killing a normal . . . *whatever* that guy had been, that would be bad enough. Killing a cop? That would ruin his life. And Carlos's.

Not gonna let that happen.

"Ready." He committed the new number that Lott gave him to memory. "Thank you."

"You're welcome. If you need to run again, I'll have both phones with me. Call me, whatever time of night or day. Got it?"

"Yes, sir. Okay. Thank you." He ended the call and punched Lott's private number into Manny's phone, preparing for a text. "Manny, can you give me your address?"

Manny was frowning. "Who was that guy?"

Carlos cursed under his breath. "What about no questions? You promised, *mano*."

"You two were running for your lives. Then X calls some mysterious dude and wants to give him my address? Come on, Carlos."

"It's fair," Xavier murmured, then cleared his throat again. "He's a lawyer from New Orleans."

Carlos blinked. "The old man's lawyer?"

Xavier nodded. "I only talked to him once. When he read me Rocky's will."

"On the phone?" Carlos asked.

"Yeah. I've never met him. He sent the inheritance money to a UPS mailbox that Rocky set up for me in Baton Rouge."

That made Carlos scowl, but his next question was interrupted by Manny.

"Who is Rocky?" Manny asked sharply.

Xavier closed his eyes. "He was a good man. Saved my life in Katrina. But I'm not going to tell you any more, so don't ask. If you know, it'll put you in danger, too."

Carlos closed his hand over Xavier's forearm. "*What happened*, X?"

Xavier shook his head. "I've put you in enough danger. If you know, you'll be targeted, too."

"I already am," Carlos hissed. "My backpack with all my books is back at your house. My books have my name in them. He'll come after me, too. And my mama."

"And your brother," Manny added dryly, but his voice shook, and Xavier knew he was rattled, too. Of course he was. Because none of them was stupid.

"I saw a murder," Xavier said. "And that's all I know."

"Holy shit," Carlos breathed. "For real?"

"Yes," Xavier snapped. "I wouldn't lie about that."

"Ooookay," Manny said. "That changes things."

Xavier nodded miserably. "You can let me out anytime."

"For fuck's sake." Manny shook his head. "I'm not letting you out. But I think the lawyer needs to tell us—me and Carlos—how to stay safe, too. Will he do that?"

"I think so." Xavier didn't know for sure.

"I'm going with you," Carlos stated. "No way am I letting you get into a car with some strange man from New Orleans. I might never see you again."

Manny rounded a corner, and Xavier stiffened. "This isn't the way to your apartment."

Manny shrugged. "I'm doing a roundabout route. I want to be sure we're not being followed."

"Fuckin' A, man," Carlos said, sounding impressed.

"You're not the only one who watches those cop shows," his brother said, amused.

Xavier's temper bubbled. "This isn't a game. I could be getting you killed."

"We know it's not a game," Carlos soothed, patting his arm. "It's how we release pressure. We make jokes. You know that."

Xavier did. He really did, but he didn't feel like jokes at the moment. "I don't want you hurt. Either of you. Not on my account."

"Then let's not get caught," Manny said with another shrug. Xavier buried his face in his hands. And started to laugh.

Then he started to cry.

Carlos rubbed his back the rest of the circuitous way to Manny's apartment.

Metairie, Louisiana
MONDAY, JULY 25, 11:30 P.M.

"I think that's it," Gabe said quietly, gathering the last of his father's papers into a neat pile on the floor. He'd managed to move out of his mother's rocking chair, then was hit with a wave of fury so powerful that he'd nearly put another hole in the living room wall.

But he wouldn't dishonor his parents' memory like that.

It was Molly who'd knelt at his feet and put disposable booties over his shoes, then taken him by the hand and led him to his dad's home office, far away from the kitchen where his father's blood still stained the floor. She'd kindly shielded him from even looking into that room as they'd walked.

"We're going to take all the papers with us," she'd told him, giving him a pair of disposable gloves. "Help me gather them."

So he'd redirected all of his fury into picking up every last paper, even the ripped ones. His father had been very organized. Several dozen empty folders had lain strewn over the floor and he'd stacked those as well.

Wearing the gloves, of course. Antoine would dust all the papers for fingerprints tomorrow. No one expected to find anything, but Gabe could hope.

The assholes had tossed poisoned meat to Shoe while he and Molly had been in his house, for God's sake. They couldn't be *too* smart.

He hoped. He was hanging on to that, because if they really were stupid, they'd fuck up and Molly and Burke would catch them.

Then a question broke into the forced calm of his mind. "Why didn't they take the papers?"

She looked up from her own stack. "Good question. I figure they either found what they were looking for and trashed the house because they were assholes or because they wanted you to think it was simple vandalism." She shrugged. "Or because they were looking for something specific and didn't find it. We might not, either, but we're going to go over every damn one of these papers with a fine-tooth comb."

He believed her. He had to. Molly was his tether to sanity at the moment and he was holding on with both hands. "What's the next step?"

"Paying a visit to your father's attorney. Do you know who he is?"

Gabe blinked. "Of course. He read the will the week after Dad died. Paul Lott. He and Dad were friends for years."

"You trust him, then?"

"Yes." He hesitated. "As much as I trust anyone right now."

"Fair enough. We'll start there and then we're going to pay a visit to the one person who threatened your father over one of his old cases."

"Just one? I thought there were three cases."

"There were, but I had one of Burke's other PIs do the background checks while we were waiting at the vet's. I'd have done it myself, but I wasn't about to be distracted in case whoever tried to poison Shoe followed us there."

Because he'd forced her into being both his investigator and his bodyguard. He figured he should let her pick which one, but not right now. Right now, he needed her. "Which is why you called Burke to meet us here? To guard me while you were searching?"

"Exactly. Anyway, two of the three are no longer available to stalk your dad. One is dead, the other's in prison. The third lives in Shreve-port. She's apparently tried to turn over a new leaf. She got sober and does a lot of volunteer work. We'll see."

"Thank you. You're going to ask Dad's lawyer about the trust that Patty mentioned?"

"Exactly," she said again, then patted the papers she'd stacked. "Some of these are bank statements. If the lawyer won't tell us about the trust, there may be something in these."

"All right." Gabe stood up, papers under one arm. "What do we do with these?"

"I'll take them out to my truck, then I'll come back for you. Antoine's nearly done processing the scene and we don't want to be here when Burke calls Captain Holmes's contact in the Jefferson sheriff's office."

Because Metairie was in Jefferson Parish, just west of NOPD's ju-risdiction. "How will Burke explain being here?"

"He'll say that you were here first, saw the mess, and called him. He sent you home because you were very upset, especially after your dog was threatened."

"Okay." He frowned. "Tell me again why we're calling the cops?"

She smiled patiently. "Because we need a record that someone trashed your dad's house. It'll improve our chances of getting a new investigation into his death once we turn up our own evidence."

He nodded. She'd told him that before, but words weren't sinking in properly at this point. "And then? We go back to my place?"

"Yes. Burke will join us after the cops are done here. We'll both sleep at your place tonight. If those assholes show up again, they'll be sorry."

"And he'll be justified in defending us because he's already shown that someone trashed Dad's house looking for something." He could do words. Mostly.

She gave him an encouraging nod. "Right again. One more thing, and you don't have to decide tonight. What do you want to do with your father's truck?"

He flinched. He hadn't wanted to do anything with his father's truck, but he figured he needed to. "Probably donate it. I'll make some calls tomorrow. Dad and Mom supported a youth shelter nearby. I'm sure they'll make good use of it."

"Would you mind if I gave it a once-over tonight? He might have left something in it that you'll want to keep."

"I'll help."

Her smile was kind. "If you're sure. I'll get Burke to cover us."

"I hope Dad didn't leave any food in it. I haven't opened any of the doors or windows yet."

She wrinkled her nose. "I hope not, too. But I've seen worse. Smelled worse, too."

He supposed she had. "Did you see your father's body?" he blurted out before he realized that he was going to ask.

It was her turn to flinch. "Yes. He'd asked me to come to his house that night. Said it was important. I got there just before the cops did. Jake, my brother-in-law, had called them. I was staring down at my father's body when I heard Jake tell them that he'd shot my dad in self-defense. That my dad was trying to . . . hurt Harper. That when he tried to stop Dad, Dad had shot at him. My father was dead, and Jake was telling all these lies . . ." She exhaled quietly. "It would have been hard enough, finding Dad's body like that, but that Jake was telling that horrible lie . . . We proved him wrong, of course. But the memory of finding my father like that? That's the image that stays with me. It's a hard memory."

He nodded. He hadn't seen his father's body in person, and for that he was grateful. "Dad's body had been removed before I got here. But his old boss, that Cresswell piece of shit, he showed me the photo."

Her expression turned murderous. "Motherfucker," she hissed.

Gabe shrugged. "He said it was an accident. Said, 'Oops.'"

Her eyes narrowed. "I hope he was involved. I want to take him down myself."

He believed she would, and that gave him comfort. He pulled a set of keys from his pocket. "These go to Dad's truck."

"Then let's have a look."

A few minutes later, after stowing the papers in a lockbox in her truck, the two of them were searching his father's Ford with flashlights while Burke stood guard.

The bed of his father's truck was completely clean—except for a single, empty jug of bleach. Gabe leaned over the tailgate to retrieve it. "It's not his brand. Dad used Clorox, because that's what Mom always swore by. This is a store brand."

Burke took it from him. "We'll check it out."

Gabe frowned at the jug, new dread piling atop the old because he knew what criminals used bleach for—to get rid of blood. "Why would my dad have bleach in his truck? He has a washer and dryer in his house and there's a full jug of bleach in his laundry room."

"We'll do our damnedest to find out," Burke assured him.

Shoving back the dread, Gabe opened the front passenger door. "We can come back tomorrow when it's daylight," he offered, shining his light into the glove box.

Molly had already checked the back seat and was checking the middle console up front. "If the sheriff's office doesn't take the truck in for an in-depth search," she replied. She made a face when she found the round can of Skoal. "Your dad chewed?"

"Yeah," Gabe said resignedly as he searched through ten years of old car registrations. "My mother hated it, but she loved him and didn't nag him too much. I didn't nag him at all. It was his only remaining vice after he quit drinking. Now I'm wishing I had nagged him. His cancer was in his esophagus."

Her gasp had him looking up in surprise. She'd known where the cancer was. It was in his father's autopsy report.

But she wasn't looking at him. She was staring under the floor mat she'd just pulled up. "Burke?"

"What did you find?" Burke asked, standing behind her, his gaze locked on their surroundings.

"Buried treasure." She straightened enough to show Gabe what she'd found. A tiny little square chip, razor-thin, was pinched between her gloved index finger and thumb.

"Is that a SIM card?" Gabe asked, stunned.

"No way," Burke said, vibrating with excitement.

She grinned, triumphant. "Yes way, boss." Bagging it, she handed it to Burke. "Give it to Antoine?"

Burke grinned back. "You bet. You guys get out of here. Antoine and I can finish checking the truck and then I'll call the sheriff. Call me when you get to Gabe's place, so I know you're safe."

"Will do."

The Garden District, New Orleans, Louisiana
TUESDAY, JULY 26, 12:05 A.M.

Lamont frowned at his phone when Stockman's number popped up. It was about time. He'd been sitting in his study, trying to read briefs, since he and Joelle had returned from dinner.

Joelle had come home drunk, as he'd hoped she would. She'd sleep until well after noon tomorrow and then wake with a hangover. Which meant that she'd be holed up in her room for most of the day.

Those were the only days he got any peace at all.

"Is it done?" he snarled into the phone. It had better be done, so help him God.

For a moment, all he heard was heavy breathing. Then a quiet moan of pain.

"No," came the whispered reply. "I'm shot. It's . . . not good."

He strained his ears, not believing what he'd just heard. "You got shot? By whom, for fuck's sake?"

"That damn kid. Morrow."

For a moment, he could only stare, shocked. "The nerdy kid? Who's always studying? The one who's going to be a doctor? *He* shot you? And you *let* him?"

Stockman grunted, and even through the phone he could hear his right-hand man's displeasure. And probably some pain as well. "I am *shot*." A shuddered exhale. "In the chest. I am *bleeding*."

Which was going to cause a whole host of other problems. "Did you get the kid?"

"No."

Lamont closed his eyes, fury washing over him in slow waves. "Why the hell not?"

Stockman coughed and he thought he heard a faint gurgle. This was bad. They covered up the murders of other people. Lamont had never needed to cover up the murder of one of his trusted men. "He ran. Shot me . . . and ran." Another cough. "Didn't know . . . he had a gun." A ragged inhale. "Not registered."

"Where are you?" he asked icily. He'd need to fetch Stockman, either to get him help or to dispose of his body.

"ER."

Lamont's mouth fell open. "You're *where*? You are *not* going to the ER. They'll call the cops on a gunshot wound."

Another grunt, this one sharper. "Not gonna die for you."

Then you'll die by my hand. He drew a breath, let it out slowly. "I understand. Which hospital?"

"No. Don't . . . trust you."

At least Stockman's brain was still working. "Don't fuck around, Stockman. Tell me where you are."

But the call had ended. Stockman had hung up on him.

He shoved a hand through his hair. "Fuck, fuck, fuck." He needed to think fast.

Crossing his office, he opened his safe and withdrew a file folder. In the folder was a list of names, phone numbers, and locations. He ran his finger down the list, wishing he had the computer skills to make a spreadsheet. It would be easier to search.

But he didn't have the skills and he couldn't trust anyone to type it for him. Not even Ashley, his assistant. She was willing to sleep with her boss, but he didn't think she'd be okay with the darker parts of his job. Plus, computers could be hacked, and this list was worth more than a ton of gold.

Especially in times like this.

Ah. There he is. The name he'd been searching for. *Tyson Whitley, Dallas, Texas.* He dialed the number and waited for the man to pick up.

"Yeah?" It was a wary greeting.

"Do you know who this is, Mr. Whitley?"

Tyson drew a sharp breath. "Yes."

"Good. I'm calling my favor due."

An audible gulp. "How did you find me?"

"You should know by now that I have many resources at my disposal. You are one of them."

A few seconds passed, then Tyson folded. "What d'ya want from me?"

"I want you to go to the hospitals closest to Mont Belvieu, Texas, and search for a gunshot wound victim. Goes by Stockman." Which wasn't Stockman's real name. He wasn't sure if he'd ever known Stockman's real name, actually. And it didn't matter now.

"All right. And when I find him?"

"Kill him."

Tyson sucked in a shocked breath. "What? I ain't no killer."

"You will be if you want to remain a free man. And if you don't want your wife to find out that you sold drugs and guns to middle school children. I can ruin your life faster than you can hang up the phone."

There was a long, long moment of silence during which he wasn't certain if Tyson would comply. But then the man grunted, "Send me a photo in case he's using an alias."

"There's the intelligent man I was looking for," Lamont said mildly. "I'll send you a photo. Once you've finished your task, text me with the words 'It's a beautiful day' then delete all of our messages and the photo from your phone."

"And then we're square?"

"And then we're square." Unless he needed Tyson again, of course. "Text me when you've found him, then again when he's dead."

"Okay. Then you'll leave me alone, right?"

"Of course," he lied, smooth as silk, then ended the call.

One down, one to go. He searched the list for another name, one he'd called before. Cornell Eckert's parents had met with a bloody end and most people thought that Eckert had done it. It was certainly probable, but because Eckert was too smart to leave evidence, he'd never been charged.

Except that one time when he'd left a witness alive. Which hadn't caused Eckert any issues. *Because I made it go away.* Stockman had taken care of the witness, and Eckert had walked away a free man.

Thus, the man owed him big-time and Lamont intended to collect. Eckert was a bounty hunter and a damn good one. He also was a hit man. Sometimes he was both at the same time, when the quarry could be brought in dead or alive.

Like the Houston kid.

Lamont dialed, then waited. Then frowned. The bastard wasn't answering. He'd almost ended the call when the line clicked and a sleepy voice answered, "What?"

"So, you're alive."

A heartbeat of silence. Then, "Fucking hell. I thought we were done."

"Nope. One more."

"That's what you said last time."

"Do you want to go to prison, Mr. Eckert?"

Another beat of silence. "No, you fucking asshole."

It was fair. "I'm so glad. And this time, I'm willing to pay you. Double your normal fee."

"I'm listening," Eckert said, sounding suddenly more upbeat.

"I'm so glad," he repeated dryly. "I need you to find a kid in Houston."

"No way. Uh-uh. I don't kill kids."

"He's twenty-two."

"Oh. All right, then. Give me the details."

"Name's Xavier Morrow. I'll send you his address, but he may not be there. You're cleaning up another operative's mess. Kid saw my other guy coming and took off."

"Where's your other guy?"

"In the hospital. Kid shot him."

"Shit."

"What was that?" Lamont asked coolly. "Don't tell me that we've switched from you getting paid to doing this for free so that your ass doesn't end up in prison."

"Nah, I'm still good. But now I'm gonna need to wear my Kevlar vest. Which sucks, because it's hotter than hell in Houston right now."

"Do what you must. I just want the kid dead. And I want proof that he's dead."

Eckert gave a low whistle. "What'd he do?"

"Not your business."

"Okey-dokey."

Lamont rolled his eyes. It was hard to believe a man who said *okey-dokey* was capable of cold-blooded murder, but such was life. "Text me when you're done."

"I know the code. How will you pay me?"

"Cash."

"I like cash."

"I figured you would. Get to work, Mr. Eckert." Ending the call, he put the list back in his safe and twisted the combination dial, checking to be sure the lock had engaged.

Then he paced for a full minute, worrying that the two men wouldn't come through—Tyson Whitley on killing Stockman or Cornell Eckert on killing Xavier Morrow.

But he hadn't had a choice, really. He needed both Stockman and Xavier gone, and he couldn't get to Houston in time to do it himself. Nor would he. One photo of him so far from home would raise all kinds of speculations and that could spell disaster. Especially right now.

He needed a distraction, and he knew exactly who to call for that. He tapped Ashley's name in his contact list and waited for her to answer.

She did on the second ring, her voice thick with sleep. "It's late, baby. What's wrong?"

"I need you tonight."

He heard the rustle of bedsheets. "What happened?" she asked sweetly.

"It's the Levinson case. It's . . . it's hard." As lies went, this one would be hard to dispute. The Levinson case *was* hard—a woman suing her employer for sexually assaulting her little boy. Levinson was safe, though, thanks to Stockman. Levinson had been a big campaign donor for years. Couldn't let anything happen to him.

"Oh." Ashley was immediately sympathetic. "I understand. Are you coming here?"

"No, I want you to come here."

"Really?"

Her surprise was understandable. He never asked her to come over to his house, because he didn't want Joelle to catch him. But Joelle was passed out drunk, and she'd never know. "Wear the perfume I gave you for our anniversary."

"Oh." Ashley's reply was flat. Disappointed. "The same perfume you gave your wife."

He wasn't aware that she'd picked up on that. "I like the scent," he said simply. "And if you wear it, she won't know you were here. The room will smell like she was here, not you."

"All right," she said in a small voice. "I'll be over as soon as I can."

"Thank you, dear. Wear the teddy I bought for you," he added. "It's your color."

It was also Joelle's color, which was a good thing, because he always bought his wives the same gifts that he gave his mistresses. Kept him from mixing things up.

"I can do that."

He smiled. "Good. I'll see you soon."

7

A RE YOU SURE I can't get you anything else?" Gabe asked, hovering in the kitchen archway.

Molly smiled at him from her seat at the table. "I'll be fine. You gave me sheets and a pillow and a blanket that I'm sure I won't need." The house had fans but no air-conditioning, and it was still hotter than Hades, despite being after midnight. "You head to bed. I'm going to sort through your father's papers and then I'll go to sleep."

But not until Burke arrived. They'd spell each other tonight, so that at least one person was awake in case the would-be dog poisoner returned.

"All right," Gabe said. "There's water in the electric kettle and the tea is—"

"In the drawer next to the sink," she interrupted, as kindly as she could. She needed him out of her field of vision because Gabe Hebert, shirtless and in his pajama bottoms, was wreaking havoc on her concentration. His chest was every bit as nice as she'd thought it would be. He wasn't cut like Burke because he didn't spend hours in the gym every week, but he was broad and muscled, his chest covered with fine red hair that she wanted to pet. He was every inch her fantasy.

She'd bet dollars to beignets that he slept nude, too, the thought of which was even more of a distraction. His pajama bottoms still had the price tag hanging from the waistband, but she was not going to bring that to his attention.

She shouldn't have been looking. Sure, when he was the handsome chef and she was his paying customer it hadn't felt wrong to ogle him a little bit. Or a lot.

But this was different. He was her client, for God's sake.

Unfortunately, that wasn't the deterrent she'd hoped it would be. It was enough, though. She wasn't going to ogle him. Not tonight. She had work to do.

Work he was paying her to do.

Besides, he'd had a series of shocks today and *that* was the nudge she'd needed to look away. She would take care of him until this was over. And then maybe she could ogle him again in good conscience.

"Go to sleep, Gabe. You need to recharge if you're going to keep up with me tomorrow." She softened the command with a wink.

He nodded once. "All right. I'll go to bed now. If you're sure you don't need—"

"Gabe?" She lifted her brows. "Go. To. Bed. Please."

He grimaced. "I'm sorry. I'm . . . nervous."

"You have a right to be. A good night's sleep will help that."

"It's not that. Well, yes, it is that, too, but . . . I haven't had anyone stay over here."

She stared at him. "Ever?"

"No, not ever."

"Not a girlfriend? A friend-friend? Not even Patty?"

He laughed, some of the tension leaving his face. "Patty demands A/C. She says she can't sleep in this heat." His laughter faded. "And I've been busy with the restaurant."

Molly put down the pen she held. He needed to talk right now, it would seem. So she'd listen. "No girlfriends, huh?"

"None that stuck around long enough." He leaned his shoulder into the doorframe, loosely crossing his arms over his chest. "They all thought that dating a TV celebrity chef would be cool, I guess."

"But the hours are harsh on a relationship."

"Yeah." He exhaled quietly. "My father kept telling me to slow down, that life was too short to work all the time. I didn't listen. And now he's gone."

Any lingering desire to ogle him faded at the pain in his voice. She understood that pain. Had felt it herself. "So often we don't listen," she murmured, thinking of her own life before that night that her brother-in-law had murdered her father. "I was busy working for the longest time. Working my way up the ladder at the SBI."

"State Bureau of Investigation," he said with a nod. "And then?"

"And then my father was gone. He'd asked me to come over that night. And I was on my way, but I was late."

His face fell as comprehension filled his eyes. "Oh, Molly. I'm sorry."

Her chest hurt and she realized she'd pressed the heel of her hand to her sternum to alleviate the pressure. Carefully she folded her hands on the table because they trembled. "Thank you. I had one more lead to follow. One more phone call to make. And so I left Raleigh later than I'd planned that night. Later than I'd promised. Dad must have decided to approach Jake on his own. Or maybe Jake made his move and Dad couldn't wait any longer."

"You blame yourself."

She mustered a smile. "Of course I do. For that and for being too busy to notice what my father had—that Harper had changed. She'd withdrawn. She was wetting the bed, throwing tantrums when she never had before. All the signs that something was wrong."

"How often did you see her?"

"Every other weekend or so. I'd started out with the SBI in Charlotte, but got transferred to the Raleigh office after a year, so my apartment was there. Chelsea and Harper—and Jake—still lived in the farmhouse with Dad. Jake liked not having to pay rent. Said he was saving for their own place, but we found out later that he'd been gambling. Chelsea didn't fight him over his being gone all the time because he was abusive to her, too. I don't know if Dad knew that. I didn't, not until it was too late to help her."

Gabe hesitated. "Did your niece see what happened? The night her father died? Or her grandfather?"

"No to both. That might be the only thing we had to be grateful about. Dad had her sleeping in another room that night. Pitched a pup tent and told her that she could 'camp out.' She heard the shot, but she didn't see anything. And then, when Jake came after Chelsea—and I shot him—she was in the bedroom. But she heard that, too, and the arguing that happened beforehand." She sighed. "She said she was glad her father was dead. That she'd wished she could kill him herself, but that she was too little."

Gabe's face constricted in a combination of anger and sympathy. "I can understand her point of view."

"So can I. It still haunts me, though."

"Why didn't your father tell you what he suspected about your brother-in-law?"

"I don't know. Maybe he tried. I wasn't mentally with them, even when I was physically there."

"Always thinking about your job?"

"Yep. And I have so many regrets, but I can't change the past. I can only be there for Chelsea and Harper now. Working for Burke allows me to set my own schedule most of the time."

He frowned. "I'm keeping you from your family. I should have allowed Burke to assign someone else to this job."

"No, you shouldn't have. Burke put Lucien on guard duty at our apartment tonight."

"I met him earlier today. He seems like a good guy."

"He is. And I'm there with them six nights out of seven. Sometimes more often. I think they need a break from me every now and again. It's hard not to hover over Harper, but we're getting better. My sister had a job interview today and it went really well."

He smiled. "I heard you talking to her. I'm glad for her. Sounds like she's getting her life on track."

Molly had called several times that day to check up on her sister and niece, until Chelsea had basically told her to stop. Kind of like Molly had told Gabe to stop a few minutes before. "She is. She's finally able to leave Harper with a sitter for a few hours at a time. The first time was rough, even though it was our office manager's daughter. We knew Louisa and we trust her, but it took Harper a while to trust, and she was the most important person in the situation. But it's better now. We all can take a little time for ourselves."

"Did you have plans with Harper this week? Am I keeping you from anything important?"

"We ride a few times a week."

"On Ginger and Shelley, right? Rescue mustang and a quarter horse."

She smiled up at him. "Right. I'm surprised you remembered. That was kind of a stressful few moments there in the truck." As she'd managed to break away from the unmarked NOPD car that had been following them. She hadn't told him that their tail had been NOPD. Only Burke and his team knew. No reason to make Gabe even more agitated.

He stared at her for a long moment, his expression suddenly unreadable, and she wondered if he could see the truth on her face. She didn't think so, but . . . "You handled it well," he said.

"I was in the military. You learned fast to handle things well. But I've always managed calm in a crisis, ever since Chelsea and I were kids." She shrugged, growing uneasy under his unfaltering gaze. "I'm the big sister. Kind of goes with the territory."

"I was impressed," he said gruffly. "And I'm sorry I didn't trust you from the start."

"You didn't know me. It's fine, Gabe. Really. I've already forgotten it."

"I haven't. I won't. Thank you, Molly."

She expected him to turn for his room, but he didn't. He didn't look tired anymore, either. So she picked up her pen and gestured to the empty chair beside her. "You want to help me go through these papers?"

His shoulders sagged, his relief clear. "Yes. Please. I don't want to close my eyes right now."

"I get it. But . . ." Desire had returned, making her cheeks heat. "Maybe put on a shirt first, though?"

He grinned suddenly, the effect on his face breathtaking. "Why?"

She rolled her eyes, because his chest had puffed out in pride. "Just do it, Gabe."

He saluted crisply. "Yes, ma'am. I'll be right back."

He disappeared, and she called after him, "Cut the price tag off your sleep pants."

His laugh rolled through the house. "Yes, ma'am."

The Garden District, New Orleans, Louisiana
TUESDAY, JULY 26, 4:45 A.M.

Lamont rarely smoked at home because Joelle didn't like it and it was easier to simply smoke on breaks at work than to listen to her bitch. He was afraid of what he'd do to her one day. She'd bitch and he'd just be done and then he'd slap her or maybe even strangle her.

It was a nice fantasy. But one that would ruin his plans for the future if he ever acted on it.

But Joelle was sleeping off last night's bender, so he lit up and in-haled, exhaling with a contented sigh.

Beside him in bed, Ashley still slept. She'd tuckered herself right out. She was a flexible little thing on an average night, but tonight had been exemplary because she'd been very horny. Something that Joelle wasn't. Ever. Well, not since she'd married him. Beforehand, she'd been every bit as interested and willing as Ashley.

It was an interview, he knew. His mistresses were usually his office administrators who wanted to be his next wife. They'd throw them-selves at him, usually growing sullen and disinterested when he didn't immediately divorce his wife and marry them. The ones who hung on the longest, who showed their loyalty, were the ones he'd weigh against the bother of getting rid of his current wife.

Ashley was getting close. Were the timing right, he'd have gotten rid of Joelle a long time ago. But people were watching him, he knew. And while being married several times wasn't a political dealbreaker, being under investigation for murder certainly was.

So he was biding his time. If Ashley stuck around long enough, he'd marry her once Joelle was history. He'd have to wait and see.

He'd never fucked Ashley here before. In his home. He knew she'd take that as a positive sign, but he couldn't help that. It wasn't like they were in his bed. He wasn't stupid, after all. He kept a bed in the room adjoining his home office, for nights when he worked too late. Or that was his excuse to Joelle. Lately, he just didn't want to share a bed with her.

He reached to his nightstand to tap his cigarette over the ashtray. It was antique decorative glassware and one of Joelle's favorite pieces, so he used it as an ashtray whenever he could. It was petty, but he didn't care. He brought the cigarette back to his lips and checked his cell phone, hoping for a text from either Tyson Whitley or Cornell Eckert.

There were none.

He tried not to be too anxious. Whitley lived in Dallas and even if he'd left the instant Lamont had ended their call, he'd only be arriving in Houston about now. And Eckert was a finicky motherfucker. He'd contact Lamont when he was good and ready and not before.

If Eckert failed in killing Xavier . . .

Well, he wasn't going to worry about that right now. He was going to wake Ashley up, have one more round of sex, then send her on her way.

He had a breakfast meeting with the DA.

Mont Belvieu, Houston, Texas
TUESDAY, JULY 26, 7:05 A.M.

"He's here," Manny said with a yawn. He handed his burner phone over the seat to Xavier, who sat with Carlos in the back seat. They were parked at the H-E-B grocery store near Manny's place, Manny not wanting Rocky's lawyer to have his home address. Which was totally fair and very smart. They'd arrived at H-E-B an hour ago, wanting to avoid any possibility of being late.

Plus, none of them had really been sleeping anyway. They'd crashed at Manny's apartment for a few hours, but Xavier hadn't closed his eyes. He kept thinking about the man he'd shot. Was he alive? Dead?

Would he come back?

And what about his mother? She couldn't go home, either. There might be a dead man in her spare bedroom. If the man was still alive, he might come after his mom.

He hadn't called her yet, because she was safe with her best friend Willa Mae in the city, hopefully still pleasantly buzzed from all the wine the women had consumed at book club. But he'd have to call her soon.

He dreaded it. Because she'd dreaded this for years.

Both of their worst nightmares had come true.

Gingerly, he took the flip phone from Manny, part of him wishing that Rocky Hebert had never found him all those years ago. If the man had stayed away, he might still be safe.

Then again, if the man had stayed away, Xavier would have been unaware that there was any danger. He would have been a lamb being led to slaughter.

He forced himself to focus on Manny's phone screen. The text from Paul Lott was simple. *Here. Where r u?*

With friends. Which is your car?

The reply was immediate. *White SUV. BMW. Parked under lamp-post, C1.*

On my way.

"He's in the white Beemer SUV over there." Xavier pointed to the sign for the C1 section of the H-E-B parking lot. It was a popular place and lots of people came and went. Way better than waiting somewhere isolated.

"You ready, *cuate?*" Carlos murmured.

Xavier's throat grew tight at the nickname. *Some brother I am, dragging Carlos into this.* "No. But Lott came like he promised. Hopefully he'll be able to help. Or at least give me legal advice."

Carlos rolled his head, making his neck crack. His friend hadn't slept much, either. "Let's go, then. Manny, you gonna keep watch?"

"Absolutely. And do not get in his car until I meet him. Got it?"

Again, totally fair and very smart. "Got it," Xavier promised. Because this wasn't Carlos's problem, and he didn't want his best friend to be hurt. Or worse.

Manny started his old junker, the engine coughing and wheezing and knocking before it finally turned over.

They rolled to a stop next to the white BMW and Xavier held his breath while a middle-aged white man exited the vehicle, standing tall, if tired.

"That must be him," Xavier whispered.

Carlos got out first. "Mr. Lott? Can I see your ID?"

Manny snorted. "He should be a cop instead of an engineer."

Xavier smiled weakly. "He really should. Thanks, Manny. For everything."

"No problem. Let's go meet your pal."

Xavier got out on wobbly legs. He had to hold on to the car door for a moment, until he could stand on his own.

Carlos turned to him. "His ID matches. I took a picture of it."

I love you, man. And he did. He couldn't have asked for a better best-friend-slash-brother than Carlos Hernandez. Swallowing hard, he nodded at the lawyer. "Mr. Lott. Thank you for coming."

"You're welcome. You've had a rough night."

Xavier had to swallow again. "Yes, sir."

"Are you calling the cops?" Carlos asked abruptly.

Lott smiled. "Nope. I'm going to take you somewhere safe."

Xavier shook his head. "I can't just leave. My mom's here. She wasn't at home last night, but she'll go home later today and see . . ." He trailed off, because he wasn't sure what his mother would see. Blood? A dead body? "What if the guy's still there? Alive? Waiting for her?"

Mr. Lott's brows shot up. "Alive? What did you do?"

Xavier glanced at Carlos, then back at Mr. Lott. "I'm not sure."

Lott frowned, but nodded. "All right, then. We'll go by your house and check. If he's still there in any capacity, we'll call the cops on an intruder. If not, you can pack a bag. And then we'll go talk to your mother."

Carlos relaxed. "That sounds like a good plan. I like that his mama is in the loop."

Xavier nodded. "Me, too. Who was that guy, Mr. Lott? What does he want with me?"

Although Xavier already knew the answer to the second question. *He wants to kill me.*

"I don't know who he was," Mr. Lott answered, and he seemed sincere. "But you know why he wants you."

"Because he saw a murder," Carlos whispered.

Mr. Lott met Xavier's gaze, steady and kind. "It's all right, son. We'll figure this out. You were important to Rocky, and he was like a brother to me."

Carlos put his arm around Xavier's shoulders. "Where he goes, I go. He's like a brother to me, too."

Mr. Lott gave them a nod. "I would be surprised if you didn't. How would you like to do this, Xavier? We can go to your house first or talk to your mother first. Your call."

"My house first. I need to know what to tell my mama to expect."

Manny spoke up. "Is it really safe to go to Xavier's place? What if that guy is still there and he's alive? He tried to kill these guys. He's not going to just give up."

Xavier gave Manny a grateful look. "I've got a—" He stopped himself before he said *gun*. Not that it was a huge deal to be carrying in Texas. Texans didn't even need a license to carry anymore, but he didn't want to announce his gun to the whole world. "I'm prepared."

Manny's jaw tightened. "I don't know about this, X."

"I'm prepared as well," the lawyer said quietly. "Would you prefer he call the cops?"

Manny blew out a breath. "No, sir. But I still don't like this. At all."

Carlos looked undecided. "We stay together."

"Together," Xavier echoed, praying that he was doing the right thing.

Mid-City, New Orleans, Louisiana
TUESDAY, JULY 26, 7:15 A.M.

Coffee. Molly had made coffee, bless her.

Gabe opened his eyes to darkness, as he did every day, thanks to the miracle of room-darkening window shades. He normally didn't get home from the Choux until two in the morning and had learned early on that the east-facing window in his bedroom was not his friend.

But coffee *was* his friend, especially at—He squinted at the clock on his nightstand. *Shit.* Seven a.m.? He never woke up at seven a.m.

You've never hired a PI to investigate your father's murder, either. He sat up in bed, scrubbing his palms over his face, trying to wake up. He'd gone to sleep sometime around three, unable to keep his eyes open another moment longer. But Molly had still been working then, still organizing his father's papers.

He wondered if she'd gone to sleep at all.

Of course, it could be Burke making the coffee. He still hadn't arrived as of three a.m., staying at his father's house to make sure the sheriffs did their jobs correctly. But Burke hadn't expected to find any prints. If the intruders had been smart enough to fake his father's suicide, they probably had worn gloves.

Still, one could hope.

Gabe pulled on the sleep pants from the night before—sans price tag—and made his way to the kitchen, but stopped just shy of the archway when he heard worry in Burke's voice.

"Are you *sure*?" Burke asked insistently.

"Am I sure that Rocky was making regular payments to someone for at least the past six years?" Molly asked. "Yes."

What the hell? No way. Gabe took another step, then froze.

"Am I sure that it was a woman in Houston?" Molly went on. "Pretty sure, yes. Do I think that Rocky was keeping a woman there? I don't know the answer to that."

No. Gabe shook his head hard, unwilling to accept that his father had kept a secret like that from him.

He didn't tell you he had cancer.

That's different.

Is it? And maybe he thought you'd object.

But six years . . . *Mom was still alive six years ago.*

"No!" The word burst from him as he barreled into the kitchen. "You're wrong. My father wouldn't have done that to my mom."

Burke and Molly sat at the table, Molly at the head and Burke on her right. She went very still at his outburst, a piece of paper in her gloved hand. "Good morning, Gabe."

"No, it's *not* a good morning," he hissed. "You're making accusations against my father. You're wrong. Burke, tell her that she's wrong."

Burke pinched the bridge of his nose. "I've only had two hours' sleep, Gabe. I'm tired and cranky and I need some of that coffee before I can think clearly. Have a cup with me while we let Molly explain what she found."

Gabe shook his head. "Not if she's going to say that my father had a mistress. While my mother was still alive and dying from cancer. Because that *didn't happen.*"

Molly set the piece of paper on the table. "I didn't say that," she said calmly.

So calmly that he wanted to scream. Until he saw the way her hand trembled.

And then he remembered how she'd comforted him the night before when he'd seen the destruction in his father's house. He remembered her compassion.

She was just doing her job. *That I asked her to do.*

So, he pulled out the chair on her left and sat, turning to face her. "What is it that you think you've found?"

She exhaled quietly, a flicker of relief in her blue-green eyes. Angling an inch-high stack of papers his way, she showed him the top sheet. "Automated deductions, same amount every month. This is the earliest that I've found, from six years ago. He kept records going back seven years, and there was no such activity during the first year of records, so I think it's safe to assume it started six years ago."

Gabe frowned. "Three hundred and fifty dollars," he read. "Where did it go?"

"To John Alan Industries." She pointed her gloved finger at the transaction.

"John Alan?" Gabe flinched, his gut twisting as a harsh shiver shook him. "That's . . . impossible."

But that was the name on the paper.

"Why?" Molly asked softly. "Why is it impossible?"

Gabe started to speak, but the word came out a croak. He cleared his throat. "My mother got pregnant when I was twenty. She was forty-four."

Molly's brows furrowed, her lips moving silently as she counted. "She was older than your father, then."

"Yes, by five years."

Molly's expression grew sad. "She lost the baby?"

He nodded. "I didn't even know she was pregnant until she lost the baby. She was waiting until she was out of her first trimester to tell anyone." His jaw clenched. "Because chances of miscarriage were higher due to her age. Turns out she was right. I remember the night it happened. We were staying with Patty's parents because our house was flooded."

Molly's startled gaze flew up to meet his. "Oh. During Katrina?"

He nodded again. "Dad was working. Every cop who could work back then, did. We couldn't take Mom to the hospital because so many of the roads were closed. She wouldn't even let me call my father. Said that there wasn't anything he could do, and he'd just worry. She didn't want him to be distracted during the storm and its aftermath. There was no . . . Well, there wasn't a body to bury. She just sat in one of my aunt's rocking chairs and cried. When Dad finally joined us after working rescue, he was devastated by all he'd seen. I'd never seen him look like that before then. But he knew, as soon as he saw Mom's face, that something was wrong. She had to tell him and he . . . broke. I'd never seen my dad cry before that night."

Molly's eyes grew shiny. "I'm sorry."

"Thank you. I felt so helpless. Nothing I could do but sit and watch and hug them."

"I think that's all you can do in those circumstances," she murmured.

"They named the child John Alan," Burke said gruffly.

Gabe stared at him. "He told you?"

"Long time ago," Burke confirmed. "We were on a stakeout, had been sitting in the car for hours. And the conversation happened to turn that direction. He told me, but I think he immediately wished he hadn't. I never would have mentioned it to a soul. I'd forgotten about it, in fact. Until just now."

Molly stared at the bank record. "So, he paid three hundred fifty dollars a month for six years to a company named after his dead son? But why?"

"Why did you say it was a woman?" Gabe asked, trying to keep the anger from his voice. She'd jumped to a conclusion that just wasn't true. Something was odd, but he'd never believe that his father had a woman on the side. Not when his mom had still been alive. Six years ago, she'd been battling cancer. Going to chemo. There was no way his father had cheated. *Never.*

That was not who Rocky Hebert had been.

"Because there's a check to a Cicely Morrow, same amount." She shuffled papers, bringing one from the bottom of the pile to the top. "It was written one month before the payments started to John Alan."

"His second son," Burke said softly.

Gabe's fists were clenched before he realized it. Flattening his palms on the table, he made himself breathe. "What are you insinuating, Burke?"

"I don't know." He met Gabe's gaze, his turbulent but mostly sad. "The man I knew wouldn't have had a secret child."

"No," Gabe snapped. "He wouldn't have."

"But it means something," Molly insisted. "These payments continue up until his death. They're the only mysterious thing in all of his bank records."

She was right about that, at least. "Who is Cicely Morrow?" he asked.

"I don't know a hundred percent for certain yet. But there is a Cicely Morrow who lives in Houston and the day he wrote the first check, he bought gas in Houston with his bank card. I ran a background check on her and she's a nurse at one of the Houston hospitals." She turned her laptop so that he could see the screen. "This is a photo of her, taken for a newspaper story about the hospital. She lives in Mont Belvieu, a Houston suburb."

A lovely Black woman was smiling at whoever had taken her picture. "I don't know her," he whispered. But his father clearly had. "Why?"

"That's one of the things we need to find out," Molly said gently. "Don't jump to a conclusion, Gabe. Your father gave money to a lot of different charities. Maybe she runs one."

He looked up at her, hopeful. "He did?"

Her smile was as gentle as her voice had been. "He really did." She pulled out several sheets of paper, lining them up, side by side. "Boys & Girls Clubs of America, Meals on Wheels, the American Cancer Society. Just to name a few. He gave away a lot of money. He was a very generous man."

Gabe found that he could smile, too. "He always said he was gonna give it all away when he died because I didn't need it, so I shouldn't count on an inheritance." He took the tissue she pressed into his hand, surprised. Then realized he'd been crying, so he wiped his face. "Some people would have thought that made him a bad person, y'know, not leaving me anything, but I knew different. There wasn't a lot left, other than his house and the truck. He really had given it all away, according to his lawyer."

"The same one you mentioned last night?" she asked. "Paul Lott?"

"The same. Dad always said his life insurance through NOPD

would go to me so that I could pay for his funeral, but that didn't happen because of the 'suicide.'" He used air quotes, the very word making him angry all over again. "Whatever someone was looking for when they trashed his house, it wasn't money, because there wasn't any."

"Maybe Mr. Lott can help us," Molly said, straightening all the papers back into a tidy stack. "I'd planned to call his office at nine."

It suddenly occurred to him that she'd organized and combed through a shit ton of papers in the hours that he'd been asleep. "Have you slept at all?"

"No, but I'm okay. I'll catch a short nap now and set my alarm for nine. Then we can pay Mr. Lott a visit." She cast a quick glance at Burke. "You okay to stay awake for an hour and a half or so?"

"Now that I can have coffee? Yes." Burke made a shooing gesture. "Go and sleep. We'll be fine."

She slid the stack of papers into a large envelope with the Burke Investigations logo printed on the top corner, then peeled off the gloves. "I think I'll take you up on the offer of the spare bedroom. If I sleep through my alarm, wake me up."

She walked as far as the archway before turning. "And Shoe is okay. I called the vet at six to check on him. He's snoring like a log and all of his bloodwork came back normal."

Gratitude mixed with shame. "I'm sorry I snapped at you."

She just smiled. "It's stressful, Gabe. And I know why you were upset. I'd have been the same way if someone told me that my father had been paying a strange woman for years. We'll figure this out. I promise."

Then she was gone. A few seconds later, he heard the creak of the bifold doors to her room.

Burke moved the envelope to his briefcase, then poured Gabe a cup of coffee. "Cream and sugar?"

"Please and thank you."

Burke served them both, then took the seat where Molly had been sitting. "For what it's worth, I don't believe your father cheated on your mother."

Relief left him feeling lighter. "Thank you. I don't think I realized how much I needed to hear that."

Burke sighed. "But this whole thing has me stumped."

"Maybe the Morrow woman runs a charity, like Molly said."

Burke shook his head. "Maybe, but I don't think so. How would she have known to name a charity after your brother? At a minimum, Rocky and this Cicely Morrow were close enough that she knew of John Alan."

"Whose name is the company in?"

Burke opened his own laptop. "John Alan Industries LLC lists . . . Okay. It's owned by another corporation. And that corporation is owned by . . ." He exhaled impatiently. "Another corporation." He was quiet for a few minutes, typing and scowling, then typing some more. Finally, he leaned back in his seat. "Your father buried this deep. I finally have an actual name. Gigi Gauthier."

Gabe blinked. "Aunt Gigi?"

Burke perked up. "You have an aunt Gigi?"

"My mother's sister. She lives in Montreal. That's where Mom was born and raised."

"Montreal's not the address provided. The address on Gigi's LLC is in Baton Rouge. Let me do a search . . ." He looked up and shrugged. "It's a box in a UPS store."

Gabe rubbed his temples. "Of course it is. Let me get my phone. We can call her." He took a bracing gulp of coffee before rising. "Not bad. Not as good as my coffee, but not bad."

"Thank you," Burke said mildly.

Gabe got his phone, then paused outside of the spare room on his way back to the kitchen. He cocked his head, listening. Then nodded when he heard a soft snore.

Good. She was getting some rest.

He found Burke peering into the fridge. "Can I help you find something?" Gabe asked.

Burke looked over his shoulder. "I'm starving."

Gabe held up his phone. "Can we call my aunt Gigi first?"

Burke heaved a put-upon sigh. "I suppose I'll survive. Maybe."

Gabe rolled his eyes. "Maybe, indeed." He found Gigi's name in his favorites list, called her, and put it on speaker. Then rolled his eyes again when he got her voice mail greeting.

"*Si vous entendez ce message, ça veux dire que je fais quelques chose de plus intéressant que de vous parler. Laisser un message. Je pourrais vous rappeler.*"

"*Salut, Tante* Gigi," Gabe said. "*Rappelle-moi, s'il te plaît. C'est très important.*" He ended the call and shook his head. "My aunt is a character, but I love her."

"My French is rusty. Did she say she was doing something more interesting than talking to you?"

"She did, indeed." He motioned Burke away from the open refrigerator. "Then she said to leave her a message and 'I might call you back.'"

Burke chuckled. "I like her already."

"Most people do. She taught me how to make pâte à choux when I was ten. I still use that pastry recipe for my cream puffs at the Choux. That—and the fact that my dad called my mom his *petit chou*—is how we named the restaurant."

"Mmmm. I love those cream puffs. Yours are some of the best I've ever eaten."

"I'll tell her that you said so."

Burke leaned against the counter as Gabe pulled out eggs, ham, and vegetables for omelets. "I didn't realize that your mother came from Montreal."

"She did. She'd come to New Orleans for Mardi Gras and asked a 'handsome police officer' for directions. Her English was not so good, and she was so frustrated that she started to cry. But then he spoke French to her, helped her find what she was looking for, then asked her out for dinner. She said that his French was so heavily Cajun that she had trouble understanding him. But they managed, apparently. It was love at first sight."

"Your dad told me that she'd come for Mardi Gras and stayed for love. He loved her so much, Gabe. He was destroyed when she died. I can't believe that there was ever another woman for him, as long as she was breathing."

"I know." Gabe focused on whipping the eggs for the omelets. Keeping his hands busy had always been his go-to method for handling stress. "I know that there's another explanation."

"And we won't rest until we find it."

And then Gabe remembered the question he hadn't yet asked. *Second son.* Gabe flinched, then stared at the omelet pan. "Does Cicely Morrow have a son? Molly didn't say."

Burke hesitated. "I don't know, and that's the truth. Let me finish my coffee and I'll look up the woman myself."

8

I DON'T LIKE THIS," Manny said for the tenth time as he pulled up to the curb in front of Xavier's house, close behind Mr. Lott's white BMW.

The blue Camry was gone.

"I know," Xavier said, hearing the strain in his own voice. "But do you have a better idea?"

"No," Manny admitted. "I don't like that he ignored you when you asked for Rocky's son."

"I agree," Xavier said. "But if you don't have a better idea, I'm gonna go with this one."

Manny growled softly. "I'm going in with you." Reaching under his seat, he pulled out a handgun and a knife.

Carlos stared at the weapons. "Jesus, Manny! Why do you have a gun?"

"Because I work the night shift at a convenience store that gets robbed at least once a month. Don't worry. I've done the safety course and I practice once a week. I know how to shoot."

"Does Mom know?"

Manny shot him a look. "No. And don't tell her. She worries enough about me as it is." He opened his car door. "Are we doing this or not?"

Xavier drew a steadying breath and opened his door, looking around for . . . he wasn't sure what. His house looked the same. The abandoned house next door looked the same. Everything sounded the same. A few birds. The dog that belonged to the lady who lived behind their property was barking, just like normal.

Then he saw the drops on the driveway. Brown. Dried.

Blood.

I hit him. But if he left on his own, I didn't kill him.

At least there was that.

Mr. Lott got out of his SUV and started up the driveway, his steps quick. When he got to the garage door, he turned and gave them an impatient come-here gesture. "Don't stand out in the open like that," he chided.

They obeyed, running up the driveway to meet him. His impatience melted away, replaced with concern. "Are you boys all right?"

Xavier shrugged. "As all right as we can be, I guess."

Mr. Lott looked around. "I didn't expect you to live in such an isolated area. Do you have neighbors?"

"No, sir." Xavier pointed at the house next door with the For Sale sign in the front yard. "They moved out a year ago." He pointed to the next-closest house, at the end of the street. "They go north for the summer. Too hot down here for them."

"So no one was around to hear your shot?"

Manny snarled. "How do you know Xavier fired?"

Mr. Lott rolled his eyes. "Because he said he was 'prepared' and that he wasn't sure if the guy was still alive. I connected the dots." He turned to Xavier. "Did anyone hear your shot?"

"Maybe the lady behind us," Xavier said. "But it was late, and she goes to sleep early. She also takes out her hearing aids at night. She says she'll sleep through the Rapture if it happens when she's asleep."

"Good to know," Mr. Lott murmured. "How did he get into the house?"

"The intruder entered through the side door," Carlos said, all professional. They followed him to the door that went into the laundry room. It was ajar, the frame splintered.

Mr. Lott pulled a pair of gloves from his pocket.

Manny's eyes popped wide. "What the hell? Is this what you meant when you said you were prepared?"

Mr. Lott handed them each a pair of the gloves. "Partially, yes. I came prepared for, hopefully, every eventuality. Suit up, boys."

They obeyed, grimacing as they gloved up. The gloves were made for someone with much smaller hands.

Mr. Lott pushed the door open with one finger. There was more blood on the laundry room floor, but it was smeared, like someone tried to wipe it away then gave up.

"Towels are missing," Xavier said quietly. "I folded them yesterday morning before I met you for breakfast, Carlos. They were still here last night."

"Your intruder has lost some blood," Mr. Lott said, sounding pleased. "We can check the local hospitals later. Your spare room is upstairs?"

Xavier nodded. "First door on the right."

They walked up the stairs, keeping to the far left because the right was where all the blood was. Xavier glanced at Manny, who'd retrieved his handgun from his waistband and now clutched it in a white-knuckled grip.

Xavier patted his pocket, making sure his own gun was still there. But of course it was. It was so heavy that it was dragging his jeans down and so bulky that there was a visible lump under his shirt, even though he wore it untucked.

He wished his father had bought a smaller gun. Although he'd been grateful for it last night.

Especially now that he knew that he hadn't completely killed the bastard. *Who was trying to kill me.*

The spare room looked almost normal. Except for the window that remained open, the curtains fluttering in the morning breeze.

And, of course, except for the pool of blood staining his mother's carpet.

"That's never coming out, is it?" he asked.

"I know a guy who can replace the carpet," Carlos said, patting Xavier's shoulder.

Xavier leaned on Carlos. "I have to call my mom."

"We will," Mr. Lott promised. "I want to check out the rest of the rooms first. He may have left something behind that'll tell us who he was or maybe who sent him."

Xavier just wanted to leave. To walk out the door and call his mother—on Carlos's phone because he'd been too afraid to turn his on.

I just want this to be over.

But he didn't think that was going to happen anytime soon.

"Is this your room, Xavier?" Mr. Lott called from his bedroom doorway.

"Yes. Why? What's wrong?" Xavier hurried to his room, but nothing looked amiss.

"Nothing. It doesn't look like he came in here. Why don't you pack a few things?"

Xavier brushed past him, feeling . . . weird.

But that was to be expected, right?

Of course it was. Everything had been weird since yesterday morning.

At least I wasn't imagining things. Someone really was trying to get me. Maybe they still are.

He opened his drawer, unsurprised to see that Carlos had found his duffel bag. Together they stuffed it full. "Take extra underwear, man," Carlos whispered. "Because if yours are still clean from last night, I'll be amazed."

Xavier snorted a laugh. "Shut up, *pendejo*," he said affectionately. He zipped the duffel and grabbed his backpack. "We're ready, Mr. Lott."

"All right, then. The two of you want to come with me? I'm sure Manny has better things to do."

"Nope," Manny said brusquely. "I'm coming and they're with me."

Mr. Lott's smile didn't dim. "As you wish. Let's go. I'll follow you. We'll let your mother decide what needs to be done about the blood. If she wants to call the police, we'll do that. At a minimum, though, the window should be shut and the door fixed."

"I'll take care of the window," Carlos offered. Shouldering his own backpack, he went to do that, then met them at the stairs and followed them outside.

Mr. Lott got into his BMW, and Xavier, Carlos, and Manny piled into Manny's rusted-out junker.

"I don't like this," Manny said again.

"Something new?" Xavier asked. "Or the same old?"

"He was watching you when you packed your bag. Like . . . I don't know. It was weird."

"Okay." Xavier didn't know what to do about Manny's concerns, but he was listening. "What do you think we should do?"

"I don't know," Manny said grimly. He handed his burner phone over the seat. "Call your mother. Tell her what happened. Let her tell us what she thinks we should do, just like the lawyer said."

"I don't know her phone number," Xavier admitted after staring at the burner's keypad for several seconds.

"I've got it in my phone." Carlos found the number and showed it to him.

"I hope she answers," Xavier muttered. "It's a strange number."

But she did, after only one ring. "Hello? Who is this?" she demanded suspiciously. "If you're calling about my car's warranty, you can go straight to Hades."

Her voice rolled over him, and his eyes filled with tears. "Mom," he said hoarsely.

"Xavier?" Fear filled her voice. "What's wrong? Why are you calling from this number?"

He blinked, sending the tears down his face. "It's . . ." He had to clear his throat. "Mama. Something happened last night. Carlos and I were going to sleep and . . ." His voice broke.

"Xavier? *Xavier!*" his mother shouted.

"What's happening?" another female voice asked. "Is everything okay?"

"I don't know," his mother said frantically. "Xavier?"

Carlos took the phone from his hand and put it on speaker. "Mrs. M? It's Carlos. We're okay."

"Oh my God," she said on a rush of air, her voice tinny coming out of the burner phone's crappy speaker. "What happened?"

"Someone broke into your house," Carlos explained. "And . . . well . . . we got out. Through the window upstairs."

"The one in the spare room?" she asked. "You all used to scare me silly climbing in and out of that window."

"You knew?" Xavier asked.

"Of course she knew," Manny drawled from the front seat. "They always know."

"Who's that?" his mother asked.

"My brother Manny," Carlos told her. "He's driving us. We wanted to meet up with you."

"And we have a visitor," Xavier added. "I called that lawyer."

She went quiet for several heartbeats. "Which lawyer?"

"Mr. Lott. Rocky's lawyer."

Her exhale was audible. "I see. Why did you call him?"

Xavier frowned. "I wanted to get in touch with Rocky's son. Rocky always told me to call Gabriel if I needed help, but I don't know Gabriel's phone number."

"Is Mr. Lott in the car with you?"

"No, ma'am." Xavier exchanged a nervous glance with Carlos. "Why?"

"Is he here? In Houston?"

"Yes. He drove all night to come and get me. But he said that we should talk to you first before we leave for New Orleans, so you don't worry."

His mother barked a laugh that did not sound amused. "I see. Magnanimous of him."

"Mom?" Xavier was confused. "What's going on?"

"I don't know yet. I don't have all the information, because you called a stranger before you called me."

Xavier winced. "I'm sorry, Mom. I was trying to protect you."

She sighed wearily. "I know you were. So tell me what happened exactly, and why you didn't call the police."

Xavier blinked hard, trying to remember all the details. He was so tired.

"Like he said," Carlos butted in, and Xavier was grateful. "We were going to bed and someone broke in. Xavier got his dad's gun—"

"You did what?" she cried.

"Dad's gun," Xavier said, amazed that his voice was steady. "And I didn't call the cops because . . . you know, Mom. Carlos and I were all alone and if they came at all, we'd get blamed."

Another sigh. "You're not wrong about that. I didn't know your father gave you his gun."

"He didn't. I found it after he died."

"He told me that he'd gotten rid of it," she said, her voice so much smaller than normal, and Xavier hated it. She exhaled again and he could picture her straightening her spine. "So, you got your father's gun."

"And I got a ball bat and a golf club," Carlos said.

She laughed, but it was a weak sound. "Carlos, you get cookies for the rest of your life."

"That was my plan," he said cheerfully, then his expression fell. "We couldn't go down the stairs, so we went out the window. But when Xavier started through, the guy grabbed him."

His mother's gasp was muted, like she'd covered her mouth with her hand. "Dear God."

"He's not hurt," Carlos insisted. "Not even a scratch. But . . ."

"I shot him," Xavier blurted. "I shot him, and I dropped from the tree and we ran like hell."

"All right," she said quietly. Too quietly. That was her I'm-freaked-out-and-trying-not-to-be tone. "Is that why you didn't call the police after it was over?"

"Yes, ma'am." Xavier cringed. "I was . . . afraid. I had a gun, and the dude was white. That's all I could see. The white hand grabbing my shirt when I turned around to shoot him."

"But the white guy had a gun, too," Carlos said. "Xavier did what he needed to do."

"All right," she said again. "I understand. So after it was over, you called this lawyer and asked for Gabriel Hebert, but the lawyer decided to come instead and wants to take you back to New Orleans with him. Am I getting it right?"

"*Perfecto*," Carlos said. "But I won't leave him, Mrs. M. I promise."

"Thank you, Carlos," she said sincerely. "To Manny, too."

"No problem, Mrs. M," Manny called. "I'm off work at the store for a few days and got nothin' better to do."

"Okay, this is what I want you to do. I want you to tell him that we're going to meet him at the Waffle House on Wallisville Road. My car will be outside. You still got the keys, Xavier?"

He patted his pocket. Keys were still there, on the key ring he'd made using the angel Rocky had left him. Maybe the angel was watching over them, he thought, then shook his head at himself. "Yes, ma'am. I have the keys to your car."

"Tell the lawyer to meet me inside. I want to talk to him. Alone. While I'm doing so, I want you to park Manny's car and get into mine. When I text you, swing around the side where the bathrooms are. I'll get out of there, meet you, and then we're going to find Gabriel Hebert. The lawyer can follow us back to New Orleans, if he wants to."

"I told you that I didn't like the guy," Manny said. "She doesn't, either."

"No, you said you didn't like the situation," Carlos corrected. "Do you think this guy isn't on the level, Mrs. M?"

"I don't know. He was nice to come all this way, but I had my own conversation with Rocky. He told me to trust no one but Gabriel. And he didn't tell the lawyer where to find you, Xavier. Mr. Lott sent the inheritance information to the UPS box because that was the address that Rocky gave him. If Rocky went to that much trouble to protect your identity and location, I'm going to do the same. If Lott truly is a nice man—which I have no reason to believe he's not—"

"Yet," Manny inserted.

"Yet," she agreed. "If he's a nice man, he won't mind a change in plans."

"Let's take my minivan," her friend said in the background. "What if he's bad news? What if he gets your license plate?"

"I'm not dragging you into this, Willa Mae."

"No, you're not dragging me anywhere. I'm coming with you. My minivan will make the trip better than your car. I just got a tune-up."

Xavier wanted to laugh, but he held it in, only because he knew he'd sound like a maniac. "Mom, are you sure about this?"

"I am. I don't have Gabriel's phone number, but I know where he works."

"At a restaurant," Xavier said. "I turned off my phone, so I can't search for which one."

"Le Petit Choux," she said. "I'll call as soon as I hang up. If I can talk to him now, I will. Call the lawyer. Tell him the Waffle House. I'll see you there."

"My van is a Honda Odyssey," Willa Mae called. "Gray. I'll tell your mama the license plate and she can text to this number. Oh, this *is* exciting. I've got a gun, too, and a carry license. I got it when I was with the prosecutor's office and some punk threatened to kill me. I might even have bullets."

"Oh my Lord," his mother said, not sounding happy about it. "I suppose we'll see you soon. I love you, son."

"Love you, too, Mom." Xavier ended the call, then gave in to the urge to laugh.

And he did sound like a maniac.

Carlos started to laugh. Then Manny joined in. They all sounded like maniacs, which was comforting in a weird way.

When Xavier was able to stop laughing, he was panting. Just in time for Manny's burner to ring. "It's Lott," Xavier said. "I'll tell him where to meet us."

Mid-City, New Orleans, Louisiana
TUESDAY, JULY 26, 9:30 A.M.

"We're fine," Chelsea assured her when Molly called to check in.

Molly stood in Gabe's spare bedroom, staring out the floor-to-ceiling window, wondering if the man who'd come so close to killing Gabe's dog would be back. She'd think not in the daylight, but there'd still been daylight last night when he'd made his move.

She wondered if the attempted dog killer had been the same person who'd trashed Rocky Hebert's house after his death. It was possible. Maybe even probable.

She wondered if she'd made a huge mistake, taking this job and putting Chelsea and Harper in danger. That was possible as well.

But at least not this morning, or so it seemed.

"Lucien stayed all night?" Molly asked. Lucien was one of Burke's trusted employees. Lucien or Val would be the only two that he'd assign to family, because in Burke's mind, Chelsea was his sister, too, and Harper his niece.

"He did. He sat outside our front door whenever he wasn't doing rounds around the building. We're fine, Molly. I swear it. What is this case that you're so afraid for us?"

Molly hesitated, trying to find a way to explain it without breaking confidentiality. "It involves people in positions of power," she hedged. "And I can't say any more than that."

"Got it. I'll worry about you, too, but I know you're careful. Harper knows not to answer the door. She's a little on edge, but nothing like she's been in the past. She likes Lucien."

"She should. He brings her a book every time he sees her. What was it this time?"

"*Charlotte's Web*." Chelsea chuckled. "She's already saying that the farmer and his wife should be more interested in the spider than the stupid pig."

"Because she's smart. Listen, I need to go. I'll call you later today. And if anything weird happens, call Burke." She ended the call, then washed up in the bathroom, which, like all the other rooms in the shotgun house, was surprisingly not claustrophobic, despite its tiny size.

The high ceilings truly added the feeling of space. She'd have to remember that for when she got a place of her own.

Because Chelsea and Harper wouldn't need her forever. Sooner or later, she'd be on her own again. She wasn't sure how to feel about that.

She found Burke sitting at the kitchen table, Gabe at his side. The two were hunched over Burke's laptop.

"What's going on?" Molly asked, making both men startle where they sat.

"We've been looking into Cicely Morrow," Gabe said grimly. "She's got a son."

"Second son," Molly said quietly. John Alan Industries. "But that doesn't mean that your father did anything wrong."

Gabe looked upset. "It's damning, though. Why give this family money all those years if he didn't have a personal connection? They're not a charity. They're a family. They live in a house on a five-acre parcel of land in Mont Belvieu, a suburb east of Houston."

Molly poured herself a cup of coffee and carried it to the table. "What's the son's name?"

Emotion flickered in Gabe's eyes. Definitely some anger, but a lot of grief, too. "Xavier. He just graduated from Rice University. Premed."

Xavier. She remembered Patty had heard Rocky Hebert talking about a trust for "X."

"Kid got accepted to med school at the University of Pennsylvania," Burke added.

"Smart young man," Molly said warily. "That's a good school."

"That's an *expensive* school," Gabe spat. "The kind one needs a trust fund to attend."

Oh my. Gabe had clearly come to a set of conclusions that—if true—were very upsetting. "What about Mr. Morrow?"

"Died of a heart attack seven years ago," Burke said. "He was a doctor, too."

"Medical family," she observed. "What else have you found on Cicely Morrow?"

"Not much." Burke looked frustrated. "Woman is a law-abiding citizen. Not so much as a parking ticket. Same with her son. He was salutatorian of his high school graduating class. Worked part-time during school months for a diner near the campus. Worked summers as a lifeguard."

"Saved some little kid's life a few years ago," Gabe added glumly. "Got a write-up in the local paper. The kid's parents wanted to pay him for saving their child's life. He asked them to donate to a shelter for LGBT youth instead. He seems like a good person."

Which would make it harder for Gabe to hate him. If he had a good reason to. *Still a big if.*

"Gabe." She waited until he met her gaze. "Look, I know this is difficult, but you need to wait until we have the full picture. Your father was a good man, right?"

Gabe swallowed. "I always thought so."

She reached across the table to grip his hand hard. "Then think so a little bit longer." She released his hand, ignoring how right it had felt to hold it. "It's coming up on ten. Maybe your dad's lawyer is in his office by now."

"He's not there," Burke said. "We called already. He told his office manager that he was taking the week off. Family emergency, or so he said."

She lifted her brows. "Or so he said? You don't believe him?"

Burke shrugged. "He doesn't have a family, as close as we can figure. He could have simply used that as an excuse, but the timing sucks for us."

"The timing is interesting, for sure," she murmured. "Gabe, is there anyone that your father might have confided in? Who was the executor of his estate?"

"His attorney, unfortunately." Gabe sighed, his hurt at not being named executor clear on his face. "But there is Aunt Gigi."

"I traced John Alan Industries to Gabe's aunt," Burke explained. "After a little untangling, she shows up as the president, but the address on record is a UPS box in Baton Rouge."

"Oh?" She straightened, feeling a little surge of energy. "I assume you already tried to get in touch with Aunt Gigi, or you would have led with that."

Burke snorted a laugh. "Got her voice mail, so we left a message. Her voice mail says she *might* call us back if she's not doing anything more important."

How rude, she thought, but was glad she didn't voice the words because Gabe's lips turned up, just a smidge.

"She's feisty," he said affectionately. "I think she'd like you all."

She was glad to see that tiny smile. It erased some of the worry lines from his forehead. "I'd love to talk to her, then, when all this is over. But for now, we should drive to Baton Rouge and check the mailbox."

Burke shook his head. "I already checked Rocky's key ring. Nothing that looks like a key to a UPS box."

"Well, shit," she grumbled. "That would have been too easy, I guess. Maybe the lawyer has a key. Has Antoine found anything on the laptop or the SIM card Rocky left in his car?"

"I called Joy at the office." Burke shrugged. "She says that Antoine told her to tell me to leave him the hell alone until he was done. That you 'can't rush the process,' whatever the hell that means."

Molly sighed. "That sounds like Antoine. Don't call us, we'll call you." The man was one of the smartest she'd ever met, but he wasn't the best at communicating with people. She turned to Gabe. "Since we're not going to Baton Rouge, when are we leaving for Houston to talk to Cicely Morrow and her son?"

Gabe glanced at his watch. "As soon as we can. I was going to let you sleep a little more, but I'm anxious to get out there. If we leave in the next little bit, we can make it to Houston by midafternoon. Definitely before dark."

"Before dark is optimal. Let me see what you've found, Burke."

Burke turned his laptop around so that she could see his screen. It was the result of the background check that she should have done herself during the night but hadn't gotten time to do before her brain crashed into sleep.

She'd seen the photo of Cicely Morrow, so she focused on Xavier. The newspaper photo they'd found was his senior picture from high school, the attached article discussing his academic achievements and the partial scholarship he'd earned to Rice University. Xavier was young, clean-cut, his hair buzzed on the sides and a neat mohawk colored blue and gold. The school's colors, she realized from another photo embedded in the article. His smile was vivid, his eyes bright.

He looked happy. He'd also volunteered like crazy throughout high school, according to the article. Key Club, Meals on Wheels, tutoring homeless teens at the LGBT youth shelter. He seemed, like Gabe had indicated, a nice young man.

"Have you found his birth certificate?" Molly asked.

"Not yet," Burke answered. "I was just about to do that."

"Race ya," she said, grabbing her own laptop and passing Burke's back to him.

"What are you doing?" Gabe asked suspiciously.

"Looking for Xavier Morrow's birth certificate," Molly told him. "Don't worry, nobody will trace this search to you. We use a VPN to maintain our privacy."

Gabe scowled. "Is it legal?"

"It's public record," Burke said evasively.

"You're hacking," Gabe said flatly.

"We're expediting the process using Antoine's search engine." Molly met his gaze. "Otherwise, it'll take a long time. I don't think we have a long time to wait."

Gabe nodded, looking unconvinced.

Molly's fingers flew over her keyboard, but Burke was a hair faster. He claimed victory seconds before her own screen filled with the image of Xavier Morrow's birth certificate.

"Huh," Burke said.

"Huh," Molly echoed.

Gabe leaned in to see Burke's screen. "Fuck," he whispered.

Because twenty-two years ago, Angel Xavier Morrow had been born in New Orleans.

"We need to find him and talk to him," Molly said. "It might yield nothing, Gabe. Or it might yield something you don't want to hear. Let me go to Houston by myself." She didn't expect him to agree, but figured it was worth a try. "I'll tell you whatever you need to know."

"No," he said quietly. "I'm going with you. I need to know the truth. If my father did make a trust for Xavier Morrow, I need to know. And I need to know why."

Molly sighed. "I figured you'd say that. Let's get on the road."

I-10, East Texas
TUESDAY, JULY 26, 9:45 A.M.

"Can you tell him it's urgent?" Xavier's mother asked, on the phone with Le Petit Choux.

Apparently, Gabriel Hebert was not in the restaurant, nor had he been any of the four times his mother had called in the last hour.

Cicely sighed. "Thank you. I left my number in case he calls in. Do you still have it?" She waited a moment, then murmured, "You, too," before ending the call.

"Maybe he'll call you," Willa Mae said from the driver's seat, reaching across the console to pat his mother's hand. "If a stranger had called me asking for one of my employees, I'd say the same thing. I'd refuse to say whether they were there or not, then take a number and contact the person myself. It's a privacy thing, hon."

"I know," Cicely said. "It's just so frustrating. Is that lawyer still behind us?"

Xavier looked up from the phone Carlos had loaned him, turning around from the captain's chair in the middle to see the white BMW SUV trailing them, a little too close. "He's still there."

"That man's kissin' my back bumper," Willa Mae groused. "I'd tan his hide if he were my man."

Cicely chuckled. "He couldn't handle you, Willa Mae, but I'd sure like to see him try."

Willa Mae laughed. "Too true. You boys need a rest stop? Some cola or snacks?"

"No, ma'am, Miss Willa Mae," Xavier said. His mother had bought them all waffles to go from the Waffle House, and they'd eaten their fill. "And Carlos and Manny are sound asleep."

"No, I'm not," Carlos muttered. "My ears are bleeding."

Xavier choked a laugh into a cough. Except for when his mama had been calling Gabe Hebert's restaurant, Willa Mae had been playing country music, of which Carlos was not a fan.

"I like it," Manny said loudly.

Carlos's head popped up, turning to the very back seat to stare at his brother. "You're lying."

Manny grinned. "Of course I'm lying," he whispered. "But *I'm* polite and shit."

Xavier rolled his eyes and resumed his search on Mr. Paul Lott. Once he'd been safely with his mother and her friend, he'd stopped to replay all the past day's events in his mind, and one thing stuck out.

Lott's voice had been different when they'd talked on the phone after Rocky had died. The man had sounded older. Less . . . New Orleans. Today his accent had been strong.

Xavier's memory might not have been accurate. He'd been so overwhelmed with grief when Lott had called him to tell him that Rocky was dead. He might not be remembering right. But last night the man had glossed over his request to talk to Gabe Hebert, like he hadn't even spoken. Which was annoying at best. Dangerous at worst.

Thus, he'd been searching for a photo of Lott. So far, he'd come up with nothing. Which was worrisome.

Of course, the man was older. Had to be forty at least. People that old didn't always have a good grip on technology like websites and social media. Paul Lott seemed to fall into that group. But there had to be a photo of him somewhere. He was a person who existed. He had to have touched the internet somewhere.

Willa Mae switched the country station back on, singing along reasonably on-key. She did sing in the church choir, after all. His mother rubbed her temples when Willa Mae sang, though.

Like Manny, Xavier's mama was not a country music fan.

Oh. A link caught his eye. He was several pages into the search results, so he'd given up hope, but here was something. *Paul Lott wins Legal Eagle tournament in a close contest.*

He clicked on the link and got sent to a page for some attorneys' association. Legal Eagle had been a golf tournament for lawyers in New Orleans, in Metairie to be exact. That was where Rocky had lived.

Xavier scrolled down, coming to a group photo. He pinched the photo to enlarge it, zooming in on the face of the guy who held the trophy.

Then gasped. "Holy shit."

"Xavier," Cicely scolded. "Language."

"But, Mom." Xavier's voice shook. "Look at this. I finally found a photo of Paul Lott. And the guy following us is not him."

His mother twisted in her seat, her expression tense, her hand out. "Gimme."

Willa Mae switched off the radio, leaving the car in total silence.

Cicely blew out a breath. "I was afraid of this," she murmured.

"I knew it!" Manny exclaimed behind them. "I knew he was shady."

"What do we do now?" Willa Mae asked. "I can try to lose him."

Which she'd probably be able to do. For an older lady, she had quite the lead foot.

"No," Cicely said quietly. "We have to assume that he's up to no good, since he's not who he says he is. He's been nonviolent up until now. If we try to get away, that might change. We still have a few hours until we get to New Orleans. I'll keep trying to reach Gabe Hebert. If we arrive before we talk to him, then . . ." She rubbed her temples. "I honestly don't know."

"We need a plan," Carlos said, his jaw tight. "This asshole is not gonna get at X."

The sound of a gun slide ratcheting echoed through the minivan. "I'm ready," Manny said grimly. "If he comes up on Xavier's side, everyone get down. Except for you, Miss Willa Mae. If he starts shooting, I'll shoot back."

"I can take care of myself," Willa Mae said tartly.

"Nobody is shooting anybody," Cicely insisted. "Anybody *else*," she amended when Carlos pointed to Xavier. "We also need to find out what happened to the man you shot, son. You keep calling Le Petit Choux, and I'll make some calls to the hospital."

"Someone will want to know why," Xavier said, ashamed that he sounded scared. But he *was* scared, dammit.

"I'll call nurses who I trust. Don't worry."

But Xavier did, because his mother didn't sound all that confident. But they did need to know what had happened to the guy. If he'd been treated and released, he could be after them, too.

Or he could be working with not-Paul-Lott.

"Wait," Carlos said, whipping out his own phone. "That guy had ID. I took a photo."

"IDs can be faked," Manny said. "One of my old girlfriends had one before she was legal so she could get into the bars. Don't ask me who or how," he added when Willa Mae perked up, interested. Because Willa Mae was a retired attorney. "I'm not going to tell you."

"Later," Willa Mae vowed, then glanced at Cicely. "Don't look at me that way. We both might need one someday. Especially if we have to go on the lam after all this."

Cicely rubbed her temples once again. "We are not going on the lam, Willa Mae. I swear to the living God, we are not going to become Thelma and Louise."

"Spoilsport," Willa Mae said, pouting. "They were cool. Except for when they died at the end."

"That was my point," Cicely snapped, then chuckled. "You sly girl. You got my mind off being scared, for just a minute. Thank you, Thelma."

Willa Mae looked at his mother fondly. "You're welcome, Louise. Now call those hospitals. *This* inquiring mind wants to know."

"You want me to call that restaurant for you?" Carlos asked Xavier softly.

Xavier had to smile at his best friend. "No. But thank you."

"You're welcome, Louise," Carlos said, his grin strained.

Xavier discreetly flipped him the bird. Then dialed Gabriel Hebert's restaurant.

"Le Petit Choux," a woman answered. "How can I help you?"

It wasn't the same person who'd talked to his mother. She'd used the speaker the first few times. That woman had sounded younger, twangier. This woman sounded like she meant business, and not in a good way.

Xavier licked his lips, his mouth suddenly dry as a desert. "Hi. I'm trying to reach Gabriel Hebert. Is he in?"

The woman huffed. "Who are you?"

Xavier was afraid to give his name. "A friend of his father's." Complete silence met his ears. Xavier had to check to see if they were still connected, but they were. "Um, hello? Ma'am?"

Suddenly the background noise increased. People and cars. The woman had taken the call outside. "You sound a little young to have been a friend of Rocky Hebert."

"I was," Xavier insisted. "Please, it's important. Life and death, even."

Another tense few moments filled with horns and traffic. "What's your name, kid?"

Xavier swallowed. "How do I know you're really a friend of Gabe's?"

She laughed, but it didn't sound too nice. "How do I know you're really a friend of Rocky's? Look, kid, you called us. Trust me or don't. I really don't care."

But she did. He could hear it in her voice. "My name is Xavier. Mr. Hebert can reach me at this number. Thank you. Goodbye." He ended the call and met Carlos's probing gaze. "She sounded like a cop."

Carlos closed his eyes. "Then let's hope she's a good one."

9

THANK YOU," GABE told the woman at the veterinarian's office, who'd called because Shoe was ready to come home. "I've had to take a quick trip out of town. Can you keep him until I can pick him up later tonight?"

"Of course, Mr. Hebert," she said kindly. "We all love Shoe here. He's been an office favorite ever since your daddy brought him home from the shelter, may he rest in peace."

"Thank you," he said again, never knowing what to say when people said *may he rest in peace*. Because his father was not resting in peace. He'd been murdered and he wouldn't rest peacefully until his killer was behind bars. Or dead. Gabe didn't really care.

No, that wasn't true. He'd like to see the killer dead.

"Shoe's good?" Molly asked after he'd ended the call. She was driving them to Houston in her big red truck. Which made them kind of a target, Gabe thought.

But also had more ramming power than her other car, she'd as-

serted. And ramming power might come in handy if someone got too
close.

That had made him feel better, although it probably shouldn't have.

"What are we going to say when we find him?" Gabe asked, trying
to plan the encounter in his mind.

"Well, we probably shouldn't lead with 'Are you Rocky Hebert's
secret second son?'" she said. "I think we should say the truth. That we
found the payments to his mother through John Alan Industries and
wanted to find out why. It's a fair question."

"And if he refuses to answer?"

"We cross that bridge when we get there." She pointed to the radio.
"Feel free to find something you like, if you want. I usually go for silence when I'm driving, but if music will help you, then go for it."

"No, silence is good for me, too." He pivoted in his seat, checking to
see if anyone was following them.

"Nope," Molly said, giving him an encouraging smile. "Nobody behind us. I've been watching."

Because of course she had. She was good at her job. He nearly apologized again for doubting her but bit it back. "I didn't get a chance to
make you a proper breakfast."

"No worries. The egg sandwich was just fine."

It was really the leftover omelet that Burke had been too full to eat,
sandwiched between two halves of a toasted bagel. He'd nearly refused
to serve it to her, but she'd grabbed it and told him to stop being a food
snob.

Which had made him laugh. Which had been her intent.

He let himself study her profile, taking the moment of quiet to admire her shiny blond hair that she'd tamed back into a bun. She was
classically pretty, wearing no makeup. He liked that. He especially liked
the curves below her pretty face. On a different day, under different
circumstances, he'd like to explore those curves.

But that wouldn't be today, he thought as his gaze landed on the gun at her hip.

She cleared her throat. "Something wrong, Gabe?"

Translated: *Stop perving on me.*

He searched for something to say that didn't make him sound like the perv she clearly thought he was. "Why do you have a holster on your belt? Why not a shoulder holster?"

Her lips twitched. "You really want to know?"

Her tone said that he probably didn't. "Maybe?"

"Shoulder holsters don't work for . . . more buxom girls like me. Anything over a B cup and you can't easily reach across your bosom to grab your gun."

His mouth fell open, his mind now wondering what she was, if she wasn't a B. And that was a really unwise train of thought. "I never would have considered that."

"Men don't," she said dryly. "It's an uncomfortable truth."

He opened his mouth to say something more, then snapped it shut, making her laugh. She let him stew in his embarrassment until he was all but squirming in his seat like a teenage boy.

"I'm sorry," she said, still laughing. "But the look on your face . . ."

He laughed, too, but was totally relieved when his cell phone rang, saving him from further discussion of her . . . endowment. But then he frowned when he saw the caller ID. "Burke?" he answered. "What's wrong?"

"Put him on speaker," Molly said, suddenly all business again.

"You've gotten a number of calls at the Choux this morning," Burke said.

Fear grabbed his gut. "Is Patty okay?"

"She's fine. Val's with her."

Okay, that's good. Val was the bodyguard who Burke had assigned to keep Patty safe. "Then who's calling me?"

"Cicely Morrow and her son, Xavier."

Molly looked away from the road long enough to meet Gabe's gaze, hers as startled as he figured his was. "Well, then," she said. "Don't keep us in suspense, Burke. What did they say?"

"Not much. I was going to call them but thought you might want to talk to them, Gabe."

"I do. Give me their number."

"I'll text it to you," Burke said. "Don't call from your own phone. Use Molly's burner."

Gabe watched Molly retrieve a slim smartphone from her pocket. It wasn't the cell with the pink sparkly case that she'd used to make other calls. This one was a plain matte gray. She handed it to him. "Code is 465329," she said.

"No face recognition?" he asked.

"Nope. Not secure, and cops can use it to get into your phone without your consent. Anything more, Burke?"

"Only that Cicely was firm but polite each of the four times she called. That was according to your assistant manager. By the time Xavier called, Val and Patty had arrived, so Val answered. She said he sounded scared and told her that it was a matter of life and death."

"Timing is interesting," Molly observed.

"Damn straight," Burke said. "I want to listen in on your call. Call me first, then I'll patch them in. I'll call the number that Xavier left with Val. He won't know that I'm there."

"Nice trick," Gabe muttered. When this was over, he was going to ask them to teach him their ways. "I'll hang up now and call you from Molly's phone."

He did so, putting on the speaker, then waited anxiously for Burke to patch them in, relaxing the tiniest bit when Molly reached for his free hand and gave it a squeeze, just as she'd done while they'd sat at his kitchen table calmly talking about whether or not his father had cheated on his mother with Cicely Morrow.

This time, though, when she started to pull away, he held on. She shot him a look that was hard to read until she smiled. "It'll be okay," she mouthed. "Relax."

He tried. He really tried. But then a tremulous male voice answered the phone. "Hello?"

"I'm looking for Xavier," Gabe said gruffly, hoping his ill feelings toward this kid weren't too obvious.

The swallow was audible. "Who is this?"

"Gabriel Hebert."

"It's him," Xavier said to someone on his end. "Gabe Hebert."

"Oh, thank the good Lord," a woman said from farther away. "Ask if you can put him on speaker."

"That was my mother," Xavier said. "Can I? Put you on speaker, I mean."

"Sure."

A second later, the background noise grew louder. They were also in a moving vehicle. He wanted to ask, but let Xavier take the lead. The guy had called him, after all.

"You still there?" Xavier asked.

"I am. Why did you call me?"

"Um . . . Well, this isn't gonna be easy for you to believe. At least I hope not. I mean . . . Never mind. I was a friend of your father's."

Not his son. A friend. "All right. But you sound a little young to be a friend of my dad's."

"You're not surprised," Xavier said faintly. "You already knew about me?"

"Not really. Why don't you tell me about yourself?" A squeeze to his hand had him looking at Molly, who was shaking her head.

"Be nice," she mouthed.

She was right, of course. "Please," he added.

"Well, I knew your dad from when I was a little kid. I, um—"

"Tell him later," another male voice hissed. "In person. When we know he's the real deal."

"Who's with you?" Gabe asked sharply.

"My mom and my best friend." He sighed. "And my best friend's brother and my mom's best friend. We're . . . well, we're kind of on the run. Someone tried to kill me last night and Rocky told me that if that ever happened, I should come to you."

"Oh." Gabe blinked, not having expected any of that. Xavier was traveling with a damn entourage. And someone had tried to kill him. *Just like someone might have done to me if Molly hadn't chased them away before they could poison Shoe.*

The timing was damn interesting.

"You have my attention, Xavier. Please go on."

"Yes, sir." The young man inhaled, then exhaled loudly. "Okay. I didn't know your number, so I called Mr. Lott. Do you know him?"

"My dad's lawyer? Yes. I've known him for years."

"Okay," Xavier said again, and Gabe felt genuinely sorry for him. He was clearly terrified. *Join the club, Xavier Morrow.* "Like I said, I called Mr. Lott and asked for your number. He kind of ignored me."

"He didn't 'kind of' ignore you," a third male voice said. Gruffer and more gravelly than either Xavier's or his best friend's voice. "He totally ignored you."

"All right, all right," Xavier snapped. "He totally ignored me, then said that he'd come and get me and take me to you."

"Did he tell you that he called me?" Gabe asked.

"No. He didn't really talk about you at all. Did he call you?"

"No. I haven't talked to him since my father died. I take it that you didn't go with him."

"No, I didn't. I told my mom about it and she said that I shouldn't go with him, that your father had told her to only trust you. So, we came in our own vehicle—well, it's my mom's friend's minivan—and he's following behind us. Except it's not him."

Molly straightened at that, briefly letting go of the wheel to twirl her finger, gesturing for him to ask more questions about that. She hadn't let his hand go, though, and that made him feel, well, not better, but at least more secure.

"What does that mean?" Gabe asked. "That it's 'not him'?"

"It's not Paul Lott," Xavier said. "I found a photo of Lott—which was damn hard to do, by the way—and your dad's lawyer looks way different than this guy. This guy is a lot younger, too. I'd thought that he sounded a little different, which is why I searched for his face."

Gabe blinked some more. "That's . . . wow. I don't even know where to start with that."

"I know, right?" Xavier said, sounding very young. "I don't know what to do now."

Molly was motioning again. "Ask if he called the cops," she mouthed.

"Did you, um, call the police?"

A very, very long silence. Then Xavier exhaled again. "No. I don't want to tell you why until I see that it's really you and not another faker."

Gabe nodded, wondering how deep the cops were burrowed into this disaster. "Understandable. Where are you?"

"East Texas, about four and a half hours from you."

Molly mouthed, "Ask if they need protection."

"Do you need protection?"

"Yes!" the best friend exclaimed. "Tell him yes!"

"Mom? I think Carlos is right. We should say yes."

"Then say yes," Cicely said with not a small amount of exasperation.

"What are you driving?" Gabe asked.

"Gray minivan," another woman called out. Probably the mom's friend. "Honda Odyssey, 2015, gray. Has a Save the Whales bumper sticker. It was there when I bought it used," she added, sounding a little embarrassed.

Gabe nearly smiled. Xavier's entourage was quite the motley crew. "I'll call you back at this number, but we're headed your way. We can meet you at a midpoint and follow you."

"Don't be obvious about it." This came from the gruff voice, maybe Carlos's brother? "If this guy thinks we're onto him, he could start shooting. He said he was 'prepared.' I assume that means he's carrying."

"Sounds like a good assumption," Gabe said, because it did.

"Wait," Xavier said. "Who is 'we'? You said 'we're headed your way.' Who's with you?"

Gabe looked at Molly, who shrugged. "My name is Molly Sutton," she told him. "I'm a private investigator. And I'll tell you why I'm with Gabe when I see that it's really you and not some faker."

"Rude, man," the gruff voice said.

"Very rude," the mother's best friend echoed. "You should have said who was with you."

"Perhaps," Gabe allowed. "But you called me. I need to be sure who I'm dealing with as well."

"It's fair," Xavier said grudgingly. "What are you driving?"

"Big-ass truck," Molly said. "Toyota Tundra. Fire-engine red. Bumper sticker says sad face plus horse equals happy face. And it wasn't there when I bought it."

Xavier snorted softly. "I guess we'll see you in a few hours. Where are you now?"

Gabe glanced at Molly. "Tell him if you want to," she mouthed.

"Just leaving New Orleans," he said. "We were on our way to see you."

"Oh. Okay." Xavier sounded as overwhelmed as Gabe felt. "Call us when you get close to Lafayette. That's about halfway between us. We can coordinate a meeting place."

"That sounds good," Gabe said. "See you soon, Xavier."

"Gabe, wait. I'm sorry about your father. He was a really, really good man."

"You'll tell me how you knew him when we meet?"

"Yes, sir. It'll all make sense then. I hope."

Gabe ended the call then turned to Molly. "Should I call Burke back?"

"He'll call you."

Molly's burner phone buzzed, and Gabe put it on speaker. "Well?" he asked.

"That was . . . unexpected," Burke said. "But you did good, Gabe. I'll prepare the office and get secure housing for Xavier and his friends. All five of them."

"What's that about?" Gabe asked. "Why bring so many people?"

"My guess is that being nearly murdered has everyone in Xavier's orbit on edge," Burke said, "but we'll find out when y'all get back to New Orleans. Drive safely."

And then it was only Molly and Gabe. And she was still holding his hand.

Gabe tightened his grip, not planning to let her go anytime soon.

Tulane-Gravier, New Orleans, Louisiana
TUESDAY, JULY 26, 10:30 A.M.

"How'd your meeting go, sir?" James asked as Lamont slid into the back seat of the town car. Thank God for A/C. The DA kept his office hotter than a sauna.

"Well enough, thank you for asking." Lamont handed a paper sack over the seat. "DA's secretary brought in beignets. Thought you might like one."

James took the bag with an appreciative nod. "Thank you kindly. Are they from Café Du Monde?"

"Nah. Some knockoff, but still pretty good." He buckled his seat belt and let himself relax. "I'm going for an early lunch, James. Take me to Le Petit Choux."

"Absolutely, sir. You must like that place. I think this is the fifth time this month that you've stopped in for lunch."

That won't do. He should have realized that James would keep track. "They've got amazing prawns in garlic butter. But maybe you're right. I don't want to become predictable."

James glanced up to the rearview, visibly dismayed. "Oh, no, sir. I shouldn't have said anything. If you like the food, you should go there."

"No, I think you're right. Don't want to get into a rut, now, do I? Take me to Remy's. I have a craving for fried chicken. I'll call in the order for both of us and you can pick it up."

"Yes, sir. Thank you, sir. With all this traffic, it'll give them plenty of time to get it ready."

Traffic was awful, thanks to that goddamn Satchmo festival. Why people felt the need to start partying a week ahead of time was beyond him.

He texted Ashley to send him a file to read to pass the time, then settled in. Only to have his phone buzz in his pocket. He looked at the screen, his pulse speeding up at the number.

It was a text from Tyson Whitley. *It's a beautiful day.*

Lamont breathed out a sigh of relief. Stockman was dead and couldn't be traced to him. He'd paid his right-hand man in cash, so there was no paper trail. Stockman had never carried ID, had paid everything with cash, and Stockman wasn't even his real name.

He had no idea if his former assistant had a family, nor did he care. Theirs was a transactional business relationship. Nothing more.

Loose end, snipped.

And, like the cherry on top, he had a missed call from Cornell Eckert. If the man knew what was good for him, he was calling to say that he'd finished the job that Stockman had fucked up. He dialed Eckert's number and the man answered on the first ring.

"Finally," Eckert snapped. "I've been trying to reach you for fucking hours."

"Be very careful," Lamont cautioned coldly. "You work at my pleasure."

A beat of silence. "Of course, sir." Except that Eckert's *sir* sounded a lot less respectful than James's *sir*.

Lamont was losing his patience. "What is it?"

"The mark's on the move, but he has a posse. Currently in a minivan, heading east on I-10."

"Why is he still—" *Breathing.* "Driving?"

"That's what I was trying to let you know when I called before. I got to his house at about four a.m. It was deserted, but someone got hurt there. There was a lot of blood. Wasn't sure if it was the mark or my predecessor."

"The latter," Lamont said flatly.

"That's what I figured. So, I waited to see if the mark would come back. And he did, but with a posse, like I said. And three of the four of them had guns, including the mark. Didn't think you'd want me to leave witnesses and I didn't want to get into a gunfight on a private street. I slid a tracker under the junker the mark was riding in. He was with two Latino dudes. And a third guy—white, about forty—who drove his own car. Fancy Beemer. White SUV."

That surprised him. "Did you get the plate?"

"Sure did. Guy's some lawyer out of New Orleans."

Lamont blinked. "Are you sure?"

"If he's not, then he stole the lawyer's car. Beemer's registered to a Paul Lott. Know him?"

Oh yes. "No," he lied, "but I know who to ask." After he was out of the town car and in a secure place, he was going straight to the source. Paul had a lot of explaining to do. "So you're—" Biting back *following them*, he glanced up at James, who was bopping his head to a tune only he could hear. *Not paying attention to me.* "You're with them?"

"Yeah. The junker with the tracker stopped at a Waffle House outside of Houston. The mark and the two Latino guys changed from the junker to a minivan, registered to Willa Mae Collins—also a lawyer, by the way. Twenty minutes later, two older ladies came out of the Waffle

House with Paul Lott. The two ladies got into the minivan with the mark and the Latino guys and Paul Lott got into the Beemer. Then they all got on I-10 and headed east. Toward you."

Lamont had figured that out for himself already. Why were they headed this way? And why the hell had Paul Lott gone to meet with Xavier Morrow? How did he even know where Xavier was? *Goddammit.*

"Stay on them," Lamont ordered. "I'll call you later with more specific instructions."

"Got it. Not in a place where you can talk?"

"Not right now."

"Then I'll stay on their tail and wait for your call."

I-10, Baton Rouge, Louisiana
TUESDAY, JULY 26, 1:45 P.M.

"Gabe?"

Gabe jolted back to reality, having been staring at the cars on the interstate all around them. He quickly turned to Molly because she sounded tense. "What's wrong?"

"I need you to text a license plate number to Burke. Now."

He grabbed her burner phone from the center console and put in her unlock code. "Ready." She fired off a license plate number, and he read it back to her before hitting send. "What's going on?"

"I have no idea," she said, not taking her eyes from the road. "But we appear to have some kind of a caravan going on. Do you see Xavier's gray minivan?"

The minivan actually belonged to Willa Mae Collins, according to Burke's earlier license plate search. Miss Collins was an attorney, which had Gabe wondering why Xavier needed one.

"I do." The minivan was about eight cars in front of them. "And I see the white BMW SUV directly behind them." The car driven by someone pretending to be his father's attorney.

They now knew that the SUV did belong to Paul Lott. Burke had confirmed this after running the SUV's plate as well. Burke had been trying to get in touch with either the attorney or his office administrator ever since, but so far, he'd had no luck.

"Do you see the grayish-green Jeep four cars behind the white SUV?"

It took him a second, but then he nodded when he focused in on the vehicle. "Yeah. Why?"

"Because he's following, too."

Gabe blinked in surprise. "What? How do you know?"

"He was waiting on the shoulder when we merged onto the interstate from the rest stop."

Gabe and Molly had met up with Xavier and his group at a gas station outside of Lafayette, where Cicely Morrow and her friend had gone inside to use the facilities. Molly had told Gabe to hunker down in the front seat. Gabe hadn't wanted to hide, but he also didn't want Xavier hurt if the Paul Lott imposter suspected they were onto him, so he'd conceded. That one time. He wasn't as big as Burke, but he was still six feet tall, and hiding in the footwell had been damned uncomfortable.

Carefully watching their surroundings, Molly had topped off her gas tank at the station while the ladies were inside. Whoever was posing as Paul Lott hadn't gotten out of his SUV. After ten minutes, both ladies emerged from the restroom, deliberately not looking at the red truck, just as Molly had instructed them.

Then they'd all gotten back on the interstate toward New Orleans. Gabe hadn't noticed the green Jeep merge from the shoulder, but he believed that Molly had.

Being around Molly and Burke made him wish that he'd honed his observational skills over the years. But he was a chef, not a former cop. He was going to have to cut himself some slack and let Molly do her job.

"You've got a good eye," he said simply, and she flashed him a tight smile.

"Thank you. Can you text Burke and ask him to run that plate? I saw the Jeep following us when we got back on the road, so I drifted back so that traffic could pass and get between us. I've been behind him for at least fifteen miles and he's glued to the same spot—four cars behind the white SUV. Every time someone pulls into the next lane, he compensates, drifting back until someone gets in front of him. He's maintaining a four-car gap and, while it could be his way of staying awake as he drives, I'm not gonna bet on it."

"Me either," he muttered, because it had been that kind of day already. Burke's reply flashed onto his phone's screen. "Burke says that he's running it now."

"Tell him the vehicle is following Xavier. And ask him if Antoine has found anything yet."

Gabe typed in her messages to Burke then waited for the man's reply.

The first text, which Gabe figured was a reaction to the Jeep following Xavier, said: *WTF!*

A minute later, the next text was not much wordier. *No.*

Molly scowled when he passed it on. "What is *taking* Antoine so damn long?"

Gabe shrugged. "How long does it usually take him to recover a wiped hard drive?"

"A few days maybe?"

"It's only been a day."

"Why are you so logical right now?" she asked with a frown.

He smiled at her. "Because you're on the job."

She laughed. "Bullshit."

"Maybe a little," he allowed. "But only a little. You saw the Jeep, and you chased away the dog poisoner. You make me a little calmer."

Her expression softened, her gaze still locked on the road in front of them. "That's nice, Gabe. Thank you."

He considered his next words, then figured why the hell not. "You used to calm me whenever you'd come to the Choux."

She startled at that. "I did?"

"You did. I'd be having a bad day, and then I'd see you having lunch with your friends or even all alone. I'd bring your meal out and after that my day would go better."

She chanced a quick glance at him, eyes wide. "I . . . I didn't think you even knew I was there."

He huffed a quiet chuckle. "Oh, I knew. Do you think I take meals out to everyone?"

"I guess I didn't notice."

"Patty did. Teased me unmercifully."

Her lips quirked up. "I guess I should say that I'm sorry, but I'm not."

"Neither am I." And then he relaxed even more because she laid her hand on the console, palm up. He slid their hands together, twining his fingers through hers.

"So why didn't you ask me out?"

"Scared, I guess. Plus, busy. And I got burned by women the last time or two. Like I said before, they think it's romantic to date a chef who's been on TV. But the reality is a lot of late nights and missed dates."

"Kind of like a cop-turned-PI?"

He wondered if she dated much but held the question for later. But he would ask if she was single. And if she was, he was taking this as fate and asking her out. They just had to get back to New Orleans in one piece first. "What's your plan on the Jeep?"

"I *was* going to create a disturbance so that Willa Mae could take our exit but the BMW couldn't. With our newest caravan member, I'm not going to be able to do that without endangering traffic. I'm going to need Burke's help."

As if on cue, Molly's burner rang, Burke's number on the caller ID. Gabe put it on speaker.

"What did you find?" Molly asked.

"You're not going to believe this. The owner of the Jeep is Cornell Eckert. He's a hit man. I recognize the name from when I was on the force. Nobody could ever get anything to stick on him. Guy was like Teflon. Word on the street was that he had friends in high places."

"Within the NOPD, you mean," Molly clarified.

"Unfortunately, yes. He disappeared shortly before I quit, and at the time nobody knew where he'd gone. And now his car shows up following behind a twenty-two-year-old who someone failed to kill last night. Surprise, surprise."

"Fucking hell," Molly muttered. "That changes my plan a little. If the Paul Lott impersonator was planning to bring Xavier back to New Orleans, it won't hurt to allow him to follow Xavier and the minivan into the city a little ways. I'd like you to take point on the minivan. Coordinate with Xavier and his entourage. Get behind them when they get into the city and block the SUV from following them. I'll make sure that Mr. Eckert the hit man doesn't exit the interstate with them."

Gabe stared at her. "How? Ramming power?"

Her grin was small and quick. "No. I'm not going to endanger the rest of the people on the highway. But he'll probably get mad at us, so I'll ask you to duck down when we get close to that point." His poor opinion of that plan must have shown on his face, because she added, "If he's following Xavier, he might have orders to take care of you, too."

A chill raced down Gabe's back, because while he had thought of that, he hadn't wanted to. "I hate that footwell."

"I know you do," she said soothingly. "I'd hate it, too, if our positions were reversed. But it'll be easier for me if I don't have to worry about you getting shot."

"Eckert's a good shot, too," Burke said. "Not sniper-level good, but it's said that he doesn't miss what he's aiming at. He's careful and leaves no trace. Or at least no trace that can't be wiped away if you know the right people."

"I'm beginning to hate those people," Gabe snarled.

"I'm already there," Burke said. "I'm going to request backup. I've got a call in to André Holmes. That's Antoine's brother, Gabe. And you'll be driving into his jurisdiction. He's the cop who made sure the right person from the sheriff's department showed up at your father's house last night. I'll let you know if he's in. Oh, he's calling now. I'll call you back."

Molly was tapping her fingers on the steering wheel. "Can you get Xavier on the phone? He and his friends need to know to watch out for the Jeep."

Gabe complied, grateful for something concrete to do. "Xavier, it's Gabe," he said when the young man picked up. "Molly wants to talk to you. Put it on speaker."

"What's wrong?" Xavier asked.

Molly told him about the Jeep, being straight with them that the driver was a hit man. Cicely Morrow made an anguished sound. "Try not to worry, ma'am," Molly told Cicely. "We're pulling together a plan. For now, it's best if Xavier isn't visible."

"I'm getting on the floor." Xavier sounded even more shaken, poor guy. "Mama, you, too."

"No, that would look even stranger." Cicely's voice firmed. "Let him try."

"Mama!" Xavier hissed. "What the hell?"

"Willa Mae had two," was all she said.

"Fucking hell," Xavier muttered.

"Two of what?" Gabe asked.

"You don't want to know," Willa Mae called cheerfully. "But we're good."

"Fucking hell," Molly muttered. "Do you guys *all* have weapons?"

"Duh," Carlos said, then yelped. "Don't hit me, X. That hurt."

"It was supposed to."

"They aren't cops!"

"We don't know *who* they are, asswipe," Carlos's brother said.

Molly shook her head. "Just . . . keep them out of sight. If you get stopped by a cop, and he finds weapons, I can't help you."

"I'm not foolish," Cicely said gravely. "But neither will I allow someone to threaten my son's life."

Molly sighed. "Fair enough. Miss Willa Mae, how well do you know New Orleans?"

"I worked in the Quarter when I was in school. Hasn't changed all that much, I don't expect."

"Probably not," Gabe agreed. "You might get a call from a guy named Burke. You can trust him, Xavier. He was also a friend of my father."

"His old partner?"

Gabe hid a flinch. If his dad had told Xavier about Burke, then they'd been closer than he'd thought. That stung and made him wonder what other secrets his father had kept. "Yeah, he's the one. Molly works with him. He's going to find a way to separate you from the white SUV."

"Okay," Xavier said. "I wish you'd told me about Burke when you first called. I wouldn't have been freaking out over Miss Sutton's Wikipedia page."

Molly wasn't able to hide her flinch, not at all. "I have a Wikipedia page?"

"Yes, ma'am, you do," Xavier said respectfully. "Just the part about what happened in North Carolina. It says that you're now a PI, but it doesn't say who you work for. I have to say, though, if Burke Broussard trusts you, then it really must have been self-defense."

"Okay," Molly said. She seemed rattled, and Gabe hated to see it. "Well, thank you, Xavier. And Miss Cicely, I totally get defending your family, but it's better if you can avoid the situation. Take it from me."

"I understand," Cicely said, so quietly that her reply was almost inaudible.

"We'll be in touch," Molly promised.

"Take care, y'all, and be careful," Gabe said, then hit end. He looked at Molly, who appeared to be miserable. "You didn't know about your internet presence?"

"I knew that there were stories. Newspaper articles and all that. But . . . dammit. It shouldn't make a difference that there's a Wiki page for me." Her lips trembled and she pursed them. "But it does."

"You can get it taken down."

"And I will. But another will pop up in its place. It really doesn't end. That's why we have to make it so that Cicely Morrow doesn't have to shoot anyone to keep her son alive."

This time Gabe made the move, taking her hand and holding it tightly. She squeezed his hand as she drove with her free one clutching the wheel in a white-knuckled grip.

He didn't let go when her burner rang again.

"I talked to André," Burke said as soon as Gabe hit accept. "As soon as I told him that someone was driving Paul Lott's SUV, he got really interested. Turns out there's a reason why I haven't been able to reach Lott's assistant. She's been at NOPD, getting questioned."

"For?" Molly asked, although Gabe figured they both already knew the answer.

Gabe was so tired. "Lott's dead, isn't he?" He should probably feel bad about that, but he was too numb to feel much of anything except total exhaustion.

"Beaten up and shot in the head in his own house, probably last night. Place was ransacked and his laptop and wallet were taken. Cops were working it as a burglary gone wrong. Needless to say, André was very interested in providing backup to make sure that Xavier gets here safely. I didn't even have to tell him why Xavier, his mother, and their friends were coming to see us, but I imagine he'll want to know."

"I guess we'll cross that bridge when we get there," Molly said, sounding as tired as Gabe felt. "This is not good, Burke. I'm grateful for André's help, but I do not want to get too beholden to NOPD or give them a reason to get their claws into our operation."

"I agree completely, but I trust André. This means that they'll pull the Lott imposter over once you separate the green Jeep. He's sending a cop he trusts to follow the Jeep. All you have to do is shepherd everyone to the exit, make sure that the minivan and the SUV veer off, and keep the Jeep from following them."

Molly nodded. "I can do that."

"I'll call you back when I have more details. You holding up okay, Gabe?"

"Yep. Molly has it under control. I'm just assisting with the phone."

Burke chuckled. "Let's keep it that way. No playing the hero."

Gabe wasn't promising anything. "I'll talk to you soon."

Molly shot him a knowing glance before returning her gaze to the road. "You planning something, Gabe?"

"Only if I have to. I'm not bad with a handgun. Like I said, I went to the target range with my dad a lot."

She was quiet for a long moment, then said softly, "There's a pistol in a lockbox in the console. Combo is four, three and two together, then one. It's a Glock, unloaded. Full magazine is in the glove box. Better be ready in case you have to defend yourself. But unless everything goes to shit and someone takes me out, you let me lead. Okay?"

He did not like the thought of anyone taking her out. "Okay."

She frowned. "Promise me."

He hesitated. "I promise." *To keep you safe if we come to that point.*

10

EXCUSE ME, SIR." Ashley stood in the doorway to Lamont's office, her expression uncertain.

Because Joelle was sitting in one of his visitor chairs, having finally roused herself from her stupor and charged past Ashley's desk and into his office to demand why he'd sprayed her perfume all over the bed in his study at home. His wife hadn't bought his excuse of wanting the room to smell like her.

Apparently, she really had been suspecting that he was having an affair with Ashley. At least Ashley had gone home to shower. She now smelled like her own perfume, lighter and less cloying than Joelle's.

Which Joelle knew because she'd sniffed Ashley on her way in. Because of course she had.

"What is it, Ashley?" he asked, grateful for the interruption.

"You've got a call on line one. I tried to let you know, but the intercom is turned off."

He glanced at the intercom on his desk. Sure enough, it was turned off and Joelle's expression had become smug. *Bitch.* "I'm so sorry, Ash. I must have knocked it by mistake. Did you get a name?"

"No, sir. The man wouldn't give one, but he said it was urgent. Something about the cold case you've been working."

He managed to control his frown. The only cold case he was currently working was his own. And as soon as Cornell Eckert killed Xavier Morrow, that case could close. Of course, there was still the question of why Paul Lott was driving from Houston to New Orleans, but the lawyer hadn't returned his call yet.

Lott wouldn't be protecting Xavier. *Unless he's double-crossed us.*

"Tell him to give me a minute to conclude this meeting with my wife."

Ashley closed the door and Joelle turned on him. "You are not dismissing me."

He wanted to pinch the bridge of his nose, because the bitch was giving him a headache, but he wouldn't give her the satisfaction of knowing that she'd gotten under his skin. "This is my place of business, Joelle. I'm happy to continue this conversation at home later, but now I have to do my job." He rose, walked around his desk, and yanked her to her feet. "You have to go."

She opened her mouth to argue, based on the set of her mouth, but he leaned in and whispered, "Don't make me call a guard to escort you out. It demeans us both. And it'll be on the front page of the society section before you're out the door."

That got her attention. Joelle hated the thought of being ridiculed by society. Funny, because those same people would have been hiring her to serve their guests at parties wearing a French maid costume before he'd married her.

She twisted out of his grip because he allowed it. "I'll see you at home." A sly smirk tilted her lips. "And I'll show you the footage."

He stopped dead in his tracks. "The what?"

She just smiled wider. He used to like that smile. Now it reminded him of a viper. "Didn't I tell you? I had security cameras installed in that little room off your study. I imagine my attorney will find it most illuminating."

He gritted his teeth. "What do you want, Joelle?"

Her smile disappeared. "I want you to break up with that whore."

Oh, you are so going to die. And I'm going to make it hurt. A lot. Divorce was way too good for her. That he had to wait until after he was elected to deal with her made him even angrier. "As you wish."

She laughed. "See? Was that so hard? I want her fired, too."

Bitch, bitch, bitch. "That may be harder to do."

She narrowed her eyes. "Find a way, Monty."

She knew he hated to be called that. He forced his clenched fist to loosen. "Yes, dear."

With a flourish, she was out of the room, closing the door behind her. He took a moment to wonder what she was saying to Ashley. Then realized that there wasn't anything he could do to help Ashley now. He'd find a nice place for her to work in one of the other offices and he'd hire himself a new secretary. A pretty one.

At least he wouldn't have to kill this mistress to keep the secret from this wife.

Pushing the whole clusterfuck from his mind, he sat behind his desk and jabbed the button for line one, picking up the receiver. No way would this call go on speaker. "Yes?"

"It's me."

Jackass. "I'll call you right back." He switched to his personal cell phone and, walking to the window, he dialed, rewinding the previous evening in his mind. He realized that he never did find out who Jackass's mole was at Le Petit Choux. "Well? Who is it?" he asked as soon as the call had connected.

"Who is which?" Jackass asked warily.

For the love of . . . "Last night. At Le Petit Choux. You texted me that your mole had seen me. You were also supposed to find out where that PI works, the one who was shadowing Gabe Hebert and his cousin."

"Oh, that. The PI works for Burke Broussard."

Well, fuckety fuck. He knew that name. That was the guy who'd nearly turned NOPD upside down with his accusations of wrongdoing a few years back. Broussard would have been right, of course, but luckily, he'd listened to reason—a.k.a. threats—and quit. *I knew that asshole would come back to bite us in the ass someday.*

Looked like someday was now. "Gabriel Hebert hired Burke Broussard?"

"His daddy was one of Broussard's old partners."

"Oh, right." He'd forgotten about that. "Makes sense, then."

"It seems that Rocky's kid suspects. Are we ready to kill him now?" Jackass's tone was filled with condescension and I-told-you-so. *Bastard.*

Lamont would deal with him later. Right now, they needed to stop Gabe Hebert from digging—and more importantly, they needed to find out what got him suspicious. There might be a few loose threads that they hadn't snipped, God forbid. "I suppose we should. Proposals?"

"You know he's gonna be harder to kill now."

"Yes," Lamont said, grinding his teeth, "I figured that out on my own."

"You've always been the smarter one." Again said in such a condescending way it was clear that the opposite was what he meant.

Goddamn motherfucker. He'd deal with Jackass after Gabe Hebert was dead. At least they hadn't agreed on anything in writing. "When?"

"As soon as I can arrange it safely. I'm not keen on gettin' caught."

"I agree." *Not that you'll have to worry for long.* He'd have to kill the man himself since Stockman was dead, but that was okay. He hadn't gotten his hands dirty for a long time and he'd rather missed it. But he would do it intelligently.

He was too close to having everything he'd always wanted to fuck it up now.

Once Jackass was out of the way, Lamont would have to take care of Lott. Or maybe he could get Eckert to do it for him. "Have you heard from Paul Lott?"

"Personally? Not since we visited Rocky. Why?"

Their "visit" to Rocky Hebert had been the night they'd killed him. "Because Paul was in Houston this morning. Visiting Rocky's young friend." And following him back to New Orleans, but he'd keep that fact in his back pocket.

"What?" The surprise was clearly feigned. Entirely fake. "That's not possible."

What are you up to? "And why not?"

"Because Paul Lott is dead."

"He's *what?*"

"He's dead. Poor fella was the victim of a burglary gone wrong last night. Perp shot him in the head. May he rest . . . in pieces."

Rage began to bubble, and Lamont thought the top of his head might actually blow off. "Why?"

"Why what?" Jackass drawled with faux innocence.

"Why did you kill him?"

"*I* didn't."

"So you hired someone else? Was it the person who was following the PI yesterday?" *Please tell me that you haven't brought an entire team into this.*

That would be a lot of people to kill. *And I have a packed calendar already.*

"Relax, for goodness' sake," Jackass said. "It's not like I have a full staff."

"Yeah, you do." That was the problem.

A chuckle rumbled through the phone. "Well, that's true enough. But don't worry. I'd never turn them on you. We're partners. But—just so you know, of course—if somethin' happens to me that's unexplainable—an accident maybe? Then they'll come after you."

"You—" *Sonofabitch.* He caught the word before it left his mouth. "You don't have a thing to worry about. Is the guy who killed Lott the same one driving his SUV right now?"

"Oh. Well, you are *full* of surprises today, aren't you? Yes, he is. Not to worry. I trust him completely."

I'm so glad that you *trust him. Now* I *have to watch my own back.*

"And I'm so glad I sent him," Jackass continued. "Especially since your man failed at the task."

Lamont swallowed his gasp, but Jackass must have heard, because the man chuckled. "You're probably wondering how I know?" Jackass said smugly.

Lamont ground his teeth. "How do you?"

"The kid called Paul Lott's phone last night. Said someone tried to kill him. Luckily, one of my men was on the scene and intercepted the call. We'll be chatting about the secrets you keep, Monty. I'll call you soon."

And the call ended before Lamont realized that Jackass hadn't told him why he'd had Lott killed. It might have been that Lott had gotten cold feet and planned to confess what they'd done. Rocky's attorney hadn't initially wanted to kill him. He'd only wanted cash for Xavier Morrow's name. Which Lott had only known was important because apparently Jackass had asked him—more than five years before—to keep an eye out for anything Rocky did that was out of the ordinary with respect to a Katrina investigation. Just in case the cop started poking into it again.

None of which Lamont had known anything about until a little over six weeks ago. He hadn't known that there had been an eyewitness. Hadn't known that Rocky had been investigating. Hadn't known the fucker had lied about the name of the eyewitness after being pressed for an ID when he'd resurrected the case on the tenth anniversary of Katrina.

They could thank Paul Lott for giving them the eyewitness's real name after Rocky had asked that he set up a trust for Angel Xavier Morrow. Paul had been surprised, and remembering Jackass's request, had searched "Xavier" against the Katrina database, found that he was the surviving child of a victim. He'd been five years old. Not old enough to be a believable witness.

Except that he'd seen Lamont's scar, the scar that he didn't really have anymore, but that plenty of photographs had documented before he'd had plastic surgery. So the kid, now a twenty-two-year-old, was a giant threat.

But that wasn't the worst of it. Not by a long shot.

That Jackass had discovered Xavier Morrow's whereabouts had not been a consideration, but he had, and now Lamont was left with too many questions. Why had Jackass had Paul Lott killed? Who was the man he'd sent to meet with Xavier? Why hadn't they just killed the kid in Houston? Why were they driving to New Orleans?

And, speaking of, he dialed Cornell Eckert. "Status?"

"Coming close to New Orleans. What do you want me to do with the lawyer's SUV?"

"Kill the driver."

"And all the other people in the minivan?"

"Kill them, too. And then, if you're interested, I'd like to offer you a job."

Eckert laughed. "I don't think you could afford me full-time, boss man."

"I think you'll be pleasantly surprised with what I have to offer. Text me when the matter is completed, and we'll talk some more. I think all of the new zeros in your bank account will speak volumes."

"We'll see. Gotta go. Coming up on the exit. Later."

I-10, New Orleans, Louisiana
TUESDAY, JULY 26, 2:15 P.M.

Molly looked over at Gabe, who was kind of cooperating. He wasn't in the footwell, but he was leaned over the console, as much as his seat belt would allow.

This was it.

"Be ready," was all she said.

Their exit into New Orleans was coming up, and traffic was moving a little too slowly to guarantee success. She had to time her move so that Xavier's minivan and the stolen BMW SUV could exit, but the Jeep carrying Mr. Eckert the hit man could not.

And not endanger anyone else on the road.

Easy peasy.

Which she was going to keep telling herself until it was over.

A glance in front of her showed a bridge looming just beyond the exit. The bridge was the reason that they'd chosen this specific exit.

A glance in her rearview showed no cops, at least none that were obvious. She worried about the cops. She trusted Burke's old friend from NOPD, Captain André Holmes, but he couldn't be everywhere during this op.

She hoped the officers he'd chosen were as trustworthy as he was, because this was going to be close.

"*Now,*" she said, pushing Gabe's shoulder down as she floored her accelerator, forcing her way in front of the Jeep as the minivan and the SUV exited, then veered sharply onto the shoulder, braking so that she was even with the Jeep. She continued driving on the shoulder through the exit, keeping the Jeep from following.

The man in the Jeep stared at her, his jaw tight. Then his arm lifted and—

"Gun!" she shouted.

Gabe looked up from where he leaned over the console, her pistol in his hand. He'd handled it like a seasoned pro, deftly loading it and racking the slide. She wasn't worried about his shooting skills.

She was worried that he'd have to shoot.

"Hold your fire," she said quietly. "Too many people around us."

"I know," Gabe said. "But is he going to hold his fire?"

They'd passed the exit and the shoulder was ending, the bridge upcoming.

"Brace yourself!" Molly slammed on her brakes, stopping a few feet from where the bridge began. In the far-right lane, the Jeep was forced to continue or crash into the bridge's railing.

"It's done," she said. "He's headed over the bridge."

Gabe quickly popped the magazine from her gun, stored the bullets in the glove box and the gun in the lockbox, which he then put back into the console.

He straightened in his seat, readjusting his seat belt. "Crisis averted. Nice driving."

"A few more feet and we'd be soaking wet," she muttered, looking at the river flowing below them, swollen and fast-moving due to a recent storm.

"Did the cops do their thing?"

She grabbed the binoculars she kept in the console, focusing on the end of the bridge. Then smiled as three unmarked police cars surrounded the Jeep, their flashers on. "See for yourself," she said, handing him the binoculars.

"Well, something went right today," he said after viewing what would hopefully be an arrest. "Is anyone going to stop us when we go over the bridge?"

"Burke said they wouldn't, but if they do, don't say a word. Both guns in the truck are registered to me and I have permits to carry, so we've broken no laws. Worst they can do is give me a citation for driving on the shoulder. If they ask to search, we ask for a warrant. Got it?"

"Yes, ma'am." He grabbed her hand and squeezed it. "So I'm going to say something and if it's inappropriate, I'm claiming adrenaline rush."

She chuckled, liking the feel of her hand in his. "Okay?"

"You were very hot, driving like that."

She grinned, pleased. "I guess I was at that."

It was his turn to laugh. "Glad to see your self-confidence is healthy."

"Still's nice to hear. Any other inappropriate-but-welcome compliments before I start over the bridge?"

He hesitated, then nodded, sober now. "When we're safe in your office, I want to kiss you."

She drew a breath, then let it out, considering her reply. Considering how he made her feel . . . enough. Better than enough.

He made her feel confident in a way that had nothing to do with her job. And when he admired her curves when he thought she wasn't looking? He made her feel desired.

The way she hadn't felt in way too long. Not since the boyfriend she'd left behind in North Carolina. The boyfriend who'd looked at her with accusing eyes after she'd killed Jake. Yes, she wanted this, wanted Gabe to kiss her. Wanted him to more than kiss her.

Beside her, he sighed. "I'm sorry. I shouldn't have said anything."

"No," she said quickly. "I want you to." She smiled at him ruefully. "I really want you to."

"But?"

"But you're my client and it's not professional."

He tilted his head, studying her. "Would Burke fire you?"

"No." The idea was ridiculous. "I'm pretty good at my job. It's more that there are lines we're not supposed to cross for a reason. If I kiss you, then . . ."

One russet brow lifted, his smile amused. "Then?"

"Then I'll want more. I'm not good at casual."

"I didn't think you were. Neither am I. Next objection?"

Her cheeks felt like they were on fire, which seemed to amuse him even more. "I can't focus on keeping you safe if I'm busy kissing you and . . . y'know . . . other stuff."

His lips twitched. "So when this case is over and you no longer have to keep me safe? Then you'll kiss me back?"

After this was over, there was no way she'd deny herself. "When this is over, I will definitely kiss you back."

He smiled. "Good. Then let's get on with the case, Miss Sutton. The sooner we clear this up, the sooner we can do all that kissing and . . . y'know . . . other stuff."

She smiled back, feeling settled. Feeling optimistic. "Yes, sir." Looking behind her, she backed up on the shoulder, enough that she could get a running start before merging into the bridge traffic. She got over into the far-left lane as quickly as she could, able to take a long look at the crime scene in progress because traffic had already slowed due to rubberneckers.

"Eckert's still in the Jeep," Gabe remarked. "What if they don't arrest him?"

"I don't know. I guess we'll find out when we get to the office. I'm debating reporting him for pulling a gun on us, but I'd prefer to keep my name out of this as best I can. I'll tell Burke and let him decide."

They passed over the bridge, Gabe turning to look behind them. "They're pulling him out of his Jeep," he reported. "And they're holding his gun."

"Good. One of the cops may have seen him pull it. I'd say our job here is done." She crossed the highway, getting back into the far-right lane so that she could take the next exit. "Next stop, the office."

"Where we'll finally get some answers from Xavier," Gabe added grimly.

I hope they're answers that don't break Gabe's heart.

The Quarter, New Orleans, Louisiana
TUESDAY, JULY 26, 2:20 P.M.

Xavier wished to high heaven that he'd switched places with Willa Mae and that he was driving now. Far from being a poky old-lady driver, the woman was channeling some secret Mario Andretti, weaving in and out of the traffic like a pro.

"Willa Mae!" his mother gasped. For the tenth time. In two minutes.

"What?" Willa Mae demanded. "I'm going exactly where that Burke fella told us to go. And if I can shake our tail in the process, all's the better."

"Don't shake our tail, Miss Willa Mae," Manny said from the back of the minivan. "Otherwise, the cops won't be able to take him down. You know what Burke said."

Burke had also confirmed that Xavier should stay down on the floor, so that his head wasn't visible through the minivan's windows. And, since Xavier liked his head attached to his shoulders, he'd obeyed.

But this made it so that he couldn't see what was happening. He was having to rely on Carlos, who, in typical Carlos fashion, was making things a whole lot lighter than they probably were. Xavier figured that it was his BFF's intention to make him laugh, so he'd obliged a time or two.

Because laughing was good in this situation. Laughing kept him from crying, and for that alone he'd be Carlos's friend for the rest of their lives. Which would—hopefully—stretch decades into the future.

This was serious. There were hit men after him. *After all of us.* Or at least one hit man. Who knew who the Lott imposter really was or why he was following them? He was probably at least a killer, seeing as how the real Paul Lott was dead.

Burke had sprung that little fact on them, intending to have them know how serious this was. Xavier thought his mother might faint, but she'd held strong. He knew his mom was amazing, but after this . . . well, he had a whole new appreciation for his mama's spine of steel.

And Willa Mae had been a constant slew of surprises. When she'd heard that Lott was dead, Xavier figured she'd make them find their own way to New Orleans. *It's what I would have done.* What most any smart person with an ounce of self-preservation would have done.

Not Willa Mae. She'd gripped the wheel tight and pursed her lips even tighter. Declared that she'd get them there safely. But she also took breaks from her take-no-prisoners persona every few minutes to quietly assure his mom that everything would be okay.

Except it wasn't okay, and Xavier couldn't see how it would be. Because the man who'd attacked them last night was dead. One of the nurses his mom knew at a different hospital confirmed that he'd died after surgery to repair damage from a gunshot wound.

That I did. I shot him. I killed him.

And I can't think about that right now.

"What's happening?" he asked Carlos, who was taking in the city with great interest. Xavier, not so much. He hadn't been back to New Orleans since he was five years old. Just being here was giving him serious flashbacks. Rain, rising water, his birth mama's hand shoving him onto the roof . . .

The time he'd sat there alone and crying. It had felt like years at the time but may have been less than an hour. Still, he remembered the terror.

And he remembered the lady in the window next door.

Which was why he was here all over again.

"We're coming up to the corner Burke told us about," Carlos said. "And traffic is crazy here. Where did all these people come from? It's insane."

"It's the music festival," Manny supplied. "Satchmo SummerFest. Good festival. Lotsa jazz. It's like a citywide block party."

Carlos twisted in his seat to stare at his brother. "When did you come to New Orleans?"

"Couple of times."

"Without me?" Carlos sounded outraged.

"You just turned twenty-one last month. You weren't old enough for the bars last year. You would've cramped my style."

Carlos turned back to face forward. "I'll cramp your something."

"Hey," Manny said cajolingly. "You're gonna see so much more in New York than I've ever seen. And next summer, we can go to Satchmo together."

From Xavier's position, he could see Carlos's lips curve, and was pleased to see the two brothers connecting like this. Manny had always been the older, cooler one, pretty much ignoring him and Carlos since forever. But he'd come through for them this time, for sure. One call from Carlos asking for help, and Manny had been all in.

"Okay, ladies and gents," Willa Mae called out. "We are approaching the rendezvous. Xavier, you scooched over enough? Don't want you to get stepped on, hon."

"Yes, ma'am," Xavier said, rolling a little closer to Carlos's chair. He clutched his dad's old pistol a little tighter. *Showtime.*

"Everyone buckled in?" Willa Mae asked and was answered by a chorus of *yes, ma'ams.*

"Xavier?" His mother's voice was pitched low and urgent. "If anything goes wrong, you run. You hear me? Do not look back. You run. All of you boys. You run."

Xavier swallowed hard. He was not going to run and leave his family unprotected. But he also didn't want her to worry, so he said, "I hear you, Mama."

"Us, too," Carlos said. "We hear you, Mrs. M."

Her sigh told him that she hadn't been fooled. "I love you all. Carlos and Manny, you're like my own sons. You all deserve a future."

"And they'll have it," Willa Mae said firmly. "Stop borrowing trouble, Cicely. It ain't helpin'."

"Are the cops in place?" Xavier asked.

"Yep," Carlos said. "At least I think so. A black car got in front of us right after Willa Mae cut in between the last two cars. A black car is beside us. And . . . yeah, I see Burke Broussard on that street corner." They'd found his photo on his PI company's website. "Jesus, he's a big guy. You should move over a little bit more, X. When he jumps in, one of his boots could squash you like a bug."

Xavier rolled his eyes, ignoring the fear coiling in his gut. "I'm not getting squashed."

"Whatever." Carlos was quiet now. Very serious. "Five, four, three, two—" His speech stuttered to a stop when Willa Mae floored it, wheels squealing as the minivan lurched forward. The black car in front of them would have cleared a path, allowing her to accelerate so that the car beside them could slip in between them and the white BMW SUV. That was the plan. "Hold on, X!"

"Oh, wow," Manny said, just as a police car siren started to wail. "Flashers and sirens. They have the Beemer completely boxed in. *Shit.*"

The last curse was due to the sharp right Willa Mae took. Two seconds later, she threw the minivan into park, the side door slid open, and Burke Broussard jumped in.

"Hi," Xavier said from the floor when Burke had jerked the side door closed, not waiting for Willa Mae to hit the button. "I'm Xavier."

Burke grinned down at him. "I'm Burke. Nice to meet you, Xavier." He looked around the van. "Manny and Carlos. And Miss Cicely and Miss Willa Mae. Welcome to New Orleans, y'all. Take a left at the next stop sign, ma'am. Then you'll see a man waving you through the gate into off-street parking."

"Will do," Willa Mae said. "And then you'll tell us what the hell is going on here?"

"We're going to wait for Molly Sutton and Gabe Hebert to join us," Burke said. "But we have lunch waiting."

Lunch waiting, Xavier thought with a mental snort. Like it was a fucking garden party. "Where are Molly and Gabe now?" he asked.

"Still on I-10, I imagine," Burke said as Willa Mae made the next turn. "There's my tech guy, ma'am. His name is Antoine. Just pull in where he's signaling to us."

"Oh, dear," Cicely said quietly. "He looks unhappy to see us."

Burke shrugged very wide shoulders. "He gets cranky when he does all-nighters. He hasn't slept yet. We've been exploring a few leads. All right, now," he said when they made another turn. "We're here and still alive. I think we're doing pretty well."

Xavier heard his mother's anxious intake of breath. "Where exactly is *here*, Mr. Broussard?"

"My office, ma'am. I'm so sorry. I'm afraid everything's been a little cloak-and-daggery up until now. We will share everything we know. I promise. And we have lunch." He repeated this last bit about lunch a little too brightly, as if hoping that giving them food would keep them from demanding answers. Xavier was about to say *hell no* to that when Manny spoke up.

"I can eat," Manny said. "You're not going to poison us, are you?"

Burke laughed. "No. I'll even eat a bite of y'all's food first, if it'll make you feel better."

"Not mine," Carlos said. "I could eat a whole cow myself. I'm starving."

"You're always starving," Manny complained. "What else is new?"

Burke looked amused. "We ordered lunch for fifteen people."

"That oughta be about right," Carlos agreed, totally serious. His BFF could put away an astounding amount of food. "Thank you, sir."

Xavier finally exhaled when the minivan stopped and Willa Mae cut the engine.

They were finally going to get some answers.

And, apparently, lunch.

The Quarter, New Orleans, Louisiana
TUESDAY, JULY 26, 3:00 P.M.

Joy, Burke's office manager, was waiting at the entry, tapping her fingers on the arm of her wheelchair when Gabe and Molly arrived. Her smile was professional, her demeanor polite but firm. "Burke's waiting in the conference room. The Houston crowd is pushing for answers, but he told them he was waiting for you. So hurry on up before the Texans revolt."

This is it, Gabe thought while following Molly into a conference room with a large table where Burke waited, looking none too patient. *This is when I find out who Xavier was to my dad.*

Gabe stopped short.

There he was. Xavier Morrow. A twenty-two-year-old Black man. *The friend that my father never told me about. The friend that my father gave a lot of money to.*

Xavier looked exhausted but appeared to be holding up okay. He was flanked on his left by his mother, who looked just like the photo he and Burke had found that morning.

Just this morning? Time really does fly when you're having fun. Or running from hit men. *Whatever.*

On Xavier's right was a Latino man who looked to be about the same age. Carlos, probably. On Carlos's other side was a slightly older man who looked enough like Carlos that to assume they were brothers was a safe bet. He'd be Manny.

On Cicely Morrow's left was a woman who appeared to be around sixty, also Black. This would be the minivan's driver, Willa Mae. She had narrowed her eyes at Gabe the moment he'd walked in. Not in a mean way, but in an I-see-you-so-don't-try-anything way.

Molly made a beeline for a nearby platter of sandwiches. She put together two plates and carried them to the table. "Gabe?"

He realized that he'd been standing there. Gaping like a fool. He joined them at the table, taking the seat directly across from Xavier. Drawing a breath, he reached his hand across the table. "Xavier. I'm Gabe Hebert. Rocky's son."

Xavier shook his hand, his grip firm. "I know. He told me all about you. Showed me your pictures. You look just like him."

Ignoring the plate that Molly slid in front of him, Gabe kept his gaze locked with Xavier's. "I'm afraid to say that he didn't tell me about you. I just learned that you exist this morning."

"How?" Cicely Morrow asked sharply. "Rocky always swore that no one could connect us. If he didn't tell you himself, how did you find us?"

"That would be because of me, ma'am," Molly said. "I'm Molly Sutton. I talked to you on the phone today. I work for Burke, and Gabe came to us yesterday, concerned about the circumstances of his father's death. I was checking into Rocky's financials and found a check he'd written to you six years ago. After that, the same amount was deposited monthly into an account called John Alan Industries."

Cicely sighed. "I worried about that check for a long time. I'd almost forgotten about it."

Xavier was frowning. "What do you mean, the circumstances of Rocky's death?"

Gabe swallowed. "He didn't commit suicide."

Xavier's whole body sagged, his eyes growing shiny with tears. "I didn't think he would. I didn't think he *could*. That means he was . . ." His voice broke. "Murdered?"

"We think so," Gabe replied, amazed that his voice was steady. Inside he was a shaking mess. "I need to know, Xavier. How are you connected to my father?"

Xavier blinked, sending a tear down each of his cheeks. "He saved my life. In Katrina. I was five."

Carlos leaned forward, clearly interested. "And that's all we know. So spill, man. I'm dying over here."

Xavier sputtered what might have been a laugh. "Okay, *hermano*. Okay." He folded his hands on the table in front of him and looked Gabe straight in the eye. "My mother—my birth mother—died in the flood. I don't remember my birth father." He straightened his spine. "My last memory of my birth mother was when she pushed me through the hole she'd chopped in the attic roof. I was safe, but she wasn't. I remember her hands, clutching at the air, trying to grab for the roof, to pull herself up. But she couldn't. She drowned."

Gabe's throat closed, and beside him, Molly gasped softly. "I'm sorry," she murmured.

"Very sorry," Gabe echoed hoarsely. Relief that his father had not cheated on his mother was eclipsed with sorrow for the horror a five-year-old Xavier had experienced while witnessing his mother's death. "You must have been so scared."

Xavier nodded. "Yeah. I was. I sat there for a while. I thought it was hours, because I was five years old. Might have been an hour. Hard to say. Other people were on their roofs, too. Help was coming, they told me. I just wanted my mother."

This was all new information for everyone at the table, except for Cicely Morrow. She laid her hand over Xavier's folded ones in silent support. The others—Carlos, Manny, Willa Mae, and even Burke—looked stricken. A glance from the corner of his eye revealed Molly wiping her eyes.

"Was my father the help that was coming?" Gabe asked.

"Yes. They came in rowboats and motorboats. Your dad was in one of the motorboats. I could see them coming down the street, which was flooded over the one-story houses by this point. Our house was one story, but it had a steep roof. That's where I was. And that's when I saw the white lady in the house next door. It was two stories, and she was in the upstairs bedroom. She was packing a suitcase."

Gabe held his breath, waiting, afraid of what he believed was coming.

"And then?" Burke prompted softly.

Xavier swallowed again. "And then a man came into the room. He was white, too. He had dark hair and a scar on his face." He traced a finger from his eye down the center of his cheek. "They were fighting, and he hit her. And hit her again. Then he put his hands around her throat . . ." His breathing quickened, and Gabe's quickened right along with him. "He ran then and left her there. Lying on the bed. Not moving. I was . . . little. And scared. Too scared to say anything or do anything to stop it."

"You were little more than a baby," Gabe said, hoping it was the right thing. "You were traumatized. Your mother had just died, and you were clinging to life on a roof. No one would have *ever* expected you to do anything."

Cicely's smile was shaky. "Except to tell Rocky Hebert," she said, her pride obvious.

Gabe exhaled, understanding dawning. "You told my father what you'd seen."

"Yes, sir. He didn't believe me at first. He tried to calm me down. Told me that everything would be okay, but it wasn't. I knew what I'd seen." More tears leaked from Xavier's dark eyes, and he wiped at them angrily. "He asked me about my mother, but she was under the water. I told him that. Then I told him that the lady next door was on the bed. She had a dog, a big, fancy dog with long hair and long ears. I'd see her walking it. The dog's name was Fluffy. I didn't know the lady's name. I just called her Miss Fluffy, and she'd always laugh."

"And then you saw her die, too," Gabe whispered. "Oh, Xavier. I'm so sorry."

Xavier waved the air, like none of it mattered. But it did. This poor young man had suffered so much that night. That he'd gone on to become such a good person, volunteering and graduating salutatorian? And he was going on to med school?

"But my father must have believed you at some point," Gabe guessed.

"He did. The neighbors told him that my mother had saved me then died, but they hadn't seen the lady next door." He shrugged. "Her window was next to where I was sitting on the roof. No one else had the right angle to see in. Anyway, your father finally went over to check, because I wouldn't be quiet about it. He broke the window and climbed in. The flood was almost up to the second-story windows by this point. When he got back in the boat, he looked sad. Told me that he'd send a doctor to take care of the lady. That he was getting me to some place that was warm and dry."

Gabe frowned, confused. "But then what happened?"

"I didn't know, not for a long time. I never saw him again, not until I was sixteen. I was taken by social services that night. I didn't have any relatives to call. Me and my birth mom were all alone. She was an accountant." His smile was small and sad. "She liked numbers. She let me play with her calculator sometimes. I don't remember that much about her. Just her hands tapping calculator keys. And reaching out of the water that last day."

Carlos covered his mouth, choking on a sob. "Why didn't you tell me?"

Xavier turned to him. "I didn't want to remember it. Took me years before I even told Mom and Dad."

"We were foster parents," Cicely said, taking up the tale. "So many of the kids were taken from New Orleans to Houston, and we ended up blessed with Xavier, although he didn't go by that name then."

"My mother named me Angel," Xavier said. "That's the name I told your dad that night."

That checked out. The name on Xavier's birth certificate had been Angel Xavier Morrow.

"Which made it hard for him to find Xavier later." Cicely shook her head. "But we're getting ahead of ourselves. We fostered Xavier, then adopted him. Got him an amended birth certificate, which is standard practice for adoptions. His original birth certificate has been sealed. We know his mother's name was Monique Johnson because her body was later recovered, but Xavier didn't remember much then. He was . . . troubled. Nightmares and such. Terrible nightmares."

Gabe shuddered. He couldn't even imagine.

"I guess so," Molly murmured. "Did you tell anyone else about the woman you'd seen, Xavier?"

"He tried to," Cicely answered. "He told us—me and my husband. He told his therapist, but she believed it was trauma from seeing his mother die. When they'd recovered his mother's body, we paid to have her cremated. Her ashes are in my husband's study, but we paid for a marker in the cemetery so that Xavier could lay flowers on her grave."

"Where is your husband?" Molly asked, even though she already knew. Gabe figured that she was checking out Cicely Morrow's story.

"My husband is deceased."

Which was also consistent with what they'd found that morning.

"So you went to school and started over with a new family until my father reconnected with you years later?" Gabe asked.

"Basically, yes. It wasn't quite that smooth." Xavier aimed an apologetic look at his mother. "I was not the easiest kid."

"You were *our* kid," Cicely said fervently. "And we loved you from the day we met you. Your daddy was so proud of you."

Xavier's throat worked and he opened his mouth, but no words came out.

"He was a little turd sometimes, though," Carlos chimed in. "Started fights in school. That's how we met."

Xavier wiped his eyes and pretended to glare. "I didn't pick that fight. You did."

Carlos grinned. "Yeah, you're right. That was me. I picked the fight and you ended it with one punch. We were in the first grade. I had to go to the nurse for a nosebleed, and Xavier was in the office getting detention, but we both had to see the principal, because zero tolerance and all that shit. By the time we made it through the first detention, we were best friends."

"*Pendejo,*" Xavier muttered, but with unmistakable affection. "You're stupid."

"Made you laugh," Carlos replied, unruffled.

"Yeah, you did. You always do. Thank you." They bumped shoulders in the way of old friends, and Xavier returned his attention to Gabe. "I thought that I'd imagined seeing the lady murdered after a while. Everyone told me that I'd imagined it, so I started to believe it. Until your father showed up. Knocked on the front door of our house and when I opened it, I recognized him immediately."

"Xavier fell to his knees," Cicely said, remembering. "He just . . . fell down. He kept saying, 'That's the man. That's the man.' He was sixteen years old, but in that moment, it was like he was five years old and traumatized all over again. But he did calm down, and we went outside to talk to your father. I'd asked Rocky to wait outside while I calmed Xavier down and he was patient with us. I was a recent widow and nervous about inviting a man into my house, and he said he understood. Besides, back then we were the only house on the street. We had one neighbor in the back, but the houses that are next to us now were just being built, so we had privacy on the porch. Rocky started talking and then the story just came out."

Xavier took up the tale. "He said he'd been looking for me. Johnson was a common enough name, but there were no Angels. Because I'd told him that was my name. Xavier is my middle name and I asked to be called that." He looked embarrassed. "Because of *X-Men.* I was only six."

"Hey, I'm good with that reason," Molly said with a smile. "But it would have made it hard for Rocky to track you down. How did he find you?"

"Through the check we wrote to pay for Xavier's mother's cremation," Cicely answered. "It took him a long time to find us, though. He confirmed that there *had* been a dead woman in the house across from Xavier's that night. He'd seen her with his own eyes. He saw the ligature marks around her neck. But when he went back after the floodwaters started to go down, she was gone."

Gabe blinked. "What do you mean 'gone'? She was dead, right?"

"No," Xavier said. "Her body was gone. Rocky told us that the floodwaters had never reached the bed and it was still in good shape. The room was waterlogged because he broke a window to get in, but he said there was no sign of the body. He reported it and tried to work the case but was told to stop."

"Told by whom?" Burke asked, frowning.

"By his supervisors," Xavier said. "He said that every time he brought it up, his bosses would give him other cases. They said he wasn't Homicide at first, back when he discovered the body. Later, when he was in Homicide, he was told that other Homicide detectives were working it. But he checked around, and they weren't."

Gabe turned to Burke. "You were his partner. Did you know about this?"

Burke shook his head. "I knew he had a case that he couldn't let go, but he'd never tell me about it. We all had that one case we couldn't let go, so I didn't pester him. I should have."

"It wouldn't have helped," Xavier said sadly. "He wasn't going to tell anyone, because it was too dangerous. That's what he said."

Cicely patted her son's hand. "He also had been threatened by his boss."

"Who?" Burke demanded. "When and how?"

"We don't know names. Rocky wouldn't tell us. But he said he'd brought it up again the year before he found us." Cicely darted a nervous glance at Gabe. "It was the tenth anniversary of Katrina, and he thought someone would care. He was ready to go to the press. He hadn't told anyone at the beginning that he had an eyewitness because he couldn't find Xavier to corroborate, but Rocky had seen the body. He knew she was dead. By the tenth anniversary he was so eager to solve the case that he told them he did have an eyewitness who could identify the killer through his scar. But then his boss told him that if he continued 'blathering' about this case, he'd lose his job, and wouldn't that be bad for his wife, not to have health insurance? So he quit asking. Publicly, anyway."

Gabe felt the color drain from his face. A warm hand grabbed his. Molly.

"Sonofabitch," Burke cursed.

"You okay?" Molly asked very softly.

Gabe jerked a nod and did the math. "My mother was diagnosed with cancer a year before the tenth anniversary of Katrina. She was still undergoing chemo a year later. If she'd lost her insurance, she would have died then."

Carlos was shaking his head. "That's wrong."

"So wrong," Manny agreed in his gravelly voice.

"That poor man," Willa Mae said sadly. "Talk about being stuck between a rock and a hard place."

Burke stood up and began pacing the room. "I wish he'd told me. Why didn't he tell me?"

"It wasn't because he didn't trust you," Cicely said. "He thought about bringing you in once you were partners, but he didn't want to drag you down with him. He figured that the cover-up went pretty high up. He told me that it was a hard decision, but he liked you. He was protecting you."

Burke sighed. "That's sounds like him. Stubborn man."

That was fair, Gabe thought. His father had been the most stubborn man he'd ever known.

Cicely made a noise of agreement. "He really was. By this point, though, he knew that the rot had burrowed deep. He didn't know who he could trust. When his boss blocked his investigation on the tenth anniversary of the flood, the man also demanded to know the eyewitness's name. Rocky was terrified that they'd come after Xavier, seeing as how they were threatening his wife. He gave his boss a fake name."

Gabe stared. "A fake name? You mean he lied?"

"He did," Cicely confirmed. "He gave them the name of another child who'd died in Katrina. He figured his boss must have been satisfied, because he stopped pressuring Rocky for Xavier's name. That's when Rocky started searching harder for Xavier, so that he could warn him. He was worried that they'd silence him, too. He believed someone in his chain of command was covering this up and at that point he didn't trust them not to try to hurt Xavier."

"Rocky was like my second dad," Xavier almost whispered. "But you were his son, Gabe. Not me. Never me. So don't you worry about that."

Gabe managed a smile. "My father was a good man. I'm glad he found you, and that you were all right."

"Well." Xavier waggled his hand. "We weren't so good when he found us. My father had died the year before, and times were rough."

"I was working two jobs to keep the house," Cicely admitted. "My late husband didn't know how to manage money, and I wasn't aware that he didn't know. Our financial situation after he died of a heart attack was a huge shock. There was barely enough to bury him. I ended up finishing my nurse's degree and getting a good job, but there was a lot of debt. We were close to losing our house. Your dad helped us. I didn't want to take it. Didn't want to take food out of your mouths, but he promised me that his wife knew and that she wanted to help us."

"Did you ever meet my mom?" Gabe asked.

Cicely smiled warmly. "We did. Just the once. She was able to travel for a short period of time and your dad drove her to Houston. They spent the night in a swanky hotel, then had breakfast with us the next morning at our house."

Gabe's heart pounded harder. "I remember that. Mom said they were having a second honeymoon while she still could. But I didn't know they were going to see you. I wondered then why they picked Houston for a trip."

"We were why." Xavier met Gabe's gaze. "We didn't want his charity, so he said we could call it a loan. We paid him back, every cent we borrowed—with interest. It took us a few years, though. Your mother had passed by then. Mom and I both put what we earned against the debt and by the time I was in college, we'd paid in full."

Cicely's chin lifted slightly. "We have receipts."

"I believe you," Gabe said simply. And he did.

"I told him to stop after we'd paid him back," Cicely said, ruefully shaking her head. "I was making decent money as a nurse by then. But he kept depositing that money into the John Alan account every month. Said it was a loan for Xavier's college. He said that he'd helped send you to culinary school, Gabe, and that he was helping Xavier, too. That Xavier could pay him back when he was a rich doctor." Her lips curved in a sad smile. "But now he won't see that."

"I had a scholarship and I worked to pay for school," Xavier said. "I was saving the loan money for medical school."

"As you should," Gabe said quietly. "And someday, when you are a rich doctor? Donate something in his name, if you don't mind. Money or time. He would have liked that."

Xavier swallowed. "I will. I like that, too."

"So do I." Cicely exhaled. "That conversation was easier than I thought it would be."

Gabe cleared his throat. "Then I guess we tackle the harder one. Once Dad found you, what did he do next? What happened six weeks ago that got him killed?"

No one answered. Because no one knew.

"We'll find out," Molly assured him, and he believed her, too. "Xavier, will you tell us about last night? You said that you called Paul Lott to get Gabe's number because someone tried to kill you."

Xavier shifted in his chair. He opened his mouth, but his mother tapped his hand.

She focused in on Burke. "Are you recording this?" she demanded.

What the hell? Gabe thought. *What happened last night?*

Burke was blinking. "No. We're not recording any of this. Why?"

Xavier suddenly looked miserable. "Because I killed someone."

11

XAVIER THOUGHT HE was going to throw up. *Because I killed someone.*

I am a killer.

"Whoa," Molly said. "Let's start at the beginning. Tell us everything. We'll help you."

He hoped that meant that they'd help him stay out of prison.

"You can't tell the cops," Cicely insisted. "They'll never believe him."

"We will keep your son safe," Burke promised. "We have friends in NOPD, but I left for a reason. I get your concerns. For now, do as Molly's asked. Tell us everything."

"Maybe he needs a break," Gabe said, sounding protective. That was one-eighty from where the man had been when he'd first walked through the door. *Because he thought that I was Rocky's secret son.*

Poor Gabe. I'd have been upset, too.

You are *upset.*

Yeah, but because of what I did. Not what Rocky did.

"Xavier?" Molly asked gently. "Do you need a break?"

"No, ma'am." His voice sounded rusty to his own ears. He cleared his throat. "But I wish that I hadn't eaten so much lunch."

Carlos got up, found a wastebasket in the corner, and set it down between them before retaking his seat. "Just in case."

Love for his best friend welled up in his heart. "*Pendejo*," Xavier muttered.

"At your service," Carlos joked, but his eyes were deadly serious.

Xavier took strength from the hand Carlos clasped around the back of his neck. "So. Last night."

He told them the whole story, from seeing the car to hearing the noise, to escaping through the window. To shooting the white man.

"Then we ran," he finished with a shrug. "When we got back to my house the next morning with whoever was pretending to be Paul Lott, the body was gone."

"Then how do you know the man is dead?" Molly asked. "Maybe he was able to leave your house on his own."

"He was," Cicely said tersely. "He drove himself to the ER. I . . . made some calls."

"And you found out that he was dead," Gabe finished.

His mother nodded, distrust in her eyes. She was poised at the edge of her seat, like she was ready to run away with her son right now. "My friend who's a nurse on another floor of the hospital checked for me. I'd been asking about anyone who'd come in with a gunshot wound the night before. It took a while because we didn't have a name or a real description. But this guy checked himself into the ER about thirty minutes after he tried to kill Xavier. He didn't have any ID or insurance. They rushed him into surgery and the doctor felt good about his chances, but the man died this morning at around ten o'clock."

"You killed him in self-defense, Xavier," Gabe said. "You protected yourself and Carlos—and he's your family. I won't tell anyone."

"Nor I." Molly lifted her hand as if taking an oath. "I'll vouch for you if anyone finds out."

"Same," Burke said. "Let us do some checking. We need to know who that man was. Did he have a gun?"

"He did," Carlos said. "I saw it in his hand when he grabbed Xavier's shirt. He had his gun out, ready to shoot." He shook his head, his voice going hoarse. "I was on the ground already. All I had was a stupid baseball bat and a golf club. I couldn't do a thing to help."

Xavier put his arm around Carlos and hugged him to his side. "You got me out of there once I dropped out of the tree. You ran with me, made me run faster, kept me calm. And then you called Manny. You saved me."

Carlos had buried his face against Xavier's side, his breaths coming fast. And he was crying. After all of this, all the joking, all the keeping things light . . . Now his best friend was crying.

Xavier had to fight his own tears. If he started crying now, he'd never finish. And he wanted to be finished with this, so damn bad. "We're okay," he murmured to Carlos, ignoring the sympathetic expressions around them. Even Manny looked like he was about to cry. "Don't, dude," Xavier told the older brother. "I won't be able to stop."

Carlos pulled away, accepting the box of tissues that Molly pushed across the table. "Damn, everybody. I'm sorry."

"It's cathartic," Molly told him. "You'd be surprised how many Marines I've seen cry."

"Zero," Carlos said, his tone self-deprecating, and Xavier hated to hear it.

"A whole lot more than zero," Molly insisted. "Go on, Xavier. Let's get this on the table."

"Not much more to tell. We went into the house and saw the blood on the floor in the spare bedroom and the laundry room. And drops down the driveway." He winced. "I think he took some of your good towels, Mom. To stem the flow."

Cicely rolled her eyes. "Towels can be replaced. You can't. So what do we do now?"

"We find out who hired the hit man," Gabe said. "My guess is when the first guy failed, whoever hired him sent Eckert the hit man after Xavier."

"He's a real hit man? Seriously?" Xavier demanded. Molly had told them while they were driving, but it was so *surreal*. "Like on TV? This is . . . This is insane."

"He's a real hit man," Burke said. "I never met him, but I knew him by reputation when I was with NOPD."

"He pointed a gun at us when we blocked the exit," Gabe said quietly. "At Molly, actually."

"Road rage," Molly said with a shrug.

"Shit," Manny whispered. "That's hardcore."

"We stopped him from following you," Molly stated as if she hadn't had a gun pointed at her face. "He was pissed off. But the cops pulled him over, and Gabe saw them with the gun he'd used. He'll get busted for that, and maybe he'll give up the person who hired him."

That was encouraging. Xavier hadn't had time to think that far out. "That would be so nice. What about the man impersonating Lott?"

"NOPD got him, too," Burke said. "My friend André, who's a captain on the force, was in one of those vehicles you saw stop the white SUV. André's brother is Antoine, who works for me. Good guys, both of them. I trust them with my life."

"Do you trust them with Xavier's if they try to charge him with murder?" Cicely asked coldly.

Burke didn't seem offended. "For now? Yes, ma'am. If that changes, you two will be the first to know."

"What are you thinking, Burke?" Molly asked. "About the guy who died in the hospital?"

"I don't know," he said honestly. "We need to find out who hired him, but we need to keep our interest low-profile for Xavier's sake. I'll get Antoine to see what he can find out. Finding out how the Paul Lott impersonator fits in is also critical." He turned to Xavier. "You're not the only one who's been attacked. Someone had planned to attack Gabe last night. They tried to poison his dog."

"Oh no." Gabe stood up and dug his phone from his pocket. "I forgot about Shoe."

"Your restaurant?" Carlos asked with a frown.

"No, my dog. His name is Shoe. Because he chewed shoes. It's a joke," Gabe finished lamely. "He's at the vet still, Burke. I want to go get him."

"I'll go get him tomorrow morning," Burke promised. "If anyone is watching the vet, waiting for you to pick him up . . . Well, let's not give them an easy target, okay? Xavier, do you have anything else you need to tell us or just want to say?"

Xavier quieted his mind and thought about Rocky, about the last time they'd seen each other. "He was worried. Rocky, I mean. He told me that he was getting closer, and that I needed to be aware of my surroundings. He didn't want me to get hurt." He frowned, trying to remember. "He said he'd make sure that Gabe understood everything, and that if anyone tried to hurt me, to find Gabe."

"But he didn't tell me anything," Gabe protested. "Not even about you."

"But he did leave a UPS box," Molly said, her voice growing excited. "Maybe he left a safe-deposit box, too. We need to check for any keys he might have hidden. Xavier, did he leave you a key?"

"Not after he died. He set a UPS box up for me when he was alive and I have a key to that, but I never got anything from Rocky after his death. Only got a letter from the lawyer, information about a trust he set up for me. I was shocked, because I wasn't expecting anything. He'd given me so much when he was alive, and this trust is on top of all of that. It's supposed to help pay for expenses in med school. I'll give it back to you, Gabe. It's rightfully yours."

Gabe shook his head. "No, Xavier. He meant you to have it. Do you know who John Alan was?"

Xavier shook his head. "No, sir. I asked a few times, but Rocky would never say. Who was he?"

"One of the nights during Katrina, my mother miscarried a pregnancy. They had planned to name the child John Alan. He was their second son."

"Oh," Xavier breathed, his eyes burning again. "He found me during Katrina."

"Maybe that same night," Gabe said sadly.

"He lost one son and found another," Cicely murmured. "Oh, Xavier. That man had the kindest heart."

"He did," Gabe agreed, his voice gone gruff. "And if he wanted you to have that trust, then you should keep it. Now, if you'll excuse me, I have to call the vet about keeping Shoe a little longer."

Molly rose with him. "I have to call home. I'll be right back, though. Do you all have a place to stay?"

"No," Xavier said.

"Yes," Burke said. "They're staying with me. We can talk about who's guarding whom once we have everyone settled."

"Thank you," Cicely said. "I've got an overnight bag and Willa Mae brought a few things, but we'll need a trip to the drugstore for toiletries."

Burke shook his head. "Joy, our office administrator, already has it covered. Tell her what you need. She'll make sure you have it."

"Xavier's got clothes at least," Carlos commented. "The guy posing as Paul Lott insisted that he pack a bag."

Willa Mae leaned forward again so that she could see Carlos. "But not you and Manny? You were all together, right? Why didn't he let you two go home to pack a bag?"

Carlos cocked his head. "That's true. Why was he so worried about your bag, X?"

"I have no idea," Xavier said. "I mean, if he meant to kill me, why ask me to pack a bag? Why take the time for that?"

"I *told* you that he was watching you funny when you were packing," Manny said.

"We need to figure that out," Molly said. "Let me call home and then we can start making a list of what we don't know. That will be first on the list. Be thinking about it, Xavier. Gabe?"

"Right behind you."

The two of them left, and Willa Mae made a dreamy sound. "How long have they been together?"

"Two days," Burke said dryly. "But I think you're onto something, Miss Willa Mae."

"I usually am," she said smugly.

And Xavier thought she just might be right.

The Quarter, New Orleans, Louisiana
TUESDAY, JULY 26, 4:45 P.M.

Gabe ended the call with the vet's office and finally relaxed into the visitor's chair in Burke's office. Joy, the office admin, had directed him here when he'd asked for a place to make a few personal calls.

He hadn't really needed privacy for the calls. He'd just needed a minute or two to decompress. And to process. And maybe to allow the tears he'd been holding to fall.

"I'm sorry, Dad," he whispered. Sorry that he'd believed the worst. Sorry that he hadn't noticed that his father carried such a heavy burden. Sorry that he hadn't been able to help.

Sorry that his father had been murdered for doing the right thing.

A light knock came a second before the door cracked open. "Can I come in?" Molly asked. "And it's okay if you don't want me to."

He didn't think twice before saying, "Yes, please. Come in." Because he needed someone who'd sit with him and simply let him be. He needed Molly Sutton.

He didn't move until she knelt before him, her palms flat on his knees. "You okay, Gabe?"

He looked up to find her blue-green eyes filled with sympathy. And understanding. "I don't know," he answered honestly.

She flipped her hands over so that her palms were facing up and he slid his hands into hers. "That's a perfectly acceptable answer. You've had a rough couple of days."

He swallowed hard, but his words still came out sounding rusty. "Thank you."

She smiled up at him. "For what?"

"Knowing that I'd need you." He hesitated, then, once again, figured why the hell not. He tugged on her hands. "Sit with me."

She eyed the chair. "I don't think there's room for both of us."

"I know." He tugged on her hands and she rose willingly, then eased onto his knee. He put his arms around her waist and tugged her closer until her cheek was resting on his shoulder. She slid one arm around his neck and then went pliant against him.

"He didn't cheat," she whispered.

Gabe's eyes burned. "No. And I'm ashamed to have thought he had."

"No," she soothed. "It was a normal reaction given the information. And I don't think you really believed it."

He considered her words, then realized that she was right. Again. "Not really, no." He was quiet for the next few minutes, taking comfort from her presence, finally close enough to smell her hair without feeling awkward. Because it wasn't awkward at all. It was . . . nice.

So very nice.

And her hair smelled like oranges.

"Why does your hair smell like oranges?" he asked, the words out before he could pull them back.

She chuckled. "It's a shampoo for swimmers. Gets the chlorine out of my hair."

He'd learned something new. "You swim?"

"Four or five times a week when I'm not on a case. Burke gives us a gym membership as an employee benefit. We're more likely to catch the bad guy—and *survive* the bad guy—if we're fit. I do the machines and swim laps and I've been taking Harper for swim lessons. Her therapist thought that getting out with other kids would be good for her."

"Surviving the bad guy is preferable," he murmured, making her chuckle again.

She didn't say anything more as the minutes ticked by, allowing him to think. His brain slowed to a mostly normal speed, and then the truth hit him hard.

"Someone killed my father to stop him from investigating a murder. A murder his cop bosses didn't want him solving."

She stroked his hair and he hoped she'd never stop. "So it would seem. Now it's up to us to finish what he started. I won't rest until we find out who killed that woman during Katrina. I give you my word."

He knew she would. "They threatened my mother."

"They did."

"I want them to suffer. I know that makes me sound vengeful."

She leaned back far enough that he could see her face. "I'm good with vengeful, Gabe. You won't hear any argument from me. You should want them to suffer. You should want them caught. You should want to see them rot in prison. And if you want to see them dead, I wouldn't blame you."

There was something in her tone, something in her eyes that gave him pause. "Did you want to see your brother-in-law in prison?"

"Oh yes. For the rest of his life."

He hesitated. "Did you want to see him dead?"

She closed her eyes for a moment. When she opened them, he saw staggering guilt. "Yes."

"Is . . . Is that why you killed him?"

She didn't look away. "I killed him because he came after me with his fists. He came after me with his fists because I taunted him to stop him from beating on my sister."

She'd used herself as bait. "You said he hit you." And Gabe was glad he'd never meet the guy, because he'd want to hurt him for causing Molly and her family such pain.

"He did. And then he pulled a gun from underneath his shirt. Chelsea screamed. I just reacted."

And, fortunately, Harper had been in her bedroom at the time. But she'd heard it. The poor baby had heard it all. Gabe wanted to say something. To comfort her as she had him, but he didn't know what to say and didn't think she was finished anyway.

She didn't blink. "I don't want to think that I planned it, but I knew he was carrying. He'd shot my father the night before. The cop took his service revolver after he killed my father with Dad's own gun, but I knew he had others. They held him for questioning, but he was a cop with a sob story and friends in high places within the local police department. He lied about my father, said that Dad had molested Harper and that Dad had tried to kill him, so they said it was self-defense and let him go without charging him. And then he came straight home. To us."

"Did you have a choice?"

"At that moment, I didn't think about choices. He had a gun. He'd used a gun. He'd already given black eyes to both Chelsea and me. He was screaming that he was going to kill me because I'd clearly lied to his wife about his molesting their daughter."

"But there was a video."

"Which Chelsea hadn't yet turned over to the police. She wanted to confront him first. I should have known that she'd do that, and maybe part of me did."

"It doesn't matter. He threatened you. You're not to blame."

"I also knew that if he did any time at all for raping his own daughter, it wouldn't be enough, and then he'd be back. He'd try it again. If not to Harper, then to some other child. And Harper would be put through the additional trauma of a trial. So maybe I could have let him go. Maybe I could have let the justice system do its job. But at that moment, I just reacted." She shrugged one shoulder. "It changed my life. People will always wonder if I really killed in self-defense or out of vengeance. I'd like for this not to change your life in the same way."

"So, it's okay for me to want them to die, but not okay for me to kill them."

"Something like that. But if it comes to you or them, choose yourself. I'm sure as hell going to choose you. I will shoot them to save you. You need to be okay with that."

"Oh, I am. Trust me. I am very okay with that." Because he'd do the same for her. It was what partners did. And for the time being, she was his partner. But it was more than that. He felt a connection with Molly Sutton that he'd never felt with any woman ever before. He wanted her, it was true.

But he wanted *this* more. This support. This . . . intimacy.

Another thirty seconds ticked by as they stared at each other. Then she tilted her head. "Xavier said that your father left you information."

"I know. I don't know what he meant."

"Then, as much as I like sitting on your lap and as much as I think you need this break, we should be getting back to the conference room. We have a lot of work to do."

He didn't want to leave the quiet and comfort of this room, but he knew she was right. Except . . . "You said I could kiss you when this was over."

She smiled. "I did."

"I wish this was over right now," he whispered hoarsely. "You don't even know."

Her expression changed, softening before her eyes became abruptly turbulent. He could feel her indecision, but even more, he could feel her yearning. She wanted him, too. Wanted this.

Whatever this was. Whatever it might become.

For a long, long moment she said nothing at all as the air between them thickened with anticipation. And arousal. Then her eyes cleared, the calm resolution that he'd seen so many times already settling his heart.

Which then nearly knocked out of his chest when she cupped his cheek and pulled his head down, brushing her lips against his. It was sweet and chaste and over far too soon. Even still, he was breathing hard.

So was she.

"What was that for?" he asked, barely controlling himself from kissing her again.

"A promise." She caressed his lips with her thumb. "So that you know you're not alone. Not in searching for answers or in wishing for this."

Chest tightening, he swallowed hard, the *thank you* stuck in his throat. But her smile said that she understood.

She slid off his lap and onto her feet, then reached for his hand to tug him out of the chair. "Come on. We've got work to do. Will the vet allow Burke to get Shoe?"

The moment itself was broken, but she'd given him some of her strength and he held on to it as he forced his brain to shift gears. "They will. Shoe knows Burke since he's visited my dad's house a lot over the past few years. They said Burke can pick him up tomorrow. Is your sister okay?"

"Yes. One of Burke's men is going to stay outside our apartment again tonight, just to be sure. I think Burke's going to be buying a company vehicle so that we can use it from now on instead of using our personal vehicles. Especially on cases like this."

Because people are trying to hurt us. Kill us. And that thought brought everything back into perfect focus.

"Let's go pick Xavier's mind," he said. "Maybe he or his mother has some idea of what my father was talking about when he said he left me information."

"Let's hope." She glanced at her phone for the time. "It's coming up on dinnertime. I'll call for pizza delivery later."

Gabe made a face. "Not on my watch. I already took care of dinner. I heard poor Carlos's stomach growling from across the table in spite of the sandwiches we all ate, and I don't think Xavier ate much at all. I know that I didn't and now I'm starving. I called the Choux and one of our cooks is bringing dinner for everyone." He had to chuckle when Molly's eyes lit up. "I assume that meets with your approval?"

She made a happy noise. "Dinner from my favorite restaurant two nights in the same week? Yes, please." She took his hand and tugged. "Come on. I'm starving."

The Quarter, New Orleans, Louisiana
TUESDAY, JULY 26, 5:15 P.M.

Standing in front of the conference room whiteboard, Molly clapped her hands and waited for the dinner chatter to quiet. She was going to concentrate so that she could keep her promise to Gabe. She was not going to think about how perfect his lips had felt when she'd kissed him. And she definitely wasn't going to think about the raw desire in his eyes afterward. "I hope everyone got enough to eat."

Everyone nodded but Carlos, but then he nodded when Xavier elbowed him in the ribs. "You ate *three* dinners," Xavier hissed.

"For fuck's sake," Manny said, passing his plate to his brother. "I'm full. You can have mine."

Carlos mumbled his thanks, then continued to eat.

"Thank you, Gabe," Xavier said, earning him a smile from his mother. "It was so good."

"So good," Carlos moaned around a mouthful of étouffée.

Manny elbowed him from the other side. "Don't talk with your mouth full."

Carlos swallowed and turned to his brother. "Sorry, *Mom*."

Cicely leaned forward. "Speaking of moms, does yours know where you are?"

"I called her," Manny said. "Told her that we came to New Orleans on a whim. Which isn't untrue."

"Give Joy her number before you leave tonight," Molly said. "Just in case." She watched everyone on the Houston side of the table flinch, so she hurried on to keep them on task. "But this is the time when we throw everything we know on that whiteboard, so everyone focus."

"My dad was murdered as part of a murder cover-up," Gabe stated baldly.

Molly wrote that down. "We need the victim's name. Xavier, you said that you didn't know her name, but what about your address back then?"

He started to shake his head, but Cicely Morrow nodded. "We have the address in our records at home, but I can't recall it. We do remember his mother's name, though."

"Monique Johnson," Xavier said, his voice choked, then he pursed his lips hard. Tears had filled his eyes. "She died the night the levee broke and the floods came."

Carlos put his arm around Xavier's shoulders. "I'm sorry I never asked."

"I wouldn't have told you," Xavier whispered. "It's hard to remember."

Molly gave him a few moments to regain his composure and pushed on. "Rocky said that the murder victim's body was gone, so somebody took her away after the rescue teams came through." She wrote: *Who took her away? Was it her killer?* She turned to the group. "What else?"

"My father had been investigating," Gabe said. "He must have gotten close for someone to kill him now, after all these years."

Molly wrote that on the board, then added: *Who knew he was investigating?*

"Good question," Burke murmured. "I didn't." He looked at Gabe. "Have you heard from your aunt Gigi yet?"

"I keep getting her voice mail. Wherever she is, she's got her phone turned off, and I don't know any of her friends or neighbors to ask them. If Dad told her anything, she didn't tell me."

"We know she knew about John Alan Industries," Molly said, then wrote: *Aunt Gigi, lives in Montreal, president —> John Alan Industries.* "We know that whoever killed Rocky has his phone, but not his SIM card."

Xavier looked up, a proud smile spreading across his face. "He hid his SIM? I told him to do that if things got bad."

· "It was in his truck," Gabe said. "Hidden under the floor mat. Burke's IT guy has it."

Burke took out his phone. "I'm texting him now to see what he's found."

"Hopefully we'll find something on that card," Gabe said. "Dad's laptop was in his house, but wiped. We don't know if Dad wiped it or his killer did. His killer also planted cocaine in his pantry with the flour and sugar."

Xavier sucked in a breath. "Sonsofbitches," he snarled.

Cicely closed her eyes. "They had to tarnish Rocky's name so that no one would believe whatever it was he either found or was on the verge of finding."

Molly wrote all that on the board, then stared at it, still wondering about who'd known that Rocky was investigating. "Paul Lott called you about the inheritance, Xavier?"

"Yes'm. But not on my cell phone. Rocky gave me a burner. It was how he'd contact me."

Gabe looked surprised. "My dad gave you a burner?"

"Yeah. He had one, too. He'd text my normal phone from his burner with something innocuous, like 'Thirty percent off sale!' I'd know then to check my burner. When he first gave it to me, I carried it everywhere, but after a while I left it at home because he contacted me so infrequently. Sometimes months would go by. Once a year went by, but that's when his wife got really sick."

"Okay, so his lawyer knew *of* you," Molly clarified, "but not necessarily where you were."

Cicely clenched her teeth. "Until Xavier called him for help last night."

"But someone already knew where to find me," Xavier said. "That guy followed me all day yesterday. Parked in front of our house."

"And the man who Xavier called wasn't Paul Lott," Burke added. "He was already dead by then or killed right around the time Xavier called."

Molly wrote: *Was Paul Lott involved? Or did killer force him to tell about X?* "That his killer just happened to be there at the exact time that Xavier called can't be a coincidence. Either Lott was cooperating or whoever killed him had bugged his phone. Still doesn't make sense, though. Why kill Lott when they already knew where Xavier was by then? It's a five-hour drive to Houston and they'd been following him all day, so they knew Xavier's location at least forty to forty-eight hours ago."

"Or," Burke said slowly, "there were two people searching for Xavier. One found him first. The other found him after he called for help."

Cicely rubbed her temples. "My head hurts."

"I'm sorry, Mama," Xavier murmured.

"Hush, son. None of this is your fault, so you stop that thinking right now."

Xavier's lips quirked up. "Yes, Mom."

"What did you pack in your duffel bag, Xavier?" Willa Mae asked quietly.

Molly startled. The woman had been so quiet, Molly had nearly forgotten she was there. "That's right. Carlos, you said the Paul Lott imposter insisted that Xavier pack a bag. What's in the bag?"

"Underwear and socks," Xavier said, bewildered. "A few clean shirts and some jeans. We each grabbed our backpacks, too. Carlos was staying overnight, so he had his with him."

"I don't think he intended for us to follow him to New Orleans," Manny said. "Carlos and me, I mean. I think he planned to kill us."

Carlos flinched but nodded. "I agree."

Xavier had closed his eyes. "Probably," he croaked, then cleared his throat. "Paul Lott knew about the UPS box that Rocky set up for me, though. That's where he sent the paperwork I had to sign for the trust. But that's in Baton Rouge."

Molly wrote that down. "Which underscores that the lawyer didn't know where to find you until you called. What about the intruder? Cicely, you said that you tracked down his body."

She nodded. "I did. My nurse friend said that he'd survived the surgery and was expected to make a full recovery, but that he'd died. Which would have been good for Xavier, because he wouldn't have . . . you know."

"Actually killed him," Xavier muttered hoarsely.

Cicely winced. "Right. But also good in that he can't come after my son again."

"I checked the news, and Houston PD's posted a sketch of the man's face," Burke said. "The police are trying to identify him. He had no ID, and his car was reported stolen. I want to get into his medical records so we can know exactly what killed him."

Xavier hung his head. "It was me. I killed him. What am I going to do?"

Carlos hugged him harder. "We'll deal with it. I promise."

Xavier shook his head. "You can't promise that."

"*I* can," Cicely said. "So try not to worry. Although I know you will."

Molly hoped the woman wasn't thinking of saying she'd shot the man instead of her son. But she wouldn't blame Cicely for wanting to save her child. *It's what I would do.*

"Did the intruder have a cell phone?" Gabe asked.

"I'm going to find out," Burke promised. "Don't ask how," he cautioned when Willa Mae opened her mouth, probably to ask.

The older woman shook her head. "Fine. I won't. What about that Eckert, the hit man? Who hired him?"

Molly wrote the question on the board. "At least the cops have him alive. Hopefully he has a cell phone and his communication can be traced."

"Your mouth to God's ears," Burke said. "And the not-lawyer, too." Then he looked at his phone. "Molly, photograph the whiteboard and erase it completely. Captain Holmes is here."

Xavier lurched to his feet. "A cop? You called a *cop*? You said you'd—"

"You lied!" Carlos hissed through clenched teeth.

Burke put up both hands. "Please. I told you I was asking NOPD for help in catching the men who were following you. I haven't lied. He wants to talk to you about the man who called you last night. He knows that you had an intruder. He doesn't know that you shot him, and he doesn't know that he's dead. Captain Holmes is the cop who caught Eckert and the other guy while you got away. All he knows is that you know the man driving the white BMW SUV wasn't the real Paul Lott. So, leave out the gun part for now, okay? And calm down if you can. If you can't, we say that you're just shaken from your ordeal. Got it?"

Xavier slowly sat down, nodding. "Got it. You trust this guy?"

"I do," Burke said. "I've known him for years. He's good. Still, keep the gun out of it. We won't volunteer that information unless we have no other choice."

Molly smiled her thanks at Gabe when he rose to help her clean the whiteboard. When she turned back to the group, Cicely was clutching Xavier's hand and Carlos looked ready to leap to his friend's defense.

"Guys, look at it this way," Molly said logically. "He has information we need. We want all the details about Eckert and the Lott impersonator, and he can help with that."

Xavier's nod was grim, his body rigid, and his eyes suspicious. "Okay."

Burke dialed Joy at the front desk. "Bring him back, please, Joy."

12

*F*UCKING HELL. LAMONT shoved his fingers through his hair, too frustrated for words. This day couldn't have gone much worse.

He'd dialed the defense attorney nine times in two hours, all the calls going to voice mail. If Hodges didn't pick up, he was paying the lawyer a personal visit to find out why.

But the man finally did answer. "For fuck's sake. Do you know the meaning of patience?"

"No," Lamont answered flatly, walking over to the window. "Where is Eckert?"

"In lockup. He's been booked. He'll be arraigned tomorrow morning. I've only just returned from the police station. Eckert said nothing, not to the cops or to me. All the cops have on him is possession of illegal firearms and aiming his gun at another driver who cut him off."

Stunned, Lamont could only gape for a few seconds. "He did *what*?"

"A truck cut him off when he was trying to exit, just before the bridge. He aimed his handgun at the driver of the truck, who then braked. It was too late for Eckert to do anything but cross over the bridge, where the cops arrested him. One of the cops saw him pull the handgun, but the person he aimed at kept going. It was a really boneheaded move, but we'll claim road rage. With a plea deal, he'll walk away with a misdemeanor."

Because Hodges didn't know that he'd hired Eckert to kill the Morrow kid. Nobody did but Eckert. He'd have to make sure the man knew to hold his tongue.

Lamont stared out of the window, watching the hundreds of tourists filling the streets, while he tried to think. "Why would he pull a gun? That doesn't make any sense."

"I agree. It's not like he knew the driver or anything. It was some random person in a pickup truck."

Pickup truck. Where had he heard about a pickup truck recently?

Oh. Right. "What color was the truck?"

"Red. Why?"

Because the lady PI who Gabe Hebert hired drives a red pickup truck. It could have been a coincidence. But if it hadn't been a coincidence . . . If the PI had been following Xavier Morrow . . .

But why would she have followed Xavier? How would she have known Xavier was driving to New Orleans?

Unless Morrow had called Gabe.

Or was she following Paul Lott's white BMW?

Did she know Paul Lott? If so, how?

What had Lott done that had gotten him killed?

Had Paul Lott told Gabriel Hebert what they'd done? Is that why Hebert had hired the PI?

Too many questions.

"Just curious," Lamont replied mildly. "I like to have the facts."

"Okay." Hodges didn't sound convinced, but Lamont couldn't have cared less.

"I may be in the courtroom tomorrow." Lamont needed Eckert to see his face so that he could warn him against saying a damn word.

Hodges didn't miss a beat. "I don't know you. Never seen you before."

"Thank you."

Now Hodges hesitated. "And now we're even? You'll get rid of the photos?"

The things a man would do to escape the ire of a betrayed wife. Unfortunately, a lot of things.

Lamont should know. That was how he'd gotten into this mess in the first place.

"We're square. It'll be like those photos never existed."

"Good enough."

He stayed at the window after Hodges ended the call and considered his next steps. With both Eckert and Stockman gone, he needed to find someone else to get rid of the Morrow kid. *Or do it myself.*

That was an option. For now, he needed to know more about the lady PI who'd been hired by Gabe Hebert.

Margaret Sutton. He'd already googled her and read the circumstances around the killing of her brother-in-law. Jackass was right—it did sound like her cop friends had minimized her role to self-defense.

It did indicate that she was willing to kill, though. He wouldn't underestimate her, especially if she'd been the one to keep Cornell Eckert from following Xavier Morrow into the city. At least he knew where they'd be.

Sutton worked for Burke Broussard, who was, unfortunately, unbribable. He'd left the force rather than get involved in anything dirty.

Lamont had always wondered why Broussard's boss had allowed him to simply walk away. There was a story there and one day he'd find out what happened. Today, though, he was more interested in Broussard's staff. If it had been Sutton's truck today, it meant that she was one step ahead of where she should be.

He'd include her in the next hit.

He would have left the lady PI to Jackass, but Jackass's plans had been blown apart today, too. Whoever had killed Paul Lott had been arrested in the Quarter that afternoon. It had been all over the news.

"At least no one can connect that shitshow to me," he murmured.

It had been a long day. He needed to get home. It was unlikely, but Eckert might be held without bail. If that happened, Lamont would have to find a replacement in the notebook he kept in his home safe.

He sighed. Joelle would be at home. She'd want to talk about Ashley, whom he'd had transferred to a colleague's office. Ashley had been devastated because the move had been a demotion. He'd had to promise to make it up to her. He'd already sent her an emerald necklace as an apology.

He had an identical necklace in his pocket for Joelle. She'd force him to view whatever surveillance footage she'd taken, and he'd do so. He'd even pretend to be sorry. He'd cry and give her the necklace. She'd pretend to forgive him and then take the necklace.

And they'd go on as if nothing had happened, leaving Lamont to focus on his real problems.

If the judge granted Eckert bail tomorrow, he'd likely be free before lunch, and if he was still willing, Lamont would put him back on Xavier Morrow. Eckert might even insist on it. Hit men were often weird that way. They had an interesting code of ethics and a real sense of pride in their work. If Eckert refused, he'd find someone else. He had a whole list of possibilities, after all.

With a last look at the throngs of people crowding the streets of the Quarter, he turned to clean off his desk, dialing James as he walked. "I'll be down in five minutes to head for home."

"Yes, sir."

The Quarter, New Orleans, Louisiana
TUESDAY, JULY 26, 6:30 P.M.

Molly flipped the whiteboard after they'd cleaned it, revealing a bulletin board with their schedules and menus from various takeout restaurants attached with thumbtacks. Then she and Gabe took their seats, Gabe taking her hand and holding on tight. He darted a concerned glance at Xavier before clearing his expression. Molly knew that he was worried about Xavier, too, which was miles away from how he'd felt about the young man that morning.

The silence was broken by Willa Mae. "Does Xavier need a lawyer?"

Burke shook his head. "I don't think so. As long as he doesn't volunteer any information."

Cicely turned to her friend. "If things go wrong, will you represent him?"

"You know I will." Willa Mae held out one hand. "Smallest you've got."

Cicely dug into her purse, producing a dollar bill. "Thank you."

Willa Mae took the money and hugged Cicely to her. "He's your son and you're my best friend. Plus, he's kind of grown on me after all these years."

"And I mow your yard," Xavier said, his smile falling a little flat. The young man was scared and, while Molly hated to see it, she certainly understood it.

Being the one who'd pulled the trigger on an attacker was not as exciting as everyone seemed to think. There was still guilt. But Xavier wasn't alone any more than she had been when she'd killed Chelsea's husband.

"Thank you, Willa Mae," Molly said. "What kind of law do you practice?"

Burke had told her that Willa Mae Collins was an attorney when he'd run her plates earlier that afternoon, but he hadn't mentioned her specialty.

"Retired a few years back," the older woman said, "but I've seen my share of courtrooms over the years. I was a Harris County prosecutor, then worked the other side as a public defender, so Xavier's in good hands. Xavier, you only answer what is asked. Stick as close to yes and no answers as you can. If things look bad, I'll call an end to things. And even if your involvement is discovered, you were well within your rights. He invaded your home. But let's avoid a courtroom if we can, okay, boys?"

Xavier, Carlos, and Manny nodded. "Yes, ma'am," they said in unison, even though Xavier didn't appear to be convinced.

Quiet descended again for the next minute and a half, until Joy pushed the door open, piloting her wheelchair into the room. She backed up so that she was still in the room, but out of the main path.

Behind her was André Holmes, a Black man with a kind face and a linebacker's shoulders. Molly had always liked him. Had always trusted him. Today she hoped her trust was well-placed.

"Can I come in?" he asked.

Burke rose to greet him with a handshake. "I hope you have good news for us."

"A little good, a little not so good," André said. He looked at the group at the table and nodded. "I'm Captain Holmes, NOPD. You must be Xavier and Cicely Morrow."

They nodded and said nothing.

André didn't seem to be bothered by their silence. "I understand that you're Carlos and Manny Hernandez and you, ma'am, are Willa Mae Collins? I hope that you all are recovering from the excitement this afternoon. It had to have been scary."

Xavier and his mother had relaxed a little on seeing Captain Holmes. Carlos still looked ready to defend Xavier. Gabe was very, very still. Barely breathing.

Molly could feel the fine tremble of Gabe's hand in hers. *Please give us some answers, André. Please.*

"We're okay," Xavier said, his voice a little unsteady. "It was scary, especially when I realized that the man who'd called me wasn't Mr. Lott."

"I can imagine." André sat next to Burke and folded his hands on the table. "Molly, always a pleasure. And Gabe, I was so sorry to hear about your father. He was a good man and a good cop. He'll be missed."

"Thank you," Gabe murmured.

"Now that introductions are done, I'll tell you what I know so far, and then I have some questions, if that's okay." André waited for Xavier and his mother to nod. "All right. We have Cornell Eckert in custody. We recovered several firearms from his vehicle. None were legally registered. We haven't yet asked him about why he was following you, Xavier. We wanted to get information out of the Paul Lott impersonator before we let Eckert know that we suspect he was hired to kill you. Eckert's been charged with possession of illegal firearms and attempted assault, as one of my officers witnessed him pointing a handgun at Miss Sutton when she was cutting him off from following you to the exit. Molly, were you in front of him at any time?"

Molly nodded. "Yes, when we first entered the interstate from the gas station. He could have noted my license plate. I suppose he could have run my plates or had someone else do it."

"We're checking his phone. We were able to get him before he could toss it into the river, thanks to your heads-up, Burke."

"Is he talking?" Burke asked.

"Nope. Lawyered himself up. LeRoy Hodges, fancy defense attorney right here in the Quarter."

"That's interesting," Burke said. "Hodges usually takes the big cases. Rich clients. Who's paying his bill?"

"That's one of the things we're going to find out. That's the good news."

Xavier stiffened. "What's the not so good news?"

"The driver of Paul Lott's BMW got away."

Protests rang out around the table. Only Molly and Gabe remained silent. Gabe's hand tightened on hers, squeezing so hard that it almost hurt. He'd paled, his lips a straight line. She covered their joined hands with her free hand, and he gave her a resolute nod.

He'd be okay. Molly would make sure of it.

"What the hell?" Burke was thundering.

"Oh my God," Cicely said as Willa Mae grabbed her free hand and held it tightly.

"*How* did you lose him?" Carlos demanded, his arm returning to Xavier's shoulders protectively.

"You had him *surrounded*," Manny added. "By four effin' SUVs."

After making a sound of fear, Xavier bowed his head. "He's going to try again."

"Maybe," André said. "I'm not going to sugarcoat it, Xavier. It's not good. But we can put you all in a safe house until we find him."

"How did he get away?" Burke asked, jaw tensed.

"We were taking him to Central Booking. Right as the officer was putting him into a patrol car, he twisted out of the officer's hold, grabbed the officer's gun, and shot him before disappearing into the crowd. It happened about a half hour ago. I wanted to let you know myself rather than having you hear it on the news. I'm . . . sorry."

"You're sorry?" Carlos asked loudly. "You're *sorry*? He's going to try to—" He cut his fury short when he saw Xavier's terrified face.

"He knows who we are," Xavier said, almost inaudibly. "He knows who came with me. He'll go after my family, Captain Holmes."

"He's not going to find you," Burke stated. "We're going to hide you. No offense, André, but we'll take care of our visitors ourselves."

André sighed. "I figured you'd say that. But the offer is open."

"Is the officer all right?" Molly asked, relieved when André nodded.

"He was wearing a vest, but the impact knocked him down. By the time his partner got around the car, the suspect had run around the corner where there was a tour group congregating. They couldn't shoot without hurting bystanders."

"No," Cicely agreed, her voice faint. "We understand."

"What are you doing to find him?" Gabe asked.

"We've sent his description to all precincts and the media and obtained security footage from the local businesses. We're asking for anyone in the public who was taking video at the moment to contact us. Of course, a number of those videos are already online, but none of them capture his face clearly enough. He hadn't made it to booking, so we didn't yet have a photo."

Carlos straightened. "I have one. I took a picture of his photo ID when he met us this morning. His picture matched his face, but the ID said Paul Lott. He must've faked it."

Both André and Burke gave Carlos nods of respect. "Send it to me," Burke said. "I'll send it to André."

"That'll be a huge help," André said, visibly relieved. "Thank you."

"All those crime shows you watch came in handy for once," Manny said, knocking his shoulder into Carlos's.

Molly studied André's face. "How did he 'get away'? He was cuffed, wasn't he?"

André looked at his hands for a moment before meeting her gaze. There was deep concern in his eyes along with a grim acceptance. "When we took him into custody, the cuffs were tight. I was there and I checked them myself. When he was being transported, they were loose enough for him to slip free. I'm investigating who had access to him during that time."

"So you've got a rat in your department," Carlos said flatly.

André exhaled. "I don't know, but I'm going to find out. Now, if it's okay, I have some questions for you."

"That depends on what you want to know," Willa Mae said calmly. "I've seen enough of these interviews bastardized into blaming the victim. Be advised that Mr. Morrow has legal representation. Me."

André's nod was respectful. "I understand. At this point, I'm asking questions of the victim of a home invasion, so he shouldn't need your services."

"Then you may proceed," Willa Mae said. "Be aware that if you stray, I will shut you down."

"So noted." André turned to Xavier. "Burke said you were running from a home intruder. Do you know who he was?"

"No," Xavier said. "I thought someone was following me yesterday. When they tried to break in, we ran. Jumped out the window."

"Following you how?" André asked. "On foot or by car?"

Willa Mae got up from her seat to stand behind Xavier. With a hand on his shoulder, she said, "You can answer that, hon."

"In a car," Xavier said. "It was a blue Camry. I didn't get the license plate."

André nodded. "That fits. A man arrived at the ER at Baptist Hospital in the wee hours of the night, victim of a gunshot wound to the chest. He died at ten a.m. this morning." He lifted his brows. "Of a *second* gunshot wound. He was shot in his hospital bed."

What? It was all Molly could do to keep her expression neutral. Inside she was so damn relieved that Xavier hadn't killed the man. For his part, Xavier gaped, looking like he'd either laugh, cry, or throw up.

"Is it possible that two people broke into your house, Xavier?" André asked.

"It's possible," Carlos said, recovering from his shock more quickly than Xavier. "I only saw the one guy's hands as Xavier was climbing out of the window. He was white and he had a gun."

"He tried to grab you?" André asked.

Xavier swallowed again. "Yes. He did grab my shirt. Tried to yank me back in through the window. But I got away, climbed down the tree outside the window, and Carlos and I ran."

"I need to ask," André said gently. "Why didn't you call 911 right away?"

Xavier gave him a sad look. "Because I didn't think they'd believe me. I'm a good student. Salutatorian of my high school class. Just graduated summa cum laude from Rice. I dress well. I'm skinny as hell. I got no muscles to beat anyone up. But some people still look at me like I'm capable of . . . anything."

André sighed wearily. "Yeah. I know about that. All right. So, you ran away, and then you did what?"

"They called me," Manny said. "I came to pick them up. And then Xavier called Paul Lott. Or he thought he was calling Lott. Xavier asked for Gabe's telephone number, but the guy ignored him, which set off my fake-o-meter. He said he'd come to get X and about seven hours later we met him in the H-E-B parking lot. That's a grocery store in Texas."

"Okay," André said. "So this is what confused me. Why did you call Gabe, Xavier?"

Xavier lifted his chin. "His father was my friend. We met when I was five years old and he saved my life in Katrina."

André's brows lifted, and he looked at Gabe. "Yeah?"

"Yep," Gabe said and gave Xavier a warm smile. "My father called Xavier his second son."

None of which was a lie, Molly thought. She still was impressed with how easily the words passed through Gabe's lips. *Note to self: he can be depended on when things get dicey.*

André tilted his head. "Rocky was a good man. I miss him."

"Me too," Xavier said.

Gabe simply nodded.

"Whose idea was it to get your mom on board?" André asked Xavier.

Xavier frowned. "The Paul Lott guy. He wanted me to tell my mom that we were headed to New Orleans. When she said he could follow us, he didn't seem too upset."

"I wouldn't say that," Cicely said quietly. "I talked to him inside the Waffle House on Wallisville Road. He was not pleased but pretended that he was just fine."

Xavier looked at his mother, eyes wide. "You never said that!"

"I didn't want to worry you. Willa Mae, what did you think?"

"I thought the same. He was . . . weaselly. Like a kid who's broken your best vase with a baseball and is hoping you haven't noticed."

"That's pretty close," Cicely agreed. "So, we got in the minivan with the boys and came to find Gabe. Why?"

André lifted one big shoulder. "Just trying to understand. I mean, I would have assumed that he intended to kill you, Xavier." He made an apologetic face when everyone on the other side of the table shuddered. "Sorry. Again, I'm just trying to understand."

Molly got where André was going. "If he didn't kill you straight out, his goal must have been to get you to New Orleans alive. That would have been easier to do if you went peacefully."

André's gaze swept all of their faces, then he clasped his hands. "Do you have any questions for me?"

"First, that you let us know when you've discovered who hired these men to harm my son," Cicely said. "Because there's no doubt in my mind that they would have."

"No doubt," André agreed. "Why, though? What motive would any- one have to hurt him? I'd say it could have been a random thing were it not for Mr. Eckert. From what we know now, someone tried to get you, failed, and a new hit man was called. Why is someone working so hard to get you, Xavier?"

Xavier shrugged. "Like I said, I'm just a premed student. I work, I study, I volunteer with Meals on Wheels, and I play video games with Carlos."

Again, no lie there. He never said that he didn't know. Just implied it. Molly kept her expression impassive but smiled on the inside. *Good job, Xavier.*

"Did the man posing as Paul Lott go into your house?" André asked.

Molly glanced at Burke, who was watching André through narrowed eyes.

"Why do you ask that?" Burke asked.

"Because after I called the Houston police to find out what they knew, they got a warrant to search the Morrow home."

Both Xavier and his mother gasped. "What?" Xavier demanded. "How?"

André met Xavier's eyes. "Partly the reason that you feared calling 911. Partly because the white guy who died was shot by someone else while *in the hospital.* You have an alibi for that time frame. You were on the road with your mother and all these other folks, so you're not a suspect. The man who shot him showed the hospital front desk a fake ID, and he may have worn a disguise. Must have also had a silencer, because no one heard the shot. Houston PD is looking for him now. The blood type found in your house matched that of the dead white guy. They'll follow up with DNA to do a positive ID. We took prints from the BMW SUV and we'll compare them to the prints Houston pulled from your house. I repeat, you have an alibi for the time of his murder, and you're not a suspect. Breathe, Xavier."

Xavier sucked in a harsh breath. "What about running and not calling 911?"

"Not a crime," André said. "You were afraid for your life. And even if you *had* shot the guy, it would have been self-defense since he broke into your home. Houston PD found the door he busted to get in. Not that I'm saying that you shot him. Just *if* you did."

Xavier's chest rose and fell as he breathed deeply. And said nothing more.

Thank goodness.

André turned to Gabe. "I'll be in touch about the break-in at your father's house."

Their Houston visitors turned to Gabe with matching glares. "You never said anything about your dad's house getting broken into," Xavier said indignantly.

Gabe blew an exhale up his forehead, making his curls dance. "I forgot. Hell. So much has happened and it was only discovered last night. I just . . . forgot."

"So did I," Molly admitted. "Someone broke in and trashed Rocky's house. Slashed cushions and destroyed paintings. They made an awful mess."

"Your mama's paintings?" Cicely asked, one hand splayed over her heart. "Oh no."

"Yes, ma'am," Gabe said, his shoulders slumping. "Not much left."

André pushed to his feet. "I'll be getting out of your hair now. Burke knows how to reach me if you think of anything else or want to take us up on the safe house."

Burke rose. "You'll update me on the search for Paul Lott's imposter?"

André met Burke's gaze directly. "I will. Heads-up, I expect Houston PD to be sending someone to talk to your guests. I told them that Xavier and Carlos were the victims here. They might be a little heavier handed in their interrogation approach."

"We'll be ready," Willa Mae said, leaving no question in anyone's mind that it would be so.

André shot her a smile. "Call me if you need any assistance." He hesitated. "I considered Rocky a friend. Helping you is honoring him, so I hope you'll trust me if things go sideways." He lifted a shoulder. "More sideways, anyway. 'Night, folks." He departed, followed by Joy, who pulled the door closed behind them.

Xavier immediately turned, pressing his forehead to his mother's shoulder. He was shaking, poor kid. He'd held it together like a pro. Molly didn't think she could have done any better.

Retaking his seat, Burke held up one hand for them to be quiet and then nodded when his phone buzzed a minute and a half later. "Joy says he's gone. I gotta say, I was not expecting that the dead white guy had been shot by someone else."

Xavier lifted his head, revealing the tears streaking his face. "I didn't kill him," he whispered. "Thank God."

Molly breathed her own sigh of relief. She hadn't wanted Xavier to carry that burden for the rest of his days, whether he'd been justified or not.

Cicely, Willa Mae, and Carlos all hugged him, Carlos looking over at Burke as he did so. "André seems all right."

Burke smiled. "He is. And he's right about the self-defense. But it doesn't look like it's going to be an issue."

"They'll have the bullet that was in the dead guy when he got to the ER," Carlos protested. "It won't match the second bullet."

"Then we need to make sure that the gun that fired the first bullet isn't found," Burke said with a shrug. "Molly?"

"I'll take care of it," she promised. "Now we need to get these folks to your place, Burke."

"Not my place," Burke said. "Not my main house, anyway. We'll use my camp. I didn't tell André because I didn't want him to accidentally tell the wrong person where they'll be."

Cicely looked uncertain. "A camp? Like . . . a tent?"

Molly chuckled. "No, it's a cabin, but folks down the bayou call their places camps. It's a really nice place and isolated enough that anyone coming for you will be seen long before they get close enough to hurt you. It's on the bayou bank, perfect for fishing and relaxing, but it's also got a satellite for Wi-Fi and a state-of-the-art security system."

"Plus, the deed isn't in my name," Burke added. "I've only taken a few people out there, so it would take the fake Paul Lott a while to even discover that it exists. I'll take you there myself and stay with you until I can assign sufficient security."

"I can make sure you stay fed," Gabe offered. "I'll get some groceries so that I can make you some meals."

"I can cook," Cicely said, brows raised. "I'm no fancy chef, but I can feed us."

Carlos winced. "Oh, man. You dissed her cooking. This isn't gonna end well."

Gabe winced as well, clearly not having thought his offer through. "No offense meant to your cooking, ma'am, but I know that I'm going to be a wreck without something to keep my hands busy. So please allow me to supplement your cooking as long as you're here?"

Cicely smiled at him. "That, I can understand. Thank you. We accept."

"Yes," Carlos hissed, fist pumping the air. "We're going to feast like kings."

Manny bowed his head with a sigh. "Our mother raised us better, I can promise you this."

Gabe's mouth curved in a genuine smile at the brotherly exchange. "I assume Molly knows how to get to wherever you're going?"

"I do," she confirmed. She hoped Gabe didn't mind boats, because that was the only way to get to Burke's camp. "We'll take care of all of you while we search for this guy, too. I trust André to do everything in his power to find this guy, but he's clearly got issues in his department, so we'll make finding him our priority."

"Thank you," Cicely said fervently. "Thank you all so much."

"Yes." Xavier swallowed hard, his eyes suddenly glassy with tears. "When everything went down last night, I didn't know what to do. Rocky said you'd help, Gabe, that we could trust you. He was right. So thank you all so much—for the protection, the place to stay, the investigation, the food. Thank you for believing me in the first place. Just . . ." His voice broke. "Thank you."

"You're my dad's second son," Gabe said, his own voice gone gruff. "And none of this is your doing, Xavier. None of this is your fault. He would have wanted us to make sure you were okay. It's the least we can do."

Tulane-Gravier, New Orleans, Louisiana
TUESDAY, JULY 26, 6:45 P.M.

"Why is traffic at a standstill?" Lamont grumbled from the back seat of the town car. "Surely the tourists have to go eat or sleep or fuck each other or *something*. This is far worse than yesterday. We've barely moved ten feet in twenty minutes."

"The road's closed up ahead by the police department, sir," James said, his tone unusually tense. "Cop got shot. Shooter's on the run."

Lamont blinked. "I didn't hear anything about that."

"It's been on the news, sir. My wife said she saw it online. Tourists posted videos of the shooting. Happened about fifteen minutes before you came down to the car. Traffic was bad before, but this road closure just snarled everything up."

A bad feeling skittered along his spine. "How was the cop shot?"

"Some prisoner was being put in a squad car. He got loose, stole the cop's gun, shot the cop, and ran. The cops just did a press conference." He held up his phone. "I've been checking the reports. Have to say, knowing a gunman is roaming out here somewhere is making me nervous."

"I don't blame you." He unlocked his phone and searched the news. Sure enough, everything James had said seemed true, but there was no word as to who this guy was.

If it was Eckert, that would be okay. But that was unlikely. Hodges had said that Eckert was already in lockup.

I don't think even Eckert could escape from there. Not without a lot of help.

Reluctantly, he typed a text to Jackass. *Who is the gunman?*

It took a few minutes for a reply to come through. *None of your concern.*

Well, fuck. That just pissed him off. *Who? Is it your guy?*

He thought of the two arrests made that day. Eckert and the man who'd killed Paul Lott. Eckert was in lockup, but he didn't know where the other guy was.

And if his gut was right, neither did NOPD. *Is your guy secure?* he added.

Another few minutes passed as he stared at his phone, willing Jackass to answer.

Yes. Stop bothering me. I'm busy.

You're busy? You'll be dead as soon as I can arrange it. Jackass really was named appropriately. *Where Is He?!?*

Not your concern.

You fucking asshole. TELL ME NOW.

Or what?

Lamont gritted his teeth and punched Jackass's number.

The man picked up on the third ring. "What part of 'I'm busy' can't you understand?" he snapped.

Lamont glanced at James. The driver was focused on the road, but he still had to be careful. "How did this happen?"

Jackass sighed. "I have my ways, Monty. I got my guy out. I'd be more concerned about the state of your own house, if I were you."

He glowered. "What does that mean?"

"It means that your boy Eckert has a message for you. He knows who was driving the red truck and he knows he was made. He says that you set him up to get arrested, and that he'd better make bail or he's gonna sing like a fucking canary. La, la, la, La*mont*."

"He won't." Lamont was sure of that. If Eckert squealed, he'd be pleading guilty to murder for hire and that was a federal offense.

"If you say so. But . . . Well, clearly you know best."

The mocking tone had Lamont grinding his teeth until his jaw ached. "But what?" he snarled.

James cocked his head but went back to watching the road. Because he was a smart man.

"He just seems like the type to burn everything down."

Unfortunately, that was accurate. He could see Eckert taking him down, too, if he felt backed into a corner. *And if he's more afraid of the Feds than he is of me.* "Thank you for the heads-up."

"You're welcome, Monty. What are friends for?"

More mocking. *Damn him.* "Indeed. What will your employee do?"

The mocking disappeared, replaced with calm, cold certainty. "Whatever I tell him to do."

Lamont swallowed his snarl. "Which will be what?"

"Not your concern. But I'd stay away from Rocky's boy's house if you like your skin where it is on your body rather than burned to a crisp. The lady PI will be with him, so two birds, one stone."

A shiver raced down his spine and across the skin that he did want to keep uncharred. "Keep me updated."

"Same goes, Monty." The mocking was back. "Eckert is due in court tomorrow morning. You should do whatever it is you're planning to do before then. I have a feeling his bail will be set sky-high. And because we're partners, if you need help handling him, you just let me know, y'hear?" He ended the call with a chuckle.

I can't pay Eckert's bail. Not without answering way too many questions. He'd convinced Hodges to represent Eckert through blackmail, pure and simple. Nothing on paper, no funds changing hands. But any money he paid for Eckert's bail could be traced and he didn't want any part of that. There were, however, other ways to deal with men threatening to sing like canaries.

Pity. He'd really hoped that Eckert could be his new Stockman.

Luckily, he had more names on that list in his home safe. He considered the possibilities and nodded to himself. He knew exactly who he'd tag next—a cop who'd have access to the holding tank where Eckert was currently hanging out until his arraignment in the morning. A cop who, while not a superstar hit man like Eckert, would suffice. *Because I'm accruing quite a list of targets.*

He wished now that he hadn't included Jackass in his plans to rid himself of Rocky Hebert, but he'd needed information that his partner had obtained. *I should have just let him handle it. I didn't need to be there.*

Except that he'd wanted to see for himself that the job was done right.

Of course, Jackass had brought Lott with him that night. Jackass's intention had been to keep Lott quiet by implicating him in the murder, but Lamont hadn't really trusted him. He'd have offed Lott himself, but Jackass's people had gotten there ahead of him.

At least Lott was no longer a worry. Unless Jackass was snipping off loose ends.

And I'm one of his loose ends.

Fear washed over him, making him angry—with himself and with his "partner." He looked out of his car window, wondering where Paul Lott's killer was at that moment. *I'm a sitting duck, stuck here in traffic.* Someone could walk by with a gun or a sniper could be waiting on a rooftop.

Suddenly, he couldn't breathe. *Goddammit.* He yanked at his tie, unbuttoned the top two buttons on his shirt collar, then sucked in a breath that physically hurt.

"I need to get some air," he said abruptly. "Please take the car to my house. I'll walk." At least he'd be a moving target.

James twisted around to stare at him. "But, sir. That's a long walk."

"I need the exercise. I'll see you tomorrow."

Grabbing his briefcase, he jumped from the car and started walking. If Jackass had plans to eliminate him, he wasn't going to make it easy.

And the walk would help him clear his mind. It was time he took matters into his own hands.

Eckert had to go.

Xavier Morrow had to go.

Gabe Hebert and his lady PI had to go. And since Burke Broussard probably knew everything they did, he'd have to go, too.

And then, when he was done with all of them, his remaining partner had to go.

13

GABE SANK INTO one of the cushioned chairs in Burke's conference room, feeling as achy as an old man. "How are you even still functional?" he asked Molly, who stood at the whiteboard in the conference room. Exactly where she'd been standing when he'd taken all the dishes to Burke's horrible little kitchen to wash and put them away.

The cook in him could not leave a messy kitchen. Even one like Burke's.

Burke had taken the Houston folks to his camp, wherever that was. Joy had bought them basic toiletries and promised to get them some clothes the next day.

Gabe and Molly had stayed behind because Burke didn't have enough room for all of them. Which was a bit of a relief if Gabe was being honest. He truly liked Xavier and his crew, but he needed some downtime to process everything that he'd learned that day.

It was a lot.

The office was very, very quiet and might have felt unsafe but for the arrival of the night security guard, who'd introduced himself only as Phin, before leaving to do his rounds. The man was scarily big and hulking—clearly former military—and, while he didn't scowl or frown, he exuded an undercurrent of tension that made the hair on the back of Gabe's neck stand up straight and salute.

He had lots of questions about that guy, but Molly had simply greeted Phin with a smile and turned back to the whiteboard.

Gabe let himself take a moment to admire the way her curvy, round ass filled out her slacks—which looked exactly as crisp as they had that morning. At this point, he was seriously wondering about her having witchcraft. The rest of them had been disheveled and exhausted, but she looked like she'd just had a nap and change of clothes.

She'd recopied their earlier notes and questions, but not in the same way. The first draft had been a free-form, stream-of-consciousness effort. The board now looked like a starburst, questions, notes, and the names of people connected to the center—which was the unnamed victim of the murder Xavier had witnessed the night of his Katrina rescue.

"I'm tired," Molly admitted. "But I needed to reorganize my thoughts, and this is the way I do it. I write it all down, then move stuff around until it starts to make sense. Everything connects. We just don't know how yet."

"What are our next steps?"

She capped the marker and took a step back to view the entire board. "I think my previous search of old police reports is a dead end." She winced. "Sorry. Poor choice of words."

He waved the air. "Don't be sorry. I know what you meant. I wish I'd known about this case of Dad's. I never suspected a thing. I wonder if my mother did. I mean, she met Xavier and his mom, so she at least knew that Dad had met him that night during Katrina, but did she know about the murder?"

"Have you heard from your aunt Gigi yet? Maybe she can shed some light on things."

"Not yet. I've left about a million messages and texts. I'm really worried." He rubbed his temples. "We were able to trace John Alan Industries back to her, so I'm thinking the bad guys—whoever they are—could have done the same. They could have killed her, just like Dad."

Molly sat in the chair beside him. "Maybe she's on vacation."

"That's entirely possible. She has a group of friends she travels with. They're pretty adventurous and sometimes go places where they don't get phone service."

"We can ask Antoine to try to trace her phone."

"Ask Antoine," a male voice said from behind them. "Everybody asks Antoine."

They turned to see a man who looked so much like André Holmes that Gabe knew this was his brother. Plus, the way Molly was rolling her eyes at the man was another clue.

"You love being indispensable," Molly said. "Don't even try that put-upon crap with me."

Antoine grinned, and there Gabe could easily see the difference between the brothers. André had been sober and, even when he smiled, he'd seemed burdened. Which wasn't a shock considering he had a bad actor in his department who'd effectively helped the Paul Lott impersonator to escape.

Antoine, on the other hand, looked carefree and happy. And a little frenetic.

"Are you okay?" Gabe asked carefully.

Antoine chuckled. "I haven't slept in nearly two days, so I'm a little . . . bouncy at the moment."

"High on caffeine," Molly stage-whispered.

"You wound me, Molly. But you're right. I am well and truly buzzed from coffee and Mountain Dew." Antoine joined them at the table, taking in the whiteboard in a glance. "I always like your diagrams. Burke called me with an update before he took the Houston folks to his camp, but you've organized it so much more clearly. You have a techie brain lurking under all that badassery."

She smiled at Antoine, charmed.

And Gabe was charmed by her. She'd been the bright spot in the last two days.

"We haven't bothered you," she told Antoine. "Well, Burke might have, but *I've* let you work. *All day.* What can you tell me?"

Antoine stretched his arms toward the ceiling, then let his hands drop to his lap. "I got something off the victim's laptop. I also discovered a few things on the SIM card you found." He stopped abruptly. "Where are my manners? And where are your manners, Molly?" He stuck his hand out and Gabe shook it. "I'm Antoine Holmes. I do the geek stuff for Burke."

"Gabe Hebert. My dad is . . ." He blew out a breath. "Was the victim."

Antoine's expression softened, making him look more like André. "I'm so sorry."

Gabe still didn't know what to say to people expressing their condolences. "Thanks. But you found something?"

"I think so. The files were wiped, but traces of data remain. It's like when Cookie Monster eats all the cookies and all that's left is crumbs. You know it was a cookie. You might even know what kind of cookie, but reassembling the cookie might not be possible."

"Shit," Gabe murmured.

"Maybe not shit, but not a clear picture. Not yet, anyway." He pulled a single folded sheet of paper from his shirt pocket, which also held an honest-to-God pocket protector filled with pens and mechanical pencils. He unfolded the paper and smoothed it on the table in front of him. "Your father was searching for a doctor."

Gabe recoiled at the thought that his father had been so sick. "Because he had cancer."

Antoine shook his head. "I found that contact on the SIM card from his phone. This was a different doctor. Not an oncologist. This was an ob-gyn."

Gabe glanced at Molly, confused. "I don't understand. Do you?"

She looked at the whiteboard. "I might. If we assume he was singularly focused on this case . . ." She uncapped the marker, and wrote something beneath the center of her diagram, which she'd labeled: *MURDER VICTIM / KATRINA.*

She'd added: *POSSIBLY PREGNANT?*

Oh. "Someone murdered a pregnant woman."

"Possibly," Antoine said. "He'd been searching for this doctor for a while. I found traces in his browser history from a year ago, but he seemed to have stepped up his search in the last few months." He hesitated. "The heightened search started around the time of his first appointment with his oncologist."

Gabe swallowed. "He was running out of time."

Antoine's nod was respectful. "You didn't know he was sick?"

"He didn't tell me." And if he sounded angry about it, that would have to be okay. Still, he felt bad about snapping. "I'm sorry. Not your fault."

Antoine held up his hands. "I'd be mad, too. In fact, after I get some sleep, I'm calling my parents and telling them if they ever consider keeping a secret like that, we will have words. Like, you know, please and thank you because my mother is scary when she's in full-on mama mode and I'd be a damn fool to disrespect her. But . . ." He shrugged. "You take my point."

Gabe almost laughed. He wondered what Antoine would be like on a full night's sleep. "I do. And thank you. No, I didn't know. I only know from the private autopsy that he had esophageal cancer that seemed to have progressed."

Antoine visibly calmed, his voice becoming gentle. "He was stage three. They were trying to shrink the mass before they did surgery. He'd had a round of chemo, but it wasn't working. He was considering stopping, but he planned to push through for you."

Gabe shuddered out a breath, grateful when Molly sat beside him and took his hand. "I wish he'd have told me."

"I think he wanted to," Antoine said with a sad smile. "I found some notes he'd written on his phone that looked like conversations he wanted to have with you. I'll print them out for you. I think he was . . . practicing."

Gabe's eyes burned. "That sounds like Dad. He was a 'measure twice, cut once' kind of guy."

"How do you know he planned to continue the chemo?" Molly asked.

"More notes on his phone. Pro/con lists. The 'pro' was reasons to stop, the 'con' was reasons to keep going. That was mostly you, Gabe, and this murder case. Which he simply called 'Katrina.'"

That was something, at least. "Thank you," Gabe murmured.

Antoine nodded. "I'll keep looking for more stuff."

"Can you track Rocky's movements from his cell phone SIM card?" Molly asked.

"Sorry, but no. He'd turned his location off in the settings. Smart of him, but bad for us. I can tell you that whoever wiped his laptop wasn't a novice, but wasn't a pro, either. I've found some nuggets of information, but it hasn't been easy."

"So they're moderately tech savvy," Molly said. "Good to know. We have to assume that they know by now that we're investigating."

"Yeah," Antoine said. "Burke told me that you were followed from the restaurant yesterday afternoon and that it was an unmarked NOPD vehicle."

Gabe swiveled to stare at her, mouth open. "What?"

She winced. "I didn't want to upset you any further yesterday afternoon. And then we got to your house and someone was trying to poison your dog . . ." She sighed. "Sorry."

Gabe tried to calm his now-racing heart. "It's okay. Just . . . I need to know this stuff, okay?"

She nodded. "Understood. I think that was the only thing I didn't share."

Antoine was watching them, a gleam in his dark eyes. "Molly?" he singsonged. He cast a deliberate glance at their joined hands. "Care to share with me?"

"No," she said primly. "Need to know only. And you don't need to know."

But she didn't let Gabe go, and that made him want to smile.

Antoine snickered. "Touché." Then he sobered. "Okay, back to this. I found what might have been a search for a location. 'Bayou' is all I could recover."

Molly groaned. "Like there aren't a million place-names with 'bayou' in them."

Antoine shrugged. "I know, I know. Just telling you what's left on the drive. Which is really not that much."

Molly frowned. "I've been thinking that Rocky wasn't the one who wiped his own laptop. Whoever killed him wouldn't have left the laptop behind unless they were sure it wouldn't be useful, so it makes sense that they were the ones who wiped it. Could they have done that while the laptop was still in his house?"

"Sure. It takes a while, though. Couple of hours at least."

She hummed under her breath. "So they were in Rocky's house for a few hours or they took the laptop and brought it back when they killed him."

"Makes sense to me," Antoine said. "He also made several calls to a number in Montreal in the days before his death."

"Aunt Gigi," Gabe murmured.

Antoine nodded. "I traced the number to Gigi Gauthier. I don't think he ever talked to her. The calls never lasted more than a minute and a half, so I think he was leaving messages."

Anxiety and fear battled in Gabe's gut. "I've been trying to reach her all day."

"That was the number you wanted me to trace?" Antoine asked.

"Yes," Molly said. "Can you?"

"Of course. The last time it seems like he actually connected with her was a week before he died. He sent her a text about his chemo. Said: 'Sicker than a dog. How did Lili stand this for all those years?'"

Gabe felt a spurt of anger mix in with the anxiety and fear. "He told her, but not me."

"For what it's worth, she fussed at him—at least in the texts I saw," Antoine said. "Said he was doing wrong by keeping it from you."

"She'd be right." Gabe's stomach was in knots every time he thought of his aunt. "Please, let her be on vacation."

"I'll see what I can dig up," Antoine promised.

"So will I," Molly added. "I can make cold calls to her neighbors if need be. I can even call her neighborhood police to do a wellness check."

"Yeah," Gabe said hoarsely, wishing that he'd thought to do that earlier. "Let's do that. The thought of her . . ." He trailed off, trying to erase the image of his aunt slumped over her kitchen table with an exit wound the size of his fist, just like his father had been.

Molly squeezed his hand. "Hey. You said she was a traveler. Let's think of her on a sunny beach somewhere, okay?"

"She's more likely to be climbing a mountain," Gabe said, forcing a mental picture of Gigi in mountaineering gear over the gruesome imaginary picture of her being dead. "She's feisty." He braced himself. "What other calls did my dad make?"

"A few to his oncologist, a few to local businesses. One to the veterinarian."

Gabe looked at Molly's whiteboard. "Dad used his burner whenever he contacted Xavier, so none of those calls would show up. It never occurred to me to search Dad's place for another phone. Was that what the vandals were looking for?"

"Possibly," Molly said, her lips pursed. "If they found it, they've destroyed it, I'm sure."

"Snipping loose ends," Antoine agreed. "First Rocky, then the attempt to poison your dog to get to you, then the attempt on Xavier's life, and finally the way that the Paul Lott wannabe tried herding Xavier to New Orleans for reasons still unknown."

"But not good," Molly said with a scowl.

"Not good at all." Antoine rubbed his face with both palms. "I'm starting to wind down. I'm going to take a nap at my desk before I drive home."

"Have Phin walk you out," Molly said insistently.

"I will. He's checked your truck for bugs and tracking devices. So far, nothing."

"I've rented a car," Molly said. "My truck is too visible and I'm afraid they'll use the truck license number to find my car's license number. I need to be able to move freely."

Antoine made a sound of approval. "Be sure to charge it to Burke."

"Already did," she said with a quick grin, then sobered. "Is there any chatter about the guy who shot the cop and got away?"

"A little. Mostly concern for the wounded officer and vows to 'make the bastard pay' when they catch him. A few wondering who loosened his cuffs. They got prints from the SUV the guy had stolen from Paul Lott." He smiled like the Cheshire Cat. "And guess what they match?"

They looked at him blankly. "What?" Gabe asked.

"Oh." Antoine gave his head a rueful little shake. "I got ahead of myself. I dusted the papers you retrieved from your father's house last night. The only prints were his own, but I've got access to the prints taken from the walls by the Metairie sheriff's people." He didn't offer how he'd gotten access, and Gabe didn't ask. "I got your father's prints from the autopsy report, and I got yours from a coffee cup you used yesterday, Gabe—I hope you're okay with that—so that I could eliminate any prints you and your dad left. I found a few of Burke's, too, but there was one that was different. It was near one of the holes in the wall."

Holes made because someone was looking for something hidden in his father's house.

Gabe sucked in a breath as he made the connection. "The print on my dad's wall matches the ones left in Paul Lott's SUV?"

"Ding, ding, ding!" Antoine grinned. "One and the same. Unfortunately, there were no prints on the meat that was used to hurt your dog."

"He wore gloves," Molly said. "I saw them on his hands when he was running away. What was the poison?"

"Rat poison. A lot of it." He looked at Gabe. "I'm so glad your pup didn't lick it. He would have been seriously sick. If he'd eaten it all, it would have killed him."

"Bastards," Gabe snarled. "Going after college kids and dogs."

"And retired cops and their sons," Molly said softly. "You are at risk, Gabe. Please do not forget that."

Gabe hadn't. Not for a moment. "I know."

Antoine pushed to his feet, swaying a little. "Whoa, that was a head rush. I am in serious caffeine decline. Gonna crash in my office for a while."

Concern creased Molly's brow. "Let us drive you home."

"Nah. Phin's here. I'll be fine. I promise," he added when she looked unconvinced. "I'll even text you to let you know I'm home safe," he added teasingly. "Mom."

She rolled her eyes. "Hush. I wouldn't be your mom for all the beignets in New Orleans. You must have been a handful as a kid."

"And a half," he agreed with a laugh. "Gabe, nice to meet you. When everything settles, I'm gonna come to your restaurant for more of that étouffée. Joy brought me some earlier, and it was fantastic. Almost as good as my mama's, but I'll never admit that to her." He waved and ambled from the room.

Molly watched him go, still concerned. "I wish he'd let us take him home. I'm going to make sure Phin checks on him." She rose to take more photos of the whiteboard, then began erasing it away.

Gabe joined her to help because she had to be every bit as tired as he was. "Tell me about Phin. He's kind of . . . intimidating."

"He can be. I've known him for about a year, and ninety-nine percent of the time he's a sweetheart—a real pussycat." She grimaced sadly. "It's the one percent of the time that he's a tiger you have to watch out for. He's a vet. He and Antoine served together in the army."

"Antoine served, too?"

She nodded. "In Iraq. All Antoine would say was that Phin came home with a shitload of PTSD and guilt. Makes my heart hurt for him. I mean, most of us came home with issues, but Phin's are . . . well, extra." She retrieved a box of whiteboard cleaning wipes from a nearby shelf, pulled one free, and began scrubbing. "But nobody here is afraid of him. He's good at knowing when he's on the edge and takes a few days off. He does handyman work around the place during his security work at night. Our hours are so iffy that Burke wanted someone on-site for the times when we might be here alone. Especially Antoine. He gets caught up when he's working and might not hear anyone breaking in. We have an alarm system, but we do make enemies in our line of work. And Burke came into this business with a fair share of his own."

"And you?" Gabe took one of the wipes to clean the board. "Did you bring enemies?"

"Not really. I left a few in North Carolina, but they're more the type to spit on the ground when they say my name. Mostly my ex-brother-in-law's family. They defended him even when they saw the tape of him shooting my father. Then there were Jake's comrades."

Gabe paused to look at her. Her profile was tense, her jaw tight. "Comrades?"

"Jake was a cop. He had lots of pals in the local PD. A few of them reached out to me, said that they wished they'd 'reined him in' years before. Most just hated me." She sighed. "Including my boyfriend at the time, who was Jake's best friend. He still blames me for killing Jake. I truly had not seen that coming. I thought he'd be supportive, but nope.

So I guess I have enemies, but I don't think they'd come here to hurt me. They do plenty of that whenever a reporter asks them questions, which still happens."

"I'm sorry." And he was. His heart hurt for what she'd lost. The pain of losing her father then having to end a life. He knew her well enough to know that she still felt guilt, even though she'd do it again. "I wish I could fix it."

She smiled at him sadly. "And I'm grateful that you do. I wish I could fix this mess for you, too."

His chest tightened, pain for what they'd each endured mixing with gratitude that she was here. With him. He stared down at her upturned face, gratitude becoming . . . need. He needed to take away the sadness in her eyes. Needed to replace it with something else. Something more. Something so much better.

His skin warmed, his pulse beginning to race. He needed her. He thought she needed him, too. He continued to study her face, watched the pretty blush creep up her cheeks. Watched as her tongue stole out to moisten her lips, as her eyes grew heated, as she swallowed hard.

She felt it, too. Felt the air growing charged. Felt the connection between them.

The need.

Here in the quiet of this room. The quiet of this building, where they were alone except for Antoine and Phin. Still, she was holding herself back.

Because she'd be distracted if she let herself go. She'd be distracted and wouldn't be able to guard him properly. He briefly considered asking Burke to give him another PI, just so she wouldn't feel so conflicted, but that wasn't right. She was the best person for this job, and he respected that.

He was about to step back when he thought, *Antoine is here. And Phin.*

He gripped her chin gently, careful not to hurt her. "Phin's here."

Her eyes widened. "What?"

"Phin's here. He's your night security, right?"

"Right," she said slowly. "And?"

"Antoine said that he'd be fine with Phin here. We are, too, yes?"

Her wide eyes narrowed. "Yes. And?"

"If he's responsible for keeping us all safe, then you're not. Yes?"

Her brow furrowed in a slight frown. "I guess. *And?*"

"And . . . if you get distracted, then I'm still safe."

Her lips began to twitch, her eyes to sparkle, the sadness gone. "How might I be distracted?"

"If I kissed you. Tell me no, and I won't." He drew a breath, quietly exhaling. "But please don't tell me no."

She held his gaze, and he held his breath, waiting as she considered all the options. All the angles. Then she smiled and he felt nearly dizzy with it. "Yes."

Swamped with relief, he took her mouth the way he'd been wanting to since the first time she'd walked into the Choux. The box of wipes she'd been holding fell to the floor with a thud, and she wound her arms around his neck, kissing him back.

Exactly the way he'd hoped. Her mouth was lush and warm and . . . smiling.

She was smiling as she kissed him and that made it even more perfect.

He wrapped his arms around her, his hands roving her back as the kiss grew heated and his body grew hard. Her soft, voluptuous breasts pressed against his chest, and he wondered how they'd feel in his hands. He wondered when she'd let him touch her the way he'd fantasized.

His hands slowed to long drags up and down her sides and she made a needy sound that brought an answering growl from deep in his chest. He was harder than he'd been in a long, long time.

He wanted her. Here and now.

He'd seen how capably she'd taken care of tense situations. He'd felt her compassion. Now he wanted to take care of her. He wanted to feel her passion.

He wanted to take her apart and see her pleasure. He slid his hands down her sides, toward her butt that he'd been admiring for two days. He wanted—

The clearing of a throat had them breaking apart like randy teenagers caught by the porch lamp. The hulking security guard stood in the doorway. But a hint of a smile quirked his lips, making him seem a little less terrifying.

"Your rental car's here," Phin said and held out the keys. "I signed for it and checked it for bugs and tracking devices. It's clean and parked inside the gate."

Gabe had to swallow a snarl. It wasn't Phin's fault that he and Molly had been making out in the conference room. *No, that's all on me.* And he had no regrets. For a few minutes, he hadn't been thinking of bad guys or murder or his father's suffering. He'd been utterly lost in her, and he couldn't be either sorry or ashamed.

Panting softly, Molly lifted her chin, her cheeks now stained a bright pink that made Gabe absurdly proud of himself. "Thank you, Phin," she said. "I appreciate you checking it." She extended her hand, neatly catching the keys when Phin tossed them over.

"That's my job," he said, clearly uncomfortable with her thanks. "Do you have your sweeper so you can recheck for tracking devices?"

"In my bag. Oh, and Antoine's gone to his office to sleep. Can you—"

"Watch over him?" Phin rumbled. "Of course. Where are you going? Burke will want to know."

"To my house in Mid-City," Gabe said, but Molly shook her head.

"Tonight, we're going to a hotel with good security. Burke already knows where. He made the reservation. I need to sleep, and Burke's running out of people to stand guard." She winked up at Gabe. "Don't worry about your virtue. Burke got us adjoining rooms and used his 'John Smith' account. Nobody will know that you're there."

Gabe considered arguing then realized she was taking care of him, just as she'd promised. And if he hoped that they wouldn't be using both rooms? *Sue me.* "Then let's go."

The Garden District, New Orleans, Louisiana
TUESDAY, JULY 26, 9:15 P.M.

Lamont made it back to his house, hot and sweaty and angry and . . . *Yeah. Not happy at all.*

"Joelle?" he called, but got no answer.

Maybe she'd gone out. If so, he could find those damn cameras she'd planted in his office and the spare bedroom. *If* she really had. He still wasn't sure that she wasn't bluffing.

If she had been bluffing, he'd fallen for it, dammit.

He stalked straight to his office, tossing his coat onto a wingback chair that was older than the United States, an item that had been passed down through wife number one's family. He turned on a single desk light, throwing the rest of the room into shadow, and turned to the bookshelf that hid his office safe.

He needed to contact that guard in the NOPD holding area. *Now.*

He'd pulled the books away from the shelf that hid the safe when the clearing of a throat had him whirling around, reaching for the pistol he kept in his desk drawer. His hand dropped when he saw his "partner" stepping from the shadows.

Goddamn him. "What are you doing here?" Lamont hissed.

Jackass looked unhappy. "We need to talk."

Lamont shoved the books back onto the shelf and sat behind his desk, discreetly drawing the pistol from the drawer.

Not discreetly enough, because Jackass lifted an eyebrow. "Really, Monty?"

"You're armed," he pointed out.

"I'm on duty." With a shrug, Jackass moved Lamont's suit jacket and sat in the old wingback chair, facing him. "As I said, we need to talk."

"Good. You can start by how you got in here."

"Joelle let me in."

So, his dear wife *was* here. He was surprised that she hadn't answered when he called. He'd figured she'd be waiting at the door to gloat over breaking up him and Ashley. "Let me see where Joelle is first. I don't want her interrupting us." He started to rise, but his partner waved him back.

"She's asleep. Really, really asleep."

Asleep as in dead? His eyes widened, hope in his heart. Maybe his partner was useful after all. He pretended to be upset. "Where? In her bed? What did you do?"

"On the living room sofa. You walked right by her. I drugged her so she'd sleep."

"With what?" Lamont snapped.

"Same thing we gave Rocky. I roofied her. She won't even remember that I was here." Jackass frowned. "What did you think I meant?"

"I don't know. You seem to be keeping a lot of secrets lately."

A shrug. "The less you know, the less you could be forced to tell."

"No. That's not how this 'partnership' works. Who killed Lott and *why*? And how did you get that bastard following Morrow free?"

"One of my men and one of my men," he answered flippantly. "That's all you need to know."

Lamont ground his teeth. "*Why* did he kill Paul Lott?"

Jackass met his gaze directly. "Paul wanted more money to stay quiet."

No surprise. Lamont had never trusted Paul Lott, the greedy little bastard. He wasn't sure why Jackass had, but the two of them had been close since high school. Lamont had considered Paul opportunistic and two-faced even then. As a teenager, Paul would've turned on them in a

New York minute if he'd gotten scared or wanted to get in good with a teacher. He'd always been a little weasel. Now he was a dead little weasel.

"Thank you," Lamont said levelly. "Now, how did 'one of your men' know to follow Xavier Morrow to New Orleans?"

Jackass's smile was not nice. Not even a little bit. "Morrow called Lott, telling him that a man had tried to kill him. Luckily, my men were in Lott's home office and intercepted the call." His voice rose, hard as steel. "Turns out that Morrow shot his home intruder and ran. Stockman found him and failed to kill him, and you didn't think I should know either of those things?"

Lamont took a page from Jackass's book and ignored the question about his having kept Xavier's location a secret. In hindsight, he'd been smart to do so. Looked like he and Jackass were both following their own agendas.

"I took care of Stockman. That's all you need to know." Flinging the man's words back in his face felt entirely too good.

"Don't be an asshole, Monty," Jackass snarled. "I can bury you."

"Do you plan to?" Lamont asked, remaining calm, even though his heart was pounding.

"No. I hadn't even considered it until now."

Years of experience had made Lamont an excellent lie detector, and Jackass was lying through his capped teeth. "Good to know. If you know so much, where is Xavier Morrow now?"

Jackass rolled his eyes. "Finally, you ask the right question. He's with Broussard, but we lost them."

"Fucking Broussard."

"At least on that we can agree."

"What about Rocky's boy?" Lamont asked. "The chef? Did you torch them yet?"

Jackass made a sound of disgust. "We lost him and the lady PI, too.

They didn't go to Hebert's house, we know that. I have someone watching the place. No point in torching Gabe's house if he's not in it."

"Seems like we both have issues with our employees," Lamont said mildly.

Jackass chuckled, his good humor seemingly restored. "How are you going to deal with Eckert?"

"I haven't decided," he lied smoothly. He'd stopped for a drink when he'd been halfway home and had decided exactly who he'd use to get rid of the hit man who'd allowed himself to get caught. "Do you have any suggestions? Because if he talks and someone investigates, we're both likely to catch some heat."

Jackass's eyes narrowed. "Only if you can't hold your tongue."

"True. But that was the purpose of this partnership, was it not? Both of us are motivated to keep the other safe. Now, answer my question. Do you have any suggestions?"

It would be better if Jackass made the arrangements. Then any snafus could be traced to him. *Not me.*

Jackass opened his mouth like he was going to rant, then drew a breath and smiled coldly. "I'm not doing your dirty work with Eckert. You're on your own there. Figure it out yourself."

It was worth a try. "Then why are you here?"

"We need to find Xavier Morrow. He's got to have told the lady PI about what he saw by now. They got cozy at Broussard's office today. Even had food delivered from Rocky's kid's restaurant. With all that time, Morrow's got to have spilled everything."

Lamont had already figured that out, minus the catering. "But if he's dead, he can't testify. It'll just be hearsay. It might get rough for a while, I'm not gonna lie. I don't relish the scandal, but there's no way they'll get a conviction without Morrow's testimony. Not against me." He'd be able to spin it. Somehow. "I've got too many allies in high places. Broussard can't hurt me. He's got no body. He's got no anything. Except for

Morrow. So I agree, he's got to go. How are you planning to do it? Considering you've got all the men, after all."

"So do you." Jackass pointed to the bookshelf. "I'd bet my next paycheck that you've got a list right there in that safe."

Lamont made a point of bringing his pistol closer, leaving his palm on the grip.

Jackass rolled his eyes. "For fuck's sake, Monty. I'm not going to make you open it. You've gotten very paranoid lately." He tilted his head. "Is that why you jumped from your car and ran through traffic like your ass was on fire tonight?"

Lamont drew a deep breath, rage bubbling up from his gut. "You were following me?"

"Of course." Jackass smiled like a crocodile. "My man followed you all the way home. I couldn't have you in danger, now could I? I was only protecting you."

Liar. Liar. Liar. It was a very thinly veiled threat. "What about Morrow?"

The smile disappeared. "I'm getting access to all of Broussard's real estate holdings. He's hidden Morrow and his group somewhere, but I don't know where. Do you know where he's hiding them?"

"No. I never socialized with the man. I don't know his hidey-holes. That would have been your domain."

"Not so. Broussard kept to himself when he was on the force. I never spent time with him. Only Rocky did. And we can't ask him."

Lamont sat back in his chair, taking the gun with him. "Speaking of. How did Gabe Hebert know to hire a PI? Did he suspect that his father didn't commit suicide? Did Paul Lott tell him? Or did Xavier Morrow contact him before this week?"

"I don't know if the Morrow kid contacted Gabe Hebert before today or not. But Hebert definitely knows that his daddy didn't kill himself. Rocky's boy got himself a private autopsy."

Lamont sucked in a shocked breath, gaping. "Fucking hell."

Jackass nodded soberly. "Yep. That about covers it."

"How do you know this?"

"The chef told his pretty cousin, who told her parents, and my mole in the restaurant overheard. My mole told me, and I investigated. Gabe suspected something weeks ago. When the coroner released Rocky's body, Gabe just made it look like a cremation occurred. In reality, the body was sent from the funeral home to a private pathologist."

"So the mortician had to know, too."

"He did. He's not around to say a word anymore."

Relief coursed through him. "And the private pathologist?"

"She's no longer a problem, either."

Lamont was reluctantly impressed. "You've been busy today."

"I have. It's your turn now. I've cleaned up enough of your messes."

"It's in your best interest to do so," Lamont reminded him mildly, trying to hide his trepidation. Yes, he'd made a mistake that night in Katrina. But Jackass had helped him get rid of her body, and in the years since, they'd assisted each other. Back and forth. And Jackass had never complained until now. "Covering up a murder—or multiple murders—plus aiding in the disposal of a body could become a real problem for you."

Jackass narrowed his eyes. "Don't push me, Monty. I swear you won't like the consequences." Lamont opened his mouth to reply, but Jackass barreled on. "Use your contacts to find out where Broussard is hiding the kid. And for God's sake, take care of Eckert before he has a chance to blab. He's spittin' mad and not nearly as good at hiding it as he used to be."

Lamont drew a breath, his face burning with rage because a shiver of fear was slinking down his spine. He could make Jackass's life difficult, but, if push came to shove, Jackass could put him in prison. Up until now, they'd scratched each other's backs. Had helped each other up their respective ladders. It didn't look like their mutually beneficial relationship would last much longer. He wondered when Jackass had turned on him, because this threat was new.

New and very serious.

Lamont forced his tone to remain calm. "I've got plans for Eckert, so you don't need to worry about that. Tell me, what were your plans for Xavier once you got him to New Orleans?"

Jackass stared at him for a long moment, then shook his head. "Truthfully, I wasn't sure. I was pretty angry when I found out that you'd found him. I wasn't sure what your game was."

Liar, Lamont thought, but smiled sadly. "I wanted to take care of him myself. So you weren't liable for my 'messes.'"

Jackass had the good grace to look uncomfortable. "I guess I can appreciate that. Just . . . don't do it again, okay?"

"Okay." It appeared that they'd achieved a détente of sorts, so Lamont pushed forward. "As for Broussard, he could be hiding Morrow in a hotel or something."

"Maybe. We're checking for any hotel activity on Broussard's credit cards—company and personal. So far, nada. But I know the man has a camp down the bayou. Rocky mentioned it once, then clammed up, like he knew he'd said too much. Broussard grew up in the swamp. He knows all the good places to hide. If he's there, I'm betting he has it booby-trapped for any trespassers."

Lamont shrugged. "Then we draw Broussard out. If he brings the Morrow kid with him, all the better. Twofer. But if it's just Broussard, we can follow him back. Put a tracker on his vehicle." Lamont considered all the possibilities, then he smiled when the perfect solution presented itself. "If Morrow's told him what he saw all those years ago, then they'll be trying to identify the victim. What if the victim's 'best friend' or a 'family member' surfaces?" He used air quotes. "What if this person tells Broussard that she's been targeted? Her life is at risk." He nodded, the idea taking shape in his mind. "She makes up a name for the victim, which sends them off on a wild-goose chase. In the meantime, we're tracking Broussard back to his hidey-hole."

Jackass's grin was very Grinch-like. "I like it. Who's our femme fatale? Has to be someone we can trust."

"I know the perfect person. My former assistant, Ashley. She even looks like . . . you know. *Her.*" Because Lamont had a type, and he wasn't ashamed to admit it.

"I know," Jackass said dryly. "She-who-shall-not-be-named. The bitch who started all this."

True enough. *Nadia Hall.* The name Lamont hadn't spoken aloud since the night he'd killed her. "I'll arrange for Ashley to contact Broussard."

"There has to be a reasonable reason for her to surface now and an even more reasonable reason that she goes to Broussard," Jackass cautioned.

"I'm aware," Lamont snapped, then drew a breath to calm his mind. *Think, think, think. Oh. Okay.* "What if Ashley claims to have gotten a visit from Rocky shortly before his death and she told him about her sister? Then Rocky gets murdered."

"But why wouldn't Ashley have contacted Broussard earlier?"

"Because someone hadn't tried to kill her until now. She first reached out to Rocky, only to find he was dead. Rocky had told her if something happened and she couldn't reach him, to call Broussard. So she does."

"Did she-who-shall-not-be-named actually have a sister?"

"No. I asked." Because Lamont preferred to keep mistresses with no family or friends. They were needy, always available, and, if they went missing, no one came looking for them. Nadia had declared that her family was dead, which had made her perfect.

She really had been perfect. He'd loved her, in fact. He'd actually gone to rescue her that night. She'd put off leaving until it was too late. The water had already covered the single-story houses on the street, forcing him to borrow Jackass's boat to go save her.

And then she'd had to go and threaten to tell his first wife that she was pregnant. Nowadays, a scandal like that would be bad, but surviv-able. Back then, though, it would have been a disaster.

So he'd had to do it. Had to kill her. He'd figured she'd be counted as a flood fatality, but the water had never reached her bed. That had been a shock, seeing the house he'd taken as payment from a desperate client on the television, the upper-story windows still visible. Luckily, his former client's name was still on the deed, but the house—and the body—still could have been traced to him.

So he'd had to go back and fetch her body. Jackass had gone with him the second time. Had helped him dispose of her afterward. And that had been that.

Problem resolved. Until Rocky Hebert had started sticking his nose into things that he should have left well enough alone. Looking for her doctor had been bad enough, but when they'd learned he'd set up a trust for a kid who'd supposedly died in Katrina? The old cop hadn't given up on solving this case. Too bad that his setting up the trust was what had led them to the kid. Ironic, that. In helping Xavier Morrow, Rocky had shined a spotlight on the one person whose testimony could have put Lamont away for murder.

"She didn't have any family," Lamont said, "so making up a sister will work. Nobody can disprove it."

Jackass nodded. "I like it. It doesn't have to hold water for long. Just long enough to flush out Broussard, who'll eventually take us to the Morrow kid. But what about your girl? Why would she agree?"

"I'll tell her that this guy is suspected in a child endangerment case. That's her trigger."

"And if she tells?"

Lamont shrugged. "There are more Ashleys in the sea."

Jackass frowned, worry creasing his brow. "Lamont, that . . . That doesn't seem . . ." He hesitated. "Prudent."

Lamont frowned back. "Of course it's not prudent. I mean, we could sit here and do nothing and let that kid spill his guts. It would be a lot more damaging if he goes to the authorities—or, God forbid, the press—and tells his story. It's far better if he dies before that can happen. Either way, if he's dead, it's just hearsay. No witness, no trial. So unless you have a better idea, we should use Ashley."

Jackson narrowed his eyes. "And if she tells? Will you kill her, too?"

"Of course not." Probably not. Not unless he didn't have another choice. "She's not going to figure it out. She's good with organization and spreadsheets, but she's not the brightest bulb in the chandelier." Which was how he preferred his women. "And if she does, I'll say she was mistaken. So? Unless you have a better idea?"

"No," Jackson admitted. "I don't."

"Then I'll get her to call Broussard first thing in the morning. Can your men follow him once we lure him out?"

"They can."

"I want to be informed the moment they find Broussard's hidey-hole. None of this 'That's all you need to know' shit."

Jackass inclined his head. "Agreed. If you'll do the same. No more keeping secrets, like the whereabouts of eyewitnesses."

Lamont nodded. "Fair enough."

Except that he'd totally keep his own secrets. Jackass had been lying when he'd said that he wasn't sure what he'd do with Xavier. Bringing him all the way to New Orleans—with a minivan full of people—still didn't make sense.

Unless . . . *Shit.*

Unless he planned to double-cross me all along. Having a live eyewitness to the murder of a woman during Katrina, a murder that Rocky Hebert had initially reported, would be quite the feather in his partner's cap. It would be easy for him to twist the story, to paint Lamont in the worst light. Once he'd accused Lamont, any allegation that Jackass had been involved would seem like a weak attempt at revenge.

Whether Jackass had sent his men to Paul Lott's house to purposefully get information on Xavier or if it really had been a coincidence didn't really matter. Jackass had been planning to take advantage of the situation.

At least now neither of them had the kid, so they still had reason to work together.

But afterward . . . *Looks like I'll be hiring more than a hit man from my list. I need eyes on Jackass's men. Whoever they are.*

"Thank you," Lamont said, knowing that he sounded sincere. He'd practiced that tone over the years. It was damn near perfect. "I appreciate you helping me out of this mess."

Jackass shrugged. "We all make mistakes. I'm just glad you've learned to wear a condom since then so we haven't had to clean up any other pregnant mistresses."

Lamont smiled tightly. *Condescending asshole.* Jackass hadn't worn a condom with his mistress. *At least* I *don't have a bastard kid running around out there somewhere.* "I promise. Shall we touch base tomorrow?"

"Sounds like a plan." Jackass got up and straightened his suit coat. "I'll let you get back to your list, Monty. I can show myself out."

Lamont rose, pocketing the handgun in a move that he meant for his partner to see. No fucking way was he letting this viper walk through his home unattended. He'd probably plant a bug or something. If he hadn't already. *Fucking hell.* "I'll walk you. It's only civilized, after all."

14

XAVIER TRIED TO relax. It wasn't that Burke's place wasn't comfortable, because it was. They'd traveled to Des Allemands, then boarded a flat-bottomed boat that two of Burke's part-time employees had waiting for them. Then they'd all traveled by water to the camp, arriving just before it got too dark to see.

Manny had been excited to see two gators slicing through the water, but Carlos hadn't been as keen. Xavier was simply too tired to care, although the swamp was beautiful with its cypress trees and hanging Spanish moss.

The camp itself was located on the bayou bank, elevated up on pilings, and seemed to kind of melt into the vegetation. The two men who'd come with them stayed to guard the place. Which made Xavier both reassured and more scared.

The camp was surprisingly nice, with three bedrooms, hardwood floors throughout, and all new appliances in the kitchen. The living room had a huge flat-screen TV and an Xbox. Which Carlos and

Manny had commandeered, of course. They sat on big throw pillows on the floor, trying to best each other in *Call of Duty*.

Burke had claimed an ancient recliner that was literally held together with duct tape. It was out of place in the room where everything else looked brand-new. The PI business must be lucrative. Burke didn't seem like he was hurting for cash.

Willa Mae sat in a rocker, knitting and occasionally humming to herself. Xavier made a mental note to buy her some pretty yarn when this was over. Her very presence had calmed him today. He'd sometimes forgotten over the years that she was a lawyer. She'd always been Miss Willa Mae, his mom's best friend, and she'd never talked about her job.

His mother sat on the sofa next to him, unusually pensive. Xavier was most grateful for her. Grateful that she'd stood with him, grateful that she was alive period. This day could have ended so differently. Hell, if she and Dad hadn't adopted him, his whole life could've ended differently.

"Thank you," he whispered.

She turned to him with a soft smile. "I was proud of you today, son. I'm proud of you every day, but today . . . Well, you've grown into an amazing man. I wish your father were here to see how well you've turned out."

Xavier swallowed hard. "Mom. Stop it."

She patted his hand. "I'm allowed to be proud. I'm allowed to be sentimental. Suck it up."

He laughed, the sound surprising him. But the lightness evaporated quickly, leaving him cold. And scared. He was so damn scared. "I'm sorry you're stuck here with me."

She swatted him. "You stop it. As if I'd be anywhere else."

"What did you tell work?"

"I told them that I had a family emergency and was taking some of the leave I have saved. That was this morning, though. If the fact that Houston PD was searching our house made the news, they'll know why I left."

That was something that they hadn't really discussed. Houston PD had been in their house. *And at some point, they'll want to talk to me.* "Will you be in trouble?"

She shook her head. "Nope. I was taking care of my son. And if there is trouble, I can find another job elsewhere. Nurses are in demand these days."

He shuddered, thinking of his mother losing her job. "What if this takes a long time? What if we're stuck here for weeks?"

"And what if we're not?" she said softly, then glanced at Burke. "You planning on throwing us out anytime soon, Burke?"

Burke grinned. "No, ma'am. You're welcome to use this place as long as you like. I mean that."

"What will Houston PD do?" Xavier asked, still scared shitless. There were so many ways this could go wrong. More wrong.

"They'll come and talk to you," Willa Mae said without looking up from her knitting, her needles moving so fast that Xavier had a hard time following the movement. "You'll tell them exactly what you told Captain Holmes. You'll tell them that you had no idea why that guy was following you—and at the time, you didn't. If they want to make a case against you, they'll have to dig." She did look up now, her eyes piercing. "They won't find anything, will they?"

"No, ma'am. I've never even smoked a cigarette. Never even bought a beer until I was twenty-one."

"I can attest to that," Carlos said. "He always said no, no matter how many times I begged."

"You are a bad influence," Willa Mae told Carlos, but she was smiling. "You're also a good friend. You're going to tell HPD that you saw the man's hands and he had a gun. And that there could have been two men, but you were so scared, you ran without finding out."

"That's true," Carlos said, uncharacteristically solemn. "I was scared shitless, and that's a fact."

"I don't plan on allowing HPD to talk to you, Xavier," Burke said quietly, "if it makes you feel better. I have no idea where you are."

It did make him feel better, actually. Except . . . "André knows that's not true. What if he tells them where to find me?"

"He won't," Burke said, seeming confident. "Not without warning me first. And if he does, it's a big bayou and I know lots of hidey-holes, so don't you waste a minute worrying."

"But what if HPD tries to hang something on Xavier even before they question him?" Manny asked. "That's had me worried all day."

"We'll cross that bridge when we get there," Willa Mae declared. "If they try, we'll fight them. You have the advantage of someone who knows how they work. I know just about all the prosecutors in Harris County, so I know what approaches they might take. I'm not worried right now. If I get worried, I will be honest with you. Trust me on that."

"Yes, ma'am." Carlos set the game controller on the carpet. "But I'm still confused about the guy who called himself Paul Lott. He went to all the trouble of making a new ID. That had to have taken him a little while. Like maybe he planned ahead or something. But Lott was only killed last night."

"Probably shortly before Xavier called him," Burke agreed. He sat reclined with his feet up, his eyes closed, and his hands folded over his stomach, looking for all the world like a dad taking a snooze. "That's a very good point, Carlos. I'm wondering if whoever killed Lott knew about you earlier, Xavier. If they'd already planned to impersonate Lott before you called."

"Like that makes me feel better," Xavier muttered.

Burke shrugged, eyes still closed. "Not trying to make you feel better. Trying to keep you alive. Had you received any other communication from Lott's office?"

"No. Just the one call to my burner cell. The one I used with Rocky. Lott told me that he was sending some paperwork to the UPS box address, except he didn't know it was a UPS box. I just let him think it was my real mailing address."

"If I was an evil bad guy," Burke mused, "and I wanted to find you because you were a witness to a murder I'd done back in Katrina, *and* I'd already made an ID with Lott's name on it, planning to impersonate him, I'd check his files for any correspondence with you. And when I found that address where Lott sent your inheritance check, I'd have checked that out, too. It would have taken no time at all to find that it was a UPS box." He was quiet for a moment, continuing to look like he was snoozing. "I'd check out that UPS mailbox location. And if I were truly smart, I'd send you a piece of mail with some kind of tracking device." His eyes popped open. "Have you checked that box recently?"

Xavier shook his head. "Not since right after Rocky died and Paul Lott called me on my burner phone to tell me that he was sending me the papers."

"Where is your burner phone?" Burke asked.

"At my house. I kept it in a lockbox in my closet."

"Maybe that man this morning was looking for that burner phone," Willa Mae said, her needles back in motion. "Maybe he was hoping you'd pack it."

Burke nodded. "You could be right, Miss Willa Mae."

She smirked. "I usually am."

Burke closed his eyes again. "I'll have Molly drive to Baton Rouge and check the box. If Lott's killer was hoping to lure you there, maybe we can get some information about him."

"What if Lott was involved?" Cicely asked.

Xavier frowned. "Rocky trusted him."

Cicely shrugged. "I trusted Rocky. But I didn't know this Lott character. I mean, he's dead now, so he's probably no longer a threat even if he was involved, but . . . what if?"

Burke made a humming noise. "It's a valid question. I'll have Molly add it to the list. She's good at lists."

Cicely smiled. "She was all about that whiteboard this afternoon."

"That's her thing," Burke said. "She's a thinker, and she organizes information in ways that make sense. It's one of the things that made her a great cop and one of the reasons I wanted her to come work for me." Abruptly he stowed the recliner's footrest and stood. "I didn't get much sleep last night myself, so I'm going to hit the hay. I think you all know where everything is. Help yourself to anything in the kitchen or anywhere else. But I don't recommend taking a walk outside. Gators, y'know. They're on the move in the night."

Carlos made a face. "I didn't need to be reminded of that, thank you very much."

Burke's grin was slightly wicked. "Wouldn't want you becoming gator food, now would we? I've got all the perimeter alarms set. If anyone comes close, I'll know, so y'all can sleep well." He sobered. "I've also got my two part-timers standing watch outside. I trust them with my life and yours. They shouldn't bother you, and they'll stay outside. So sleep well."

"'Night, Burke," Xavier called as the man headed toward his room at the back of the house. "Thank you."

Burke just waved.

Xavier sighed. "I know I need to sleep, but my brain is too wired."

"I'm going to try," Manny said. "At least Burke didn't ask me to give up any of the weapons I brought with me. If anyone comes after us, I'll be ready."

Xavier didn't want to think about using his father's gun again. Even if Molly hadn't taken it so she could get rid of it, the memory of using it the night before had left him queasy. "Maybe we should find a baseball bat or a golf club for Carlos. He was badass with those things. Wielded them like freaking swords."

Carlos laughed. "All that playing Luke Skywalker with a light saber paid off. Sometimes being a geek works out. Come on, X." He stood up and held out his hand, tugging Xavier to his feet. "Let's try to sleep. Manny and Burke have us covered."

"Don't count me out," Willa Mae said. She leaned down to rifle through her yarn bag, taking out her handgun. "So your mama's safe, too."

"Thank you, Miss Willa Mae." Xavier leaned over to kiss her cheek. "'Night, Mama."

"Sleep tight, son. Things will be better tomorrow."

Central Business District, New Orleans, Louisiana
TUESDAY, JULY 26, 9:15 P.M.

"We're here," Molly said, parking the rental car in the hotel's underground garage. Turning in her seat, she nudged Gabe, who'd fallen asleep a half hour into their drive. She hated to wake him. He looked so peaceful. And handsome.

Lord help her, the man was hot. She caressed the hard line of his jaw, his stubble scraping her skin in the most pleasant of ways, before brushing a loose red curl from his forehead.

And she needed to stop admiring her client and get him up to his room where he'd be safe. This garage had 24-7 surveillance by the hotel's security, and she'd driven a long time to ensure that no one had followed them, but it still wasn't safe for Gabe.

She shook his shoulder harder. "Gabe? Wake up."

He grumbled something she didn't catch. "Gabriel Hebert, wake up this instant," she commanded sharply.

His eyes opened slowly. "Where are we?"

"Hotel in the Central Business District."

Gabe straightened in his seat, glancing at the car's clock in confusion. "That's, like, ten minutes from your office. We've been driving for an hour."

"Needed to make sure we weren't followed. Let's get upstairs and then you can sleep for real."

She needed to, for sure. She hadn't been this tired in a very long time.

She forced her feet out of the car and shouldered her duffel bag. Gabe followed, still blinking. She linked her arm through his and guided them toward the elevator to the lobby. "We're all checked in. We can head straight up to our rooms."

"Rooms?" he asked, disgruntled. "Why two?"

She grinned up at him, all while she kept watch. She'd spotted one security guard at the entrance and another deep in the shadows of the garage. No one else seemed to be down here, which was just the way she liked it. "Why, Mr. Hebert. Are you saying you want to share a room with me?"

His lips quirked. "I'd like to share more than a room. But I'm a gentleman, so I won't push."

"I'm a lady, but I'll push if I want to."

He chuckled at that, then stiffened when a shadow moved in front of them. Molly went on full alert, her free hand moving to the gun holstered at her hip. Gabe had come to a halt, his body moving into a stance she recognized from her own martial arts training. *Good to know.* Even sleepy, he had good instincts.

But their vigilance wasn't necessary. It was only a third security guard.

"Sorry," the man said, eyeing Gabe's attack-ready posture. "Didn't mean to scare you."

"Quite all right," Molly said smoothly, even though her pulse was now racing. "Maybe don't sneak around in the shadows, though."

"Yes, ma'am. Have a good evening, ma'am," he said with enough sarcasm to make Molly wish that Gabe had attacked him.

"Asshole," Gabe muttered when they were in the elevator. "Yes, ma'am," he mimicked.

"I'm used to it," she said, then rose on her toes to give his cheek a peck. "Still, it's nice to see you ready to defend me. Nice moves."

He grumbled under his breath, but she could tell that he was pleased. "Better than last night. I nearly had a panic attack when that guy tried to hurt Shoe."

She hated the self-deprecation in his voice. "You were shocked, Gabe. I never thought less of you. But I'm glad that your instincts were good just now. That might save your life someday."

His jaw tightened. "*I* thought less of me."

The elevator doors opened, saving her from a response. Which was good because she didn't know what to say to make him feel better.

"Come on," she said, tugging him away from the front desk and toward the main bank of elevators. "This way."

"We don't need a key?"

"Not tonight. Just . . . wait till we're behind closed doors. I'll explain."

He fell silent as they entered another elevator, watching as she pushed the button for the sixteenth floor. When the doors opened, she led him toward the room number that Burke had texted her.

She rapped twice on the door, paused, then rapped twice more, and the door opened.

Molly breathed a sigh of relief at the sight of the six-foot, blond Norwegian woman whose skin was three shades paler than even Gabe's.

"You look like crap, girl," Val said in her typical brusque way, stepping back to let them inside, then shutting the door. "And . . . OMG, is that a wrinkle I see on your shirt?"

Molly chuckled. "Shut up. Gabe, this is Val Sorensen, one of Burke's PI-slash-bodyguards, and one of my very best friends. Val, Gabe Hebert."

Val stuck out her hand. "I have heard so much about you. Most of it good."

Gabe blinked. "Um, thank you? But if you're here, who's guarding my cousin?"

"Gabe!" Patty flew from the adjoining room, throwing her arms around Gabe's neck. "You're okay. I just heard about today. About the guy on the highway pointing his gun at you."

Gabe looked at Molly, confused again. "What's happening right now? Why is Patty here?"

"Val's going to stand guard tonight so I can sleep. Patty can't be left alone, so she's here."

A slow grin brightened his face. "Adjoining rooms?" he mouthed.

She grinned back. "Yep," she mouthed back.

Val just snorted. Patty missed the entire exchange because her face was buried against Gabe's neck.

Gabe pried Patty's arms from his neck so that he could look her in the eye. "I'm fine. The gun was pointed at Molly, not at me. But we're fine."

Patty stepped back. "I kept imagining the worst when it took you so long to get here."

"I'm sorry," Molly said quietly. "I was making sure we weren't followed."

Patty nodded, flicking a glance at Val. "That's what Val said. I still worried."

"Who's minding the Choux?" Gabe asked.

"Donna Lee has everything under control." Patty braved a smile. "We might come back and find that we're not needed at all."

"Not true, and you know it," Val said. "Sit down and rest, guys. There's a minibar if you need a drink."

"Not me," Molly said. "I just need to sleep. I can't run on two hours' sleep like a college kid anymore." She dropped her duffel bag on one of the two queen-sized beds in the room, toeing off her boots and arranging them next to the bed as she always did.

At least she wasn't sleeping in her boots like she had in the Corps. That had sucked royally.

"Anything new?" Val murmured, sitting on the side of her bed while

Gabe answered Patty's flurry of questions on the other side of the room.

"When did Burke brief you?"

"He called me fifteen minutes ago."

"Me too." To tell her that HPD might show up tomorrow, expecting to interview Xavier, but that he didn't plan to allow it. There was no reason to give HPD the opportunity to haul Xavier in for questioning where he might be in danger. Burke also told them that the Paul Lott impersonator might have been looking for Xavier's burner phone. "So we're both up to speed."

"Plans for tomorrow?" Val asked.

Gabe and Patty sat on the edge of the other bed. "Yes," Gabe said. "I'd like to know, too."

Molly was afraid to sit. Exhaustion was already shutting her body down. If she sat, she'd be out in a second. "I want one of us to be present when Cornell Eckert is arraigned tomorrow."

"I will," Val said. "You can stay here with them. If Eckert pulled a gun on you yesterday, he'll recognize you tomorrow in court. I don't want whoever hired him to be able to follow you back here."

Molly weaved on her feet. "I was thinking the same thing."

Val arched a brow. "Anything else before you fall over?"

"Yeah. I want to take Xavier back to his old neighborhood tomorrow. We need to know where the victim lived. I know he was young when it all happened, but he might remember."

Val winced sympathetically. "That's going to be hard on him. Pictures won't suffice?"

"A lot of those areas have changed since Katrina," Molly said. "Xavier might not recognize it from photos."

Val frowned. "He might not recognize it in person, either."

"I know," Molly said. She'd thought of that already. "But the victim is the center of everything. Once we find her, the connections to all the other players will be clearer."

Val nodded, but looked skeptical. "It's worth a try, I guess. You'll have support?"

"I think just me. It'll be better if Xavier's not with an entourage. He'll attract attention."

Val frowned. "Burke's not going to let you go alone."

"I'll talk to him tomorrow, after I've slept." Molly rubbed her forehead. A headache had taken root. "I'm not sure when Eckert is scheduled to be arraigned, but it's normally first thing."

"I know," Val said gently, then lifted her voice to call to Patty. "Let's let these two sleep."

Patty kissed Gabe's cheek. "I'm next door if you need me." She waved at Molly on her way out. "Thank you for keeping him safe."

Molly smiled. "My job and my pleasure." She waited until the door to the adjoining room closed behind them, then sank to the bed. "I'm running on fumes. If you don't mind, I'll take the bathroom first."

Gabe made an after-you gesture. "Molly? Where do you want me to sleep?"

She paused in midstride. And really thought about her answer. She could say that sharing a bed would help her protect him better, but they both knew that was a big ole lie. So she went with the truth. "With me? I can't promise anything's gonna happen, but it would be nice to hold you and—"

He was at her side in a moment, his finger pressed to her lips. "Holding you is exactly what I want, too." Moving his finger from her mouth, he cupped her cheek in his palm. "And when you wake up, maybe to kiss you again. That's all."

She nuzzled into his palm. "That sounds perfect."

Fifteen minutes later, under the covers and nearly asleep already, she felt his arm curling around her waist, his body spooning her. He smelled of minty toothpaste, the hotel's vanilla-scented soap, but mostly of himself, all spicy and clean. He kissed her temple, slipping his hand under her T-shirt to rest on her stomach while murmuring in her ear. "Sleep. Val is on guard duty. Let go and sleep."

The rumble of his voice and the touch of his hand sent a shiver across her skin that was a wake-up call. Plus the reminder that Val was—at the moment—responsible for standing watch had her remembering that kiss in the office. That she wasn't technically responsible for Gabe's safety—at the moment—was a really flimsy technicality for excusing what she was about to do, but she couldn't make herself care. Gabe made her want . . . all kinds of things.

Suddenly sleep was the furthest thing from her mind.

"Don't want to now," she murmured back. "Got a sexy man in my bed." She rolled to her back, staring up into his face. His hand had splayed wide over her stomach, his thumb tantalizingly close to the curve of her breast. *Just a little higher, Gabe. Please?* "You're perfect, you know that?"

"I'm far from perfect. You're pretty damn close, though."

She rolled her eyes. "Shut up and kiss me, Gabe."

And he did. Sweetly at first. Chastely. More like the first kiss they'd shared. But then he made a needy sound deep in his throat.

Or was that me?

It didn't matter, because he changed the kiss, covering her body with his own, going from sweet to full-on sex in a heartbeat. She reached for him, one hand threading through his curls on his head, the other the curls on his chest. So soft, both places. Just as she'd hoped they'd be.

His skin against hers was warm, his lips firm and insistent, and she cursed that she needed air. She pulled away just far enough to draw in a breath. "You're good at this."

His lips curved against hers. "You're good for my ego. I was afraid I'd be out of practice."

His thumb brushed a sizzling path a fraction of an inch closer to her breast, making her want to grab his hand and move it herself. But this was seduction, and she hadn't been seduced in a very long time. "Practice never hurts."

She bent one knee, bracketing his hip, lifting her own hips to feel how much he wanted her. She shivered, because, if the rigid length in his boxer briefs was any indication, he wanted her very much. Despite her exhaustion, her body flared to life, and she needed more. She slid her hand beneath the elastic waist of his underwear, wanting to learn his body more intimately, exhaling on a hiss when she wrapped her fingers around him. He was big and hard and ready. Very ready.

With a quiet groan, he thrust into her hand. "The things I want to do to you." He thrust again. "With you."

"Tell me," she whispered.

"I want to touch you," he whispered back, his voice gone deeper, his accent thicker. Richer. His fingertips brushed the underside of her breast, making her shiver in anticipation. "Can I touch you, Molly?"

There was only one answer for her, here in this moment that was just for them. "Yes. Please."

His hand finally cupped her breast, his thumb lightly flicking her nipple. "I want to touch you all over. I want to learn what you like. I want to taste you. I want to be inside you, and I want to hear you moan for me."

She couldn't have silenced her moan if she'd tried. "Yes. Yes, please."

Central Business District, New Orleans, Louisiana
TUESDAY, JULY 26, 9:55 P.M.

Yes. Yes, please.

Molly's words echoed in his mind and it was all Gabe could do to keep his touch gentle. He'd held himself in check all this time, ever since she'd first walked into the Choux, contenting himself with only looking.

Not touching. Not tasting.

Not having.

But she'd said yes.

Hands trembling, he urged her arms over her head and pulled her T-shirt up and over her breasts. And let himself take a moment to stare. "You're beautiful," he whispered.

"So are you," she whispered back, then made a needy little noise. "Gabe, come on."

He flashed her a grin. "Impatient."

"Damn straight."

"I thought of you," he confessed. "Every time you'd come into my place, I'd watch you and then I'd think of you later."

Her lips curved slyly. "Did you jerk off when you'd think of me?"

His eyes widened, his cheeks heating. Hell, they were on freaking fire. But he nodded. "I did."

She licked her bottom lip. "I might have thought of you a time or two. When I was lying in my bed. All alone."

Shuddering at the mental image, he kissed her lips, then kissed the curve of her jaw. "You're not alone now."

"No, I'm not." She rocked her hips, rubbing herself against him, and he groaned softly, conscious that her friend was on the other side of the adjoining door, likely listening for anything that sounded like trouble. "Kiss me, Gabe. Stop thinking and kiss me."

Not waiting for him to comply, she shoved her fingers through his hair and pulled him down, crashing their mouths together.

He stopped thinking, drowning in the taste of her. It had been so long. Too long. But anyone who'd come before had faded into a distant, fuzzy memory. He ripped his mouth away, panting. "I want you."

She was panting, too. "Then hurry."

He wished there was more light so that he could see her better. *Next time*, he thought. Kneeling between her legs, he pulled her T-shirt over her head and dropped it on the floor, next to the bed. He reached for her sleep shorts, but she distracted him, lifting up enough to run her hands over his pecs.

"I like your chest," she murmured, leaning in to kiss his collarbone. "Is this okay?"

"Yes." The word came out strangled, but clear enough that she kept going, kissing across his chest until she got to his left nipple, giving it little licks that sent a jolt of sensation right to his cock. "Good."

It felt so good. Better than good.

He felt her lips curve against his skin, her chuckle a puff of warm breath that made him shiver. "Mmm. We're down to one-word utterances. I think you like this."

She made her way to the other side of his chest, sometimes kissing and sometimes sucking so hard that he was sure he'd have marks. Finally, she got to the other nipple, this time interspersing the little licks with light bites that sent jolts of pleasure down his body.

"Fuck." The word came out on a shudder and his body was in motion, driven by instinct and the desire to see her completely bare. He grabbed the waist of her shorts. "Lift."

She did and he yanked the shorts down her legs, taking her panties with them.

"Molly." He stared down at her, taking in her luscious curves, the flare of her hips, the neat patch of blond hair between her legs. He swallowed hard, unable to find the words. "Molly," was all he could say.

She didn't give him any more time to look, though. "Off," she muttered, pulling his boxer briefs to his knees, making his cock bounce against his stomach. She drew in a breath. "Oh yeah." She leaned in and licked him, base to crown, and he couldn't control his shout.

"Fuck."

She glanced up, meeting his eyes in the darkness. "Is that what you want?"

He swallowed again, his mouth watering with how much he wanted. "I have a condom."

He was afraid she'd wonder why. Afraid she'd think him forward. Presumptuous.

But she didn't, flopping back to the pillow in a move that sent her breasts bouncing hypnotically. "Then get it."

Blindly he reached for his wallet on the nightstand and fumbled for the foil packet he'd stored there more than a year ago. His hands no longer trembled, thank God. With sure, deliberate movements, he tore the packet, retrieved the condom, and slid it down his length.

All while she watched him hungrily.

He settled himself between her legs, his heart pounding so hard it was a wonder it didn't leap from his chest. *Be a good man. Make sure this is what she wants.* "Are you sure? We don't have to—"

She hooked her legs around his hips. "I'm sure." A moment later he was blinking up at her, having been rolled to his back. "Are you?"

He grinned so wide that he thought his face would break. "Yes. Are you gonna ride me, Molly?"

She braced her hands on his chest. "That's my plan."

They both groaned as she took him inside her body. She was warm and tight and . . .

"Ohmygod," he muttered, his words running together, and she laughed, her happiness filling the space between them. Filling his heart.

He could fall for this woman.

Maybe he was already starting to.

Then she was moving, sex and grace and . . . joy. Watching Molly Sutton taking her pleasure, uninhibited, was something he didn't ever want to end. But all too soon his body got caught up in the moment, in the pleasure. He gripped her hips, thrusting up to meet her every downward bounce.

So good. But he wanted more. More contact. More skin. More of her. Crunching his abs, he sat up halfway, sucking her nipple into his mouth, feeling her fingers digging into his shoulders. Hearing her gasps and pleas for *more, more, harder*.

He was barely aware that she was no longer gripping one of his shoulders until she gave a keening cry. Looking between them, he saw her touching herself, furiously rubbing her clit. He barely had time to register how damn hot that was before her back arched, her head falling back as she moaned, long and low.

That was it. That was all he could take. Wrapping his arms around her, he rolled them back over and began thrusting in earnest. It wasn't graceful, it wasn't neat, but he couldn't care. He didn't know when he'd felt so good.

His orgasm hit him like a crashing wave, pulling him under as his body spasmed and he thrust one more time. Then he exhaled, careful to keep his weight on his forearms as he lowered his body. He shuddered as a final spasm rocked through his body.

"Mmmm," she murmured. "You okay?"

He chuckled tiredly. His whole body felt limp and . . . good. So good that he was still thinking in—what had she said? *Oh, right.* One-word utterances. "I think so. You?"

"I know so. If that's you out of practice, I can't wait to see how you improve."

So they'd do this again, which was a relief. He wasn't sure what he'd do if he didn't experience this again. But he was crushing her, so he carefully pulled out, tied off the condom, and tossed it in the trash can next to the bed.

She snuggled up against his side. "I think we should sleep now."

He just might be able to now. His mind was shutting down, too tired to worry about what tomorrow would bring. He pulled her closer, content when she rubbed her cheek against the coarse hair on his chest.

He could get used to this. Holding her while she slept.

"You're a nice pillow," she murmured sleepily. "I like this. Like you. More than I should."

He kissed the top of her head. "Sleep, Molly. I'll be here when you wake up."

The Quarter, New Orleans, Louisiana
TUESDAY, JULY 26, 10:30 P.M.

Sitting on the edge of the bed, Ashley bit her lip, looking around the plush hotel room as she contemplated his request. Lamont had arranged for her to meet him there, saying he needed her help to save some children. Which was exactly the right thing to say, because punishing child abusers was the reason Ashley had given when he'd first interviewed her for his assistant. Having endured abuse herself as a child, taking abusers down was her passion.

But she wasn't fierce. Joelle would have jumped at the opportunity to role-play before his money had spoiled her. Ashley, however, was deep in thought.

"If you can't help me," he murmured, "I'll understand. This isn't your job. But there's really no one I trust more than you to help me pull this off."

Again, that was the right thing to say, because her cheeks tinged pink, her smile shy but bright. "I want to help you, and I will. I'm just thinking about the questions I need to ask first."

He sat back in the chair next to the bed. "Ask away. Your safety and comfort with the situation are my priorities."

"Well, okay. Why aren't the police handling this?"

"Good question." It really was. *Dammit, Ashley.* "They are. They'll be backing you up."

Her forehead wrinkled. "But don't they have undercover policewomen?"

Her questions came as a surprise. He'd honestly expected her to say yes without the third degree. If she said no to his request, he'd have to kill her tonight. That he'd end up killing her at some point was a foregone conclusion, despite what he'd said to Jackass. What else could he have said, what with the man looking at him like he was crazy?

I'm not crazy. In fact, I might be the only sane one in this mess. He might be the only one truly thinking.

Once he'd presented his dilemma with Burke Broussard to her, she had information that could hurt him. But he'd really hoped for at least one more roll between the sheets.

Ashley was very enthusiastic in bed, and he'd miss that.

He frowned at her. "If you're not willing, I can find someone else."

"No, no, no," she said hastily. "I never said I wasn't willing. Just asking why a policewoman isn't handling this. I'm just an office assistant." She grimaced. "I'm not even *your* office assistant anymore."

Ouch. Nice aim, Ash. "The policewoman involved was compromised," he lied. "Her cover was blown. I've been working with NOPD, and they asked for my help."

Which was also a total and complete lie, of course. Not that Ashley would know that. She was a genius with spreadsheets, but her common sense was lacking.

"Okay," she said, clearly still doubtful. "All I have to do is call this Broussard guy first thing in the morning and tell him that I need him to investigate a case for me. That someone tried to kill me, and I think it's related to the murder of my sister JoAnn back during Katrina."

"Exactly." He smiled the way she liked best. "That's my girl."

She smiled back, happy to be useful to him. "And this will lure him out of hiding so that you can grab him?"

"It will." It had to. If Broussard suspected, it would be even harder to lure him out.

"And this Broussard is guilty of trafficking kids?"

"He is. But he's never harmed a woman, so you're in no danger. You'll wear a wire and we'll be waiting outside." That much was true.

He'd already made calls to the most reliable names on his list, both as personal security for himself and to take care of Eckert. One of his men would be waiting outside so that they could follow Jackass's men when they tailed Broussard, because his partner could not be trusted. "As soon as you come out of his office, we'll whisk you away."

Her brow furrowed again. "What if Broussard asks me why I chose him? He might be suspicious."

"Tell him that you were visited by a cop named Rocky who was investigating your sister's murder. You tried to call Rocky, but he's dead."

Her eyes widened. "He's dead? How?"

"Shot himself. Very sad. He was a good cop. Tell Broussard that Rocky told you that if anything bad happened to you, to go to Broussard because they were partners in the NOPD."

Her eyes widened further. "Broussard was a cop?"

"He was."

Her jaw tightened, rage filling her normally placid expression. "Then he deserves to be thrown in jail. Maybe one of the criminals he arrested will give him justice."

He smiled, this time sincerely. "I like the way you think, Ash. So you'll do it?"

"I will."

"You can't use your real name. You're Alicia Rollins and your sister was JoAnn." Not Nadia Hall, because he'd never say that name again. Plus, there really had been a JoAnn Rollins who'd died during Katrina, so if Burke checked, his suspicions would be satisfied. Kind of fitting since Rocky had done the same thing—giving his boss the name of a Katrina victim instead of Xavier Morrow when he'd been pressed for the eyewitness's identity. "Got it?"

"I do."

"I'll send you a fake address that you can give him when he asks where you live."

Lamont had received both the names to be used and the address from Jackass an hour before. It was a house in a small South Carolina town, not too far from where Gabe Hebert's lady PI used to live. If Margaret Sutton got curious and went to investigate, she'd receive a little present, courtesy of one of Jackass's trusted operatives.

Lamont hoped it worked. And if it didn't, none of it could be tied to him. No harm, no foul.

"And," he added, "you can't give Broussard any details over the phone except for—"

"Except that someone tried to kill me and it's due to the murder of my sister during Katrina. I got it. I promise." Her lips curved seductively. "And now that we've taken care of business . . ."

He pushed away the irritation at being interrupted and glanced at his watch. "I can stay for a little while."

She tilted her head, trying—and failing—to look nonchalant. "And your wife?"

"I'm going to divorce her." More or less. "But I have to wait until—"

She sighed. "After the election. I know, I know."

He reached for her hand. "She's watching me too closely. I can't risk her having any ammunition against me. Against us. She's not a nice person."

Ashley laughed bitterly. "I figured that out for myself."

"Let's not think about her right now. We have this lovely room and complete privacy."

She nodded firmly. "You're right. Let's have some fun."

15

*C*OFFEE. GABE ROLLED toward the aroma, vaguely cognizant that he wasn't lying on his own mattress. Memory rushed back in a flash as he opened his eyes to the hotel room that was standard in every way except for the woman currently doing a kata in the small open area near the bathroom door.

She was wearing a loose-fitting pair of pants that hung low on her hips and a T-shirt that hugged every one of her gorgeous curves. He remained still, watching as she went through the moves of the kata. Her body flowed slowly and fluidly, but with visibly restrained power.

She was breathtaking.

He didn't recognize the sequence of blocks, kicks, and strikes. The routines he'd learned in his Brazilian Jiu-Jitsu training were very different. This looked more like karate. She'd said she was a black belt in three different schools, and he could believe that, just by watching her move.

She was calm and strong and the most capable woman he'd ever met. Which was good, because now that he was awake and his mind clear, the blanket of dread descended once again.

He'd been much happier when his brain had been clouded and sex-drunk.

He sucked in a breath when she did a roundhouse kick, spinning in the air to land on the balls of her feet almost silently on the hotel room floor. Also good, because they were on the sixteenth floor.

He doubted the people below them would have heard even the slightest of thumps. She was agile like a cat.

Waiting until she'd placed her hands together and bowed, he cleared his throat. "Good morning."

She smiled over at him. "Good morning to you. I hope I didn't wake you up."

"Nope," he said cheerfully, trying to shove the dread aside. "That would have been the coffee."

"It's not Choux-quality coffee, but it's caffeine."

Molly Sutton had looked beautiful in the dark the night before, but, if it was even possible, she looked even more so in the early-morning light.

He pushed himself up to sit against the headboard, gratified to see her gaze drop to his bare chest. His morning wood definitely sat up and took notice. "Caffeine is caffeine. I'm not picky this morning."

"I'll get you a cup."

He would have argued that he could get it, but she was already walking to the coffee machine. So, he shut up and watched her round ass in those loose pants, remembering how she'd felt in his arms. Wishing that he'd been able to wake up still holding her.

"What were you doing?" he asked, noticing her laptop open on the other bed.

She turned to glance at him and it was impossible to miss the sway of unfettered breasts. Very nice unfettered breasts. He tried not to stare but couldn't stop himself.

Not until she answered his question. "Looking at police reports of murders that happened during Katrina. I was hoping to find one that matched what Xavier saw, but so far, I've come up with nothing."

Her words were like a cold shower. Okay, more like a lukewarm shower, because he was still aroused. "How long have you been awake?"

She doctored his coffee, and he was relieved to see the hotel provided real cream. That powdered stuff was an insult to humanity. "A few hours. I needed to give Val some time to sleep. She's heading to the courthouse in an hour or so for Eckert's arraignment. I'll guard both you and Patty until she gets back."

"And then?"

She set his coffee on the nightstand and perched on the edge of the bed they'd shared, her ass against his knee. "And then I'm taking you both to the office, where you'll be safe while I take Xavier to his old neighborhood."

Gabe frowned. "No. We agreed that we'd go together."

She lifted her own cup to her lips and sipped, but the set of her jaw told him that they were about to vehemently disagree. "Gabe, I—"

"You're the trained one," he interrupted. "I get that. But you promised."

"No, Burke promised."

He huffed. "Molly."

She tilted her head. "Gabe. It's too damn dangerous. It's bad enough that I'm taking Xavier. I can't worry about both of you."

"Do you plan to get out and walk the street with him?"

"Of course not. I'm going to drive up and down the street until he gets his bearings."

He lifted his brows. "And that won't elicit any suspicion?"

"Not if I have a real estate agent sign on my car door," she shot back. Then her shoulders sagged. "That guy yesterday, Eckert, he pulled a gun on us. If he'd seen you . . ."

"He might not have even known to look for me," Gabe protested. "He was following Xavier."

"True. But even hit men can multitask," she said tartly.

She was right about that. "What if I sit in the back seat of the car with your spare handgun? If we have any trouble, you're going to need backup."

"No."

He decided to approach from a different direction. "Look. You said yourself that Burke's running out of people to be bodyguards. Why would I take up his valuable resources?"

She looked him straight in the eye. "No."

Fine. The gloves are coming off. "You realize that I could just follow you, don't you? Unless you plan to tie me up. Which could be fun, too." He waggled his brows, and she snorted.

Then sighed. "Would you really follow me? Knowing how dangerous this is?"

"I would. You are the badass PI and I'm just a chef, but . . ." He swallowed hard. "These people killed my father, Molly. I don't want them to hurt you, too. I'm not useless."

Her expression softening, she slid her hand from his knee to the middle of his thigh. He figured she intended it to be a comforting gesture, but it just made him more aroused.

"You're far from useless," she murmured, and he knew that he had her. Then her eyes narrowed, and she yanked her hand back. "You little shit. You played me."

"Did it work?"

"Maybe," she said grudgingly. "Let me figure this out with Burke."

"I'll take that. For now."

She shook her head. "You're impossible."

"And you like me," he said smugly, taking her hand and putting it back on his thigh. "You said so last night."

"That's the problem," she said soberly. "I like you a lot. Maybe even too much. I've gone three years without even looking at a man, and then you come along."

"Not true." Setting his cup on the nightstand, he tipped up her chin, making sure that he had her attention. "I saw how you watched me, every time you came into the Choux."

A blush tinged her cheeks. "I did."

He dropped his voice an octave. "I watched you, too. Every time you came in."

"And?" she asked, her voice gone breathless.

Now I'm hard, and I want you. "Now I see that my assistant manager is very capable and running the place perfectly in my absence. When all this mess is over, I can ease back a little. Have some 'me' time. I'd like to spend that time with you. If you're willing."

"Very," she whispered. Blindly she set her cup next to his, her eyes already closed as she leaned in to kiss him. "I'd say we should take some of that time now, but I'm on duty. Val should be waking up soon and going to the courthouse. Patty will probably want to have breakfast with us."

He sighed dramatically. "Which means I should get dressed."

Her blue-green eyes danced. "Unless you want her to see you buck naked."

"Um, no." Swinging his legs off the bed, he started for the bathroom, but paused at the door. "What is this?" He studied the contraption—a harness of some kind that was fixed over the bathroom door. He looked over his shoulder with a grin. "A sex toy?"

She laughed. "No. It's my exercise pulley. I keep it in my bag for when I'm on duty and can't go to the gym. I can get a limited workout with it."

"Did you do that already?"

"Yes," she said warily. "Why?"

"First, so that I could have watched you, but mostly because I might have worked out, too. I haven't been exercising regularly since Patty and I opened the Choux. I walk to work, but it's not enough."

"I'll show you tomorrow."

"It's a date," he said before going into the bathroom and closing the door. Standing in front of the mirror, he touched the places where she'd sucked hard enough to mark him the night before. He'd never had a woman do that before and he'd liked it. A lot.

Molly Sutton didn't do anything halfway. He grinned at his reflection. *May the good Lord bless her.*

I definitely look . . . debauched. He'd always wanted to look debauched. *Patty will know.*

I don't care. I'm happy.

He'd reached for the shower fixture when he heard a French woman's voice singing "Le Festin" from *Ratatouille*—his ringtone. He was tempted to ignore it but knew he couldn't. It might be Burke.

Shit. It might be Burke.

His happiness drained away, replaced by the dread that hadn't been too far away. Burke wouldn't be calling them this early if it weren't important. Something was wrong. His brain immediately thought of Xavier and his mother and the others.

He rushed from the bathroom and headed for his pants because he'd left his phone in his pants pocket. His phone had stopped ringing, but he'd check the call log.

Molly was no longer smiling. Now she was grim. And mostly dressed again, wearing a bra, dark trousers, and . . . her belt holster. Complete with gun.

Yes, something was very, very wrong.

"It's Burke," she said, sliding her arms into a white blouse and buttoning it up. "He texted me while he was dialing you."

"Is it bad?" he asked, fishing his now-silent phone from his pocket. He had a new voice mail from Burke.

When he straightened, she met his eyes from across the room. And nodded. "Yeah." She patted the bed beside her and for a moment, Gabe had the childish urge to run back into the bathroom to hide.

He didn't, of course. Instead, he drew a breath and pulled on his pants. He didn't want to receive bad news while he was naked. "Are Xavier and the others all right?"

"Yeah. They're okay." Sitting on the bed, she waited until he sat beside her, then took his hand. "This is not your fault, Gabe."

Dread had him swallowing hard. "Tell me."

"The private pathologist you hired. Phyllis McLain. She's dead."

Gabe stared at Molly's laptop screen, a news story on one of the internet sites. *Pathologist murdered, lab destroyed.* And below was a photo. It was her. Dr. McLain. She was dead.

He was . . . numb.

"Oh my God," he whispered, then winced when Molly squeezed his hand harder.

"Not. Your. Fault," she whispered fiercely.

But it was. It was totally his fault. He shook his head, the words refusing to come. Not that he knew what to say. He cleared his throat. Forced his mind to *think*, for fuck's sake. This had happened because McLain had done his father's autopsy. This had happened because whoever killed his father was covering their tracks. He swallowed past the thickness that nearly choked him. "How did they know about her?" he rasped.

"We don't know yet." Molly's voice was steady, her grip hard enough to anchor him. "We will find out. I promise."

He brought his free hand to his eyes, then down to cover his mouth. Then his heart stuttered. *Oh shit.* "Dusty." He grabbed his phone and redialed Burke. "Dusty Woodruff," he said as soon as Burke answered.

"He's my friend. The owner of the funeral home. If they got to Dr. McLain . . ."

"I'll check," Burke said. "Stay where you are, both of you."

Gabe stared at his phone. Burke had ended the call. He hadn't told Gabe not to worry. He hadn't said Gabe was imagining things.

He'd simply ended the call. So that he could check.

"Gabe," Molly murmured.

"Don't tell me that it's not my fault." His heart was beating so hard, it was almost all he could hear. "I involved them. Dr. McLain *died*."

"Could she have filed the autopsy report with the police as evidence that your father didn't kill himself?" she asked gently.

"No. I don't think so, anyway. I asked her to give me some time. A few days. She said she would. I came straight to you. I didn't—" His voice broke. "I didn't warn her. I didn't warn Dusty. Oh my God. I didn't warn them."

She said nothing. Uttered no platitudes. Just sat with him, holding his hand.

Time passed. It felt like hours, but his phone told him it was only minutes until Burke called again. "I'm sorry, Gabe," he said heavily.

No. No. No, no, no. Gabe wanted to throw his phone against the wall. He wanted to scream. He wanted to find whoever killed his father and—

He blinked, unsurprised when hot tears streamed down his cheeks. Tears of horror. Tears of shame. But mostly tears of rage. "I've never truly hated someone before this whole thing started," he said, not recognizing his own voice. "But I do now."

"I know," Burke said. "Trust me, I know."

So does Molly, Gabe thought and waited for her to say so. But she didn't.

"How did Mr. Woodruff die?" she asked quietly.

Gabe turned to look at her, to find her staring at him, her blue-green eyes full of pain. For him. It should have helped. Maybe it would later. Right now . . .

Two people are dead because of me.

"He was found in his car yesterday evening. He'd run into a tree."

Molly didn't look away, holding Gabe's gaze. "Has anyone checked to see if Rocky's body is still in Dr. McLain's lab?"

Burke made an anguished, strangled sound. "No. I didn't . . . Dammit, Molly. I didn't even think of that. We need to find that out."

Rage erupted in Gabe's chest and he sucked in a breath from the impact. That they might have taken his father's body on top of everything else?

"I'm . . ." Burke sighed. "I'm going to have to level with André. Tell him what we know."

Something inside him broke. "So that's it?" Gabe shouted. "You're quitting?"

"Absolutely *not*," Burke snapped. "We're going to keep on this until we get justice for your father and for these latest victims. I give you my word, Gabe. But we have to share information with at least André. Before, when the police had declared Rocky's death a suicide, we could investigate on our own, to prove them wrong. But this is bigger now. We have information that could aid investigators in solving two more homicides."

Gabe closed his eyes, grateful that Molly hadn't let go of his hand. "I know. But I don't trust them."

Burke sighed again. "Neither do I. Except for André and a few others that I know personally. I don't know how high this goes in the NOPD, but somebody knows something."

"What are the chances that we can pay Mr. Eckert a visit in jail?" Molly asked.

Gabe opened his eyes to study her. She was calm, cool, collected, and . . . coldly furious. Something eased in his chest. He wasn't alone in his rage. The only difference was that she wasn't too angry to think. It was a small comfort.

"Nil," Burke answered. "Eckert's a known hit man. Cops just weren't able to get anything to stick in the past. They're going to keep him to themselves."

"And let him go?" Molly asked sarcastically. "Like they let the Paul Lott impersonator go?"

"If they do, we'll be waiting to scoop him up. I promise you that."

Molly's throat worked as she swallowed. "Okay. I want to take Xavier to his old neighborhood today. I need to know where his neighbor lived. Is that too dangerous now?"

Burke was quiet for a long moment. "Probably," he finally answered. "His mother tried to remember Xavier's old address, but she could only recall the street name. It was on Center Street near the intersection with West Judge Perez in Chalmette. I'm going to show him photos of the current neighborhood on Google Earth. If he can't remember from the pictures, you can take him. But you won't go alone. I'll find someone to go with you."

Molly met Gabe's gaze and for a moment he thought she would tell him that he couldn't go. But she didn't, surprising him yet again. "Gabe will go with me. I'm not leaving him alone."

"You could bring Gabe to my cabin," Burke suggested.

"I might afterward. For now, he stays with me."

Burke was quiet again, then sighed. "Everyone wears Kevlar. No exceptions. I'll have Val bring it to you after she goes to court for the arraignment. I want eyes in that courtroom."

"Will they close the arraignment to the public?" she asked.

"Possibly. But given these charges are technically only road-rage and weapons related, probably not. If they do, I'll contact André. I also want to know who's financing Eckert's attorney. And, if he makes bail, who paid it."

"All right," she said, her tone quiet but steely. "But I'd prefer not to wait too long for the Kevlar. I've got a vest with me. Can you send Phin over with vests for Gabe and Patty? We don't have any idea of how long Val will be in court. I don't want to waste time that I could use searching for the Katrina victim."

"I'll tell him. He can bring you what you need."

She nodded once. "Thank you. Where are you?"

"At the camp. I'm with Xavier now. He couldn't sleep. We'll try to get an address for the Katrina victim. Hold tight until we call back."

"Burke, wait." It was Xavier. "Don't hang up yet. Gabe, it's me. I was upset yesterday that I'd dragged my friends and family into danger. What did you tell me?"

Gabe exhaled. *Damn the kid.* "That it wasn't your doing. That it wasn't your fault."

"Yeah. Same goes. This isn't on you. This is on the assholes who killed them."

"I know," Gabe said hoarsely. "But knowing it and *knowing it* are two different things."

"I get it, Gabe," Xavier said, his voice heavy with regret. "I really do. Molly? Don't let him feel guilty."

Molly's smile was small but genuine. "I won't, Xavier. Thank you."

Gabe ended the call and sat, clutching his phone while staring into Molly's calm eyes. "I don't know what to feel right now."

She brushed his hair from his forehead, then cupped his cheek. "I know, baby. I can't make it better right now. But we will not rest until the assholes who killed them are either dead or rotting in jail."

He believed her. He had to believe her. She was all that was holding him together right now.

"I need to do something for Dusty. We were friends since high school. He has a wife and two little kids. I need to call her."

"Not just yet. As soon as it's safe, you can do whatever you think is right. And I'll go with you, if you want, to pay your respects to his family in person. You aren't alone, Gabe."

He bowed his head, resting his forehead on her shoulder. "Thank you."

She kissed his temple. "Stay here. I'm going to check on Patty and tell Val what's happened."

He shook his head, following her when she rose. "No. We stay together."

He thought she'd say he was silly because she was just going to the adjoining room, but she simply gripped his hand harder. "Together."

16

G ABE'S STILL GOING to feel guilty, isn't he?" Xavier asked when Burke ended the call with Molly and Gabe and tossed his phone to the kitchen table. It was just the two of them for now. Everyone else had had breakfast and were off doing other things. Carlos and Manny were playing video games, Willa Mae was knitting, and his mom had found a romance novel in the bag of stuff that Burke's office manager, Joy, had bought for them the night before.

Xavier himself had been trying to read his textbooks but had kept nodding off. He hadn't slept much the night before and needed caffeine. He'd entered the kitchen in time to hear Burke on the phone with Gabe, confirming that the mortician was dead along with the pathologist who'd done Rocky's real autopsy.

Poor Gabe. His dad was dead and now two more people were as well, one of them his personal friend. Because Gabe had asked them both for help. It made Xavier's gut clench at the thought of anything happening to Carlos. Or his mom. Or Manny or Willa Mae.

"Probably," Burke said with a regretful shake of his head. "Involving others in your personal drama, even when it's not of your own making, puts a huge weight on the shoulders."

"I know," Xavier said, miserable to even consider it.

"I know you do. That's why I said it. It's not of your own making. Not your fault. Not Gabe's fault. That's why therapists exist. For the aftereffects."

Xavier studied the older man. Burke had to be forty, maybe older. He was still in great shape for a guy his age, but his eyes had little wrinkles at the corners and held a lot of sadness when he thought no one was watching.

He wanted to ask about Burke's story, but he understood keeping one's personal history private. He loved Carlos like a brother, and he'd been an amazing support the past few days, but he didn't think that Carlos could have held on to his secret all these years.

"For a long time," Xavier said quietly, "I thought that I'd made up what I saw."

"The woman getting murdered."

Xavier nodded. "I'd have these awful nightmares. Wake up screaming."

"I know those nightmares. I have them myself from time to time."

He really wanted to ask more, but Burke didn't look in the mood to share any more. "When Rocky came into my life—back into my life—I wasn't sure what was worse. I mean, it was awful thinking that I was so screwed in the head that my imagination made up the woman getting killed. But then . . ."

"You found out that it wasn't your imagination."

"My mom and dad took me to therapists when I was little. They're the ones who said it was all in my head. A product of my trauma."

"Well, you *had* just seen your mother die," Burke said pragmatically.

Still, Xavier shivered. "I can still see her hands on the hole she'd chopped in the roof. She'd shown me the hatchet in the attic, told me what to do in a flood. Her mother had told her about a hurricane in the sixties, how people got trapped in their attics trying to outrun the flood, so they started keeping hatchets in case they needed to escape through the roof."

"Hurricane Betsy," Burke murmured. "Back in '65. My uncle told me about it, too. He also kept a hatchet in the attic. Your mother was wise to have done so."

Xavier pressed his lips together, trying not to give in to the fear he felt every time he remembered. "I know, but the water came too fast. We heard a loud noise—that was the levee breaking—and within a few minutes the house was filling up. She barely had time to cut through the roof. She shoved me out through the hole, but she . . ." He swallowed hard. "She was trying to get out, trying to lift herself out, but the roof kept breaking away. Her hands would disappear, then reappear and grab the roof. Then disappear again."

Burke sighed. "That is enough to give anyone nightmares. And then to see a woman murdered on top of that? Hell, Xavier."

"I know. Trust me, I know. But the therapists never listened to me. I was just a traumatized little kid, making stuff up. It's hard not to be bitter."

"I get that. But do me a favor? When this is over, I'll give you the name of a therapist who can help you. Please call her. She's very good."

"She helped you?"

"Immensely."

Xavier waited for him to say more, but he didn't, which was his right. "What's next?"

"Next we look at photos of your neighborhood as it exists today. I looked at Google Earth last night and at the neighborhood's recovery and renewal website. Gotta say, I'm not hopeful. The neighborhood looks different than it did before Katrina, and you were so small."

Xavier's gut churned some more. "If I have to go back there, if it'll help y'all identify the original victim, then I will."

Burke gave him a smile. "I know. You're a good person, Xavier, and a helluva lot stronger than you think you are." He started to bring the screenshots up on his laptop, but was interrupted by the buzzing of his cell phone. "It's Joy. Let me take this."

He picked up the phone, not putting it on speaker. "Good morning, sunshine," he said with a smile. A smile that abruptly disappeared. "Play it," he said tersely.

What now? Whatever it was, it wasn't good.

A minute passed during which Burke's jaw got tighter, his teeth clenching hard. "Fucking hell." He glanced at Xavier, seemed to be considering, then exhaled. "Play it again. I have Xavier here. I want him to hear this, too."

From the corner of his eye, Xavier saw Carlos appear in the kitchen doorway, followed by Cicely. Followed by Manny and Willa Mae, who pushed to the front, coming into the kitchen to take a seat at the table.

"Okay," Burke said. "I guess we're all hearing this." He put his phone on speaker. "Play it again, Joy."

"Hello." It was a woman's voice, soft and quavering. She sounded scared. "My name is Alicia Rollins and I need to speak to Burke Broussard as soon as possible. It's urgent. It's . . . It's a matter of life and death. Someone tried to kill me last night and I think it has something to do with a conversation I had with Rocky Hebert. He said I should call Mr. Broussard. I'm in New Orleans and can be in your office as soon as you can see me."

She left her number, then added, "Please help me. I'm really scared."

Then the call ended.

Xavier realized that he'd stopped breathing and sucked in some air. "Can she play it again? I don't think I recognize the voice, but I want to be sure."

Joy complied and Xavier shook his head when the message ended a second time. "I'm pretty sure that I don't know her."

Burke looked over at Willa Mae. "Your take?"

Willa Mae made a face. "I don't know. She *sounds* scared, but . . ."

Cicely sat next to Willa Mae. "Can you call her at that number? Find out what she wants?"

Burke nodded. "I will, but I want a game plan first."

"You and Willa Mae don't believe her," Carlos said. "Why? She does sound scared."

Burke hesitated. "I don't *not* believe her. But . . ." He sighed. "Two more people are dead. The private pathologist who did Rocky's autopsy and the mortician friend of Gabe's who transported the body." He waited until everyone had gasped and uttered words of shock. "Gabe is devastated, as you can imagine."

"More loose ends taken care of," Willa Mae said quietly.

"So it would seem," Burke agreed. "It's very possible that this woman was targeted. And I want to hear what was said in her conversation with Rocky."

"But you're suspicious," Xavier murmured. It wasn't a major deduction on his part. It was written all over the man's face, and Willa Mae was nodding.

"The timing seems convenient," Burke said.

"You think she's luring you out?" Carlos asked.

"To follow you back to us," Manny finished grimly. "To Xavier."

Burke shrugged. "I have to think of your safety. One thing's certain—no way are you leaving this cabin, Xavier. If she's legit, I'll find her a safe house. If she's not, I don't want you anywhere near her."

"Thank you," Cicely whispered. "I was scared to let him go with you. I lay awake last night, wracking my brain for the address of Xavier's mother's house, but all I could remember was the street, not the house number."

"I know," Burke said kindly. "Now you don't have to be scared, at least."

"Not any more scared," Willa Mae observed wryly.

"Sorry," Cicely muttered to her friend. "I kept her awake, tossing and turning last night."

Willa Mae patted his mother's hand. "It's all right. I just wish I could help you."

"When will you leave, Burke?" Xavier asked.

"As soon as I have an escape plan and more coverage for this place. If you'll excuse me, I have to make some calls." He pushed away from the table and headed toward the back door.

"Be careful, Burke," Cicely called.

He threw a grin over his shoulder, making him look years younger. Still old, Xavier allowed, but younger than before. "Yes, ma'am. Thank you for breakfast, by the way. It was a real treat."

The door closed behind him and, for a moment, there was silence.

Then Carlos and Manny joined them at the table. "This sucks donkey balls," Carlos muttered, then winced. "Sorry, Mrs. M, Miss Willa Mae."

"It's all right," Cicely said resignedly. "I've heard much worse."

"And I've heard much worse than that," Willa Mae added, then smacked the table, making them all jump. "Enough of this worrying. Everyone come into the living room with me. Xavier, Carlos, and Manny, I want you to move the furniture back. I want as large a space as possible."

"Why?" Manny asked warily.

Xavier nearly snickered at the look of fear on his face.

"Because we are going to do tai chi. It's calming, meditative, and will work out some of this muscle stiffness that's making me cranky."

Carlos grinned. "I like it."

"Suck-up," Manny muttered.

Willa Mae arched one eyebrow. "What happened to being nice to old ladies? I mean, I could play country music and make you line dance, if you really want me to."

Manny cringed. "Tai chi is fine."

"I thought so. Come along. Move."

They moved. And, after their first tai chi lesson, Xavier did feel a little better.

He was still scared as hell, but he was able to breathe. His mother looked calmer, too. He kissed his mother's best friend on the cheek. "Thank you, ma'am."

Willa Mae patted his face. "Nothing to thank. I know you're scared. I know your mama's scared. I'm scared, too. But we need to stay calm and centered so that we can think if something goes wrong."

"More wrong, you mean." Because something was going to go more wrong. He knew it.

"Fine. More wrong. Now." She clapped her hands once. "Fix the furniture. This is Burke's house and we're going to keep it nice. When we're done with that, I'm making a list of chores. We will be good guests."

Cicely bit back a smile. "You're right, Willa Mae."

Willa Mae nodded smugly. "I usually am."

Central Business District, New Orleans, Louisiana
WEDNESDAY, JULY 27, 8:45 A.M.

"Gabe." Patty's voice was tense. "Stop pacing, or I'll tie your feet together."

"Sorry." Gabe dropped into one of the hotel room chairs at the small dinette table, surprised it had taken Patty as long as it had to yell at him. He'd been pacing for at least twenty minutes.

He felt like a trapped animal. Patty had watched him pace while Molly had been glued to her computer screen.

Val, the other PI, had gone to the courthouse. Arraignments were supposed to start soon.

They were stuck here until Burke's night security guard brought them Kevlar.

How is this my life?

"I feel so damn helpless," he confessed. "I can't even cook anything."

Patty reached across the small table to squeeze his forearm. "I know. I feel helpless, too. At least Mom and Dad are okay. I checked in with them."

Gabe frowned. He hadn't even thought of his aunt and uncle. Just one more thing to feel guilty over. "Where are they?"

"I suggested that they take a trip. They decided to visit my grandma in Florida."

At least they were out of harm's way. Unlike Dr. McLain and Dusty Woodruff.

He couldn't think about them. Not right now. He turned to Molly, who was once again sitting cross-legged on the bed. "What are you doing?"

"Looking at property records," she said without looking up.

"For?" he pressed.

"The street where Xavier lived with his biological mother before Katrina. That area was underwater for days. None of the houses were spared. Everything there was built post-Katrina. Even if Xavier did go back to see the neighborhood, it won't look the same. Burke and I agreed that it doesn't make sense to put Xavier in danger for no good reason, so he's staying put today."

Gabe breathed a sigh of relief. He hadn't realized how tense he was over Xavier leaving Burke's safe house.

"So why are you still looking at property records?" Patty asked.

"I'm looking to see which owners are the same as pre-Katrina. Old neighbors might remember the woman Xavier described."

"That's a good idea," Patty said. "A lot of people left the city and never came back, but there were some who rebuilt in the same place."

Gabe studied Molly with renewed appreciation. "That's a smart approach."

She looked up then and smiled at him. "Thank you. We don't know the exact house where Xavier's mother lived because she rented the place, but I have found three property owners so far who're still there. We've got Xavier's description of the woman—tall, with long blond hair down to her butt—so I figure we can ask them if they remember a woman who'd walk her dog. His description of the dog was even better than his description of the woman."

"What kind of dog?" Gabe asked.

"He searched a dog breed page until he found the animal. It was an Afghan hound."

He gave a low whistle. "Those are pretty rare, aren't they?"

She nodded. "They are. Neighbors might remember it."

Patty frowned. "What does one of those even look like?"

Gabe did a quick search on his phone and showed the photo to his cousin. "Like this." The dog was tall with a long, glamorous coat and long silky ears. "I saw a commercial once where the dog was in the passenger seat of a convertible and looked like a blond woman with her hair blowing in the wind until it turned around."

"I've seen them," Patty said, "but only on TV. Never in person."

"Me either," Molly said. "I can't imagine that it was a dog people saw too often. Especially with all that coat. They'd roast in the summer here."

"So we're going door to door?" Gabe asked.

Patty gave a worried sigh, but said nothing. They'd already argued about it, and Gabe wasn't budging. He was not going to hide while Molly took all the risks.

"I guess we are," Molly said resignedly, because she still wasn't keen on exposing him to danger. "We can leave as soon as Phin gets here with the vests. Patty, I'll drop you off at Burke's office to wait until Val is done in court."

"Val is done in court," Val said from the adjoining doorway. She reminded Gabe of a Viking warrior, minus the armor and sword. At the moment, she was leaning against the doorframe, looking frustrated and grim. She held what appeared to be their Kevlar vests, one in each hand.

Molly set her laptop aside and slowly came to her feet. "What happened?"

"I couldn't get anywhere near the courthouse," Val said. She pushed away from the doorframe and sat on the bed that Gabe and Molly had shared. "There was a stabbing in Holding sometime during the night."

"Well, shit," Molly breathed. "Is Eckert dead?"

"As a doornail," Val said. "The courthouse is a media circus. I got close enough to hear the news from one of the reporters and gave up getting any closer and just headed back here. I passed Phin in the parking garage of the hotel. He gave me four vests and headed back to the office because Joy's there by herself. He doesn't want her to be alone."

Patty was so pale that Gabe worried she'd pass out. "What is happening?" she whispered, horrified. "Gabe, what did your father stumble into?"

"Someone is snipping off loose ends," Molly said flatly. "Which means we have to work faster. Val, what do you want me to do with Patty? Leave her here with you or take her to Burke's?"

"Leave her here with me," Val said wearily. "I need to sleep, but she'll be safer with me than she will be with you."

"What does that mean?" Patty insisted, the words coming out a terrified screech.

Molly crossed the room and laid her hand on Patty's shoulder. "It means that whoever killed your uncle is trying to take out anyone who either witnessed him murdering a woman or who knows anything about it."

"Which is us," Gabe said, surprised that his voice was steady. "This is why I tried to keep it from you."

Patty shuddered. "I'm kind of wishing I'd listened to you."

Molly's smile was rueful. "Will you stay with Val, Patty? I'll take you wherever you want to go, but I think you'll be safest here for now."

Patty nodded. "I'll stay. Gabe? Stay with me?"

Gabe shook his head. "I'll text you every hour if you want me to, but I'm going."

"Every hour," Patty said fiercely. "Promise me."

He hugged her hard. "I promise."

"Be careful," Val said, then went back to her room, pausing in the doorway to give Patty a meaningful leave-them-alone look. "I put your vest on your bed, Patty. Come on. I'll show you how to put it on."

Reluctantly his cousin followed the tall blonde to the adjoining room, shutting the door behind them. Leaving them all alone.

Alone, but unfortunately, with somewhere to go. Somewhere he had to wear bulletproof gear. He picked up his vest from the bed. "How does this fasten?"

"Under your shirt."

He unbuttoned his shirt, noting the way Molly's eyes followed his hands down. When he tugged his shirttail free, he heard her sigh.

A very nice sound indeed. Even if things were crazy all around them, she liked his body and he'd cling to that for a while. He tugged off his shirt and slipped his arms into the vest.

Molly stepped into his space, fastening the Velcro tabs at his sides before he had a chance to do it himself. "Like this."

"I probably could have figured it out," he said mildly.

She looked up at him, worry in her eyes. "I know. But now I know it's on right. I've got a tactical helmet in the trunk of the rental car. If things go south, you'll wear it, too."

He vaguely remembered her transferring the equipment from her truck to the rental the night before. She'd scanned each item for tracking devices and bugs before storing it in the trunk. She was smart and she was careful.

The knowledge made him feel far safer than the Kevlar vest ever could.

She took her shirt off and pulled her vest on over the serviceable bra that he hoped he'd see again later. But now was not the time. Soberly, he followed her example, fastening her Velcro tabs. It was affirming. She'd keep him safe, and he'd do the same for her.

She buttoned up her shirt and shrugged into her gun-concealing jacket. "Ready?" she asked.

"Yep. Let's go."

Chalmette, New Orleans, Louisiana
WEDNESDAY, JULY 27, 9:50 A.M.

"What's wrong?" Gabe demanded as Molly checked her phone for the hundredth time since they'd left the hotel.

She took another long look at the houses that lined Xavier Morrow's old street, where he'd lived before Katrina.

The Lower Ninth Ward had been the focus of media coverage of the boat rescues, and that was what Molly remembered from that time. But Burke had schooled her on the neighborhoods of New Orleans when she'd first agreed to work for him. There had been boat rescues in several of the other neighborhoods—this one and others along the river to the south of the city.

Chalmette—and the entirety of St. Bernard Parish—had been devastated by the hurricane, no homes spared by the floodwaters. Much of the neighborhood had not been rebuilt, vacant lots where homes had been.

The post-Katrina houses were mostly single-story, with a few two-story homes here and there. There were no other cars on the street, unless they were parked. Anyone who was going to work was gone by

now. A few children played in one of the backyards, periodically running around to the front to retrieve a ball, which normally would have
made her smile. She was too anxious at the moment, too aware of the
danger hanging over Gabe's head.

She was also aware of the older woman weeding her garden—while
she watched them.

Molly had caught her sneaking peeks at them from beneath her
wide-brimmed hat. She would be the first person they'd talk to. She
was one of three original residents on this portion of the street.

"Just checking the time," Molly said, not sure why she hadn't told
Gabe what Burke had shared that morning. Maybe she didn't want him
to get his hopes up.

But more than likely it was the really bad feeling she had about it.
Gabe would want to be there, to talk to the woman who'd contacted
Burke first thing, who was likely still in Burke's office, asking for his
help.

Molly didn't want Gabe anywhere near the office. She didn't want
him anywhere near Xavier's old neighborhood, either, but she was
learning to choose her battles with her chef.

My chef.

He wasn't really hers. But he could be.

Her chef was currently staring at her, his arms crossed over his
broad chest, hazel eyes narrowed. "I thought you weren't going to lie
to me."

"I wasn't. I really was checking the time. This time. It's rude to call
on people before ten o'clock."

He shook his head. "Molly, just tell me."

She sighed. "All right. There was a call on the office voice mail this
morning when Joy arrived, a message from a woman who said she
needed to speak with Burke urgently and that it had to do with your
father."

Gabe gasped quietly. "I want to see her."

"I figured you would," she admitted. "But I have a bad feeling about this. It's too convenient. We find out that your father was investigating a murder, and, alakazam, this lady shows up."

"Xavier did," Gabe pointed out.

"True. That's why Burke is meeting with her. He said he'd call me when he's done."

Gabe frowned. "Why would someone fake this? How would they know—" He exhaled. "Oh. You think it's some kind of a trap laid by the killer or killers."

She had to smile. "You're sounding more and more like one of us." She sobered. "Yeah, that's exactly what I think. It's what Burke thinks, too. He didn't want us anywhere near the office this morning. And if he had, I would have said no. I won't put you in danger like that."

"You think they're trying to get to me?"

"Well, yeah," she said, trying to keep the *duh* from her tone and failing spectacularly. Gabe didn't seem to mind, though. He kept studying her face with the same fatalistically curious expression. "Either to get to you directly or to tail Burke afterward."

Gabe's mouth tightened. "To find Xavier."

She lifted a shoulder. "He's the eyewitness."

"He was just a child," Gabe said, frustrated. "It's unlikely anyone would take him seriously, even if he did come forward. Why is this happening?"

"That is a very good question," Molly said. It was one that she'd considered often over the past forty-eight hours. "My best guess is that Xavier saw the man's scar and that makes him identifiable today."

"True. I guess we can't google 'New Orleans men with scars.'"

Her lips curved faintly. "I did. Didn't get anywhere. Especially since I think this guy is high-profile. For the kind of obstruction you experienced, a poorly done autopsy and the attempt to frame your dad with cocaine planted in his pantry, there has to be some kind of high-profile exposure."

"You're saying that whoever killed the woman during Katrina is afraid of scandal."

"That's my guess, anyway. Trouble is, it might not even be the killer. It could be whoever covered it up back then. Your father saw the body, but when he came back, it was gone. The residents weren't allowed back for days afterward, but somebody came to retrieve that body."

"And Dad was actively discouraged from investigating." He bit his lip, worry in his eyes. "Call Burke. Please?"

"Okay." Cautiously, she looked up and down the street again, on alert for anyone or anything that looked remotely out of place. She dialed Joy's extension and put it on speaker. "Hi, Joy, it's Molly. Is Burke available?"

"He is," Joy said, a thread of tension in her voice that Molly did not like at all. "I'll patch you through."

"Joy, how's the coffee this morning?" Molly asked before Joy could transfer her call.

"Shitty," Joy said, and Molly breathed a sigh of relief.

"It's a code," Molly said to Gabe, because his brow was furrowed in confusion. "She's okay. If she'd said the coffee was delicious, I'd have known something was wrong."

"It's just been a morning," Joy said. "None of us trust that woman who met with Burke today and Antoine's doing a sweep of the office to make sure she didn't bug us. Phin's been sweeping for any kind of bombs. But that's just Phin."

"Yeah, bombs would be his go-to," Molly agreed. "You'll allow him to escort you home tonight?"

"I will," Joy grumbled. "I've been schooled by everyone here who *worries* about me. Like I'm not a woman grown and an ex-cop. Let me patch you through."

Gabe's brows raised. "Ex-cop?"

"She took a bullet to the spine when she responded to a robbery," Molly explained. "Joy was and continues to be a badass."

"Molly." Burke had come on the line. "I was getting ready to call. We've been sweeping for bugs."

"That's what Joy said. I told Gabe about the call on the voice mail this morning. If you've learned anything, it'd be nice to know before I bother the woman who's glaring daggers at me while she weeds her garden."

"What are you talking about? What woman?"

"She's the first name on my list of pre-Katrina homeowners on Xavier's old street. She does not appear happy to see us."

"Oh, okay." Burke exhaled wearily. "The woman who called claimed to be Alicia Rollins. She was really young. Early twenties, I'd guess. She said her sister was JoAnn Rollins, who'd disappeared during Katrina. Alicia searched for her for years but found nothing."

Molly did the math. "If Alicia's in her early twenties, she'd have been between five and seven years old during Katrina. Not sure how *she* could have searched for her sister."

"I know," Burke said. "It was one of many things wrong with her story. I asked her why she'd come to me and why now. She said that someone tried to kill her yesterday."

"Oh." Molly hadn't expected that. "How and where?"

"She said they fired shots through the window of her bedroom last night."

Molly opened the note-taking app on her phone. "Her address?"

"I'll text it to you. It's in Rock Hill, a town in—"

"South Carolina," Molly said. "Only about thirty minutes from where I lived when I was working in Charlotte."

"I know," was all Burke said.

"More coincidence?" Molly asked.

"Hard to believe so. She said she left immediately and drove straight to New Orleans."

"She didn't call the police?" Gabe asked.

"Nope. Said that she didn't know who she could trust, and that Rocky had told her to come to me."

Gabe's eyes closed, grief flitting across his face. But when his eyes opened, they were cold with anger. "She has nerve, using my father's name."

"I agree," Burke said. "But I let her talk. I hoped she'd drop some hint about who'd sent her, but she didn't. Her story was that Rocky came to see her seven weeks ago and that he'd asked her about JoAnn, her sister. She told him that she hadn't spoken to her sister since before Katrina. Rocky thanked her and said that if anything happened or anyone threatened her, she should call him. And if he wasn't available, to call me. She called Rocky first, but he didn't answer his phone. She googled and found he'd passed away. So she called me."

"But not until this morning. I would have thought she'd have called before driving ten hours." Molly considered the woman's story. "Did you ask for ID?"

"She claimed she'd left it at home. That she was so flustered after nearly being killed."

Molly rolled her eyes. "Convenient. You get prints?"

"Of course. Antoine's working on putting them through AFIS."

Gabe looked surprised. "You have access to the federal fingerprint database?"

Both Molly and Burke went silent. Accessing government databases was something Antoine did, and they didn't ask questions. Like with most of the stuff Antoine did. He might hack, but then again, he might have an internal resource running the scans for him. Molly didn't know and didn't want to know.

Gabe sighed. "Ask me no questions, I'll tell you no lies?"

"Rocky didn't raise no fool," Burke drawled lazily, but there was an undercurrent of terseness that Gabe apparently didn't miss.

He nodded. "Shutting up now."

Molly patted his hand. "It's better that way. So, Burke, what's your plan? How will you evade the tail that they've most definitely placed on you?"

"I worked it out with Antoine, Joy, and Phin before I left for the office this morning. As for the woman, I want to check out her story. JoAnn Rollins did exist, and she did die in Katrina. She would have been in her early twenties. There were no incident reports at the South Carolina address the woman gave me, but she said she didn't call 911. She was . . . sketchy on the details."

"Smart," Molly said. "Less to disprove that way. What did you think of her, Burke? Of the woman herself? Clearly, she's involved, but in what capacity?"

Burke hesitated. "I believed her," he finally said. "Not her story, because that was a crock of shit with holes big enough for a locomotive to drive through. But I believed that *she* believed in whatever it was she was doing. Most of the time she played shy and even a little mealy-mouthed, but every so often, I'd catch her glaring at me. Like if looks could kill . . ." He trailed off. "She hated me, and I don't know why."

"Did you follow her out?"

"I watched the feed on the surveillance camera. I wasn't sure that they didn't have a gunman waiting on the street. Which is not a feeling that I like to have."

Molly glanced around again, feeling too exposed even though she was certain that she hadn't been followed and she'd checked her rental car for any tracking devices before they'd left the hotel. "I get that."

"She got into a car that I traced to an Uber driver. I dropped a tracker into her handbag when she wasn't looking, but it stopped moving shortly after she left. Phin found it in a garbage can a block away."

"The tracker?" Molly asked.

"The whole handbag," Burke said dryly. "No ID inside."

"So, what's her goal?" Gabe asked. "Distraction?"

"Yes," Burke said. "I think we're supposed to chase our tails, checking this new ID just in case it proves truthful. And I think I'm supposed to lead them to our guests. Which isn't going to happen."

Molly watched the woman in the wide-brimmed hat gather her garden tools and go back into her house. "Okay. We're going to chat with the lady with the sharp garden implements. I'll call you back afterward."

"Thank you. Be careful."

"We will." Molly disconnected and met Gabe's eyes. "Ready to speak with Mrs. Nancy Royce?"

He nodded once. "Yep."

"She's a retired schoolteacher, recently widowed."

Gabe's brows crunched. "How did her husband die?"

"Liver disease." She squeezed his hand. "His death was not related to this case."

His relief was visible. "Good. I don't think I can handle any more people dying because of what my dad uncovered."

"Stick close to me. I don't want you dying, either."

"Yes, ma'am."

They got out of the rental car, Molly keeping an eye on their surroundings as they approached Nancy Royce's front door. She'd lifted her fist to knock when the door opened, sending a wave of deliciously cool air wafting across her face, courtesy of the woman's air conditioner.

"Good morning, ma'am," Molly said. "I'm sorry to bother you."

"Yet here you stand," Nancy said tartly.

"Yes, ma'am. My name is Molly Sutton. I'm a private investigator. This is my partner, Gabe."

Nancy's eyes narrowed as she looked up at them. She was about five foot two, her tanned skin leathery with deep wrinkles. She was only sixty-four, but her worry lines spoke of hardship.

"Gabe who?" the woman asked.

"Gabe Hebert, ma'am," Gabe answered, and Molly wanted to sigh, irritated with herself.

Should have told him that I didn't want him to give his name. But she'd forgotten, the murder of Cornell Eckert having shaken her more than she'd wanted to admit aloud.

Nancy scrutinized Gabe for a long moment before cocking her head. "Come in," she ordered, turning to walk deeper into her house.

Molly gave Gabe a nod and they followed her in.

17

W ELL?" JACKASS DEMANDED.

Burner phone in hand, Lamont shut the door to his office and walked to the window for better reception. "Ashley talked to Broussard. She said he bought it, but we'll have to see."

"Has he left the building yet?"

"No. He's still in his office."

The men he'd hired from his list were in place around Broussard's office, checking in every hour. He'd decided to pay these men rather than blackmail them, as he'd done with the guard in the prison. The guard hadn't been a hit man, had never killed for money. His sin had been the accidental murder of the man's own wife when he'd hit her a little too hard. To keep her in line, of course. A man like that could do violence but had needed a little incentive to kill a prisoner like Eckert. A threat to reveal the file containing the evidence of the guard's manslaughter had been incentive enough.

The exposure of the guard's role in the death of his wife would cost him his job and his children. Plus, it would put him in prison with the very people he'd abused when they'd been awaiting trial.

Lamont had been judicious over the years, choosing who to save from prison by virtue of how much future value they'd be. Or how much money they'd paid him. Either worked.

Everything was going to plan. Eckert was dead. It was all over the news, and it appeared that the guard had been sufficiently stealthy. No one had any idea who'd gutted the hit man.

"It's early yet," Jackass said. "Broussard's probably checking out the name we gave him."

"I certainly hope so."

"You hired men really fast," Jackass said with that fake nonchalance that had been his tell for more than thirty-five years.

"I did."

"And you trust them?"

"I paid them well, and I can track them."

"Oh yeah?" Now Jackass was overtly suspicious. "How?"

"I sent them texts with links to the address they were to surveil. When they clicked to open the address in their phone's map app, the tracker downloaded. I know exactly where they are."

Technology really was a beautiful thing. And saving a few hackers from prison had netted him his very own computer experts. Blackmail was even more beautiful.

"Slick. You'll have to show me how to do that."

I don't think so. When this was over, when Xavier Morrow, Gabe Hebert, and Broussard were dead, Jackass would be the next loose end he'd snip.

"I'll be happy to show you," he lied smoothly. "Now, for new business. How did Rocky's boy know to do a private autopsy?"

"I'm not certain, but I think he was suspicious because of Cresswell."

Lamont sighed. The cop was a thorn in everyone's side. Not that he was a goody-goody. Quite the opposite. He'd been taking bribes from pimps and skimming drugs from busts and selling them back to dealers for decades. But he knew where a lot of bodies were buried, so they kept shoring him up.

"What did Cresswell do?"

"He found the coke we left in Rocky's house. Had it tested."

"Which we planned for," Lamont said, trying to hide his impatience. "And?"

"And he told Gabe."

"Which we planned for," he repeated more sharply. *"And?"*

"He's a smarmy bastard. Gabe didn't believe him. He went to the ME and pushed harder."

"Still not enough to prompt him to hire his own pathologist."

"I know. I think someone tipped him off. I'm checking."

"Shit. Who do you suspect?"

"Don't know yet. But you know André Holmes?"

"Yes, I know Captain Holmes." He was also a thorn in their side— an ethical cop. "What about him?"

"His little brother is working in the ME's office now. If anyone would snitch, it'd be DeShawn Holmes. I'm having someone check his work email account today."

"How?"

"I got my tech experts, Monty, just like you do."

Asshole. "Fine. Just tell me when you know."

"Will do," Jackass promised, his tone changing from intense to breezy, which meant someone had come in. "Talk more soon."

The call ended and Lamont turned from the window, sinking into the chair behind his desk with a sigh.

Chalmette, New Orleans, Louisiana
WEDNESDAY, JULY 27, 10:15 A.M.

"Close the door behind you!" Nancy Royce bellowed. "I'm not paying to cool the whole neighborhood."

Molly smiled at that. "She sounds like my mom did," she whispered.

"Mine, too," Gabe whispered back.

Nancy already had set a tray of lemonade on the coffee table, complete with three glasses. She sat in an easy chair, watching them.

"You expected us," Molly said, gesturing to the tray.

"I'm not stupid," Nancy snapped. "Say your piece, then leave. I've got things to do."

Molly suspected the attitude was left over from a career of teaching because there was open curiosity in the woman's face.

"We'd like to ask you about a woman who lived on this street before Katrina," Molly began.

Nancy tilted her head, resembling a very weathered bird. "So, ask. And be quick about it. My soap comes on soon, and I'm not missing it for anything."

Molly studied the woman's eyes. "Why aren't you surprised to see us?"

Nancy leaned back, studying Molly right back. "Because you're not the first people to ask about a woman who lived on this street before Katrina."

Gabe sucked in a breath. "Who else?"

"A man named Rocky Hebert." Another head tilt. "You favor him."

"My father," Gabe said. "When did he talk to you?"

"The first time or the second?"

Molly blinked. Then understood. "You met him during Katrina."

Nancy nodded solemnly. "He saved our lives. I will never forget that man's face or his bravery. Or his kindness." She smiled, softening her features. "I was stunned, because he remembered me, too. My husband and I and all the others were so damn scared that night, and Rocky was patient and gentle with us. Helped me into that little boat like I was made of fine glass. You should be proud of your dad."

Gabe's swallow was audible. "I am. He was the best father a man could have."

Shock flickered over Nancy's face. "Was? He's passed?"

Gabe nodded. "Six weeks ago, ma'am."

"I'm so sorry, son. Really." She drew a breath, then let it out. "He was here about four or five months ago, also asking about the woman who lived on our street. I didn't know her well, but I remembered her name. Forty-some years of teaching has made me very good at remembering names. Hers was Nadia Hall."

Molly's pulse kicked up. *Yes.* "Did she have a dog?"

"Oh yes." Nancy smiled again. "Madame Fluffy. Fancy dog, all ears and hair with a long snout."

That fit. "An Afghan hound."

Nancy seemed amused. "If you say so. Never had much use for those fancy pooches. All my dogs came from the pound." She sobered. "I hope the dog survived the flood."

"What happened to Nadia?" Molly asked.

Nancy's eyes narrowed. "Now, don't be playing innocent with me, young lady. I'll tell you what you want to know, but I don't countenance false innocence."

"She died," Molly said baldly.

"I think so, yes." Nancy's gaze moved to Gabe. "Your daddy was looking for her, too. I got the impression he knew what had happened to her."

Don't tell her about Xavier. Don't tell her.

"Dad thought that she was murdered. He was going door to door that night, searching for people to rescue."

"More like window to window," Nancy corrected. "My husband and

I were on our roof and the water was rising so fast, we both thought that we were goners. Your daddy came along in the nick of time."

"I can't even imagine," Gabe murmured. "Anyway, Dad was searching for survivors and found her body."

Nancy nodded slowly. "That's what he told me, too."

Molly let herself relax. *Nicely done, Gabe. Nicely done. No mention of Xavier.*

"I didn't understand what had happened at the time," Nancy went on. "Not until he showed up on my doorstep this past spring and we reminisced. He said he'd come by a time or two before, but we weren't living here then."

That was news. "Where were you then?" Molly asked.

"In Huntsville. My husband was being treated at the hospital there. Our daughter lives there, and I needed the help. I rented the house out while we were there. Three long years. But the treatments weren't working, and my husband didn't want to continue." Her lips curved sadly. "He wanted one more Mardi Gras. So we came home. That was last year. He got his Mardi Gras, and then he let go."

"I'm so sorry," Gabe said quietly.

"I know you are, son. You know grief. You, too, Miss Sutton. I can see it in your eyes."

It was true. Molly's heart had been cracking, her eyes filling, and she hadn't even been aware.

"I guess grief is a part of life," Gabe said philosophically. "It still sucks."

"It does, indeed." Nancy studied their faces, then sighed. "Why are you searching for Nadia Hall now?" Then she tensed. "How did your daddy die?"

Gabe tensed as well. "The official cause of death was suicide."

Nancy frowned. "But you don't think so. You think it's connected to Nadia."

Gabe glanced at Molly, his eyes pleading for her to warn this woman.

She made a decision. "We think so." If Rocky's killer tracked them to Nancy Royce . . .

"And me?" Nancy asked, her voice quivering. "Am I in danger for talking to Rocky?"

Molly met her gaze head-on. "Can you visit your daughter in Huntsville for a little while?"

Nancy drew a shocked breath. "I expect so. Haven't seen my grandkids in a month. My car's all gassed up. I'll leave today."

Molly put one of her business cards on the coffee table. "Please call me when you get there. We'll sleep better knowing you're okay."

Nancy smiled wryly. "Then it must be pretty bad."

"Yes, ma'am," Molly said. "It is. Can you tell me what you remember about Nadia Hall? What did she do for a living?"

"She worked in an office somewhere near the Quarter, I think. She rode the bus and used to complain about traffic all the time. But she was cagey. Didn't give many details about her life."

"Was she married? Or have a boyfriend?" Molly asked.

"Rocky Hebert asked the same thing, and I'll tell you what I told him. She must have had a boyfriend at some point. She was pregnant." She lifted her brows. "He wasn't surprised. You're not, either. Why?"

Molly winced. "No disrespect, ma'am, but I'd like to keep some of the details to ourselves. The more you know, the more in danger you might be."

Nancy rolled her eyes. "Fine. I suppose I'll read about it in the newspaper sooner or later. The only other thing I remember about Nadia is that she was a hard worker. Left early in the morning and didn't get home till late. Sometimes after midnight."

"Did you ever see the boyfriend?" Molly asked.

"No. If he came over, it was after we went to bed. Or while we were at work."

Dammit. But what they'd learned so far was still far more than they'd known when they'd knocked on Nancy's door. "What did she look like?"

"Young. Early twenties, maybe. Blond. Long hair, down to her butt. Real pretty. She smiled a lot, as I recall. She seemed . . . grateful. Like she hadn't had much and couldn't believe how well she was living."

Molly mentally crossed her fingers. "Would you have any photos?"

"No," Nancy said with a sad slump of her shoulders. "If I'd had any, they were destroyed in the flood. Everything was destroyed. My kids' baby pictures, my wedding pictures. Everything." She shrugged. "If I had some, I'd give them to you, but I know I don't."

"I'm sorry," Molly murmured. "This is bringing back a lot of pain for you."

"If it helps get justice for Rocky, I don't mind. That man saved us."

"Who took care of the dog when she was at work?" Gabe asked. "Did she have a friend or a family member walk the dog?"

Molly felt a little thrill of pride. *Good questions, Gabe.*

Nancy shook her head. "She hired a dog walker. High school girl who lived down the street. The girl's family relocated after Katrina. We didn't hear from them again. We've lost touch with most of our old neighbors," she added sadly. "It was so crazy then, getting out of the flood, living in a tent in the heat. God, it was hot. And the smell . . ." She shuddered. "I still remember that, way too clearly. So many people didn't make it. The ones that did scattered. Some went to live with family, some went to Houston. Others lived in government housing. We went to Huntsville to live with our daughter until we'd rebuilt. After that, we contacted folks whose phone numbers we had. Mourned the ones who died. We didn't know what happened to Nadia. Not till your daddy came by and asked about her. I assumed she'd gotten out with the dog before the waters rose." She paused. "Did Rocky find the little boy?"

Molly was startled but kept her expression bland. As did Gabe. If he ever decided he was done with chefing, he could have a real future as a PI. "What little boy?" she asked.

"There was a little boy. Sweetest kid. Named Angel. His mama died that night. Died saving him, in fact. I was holding him on my lap in the boat. He was the one who insisted that Rocky check Nadia's place. I didn't even think about the look on Rocky's face when he got back into the boat. I was too terrified that we were going to die. But now, thinking back, I think that was when he saw her body. When he was here a few months ago, he said he was still looking for Angel." She stared at them shrewdly. "I didn't believe him then. I don't now. I just want to know that little Angel's okay."

"We'll do our best to find him," Molly promised. "And then we can give him your information if you like."

"I'd like," Nancy said knowingly. "Is there anything else?"

"How did you know Nadia was pregnant?" Molly asked. "Did she tell you?"

"Nah. I had kids. I knew the signs. She'd cover her belly with her hand and ask what ingredients were in foods we shared at neighborhood barbecues. Also, the kid who walked her dog said that she heard Nadia puking when she came by to get Madame Fluffy."

"Do you know if she was seeing a doctor?" Molly pressed. "Like an ob-gyn?"

"No, I'm sorry. I can't help you with that."

Hiding her disappointment, Molly smiled at her. "No worries, ma'am. What about her address? Which house was hers?"

"I don't recall the house number, but Angel and his mother lived in the house directly across from ours. Standing in our front yard, Nadia lived in the house on the right."

Antoine could work with that, Molly thought. "Thank you. You've been a big help. How long will it take you to get packed?"

"Thirty minutes or so. Why?"

"If you'd like, we can wait and follow you to the highway. Just to make sure you get out of the city all right."

Nancy went still. "It's that dangerous?"

Molly didn't want another private pathologist or mortician on Gabe's conscience—or her own. "Yes, ma'am."

"Then I accept. I watch a lot of crime shows. It's always the stupid ones who refuse the help that end up gutted in an alley somewhere."

Molly grimaced. "Heavens. What a thought." And not terribly inaccurate.

Gabe rose when Nancy did. "Can I help you with anything, ma'am?"

"Unplug my appliances and turn off the water? And maybe carry my bag to the car?"

"Absolutely." He looked down at Molly. "Anything you need me to do?"

"No. I'm going to message the office. Don't go outside."

"Mercy," Nancy murmured as she disappeared into a bedroom.

Molly pulled out her phone and texted Burke. *Victim was Nadia Hall.* She added Nancy's address. *Nadia lived one house to the right of house directly across the street. Don't have exact address.*

??!!!, was Burke's reply.

Yep. Rocky was here 4–5 mo ago. Talked to a neighbor.

WTF???

What the fuck, indeed. *Can you have Antoine trace the victim? Any surviving family? CC/phone records?* Although she'd be shocked if any credit card or phone records existed after all this time. She'd never worked a cold case like this before. But if the information existed, Antoine could find it.

Just sent him the name. He can def check property records for owner of Nadia's house. Where are you going next?

Molly thought about that. *Did you get Shoe?* The talk about Nadia Hall's dog made her remember. Gabe had, too. She'd seen the guilt on his face.

Shit. No.

No problem. We'll do it.

Tell G that I'm sorry.

He'll understand. Talk later. She closed her texts, then reconsidered.

Clearly the woman who'd visited Burke that morning had been lying. *Duh.* But why?

She started another text to Burke. *Why did lady visitor this am drop a SC address? Bait for me?*

Maybe. Don't go up there.

I won't. But I can ask my old boss to check on the QT.

There was a long pause. Then, *I trusted him. He fought for you back then. Yes. Ask him. Warn him. Maybe a trap.*

I will.

She moved to Nancy Royce's front window so that she could keep an eye on her car. She'd set the alarm, but a skilled operator could slip a tracker in a hubcap without setting it off.

Drawing a breath, she found her old boss in her contacts list. It was his personal cell, not the office phone. *I should have kept in touch.* But he wouldn't be upset. He'd understood why she'd fled town three years before.

She tapped his name and held her breath, waiting for the call to connect.

"Thatcher," he answered.

"Hi, Steven. This is Molly Sutton."

She could hear the creak of his chair and pictured him leaning back as he always did.

"Well, well," he said, warmth in his voice. "How the hell are you guys?"

"I'm okay. Chelsea and Harper are doing well. And you and yours?"

"Jenna's great, as are the kids. Nicky's headed off for college in a few weeks and Jenna's already crying."

Molly smiled. That sounded like Jenna. "Where's he off to?"

"Duke, so he's close enough to come home for supper sometimes. Seth is about to start middle school and has a girlfriend. That's fun." Clearly it was not fun. "Matt's finishing his final tour in Iraq and will be coming home soon, which will be a huge relief. And Aunt Helen is still traveling. She's in Egypt, having the time of her life."

Molly missed them all. "And Brad?"

Steven hesitated. "He's . . . engaged."

She understood his hesitation, but there was no need. "I'm so happy for him." And she was. "You know we were better as friends. I think we put off breaking up because we didn't want to disappoint you guys." And because she hadn't wanted to give them up. Luckily Steven's oldest son was as generous as his father. He'd understood that she'd fallen for his family, maybe more so than she'd cared for him. "Tell him that I can't wait to meet her."

"I will. We miss you. Maybe take a few days' vacation and come see us."

"I will. But now's not the best time."

"Okay. I'm guessing you didn't call to catch up. What's going on?"

She explained the situation, glossing over some of the details. "So I think this may have been a ploy to get me up there to take me out."

"Assholes," he grumbled. "So, you want us to check it out on the down-low, no records, and maybe we'll get shot at. That about sum it up?"

She winced. "Yep. You can say no."

"As if I would. I'll do it myself. It'll be good training for my newbie. I'll let you know what we find. Be careful, Molly. You're important to a lot of people."

She swallowed hard. She'd loved her job with the North Carolina SBI. Loved her work family. Had hated to leave. "Miss you."

"Likewise. You'll always have a place here, but I get why you left. Next time, call me to shoot the breeze, okay?"

She smiled. "Yes, sir."

She ended the call and nearly squeaked when Gabe moved in behind her and put his hands on her shoulders. "You okay?"

She looked over her shoulder. "I'm fine. Is the water off?"

"Yep. Just waiting on Mrs. Royce to finish packing her suitcase." He looked uncomfortable. "Can I ask who Brad is?"

"Yes. He's an old boyfriend—the one before Jake's best friend. Brad's the son of my old boss. He's also with the SBI, and we met when I was assigned to a team in Charlotte. We decided that we weren't cut out for romance and we parted as friends. He's getting married."

Gabe visibly relaxed. "Thank you for telling me. So your old boss is going to help?"

"Yeah. We'll see what happens when he shows up at 'Alicia Rollins's' house."

"You're *those* kind of partners?" Nancy asked, startling them both.

They turned to find the older woman giving them an interested stare. Gabe hurried to Nancy's side, taking her suitcase. Which was enormous.

Nancy was grinning. "I knew it. I picked you two as sweethearts." She snapped her fingers. "I still got it after all these years."

Molly laughed. "How long are you staying in Huntsville, ma'am? Six months?"

Nancy shrugged. "Until you say it's safe for me to come home." She wagged her finger. "And don't you leave me hanging, young lady. I expect an update."

"Absolutely. I promise."

Tulane-Gravier, New Orleans, Louisiana
WEDNESDAY, JULY 27, 11:45 A.M.

On the downside, Broussard hadn't left his office yet. On the upside, the reporters were having a field day wondering who could have been behind the murder of "alleged hit man Cornell Eckert." So far, they were looking at all of Eckert's past misdeeds. Or ones he'd been rumored to have committed.

Eckert had been pretty smart. Had never left evidence behind that could convict him. Except for that one time. *And then I had him exactly where I wanted him.*

Of course, now he'd lost Eckert permanently, but it was what it was.

Lamont closed the browser, silencing one of the reporters in mid-sentence. They didn't know their heads from a hole in the ground. *Lucky me.*

"Sir?" A young woman stood in his doorway uncertainly. It took him a moment to place her. *Oh, right. Ashley's replacement.* "Just a reminder that you have lunch with the senator today. Your driver phoned to say he was downstairs waiting. He's afraid that you'll be late, what with the traffic and all."

Shit. He'd forgotten. That wasn't like him at all. "Thank you, Carrie. I should be back by midafternoon."

"Very good, sir. Your next appointment isn't until four."

He shut down his computer and cleared his desk, feeling rattled. He hadn't prepared for this meeting and it was important. Like, life-changing important.

This was one of the men he needed on his side for his own Senate run. Drawing a breath, he glanced in the mirror next to his door as he left his office. He looked good.

He looked normal.

He looked senatorial.

Grabbing his briefcase, he left his office, only to run smack-dab into the new guy. The man stepped into his path, forcing him to either shove him out of the way or stop.

Lamont stopped, but let his irritation show through. "Jean-Pierre," he said evenly. "I'm in a bit of a hurry."

Jean-Pierre was from New York City, which made him despicable enough, but add to that the earnest way the man looked at *every single case* and it made Lamont want to vomit.

Lamont had never been that earnest, even when he was just starting out. He'd pretended to be that earnest so that he could snag wife number one, but it had all been a lie. Jean-Pierre was like a damn puppy, panting for scraps. The man had no self-respect at all.

Of course, I might be feeling a little tetchy because he's Ashley's new boss. For all of her naivete, she'd kept his office spinning like a top. And she fucked like a porn star. He was going to miss that.

"Lamont." Jean-Pierre smiled like a movie star. "I won't keep you. I just wanted to thank you for sending Ashley my way. She's already organized my schedule and created a database for my cases."

Lamont forced his lips to curve. He had to be sociable. He hated being sociable. Especially to slick, save-the-world phonies like Jean-Pierre. The man's name wasn't even Jean-Pierre, anyway. It was his middle name. His first name was Kaj. *What kind of name is that?*

Lamont nodded graciously. "You're most welcome. She was an excellent assistant."

Jean-Pierre tilted his head, his smile dimming. "Then why did you transfer her to me?"

Oh, so the city slicker has him some teeth. Good to know. He decided to be honest. "Because she's young and pretty, and I have a jealous wife," he said ruefully. "There was never anything going on, y'understand, but wives . . ." He shrugged. "You know how they can be."

Jean-Pierre's smile disappeared completely, something flashing in his eyes that looked a lot like loss. "Not recently. I'm a widower."

Lamont blinked, having not expected that. "I'm sorry," he said and almost meant it. "Look, I hate to run, but—"

Jean-Pierre stepped aside. "No, the apology is mine. I've kept you when I said I wouldn't. Please, have a nice afternoon."

Feeling off in a way that he didn't like, Lamont made his way to the car. "Thank you for the reminder, James," he said when he was buckled in. "I'd gotten caught up in some work."

"No problem, sir," James said and pulled away from the curb. "I'll get you there in time."

If James didn't, it wouldn't be the driver's fault. Stupid festivals. Stupid traffic.

He glanced at his phone to make sure his new hires watching Broussard's building were still where they were supposed to be. And they were. *Dammit, Broussard. Go home already. Or wherever it is you've stashed that kid.* This was taking a lot longer than it was supposed to.

He startled when his phone buzzed in his hand, muttering a curse.

"Sir?" James asked.

"Nothing. Never mind. I'm fine." Maybe better than fine. It was Ashley. Maybe she'd heard from Broussard. He put the phone to his ear. "Hello, Ashley."

And what the fuck? He hadn't just seen James's mouth twist in a frown, had he? A judgmental frown at that. James didn't even like Joelle. What business was it of his that Ashley called him? The man better watch his step. Drivers were a dime a dozen in this town.

But James had been with him for at least twenty years, so he'd let it go. This time.

"Hi," Ashley cooed. "I just got it. Thank you!"

Got it? Oh, right. "The bag. You're welcome."

"You really shouldn't have. It's too expensive."

But what she really meant was *of course you should have* and *please, do it again.* "It was the least I could do considering you had to throw yours away." Hers had been a cheap handbag. Maybe from Target. The one he'd had sent to her new office had cost five hundred bucks. "But that's—" He glanced at James, who'd straightened out his face and now listened placidly to the radio softly playing jazz. "That's part of the assignment. Confidentiality, you know."

"Oh, I know. I won't tell anyone. Hell, I don't have anyone to tell."

It was true. Like all of his previous mistresses, she had no family. No friends. She really would have made a very nice replacement for Joelle.

"Well, enjoy it. I need to go now."

"Wait! Did he . . . you know? Did he leave his office? Have you followed him?"

He frowned. "What part of 'confidential' did you miss?" Then he realized how it sounded. "I apologize. I've had a busy morning."

"It's all right." Although she sounded a lot less bouncy than she had a minute ago. "I was just hoping you caught him. To stop him."

"We will," he said, infusing warmth into his voice. "And I'll keep you informed, okay?"

"Okay," she said, then hung up.

His frown morphed into a scowl. *She didn't just hang up on me.* But she had. Maybe it was better that he'd hired a new assistant. With that attitude, Ashley wouldn't have worked out after all.

With a last check on the men guarding Broussard—still no movement other than brief periodic walks up and down the block—he slid his phone into his pocket and closed his eyes. He pushed all thoughts of Broussard, Xavier Morrow, and Gabe Hebert from his mind, mentally picturing how this meeting would go.

It would go well, just like all the meetings that had come before. He was well-liked. He looked good on camera, sounded even better. He had an amazing career record. He was senatorial.

He might even be presidential.

He smiled. He definitely liked the sound of that.

Mid-City, New Orleans, Louisiana
WEDNESDAY, JULY 27, 12:05 P.M.

"Oh. Oh, wow." Molly stared at her laptop screen, disbelieving. *Holy fucking shit.*

"What?" Gabe asked.

She glanced at him from the corner of her eye. He sat on the plastic chair next to hers, squeezing the rubber ball he'd just bought from the little shop in the corner of the veterinarian's waiting room. It was a present for Shoe, because he felt guilty for forgetting about him. The woman behind the counter had informed them that they'd had a medical emergency with one of the animals, but that Shoe was fine and if they'd please wait, someone would bring the dog out as soon as possible.

Which was okay. No one had followed them in the rental car. There were no windows in the waiting room, and Molly was seated facing the only exterior door. Unlike the night they'd brought Shoe to the after-hours emergency vet, the waiting room was crowded with people—plus five big dogs who looked like they'd show an intruder who was boss.

Unless the intruder had a gun. But so did Molly. So did Gabe, for that matter. So she'd felt safe enough to open her laptop and research Nadia Hall. And she'd hit pay dirt.

Most of the fellow pet owners were looking at their phones and not paying attention to them, but she kept her voice pitched low. "It was just a whim," she murmured. "But, look."

She turned her screen so that Gabe could see.

"Whoa," he whispered. "I thought Myspace was dead."

"Me too. And a lot of the personal accounts *are* dead. Or left for dead, anyway."

Including Nadia Hall's account. It was a name only. No photo. No profile except New Orleans as a location. But her account still listed "connections." She was connected to 98 people and 152 were connected to her.

The site listed the "top eight" connections for most users.

Enter the holy fucking shit.

Molly had tried Myspace as a last resort, because Antoine hadn't found any records on Nadia Hall. No employment record, no tax records, no driver's license. He had only found a birth certificate.

She'd been twenty-one years old when she was murdered.

And her top connection was a woman named April Frazier.

April Frazier had a Facebook account.

Molly toggled to the open Facebook tab in her browser. "Look. It's current. Her last post was this morning."

"Oh my God, Molly," Gabe breathed. "Look at the photo of her daughter."

"I know." April Frazier had named her oldest daughter Nadia.

A quick search of the white pages yielded a current address in Biloxi, Mississippi. No phone number, which wasn't a surprise. Very few people had landlines anymore.

Quickly she texted Burke, with screenshots of what she'd found. *Look. NH's BFF.*

NICE, was Burke's reply. *Well done, grasshopper.* ☺

Molly snorted. *She lives in Biloxi. Going there after we get Shoe from the vet.*

Will have Antoine run background on the BFF, Burke texted back. *Check in before you knock on her door.*

Yes, sir. Anything new?

Just you, superstar. Antoine will be so annoyed he didn't think of it.

Leaning over to read her screen, Gabe laughed. "I bet he will be."

"Mr. Hebert?" a woman called from the doorway to an exam room. "Shoe's ready to go. The doctor will see you now."

Gotta go. Gabe just got called by vet. Later.

She slid her laptop into her handbag and followed Gabe into the office, feeling elated.

Finally. Now they were getting somewhere.

18

G OOD BOY," GABE soothed, stretching over the console to the back seat so that he could give Shoe a scritch behind his ears. They'd been sitting in their new rental car for two hours, waiting for April Frazier to come home. "You're being such a good boy."

Shoe really had been a good boy. He'd waited patiently while Molly had switched out the rental sedan for an SUV, paying with Burke's "John Smith" credit card.

It wasn't really in the name of a fake person named John Smith. It was a company Burke had set up specifically for situations such as this—allowing his PIs to rent vehicles, reserve hotel rooms, and buy food that couldn't be traced to any of them or to the company as a whole.

The driver's license she'd used, on the other hand . . . That was not as legit. She was listed as Jennifer Arnold, which were the first names of her grandparents.

Gabe wasn't going to think about the legality of her fake ID right now, because he'd been relieved to switch vehicles. First, they couldn't be tracked if his father's killer had managed to slip a tracker into the previous car while they'd been waiting at the vet's. Second, the sedan had been small for anyone approaching six feet tall, which he was. The SUV was much more comfortable, plus it had room for Shoe to stretch out in the back seat.

The dog seemed no worse for his near-death experience. He'd had a vacation at the vet's, in fact. Everyone there loved Shoe.

Gabe hoped no one would use his relationship with the veterinarian to hurt anyone who worked there. Or any of the animals.

I couldn't stand that. He wanted to warn everyone with whom he came into contact. *Be careful. Don't walk alone in the dark. Lock your doors. Watch for shadows in the night.*

But he couldn't. And he probably shouldn't, because ninety-five percent of the people he talked to weren't in any danger. He'd cause hysteria.

Except he hadn't warned Dr. McLain or Dusty Woodruff. They'd helped him. They'd helped his father. And now they were dead, too.

"Stop," Molly murmured.

He met her gaze with a frown. She sat behind the wheel, looking as crisp and calm as she usually did, despite the oppressive heat. The SUV's air-conditioning simply couldn't keep up and the Kevlar vest was like an oven all on its own.

"Stop what?" he asked.

"Stop feeling guilty about the pathologist and the mortician."

"How did you know I was doing that?"

"You get this little line in your forehead when you're upset." She traced a fingertip between his crunched brows. "Right here. It was not your fault, Gabriel Hebert. So stop. Think instead about getting them justice."

"What will that look like?" he asked, genuinely needing to know.

"Depends. Prison at best. A gruesome death at worst. Or flip the two, if you want. Best and worst are relative to the perpetrator."

She knew what she was talking about, so he nodded. "I'll try."

She lightly squeezed his forearm. "That's all we can do."

He pointed to her phone when it buzzed. "Incoming."

She snatched it up, unlocking the screen to read the text. "Antoine says that April Frazier is headed our way."

"How can Antoine possibly know that?" he asked.

"He's tracking her cell. He was able to find her number while we were waiting."

"What? He can do that? Track people's phones without their knowledge?"

Molly shrugged. "Antoine can do a lot of things. Most of the time I can't understand even when he tries to explain. I just accept it. Like . . . I don't know. Like the miracle that is bacon."

Gabe shook his head. "Bacon is not a miracle. It comes from pigs."

"Hush. I don't want to know that."

"You grew up on a farm!"

She looked guilty. "It was hard. Pigs are cute. But bacon is delicious. It's a real moral dilemma."

He smiled, which he suspected was her end goal, because she looked pleased with herself.

"He's also tracked your aunt's phone," she added, scrolling through the messages from Antoine.

"Oh?" Gabe leaned over to see the screen. "Aunt Gigi's in Fort Lauderdale?"

"She was sixteen days ago. That was the last time her phone was in use. It's been turned off since then. I'm betting she's on a cruise."

"That makes sense. She takes a lot of cruises with her friends." And that made him feel so much better. He relaxed, drawing, if not an easy breath, then an easier one, at least.

"I'll ask Antoine to run checks on her credit cards. If she is on a cruise, she'd probably be using them for buying souvenirs in whatever ports they stop in." She looked over her shoulder. "That's April's car. Cross your fingers, Gabe."

"Fingers and toes."

She took his hand and held fast. "We don't mention Xavier, okay?"

He huffed, offended. "I didn't! I didn't even blink when Mrs. Royce asked about him."

"And I was very impressed." She brought his hand to her lips for a quick kiss before letting him go. "It's showtime. Let me talk to her first. She's alone, and I'm less intimidating."

Antoine had outdone himself, getting them all the details of April Frazier's life. She worked for an insurance broker, was married to a pharmacist, and had three children—Nadia, age thirteen, Josephina, age ten, and Hanna, age eight—and she'd apparently stopped at the grocery store on her way home from work.

The latter was Gabe's own observation, as he could see the grocery bags in the back seat of her car as she pulled past them into her driveway. "Tell her I'll carry her groceries," he offered.

"You're sweet." Molly approached April's car as the woman was getting out. "Hi," she called. "My name is Molly Sutton. I was hoping I could talk to you for a moment."

Gabe got out, shut the door, and leaned against it. He'd let her take the lead, but he would be her backup if things went south, as she would say.

"I'm not interested in whatever you're selling," April said with frosty politeness. She was about forty, tall, thin, and angular. Her medium brown hair was pulled into a ponytail and she wore yoga pants. "Please go away." She started toward her house, her cell phone in hand. "I have 911 ready to dial, so leave."

"I'm not selling anything. I'm a private investigator. I'd like to ask you about Nadia Hall."

The woman stopped abruptly, then turned slowly, her mouth open in shock. "What?"

"I'm investigating a murder, and I think the victim was Nadia Hall."

April lifted her hand to her mouth, her eyes filling with tears. "Oh my God. Oh my God."

"You knew her?" Molly asked.

She lowered her hand and nodded. "Yes. She was my best friend in the world. I . . ." Her eyes narrowed. "How did you know about her, and how did you find me?"

"How I know about her is a long story. How I found you is a shorter one. Both you and Nadia still have Myspace accounts. I tracked hers to yours, then used Facebook and the white pages."

April blinked. "Wow. That's . . . Wow. I didn't realize Myspace still existed."

"Well, I'm grateful that it does." Molly gestured toward Gabe. "This is Gabe Hebert. He's my partner. His father was the police officer who found Nadia's body."

April leaned to one side, giving Gabe the once-over. She must have been satisfied, because she nodded at him. "Why isn't your father investigating?"

"He did," Gabe said. "But he died recently, and I've taken up his investigation."

"You're a cop, too?"

Gabe shook his head. "No, I'm a chef. I have a restaurant called Le Petit Choux in New Orleans. My photo is on the website if you want to check."

"And I have my PI license," Molly added. "Please, feel free to check us out."

April studied her screen, then his face, repeating the motions with Molly's license. "I remember you from the TV, Mr. Hebert. Would you like to come in? It's hot out here."

"If you're comfortable inviting us in," Molly said. "We're not here to pressure you. We just want to understand what happened to Nadia."

April nodded gravely. "Me too."

"Um." Gabe pointed to the SUV. "Shoe."

Molly grimaced. "We have a dog, and we can't leave him in the SUV unless I leave the engine running."

"Somebody will steal your car," April declared. "We like dogs. Is he friendly?"

"Very," Gabe assured her. "I'll keep him on a leash."

"Then come in. I'm very interested in what you have to say."

"What about your groceries?" Molly asked.

"Oh. Right." April reached into her back seat and pulled out a small cooler bag. "This stuff needs the fridge. Everything else can stay out here until we're finished."

Gabe got Shoe from the SUV and, keeping a hold on his leash, followed Molly and April. Or he tried to. Shoe was distracted by the shrubs in the front yard. "We've been driving for a few hours," he said apologetically as Shoe peed every three feet.

April chuckled. "I've had loads of dogs. I get it. No problem."

Gabe finally got Shoe into the house, which was blissfully cool.

"Ah," they all said in unison.

"This way." April led them to the kitchen, which was very nice. "Please sit down. Can I get you something to drink?"

"Water would be great," Molly said.

Gabe nodded. "Same. Thank you." They waited as April put her groceries in the fridge and filled glasses of water for them and a bowl for Shoe. "He says thank you, too."

April patted Shoe's head, then joined them at the table. "So. Tell me your story."

"Gabe's dad died six weeks ago," Molly began. "Full disclosure: we think he was killed because he was investigating Nadia's death."

April gasped. "Oh my God."

"Has anyone come asking about Nadia?" Gabe asked.

April shook her head. "No. I yelled and screamed at the police after Katrina because Nadia had simply disappeared. But there were so many other things going on. So much death. They brushed her case aside. I was so frustrated. I kept asking and asking, but years passed, and I finally gave up. How did your father find her body?"

Gabe told her about his father's rescue of the people in Chalmette. "He came back afterward, and her body was gone. He tried to investigate, but was discouraged by someone higher up. Like you said, so much was going on back then. It was chaos."

"I remember," April murmured. "Nadia was my roommate. Well, she was up until about six months before Katrina. We went to high school together, here in Biloxi. She was a foster kid. She spent more time at my parents' house than she did any of the foster homes. We always dreamed of going to New Orleans when we grew up. So when we graduated high school, we did. We got this awful little apartment in the Quarter. It was tiny and moldy, but we could open the windows and hear the music. We loved it. We were waiting tables mostly. We'd both turned twenty-one the year before Katrina and could finally tend bar. Tips were good. Nadia's tips were better." Another sad smile. "She was stunning."

"Do you have any photos?" Molly asked.

"I do. I'll get them when we're finished if you like."

"That would be great." Molly traced her finger through the condensation on the water glass. "What happened six months before Katrina?"

"She met someone."

A shiver raced over Gabe's skin. He wanted to ask who, but April was looking straight ahead, focused on nothing. Except her past.

"He was rich and, according to her, sexy as sin. I never met him, and I don't know his name."

Gabe had to breathe through his disappointment.

"If you'd known, you'd have had a place to start when she disappeared," Molly said.

April nodded. "Exactly. She met him about seven months before Katrina. Within a month, he'd rented her a house." Her smile turned bitter. "I wasn't allowed to visit. She wasn't even allowed to tell me the address. She slipped once and told me the basic neighborhood and I thought she'd have a heart attack. Begged me to forget she'd ever told me that much. He was older and very controlling. She didn't even tell him about me at all. I tried to talk sense into her, but she'd cut me off. She said I didn't understand, because I was still single."

Molly winced. "Ouch."

"I know. Finally, she threatened to stop seeing me at all. She'd quit her jobs and was his 'personal assistant.' She'd get his dry cleaning mostly, from what I could tell. I think he wanted her isolated and available. And secret. I figured he was married."

"That makes sense," Molly murmured. "Did he buy her things?"

"Oh yeah. Diamond necklaces, fancy clothes, designer shoes and handbags." She frowned. "And a dog."

"Madame Fluffy," Molly said.

April looked startled. "Yes, that was the dog's name. How did you know that?"

"We talked to one of her old neighbors." Molly hesitated. "Did you know that Nadia was pregnant?"

April nodded slowly. "She was devastated and absolutely terrified to tell the guy. He'd made no promises. She was his side piece." She sighed. "Nadia wanted the baby desperately, though. She was raised in foster care and had always wanted a husband and a child."

"Someone to love her unconditionally," Gabe said quietly.

"Exactly. I didn't understand then. I just knew that I'd lost my best friend. I was angry." April sighed again. "And hurt. And not mature enough to handle my emotions. I lashed out. Told her that she should demand he marry her or she'd walk away. That if she let him convince her to have an abortion, I'd never speak to her again. I don't know if she did or not. Our last conversation was the morning before the storm. I never saw her again."

"Oh, April," Molly whispered. "I'm sorry."

April blinked, sending tears down her cheeks. "Thank you. I've never forgiven myself for that fight."

"Twenty-twenty hindsight," Molly said with a sad smile of her own. "We all do things we regret. But I know it's hard to get past traumatic events like that. No matter how old you are."

April smiled through her tears. "That's what my husband says."

"Smart man." Molly found a pack of tissues in her handbag and passed them to April. "Where were you when you had the fight?"

April dabbed at her eyes. "In a coffee shop in Bywater, near the river. Neither of us had a car and it was close to the bus stop. I begged her to come with me, told her that my father was telling me to come home, to get out of the city. That the hurricane was going to be bad." She shrugged. "Biloxi got it bad, too, but at least I wasn't alone. I was with my folks."

"Nadia wouldn't come with you?" Gabe said, already knowing the answer.

"Nope," April said sadly. "She said her man would come and get her and take her someplace really nice to ride out the storm. She was going to tell him about the baby, though. And demand he do the right thing." She exhaled. "Do you think he killed her?"

Gabe thought of Xavier's story, how a man had strangled her. "Maybe. That's what we're hoping to find out."

"Your dad got close?"

Gabe nodded. "I think he did. He'd been investigating off and on— on his own time—for years. Some years he had more time to give. Some years he didn't. My mom had cancer and that was a hard time for all of us. Dad worked and took care of her. I'd get him to let me take over sometimes so that he could sleep, but he was stubborn. I don't think he had much opportunity to investigate in those years."

"I'm sorry," April said softly. "What else do you know about Nadia?"

"Not much," Molly admitted. "We just found out Nadia's identity today. Did she have an ob-gyn?"

"Yes. I mean, I think so. I gave her the name of one."

Gabe straightened, his heart starting to pound. "Do you remember it?"

"Is it important?"

Molly lifted a shoulder. "We don't know. But we believe that Gabe's dad was searching for him. At this point, we're just trying to reconstruct his investigation."

April frowned. "It's been a lot of years. I got the name from one of the other bartenders whose girlfriend was pregnant. Give me a minute. It started with a *B*." Her lips moved as she soundlessly tried different names. Then her eyes flew open. "Benson. I don't remember his first name. He had a practice near Tulane. I hope that helps."

"It's a lot more than we had when we got here," Molly said fervently. "Thank you."

"Thank *you*. I'd given up hope of ever finding her. I think some part of me has always known she died. Her neighborhood was underwater. I thought she'd drowned. At least now I know what really happened. Or at least some of it." She rose, waving Gabe to stay put when he started to rise with her. "I'm going to get my photo album. It's just in the living room."

Molly was already on her phone, texting Burke. *Dr. Benson. OB-GYN.*

SUPERSTAR, was his reply. Then, *On it.*

Molly was stowing her phone when April returned with the photo album. She set it on the table and flipped pages until she found what she was looking for. "Here we are. We were maybe fifteen in this one."

"Oh," Molly murmured. "You two were so cute."

The two teenagers stood arm in arm, smiling for the camera. They wore shorts and matching NSYNC T-shirts. April was easily identifiable—she hadn't changed much over the years.

Nadia was stunning. Blond shiny hair that fell halfway down her back, big eyes, a classically beautiful face, and a figure that made her look twenty-one instead of fifteen.

"I was cute," April said with a self-deprecating smile. "Nadia was gorgeous, even then. My mother was so worried about her virtue. Men would stare at her whenever we were out together. My mom would say, 'Hey, she's fifteen!' and they'd scatter." She chuckled sadly. "We were going to change the world."

She flipped another few pages, then sighed. "This was the last photo I have. Mom took this one on the Mother's Day before the storm. It was one of the few times Nadia got away from the man to spend time with my family. All my photos were destroyed in Katrina. My mom still had this one in her camera when the storm hit. She got it developed weeks later. By then . . . well, chaos was still everywhere and I had started begging the police to help me find her." She removed the photo from its protective plastic sleeve. "Can I get it back?"

"Let me scan it to my phone," Molly said. "This photo isn't re-placeable."

"I should do that," April mused as Molly opened her scanning app. "I keep telling myself to digitize the family photos. You know, in case Katrina ever happens again."

Gabe frowned. "My father said he was going to do that. He even bought a scanner." But it hadn't been in the house when they'd searched on Monday night.

He looked at Molly to find that she was staring at him, probably thinking the same thing. She gave her head a little shake and refocused on scanning the photo. She handed it back to April, who replaced it into the photo album with care.

"I couldn't even bury her," April whispered, new tears streaking down her cheeks.

"I'm so sorry." Molly touched April's shoulder briefly, then sighed. "If you need anything, please call me." She gave April her card. "And I hate to say this part, but it needs to be said. We were careful coming here. We changed vehicles and used either cash or credit cards that couldn't be traced to us. But the people who killed Gabe's dad are dangerous. If you see anything out of the ordinary, call 911. Please."

April nodded unsteadily. "I understand. But I'm not sorry I talked to you. Nadia was like a sister to me, and I want whoever took her life to pay."

"As do we," Gabe said quietly.

"Because they killed your father, too." April bowed her head for a moment. When she looked up, her eyes were determined. "You'll keep me updated?"

"Absolutely," Molly promised. "Please don't mention this to anyone. For now."

"Not even my husband?"

"Tell him," Molly said, "so that he's aware and can help you stay alert. But no media."

April scoffed. "Not on your life. I'll keep quiet."

Molly smiled. "And we'll keep in touch."

Gabe was quiet as they walked to the SUV. He put Shoe in the back seat, then waited outside while Molly checked the SUV for tracking devices with her handheld scanner. He kept watch, making sure she was safe while she worked.

Finally, she looked up. "We're clear. Let's go."

They buckled up and made it to the end of April's street when Molly's cell phone buzzed with an incoming call.

"It's Burke," Gabe said. His own phone buzzed with a text, also from Burke. "He says to answer because it's urgent."

Molly pulled over and hit accept. "What do you have?"

"Dr. Curtis Benson is dead," Burke said tersely.

Molly's mouth fell open. "How?"

"And when?" Gabe asked.

"His throat was slit, and he was disemboweled." Burke made an angry sound. "His body was discovered by police the same night your dad was killed, Gabe."

"Oh my God," Gabe whispered.

Molly grabbed his hand and squeezed. "How was he discovered?" she asked. "By whom?"

"By the Lafourche Parish sheriff. They were responding to an anonymous 911 call."

"Breathe, Gabe," Molly murmured. "Please, breathe."

Gabe forced himself to exhale the breath he'd been holding. "Dad either found him before they killed him, or they knew Dad was close."

"That's what I think," Burke said grimly. "Come on back to New Orleans. Call me when you're twenty minutes out. I'll have a location for you to meet up with André."

"Did you tell him everything?" Gabe asked, still uncertain about the cop.

"Everything but Xavier shooting his home intruder. André's got a boat and will bring you to my cabin. We'll all sit down and figure this out."

"Okay." Molly looked shaken. "We'll hurry. Tell him that we have Shoe."

"André knows about the dog. He'll be ready for you all."

Gabe had a sudden, terrible thought. *Oh no. I forgot about Harry.* "Wait," he said sharply when Molly moved to end the call. "Burke, have you checked on Harry Peterson? The ME's assistant who helped me?"

Burke cursed softly. "Not since yesterday evening. I'll do that now. Drive safely."

Molly ended the call and Gabe shuddered out another breath. "Motherfucker," he choked.

"I know," she murmured. "We'll find them, Gabe. We won't let them escape justice."

"I know."

She pulled back into traffic and pointed them toward home.

Tulane-Gravier, New Orleans, Louisiana
WEDNESDAY, JULY 27, 6:15 P.M.

"What do you mean, he's gone?" Lamont thundered, then turned from his office window, lowering his voice to a hiss. "How the *hell* can he be *gone?*"

It was quiet in the building, most everyone having gone home for the day. He could hear the quiet roar of a vacuum, so the maintenance crew was around. He'd locked his outer door so that no one could surprise him, but he still didn't want to be overheard shouting about anything.

"We've been watching the doors all day," one of his new men said defensively. "He did *not* come out. I swear it."

"Then how do you know he's gone?" Lamont asked through clenched teeth.

"One of the guys that works there—we saw him leaving this morning. I think he's their night guard. Anyway, he arrived an hour ago, then a half hour later walked a lady in a wheelchair to her van. Then, just now, he walked a Black guy with three computer bags to his car. We heard the night security guy ask the guy with the computers if Burke made it out okay. The computer guy said that he had, and that some guy named André helped. They smuggled him out in a delivery truck. The listening device you gave us to plant near their front door really works," he added in an attempt to be upbeat.

Lamont leaned against the window and pinched the bridge of his nose. *Jesus, Mary, and Joseph.* It had all been for nothing. Broussard had suspected the whole time and had planned a way out. And that bastard André Holmes helped him. *Motherfucking sonofabitch.* "Okay. Take off for now but watch your phone. I may need you later."

"You're the boss."

He ended the call and closed his eyes. *Some boss.* He could feel a headache coming on. Probably from clenching his teeth so hard. "Fucking hell." He did not want to tell Jackass this news, but he didn't really have a choice. He dialed and waited, his gut churning.

"Do you have Broussard?" Jackass asked.

"No. He was onto us. He hitched a ride out on a delivery truck, aided by André Holmes."

"Fucking hell."

Lamont rubbed his temple where he could feel his pulse pounding. "I know."

"All right, let me think."

Lamont started to make a nasty remark, then stopped himself. He had not performed well today and wasn't going to give Jackass an opening to tell him so.

After a moment of silence, Jackass said, "Broussard's going to be on the defensive now and we tipped our hand by having your girl show up on his doorstep."

"So it would seem."

"Don't take that uppity tone with me, Monty," Jackass snapped. "This is serious. If they trace any of this activity to us, we are fucked."

"I know that," Lamont snapped back. "Don't you think I know that?" He drew a breath and let it out. Turned to the window and stared down at the people drifting by in hordes. "I'm sorry. I have a headache from hell, and I'm frustrated."

"Sorry, too," Jackass muttered. "We can't be fuckin' with each other. That's how they'll get us."

Oh, right, Lamont thought snidely. *Like you weren't planning to serve me up on a damn platter with Xavier Morrow as an eyewitness.* "You're right," he said calmly. "What do you think we should do?"

"I think we need to start going after Broussard's people. He's got relationships with all of them. They're all friends."

"And this accomplishes what exactly?"

"We grab his people, he'll either come after them or he'll trade the kid."

"I don't think he'll trade the kid." Broussard was far too *honorable* for that. *Dammit.*

"Then we lure him out and make sure he doesn't get in a goddamn delivery truck again. We actually follow him home. Or wherever the fuck he's holed up."

"Fine. Where do we start?"

"With the lady PI. That way we get Rocky's boy at the same time. We kill Hebert and use the woman to draw Broussard. Broussard and the woman served together. They're real tight. He'll come after her."

"What if he doesn't go back to Morrow? What if he has Morrow stashed in a safe house miles away?"

"Then we cross that bridge when we have Broussard in our hands."

"Okay." Lamont wasn't going to argue. He didn't have the energy for that right now. "Where are the lady PI and Hebert?"

"Probably still at the office. Her truck is still parked outside."

"As it has been since long before dawn," he said, feeling a spurt of satisfaction at Jackass's surprised grunt.

"Well, fuck."

"I thought you had eyes on the woman?" Lamont asked, controlling the urge to taunt.

"I did. She must have slipped out."

"Some good we've done hiring men to watch them, then," Lamont said mildly. "How do we draw her out?"

"That's easy. She's got a sister. And a niece. Right now, one of Broussard's men is guarding them. If we send in enough firepower and walk away with Margaret Sutton's family? Even if we don't get her with her family, she'll come to us to get them back. If she won't tell us where the Morrow kid is hiding, we lure Broussard. Sound good?"

It actually didn't sound horrible. "As long as you kill Gabe Hebert right away. I don't want him getting away."

A gasp caught his attention, and he turned in time to see someone darting out the door. *Shit.*

"Will do," Jackass was saying. "Later."

Motherfucking shit. Ending the call, Lamont raced to his outer office. In time to see Ashley grabbing for the door to the central hall.

Of course she'd heard. Of course she was trying to get away. Of course she'd tell.

"I'm sorry." She whimpered when he grabbed her arm. "I just wanted to thank you in person for the bag."

She'd used her key. The one that he'd neglected to take from her. *Dammit.*

"I'll just go. I'm sorry." She tried to yank free of his hold. "Lamont, you're hurting me."

He'd have to do worse than that, he thought as he dragged her back into his office, clamping his hand over her mouth when she drew a deep breath to scream.

Fucking hell. This day just kept getting better. Holding her against him, he covered her nose and mouth, waiting until she stopped thrashing. Her new handbag slid off her shoulder to the floor with a muted thump. When she went limp, he held her for another minute. Then he eased her quietly to the floor and pressed his fingers to her throat, nodding when he felt no pulse.

That had been easier than he'd remembered. Like riding a bike.

Now, how was he going to get her out of the building? He sank into the visitor chair, the adrenaline rush quickly fading, leaving him shaking.

Okay, maybe not quite so much like riding a bike. He'd never killed someone in his place of business before. *Dammit to hell.*

But he had sneaked bodies out of places before. He did have a private washroom. The washroom did have a shower. And they only x-rayed them on their way in, not their way out.

He needed a sharp knife. Or maybe a cleaver.

He bet Gabe Hebert had a cleaver. A really fancy one.

The thought sent hysterical laughter bubbling from his gut, but he tamped it down. *Don't be weird. Don't act different.*

He'd go out, avoid James, who waited downstairs with the town car, and find a place where he could buy a cleaver. With cash. Then he'd come back and make Ashley much smaller.

It would be all right. He'd done this before.

He knew exactly where to dump her body. The gators would finish her off, just like they had Nadia. Nobody would ever find her.

It would be all right.

19

XAVIER WANTED TO scream. Everyone looked so normal. Was acting so normal. Carlos and Manny still played video games. Willa Mae still knitted. His mother was reading a book. Burke was reclining in his chair, eyes closed, his hands folded over his belly. The two guards outside were doing their rounds.

Just like normal.

Except that *nothing* was normal. Nothing was even remotely *approaching* normal.

Xavier was the only one moving. Pacing. Nervous. *Terrified.*

The doctor was dead, too. The one that Rocky had been searching for. Why? Why would they kill him? What had the doctor known? What had Nadia Hall told him?

Xavier had turned it over and over in his mind and the only thing that made sense of the doctor's murder, the only relevant connection, was the identity of the father of Nadia's unborn child.

There didn't seem to be any other reason to eliminate him.

Eliminate. It was such a sterile word. The doctor hadn't been merely eliminated.

His throat had been slit. His gut slashed open.

He'd been disemboweled.

Xavier couldn't get the image out of his mind. Why would someone *do* that?

And what do they plan to do to me? And my mom? And Carlos and the others?

And when would Molly and Gabe get here? Every moment that ticked by was another moment that they were out there, ripe to get grabbed. Killed. Mutilated.

Abruptly Willa Mae put her knitting aside and rose, went to the kitchen, and returned with a chair. Xavier was distracted enough to stop pacing.

"Miss Willa Mae?" he asked. "What are you doing?"

"Giving you something to do," she snapped. "You're driving us all crazy, but we feel too bad for you to tell you so."

His mother put down the book she'd been reading.

Or not been reading. Now that he really looked at the book, he realized that she hadn't turned many pages.

"Is that true, Mama?"

"Of course it is," she said with more kindness than he probably deserved.

Carlos paused the video game and turned, interest on his face. "What're you gonna have him do with that chair? Tame some lions?"

Manny snorted. "Or gators."

Burke had opened his eyes, watching them all. "Or maybe it's a prop. Like for a dance sequence."

Willa Mae shook her head, a fond smile on her lips. "I wish. Xavier can't dance."

"I can too."

"No, you really can't," Carlos said helpfully.

Xavier flipped him the bird.

Carlos just grinned. But when Xavier really looked, he saw that it wasn't a real grin. There was tension in his best friend's face.

They were all nervous. *It's not just me.*

It's just me that's acting like a fool about it.

His shoulders slumped. "What do you want me to do, ma'am?"

Willa Mae took one of those . . . things of yarn from her bag. It was twisted, looking like a fancy loaf of bread. She shook it, revealing it to be a big circle of yarn. Which she then draped over the chair's back, then held out one end to Xavier. "Wind it into a ball."

Xavier stared. "Wind it into a ball? Why?"

She nodded. "Because it's soothing."

Xavier looked around the room. His mother was hiding a smile behind her hand. Carlos, Manny, and Burke weren't even trying to hide theirs.

"Soothing for who?" Xavier demanded.

"Whom," Willa Mae corrected. "And soothing for *us*. You can worry all you like, but take out your energy on the yarn. If you keep pacing, you'll need to buy Burke a new rug because you'll have worn a hole in the one he has now."

Sighing, Xavier took the yarn and began to wind. And, like the tai chi, it was surprisingly soothing.

Willa Mae sat back down and resumed her knitting.

And the clock ticked.

"It's a hard thing to strike from your mind," Willa Mae murmured. "The image of that poor doctor." She sounded like she spoke from experience.

"You've seen murders like that?" Xavier asked.

"Pictures," she confirmed. "More than I want to recall. Especially when I was a prosecutor. Burke probably saw them in the war and with the NOPD. Your mama sees them, too, in the ER. The victims that are still breathin', anyway."

He glanced at his mother, making sure he continued to wind the yarn. It was blue like the sky, and that was soothing, too. "You do?"

Cicely nodded. "Stabbings, shootings, and beatings. I have to compartmentalize away the horror so that I can save their lives. You'll have to do that, too, when you become a doctor."

He'd known that but had never really stopped to contemplate it. "Oh. Wow."

"I won't," Carlos said with a shudder. "I'll just see wires and conductors and shit." He winced. "Sorry, Mrs. M, Miss Willa Mae."

"Burke?" Xavier hesitated to ask, but he was curious about the man. "Did you see wounds like that in the war?"

"I did," he confirmed, then closed his eyes again.

All right, then. Conversation over. They went back to their activities, the tension in the room no longer as high as it had been. It was still tense, but Xavier could breathe once more.

The silence was broken by the barking of a dog.

Burke abruptly closed the recliner and leapt to his feet, startling Xavier's mother into a gasp. "Sorry, Cicely. They're here. That's Rocky's dog." He faltered, grief flickering over his face. "I mean Gabe's dog." With a sigh, he stalked to the front door and slipped out.

Xavier kept winding the yarn because he didn't want to look at any of the others' faces at the moment. Not until he could clear the tears from his own eyes. There were some times that he also forgot that Rocky was dead, only to remember. It had been like that for the longest time when his father had passed. His birth mother, too.

Grief sucked.

The door opened and a brown-and-white dog bounded in, wagging its tail like there was no tomorrow. It was medium-sized and might have been a Lab with a bunch of other breeds thrown in. He ran straight for Xavier, tongue lolling.

Xavier's chest constricted. He recognized the dog. Rocky had brought him when he'd visited them in Houston. He dropped to one knee. "Come here, Shoe. There's a good boy." He buried his face in the dog's neck, letting his tears seep into his fur. Then let Shoe go when the dog started wiggling eagerly. "Go on. Say hey to everybody. Everybody, this is Shoe."

Everyone in the room smiled as the dog made the rounds, getting pets from them all. Shoe had settled into Burke's old recliner when the door opened again and Burke appeared, holding three grocery sacks in each hand. Behind him were Gabe and Molly, also carrying groceries. Antoine was next, but he had computer bags hanging off of him. André brought up the rear.

The cop held a semiautomatic rifle. Because someone was trying to kill them.

And just that fast, Xavier felt the respite the dog had offered simply fizzle away and realized that he'd pressed a hand to his chest. Trying to hold on to the happiness a moment longer? He wasn't sure.

Carlos and Manny went to help with the groceries while Xavier held back, watching the cop with the rifle. André took a last look outside, then secured the door. Including the dead bolts.

"What happened?" Xavier demanded.

"Let's wait for the others so everyone hears everything at the same time," André replied.

A few minutes later, the groceries had been put away, and the newcomers crowded into the living room. Gabe and Molly joined Cicely on the sofa, and Burke ousted Shoe from his chair, then picked the dog up and settled him on his lap like he was a toy poodle.

Everyone else sat on the floor, Antoine busily unpacking his laptops. He had three.

Xavier wanted to ask why he had three laptops, but he suddenly didn't have the energy to care. "What happened?" he asked again.

Gabe looked positively gray. Molly just looked exhausted and Burke looked a lot grimmer than he had before he'd met Gabe and the others outside. So, somebody had shared something already.

Molly sighed. "André and Antoine's brother—DeShawn is his name—is doing his residency at the ME's office. We asked him to keep an eye on the ME's assistant who told Gabe that the ME hadn't done the autopsy correctly."

"Prompting Gabe to get a private autopsy," Xavier said, dread mounting because he sensed what was coming. "Is the assistant dead?"

"No," Gabe said, guilt plain on his face, "but he's in the hospital, in critical condition."

"He took a beating," André said. "A bad one. They were waiting for him when he got home from work. They left him for dead, but my little brother DeShawn had also gotten a visit from the cops that day at work. They were asking questions about Gabe and his dad. Did he know Gabe? Had he talked to Gabe?" He waved his hand in a yada-yada gesture. "He told the truth. He didn't and he hadn't. Then they asked him if he knew Burke. He lied about that and they left him alone. D went to Harry's office—that's the assistant—but he couldn't find him to warn him, so he called him. No answer. He went to his house and found him." His mouth tightened in anger. "Behind his house amid the garbage cans."

A chill went down Xavier's spine. "That was a message."

André nodded once. "It certainly was. DeShawn called 911 and bandaged some of the wounds on Harry's arms and legs. There was a ball bat nearby with bloodstains. They'd used that on his head. They'd stabbed his extremities."

"Oh my Lord," Cicely murmured. "That poor man."

Willa Mae had stopped knitting altogether, her hands trembling. "I'm glad your brother found him in time."

"I called Harry," Burke said. "Warned him. I don't know why he went home alone."

"We're investigating that," André said. "DeShawn said that Harry was supposed to wait so that they could leave together, but something happened that had him racing home alone."

"Where is your brother now?" Cicely asked.

"At home with our parents," André said. "He can take care of himself, so I'm not worried about him. He's worried about our folks, though, so he'll stick close by them as long as he can."

Xavier bowed his head, all of his earlier frantic energy gone. "What are we gonna do?"

"*You're* going to stay right here," Burke snapped.

Xavier glared at him, welcoming the irritation he felt at the words. Irritation was better than helplessness and fear. "I *get* that. What are *you* going to do? We can't stay here forever and too many people have died already. So, Mr. Broussard, what are *you* going to do?"

"Sorry." Burke exhaled wearily. "We're here to figure that out."

"We'd hoped that Nadia Hall's doctor could give us the name of her lover," Molly said. "You know, work from the past to the present. Now we need to track back, present to the past."

"I'm going to talk to Cresswell again," Gabe said, glaring at Molly.

"No, you're not." Molly glared right back. "That'll be a big fat trap and you know it."

André held up a hand. "For what it's worth, I agree with Gabe, but not just yet. We need to know what to say to the man."

"Who's Cresswell?" Carlos asked.

"My dad's old boss," Gabe said. "He's the one who told me that they'd found cocaine in Dad's pantry and that they 'didn't want to ruin Dad's reputation' by making that public, but they would if I kept pushing."

"Sonofabitch," Xavier muttered.

"Sonofabitch," his mother echoed, then sighed. "What do you hope to gain, Gabe? I'm not being judgmental. I really need to understand."

"He knows something," Gabe said, his face pale and strained. "The day I went to see him, to ask why they weren't investigating, he was smug and cocky. I wanted to hit him. I still do."

Shoe jumped off Burke's lap and climbed into Gabe's, whining softly. Gabe stroked him and the dog quieted. "He knew that coke wasn't my dad's. He knew someone planted it there. He has to know who."

"Put a pin in that for a little while," Burke urged. "Let's get our ducks in a row, first. What we do know, what we don't know, what we need to specifically find out. Molly, will you take us through it?"

Bayou Gauche, Louisiana
WEDNESDAY, JULY 27, 10:30 P.M.

Molly held up her hand, counting on her fingers all the things they knew so far. "We know that the original victim was Nadia Hall. She had a lover. She was pregnant. He was likely married. She was supposed to see him the night of the flood. Xavier saw a man strangle her. She had a doctor—Dr. Curtis Benson—who is now dead."

"I found the police report on the doctor," Antoine said, typing something on one of his laptops. The other two he'd set up nearby and they were doing something. The screens kept changing, with streams of letters and numbers. Carlos was going to get a crick in his neck the way he was leaning over to check them out.

"Dr. Benson had been dead about a day when his body was discovered after an anonymous 911 call, placed a few hours before Rocky's death." Antoine paused, glancing at Xavier. "The anonymous call came from a burner—904-555-4930."

Xavier sucked in a breath. "That's Rocky's number—the one he used to call my burner."

"I know," Antoine said. "So we can only assume that Rocky found Dr. Benson's body and called it in. The police report lists Benson's visible injuries and says that no usable fingerprints were discovered at the scene. His phone was missing, as was his laptop. He was retired, so he no longer saw patients or had a practice, but whatever files he'd kept in his house appeared to have been stolen as well." He glanced at Burke. "The sheriff's team took samples of the blood on the floor and some vomit found in the rosebush outside. They detected bleach on the rosebush, which would have rendered the DNA unusable."

"The empty jug we found in the back of Rocky's truck," Burke murmured. "He found the body and threw up but didn't want to leave any physical evidence behind. Can you get into the doctor's cell phone records?"

"I can and I did," Antoine said. "Rocky's burner number first appears nearly a month before they died. The doctor texted him as well, but to get the content of the texts, I'd need his actual phone. Most carriers don't keep the content for very long, if at all. Rocky's last call to the doctor's phone was the day of his death."

"How did Rocky find the doctor's name?" Molly asked. "He never contacted Nadia's friend."

There was a beat of silence. "That," André said, "is a damn good question. Antoine? Did you find anything more on his hard drive?"

Antoine shook his head. "Not yet. I'm still working on his hard drive. Rocky wouldn't have called all the doctors who had practices back then. It wouldn't have been legal for the doctors to share their patients' names."

"Someone else may have known about Dr. Benson," Molly said. "I'll ask April Frazier—that's Nadia's best friend—if anyone else knew about the pregnancy."

"A nurse might have known," Cicely said slowly. "Or a midwife, or even a doula, if she was planning ahead. Her pharmacist might also have known, especially if she was taking prenatal vitamins."

Molly made notes on her phone. "Good ideas." They were brainstorming, after all. Even if an idea wasn't actionable, it could lead them to a better idea. "Finding those people now, after all this time, might be a problem, but it seems like Rocky managed to find someone." It wasn't a problem—it was a needle in a freaking haystack, but they had to try something new.

Gabe drummed his fingers on his knee. "She had terrible morning sickness. That's what Mrs. Royce said. Remember?"

Molly nodded. "I remember."

"Who is Mrs. Royce?" Cicely asked.

"She's the woman who still lives on Xavier's old street." Gabe turned back to Molly. "Maybe Dr. Benson gave Nadia something for the nausea. Maybe Dad found her pharmacist."

Molly winced. It was an even smaller needle in a bigger haystack, but she wouldn't hurt Gabe's feelings for the world. "I'm noting it, but it's a very, very long shot."

"I'll search Rocky's hard drive for anything related to a medication," Antoine promised. "I'm finding crumbs of information, but so far, nothing has jumped out as important."

"It's unlikely that she would have confided the identity of the baby's father to a pharmacist," Molly said. "Especially since her lover had sworn her to secrecy about their relationship in general. But again, I've written it down."

Gabe stroked Shoe's back. "What about the dog?"

Molly looked at him. "The dog? You mean Madame Fluffy?"

"I *knew* the dog's name was Fluffy," Xavier said. "What about her?"

"She was a gift from Nadia's lover," Gabe said. "Did my dad mention finding the dog in the house when he told you about how he'd found her body that night of the flood?"

Cicely shook her head. "No, not that I recall. Xavier?"

"No, sir. He definitely didn't. I told him about the dog that night. The rescuers were taking some of the pets in the boats, too. If he'd seen the dog, he probably would have taken it."

"So . . . I'm assuming the father of Nadia's unborn child killed her,"

Gabe said. "April said that Nadia was going to demand he marry her. And if he was already married, that wouldn't have ended well. What if she made the demand, they had a fight, and he killed her?"

"With you so far," Molly said. This was a better train of thought. "And then?"

"And then he took the dog back. He'd given it to her as a gift. It's an unusual breed. It can't hurt to ask a few veterinarians what they remember."

Molly noted it. "Not bad. We can make some calls, ask vets who were around back then if they remember anyone bringing in a new Afghan hound after Katrina." Still a long shot, but a fancy dog like that might be remembered.

"Wait." Cicely held up a hand. "Xavier saw that man murder that woman while he was *sitting on the roof.* That means the water was at least over the first story of Nadia's house. How did her killer get in to kill her?"

There was a long, long moment of complete silence and a lot of open mouths.

How indeed? Molly thought, irritated with herself for not having thought of that earlier.

"Well," Willa Mae murmured. "That is another very good question."

"He had to have had a boat," Gabe said slowly. "Maybe her killer was posing as a rescuer."

"There were rescues going on everywhere," André recalled. "Ordinary folks who had a boat. Some even stole boats to do the rescues. Then there was the Cajun Navy, NOPD, and the Coast Guard. It was less than organized. I was doing rescues down on Tchoupitoulas Street, in the Lower Garden District. There were rowboats and flat-bottomed bayou boats, shrimp boats and . . . well, anything that floated. If her killer had a boat, he wouldn't have stood out."

"And he probably can't be traced, either," Burke said grimly.

Molly sighed. "I'm still writing it down. Knowing he had access to a boat could help later. André, what about the murders of the pathologist and the mortician? What do you know?"

"Not much. The pathologist's office was trashed, files stolen, computers destroyed." André hesitated, and Gabe visibly tensed. "Her lab was burned and all the drawers in cold storage were opened. The bodies burned. Not to ash, but enough to make further autopsy very difficult."

Poor Gabe. He'd gone pale, so Molly took his hand. It trembled. *Goddammit.*

"Oh no," Cicely murmured, taking Gabe's other hand. "I'm so sorry, Gabe."

Gabe swallowed hard. "Thank you, Cicely. I mean . . ." He trailed off, staring at the ceiling while a few tears trickled from the corners of his eyes. "I know he's gone and that he wouldn't have cared what happened to his body, but *I* care. I wanted to put his ashes with Mom's."

"You should still be able to do that at some point," André said softly. "And it's still likely that another autopsy could be done confirming Dr. McLain's findings. But right now, it's a mess. Physically and legally. It could be a while before your dad's body is released to you."

"But wait," Carlos said with a frown. "That seems really obvious, doesn't it? Trashing the pathologist's office was like they're saying that they're guilty. Wouldn't that make investigators look *harder* at Rocky's death?"

"If we're all still around to push it," Burke said grimly.

Molly frowned. *What the hell, Burke?*

Carlos flinched as if he'd been struck. "Oh. Okay."

"What the hell?" Manny exploded. "We're not just giving up and letting them kill us!"

Xavier dropped his head to his hands. "Fuck."

Molly glared at Burke. "We *will* be around. We will *all* still be here to push it."

"Of course we will," Burke fired back. "That's not what I meant. I *meant* that *I* know it and *you* know it, but that's not what Rocky's killer is thinking. Trouble is, too many of us know now. They—whoever they are—are going to be getting desperate."

Xavier looked up. "And make mistakes?"

"I sure as hell hope so." Burke rubbed his face. "Okay. André, who's investigating the murders? Which department?"

"Dr. Benson lived in Lafourche Parish, so that's their sheriff's department. Mr. Woodruff, the mortician, died on his way home. He lives in Mid-City, but his car went off the road in Belle Chasse, so that's Plaquemines Parish sheriff's department. Dr. McLain was in Baton Rouge, so that's BRPD. My boss knows that they're connected, so I'm coordinating. It's too early for any sizable amount of evidence to be processed, and Dr. McLain's lab, as I said, is a mess. They're proceeding very carefully there so they don't corrupt any evidence. The sprinklers came on when the fire started." He shrugged. "It's not going to be quick."

Molly swallowed another sigh, conscious of Gabe rigidly holding himself together. This was a disaster. "André, what do you know about Cornell Eckert's death? Who are you questioning?"

André scowled. "That's not my case, and I've been blocked from the information."

That shouldn't have surprised her, but it did.

Burke narrowed his eyes. "By whom?"

"By someone higher up the pay scale than me. My boss is trying to wade through the red tape. The Feds might even be getting involved, because Eckert had some prior warrants. They were there this morning, waiting for the arraignment."

Burke groaned. "Lord have mercy. If the Feds get involved, we'll never get any information."

"That's not fair," André cautioned. "We have a mostly decent relationship with the Feds. I think the obstruction is on our end. But, to answer your question, Molly, I don't know much. It had to be someone around the holding area. The logs don't show anyone having visited him after his attorney left once he was booked. All I know is that it happened at the shift change. New guard came in to get him for court and found him dead."

Molly rubbed her forehead wearily. "What about the guy posing as Paul Lott?"

"He's gone under," André said, clearly frustrated.

"His prints aren't in AFIS, either," Antoine added.

"And I did not hear you say that," André stated.

Antoine put on his innocent face. "Say what?"

"But we *do* suspect he killed the real Paul Lott, right?" Molly pressed. "What evidence do you have from that crime scene?"

"Not much," André admitted. "No usable prints. Lott had cameras around his home, but they'd been spray-painted over. All they caught was a guy in a hoodie. All of his skin was covered. No discernible features or traits."

"So . . . nothing," Molly said, feeling exhaustion creeping in. "Okay, so the route from present back to the past isn't looking so good." She eyed Gabe ruefully. "Tracking Nadia's dog is looking better and better."

Xavier glanced around the room. Everywhere but at his mother. "What if we lay bait?" He drew a breath. "Like me."

"*No!*" The word exploded from Cicely's throat, sounding terrified and final.

Molly could understand Cicely's reaction, but this was the first proactive idea anyone had put forward.

Burke was tilting his head thoughtfully. "What do you mean?" he asked.

"Burke!" Cicely shouted. Actually shouted. She pushed to her feet, planting both fists on her hips. "*No.* That is simply out of the question."

"Probably," Burke allowed, "but let's hear him out. You raised a smart young man. Let him talk."

Cicely shook her head but sat down slowly. "You're going to get my son killed."

Gabe put his arm around her. "Let's hear him out, like Burke said. Then we'll say no."

Cicely chuckled, but it came out as a sob. "Fine. Talk, Xavier."

"I'm not keen on getting killed, Mama," Xavier started. "But our options don't sound so good. Especially if we ever hope to go home. I'm thinking that we create a situation that I wouldn't be able to resist. Kind of like they tried to do with you today, Burke. Luring you out with the woman who claimed to be the victim's sister."

"We're listening," André said. "I'm inclined to agree with your mother, but keep talking."

Cicely crossed her arms over her chest mutinously and said nothing.

"What if you call the lady back from this morning?" Carlos offered. "Tell her that X wants to talk to her? Because he saw her sister die and he needs closure or something."

"But X won't be there," Manny added, "because it would be fucking stupid otherwise."

"Thank you," Cicely muttered.

Xavier nodded eagerly. "He wanted to follow you here, Burke. To us. So maybe after you talk to the lady again, you let them follow you. Try to lose them, so they're not suspicious, but let them follow you to somewhere that isn't here. Have a bunch of cops waiting for them. Catch them that way. I mean, they probably will send underlings to get me, but at least you'll have someone to question."

André tilted his head, considering. "My boss might go for that. We might even get an undercover officer that looks like you, Xavier, to ride with Burke. That way you stay safe."

"Gee, thanks," Burke said dryly. "*I* don't need to stay safe."

André grinned. "No problem. Let me work on it. The place would have to have some connection to Burke for them to buy the location."

"Have him rent an Airbnb somewhere," Willa Mae suggested. "If they're watching Burke that closely, they may have an alert on his cards. Especially if one or more of 'them' is NOPD."

André sobered. "True enough. I like that idea, ma'am. Let me work on it tonight. I'll get back with you later." He rose but paused when Molly held up her hand.

Her phone was buzzing with an incoming call from Steven Thatcher. "Hold on. This is my old boss. He said he'd check the address the woman gave in South Carolina." She tapped her phone and held the phone to her ear. "Steven?"

"It's not good," he said.

She hadn't thought it would be. "Can I put you on speaker? My group is here with me." She did, then held the phone so that they could hear. "This is my old boss, Special Agent Steven Thatcher."

"Hey, everyone," Steven said. "The short version—we found the door ajar and a bullet hole in the window. We announced ourselves and entered. Then the place blew up."

Holy shit. Everyone gasped, including Molly. "Was anyone hurt?" she asked.

"My newbie was thrown to the ground. She has a mild concussion, but she'll be okay. The good thing is that she kind of resembles you, Molly. Not a ringer, but someone could mistake her for you if they were watching from far enough away. So we said it was you, that you had come to South Carolina to check it out and I'd gone along as backup. You're in serious but stable condition and there's an officer standing guard at your door in the hospital. Sorry. I had to think fast. But hopefully it'll give you some cover for a little while."

Molly blinked, stunned. Her first thought was for Chelsea. "I need to call my sister in case someone informs her as next of kin. She'll be beside herself with worry."

"Already called her," Steven assured her. "She's good. But you need to lay low for a while."

"We're doing that anyway," she said. "Too many people are trying to kill us."

Someone said something in the background, and Steven told them that he'd be right with them. "Molly, I gotta go. I'll be in touch when I have something I can share from the crime scene. Stay safe, y'hear?"

"You, too. Thanks, Steven." She ended the call and fixed her gaze on Burke. "That bomb was meant for me."

Gabe had grown even paler. "Fuck," he whispered.

Burke nodded grimly. "They take you out and Gabe would be alone. Or if he'd gone with you, he'd be hurt, too."

The thought of Gabe being injured made her chest hurt. "Xavier's bait plan just got better," she said. "And it gives you another reason to contact her—you can tell her that her house was booby-trapped in case she came back. Warn her that she's still in danger. I mean, *we* know she was leading us to a trap, but we don't have to let *her* know that we know."

"I agree," Burke said. "Xavier's bait plan is plan A."

"*My* plan," Carlos muttered under his breath, and Manny elbowed him. "Ouch!"

Molly shook her head although she had to admit to being a little bit grateful that Carlos was trying to lighten the mood. "The Carlos-Xavier-Manny-and-Willa-Mae plan, then."

Cicely turned to Burke. "You won't put Xavier in harm's way, will you?"

"Not if I can help it," Burke promised. "Molly and Gabe, are you staying here tonight?"

Molly shook her head. "Gabe, you can, but I want to go home. If they came after DeShawn because he's connected to André and actually left a bomb in South Carolina for me, I don't want my sister targeted."

"Lucien is still there with her," Burke said.

"I know and I trust him, but I still want to go home." *Don't fight me on this, Burke. Please.*

"I'll stay with her," Gabe said. "We'll keep our heads down. I promise."

Burke sighed. "Then go with André. Do not let anyone see you or you'll ruin the cover your old boss has provided for you."

"We won't," she assured him.

Burke looked unhappy, but he nodded. *"Be careful."*

"We will." Gabe stood up and pulled Molly to her feet first, then offered a hand to Cicely. "Ma'am?"

"No, I think I'll sit a bit longer." She smiled up at him, but there was fear in her eyes. "Come back to us soon."

"We will," Gabe said again.

André shouldered his rifle. "Come on. I need to get back to the city."

20

LAMONT STOOD BEFORE the mirror in his office, straightened his tie, and decided that he looked fine. He looked normal. Dressed in one of the spare suits he always kept in his office, he looked like the dignified public servant that he wanted the world to see.

He surveyed the small washroom, wishing he had a black light so that he could be sure that he'd cleaned up all the blood. Using the cleaver, he'd taken care of Ashley's body in the shower stall, so none of her blood should be anywhere on the washroom walls or floor.

He'd scrubbed the shower stall top to bottom, but he'd known of enough cases where the killer got careless or cocky and missed a drop of blood somewhere. Those guys were currently serving life terms.

Not me. He'd cleaned everything with bleach, including the very expensive knife set he'd purchased from a kitchen shop in the Quarter—with cash, of course. *A gift*, he'd told the cashier.

A very nice gift, she'd replied with a smile.

He'd get another set, just in case someone came looking. Another set that didn't have Ashley's blood all over it. Again, he'd known of too many killers who'd thought that they'd cleaned all the blood off their weapons.

They were serving life sentences, too.

Not me. He'd triple-bagged everything, including the clothing he'd been wearing when he'd killed her. The clothing he'd burn. Everything else was going into the bayou.

He inspected the two boxes into which he'd packed the triple-bagged remains of his former assistant. They looked professionally wrapped, the silver foil paper gleaming in the overhead fluorescent lights. The bows were a nice touch, if he did say so himself.

Presents for Joelle, he'd tell James, if his driver asked.

He loaded the boxes on the dolly that he'd grabbed from the mail room on his way back from his little shopping trip that evening. Carting them out of his office and down the elevator to the lobby was easy as pie. He met no one along the way and that was just fine with him.

James got out of the car when he approached. "Good evening, sir. You're working mighty late tonight."

"I have a big case next week. Can you give me a hand with the boxes?"

Because he never would have put them into the car himself. *See? Normal.*

"Certainly, sir. They're very pretty."

"Something for Joelle."

"I'm sure she'll be happy to get whatever it is," James said, hoisting the boxes into the more-than-ample trunk of the town car. Luckily Ashley hadn't weighed all that much. Then James opened the back passenger door. "Sir?"

Lamont slid into the back seat and let himself relax. *Almost there.*

James got behind the wheel. "Home?"

"Yes, please. It's been a very long day."

He'd have James place the boxes in the garage when they got home. Joelle would probably be in bed already, so she'd never know they were there. James would be too discreet to mention them to her, even if he had any opportunity to do so. Which he probably would not.

James was not a fan of Joelle. *Join the club, buddy.*

Lamont checked his phone, hoping for a text from Jackass saying that Margaret Sutton's family was in their hands. Nothing so far, and he wondered what the man was waiting for. How hard could it be to kidnap a woman and her child?

He thumbed out a text. *Anything?*

The reply came a few minutes later. *Waiting for the lights to go out. Easier that way. We have time. The lady PI checked out the house in SC. It went boom. She's in the hospital tonite. Should be released tmw. She'll take us seriously now. She'll be cooperative when she learns we have the sister.*

Lamont exhaled a sigh of relief. Finally something was going right. *Just let me know.*

A thumbs-up emoji buzzed, and he pocketed his phone, leaned back, and closed his eyes. He was exhausted, and he still had a long night ahead of him. He'd grab a quick nap as James navigated the still-crowded streets. Then, off to the bayou.

Lake Salvatore, Louisiana
THURSDAY, JULY 28, 12:30 A.M.

André docked his boat behind a little cabin. Antoine scrambled up to the small platform and grabbed the rope that André tossed him, securing the vessel.

"Where are we?" Gabe asked, looking around but seeing nothing but a single light in one of the cabin's windows. It was pitch-dark out, cloudy without a star in the sky. Perfect for stealth. Not so perfect for getting a feel for the place.

"My fiancée's family's cabin on Lake Salvatore," André said. "The Romeros have owned this land for two generations. It's nice and quiet and we can see people coming down from the road half a mile away. Her folks are very generous about letting Farrah and me use it as a getaway whenever we get a chance."

Molly shouldered her bag, still gripping her gun, just as she had the entire way back from Burke's cabin. She'd been tense and quiet and very, very watchful. "Tell them thank you. And give Farrah my best."

André jumped to the dock and extended his hand to her. "You can tell her yourself. She's waiting inside."

Molly was smiling when Gabe stepped onto the dock. "I'm so glad," she said. "I haven't seen Farrah in way too long."

Gabe snapped his fingers for Shoe and the dog leapt from the boat like he'd been doing it for years. He might have, actually. Burke had told him that his father would bring Shoe to his cabin from time to time. They'd fish and the dog would sniff around, smart enough to stay away from the water's edge.

Way too many gators in that water. Gabe didn't even want to think about it.

He attached a leash to Shoe's collar and followed the others up a small hill to the cabin. The back door opened, and a woman came out to meet them, looking worried until she saw André.

"Took y'all long enough," she called.

André just grinned and gave her a rather boisterous kiss when he got to the door. "You missed me."

"Always," she said, tugging at the hem of her blouse when he let her go. And maybe panting a little. Gabe couldn't blame her. The kiss was hot and made him want to do the same to Molly.

Made him want to do far more than kiss her.

When it's safe. When we're safe.

"Who *do* we have here?" Farrah continued with a smile. "Molly Sutton, I have missed you."

"I've missed you, too," Molly said and hugged the woman like they were old friends. "I love your blouse. This color is . . . so you."

It was bright yellow, like a Post-it Note. Nearly neon. And Molly was right. It did look amazing on her. He stepped forward, holding out his free hand. "I'm Gabe Hebert, and this is Shoe."

Shoe wagged his tail and Farrah bent to give him a head scratch before shining her smile on Gabe. "Oh, I know who you are. I have been known to dine in your restaurant simply for that sinful chocolate cake."

"On the house forever," Gabe said, charmed.

"He's supposed to be teaching me to bake it," Molly said.

"No," Gabe corrected. "That was your ploy to distract my cousin Patty. My mama would haunt my ass if I just gave out her recipe to everyone."

Molly just raised her brows. "We'll see."

"Do you even bake, Molly?" Farrah asked.

Molly laughed. "Well, no, but I like a challenge and hate a secret." She looked around and sighed contentedly. "I didn't know you had a place out here. This is nice. Wish it was daylight so I could see it better."

"When all this is over, you'll have to come back out. You, too, Gabe. My dad's got a barbecue pit and he'll roast a brisket for two days. It's not Choux quality, but it's damn good."

"Ma'am, two-day brisket is heaven's fare," Gabe declared, and he meant it. "There's little better than a properly barbecued brisket."

"Truth," Antoine declared, then hugged Farrah tightly. "I'm going home. I have scans to run and the internet here is not so good."

"It's late," Gabe said, remembering his manners. "We've kept y'all far too long. How do we get back to our rental car?"

"You don't," André said. "It's best to keep the bad guys guessing. Farrah drove our extra vehicle out here tonight so that you could borrow it."

"Oh!" Molly looked like she might cry a little. "That was so nice of you."

"Think nothing of it." Farrah motioned for them to follow her as she started walking around to the detached garage. "We hardly ever use it, and it needs to be driven. It belonged to my best friend. She left it behind when she moved to California to live with her fiancé. She'd be happy that you were using it to keep safe."

"And you don't need to worry about pampering it," André added. "If you need to grind some gears to make a getaway, do it. The engine will do you right. We just had it tuned up. And if you have to ditch it somewhere, that's all right, too. It's just a car."

Gabe was overwhelmed with gratitude and slightly ashamed that he'd mistrusted André at the beginning. Which was only like, what? Two and a half days ago? *Hell.* "Thank you. Truly."

"We all loved your dad," André said simply. "It's our way of honoring him." He gave Molly the keys. "Be safe and you have my number. Call if you need anything at all."

Molly hugged him hard. "Thank you. Thank you so much." She stepped back, looking concerned. "Are we putting you in a bad position?"

"No," André assured her. "Someone in the department is involved in a murder. Several murders. We need to find him—or them—and dig them out. Keeping you safe is my job *and* a way to clean up my own house."

They took leave of the couple, who stood hand in hand, watching as they drove away.

"That was nice," Molly murmured. "I really love those two. Farrah's some sort of genius, but you'd never know it. She's just plain people."

"You're no slouch," Gabe said, feeling an inexplicable need to defend her.

She grinned. "You sweet-talker, you. Hey, I'm sorry you didn't get a chance to cook at Burke's place tonight. I know you were hoping to let off some steam."

He felt his lips curving into an answering smile. "I can think of other ways to let off steam."

"My bed at home is really soft."

He studied her profile. It was too dark to see if she was blushing, but she was biting her bottom lip and he'd noticed that the two often happened together. "I don't care if it's a slab of rock. If I get to sleep with you, it'll be perfect."

"It's no slab of rock, and thank you. My sister will want to meet you. She'll likely squeal and ask for chocolate cake or maybe your profiteroles. They're real favorites in our house."

"I'll make either for her, or even both. And your niece? Harper? Will she be okay if I'm there? I mean, do men scare her?"

Molly's expression softened. "It's thoughtful of you to ask. For a long time, she was afraid of men, but she's coming around. I know she likes Lucien, the guy who's been standing watch over them at night. She knows him from get-togethers with all of us from Burke's. He does some amateur magic and she's a fan. She's always trying to figure out how he does the tricks. She's very analytical."

"She gets that from her aunt."

Another smile was his reward. "And you? I know you're an only child. Is Patty your only family?"

"Kind of. Patty's other side of the family is bustin' with cousins, and they call me one of their own. Of course, it doesn't hurt that I make them the famous chocolate cake for birthdays and such."

"That cake is better than gold as currency," she declared. Then frowned. "Your aunt and uncle—Patty's folks—are in Florida, right?"

"That's what Patty said. They went to visit her granny on her mother's side. Why?"

"How much did Patty tell them?"

"Most of what I told her. She told me that they'd wanted her to come, too, but Val convinced them that Patty would be safe with her around. They must have believed Val, because they took off."

"Val is very convincing."

"Val is very intimidating," Gabe corrected.

Molly's lips twitched. "She's Val-Killer-Rie."

"She's what?"

"Val-Killer-Rie—a takeoff on Valkyrie. It's her roller derby name. She's part of the New Orleans QuarterMasters."

Gabe stared for a moment, then laughed so loudly that it startled Shoe in the back seat. "Get outta town. Really?"

"Really. When Harper saw her skate? Well, let me tell you. After seeing Val on the track, she now wants to do roller derby when she grows up. Chelsea was beside herself, but I told her to chill. Harper's only eight. She'll change her mind a million times before she's grown."

"I didn't," Gabe said. "I always wanted to be a chef."

"I'm glad. Your dream is delicious."

Something wistful in her tone had him regarding her thoughtfully. "What's your dream, Miss Molly?" he asked, making his tone teasing enough that she didn't feel too obligated to share if she didn't want to.

"I wanted to be a farmer, like my dad."

That was not what he'd been expecting. "Really? Why didn't you?"

She shrugged. "My mom wanted me to go to college because she and Dad never were able to. To do that, I needed money from Uncle Sam, so I did my time in the Corps. By the time I got back, Chelsea had met Jake and they'd moved into the farmhouse."

"They didn't get their own place?"

"Nope. Jake said he wanted to save money so that they could buy a place, but he was always gambling it away. Then, by the time I graduated from college, Harper was born, and the house was a little too full. I needed to find a place for myself and law enforcement was the route Burke had taken, so I . . ."

"So, you kind of fell into it."

"More or less. My first assignment was in Charlotte, which meant I was far enough away that I wasn't tripping over Chelsea's new family but close enough that I could be part of Harper's life."

He read between the lines. "You didn't like Jake."

"No, I never did. I liked his best friend. Thought I could grow to love his best friend, in fact, but I never could stand my brother-in-law."

"The best friend who you dated after your old boss's son." And he hated that she'd had those relationships. Which wasn't fair. He'd dated people in the past. *But this feels different somehow.* It felt like . . . more.

"The best friend who I'd briefly considered marrying one day."

He frowned, his thoughts veering from his own jealousy to how abruptly her life had changed. "You lost a lot that night. Your dad, your job"—because she'd killed the fucking brother-in-law—"and your boy-friend."

"And my home. The farm had been in my family for almost a hundred years. But we were the last of our line and we couldn't stay. Even if Harper hadn't been traumatized and molested, we couldn't stay. Dad was murdered there."

"I'm sorry."

She shrugged. "It happened. Can't change it. And I wouldn't change anything I did. Except for maybe getting to the farmhouse earlier. It wouldn't have changed Harper's reality, though. The damage Jake did to her had already been done." She drew a breath and gave herself a little shake. "The break's been good for us. I like working for Burke, and I'm good at it. And I can grow some flowers and veggies in pots on the balcony. So, it's fine."

He almost offered her part of his backyard for a garden but bit it back in time. *Too soon.* He'd see how it went between them. If it be-came permanent when all this was over, he had a plot of land he'd been planning to till. Until then . . . "How about a community garden?"

She glanced over, startled. "I never considered that."

"There are several in the area. And one of my suppliers runs his own organic farm north of Lake Pontchartrain. They probably couldn't pay you, but if you get a yen to get your hands dirty, they most likely wouldn't say no to some volunteer work."

The smile she gave him seemed to brighten the dark interior of their borrowed car. "When this is over, I'll get their names. Thank you, Gabe. I mean it. Thank you."

He reached over to stroke a finger down her cheek. "You're very welcome."

They quieted then, Molly becoming more on edge as they approached the city. She was alert, vigilant, her gaze always searching, one hand white-knuckled as she gripped the steering wheel. The other held her handgun in her lap.

Just in case.

Gabe remained silent, not wanting to distract her. He found himself searching as well. He wasn't sure what he was looking for, but if there was a strange movement maybe he could warn her before it was too late. And he did have her extra gun. He removed it from its lockbox and followed her lead, holding it on his lap, his hand clutching the grip.

Just in case.

The pace of the city had wound down a little as they exited the highway and passed the Superdome. It was the time of night that he was usually just finishing up at the Choux. Which he hadn't thought of in . . . he couldn't remember.

Thank the good Lord for Donna Lee. She was keeping their business running so that he and Patty could stay safe. Speaking of Patty, it was time to text her, just as he'd been doing every hour as he'd promised. He took his phone from his pocket and typed: *You okay? I'm good.* He waited for a reply, but none came.

Odd, because Patty kept the same hours that he did. She shouldn't be asleep yet.

Maybe she's busy watching a movie. Or cooking something. Lucky her.

He'd really missed cooking things the past few days. He typed another message. *Hello? Patty?*

He looked up from his phone when Molly's started to buzz. "It's Burke," he said after checking the screen. "Want me to answer it?"

She grew visibly tenser. "Please. Speaker, if you would."

"Molly, you need to get home," Burke said without saying hello.

Gabe felt sick. There was fear in Burke's voice.

Molly stepped on the gas. "What's happening?"

"Lucien called. They're under attack. Four men. Luc's hurt. Hurry."

Molly floored it, passing the other cars like they were standing still. "I'm a minute out."

"Don't hang up," Burke ordered. "Gabe? You armed?"

Gabe swallowed. "I am."

"Good. Try to take them alive."

Molly gripped the wheel even harder, twisting her fist like she was riding a motorcycle. "Making no promises," she gritted out.

"I've called the cops, so you'll have backup soon. André's on his way."

"Got it." A minute later, she took a right-hand turn at full speed into a darkened garage. Shoving her phone into her pocket, she dug something from her other pocket and screwed it onto the barrel of her gun—a silencer, he realized. "I don't want Harper to hear if I have to shoot," she said, then leapt from the car, gun in her hand.

To Gabe's horror, Shoe jumped from the back seat to the front and disappeared out of the door behind her.

Central Business District, New Orleans, Louisiana
THURSDAY, JULY 28, 1:20 A.M.

Gabe got out of their borrowed car, his gaze darting around the garage of Molly's apartment building while his eyes got used to the darkness.

Molly had run to a door that led to a flight of stairs, but as soon as she flung it open, she began backing up.

One of the intruders was forcing her backward, his gun pointed at her chest. *Oh God. Oh no. No, no, no.*

"Drop the gun," the man commanded. "Do it *now*, or your sister and the kid die tonight."

Molly's back was rigid, but Gabe couldn't see her face. He could, however, see her hand and watched, horrified, as she dropped her gun to the floor. *Maybe she has a backup gun.*

You have her backup gun. Do something!

The man shoved the barrel of his gun harder, and Gabe heard Molly's grunt of pain.

She was still wearing the Kevlar vest. *As am I.*

But at that range, she'd still be hurt if the man fired. Still, the thought of the Kevlar quieted his mind, and he crept quietly around the other cars so that he could get a better view of the intruder, all while wondering where Shoe was. *Just stay down, boy. Please.*

"We didn't expect you here," the man said. "We thought we'd only get your sister and the kid." His teeth flashed in the darkness as he grinned. "Bonus. Hey!" he yelled over his shoulder. "Got the—"

I don't think so. Gabe lifted the gun and fired, aiming for the man's shoulder. The noise echoed in the garage, and Gabe pressed his free hand to his ear. *That hurt.*

The man seemed to be hurt worse, though, slapping his hand to his neck as his knees folded, sending him to the floor.

Oops. Gabe had missed. But he couldn't care. The man was down. He might even die from such a wound.

Gabe found that he didn't care about that, either. This man had invaded Molly's home. Held her at gunpoint.

Not even hesitating, Molly scooped up her gun, grabbed the intruder's, and disappeared again into the stairwell. Gabe ran to catch up, relieved when Shoe popped up from behind one of the cars to follow them.

They passed another body as they climbed the stairs, a bullet hole between his eyes.

Please don't let that be Lucien, Gabe thought. *Please.*

Molly looked over her shoulder. "Shhh," she whispered without stopping, because there were sounds of an altercation coming from farther up.

He and Molly came to a landing and started up a second flight. When they rounded the stairs to the next landing, they found two men fighting hand to hand. The floor was covered in blood, the plaster on the walls chipped and broken with small holes everywhere.

Gun battle, Gabe thought grimly.

Molly ran soundlessly to the two men, grabbed the one on top by the collar and yanked him hard, sending him flying to his back. The man's clothes were soaked with blood. She went to grab him, but a flash of metallic black in the man's hand had her stepping back.

The bastard was pointing his gun at Molly's head, his finger on the trigger.

Before Gabe could make a sound of warning, Molly raised her gun at the man she'd thrown and shot him in the head.

Gabe ran to her side in time to see her murmur to the man who was still alive.

The injured man shook his head at whatever she said. He lifted one finger, then pointed at the apartment door. "One more. He has Chelsea. Hurry."

Molly ran to her apartment. Gabe started to kneel next to the man, who he assumed was Lucien, only to be waved away.

"I'll live. *Help her.*"

Gabe obeyed, following Molly into the apartment, where he stopped, stock-still. A fourth man had his gun pointed at a woman who stood at an interior door, a gun in her shaking hands, her face a mask of desperate fear mixed with determination. Molly's sister. Gabe remembered her from Molly's birthday dinner Sunday night, but even if he hadn't, the resemblance was clear. The door Chelsea guarded must lead to Harper's room. Fury boiled up from Gabe's gut and it was all he could do not to charge forward.

"Put the gun down, Chelsea," the man said smoothly, then called over his shoulder. "Mason! Get your ass in here. How many bullets does it take to put that damn dog down?"

Gabe froze. *Dog? Shoe? Shoe's dead?* No, he realized, nearly collapsing with relief when Shoe brushed up against him. The man didn't know about Shoe. The first guy hadn't seen the dog, hadn't mentioned him. *Didn't mention me, either.*

He must have meant Lucien.

"No," Chelsea said. "You won't touch my daughter. I will *kill* you."

The fourth intruder took another step forward. "We won't hurt you. Not if you cooperate."

Chelsea was deathly pale, her chest heaving as she struggled to breathe. She looked like she'd start hyperventilating any moment.

Molly had been standing frozen, watching. Calculating, Gabe realized. She crept forward, one finger pressed to her lips to silence Chelsea as she approached the man, her gun pointed up at an angle.

An angle that would bring it flush with the man's head when she got close enough.

Chelsea stiffened when she saw her sister, but rallied so quickly that the man didn't notice. "No, you aren't going to hurt me," she said. "I *will* kill you if you take a single step closer."

The man chuckled. "No, you won't. You can't." To prove it he took another step, then another. "See, Chelsea? You won't kill me."

Molly shoved her gun against the base of his skull. "No, but I will. Drop your fucking gun."

The man's body went rigid, but he didn't drop his gun. "You won't kill me, either."

"I've killed before to protect my family. I will do it again. In fact, all three of your men are dead. *Drop the fucking gun.*"

An ominous growl rumbled beside him and, before Gabe could grab him, Shoe darted into the room, teeth bared, going straight for the man and sinking his teeth into the bastard's leg.

The man screamed, contorting his body and kicking his leg to try to escape the dog's bite, but Shoe held on. Molly grabbed the wrist of his gun arm and twisted it, making him scream again. The gun fell from his hand to the hardwood floor and Molly brought his arm up behind his back, shoving him to his knees. Shoe followed the motion, going down on his belly, teeth still firmly planted in the man's calf.

Good boy, Gabe thought. *Such a good boy.*

"Other hand where I can see it," Molly commanded, the gun in her hand never wavering, still pressed to the man's head. "Gabe? He's got tactical restraints in his back pocket. Can you retrieve them?"

"Yes." He tried to move, only to find his legs had become like rubber. *Fall apart later. Move it now.* He took a step, then another until he was walking normally. He was a foot away, about to reach for the restraints, when the man twisted again, knocking Molly back. His free hand moved, something flashing silver.

Knife.

"Molly!" Gabe yelled and she jumped back in time to avoid the wide swipe of the blade. The man turned the knife on Shoe, but Molly was faster, shooting him in the arm. The blade fell to the floor just as the gun had.

"Shoe, release," Molly said and, surprise of surprises, Shoe obeyed.

Dad trained him well, Gabe realized, pride for his father warming his chest.

Molly simultaneously grabbed the zip ties from the man's pocket and planted her boot against the man's side before shoving him to his back. "Arms to your sides, asshole." Then she exhaled when he obeyed. "Well, shit."

Well, shit, indeed.

It was him. The man who'd impersonated Paul Lott. Who'd probably killed him. Who would have killed Xavier. *Who would have killed all of us.*

The man's eyes widened in shock before narrowing. "You," he hissed. "You're not supposed to be here."

Molly frowned then nodded briskly. "Because I'm supposed to be in the hospital? Surprise, asshole. I'm just fine."

So much for keeping a low profile. Pushing his own shock aside, Gabe knelt to gather the man's weapons and stepped back, giving Molly room to operate.

"Cover me?" she requested. "And shoot the fucker in the head if he so much as twitches."

"Gladly." Gabe aimed at the man's head, not allowing his gaze to wander at all.

"Roll to your stomach," she commanded, giving their captive a hard kick in the ribs when the man didn't comply. "Roll. Now."

"Fucking cunt," the man muttered, but he obeyed.

Gabe wanted to shoot him for the slur alone, but he managed to control himself. *Go, me.*

"Arms out," she snapped, then dropped to her knees when he did. One of her knees landed in the man's kidney, making him grunt, then moan.

She did that on purpose, Gabe thought, incredibly impressed.

Quickly she restrained his hands, then roughly flipped him to his back. "Who are you?" she demanded coldly.

The man pursed his lips, saying nothing. She gripped her gun and shoved it to his temple. "All three of the others are dead. Start talking or you're next. *Who. Are. You?*"

"Maybe he has ID in his wallet," Gabe said mildly.

Molly's gaze flicked up to him, then she laughed. "Shit." Gripping the shoulder of the arm she'd shot and making the man moan, she rolled him to his side so that she could get his wallet. "Here's his license. Gabe, you're a genius. He used a fake ID when he posed as Paul

Lott, so who knows if this one's real—but if it is, he's Nicholas Tobin."
She set the license aside. "Never heard of you. Who hired you?"

Tobin shook his head. "Kill me if you want."

But there was fear in his eyes. Molly hadn't missed it, either. "Gabe, can you check on my sister? You okay over there, Chels?"

"Yes," Chelsea said, the word coming out on a sob.

Now that the danger had passed, Gabe focused his attention on Molly's sister. She'd slid down the door and was huddled on the floor, her face pressed against her knees, her arms wrapped around her legs. The gun was on the floor at her side, and her body shook with sobs that broke his damn heart.

"Chelsea?" He knelt beside her, afraid to touch her. "I'm Gabe. Are you hurt?"

She shook her head without lifting it. "No. He . . . Oh my God."

He chanced a touch, gently stroking her hair, the same golden color as Molly's. "I know. I'm so sorry."

"Not your fault," she choked. Then shuddered out a breath and lifted her chin. And stared. "You're . . . Are you . . . Are you the chef?"

He had to smile. "I am. Gabe Hebert. I'm . . . well, I'm working with Molly."

She braved a smile back, but it was faint. "Nice to meet you, Gabe. I'm Chelsea."

He stroked her hair once more. "Where's Harper?"

She swallowed hard. "Behind the door." She tried to stand but was apparently suffering the same rubbery legs that he had. He extended a hand and helped her to her feet, waiting as she opened the bedroom door and rushed inside. "Harper? Baby?"

There wasn't a sound. Then Gabe heard it.

"Mommy?"

It was coming from the closet. Chelsea ran and flung the door open and once again, Gabe thought his heart would break. Harper had hidden herself under a pile of clothes. The clothes were shaking. Chelsea began pulling them off her until she revealed a small girl with golden curls, her eyes clenched shut, her little tearstained face scrunched up in fear.

She held a steak knife in her trembling hands.

"Honey," Chelsea murmured. "It's Mommy. Give me the knife." She slowly reached for the utensil, and the child gave it up willingly.

She'd had the knife in her room, Gabe realized, and his breaking heart cracked wide open. She'd been assaulted before and was prepared to defend herself.

She was only eight years old.

Suddenly the rage geysered out of him and he stalked from the room, ready to kick the sick sonofabitch Tobin in the head. Bad enough that the child had been hurt by her own father, but to be terrorized by this asshole . . .

Molly wasn't in the living room. But Tobin lay on his side, hands still restrained. His ankles had been bound as well and Molly had trussed him up with what looked like a phone charging cord.

"Molly?" Gabe called.

"With Lucien," she called back.

Good. No one was around to see him kick Tobin's brain in.

But then Molly rushed back into the room and his cell phone began to buzz. It was a number he didn't recognize, so he let it go to voice mail.

"We need to go," Molly said grimly. "Burke called 911 and the cops still aren't here. Something's wrong, and I don't want to wait around for more of these goons to come for Chelsea and Harper."

"What about Lucien?"

"He says he'll be okay, and André is on his way."

"But Lucien's bleeding."

Molly stopped in front of him, meeting his gaze squarely. "Lucien will last until André gets here and the medics come. He's sitting up, he's lucid, and he's telling us to go. With all of these gunshots, someone else will have called 911 by now. The cops are coming, and I don't know if they'll be good guys or not. We need to go. *Now.* Once we get Chelsea and Harper to safety, I'll come back for Lucien."

Gabe pointed at Tobin. "What about him?"

"André will take care of him. Come on. There's a fire escape in the back. I might need help getting Chelsea and Harper down it." She rushed to the bedroom, ignoring Tobin like he didn't exist, Shoe at her heels. "Chels, pack your meds. We're getting out of here. Now."

Gabe stopped, though, kneeling to whisper, "I would have killed you and not lost a wink of sleep." Although he wasn't so certain that was true. It was one thing to want to and quite another to have to live with having done so, as Molly could attest. He might have actually killed the guy downstairs, but adrenaline had the thought muted for the moment. He'd have to deal with that later. "Who are you working for?"

The man just grinned. "Enjoy the hours you have left, Hebert. There won't be many."

Gabe didn't answer, but knew they had to do something in case Tobin escaped again. He dug Tobin's cell phone from his pants pocket and held it up to the man's face before he could close his eyes.

The phone unlocked, and Gabe went straight to his texts. The most recent was the most damning, with instructions to head to Molly's address and invite the sister and niece for a "ride."

"Who's Jackass?" he asked, noting the name attached to the sender.

"None of your fuckin' business," Tobin snarled, struggling against his bonds, but to no avail. "Put my phone down. You're not allowed to look at it."

Ignoring him, Gabe took screenshots of the text, the sender's contact information, and the screen in Tobin's settings that listed all of the model numbers and stuff. He thought about what else that Antoine might need. *Oh.* Tobin's phone number would be nice.

He found that screen, took a screenshot, then sent all of the screenshots to Molly's burner. Then he wiped his prints from the phone. Using Tobin's own shirt to grip it without leaving more prints, he shoved it back into Tobin's pocket.

He knew that Antoine could probably unlock the phone without Tobin's face, and that they'd get a lot of information from it, but he didn't want to tamper any more with a crime scene than he'd already done. He didn't want to do anything that could corrupt the DA's case against the bastard. His father had drilled that into him. Good police work resulted in solid cases, which delivered unappealable convictions.

He'd have to trust that André would do the right thing. That the system would still somehow work. His father had given his entire life in the service of others. Surely that had to count for something.

Surely there were other cops who would do the same.

"Gabe?" Molly called urgently. "We need to go."

He took one last look at Tobin, allowed himself one last fantasy of killing the man, then he followed Molly to the fire escape.

Chelsea was waiting at the fire escape, balancing a trembling Harper in her arms along with a small overnight bag. Shoe hovered at her side, his nose pressed to the back of Harper's leg.

Gabe took the bag. "Can I carry Harper?" he asked.

Chelsea shook her head. "She's too scared."

Molly went down the first few steps, her gaze searching the darkness, her gun clutched in her hand. "Come on," she hissed. "*Now.*"

Chelsea started down the fire escape, but the stairs were steep and she wobbled. Spurred by Molly's urgency, Gabe scooped the child from Chelsea's arms. "Go," he told her. "Harper, I'm a friend of your aunt Molly's. My name is Gabe. This is Shoe. He's a good dog. We're going to get you downstairs, then I'll give you back to your mom. Okay?"

Harper's nod was faint, but clear, so Gabe hefted her to his hip and started down the stairs. Shoe followed, slowing when his paws skittered on the grated steps. "Good boy," he murmured when Shoe took the final four stairs in a single leap, his tail wagging.

When they got to the bottom of the stairs, he looked for Molly, who emerged from the garage, scowling. "Our borrowed car is gone," she said harshly.

"Somebody stole it?" Gabe demanded. "Who was left to do that? We took care of all of them."

"I don't know, and I don't want to take my chances that there's someone down here to catch us. Come on. We'll take Chelsea's car and hope they don't know our license plate numbers."

21

GABE HAD TAKEN only two steps toward the garage when he heard the quick tap of a car horn. Spinning toward the street, he saw their borrowed car—and Farrah getting out of the driver's seat to wave them over.

Molly put her arm around Chelsea, urging her along. "It's okay. She's a friend."

Gabe followed, poor little Harper's arms wrapped around his neck so tightly that he was having trouble breathing. But he let her. She was eight years old, and she was terrified.

She was just recovering from the last bastard who'd touched her. Her own father. She'd already heard two gunfights—when her father shot her grandfather and when her father had been shot by her aunt, who'd been protecting her mother. Now this? How would she ever feel safe again? He hoped like hell for a miracle, for Harper's sake. He knew few children her age and had no idea how their minds worked. Had no idea how much they could experience and . . . bounce back? Was that even possible?

Molly helped Chelsea into the back seat and Gabe handed Harper over as gently as he could. The child clung for a heartbreaking moment before leaping into her mother's arms. Molly got in after them and Shoe jumped in, all on his own, quickly moving over their feet to be closest to Harper. By the time Gabe was in the front seat, the dog had laid his head on Harper's knee.

Such a good dog.

"Buckle up," Farrah said. "We're out of here." She pulled away from the curb as a call came through on her phone. She answered, putting it to her ear. "I got them. They're okay. They came out down the fire escape." She glanced at Gabe, with a slight shake of her head. "Made more noise than a herd of elephants. I could hear them over the car's engine, but I didn't see anyone around, so I don't think anyone else did."

Gabe winced. "Sorry," he muttered.

Farrah just smiled, handing him the phone. "André wants to talk to you. Take a deep breath, Gabe. Everyone is okay."

Everyone but the bodies they'd left behind and poor Lucien, Gabe thought with a flutter of fear now that they were away from the scene. He thought about the man he'd shot. How he'd fallen. How much he was bleeding.

He suddenly knew exactly how Xavier had felt Monday night. *I might have killed someone.*

In fact, it was highly likely he'd done so.

But he didn't regret it. Not for a single moment. Because Molly was still breathing. "Hey," he said to André. "Where are you?"

"In Molly's apartment. I must have come up the stairs as you went down the fire escape. I nearly had a heart attack when I found the place empty. Do you have any injuries?"

"No. Thank God."

"Ask him about Lucien," Molly said from behind him.

"He's fine," André answered, evidently hearing her. "He's still bleeding, but Molly got the worst of it stopped before you guys ran."

Gabe should have known Molly wouldn't leave her colleague injured without trying to fix him up. "Good. I've been feeling guilty for leaving him."

"You did the right thing. Lucien can't make it down the stairs without a stretcher. Don't worry, I've got medics coming. Tell Molly that I found him on his hands and knees in her living room, holding his gun on that bastard she left hog-tied. He'd crawled in from the hallway."

"I'll tell her. What happened, André? Burke called the cops. Why didn't they come?"

"Good question," he said grimly. "I'm going to find out. And Mr. Tobin won't be escaping again. I promise you that."

Gabe really wanted to believe him. He knew that if it was at all under André's control, it would be true. "Thank you. Where are we going?"

"Back to our camp," André said. "I've called on a few guys I trust to stand guard. And Farrah's become very proficient with a rifle recently. Don't let her sweet smile fool you. That woman of mine is brave."

"Never a doubt," Gabe said truthfully. "Does Burke know where we are?"

"He will. I'm calling him as soon as I hang up with you. I'm waiting for my team to arrive to secure the scene. There's quite a lot of blood here."

"None of it ours. Just Lucien's and the pr—" He cut himself off from saying *pricks* because there was a child in the car, and his mother had raised him right. "And the men who came after Chelsea and Harper."

"I'll need your statements soon, but for now take a breath and try to relax. I'll make sure that Lucien gets to the hospital, but after that I have a lot of work to do. I may not call you for a while. And I'll need to interview you and Molly sooner versus later. I'll try to do it at our camp, but I may have to bring you two downtown. Can you ask her if there are security cameras?"

Gabe turned in his seat to see Molly stroking Harper's hair with a hand that trembled. "André wants to know if there are any security cameras in your building."

She nodded. "Several. One in the garage, one in the stairwell, and one at each landing. The feed is saved to a hard drive in the building owner's apartment, which is the unit below ours." Her hand abruptly stopped stroking Harper's hair, flying to cover her own mouth. "Oh God. Mr. Wilkins. I didn't even check on him. He's an old man. Can you have André see if he's okay? If he'd heard the gunshots, he definitely would have tried to help us. That he didn't? I . . . Please, just ask André to check on him."

"I'll do that right now," André promised when Gabe relayed the information. "So that I'm prepared, who is responsible for the three bodies I had to step over on my way up the stairs?"

Bodies. *Shit.* "Is the man in the garage—" He broke it off, not wanting to say *dead* around Harper.

"Dead?" André asked. "He is."

Shit. Shit. Shit. Gabe swallowed hard, bile burning his throat. *I killed a man.* "The, um, the man in the garage was mine, but I was aiming for his shoulder."

"Damn, Gabe." André sounded impressed. "The guy on the stairs?"

"Lucien."

"And the guy on the landing outside Molly's place?"

"Molly."

"That she didn't kill the bastard on her living room floor was a testament to her good nature," André muttered.

"His ID says he's Nicholas Tobin."

"I know. I saw it. He said that you tampered with his phone."

"I did not." He wasn't going to admit what he had done. He wasn't sure if texting screenshots from a killer's phone was illegal—although he'd killed a man, so how could anything be worse than that?

I killed a man. Oh my God.

"Okay," André said simply. "I'll check on the building owner down-stairs and let you know. Is there anyone living upstairs?"

Gabe asked Molly, and she shook her head. "Tell him that the third-floor unit is unoccupied right now."

Gabe relayed it, then thanked André again when he said the medics had arrived for Lucien. Ending the call, he gave Farrah back her phone. "He said he'd call when he could."

"I know the drill," Farrah said with the sweet smile that André had mentioned.

Pressing his fingers to his temples against a headache, Gabe looked to the back seat and found a little pocket of peace. Shoe had all but climbed into Harper's lap and she was petting him, her face pressed into the fur at his neck.

"Good boy," Gabe said softly, and Shoe's tail wagged. "He bit the man who was in the apartment."

"Good boy," Farrah echoed. "He's a hero."

Molly managed a tired smile and stroked Shoe's back. "He really is."

Gabe was startled by a buzzing in his pocket and retrieved his cell phone. Three missed calls, all from the same number that was calling him now. New dread settled on him like a shroud. "Hello?"

"This is Val, and Patty is okay."

Tears stung Gabe's eyes. *No more, please.* "What happened, and what number are you calling me from?" Although he was afraid that he already knew.

"We're at the hospital. Patty has a mild concussion."

Gabe scrambled to sit up straighter. "I'll come there now."

Farrah shot a concerned glance his way. "Go where?"

"Patty's in the hospital," he said, hearing his own fear.

"No, you will *not* come to the hospital," Val snapped. "For all we know, that's what they're hoping you'll do so that they can shoot you on your way inside. I said that she's okay, and I'm not lying to you. She's had a CT scan and everything."

"A CT scan?" Gabe asked, his voice ratcheting higher. "What happened?"

Two hands covered his shoulders, kneading softly. *Molly.* Hell of it was, her touch really helped. She was uniquely able to settle him.

"They sent two men after Patty," Val said. "I stopped them."

There was so much to unpack from those two sentences. "Where are they now?"

"On their way to the morgue," Val said flatly. "Like I said: I stopped them."

"Holy shit," he whispered, then remembered that Harper was listening and bit his tongue. "They sent four to Molly's."

"Holy shit," Val said, much more loudly. "That's discrimination!"

Gabe barked out a shocked laugh. "What?"

"They thought they could get by me with two and sent four to Lucien? That is gender discrimination, pure and simple."

Gabe blinked hard. "This night has been surreal."

"I guess it has," Val said quietly, and he realized her outburst had been to distract him. *Nicely done.* "Patty's sleeping. I'm in her room and nobody will touch her. I promise you."

"Do you need the hospital, Gabe?" Farrah asked.

"No, you do not," Val answered, having overheard. "I'm serious. One of those calls you missed was from Patty, because she wanted to tell you not to come. She did well, Gabe. Smacked one of the intruders with a frying pan upside his head. It was art in motion. I need to go now. Tell Molly that I'll call her later. You're all okay?"

"We are. Lucien is on his way to the hospital."

"Shit. Poor Burke. We're dropping like flies."

Gabe blinked. "We? What happened to you?"

The hands massaging his shoulders abruptly tensed, but Molly waited silently for him to relay Val's answer.

"Flesh wound," Val said dismissively. "Needed a few stitches and an antibiotic shot. The shot was the worst part. I'm fine. Patty's fine. Don't make Molly have to protect you here. Go somewhere safe and I promise to call you as soon as Patty wakes up. They'll have to wake her frequently anyway for the concussion, so it shouldn't be too long."

Gabe's throat tightened. *Not your fault,* he tried to tell himself, and logically he knew it was true. But too many people had nearly lost their lives tonight.

Because some fucker killed Nadia Hall during Katrina and is now trying to hush it up.

"Thank you, Val," he said hoarsely and ended the call. "Farrah, take us to the camp, please. Val says that Patty is resting, and that I'll create more danger if I visit her in the hospital."

"She's right," Farrah said firmly. "Close your eyes, Gabe. You, too, Molly. Rest a bit."

"In a minute." He twisted around in his seat so that he could see Molly. "I texted some screenshots from Tobin's phone to your burner. Can you send them to Antoine?"

Interest—and admiration—sparkled in her eyes. "Very nice, Gabe." She gasped softly when she checked her texts. "Motherlode. I wish we had his phone."

"I thought about taking it, but I didn't want to disturb the crime scene any more than we already did."

"Honey," Molly drawled, "we *made* the crime scene. Seriously, this is good stuff." She tapped on the phone's screen then nodded. "Sent them to Antoine. Hope he can work his magic." She sat back in her seat and resumed stroking Harper's hair. "Now we rest. I think we've all earned it. Chels, I was super proud of you tonight."

Chelsea's sigh was tremulous. She opened her mouth to say something, but, glancing down at her daughter, she closed it. "Thank you," was all she said, then chuckled wetly. "To you, too, Shoe. I think you made a friend in Harper."

Gabe felt suddenly exhausted. *Adrenaline crash.* He'd just close his eyes for a little while.

Lake Salvatore, Louisiana
THURSDAY, JULY 28, 3:15 A.M.

"Is she asleep?" Farrah murmured as Molly sat next to Gabe at the kitchen table of the cabin that they'd left only a few hours before.

Molly gratefully accepted the cup of tea that Gabe slid her way. It was good. It would have been even better with a healthy shot of whiskey, but this would do for now. "Yes. Chelsea's with her. They're both asleep. Shoe's lying next to their bed."

"That is one good dog," Farrah said with a smile.

"My dad trained him well," Gabe agreed. "He went after Tobin like he was a pork chop."

"And then he comforted Harper," Molly added. She rested her head on Gabe's shoulder when he put his arm around her. Despite the terror of the evening, she still had him by her side. It gave her comfort. "I'm so sorry, Farrah. We're putting you in danger."

Farrah waved a beautifully manicured hand. "I'm marrying a cop. Comes with the territory. It wouldn't be the first time I've been in danger, and it's unlikely to be the last. Your clothes are in the dryer, by the way. I didn't get all the bloodstains out, but they aren't too obvious."

Farrah had been generous, loaning them clothes while she washed the ones they'd been wearing. Now they wore T-shirts and sweats. André's clothes were a little big on Gabe, but Farrah's fit Molly pretty well. It was always nice to borrow clothes from another buxom woman.

She and Gabe had set their Kevlar vests aside to air out. They'd become ripe over the course of the day. But they'd put them on again when they left the house, no matter how bad they smelled.

Smelling like ass was way better than being dead.

"Thank you," Molly said, then turned to Gabe. "How's Patty?"

"She's good. I talked to her for a little while. Farrah let me use her phone so that no one would be able to trace the call to me. André put someone he trusts at her door and they'll escort her and Val back to Patty's house tomorrow when she's released. She was lucky. The bastard who grabbed her hit her head with the butt of his gun."

"Well, she did hit him with a frying pan first," Farrah commented dryly. "I can't wait to meet her. I think we'll be great friends."

"I think you will, too," Gabe said, then sobered. "She said that the leader of the two said that they needed to take her alive, but that they could kill Val."

Molly shuddered. "That's what Val said when I talked to her. But, then again, I guess they learned not to mess with a roller derby queen."

Farrah smiled. "That is *so* very satisfying. I hope Val hurt them both."

Molly sighed. "They're both in the morgue, so I'd say so. I mean, I'm not going to mourn them any more than I'm going to mourn the guys we took out, but now we can't try to turn them on each other in exchange for information. I hope Antoine's able to trace that phone number you got off of Tobin's phone."

Gabe scowled. "I should have just stolen it. I've been kicking myself ever since."

"You did the right thing," Farrah told him. "André will get it all sorted."

Molly personally agreed with Gabe's current assessment, but she wasn't about to disagree with Farrah in her own home. Or in her family's camp, anyway. Plus, Gabe's logic had been sound. If they tampered with evidence, Tobin might escape justice. Again.

Gabe shook his head. "I sure hope so." He glanced at the time on his phone. "Can we check in with Burke? I need to know that I didn't colossally fuck up by not taking that phone."

"He's in the waiting room at the hospital," Molly said. "Lucien's still in surgery and he doesn't have family except for us, so Burke's staying until the surgeon comes out with an update. Let's call Antoine instead. He'll be doing the real work on this anyway."

Farrah took out her own phone and dialed her soon-to-be brother-in-law. "Hey, it's me. I've got Molly and Gabe here, and they'd like an update."

"I might have been asleep," Antoine grumbled. "You should apologize for calling so late."

"But you weren't asleep," Farrah replied lightly. "You're on speaker."

"Hey, guys," Antoine said. "I was actually just about to call you. Let me link Burke in. He said to call him when I had info. He'll find a room there at the hospital that's private."

A minute later, Burke was on the line. "I need some good news," he said heavily. "Lucien's surgery's taking a lot longer than they thought. I don't know how he was able to make it into your apartment, Molly. Not with a bullet hole in his gut."

And she and Lucien would be discussing that later. He'd made it seem like his injuries weren't all that bad. Gabe might be second-guessing leaving Tobin's phone behind, but she'd been second-guessing leaving Lucien behind.

"I have some new connections," Antoine said. "First, good job, Gabe. I was able to use all the information you gave me to get into Tobin's cloud account."

"Oh, thank God," Gabe said on a rush of air. "I've been cussing myself to hell and back over that damn phone."

"No need, my man," Antoine said cheerfully. "It's all good. So . . . first, Nicholas Tobin has no priors and no criminal record. He has, however, been linked to several crimes. Because he's never been arrested, there are no prints on record. He didn't have his wallet the day he was caught following Xavier into the city. He must have been confident to have it on him today."

"Cocky bastard," Molly muttered.

"Lucky us," Antoine countered. "We'll have to see what the cops turn up when they search Tobin's apartment. He might still have Paul Lott's phone and laptop, so that would be evidence toward a murder charge. But again, luckily for us, I am awesome and have obtained both Tobin's *and* Paul Lott's cell phone records."

Farrah mimed putting her fingers in her ears. "I don't want to know, Antoine."

"No, you really don't," he said good-naturedly. "Okay. The texts you copied, Gabe, showed that Tobin was taking orders from someone else to kidnap Chelsea and Harper. The number those orders came from . . . wait for it . . ." He paused dramatically. ". . . *also* called Paul Lott's phone. Several times, in fact. Specifically, whoever ordered Tobin tonight also talked to Paul Lott for nearly thirty minutes on the night that your father was killed, Gabe."

"Oh my God," Gabe breathed. He pressed the back of his hand to his mouth, then looked down at Molly. "It's the first real *actionable* link we've had to Dad's death."

She took his hand and kissed it, feeling his excitement bubble through her as well. "I know. We're getting closer."

"Do we know who owns the phone that gave the orders for tonight's attempted kidnapping?" Burke asked.

"No. It's a burner. All we know is that Tobin had him listed as 'Jackass.'"

"*What?*" Burke nearly shouted, then muttered an apology for yelling. "Did you say Jackass?" he added in a whispered hiss.

"Yes," Gabe said. "That was the name on the text message. Do you know him?"

"Oh yeah," Burke said bitterly. "His name is Jackson M-u-l-e. Last name is Italian—pronounced 'Moo-lay'—but most of us grunts just called him Jackass. Though not to his face."

"What horrible parents," Farrah murmured, "to give him that name. 'Mule' was bad enough, but to add 'Jackson' to that was just irresponsible."

"How do you know him, Burke?" Molly asked.

"He's Cresswell's freakin' boss."

Molly was momentarily speechless, and she wasn't alone. She'd figured Mule was a cop, just not one of NOPD's brass. She shared a stunned
look with Gabe, then Farrah. "When I said I'd be looking for high-profile
connections in Rocky's cases, I had no idea it went that high up."

"Yeah," Burke said wearily. "We need to get this info to André right
away. He'll want more proof before he accuses one of their own, especially Mule, so I don't expect anything to happen quickly. If it happens
at all. I had no idea Mule was involved in anything dirty. He appears
squeaky-clean. Pinning anything on him is gonna be a hard sell."

"Don't underestimate André," Farrah said quietly.

"I never do," Burke said sincerely. "I trust him. I just hope that him
going after Mule doesn't tank his career."

Farrah looked troubled, but resolute. "He'll figure it out. And if it
does tank his career, he probably wouldn't have wanted it anymore,
anyway."

"Can we put someone on Mule?" Antoine asked.

"Yeah," Burke said. "Let me think. I'm going to have to move some
people around."

"I'll go," Molly said. "Give me his address, and I'll wait outside his
house and follow him if he leaves."

Gabe shook his head. "You're exhausted."

She shook her head. It didn't matter if she was exhausted. She was
going to surveil Mule. It was the right thing to do. She could feel it in
her bones. "We're close, Gabe. I can feel it. André is busy with Tobin,
and Burke doesn't have any more staff. Val and Lucien are in the hospital and his part-timers are guarding Xavier. It's going to be me."

Burke sighed. "Dammit, Molly. You're throwing logic my way again."

"No," Gabe insisted. "What about Phin?"

No, she thought, *not Phin. Not yet.* The man was still too volatile in
situations outside of his firm control. She didn't think he'd hurt anyone,
but he might have to take off to avoid doing so. Leaving himself vulner-
able and Mule unsupervised.

"Phin's . . . not ready," Burke hedged. "Molly, you go and watch Mule's house. He'll be at home this time of the night. Guys at his level don't do shift work. Once Lucien's out of surgery, I'll relieve you. Is that better, Gabe?"

Gabe grunted. "No, but if it's the best I can get, I'll take it. I'm going with you."

Molly considered protesting, then remembered how calm and collected he'd been earlier. He'd saved her life when he'd shot that first thug in the neck. "I'd like that," she said, then stopped herself. *My family.* She couldn't leave them. *What was I thinking?* Slowly she shook her head. "But I can't leave Chelsea and Harper alone."

Farrah harrumphed. "What am I? Chopped liver? They can stay here. I've got a rifle and André's trained me to use it. We ran into some trouble last year and I decided I needed to know how to defend myself. I'm no sniper, but I am a decent shot. Plus, André's got three of his own officers on their way. They'll be here within the next thirty minutes. We'll be fine."

Molly studied the other woman's face. "Are you sure?"

Farrah met her gaze. "Very sure. You're Burke's family, so you're our family, too. We'll keep Chelsea and Harper safe."

"Then thank you," Molly said fervently. "Thank you so much."

Farrah patted her hand. "You're welcome. I'll make some coffee and put it in a thermos. It'll help you stay awake."

Molly tugged on Gabe's hand. "Come on. We need to put our vests back on."

Gabe followed her to the room they'd been given and picked up the vest, wrinkling his nose. "We're not going to be able to hide from anyone. They'll smell us a mile away."

Molly chuckled. "Take off your T-shirt, Mr. Hebert." He did so, and she let her mouth water. Just a little. "You have a very nice chest," she said as she helped him into the vest and fastened the Velcro flaps.

He pulled her T-shirt over her head and looked his fill. She was completely bared to him, her bra in the wash. "So do you. Seems a shame to cover up such pretty breasts." But he followed her lead, helping her into her vest and fastening her up.

She moved her shoulders, trying to get more comfortable. It felt weird wearing the vest without a bra, but she wasn't about to ask Farrah to borrow one of those.

Boundaries, after all.

She handed him his T-shirt and they redressed. "You'll wear a helmet," she said. "I don't want to lose you."

He cupped her face in his hands and kissed her. "Same goes. No charging off by yourself like you did tonight. I nearly had heart failure when that guy pulled a gun on you."

She started to argue, then sighed. "I promise. You were pretty awesome there. You saved my life."

He kissed her again. "I'm glad you noticed. Now let's go. I want this whole nightmare over with."

She held on to his wrists, holding him in place for another few seconds before letting him go. *And then?* she wanted to ask. What would happen then? What would happen to *them* then?

But this wasn't the time to ask. This was the time to do her job. To keep assholes from trying to kill him and Xavier and all of their families.

Then. Then she'd ask and hope that he wanted *them* to continue.

The Garden District, New Orleans, Louisiana
THURSDAY, JULY 28, 5:00 A.M.

"It doesn't seem fair that Mule gets to sleep and we're sitting outside his very fine house not sleeping," Gabe grumbled. He was tired and cranky and—although he was really trying—unable to keep his thoughts to himself.

Mule's house was very fine. A mansion, in fact. With pillars in front and everything. The house had to have five or six bedrooms. It was too fine for a cop to afford, even one of the brass. Gabe's own father had lived in the same small house for Gabe's entire life. It didn't seem fair that a crooked cop got to live in a place like this.

Bitterness might have been adding to the crankiness, if he were being honest.

"So you've said," Molly said dryly. "Several times."

"I'm sorry," Gabe said on a sigh.

She reached over the console and patted his thigh. "It's okay. It's actually kind of nice to know that you have a flaw."

He smiled at her. "Just the one?"

"I haven't seen any others."

"There's still time," he said cheerfully.

Her smile bloomed into something so beautiful that he had to swallow hard to dislodge the sudden obstruction in his throat. "I'm glad," she said softly. "I was hoping that you'd want to . . . you know, continue after all this was over."

He grabbed her hand and squeezed it lightly. "Is that what the kids are calling it these days? If so, I definitely want to, you know, *continue*."

She grinned. "Good. Now that that's settled, sit back and close your eyes. I'll wake you up if anything exciting happens."

"No, I'll stay awake with you. Who knows if I'll have to save your life again?"

She snorted. "Rude." Then she jerked upright. "Shit. Here he comes."

Sure enough, Mule's garage door was opening, the taillights of a Range Rover glowing in the darkness.

She handed Gabe her burner. "Text Burke, please. Tell him that the target is moving, and we are in pursuit."

Gabe did as she asked, then waited for a reply, wincing when it came.

Goddammit. Of course the prick couldn't wait 15 more mins. I'm just leaving the hospital. Lucien is out of surgery and drs expect full recovery. Keep me updated with your location. BE CAREFUL.

Will do, Gabe texted back. "First, Lucien's going to be all right."

"Oh, thank God," she breathed.

Gabe had told her that first because he'd sensed how guilty she'd felt leaving him behind. "Second, Burke's annoyed that Mule didn't wait a little longer. He's on his way and wants us to leave bread crumbs so that he can follow us."

Molly lifted a shoulder, her gaze fixed on the Range Rover, which was now halfway down the street. She started the car, keeping the lights off as she began to follow. "Burke can track my phone. He's just being dramatic."

"He can track us?" That made Gabe feel much better. Not so alone.

"Antoine can. That was one of the purposes of the company burners. Antoine hands them out like candy on Halloween, and they're all tricked out to be little homing beacons."

"No pun intended?"

She frowned, then laughed. "Right. Halloween, tricked out. Got it. Definitely not intended. Apparently, exhaustion makes you cranky and brings out the horrible puns in me."

"Your one flaw," he said with a flourish, and she laughed again.

"Hush, now. I have to concentrate."

He hushed, watching how she pulled to the side of the road when Mule turned onto a more crowded road. She switched on her headlights and maneuvered them back into the traffic flow.

Mule drove straight through the city to one of the state highways and headed south, the surroundings already becoming more remote.

"He's headed into the bayou," Molly said, her jaw stiff. "Not sure if anything good comes from a trip into the bayou before dawn."

"Maybe he's going fishing?" Gabe asked sardonically, knowing that wasn't the case.

Molly's lips quirked up. "You sweet summer child. I'm thinking more along the lines of a clandestine meeting or a drug handoff or a body dump."

"I figured as much. I'll text Burke our location."

He did so, keeping the other man updated as Mule's Range Rover continued down the lonely road, abruptly pulling onto a side road. Molly kept going.

"We're not going to follow?" Gabe asked.

"Nope. He turned too suddenly. I think he's faking it. He'll be back behind us soon. If he's not, I'll backtrack."

Gabe's anxiety climbed a little. If they lost him . . .

But Molly was right. Soon enough, the Range Rover reappeared behind them, driving faster than the speed limit until it overtook them, passing on the left. Then they were following again.

Gabe checked the speedometer of their borrowed car. "He's in a hurry."

"Yeah, he is. I'm trying to keep up without being too obvious about it. I'd turn off my headlights, but it's going to be dawn soon and he'll see me anyway."

Gabe didn't say any more. They were driving entirely too fast for this road. This was how accidents happened.

He thought about Dusty Woodruff. The mortician had died after running off the road and hitting a tree. Had he been followed? Forced off the road?

Pain in his chest had Gabe pressing the heel of his hand to his sternum.

"You okay?" Molly asked quietly.

"Yeah. Just thinking about Dusty. I hope he didn't suffer."

"I hope not, too. I meant what I said, Gabe. I'll go with you when you pay your respects to his widow. You're not alone in this."

Another lump lodged in Gabe's throat. "Thank you." Then he leaned forward. "The road ends up here. There's a gate blocking anyone from going farther."

"He's going off road." She glanced at the map on her phone, then turned into the parking lot of the last local business on the road before it ended at the old gate. "I'm going to wait here for a few minutes."

She turned off their borrowed car's lights and they watched as Mule got out of his Range Rover and pushed at the gate. It swung open easily.

"He's got to be meeting someone," she murmured. "I wonder who."

"Are we going to find out?" Gabe asked, not sure how he hoped that she'd answer.

"You bet your fine ass we are," she said without moving her gaze from Mule, who had gotten back into his Rover and was going through the gate. He didn't bother closing it.

"He wants a quick getaway," she said. "Which is fine by me."

Leaving her lights off, she waited until Mule's lights were no longer visible before pulling out of the parking lot and following. "I needed to give him time to get a little ahead of us," she said. "Always a tightrope, following someone like this. Need to give them enough space to confidently get where they're going without arousing any suspicion."

The road had disappeared, becoming more of a beaten path, and Molly slowed their speed, rolling down the windows as she inched along. The air smelled earthy, already thick with humidity. They were very close to the bayou, yet Gabe could hear the roar of the Range Rover just up ahead, still driving way too fast.

He didn't say a word. He could barely even breathe.

This was significant.

This could be it.

We'll catch them, Dad.

He only hoped that he and Molly walked away once they had.

22

LAMONT GOT OUT of the car he'd stolen, looking east with a frown. The sun had started to rise. He'd hoped to finish this under the cover of darkness, but stealing a car to make the trip had taken more time than he'd expected.

He'd chosen a name from his list—a meth dealer that he'd helped evade charges a few years before. The man lived close enough to the bayou that it would be quick and easy to borrow his car, dump Ashley's body, then drive back and get his own vehicle. If anyone saw the sedan near the water's edge, it would fall back on the meth head.

All he'd wanted was the man to leave his keys in the car, which he'd told him when he'd called him shortly before his arrival. Unfortunately, the meth head had met him with a rifle and a demand for hush money.

So he'd had to take care of the idiot before taking his car and heading here, to the bayou. Now he needed to hurry.

It was still dark enough to hide his face, but he donned the zip-up hoodie anyway, snugging the hood over the ball cap he wore. One never knew when he'd encounter a fisherman out this early. Those guys were far too common in these parts.

And even if he didn't meet up with a fisherman, his skin would be mostly covered by the hoodie, keeping the worst of the gore out of his hair and off of his face. He'd discard the hoodie afterward. It would be pretty disgusting by then.

His hands were sweating from the leather gloves he wore, but there was no way he was taking them off and leaving fingerprints on the stolen car. He hadn't come this far to be stupid.

Instead, he pulled a pair of disposable gloves on over the leather ones so that they didn't get messed up. He liked his leather gloves. They were formfitting, allowing him to fire a gun while wearing them. He'd prefer not to have to throw them away, too.

Opening his trunk, he took out the smaller of the two boxes that he'd wrapped in silver paper. Ripping the paper away, he examined the box, top, sides, and bottom.

It was clean. No leaks. Triple-bagging had done the job.

He took the bag from the box and carried it to the water's edge. It was still quiet, but the bayou was waking up. Birds were starting to rustle, and fish were feeding on the bugs that swarmed on the water's surface.

It was deep here. Or, at least, it had been.

He frowned at the exposed roots of the trees, not remembering them from the last time he'd dumped a body in this waterway. It had been after Katrina, though. They'd come in a boat that night, but he'd returned once the floodwaters had receded.

Just to make sure that Nadia's body was truly gone. Luckily, it had been.

He hoped the water was still deep enough for what he needed it to do.

The first bag wouldn't be a problem. Ashley's fingers and toes would soon be fish food. He'd picked up a loose brick from a construction site after buying the knife set and had tied it to her torso, so it would sink. The gators would feast today.

Holding his breath, he opened the bag, held it over the water, and dumped it. Grabbing a downed tree limb, he pushed the torso into the water like it was a shuffleboard disc, then watched as it slowly sank.

One bag down, one to go. The next bag would be harder.

He got it out of the box, again making sure that he'd had no leakage. No leakage meant no fluids had soaked into the trunk's upholstery—in this car or in the one he'd taken from his own garage and left close to the home of this car's dead owner. Which meant that the cops would find nothing even if something terrible happened and he was suspected and investigated.

He might be. He didn't think that anyone at the office suspected that he'd been having an affair with Ashley, but Joelle had known, and she had proof. She hadn't been lying about the cameras in his study and the adjoining bedroom. He'd found them the night he'd walked Jackass from his study to the front door.

The cameras had been well hidden. Whoever she'd hired to install them had known their stuff. The cameras were still there, but no longer operational. He'd yanked the wires from each one. But if Joelle went looking, she'd see the cameras and wouldn't suspect a thing.

So, because of his dear wife, he needed to cover his tracks very carefully. He opened the second bag and had to turn his face away when he took an ill-advised breath through his nose. It had only been twelve hours, but the body had started to stink.

All the better for the gators. They'd come for the stink and stay for the buffet.

He reached into the bag, pulled out an arm, and flung it into the river. It made a satisfying splash, bobbing on the surface for a second or two before sinking.

Keep going. Just don't breathe. He didn't want to puke. That would leave DNA that he'd have to destroy.

Quickly he tossed another arm into the water, following it with all the pieces of her legs.

Now it was just her—

He hesitated, grimacing again. He didn't want to look at *it*, didn't want to see her face in its death rictus, but he couldn't just shove it into the water as he'd done her torso and he wasn't sure he had the stomach to fling it in like he had her limbs.

He reached into the bag and immediately yanked his arm out. *Gross. So gross.*

Stop being a pussy. Just do it.

He'd reached into the bag a second time when he heard a vehicle's engine, roaring through the quiet air. *Fucking hell. Shit, damn, fuck.* Someone was coming. Someone would see.

Gripping the bag, he moved back toward his car. To where he'd left his gun.

He grabbed the gun, cursing when his gloved hands, now slippery with Ashley's blood, slid uselessly over the gun's slide. Heart beating way too fast, he ripped the surgical gloves from the leather gloves he wore. He threw the surgical gloves into the bag along with the rest of Ashley's . . . remains.

Her head. Just say it.

Then he exhaled. It was Jackass's Range Rover. But then he tensed again.

What the hell was Jackass doing here? *And how did he know I was even here?*

Lamont racked the gun, chambering the first bullet as Jackass slowed to a stop. The man should not be here. He couldn't trust that this was anything good.

Grabbing the bag in one hand, he edged toward the water's edge once again. If worse came to worst he'd fling the whole damn bag in.

"Mornin', Monty," Jackass called, getting out of the vehicle. "Whatcha doing?"

None of your fucking business. "Fishing," he called back. "Why are you here?"

Leaving his engine running, Jackass sauntered closer, his eyes on the bag. *Not on my hand.* Which clutched the gun, ready to shoot if he needed to.

"What's in the bag, Monty?" The question was asked smugly, like he already knew.

"Supplies. Bait. You know."

"I think I do." Jackass stopped a foot away. "She heard you talking, didn't she?"

He blinked. "What?" How had he—

"You had to go and kill her, didn't you?" Jackass continued, shaking his head. "Even after we talked about it. It wasn't smart, Monty." And suddenly, Jackass held a gun.

Pointed at me.

"You're under arrest for the murder of Ashley Resnick," Jackass said calmly. "Drop the gun you're holding behind your back and put your hands behind your head."

Lamont took another step back. "How did you know?"

Because when he walked away from this, he'd need to know which leak to plug.

"I didn't until now, not for sure. I heard a gasp, right there at the end of our conversation, so I followed you once you'd left your house. I was really hoping that you hadn't killed her, but I figured you had. You're becoming predictable, Monty. But you did stump me when you switched vehicles, I have to say. Wasn't expecting that. But this was where we dumped she-who-shall-not-be-named. That this here"—he gestured to the bag—"was Ashley isn't that big a leap. Neither was my guess that you'd bring her here. You're nothing if not a creature of habit, Monty. So drop the gun."

"How did you follow me?"

"Trackers on all of your vehicles. For years. I know everywhere you've been, old friend. And everything you've done. Shame you had to kill the girl. She was an animal in bed."

"How—" His brain whirred as he processed this smug pronouncement. "You saw us?"

The man grinned. "In your very own home."

"You saw the video Joelle took."

Jackass laughed. "Who do you think installed the cameras? I did it as a favor to a good friend because she was *so* devastated that her husband had strayed." His expression became grim. "You've become a liability, but killing your mistress *again* is crossing the line. You were useful to me for a time, but cleaning up your messes has become inconvenient for my career." He gestured with the gun. "Drop your gun."

Fucking bastard. No way am I dropping my gun. I'd never make it out of here alive. He'll kill me, saying that I was "resisting arrest." Instead, he flung the bag at Jackass, hitting him square in the chest.

And the . . . *thing* . . . the *head* . . . rolled out, landing on the ground with a wet squelch.

Jackass was distracted—for just a moment, but that was all the time Lamont needed. He brought his arm up and fired.

Jackass staggered back, but no blood appeared on his white shirt.

Fucking Kevlar.

The man was righting himself, shaking off the pain of the impact, so Lamont fired again.

Right between the eyes. *Yessss.*

Jackass dropped like a rock.

And now he had to dispose of his body as well, dammit. At least he'd kept the cleaver. He'd planned to bury it somewhere when he'd finished disposing of Ashley's body.

Better get started. Day's a-wastin'.

Ignoring the shaking of his hands, he went back to his trunk for another pair of surgical gloves. There was no way he was touching that . . . *head* without them. His leather gloves were expensive, after all. He set the gun down, then pulled on the second pair of gloves.

Then spun when a twig snapped behind him.

Two people stood there, a man and a woman. The man he recognized, and for a moment he flinched. *Rocky Hebert.*

No. Not Rocky. Rocky was dead. This was Gabe, the son. That meant that the woman had to be the lady PI, Margaret Sutton.

He blinked in shock for a long moment. She couldn't be here. She was supposed to be in the hospital. With a concussion. Jackass had said so.

It appeared that Jackass had been wrong, because here she was.

This wasn't good.

Both Sutton and Hebert held guns. The woman had hers pointed at Lamont's heart, and he wasn't wearing Kevlar, dammit. The man was more of a threat, however. Gabe Hebert held a gun in one hand, his cell phone in the other. And he seemed to be recording.

At least I'm wearing a hoodie. He lowered his head, making sure his face wasn't visible.

Run. Run. Run.

"Put your hands on the back of your head," the woman said, her eyes narrowed. "*Now.* Gabe, step back and give me some room. And keep recording, please."

Rocky's boy complied, his lip curling in an angry sneer. "You fucking *killed* him. That wasn't yours to do."

"And whose was it, boy?" he asked in a tone much deeper than his normal, watching the woman from the corner of his eye. Waiting for her to be distracted.

Her eyes were still narrowed. No . . . they were squinting. The rising sun was right behind him. She could probably see well enough to shoot him, but she was concentrating really hard.

Distraction. He no longer held the bag with Ashley's head. He needed something else. Something that would make her flinch. *Just for a second.*

"No one's," Gabe spat. "He killed my father. He should be in prison, and now you've ruined it."

Well, that was one bright spot. *Rocky's boy doesn't suspect me of killing his daddy. And if I have my way, Gabe will have no idea of who I am.*

All of his co-conspirators were dead. All he had to do was get away, and he'd be fine.

Everything would be fine.

"Hands behind your head," the woman said again. "I've already shot someone tonight. I really don't want to make it a habit."

Oh, isn't she simply hilarious? She wasn't looking away from him, her concentration fierce. If she'd meant to shoot him, she would have.

She was waiting for backup. *Fucking hell.*

He was going to have to create his own distraction. It was Hail Mary time.

He bowed his head and . . . charged, knocking his head into her torso. She stumbled back, her gun firing, but the bullet went straight up.

He heard Gabe shout, "Molly!" before running to her side.

It was the only opportunity he'd have to escape, and it wasn't a big one because Molly was already getting up. He grabbed his gun from the car's trunk but didn't have time to get out his keys and start his own damn stolen vehicle, because the woman was now firing at him.

He zigzagged as he ran for Jackass's Range Rover, with its still-running engine, avoiding her first two shots. He turned and fired back, his shot going wide, but it bought him the few seconds he needed to get to the far side of the Rover, which was pointed toward the water. Using the vehicle as a shield, he shot back, missing again.

And again. He kept missing while her bullets kept coming closer and closer.

He fired again and . . . nothing happened. Just an ominous click. A jam. *Goddammit.*

For a few seconds, he tried to clear the chamber, but his hands were shaking and she was coming closer.

Run. Just run.

He'd climbed into the driver's seat when a bullet shattered his front passenger window.

He threw Jackass's SUV into reverse and floored it, escaping the next four bullets. He turned the wheel, swerving toward the road before shoving it into drive, flooring it again, hunching down again as a final bullet shattered his back window.

Could have been a helluva lot worse.

He careened around the curves, spotting a sedan parked on the side of the road. That had to have been the car that Hebert and Sutton had driven here. If he'd had time, he'd have shot it to pieces. But he didn't have time, so he kept driving like a bat out of hell until the highway approached.

Freedom. He fought the urge to holler a triumphant whoop, focusing instead on the road.

And then he scowled. "I should have run them over," he snarled aloud. *Why didn't I run them over?* But it was too late now.

Especially since two SUVs were headed the way he'd come. The SUV in front looked like a cop car. If the driver had seen his broken windows, he was sunk. Quickly he switched off his headlights and pulled into the parking lot for a swamp tour company—the last business on this road. There were already a few cars parked in the lot, so he wouldn't stand out. He rolled down the side windows, hiding the damage they'd sustained, but there wasn't anything to be done about the back window that was pebbled to hell and hanging on to the frame with a prayer.

Holding his breath, he watched as the SUV and the truck passed him by and turned onto the side road.

Guess it was a good thing that I didn't linger. But they'd figure out soon enough that they'd let him escape. Gabe and the woman he'd called Molly would tell them. The driver of the SUV would put a BOLO out on the Rover and every cop in the area would be looking for him.

He'd killed their boss. They'd be frothing at the mouth for a chance at him.

Gotta ditch the Rover. Luckily, he wasn't too far from where he'd stolen the car that he'd left at the water's edge with Jackass's body.

Everything was going to be fine.

Bayou Barataria, Louisiana
THURSDAY, JULY 28, 6:40 A.M.

"Well, shit," Molly muttered, as the Range Rover's taillights disappeared. "This sucks."

"At least you're okay," Gabe said. "Better than that guy over there."

"True. You still recording?"

Gabe checked his phone. "No. I must have stopped it when I ran to you. Should I restart?"

"Maybe in a minute." Molly turned to study the body, not taking any steps closer. "The ground's wet here. There might be footprints."

"For who to collect?" Gabe asked. "André or Antoine?"

Their answer came a moment later as two cars came speeding down the road. One was a black SUV, the other, Burke's blue Escalade.

"I think the first SUV is André's," she said. "So . . ."

"Once again we're caught with a corpse," Gabe said heavily. "And this one's a cop."

Indeed he was. One of the top cops, in fact. "Mule's corpse isn't ours, though. The security cams in my building will show that we shot the others in self-defense. Your video will show that someone else shot Mule."

Gabe's gaze turned a fraction, his eyes widening as he grew frighteningly pale. "Oh my God. Molly."

She pivoted to look to where he was focused. *Oh dear Lord.* She fought the urge to gag at the remains the man in the hoodie had flung at Mule. "Just . . . don't look at it, okay?"

But Gabe didn't move. "Is that a . . ."

"Yes. It's a head." A female's head, if the hair was any indication. Hoodie Guy had clearly been disposing of a body. She gripped Gabe's biceps, tugging until he turned away from the grisly sight. "Stay here and try not to pass out, okay? But if you do, no one will blame you."

Molly walked toward the two new vehicles, squaring her shoulders.

She holstered her gun and met André and Burke halfway. "Mule's dead. We didn't do it. The shooter got away in a Range Rover."

André's jaw clenched. "Dammit. Give me a second to call in a BOLO."

She waited until he was done before explaining. "Some guy in a hoodie shot Mule. The two were arguing about something, then Hoodie Guy flung a bag at Mule, distracted him, then shot him twice— once in the chest and once in the head. We approached then, but . . ." She sighed. "It's my fault he got away. I had my gun trained on him, but he charged, and I wasn't expecting that. He knocked me down and . . . I guess I'm tired. My reflexes weren't what they should have been. I shot at his tires as he was driving away, and I hit them, but he kept driving."

"Probably had run-flat tires." Burke lightly grabbed her shoulders and checked her over. "But you're okay? You and Gabe?"

"Yes," she said with disgust. "Hoodie Guy grabbed a gun from the trunk of that car parked over there and ran."

André was shaking his head. "Fucking hell, this is a mess. I'm glad he didn't shoot you, Molly, but why didn't he?"

"He did shoot at me but kept missing, and then he stopped. I was shooting at him as he ran. I don't know. Maybe he lost his nerve?"

"His gun jammed," Gabe said. "I saw him trying to clear it right before he got in the Range Rover. At that point I was more afraid he'd use the SUV to run us down."

"Or to force you into the water," André agreed. "All right. Y'all stay back here, and I'll take a look at Mule. I need to be sure he's dead and doesn't need the medics." His body was rigid as he approached the dead cop.

"Oh, he's for sure dead," Molly muttered, then smacked her forehead. "André, Gabe got the whole thing on video."

André stopped short and hurried back to them. "Let me see."

Gabe hit play, turning the screen so that Burke and André could watch. When it was over, both Burke and André looked relieved.

"This is gonna save y'all's bacon," Burke declared.

André nodded. "Absolutely. Too bad we can't hear what they were saying, though."

"We didn't want to get any closer," Gabe said apologetically. "But then he was going to . . ." He grimaced, swallowing hard. "That thing he threw at Mule was a woman's head. He was going to throw it into the water."

"Of course he was," Burke murmured, his voice gone thick. "We need to find out who he was disposing of."

André made an unpleasant face. "Yeah. Stay here. Just so you know, I have backup coming. Send that video to the cloud. I wouldn't want it 'accidentally' erased before we can use it to clear you of any suspicion here."

Molly watched as André knelt by Mule's body and pressed two fingers to his throat.

"It's my fault the man in the hoodie got away," Molly said quietly to Burke. "I was too tired to do this, and my reflexes had gone to shit."

"Shut up," Burke said, putting an arm around her in a brief side hug. "You stopped him from disposing of evidence. Don't be so hard on yourself."

"Thank you," Gabe said, with a hint of sharpness. "She'll be blaming herself from now till doomsday."

One side of Burke's mouth lifted. "You know her pretty well already."

Molly felt her cheeks heating, which was ridiculous under the circumstances. "Did you send the video to your cloud account, Gabe?"

"Already done. And I sent a link to Antoine so that he could view it."

Burke's half smile became a grin. "Damn, boy. You'd make a good PI."

Gabe shook his head. "No, sir. I'm going to be a boring chef for the rest of my natural life."

Molly caught a sudden movement in André's direction and barely stifled a shriek. "André!"

Because a gator—a fucking big gator—was climbing out of the water and headed for the head.

André whirled and fired, his shots intentionally going wide, all hitting the water around the gator. Burke ran to André's side and added his own fire.

The gator slithered back into the water and André stumbled back, Burke righting him with a hand to the cop's back.

"Holy hell," Gabe whispered weakly. "Just . . . goddamn. This day keeps going on."

"I should have helped them," Molly said, trying to ignore the way her entire body was now shaking. "But I can't seem to make my legs move."

It had been a fucking long day, and she was spent, her legs like jelly.

"Then stay here with me." Gabe put an arm around her waist, encouraging her to lean on him. Which felt so nice. "You've saved enough people for one day."

They stood there together, watching as André gingerly pulled the victim's remains away from the water's edge. Then he seemed to freeze.

Molly took a step forward. "I wonder if André knows the victim. Or Burke," she added when her boss crouched at André's side.

Gabe followed as she walked toward the scene, her steps careful so that she didn't contaminate any other evidence that the man in the hoodie might have left behind.

"You know her?" she called.

"Yeah," Burke called back over his shoulder. "Stay where you are." She and Gabe stopped, waiting until Burke joined them. "Well, Xavier and Carlos's plan of calling yesterday's visitor is now toast."

Molly sighed. "The woman who claimed to be Nadia Hall's sister, but who gave you all the wrong names?"

Burke's nod was short. "Yeah. Her."

Molly leaned her head on Gabe's shoulder. "I'm really tired, Burke." And she might even have a bruised rib or two. Hoodie Guy had a hard head.

André pointed to his SUV. "Get in the back seat and take a load off. I'd planned to interview you at the camp, but I'm gonna need to do this by the book. Give me your phone, Gabe. I'll keep it safe."

Unsaid was the alternative. If cops swarmed this place, someone who was not their friend might take Gabe's phone, and he'd never see it again.

Gabe gave the phone to André, who pocketed it. Then the chef turned crime fighter gave her his arm and helped her into André's SUV.

"One of these days we'll have us a real date," Gabe said lightly as he put his arm around her shoulders and pulled her close. "I'm pretty sure we can do better than this."

Surprised, she huffed a laugh. "I'm pretty sure that's true." She sobered, trying to think clearly. "We're going to be interrogated. André calls it an interview, but let's be honest—they're going to hit us hard with questions we're going to have to answer. I wonder if we should call Willa Mae to represent us, just in case."

Gabe kissed the top of her head. "Might not be a bad plan. Give me a minute to catch my breath and I'll make the call."

"You can't. André took your phone."

"Oh, right. Then you make the call. You've still got your burner, don't you?"

"I do." She distanced herself from Gabe only long enough to find her burner. "I don't have her number, but I do have Antoine's. Someone's going to have to get her from Burke's place if she's able to legally represent us. I don't know if she's licensed to practice in Louisiana, or if that was just theater the day she took the dollar to represent Xavier."

"Which was only Tuesday," Gabe said glumly. "Feels like a year ago."

She patted his thigh. "Don't get discouraged, Gabe. We're figuring stuff out."

He sighed. "Not fast enough."

Bayou Gauche, Louisiana
THURSDAY, JULY 28, 9:00 A.M.

"No." Cicely turned on her heel and walked into Burke's kitchen, a woman on a mission.

A mission to avoid her son, who was just about going out of his damn mind.

Xavier looked at Antoine, who'd arrived in a boat to escort Willa Mae to the police station where both Molly and Gabe had been detained. *While I sit here doing abso-fucking-lutely nothing.* "Come on, man. Take me with you. I need to help."

Antoine gave him a look of sympathy. "I get it, but I'm with your mom on this one. At this point, you are too valuable a witness to lose. You are not safe out there. I'm sorry."

Xavier crossed his arms over his chest, fighting the urge to pout. "I was five years old when I saw Nadia Hall murdered. Nobody's gonna take my word for it anyway."

"You'd be surprised," Willa Mae said, pausing in the hallway. She wore a suit. And heels. And pearls.

"You look nice, ma'am," Xavier told her. "Very lawyerly."

She snorted. "I should. I was a lawyer for more years than you've been alive."

"How did you know to bring a suit, Miss Willa Mae?" Carlos asked. "We just ran from town with the clothes on our backs."

"Yeah," Manny chimed in. "Are you clairvoyant or something?"

Willa Mae gave them a fond smile. "No, although I wish I were. I just figured that you boys might need an attorney after the fine mess y'all've gotten yourselves into."

Xavier's brows shot up. "We didn't *get ourselves* into any—" He cut himself off when he saw the sparkle in the older woman's eyes. "You're just messin' with me."

"Only a little. Now, you listen to an old lady. Your mother needs you. She needs you alive, she needs you whole, and she needs you to sit with her and hold her hand. I know you feel like you need to do something. At this point, *that's* what you can do. You can help your poor mama get through this. She's keeping a stiff upper lip, but she is falling apart inside." She gave his cheek an affectionate pat. "Be the man that I know you are and take care of your mother. Stop this feeling sorry for yourself. Not that you don't have a right to," she added. "But it isn't going to help you or the woman sitting at Burke's kitchen table trying her best not to cry."

Xavier bowed his head for a moment before nodding because Willa Mae was right. "Yes, ma'am. But please let us know what's happening."

"Kid, you know everything we do," Antoine said. "That Lott's impersonator is Nicholas Tobin, that the *grand fromage* was Mule, and that some dude in a hoodie offed him, then ran."

"*Grand fromage?*" Manny asked.

"Big cheese," Willa Mae supplied, and Manny laughed while Xavier shook his head.

"And the dude in the hoodie was feeding a body to the gators," Carlos inserted helpfully. "You can't forget that part."

"I was trying to," Antoine said with a grimace. "This is why I'm not a cop. I don't have the stomach for such things. You ready, ma'am?"

"I am, indeed. I'm leaving, Cicely," she called over her shoulder. "I'll call you when I know something. For now, don't worry. They're just being interviewed. André said that Gabe has video evidence that they didn't have any part in this morning's murder."

"This morning's murder," Xavier said with a sigh. "Now we're labeling the murders to keep track. I don't even know how many there've been."

"I know," Carlos said. "I've been keeping a list."

"Of course you have," Xavier muttered. "So? How many?"

Carlos took out his phone and counted. "Fifteen, starting way back at the beginning. Nadia Hall, Rocky, Dr. Benson, and Paul Lott. Then the guy who you shot, Xavier, but who somebody else—who was *not* you—actually killed. Eckert the hit man, the pathologist, the mortician, the three guards who attacked Molly's family, the two that Val took out, the lady who pretended to be Nadia's sister, and Mule. Fifteen."

"Text that list to me, Carlos, if you would," Willa Mae requested. "I've got to go now. Gabe and Molly are waiting for me." She gave a little wave, then followed Antoine to the boat.

A minute later, the boat's engine roared to life and they were gone.

Xavier went to the kitchen, where his mother sat with her hands folded on the table. Sure enough, her eyes were red and wet, and Xavier felt about three inches tall. "I'm sorry, Mama."

"So am I." She patted the chair beside her, and Xavier sank into it. "I'm proud that you want to help, and I'm sorry that I cut you off with no explanation."

"It's okay. Miss Willa Mae explained it all just fine."

Cicely smiled weakly. "She's good at that. I didn't know that she'd kept up her license here and in Texas, but I'm glad she did, for Molly and Gabe's sake."

"I hate that they're in trouble because of—" He stopped himself from saying *me*. "Because of all this."

His mother was not fooled. "Good catch there, son. You are as much a victim of all of this as anyone else. Probably more. You think you're not helping, but you are. Without you, nobody would have known to look for Nadia Hall. And your turn is coming, Xavier. When Molly and Burke and André unravel all of this craziness, you're going to be called on to testify. That's not going to be easy."

"Testify against who?" Xavier asked, so very frustrated. "Everyone's dead."

"Not the man who killed Mule," Cicely said quietly. "If that man wearing the hoodie was disposing of the body of the young woman who came to see Burke—who was definitely involved in some way—then he's involved, too. We just don't know how yet. And we don't know who Nadia's lover was back then. It might have been Mule or someone else. We just don't know."

No, they didn't know. But they might be able to help find out. "I have an idea about what we can do while we're waiting. Carlos! Manny! Can you come in here?"

Seconds later, the brothers were crowded around him. "What's up?" Carlos asked.

Xavier motioned for them to sit. "I was just thinking that there's something we can do. Remember when we were brainstorming last night?"

Carlos blinked. "Yeah, that really was just last night. Yes. I remember. Why?"

"Remember when Gabe was petting Shoe and asked Molly, 'What about the dog?'"

A slow smile spread over Carlos's face. "We're going to call all the veterinarians in New Orleans."

Xavier nodded. "Yes, we are."

Manny took out his phone. "I got my burner and it's got a full charge. Let's do this."

Xavier glanced at his mother to gauge her reaction. She was nodding. "I'll look up the names and numbers on my phone," she said. "You boys can make the calls."

Xavier held up a hand. "Hold up. We know now how easy it is to trace our calls."

"I already knew," Carlos said smugly.

Xavier found he could still smile. "I'm sure you did. Those crime shows you love have served us all well. Do you know how to make it look like we're calling from different numbers?"

"Spoofing," Cicely said, and they all stared at her. She frowned. "What? You don't think I know stuff? Spoofing is when you fake the number you're calling from. One of the nurses did it when she was harassing her ex-boyfriend. She got in trouble for doing it, just so you know."

"But we wouldn't be doing it for any illegal reasons," Manny said. "Plus, they'd have to catch us first, and this is an untraceable phone. Let me pull up a spoofing website." He gave Cicely a nod. "Nice job, Mrs. M."

She reached across the table to pat his arm. "Thank you, Manny. It's nice to be appreciated."

Xavier tapped the table until she met his eyes. "I appreciate you, Mama. More than I can ever say."

Her eyes filled again, and she waved him away. "Hush, now. We have work to do."

23

LAMONT STRAIGHTENED HIS tie, his hand pausing on the doorknob. He stared at his office door, psyching himself up to enter. He was showered, dressed, and ready to start the day.

Usually that meant paperwork and a slew of meetings.

Today that meant first figuring out how much the cops knew. How much of his face had been captured on that video?

Damn that Gabe Hebert and damn his fucking phone.

Damn his own gun, jamming on him when he'd needed it most.

I should have run them over. Why didn't I just run them over?

He'd panicked, pure and simple. He couldn't fight, so flight had taken over. And if he didn't figure out a way out of all of this, his fit of panic would be the thing that ended him.

The murder of Jackson Mule was all over the news, but the details were scant. City movers and shakers were crying crocodile tears over the "loss of a great man."

Bullshit. Jackass had been nothing more than a bully. A stupid, ham-handed bully.

He got the drop on you, so maybe he's not so stupid after all?

Shut up. Just . . . shut up.

"Lamont? Got a minute?"

He turned toward the man moving toward him. Jean-Pierre, Ashley's new boss. He hated dealing with him, because he knew all that squeaky-cleanness had to be a front. Other than using his more suitable, French-sounding middle name to get in good with the locals, *Kaj* Jean-Pierre was a damn choirboy. *That boy is no more squeaky-clean than I am.* Trouble was, Lamont had never been able to find proof to that effect.

"Jean-Pierre. What can I do for you?"

"I'm looking for Ashley. She's late to work and I desperately need the brief that she was working on yesterday. She must have saved it to her hard drive, because it's not on the server. If I can't find her, I'll have to get a network admin to unlock her computer. Have you seen her?"

"I sure haven't," Lamont lied smoothly. He entered his office, Jean-Pierre on his heels.

Carrie looked up from her computer, her mouth curving in a polite smile. "Good morning, sir." She rose and took Lamont's jacket, hanging it on the back of the door. "Coffee?"

"Yes, please." He'd have preferred a bourbon to relax his tense muscles, but not here at work. He turned to give Jean-Pierre a pointed glare. "She's not here. You should look elsewhere."

The other man ignored him. "Carrie, have you seen Ashley?"

"No, sir. Not this morning. If I see her, should I tell her that you're looking for her?"

"Yes, please," Jean-Pierre said, sounding frazzled, then left muttering, "Dammit."

"That man is rude," Lamont said dismissively.

"He's not so bad," Carrie said with a fond smile. "Once you get to know him, anyway. He's just intense. He'll calm down once he's more used to the pace down here."

Because *Kaj* had come from New York City. That was enough reason to distrust the man.

Putting Jean-Pierre out of his mind, Lamont gave Carrie a list of the
briefs he needed for the day and shut the door to his office. Finding it
empty, he sighed quietly in relief.

He'd feared, deep down, that someone with a badge would be waiting for him, but so far, so good. If they had seen his face on that damn
video, they'd have been here with handcuffs.

He remembered the way the woman's eyes had squinted. The rising
sun had blinded her. Hopefully it had cast any visible part of his face
in enough shadow that the video was useless.

Should have run them over.

Shoulda, coulda. You didn't. So move on.

He turned on his computer and checked the news feeds. The media
didn't have a copy of the video, thank the good Lord. Jackass's little
toady, Cresswell, might know something, though.

And it would look weird if he didn't call, right? Seeing as how he
and Jackass were known to be friends.

Using his desk phone, Lamont dialed Cresswell and, surprisingly,
the man answered.

"Lamont, what can I do you for? If you can make it fast, I'd appreciate it. I don't have much time. Everything is nuts here this morning,
what with Mule's murder and all."

"I expect so," Lamont said, laying the sadness on thick. "That's why
I'm calling. What the hell happened? Do you know who did this?"

"No. Just a guy wearing a hoodie. Looked like he was covering
up another murder. But we'll be pullin' out all the stops, I promise
you that. We'll find who killed Mule and may God help him when we
do. Everyone here is so angry that I doubt the bastard will make it to
trial."

"I hope you find him," Lamont said with a heavy sigh. "I'll let you get back to it. If you could update me when you hear anything? I'd be appreciative."

"Of course. And look. I'm sorry about Mule. I know y'all go way back."

Went way back. Because Jackass was no longer the albatross hanging around his neck.

"Thank you. I . . . Well, I just haven't processed it yet. It doesn't feel real."

"I know," Cresswell murmured. "Things are gonna change around here."

It didn't sound like Cresswell was too excited for those changes, and why would he be? The man had been permitted to do whatever he'd wanted for too many years. Depending on who replaced Jackass, someone might be riding herd on Cresswell for once in his miserable career.

"I'll let you go," Lamont said. "Stay strong."

"You, too. See ya, Lamont."

He ended the call and breathed another sigh of relief. Cresswell might not be privy to everything, but he had worked for Jackass for a lot of years. The man would know if a killer was suspected.

Home free.

Except for Xavier Morrow and Gabe Hebert. He'd allowed Ashley and Jackass to distract him from the real goal—eliminating all witnesses. Gabe Hebert hadn't seen him kill she-who-shall-not-be-named, but he knew altogether too much about the murder of his daddy.

He needed to find Morrow and Hebert, and he needed to do it quickly.

They'd be on double alert, especially if the lady PI had gotten a look at Ashley's head. They already suspected that Ashley's visit had been a ruse. Hopefully they were still chasing their tails when it came to the bogus ID of the woman Morrow had seen being killed.

Then he frowned. *Wait just a damn minute.*

Why had the Sutton woman been there this morning? Beyond the fact that she was *supposed* to have been in the hospital, how had she known to follow Jackass into the bayou? That didn't make any sense.

Unless . . .

He checked the arrest reports from that morning, then closed his eyes, struggling to hold his temper. *Fucking hell.*

A man had been arrested in the wee hours of the morning for breaking and entering with intent to kidnap. The address was an apartment in the Central Business District.

Home to one Chelsea Sutton. Same last name as the lady PI. What had Jackass said? *She has a sister and a niece.* Jackass was supposed to have sent in enough men to overpower the guy Burke had installed as their bodyguard.

Lamont checked the local news website, then dropped his head back with a sigh. The break-in at Sutton's apartment was right under the headline about Jackass's murder. Three dead outside Sutton's apartment, one man arrested. Nicholas Tobin.

Lamont had never met the man, but he knew the name. He'd made it a point to know everything about Jackass over the years. Tobin was Jackass's son with his own mistress—one he hadn't killed for getting pregnant because the woman had been paid for her silence.

Not like Nadia. Nadia hadn't accepted his money. Nadia had insisted that she'd tell. Which was why Nadia was dead. If she'd just been reasonable, he wouldn't be in this mess now.

Lamont returned to the search results on the local news website and, teeth grinding, clicked the next headline. *Two men killed in attempted abduction.* The two men had broken into the home of local restaurant owner Patience Hebert. Both men were found dead upon arrival of the police.

Jackass's men had fucked up royally.

I would have liked to have rubbed it in his ugly face. Too late for that now.

It seemed no one—at least in the news—had made the connection between the two break-ins. Margaret Sutton—Hebert had called her Molly—was the link between the two, but it didn't look like the media was aware of that.

Not yet, anyway.

The cops had to know. They were just keeping it close to their vests for now.

On the bright side, they'd be investigating Jackass's connection to those break-ins and the five dead bodies. Jackass had tasked the kidnappers, so the deaths would connect back to him somehow. Even if Tobin had assigned them, it still pointed back to Jackass.

Leaving me completely out of it.

Hell, if Broussard and his group knew about Nadia Hall, they might even think that Jackass did it. There was no one to refute it.

Except for Xavier Morrow, but who'd even believe him? Kid couldn't have been older than five that night during Katrina.

Five-year-olds were notoriously poor eyewitnesses.

Except for the fact that Xavier Morrow had seen his scar. Jackass had never had a scar.

Dammit.

Xavier Morrow still had to die. And he would.

At least no one can connect me to Jackass's death. He'd tossed the burner that he'd used to communicate with the cop. It now lay at the bottom of the Mississippi. Luckily, he'd owned several, using separate phones for various contacts. He now had a fresh new untraceable phone in his pocket. There was no other evidence connecting them, right?

Right.

Except for . . . "Ashley," he muttered. Once her body was identified—and it would be, because he hadn't destroyed her face when he'd made her smaller—they'd wonder why Jackass had been found near Ashley's remains. They'd wonder how she and Jackass connected.

But Jackass and Ashley didn't connect.

Ashley could only be connected to me.

By Joelle, who had incriminating video.

Goddammit.

Joelle needed to be dealt with. Maybe he could take the surveillance video from her. But she'd said she'd sent a copy to her attorney.

Dammit. Killing her now would be too obvious. Lamont closed his eyes, trying to get a handle on exactly what he needed to do. The goal was ever-shifting. He needed to find a way to silence Joelle without triggering suspicion.

It was ironic, really. Joelle would be so happy right now. She'd hated Ashley and—

Oh. Oh. His eyes flew open as he abruptly sat up straight. "Oh," he whispered aloud, because the perfect solution had just crossed his mind. What if he could do away with Joelle and deflect attention away from his involvement with Ashley all at once?

Joelle had hated Ashley. Hated her with a passion.

Hated her enough to kill her herself.

But was depressed enough afterward to take her own life. Poor Joelle.

Lamont wanted to make it hurt, but if he staged her suicide, it would be by pills. Joelle didn't have the guts to shoot herself in the head like Rocky had.

Or like his first wife had. Lucille had been an avid hunter. She'd known her way around guns. Joelle wouldn't know the first thing about firing one.

He'd have to admit to having fucked Ashley, because Joelle would mention this in her "suicide note," but while a sexual scandal might look bad, it would soon blow over.

Joelle was the focus now. Then he'd finally be able to focus on his future. He'd gather his donors, throw his hat into the political ring, and his next wife would have to call him "Senator" in bed.

Tulane-Gravier, New Orleans, Louisiana
THURSDAY, JULY 28, 1:30 P.M.

"Mr. Hebert?"

Gabe jerked awake and lifted his head from the table in the interrogation room, blinking at the bright light. He'd fallen asleep. How the
hell had he let himself fall asleep in the police station?

Maybe because he was fucking exhausted and had been questioned
three times by different detectives, all playing good cop/bad cop until
he wanted to scream? Yeah, that was it. He needed to cut himself a
little slack because he'd had a really bad evening.

And an equally bad morning. On top of being interrogated for
hours, he had no idea where they'd taken Molly. The cops had sepa-
rated them as soon as they'd arrived at the scene at the bank of the
bayou. Was she all right? What had they done to her? *How could I have
let myself fall asleep?*

Then he saw the officer standing in the corner. Officer McCauley
was one of André's and had been standing guard for hours—ever since
Gabe had been taken to this room. André said that he trusted him.
So did Burke, which was the only reason he would have felt safe
enough to sleep. The officer gave him a kind nod, which Gabe returned
before twisting toward the door to study the man who'd called his
name.

The new arrival was dressed in a snazzy gray suit with a black tie
covered in . . . Gabe squinted. "Saxophones?" he asked blearily.

The man tilted his head in confusion before glancing down at his
tie. "Oh, right." He chuckled. "A gift from my son," he said. The man
placed his briefcase on the table and took the seat across from Gabe.
"Your attorney will join us in a moment and then we can get started."

My attorney? Oh, right. Willa Mae had been at his side during his
interrogations. He must have fallen asleep right after she left, because

that was the last thing he remembered. He rose when Willa Mae walked in. "Miss Collins."

She smiled at him. "Mr. Hebert. How y'doing, Gabe?" she added softly.

He rubbed his neck. "I've slept better."

"Then please sit down before you fall down." She sat beside him and leaned in to whisper in his ear. "Molly is fine. You will be, too. Just follow my lead, and only answer what you're asked, just like before."

"Yes, ma'am."

The man with the saxophone tie cleared his throat. "I'm Assistant District Attorney Cardozo. I'd like to ask you a few questions."

"Fine," Gabe said wearily. "Then can I leave?"

"Let's get through the questions first, shall we?" Cardozo said, which would have sounded ominous except that Willa Mae was patting Gabe's arm encouragingly.

Gabe sighed. "Fine. Go ahead."

"Can you start at the beginning?"

Gabe wanted to groan. "I've told my story three times already. I'm pretty sure they taped it. Can't you just catch the highlight reel?"

Cardozo's lips twitched. "I could, but I'd like to hear it from you. I know you've had a rough night, so I appreciate it."

Gabe rubbed his palms over his face, then shoved his hands through his hair, yanking gently to wake himself up. "Well, just because you appreciate it," he muttered and started from the beginning, leaving out only the part where Xavier shot his intruder before fleeing. "And then we came upon the guy with the hoodie, and he shot Mule right in the chest, then in the head. We approached, Miss Sutton and I, to try to keep him from disposing of any more evidence. He shoved Miss Sutton down, grabbed his gun, then ran for Mule's Range Rover. He drove away."

"With several bullet holes in the Range Rover, as I understand,"

Cardozo said mildly. He was a nice-looking man with nearly black hair, a tanned complexion that spoke of a lot of time in the sun, and dark brown eyes. Those eyes seemed kind, but Gabe couldn't trust him.

"Miss Sutton tried to stop him from leaving the scene. She shot his tires first, but he kept driving."

"And what were you doing while all of this was happening?" Cardozo asked.

"Recording the entire thing, from when we approached through the trees to right after the man in the hoodie charged into Miss Sutton." His heart stuttered a little, just remembering how terrified he'd been when Molly went down. And how proud he'd been when she got back up and started shooting.

She blamed herself for the man's escape, but she wasn't to blame at all. She'd been brave and he couldn't wait to tell her so again so that maybe she'd start believing it.

"And where might we find the video?" Cardozo asked.

Gabe narrowed his eyes. "Like you haven't seen it already?"

Willa Mae squeezed his arm. "Just answer the question, Gabe. Cardozo's simply connecting the dots."

Gabe exhaled impatiently. "It's on my phone. Which is in Captain Holmes's custody."

Cardozo nodded. "Thank you. Now, did you hear any of what the two men were saying to each other?"

"No."

Cardozo didn't seem offended by the brusque answer. "Did they seem friendly with each other?"

"Before one of them shot the other?" Gabe asked sarcastically, then sighed when Willa Mae surreptitiously elbowed him. "Sorry. I'm tired. I'm not sure how to answer that. We couldn't see the shooter's face. Between his hoodie and the sun behind him, he was pretty well hidden. Mule seemed relaxed enough, right up until the end, that is. They were talking at a normal volume, I guess. They never yelled." He glanced at Willa Mae to make sure he'd said the right things, and she nodded at him. *Well, at least I haven't incriminated myself.*

"You were carrying a gun," Cardozo commented.

"Yes."

"Did you fire at the man in the hoodie?"

"No."

Cardozo smiled, like they were playing a game. "Did you fire earlier in the evening?"

"Yes."

"How many times?"

"Once."

"When was that, Mr. Hebert?"

Willa Mae patted his arm again. "You can answer that. They have the security footage from Molly's apartment. Your action of defending Molly has been noted as such."

"It was somewhere between one fifteen and one thirty this morning."

"Who did you shoot?"

"I don't know his name. He had a gun pointed at my . . ." He frowned, unsure of how to label Molly. *My girlfriend? My partner?* "My private investigator's chest. He'd forced her to drop her weapon by threatening her family, then started to call to his partners that he had her."

"You thought he'd harm her?"

"I had absolutely no doubt that he would have."

"At that point, why did you think the men were there?"

"To harm—or possibly abduct—Miss Sutton's sister and niece."

"What purpose would that have served?"

Gabe wanted to scream but reined in his temper and forced himself to remain civil. "To force Molly into the open so that they could use her to either lure Burke or to follow her to where key witnesses were hiding."

"When you shot the man in the garage, did you intend to kill him?"

Gabe couldn't control his flinch. "No. I was actually aiming for his shoulder. I would have accepted an arm or a leg or even a torso, but I hit his neck."

Cardozo nodded again. "It was a kill shot."

Gabe swallowed. He'd have to deal with the fact that he'd killed a man later. He couldn't let himself be distracted now. "I guess so."

"Your father was a cop. Did he teach you to shoot?"

"He was and he did. Not necks, though. That was an accident."

Cardozo's smile was kind. "I never met your father, but I've heard good things about him."

Gabe glanced at Willa Mae, unsure of how to respond.

"Just say thank you, Gabe," she murmured.

"Thank you?"

Cardozo chuckled wryly. "You're welcome?" He propped his arm on the table and leaned forward, sobering. "Do you know who it was wearing the hoodie?"

"No. If I knew, I'd tell you."

"Who do you think killed your father?"

Gabe hesitated, then figured why the hell not? "Do you accept that he didn't commit suicide?"

"I do. Miss Sutton told me about the private autopsy you had done. We'd already found the record in Dr. McLain's cloud account—her husband knew her passwords and has been very cooperative in our investigation into her murder."

Gabe started to relax. Maybe this really would be okay. "Why didn't you ask me earlier about my father's murder? Like yesterday?" *Before I was forced to kill a man.*

"Because we just got the files last night. We'd intended to discuss it with you today, then events happened and here you are. Last question: do you intend to keep looking for your father's killer?"

Gabe didn't look at Willa Mae. He kept his gaze locked on Cardozo's. "Yes."

"I figured as much. If you'd said no, I would have doubted every-thing else you'd told me. But this is the deal, Mr. Hebert. I'd like to let you go home—or wherever you choose to go here in the city. But I can't have vigilantes out there hunting down killers and shooting up SUVs. Or even shooting men attempting abduction."

Gabe studied the man for a long moment, then nodded. "I under-stand your position."

"I hoped you would. Thank you for your time and your candor. And thank you especially for the video. It will come in handy, I expect."

"I hope so. Do *you* know who the hoodie guy is?"

"No. But I will."

"Do you know who the victim was? The one whose . . ." Gabe swal-lowed. "The one whose head we found?"

Cardozo didn't speak for at least five seconds. He just held Gabe's gaze, blinking in time with the ticking of the clock on the wall.

Gabe didn't know how to feel about that. The man did know who the young woman had been. And he wanted Gabe to know that he knew. "I'm glad," Gabe finally whispered. "I hope her family gets closure."

Cardozo rose, smoothing a hand down his saxophone tie. "You're free to go, Mr. Hebert. If you wouldn't mind, please stay in town. Your phone will be returned to you, and Miss Sutton is waiting for you in the lobby."

Then the ADA took his briefcase and walked out, leaving Gabe star-ing at the door. "What the—"

"When we're alone," Willa Mae murmured. "Not a word until I tell you to. Now let's get out of here."

Gabe held his tongue but stared at the one-way glass that made up one of the walls. There were people back there, he knew. Apparently, Willa Mae didn't trust them.

Saying nothing, he followed Officer McCauley out of the room and through the halls to the lobby, where Molly was pacing the floor. She ran to Gabe, throwing her arms around his neck and holding on for dear life.

"I'm okay," he murmured, his arms closing around her as he breathed her in. Her hair smelled like the shampoo in Farrah's bathroom, and he missed the scent of her own orange shampoo. She was still wearing Farrah's sweats, complete with the mud stains from when the shooter had knocked her down. But she was alive and whole and appeared unhurt by the cops. He honestly wasn't sure what he'd expected them to do, given that one of the NOPD brass was dead. "You?"

She tightened her hold, pressing her face against his neck before letting him go. "Me too."

And that was all they said until they were outside, where Burke waited with his truck. "Get in," he said. "And buckle up."

They obeyed, Willa Mae in the front and Gabe and Molly in the back. Molly was clutching his hand so hard that it hurt, but he wasn't about to tell her to stop.

"Miss Willa Mae, can we talk now?" Gabe asked.

Willa Mae looked at Burke. "We clean?"

Burke nodded. "Yeah. I never stopped long enough for anyone to mess with my truck." He handed Molly's cell phone and her burner back over the seat. "Here you go."

"Thank you for holding on to them for me," she said. "Where are we going? Your camp?"

"No, it's too crowded now. No spare bedrooms and five extra people make a lot of noise, even when they're trying to be quiet. We're going back to Farrah and André's place on the river so that you can rest."

"Thank God," Gabe muttered.

"Chelsea?" Molly asked. "And Harper? Are they still there?"

"They are," Burke confirmed. "Last I heard, they were baking with

Farrah so that you could have something sweet when you got back. So . . ." He let a few seconds pass. "Busy day, huh?"

Molly laughed, a brittle sound. "Yeah, it was. What more do we know?"

"The ADA knows who the victim is," Gabe said. "The one whose body the hoodie guy was throwing in the water."

"He does," Willa Mae confirmed. "But he's not telling. Not that I thought he would."

"I wonder how they identified her so quickly?" Molly mused. "Did they send divers in after the remains? If they found a finger or two and if she was in the system, they might have ID'd her through her fingerprints."

Gabe closed his eyes, fighting back a wave of nausea at the thought of finding fingers in the bayou.

"I don't know," Burke said. "Her face was recognizable—you know, through the blood, so I'm wondering if she was someone he knew."

"I vote for the second one," Gabe said weakly. "How about them Saints?"

"I'm sorry," Molly said, bringing his hand to her lips for a quick kiss. "I forget that you're a civilian. You were pretty wonderful today."

"Thank you." He leaned back and closed his eyes. *So tired.* Almost too tired to feel pride at her words. *Almost.* "Do we know anything more?"

"André said that they found Mule's Range Rover," Burke offered. "It was parked in some woods near the home of the stolen car's owner."

"Stolen car?" Gabe asked, shaking his head hard, worried that he'd slept through some part of the explanation.

Burke glanced at him through the rearview mirror. "Oh, sorry. The car that the shooter left at the scene had been stolen. The cops went to the address on the registration and found the stolen car's owner on the ground a few feet away from Mule's Range Rover."

Molly sighed. "The car's owner was dead?"

"Yeah," Burke said. "The guy had a rap sheet, so he was known to NOPD. Drug dealer. Made some meth, that kind of thing. He'd been dead for at least a few hours when they found him. There was a set of fresh tire treads in the ground near the Rover. Probably from a sedan. The treads didn't match those of the stolen car left at the scene. That's all I know right now."

"Okay," Molly said slowly. "Hoodie Guy brought his own vehicle, switched it for Meth Guy's car, drove it to the bayou to dispose of a body, killed Mule, then got away in Mule's Range Rover, and drove back to where he stole the car, switched back to his own vehicle, then drove away?"

"Close as I can figure," Burke said.

Molly yawned. "I'm wondering if Hoodie Guy knew Meth Guy or if it was a random theft of opportunity?"

"Good question," Burke said. "I wondered the same. And if they did know each other, from where?"

"I'm wondering how you're all still conscious," Gabe muttered under his breath.

Molly leaned into him as much as her seat belt would allow. "Just used to long hours, I suppose. But my brain is winding down, for sure."

"Close your eyes," Burke said. "We'll be back to Farrah's place soon."

Tulane-Gravier, New Orleans, Louisiana
THURSDAY, JULY 28, 6:30 P.M.

"Evening, sir," James said.

Lamont settled into the back seat of the town car. "Evening, James."

James pulled away from the curb. And stopped.

"Traffic, sir," James said apologetically. "Seems like half the country's here."

Lamont found himself unbothered. "Not a problem, James. I'm in no hurry tonight. Just take me home."

James glanced at him in the rearview mirror. "That's a switch. Seems like you've always got some place to be. Did you have a good day?"

"I did, thank you." So far, so good, anyway.

They hadn't identified Ashley's body yet and he'd checked. Multiple times. But discreetly. He didn't want anyone to know that he was the one asking.

It was possible that they wouldn't ID Ashley's body for a while. Maybe ever. And if that was the case, he was home free.

But he wasn't going to depend on it. Rocky Hebert had gotten close. He may have even ID'd Nadia as the woman whose body he'd seen during Katrina. He'd certainly known enough to go hunting for her doctor.

But he didn't ID me. If he had, I wouldn't be sitting here right now.

Rocky Hebert hadn't known who killed Nadia. Lamont knew he was damn lucky that they'd killed Rocky before he'd discovered the truth. There was no way that he was going to depend on luck again. While it was *possible* that Ashley's body might never be identified, it was likely that it would. She had no family to miss her, but her new boss, Jean-Pierre, had come by his office yet again that afternoon asking after her.

"Have you seen Ashley?"

"No, I have not."

"I'm worried, Lamont. She might be hurt somewhere. Is this like her? To just not show up for work?"

"Maybe. She'll call in sick sometimes. Y'know, after a busy night." He'd mimed guzzling liquor. *"Wicked hangovers."*

The other man had frowned. *"You didn't mention that when you sent her over. I don't want an alcoholic working for me. Or not working for me, which is more in line with what happened today."*

Jean-Pierre had finally given up, returning to his office. Or maybe to the network admin's office to get into Ashley's computer.

I really don't care.

What he did care about was that eventually Ashley would be ID'd, if for no other reason than that damn Jean-Pierre wouldn't back off. And when she was ID'd?

They're gonna come looking at me. Joelle would make sure of it.

He'd thought a lot about how to neutralize Joelle over the course of his workday and now he had a plan. He had a script. He'd picked a fall guy who'd be ID'd as the "man in the hoodie"—a guy on his list who'd killed for hire in the past.

Lamont had even practiced his sad face for when Joelle's body was discovered.

Poor tortured Joelle. Couldn't live with the guilt after killing her husband's mistress.

He'd have to navigate the fallout of sexual scandal, but that was nothin' these days. In some circles, it'd be considered a plus.

"So, how'd the missus like those presents?" James asked, breaking into his thoughts.

Momentary panic swept through him. Ashley's body. The presents wrapped in silver paper. The silver paper that was in police evidence right now because he'd left it in the trunk of that stolen car. *Goddammit.*

At least there'd be no prints on the silver wrapping paper. He'd meticulously scrubbed it clean of both his and James's fingerprints.

But James had seen the gifts and if anyone asked, he'd have to tell.

I don't want to kill James, too. He's a damn good driver. But if he had to, he would.

"I haven't given them to her yet," he said, relieved that his voice didn't tremble. He'd have to get new boxes, fill them with presents, wrap them in silver paper, then leave them in the garage. Just in case.

"I'm saving them for the next time she gets mad at me," he added, chuckling ruefully.

"I know how that goes," James agreed. "Never thought about having a gift at the ready, though. That's a really good idea. I might borrow it."

"Be my guest."

Thankfully, James shut up, and Lamont spent the next forty-five minutes with his eyes closed, mentally rehearsing his lines. When James stopped in the driveway, he was ready.

"Thank you, James. I'll see you tomorrow morning, normal time. Oh, and I have a business dinner tomorrow night at the Monteleone. I need to be there by seven."

"I know, sir. That one's been on the schedule for weeks."

Because it was the most important dinner of Lamont's career—so far.

He got out, waved at James, then squared his shoulders and let himself into his house.

He really loved his house. It had belonged to wife number one, had been in her family since just after the Civil War. As she was the last of her line, the house had passed to him after her death.

Poor, poor Lucille. He'd been happy to be rid of her, too.

He might wait a while before marrying again. Play the bereaved bachelor. Focus on his election and his soon-to-be constituency.

Enjoy his house again. He hadn't, he realized. He hadn't enjoyed coming home in a very long time.

That was about to change.

"Joelle?" he called.

The front of the house was dark, but something smelled good, which meant that Joelle wasn't doing the cooking. She was a terrible cook. Too bad that he hadn't thought to ask before marrying her. She'd been good in bed, and he figured that she could learn to be a home-maker.

Ha. That had not worked according to plan.

He made his way to the kitchen, noticing the dining room table set for two. China, candles, and his best crystal. He wondered what Joelle was up to.

The kitchen was empty and sparkling clean. There were covered dishes in the warming tray with a scribbled note from their regular cook. The woman had gone home, thankfully.

He and Joelle were all alone.

"Joelle?" he called again.

"In the front parlor."

He frowned at that. Returning to the living room—which Joelle liked to call the "parlor" because it sounded fancier—he saw her lounging on the sofa in a negligee. He'd walked right past her like she hadn't even been there.

Wishful thinking, I suppose.

She rose fluidly, the sheer fabric clinging to her curves. She was a very beautiful woman. That hadn't changed. But he'd rather touch a cobra.

"How was your day?" she all but cooed.

He sat on the sofa, spread his arms along the back, and propped an ankle on his knee. "Same old, same old. And yours?"

She settled on the middle cushion, tucking one foot beneath her so that their knees touched. "It was nice." She ran a fingertip over the emerald necklace he'd given her two days before—identical to the one he'd given Ashley. "I went to the spa. Had Cook make your favorite meal. And then I got ready for you."

Translation: she got ready for sex.

But that's not going to happen today. "Excuse me," he said. "I just got a text."

She frowned when he took out his phone. "I think we need to have some phone-free time."

Instead of checking his texts, he brought up his recording app and hit start. Then made sure his home screen was showing before placing the phone on the table. "I agree. We should talk."

She scootched over a little closer and trailed her fingers up his thigh. "Or not."

He placed his hand over hers, halting her explorations. "I want to talk about Ashley."

She flinched, grabbing her hand back as though he were infectious. "What? Why?"

"Because she's important to me."

Joelle lifted her chin. "She's just a two-bit whore."

"So were you," he said smoothly, and her hand swung as if to slap him, but he caught it before she made contact. "I wouldn't do that if I were you, Joelle."

"Why not? Are you going to have me arrested?" she mocked.

"Maybe. Don't push me."

"Don't push you? Don't *push* you? I *will* push you, husband dear. I will push you all I want to. I am your *wife*."

"For now."

She gasped, but it sounded rehearsed. "Are you threatening me with divorce?"

"No, I'm saying that I want one."

She drew herself to her full height. "No."

He laughed quietly. "What did you think would happen, Joelle? You put cameras in my office. You invaded my privacy. I do business in that office. You may have breached the privacy of any number of innocent people."

"You don't deal with innocent people."

That was pretty much true. "It doesn't matter. What did you think would happen?"

"I thought you'd get rid of her. I thought we'd be free of her. Now she's gone. The whore is gone. Now we can get back to normal. We can work on our marriage. It'll be like it was at the beginning."

That was good. He'd be able to use a few of her words to his own advantage. He needed more, though. "Our marriage is over."

She lurched to her feet, her hands balled into fists. "It's not over until I say so. How dare you? You cheated on me."

"As I've done before with previous wives, as you well know. Did you think you were special?"

Another gasp, this one seemingly sincere. "I did, and I was the fool. I thought you loved me."

"I did. Once."

"But you don't love me anymore?" she asked, her lip trembling.

If he hadn't seen the twitch of her left eye, he might have thought that she was genuinely brokenhearted. But the words themselves were gold. "I do not. I haven't for a long time."

She stomped one foot. "You will not divorce me. You will not leave me. I will fight you."

"You will lose."

"I have the videos," she said smugly. "We have a prenup."

"Which stipulates that you can't cheat. It doesn't say anything about me."

Horror filled her eyes. "What?"

"You heard me." And it was mostly true. Their prenup didn't explicitly say that he could cheat, but he doubted a judge would make the distinction. Even wife number two got a little alimony. With video proof that he'd been fucking his assistant, Joelle wouldn't get half of his net worth, but she would get a lot more than a little alimony. If she lived. Which she wasn't going to. "I don't want the scandal of a divorce, but you've left me no choice. I can no longer trust you in my home. I'd like you to pack your things and be out of here by tomorrow evening."

Horror became shock. "You're throwing me out?"

"I am."

"You can't do that!"

He actually couldn't, but he wasn't going to let her know that. "Watch me."

"No." She shook her head vigorously, sending her diamond earrings swinging. "You will not divorce me. I won't let you. I'll fight you in court and I'll win. I will destroy you. Your reputation will be in tatters by the time I'm through with you."

Yes. This was what he wanted.

"Don't make empty threats, Joelle."

"They're not empty threats! I will crucify you in the press. You'll wish you were dead by the time I'm through with you. You'll be sorry you ever crossed me."

"I'm going to marry Ashley."

Her eyes narrowed. "You can't marry her."

"Watch me."

"Over my dead body," she said, then flounced out of the room and up the stairs.

He winced when the bedroom door slammed hard enough to knock pictures off the walls, then he took his phone and stopped the recording. It wasn't perfect, but she'd given him a fair bit to work with.

He wished she'd threatened to kill herself. She'd done that before. Unfortunately, she had not done so today. But there were a few gems he could use.

The whore is gone. Now we can get back to normal. Both of those were good.

All the talk of destroying his reputation and him being sorry he'd crossed her was even better.

He could cut and paste and create a conversation that had actually never happened. But to someone overhearing, it would sound like Joelle was frantic, hysterical, and—hopefully—suicidal. Pair that with a convincing note—printed on the home printer, of course—and an electronic payment from her account to her "hit man"—a.k.a. the fall guy he'd chosen from his list?

The cops would conclude that Joelle had hated Ashley enough to have her killed, her body dismembered, and her remains thrown to the gators.

Problem solved.

Now for the fun part. He got to kill her himself. But he'd do that tomorrow afternoon.

No one suspected him yet. He had time to do this right.

24

Lake Salvatore, Louisiana
THURSDAY, JULY 28, 8:30 P.M.

MOLLY WOKE UP with a jerk, bolting upright in bed. A strange bed.

She'd already grabbed her gun from the nightstand before inhaling deeply. *Peanut butter cookies.*

Slowly she returned the gun to the nightstand, clarity returning. Her sister and niece had been making peanut butter cookies in Farrah's kitchen when Molly and Gabe had fallen asleep, and the delicious scent still hung in the air, hours later.

It had to be hours later. When they'd gone to sleep, the sun was still high in the sky. Farrah's spare bedroom was already semi-dark, sunset approaching.

"You okay up there?" Gabe asked, his voice a little thick with sleep.

She glanced down to see that he'd rolled to his back and was staring up at her, amusement in his hazel eyes, the last rays of daylight making his dark red curls glimmer like fire. "Just that moment when you wake up and realize that you don't know where you are."

"You're right here with me," he drawled, and she smiled.

"Yes, I am."

"And nobody's shooting at us," he added lightly.

"For now."

He chuckled. "There's my eternal optimist. Come back down here. Your energy is making me tired again."

She complied, resting her head against his shoulder, sighing as his arms came around her. They were mostly dressed. Molly was wearing an oversized T-shirt that probably belonged to André. Gabe had on a pair of athletic shorts, his chest wonderfully bare and warm, smelling of soap and sleep and clean sweat. This was nice. More than nice. This was the feeling that smart people fought to keep forever.

They'd initially been put in separate rooms, but they'd met in the hallway when they'd both tiptoed out to find the other. They'd agreed on Gabe's bed, because it was bigger.

Neither of them had wanted to sleep alone, and he'd held her almost desperately before his body had gradually relaxed into slumber. He'd held her like she was his lifeline.

She got the feeling. He was quickly becoming hers.

She didn't want to think about what would have happened had he not been there in her apartment building's garage. She'd acted rashly, charging ahead without scoping out the scene, her mind focused on the danger to her family. Gabe had been slower, more cognizant of their surroundings. Of the threats.

And he'd saved her life. By killing a man.

She'd killed the night before as well, and while she'd probably have a nightmare or two, she'd mostly made her peace with it. The man had been coming after her family. He'd tried to kill her and, if he'd succeeded, he would have killed Lucien and Gabe. And then he and Tobin would have taken Chelsea and Harper and who knew what would have happened next? She shuddered at the thought.

Besides, that first kill was usually the hardest. She remembered the first time she'd killed a man, back in Iraq. She'd had violent nightmares every night for nearly a year thereafter. Sometimes she still did, even now. And Jake . . . Killing her brother-in-law had been one of the lowest moments of her life.

She'd do it again without hesitation, but she'd emerged from the experience with scars on her heart that might always remain. She worried that Gabe wouldn't be able to accept what he'd done.

"Are you okay?" Molly murmured, nearly purring when he began stroking her hair, struck by the fact that *he* was comforting *her*. "This has been intense."

"We only slept," he said dryly. "Despite what your sister is probably thinking that we're doing back here."

She looked up to see him smirking and the sight made her heart lighter. If he could still joke after everything that had happened, he was far stronger than she was. She still had trouble seeing the brighter side of life. It seemed safer somehow.

She lowered her head, loving the feel of his warm skin and soft chest hair against her cheek. "I meant the last twenty-four hours have been intense."

He said nothing for a moment, then sighed. "Not to complain, but the last six weeks have been intense."

He had every right to complain. She petted the hairs on his chest, keeping her touch soothing rather than sexual. "I'm *optimistic* that it'll be over soon."

She felt his chuckle more than she heard it. "I see what you did there. I hope you're right. I don't think I can keep up this pace much longer. It's physically exhausting, but more mentally draining. I don't know how you guys do it."

"I'm wrung out, too. Usually, we're helping strangers. This . . . well, it's not usually this . . . *personal*." They were sleeping together and, even if today was only sleeping, they'd already had sex once. They'd talked about continuing their nascent relationship when this was over. She wasn't sure how much more personal it could get.

He flinched. "I'm sorry. I never wanted your family to get hurt."

Once again, she pulled back to look at him, needing him to understand. "Well, that, too, but that's not what I meant. Yes, I'm terrified for my family, and I *hate* that they were terrorized last night, especially because they were just getting over what happened before. But right now, I meant that I've never gotten involved with a client before. Not until you. *This* is personal, Gabe. This right here. *Us.* We are personal."

He went very still, holding her gaze. "Why didn't you get involved with clients before?" he asked, his voice dipping low.

"I never wanted to. Nobody even made me think about it, not until I walked into the Choux that first time and saw you behind the kitchen glass. I wanted to talk to you, to maybe ask you out for coffee or something, but . . . I don't know. Maybe I wasn't ready. Maybe I shouldn't have gotten involved with you right now, but I couldn't seem to help myself. I could have kept you safer had I kept you at arm's length, but . . ." She lifted a shoulder and let it fall. "I couldn't seem to help myself."

"I'm glad," he murmured, sending chills racing across her skin. "Because I can't seem to help myself, either. I want you, Molly Sutton. May I have you?"

Her cheeks heated in pleasure at the polite request. "I've been hoping you would."

He kissed her then, long and . . . calm. There was a possessiveness in his touch, but it wasn't the frantic grasping and stroking of their last time together in the hotel room.

This was confident and sure. The question in her mind wasn't *Does he like me*, but more *What will make him feel good?* She swept her palm over his chest, teasing his nipples, feeling the harsh intake of his breath against her lips.

"Like that?" she whispered.

"Mmm. Yes. Please." He rolled closer and his body was hot and hard . . . and ready. Very ready. His hands were relaxed but sure as he stroked up her thigh, urging her leg over his hip.

She continued the caresses, drifting lower and lower with each sweep of her hand. This felt lazy. Decadent. Like they had all the time in the world as the sun set over the water and the ceiling fan slowly turned.

But what if we don't? What if the next shooter—

Stop it. Stop thinking. Just be. She banished the dark thought of *what if*, slipping her fingers beneath the waistband of his shorts, questing. He interrupted her journey when he slid his palm under the long T-shirt, cupping her butt, his hand freezing when he touched bare skin.

He reared back, eyes wide and full of old-fashioned lust. "No panties? Molly Sutton, you're a bad girl."

"Wasn't wearing any earlier, either," she said with a grin. "Not all day." Her panties had been in the dryer when they'd left that morning to follow Mule, and borrowing underwear . . . *Just no.*

He groaned softly, sending shivers rippling down her body straight to her core. "I'm glad I didn't know that then. I wouldn't have been able to concentrate on anything but your ass." He groped her butt with a salacious waggle of his brows, making her giggle. "It's a very, very nice ass, by the way."

She pushed past his waistband, finding him bare beneath. Sliding her hand over his hip, she gave his butt cheek a squeeze. "Pot meet kettle," she said, then returned to the part of him that really held her interest, wrapping her fingers around his erection. He was hard and hot, pulsing in her hand.

He let go of her ass long enough to shove his shorts down and tried to tug her shirt off. "You have to let go of me for a second," he whispered, brushing another kiss over her lips.

She smiled. "But what if I don't want to?"

"Then I can't touch you and—" He made a startled sound when she let him go, yanked the shirt off herself, then fused their mouths together while gripping his cock once more.

He groaned again, deep and rumbly, before rolling her to her back and sliding down her body, kissing her neck, her collarbone, the swell of her breast. Then he sucked her nipple into his mouth, and she arched, her back coming off the mattress. She wanted to cry out, but there were people in the kitchen, close enough to hear her.

And this was private. This was for them. This was a brief oasis where they could take what they needed from each other, filling the places deep inside that had been so empty. So lonely.

They were lonely no more. Not right this minute, anyway, and for now, that was all that mattered.

She tunneled her fingers through his loose curls, soft between her fingers, tightening her grip on his hair when he started to lift his head. "No, don't stop."

"Not plannin' to." He gave her a wicked wink, then switched breasts, his hand curving over her hip on his way to her ass, which he gently squeezed again. He looked up, his mouth wet, eyes burning. "You have a beautiful body."

"Mmm, so do you." She ran her hands over his wide shoulders, lifting her knees to hug his lean hips and tilting her own higher to put his hard cock right where she needed it most. She shuddered, biting back a groan.

Well, not exactly where she needed it most. "Condom," she whispered.

He raised to his elbows and reached for the packet on his nightstand. She'd placed a gun on hers. *Protection, either way.* The chuckle on her lips dissolved into an impatient sigh when he reared back, kneeling between her legs to roll the condom down his length.

She trailed her fingertips down his chest, across his abs, veering from his cock to lightly brush his balls. "If I'd known what you were hiding under that chef's coat, I would have climbed you like a tree the first time I ate at the Choux."

Breathing hard now, he grinned down at her. "Better than my chocolate cake?"

"I'm not sure," she said tartly. "Best to make an informed choice."

He laughed, then slid his finger into her heat, and both of them groaned quietly. "I want our next time to be somewhere that we can be loud as we want," he whispered.

"Agree. Just . . ." She arched again when he curved his finger inside her, covering her mouth to muffle what would have been a shout. "Hurry, Gabe. Please."

"No. No hurrying this time. I'm going to . . ." He sucked in a breath as he slid into her in one smooth stroke and hummed, the sound vibrating along her skin. "Gonna take my time." His next kiss was sinful and left her seeking more when he lifted his head enough to whisper, "Gonna savor what's mine."

Mine. God, she wanted to be his. She was almost afraid of how much she wanted it. She cupped his face with one hand, loving the feel of his stubble against her palm, and threaded the fingers of the other through his curls. "I like that. Being yours."

He met her gaze. Held it for just long enough. "Thought you might."

He was quiet then, the only sound that of his skin on hers, her sigh, his soft groan. The quickening of their breaths. Her gasp when he did something with his hips that made her arch once again and her whispered pleading. "Please, Gabe. More. Please. I need—"

"I know what you need." He kissed her hard, then lifted his body, framing her shoulders with his capable hands. Then he gave her what she wanted, what she needed, lunging harder and faster and way more intensely. She met him thrust for thrust until her body stiffened.

She threw back her head and, biting her lip to stay quiet, came harder than she ever had in her life.

And after the last time, that was saying something.

She collapsed back to the mattress, staring up at him as he shoved up on his arms, his head thrown back, his body one long, solid, beautiful curve of muscle. His groan was muffled, but not very quiet.

Molly didn't care. Watching him come apart . . . He was so beautiful.

His shoulders sagged and he caught himself before he landed on her too hard, lowering himself slowly, carefully. Then made everything even more perfect when he nuzzled his face against her throat, his chest heaving as he tried to catch his breath.

"Mmmm," he hummed.

She smiled, stroking his back. "Mmmm, indeed."

He stayed there for long minutes while the ceiling fan spun, gradually cooling their skin. Then he pulled out, every movement deliberate and gentle.

He flopped to his back with a low laugh. "Damn, woman. You done tired me out."

She rolled to her side, caressing his chest again. Unable to stop touching him. "Good cardio."

He snorted. Then sighed. "It's dark outside now. I think they'll be waiting for us so we can leave."

They'd be going to Burke's soon, taking Chelsea and Harper with them. They'd be shoved together like sardines in a can, but it would be easier to guard everyone all together and they'd taken enough advantage of Farrah's hospitality.

"It's gonna be noisy and crowded at Burke's," she murmured. "I'm glad we got this time for ourselves."

"I think we more than earned it. Let me clean up, then the bathroom is yours."

That had been the other advantage of choosing this guest room— the en suite bathroom. Nothing like sneaking to the bathroom after sex in someone else's house.

Twenty minutes later, they left the bedroom wearing the clothes they'd first arrived in. Farrah had washed, dried, and folded them at some point during the day. There were still stains, but at least the clothes were no longer bloody.

Taking their sheets to the laundry room down the hall, Molly dumped them in the washer and started the cycle. Then, hand in hand, she and Gabe made their way to the kitchen.

Chelsea was sitting with Farrah, both sipping from coffee cups, both wearing ridiculous grins. "Hey, there, big sis," Chelsea drawled. She nodded at Gabe. "And *bonsoir* to you, Chef Hebert. Hope y'all had a good 'nap.'"

"We did, thank you," Molly said with as much dignity as she could muster.

Chelsea chuckled and Harper looked up from the tablet on which she'd been playing. "What's so funny?" her niece asked, eyes narrowing.

"Absolutely nothing," Molly said firmly, then sat next to the child. "How you doing, kiddo?"

Harper shrugged, her eyes downcast. "Shit happens."

Chelsea gasped, and it was Molly's turn to chuckle. "So it does. But I don't think your mama appreciates such language."

"It was the best word for the situation," Harper said in a way that was far too adult, then looked at Gabe, who still stood, looking uncertain. "Are you a cook?"

He coughed. "More or less. They call me 'Chef,' though."

Harper shrugged again. "Chef, cook. What's the difference?"

He slid into the chair across from her. "About four years of school. Are there any of those cookies left? They smelled so good."

Harper nodded soberly and Molly missed her niece's spark. *Please let it come back. Please.* "I'll get you some," Harper said. "Cookies for everyone."

Chelsea looked like she'd argue, then shook her head. "Cookies for everyone," she echoed. After her laughter at Molly's expense, her sister looked drawn out and exhausted. Molly wished she'd make some more fun of them, just to see her smile.

Farrah got up with Harper, fixing them plates of the chicken they'd had for dinner while Harper slid a plate full of cookies to the table. The child waited silently until Gabe had tried one.

"Oh, this is good," he said with a little moan that made Molly wish they were alone.

"On that note." Farrah placed their dinner on the table, then pressed a small canister of balm into Molly's hand. "For the beard burn," she said in a stage whisper, patting Molly's cheek. "It's really red, hon."

Chelsea started laughing again, and Farrah gave Molly a knowing wink before cocking her head to one side. "I hear a boat."

Farrah walked to the back door, casually grabbing her rifle in a move that Harper missed, though Molly did not. But then her phone buzzed with a message from Burke.

Wake up, sleepyhead. Time to work. We're 1 min out so b decent.

"It's Burke," Molly said, and Farrah relaxed, quietly placing her rifle by the door.

Chelsea stood and began wiping the crumbs from the table, but Farrah stayed her hand. "I'll do it," their hostess said with the warmest smile Molly might ever have seen. "You get Harper's things together while I put Gabe and Molly's dinner into plastic containers. I'll clean the kitchen before I leave."

Burke appeared in the doorway, studying Molly before giving her a quick glance that said that he knew what she and Gabe had been up to. She wanted to blush, to deny, to say something, but he just grinned at her. "You and Gabe look . . . rested."

"They took a nap," Harper told him soberly.

He smiled down at her. "Naps are good. Time to get going. We have places to go, people to see. Oh, and cookies to eat. Are those for me?"

"They are, Uncle Burke," Harper said. "I made them all by myself."

"Then we shall have ourselves a true feast on my boat." He lifted Harper to his hip and kissed her cheek. "You ready, princess?"

Harper's nod was grim. "Yes, sir. Aunt Molly, you're gonna find who tried to hurt us, right?"

Molly brought Harper's face close and pressed a kiss to her forehead. "I promise." Then she turned to their hostess. "Farrah, I don't know how we'll ever thank you."

"Just stay safe and trust my André. He'll do the right thing."

"Of that we have no doubt." Gabe extended a hand to Farrah, but she grabbed him for a hug before walking them to the dock.

"Be safe. Watch out for gators. I'll be by the Choux soon for chocolate cake!" she called as the boat pulled away.

"I'm going to give her the freaking recipe," Gabe muttered. "Such hospitality—and soft beds—cannot go unrewarded."

Molly faced the darkness over the river with one of Burke's rifles in her hand and a smile on her face.

Bayou Gauche, Louisiana
THURSDAY, JULY 28, 11:15 P.M.

"Have we become nocturnal?" Willa Mae asked when everyone was settled in Burke's living room, including Antoine, who sat on the floor, his three laptops placed in a semicircle around him.

"Seems so, ma'am," Burke said, sitting in his recliner.

They were seated much as they had been before—Gabe and Molly sitting with Cicely on the sofa, Willa Mae in "her" rocking chair, her knitting needles in motion. Xavier sat on the kitchen chair beside her, and Carlos and Manny were on the floor with the Xbox. Molly had her tablet, prepared to take notes.

Only André was missing, focused on the investigation into Mule's murder.

Chelsea had taken Harper and Shoe into Burke's bedroom, which he'd insisted they occupy until it was safe for them to go home. The two were watching a movie, Chelsea having given up on keeping Harper to a schedule. Harper was wired on sugar from the cookies. And far too grim and tense for an eight-year-old girl.

Gabe hoped the volume of the movie would keep Harper from overhearing anything they'd be discussing. "Thank you again for coming to help us today, Miss Willa Mae. It was nice having a lawyer we could trust."

"Don't you think another thing about it," Willa Mae said. "It was the least I could do, since you're helping Xavier and Cicely out of this mess that Xavier's gotten himself into."

Gabe blinked, but the slow grin on Xavier's face said that this was welcome banter, so he turned to Burke. "What do we know?"

Burke motioned to Antoine. "You want to do the honors?"

Antoine looked up from his three laptop screens. "Houston PD has identified the man who killed Xavier's home invader. He's Tyson Whitley, who lives in Dallas, but he's originally from New Orleans."

"Connection," Molly murmured.

Antoine nodded. "Exactly. He was arrested and charged for selling drugs to middle school students in the Eleventh Ward when he was eighteen. That was five years ago. Did four months of a one-year sentence before he was released for good behavior. He was brought in for questioning again a few years later, this time for selling drugs and weapons to a different group of kids in St. Bernard Parish. He claimed he was innocent, and he was never charged. There's really nothing to indicate why Whitley was let go back then."

"How did they ID him this time?" Carlos asked.

"Houston PD used facial recognition," Antoine said. "Even though he wore a fake beard, he didn't change his eyes and the software's gotten good at just using eyes. When HPD arrested him, Whitley claimed that he was innocent and hadn't ever been to Houston, but a gas station security camera has him in the city just thirty minutes after our mystery man breathed his last."

"How do you know all—" Gabe cut off the question. "Never mind. I don't want to know."

Antoine grinned. "You learn quick, Hebert. So far, Whitley's not talking, so we don't know why he was there and what connection he has to either the man he killed or all our goings-on."

"Hm," Molly murmured. "Meth Guy, whose car was stolen this morning—the car the hoodie guy used and then left at the bayou scene— he was also in trouble with the law in New Orleans and walked away from a drug charge."

"Good point," Burke said. "Your"—he coughed—"*nap* did good things for your brain, Molly."

She flipped him an unoffended bird. "I wonder if there's a connection between Meth Guy and Tyson Whitley."

"Could be," Antoine said. "I'll look into it. Mule is loosely connected to both George Haslet—that's Meth Guy—and to Whitley through this case. But I'll see if the two are directly connected. Hold on one second. Let me get back into HPD's case file . . ." They waited in silence, then Antoine did a double take. "Huh. You're right, Molly. I'm looking at Whitley's cell phone records now. The number that called him just hours before he killed Xavier's intruder was the same number that called Meth Guy, a few hours before Mule was murdered. So they might not be directly connected to each other, but they are connected through whoever called them."

Yes, Gabe thought. A few more dots connected.

"Called it," Molly told Burke, who nodded his respect.

Xavier leaned forward, excited. "Mule called them both?"

Antoine shook his head. "Nope. Not unless he used a different phone than the one he used to text Nicholas Tobin instructions to abduct Chelsea and Harper last night. I mean, it's possible that Mule had multiple burners. I do. The big takeaway here is that the same person contacted both Whitley and Haslet."

"What about the hit man?" Carlos asked. "Eckert?"

Antoine scowled. "I can't get into that report. It's not being kept in the same database as Haslet's information. I've been trying to get in, to look at what they know, but I keep coming up against a brick wall. I will get through, but I'm not sure how long it'll take."

Molly tilted her head, frowning in confusion. "Wait. Let's assume that whoever stole Meth Guy's car and killed him was the same person who then drove to the bayou, dumped most of the woman's remains, and then killed Mule."

"Reasonable assumption," Burke allowed. "So?"

"So," Molly continued, "Mule is brass, so I'd think his case would be blocked. Why are you able to get into Meth Guy's information, but not Eckert's?"

Antoine touched his nose. "*That* is the one-million-dollar question. Although Burke won't pay me a million to break into the case file."

"I pay you enough," Burke grunted.

"More than," Antoine agreed. "But a man can dream, right?"

"Dream cheaper," Burke said. "But Molly's right. What's Eckert got in his file that's so damn secret?"

"Maybe not a what," Molly said. "Maybe a who."

"Lotsa maybes," Willa Mae observed. "Do we know who that poor woman was? The one that ADA Cardozo knew but wasn't gonna tell us?"

"Nope," Antoine said. "If her identity is known, it hasn't been recorded anywhere. Not that I can find."

"So, Eckert the hit man and the female victim—who lied about being Nadia Hall's sister and set Molly up to be injured in a house bombing—they have the *same* level of security?" Gabe asked.

Antoine shrugged. "Maybe. I haven't even found a reference to her remains being found yet. It's possible that it's also being locked down."

"Interesting," Molly murmured. "What else?"

"I've found more info on your father's hard drive, Gabe," Antoine said. "I've had my artificial intelligence software piecing together all the fragments I found. The program guesses the letters and words in the gaps based on normal language patterns."

Carlos perked up. "Like predictive text in reverse?"

"More like predictive text came from the software," Manny said.

Antoine looked impressed. "Exactly right, Manny."

Manny smiled smugly, and Carlos shot him a pointed glance. "How do you know this?" Carlos demanded.

"You're not the only smart one in the family, *pendejo*," Manny answered, avoiding Carlos's punch.

"What did you find, Antoine?" Gabe asked, trying to be patient.

"Oh. The name of the doctor he was looking for, actually, but we figured it out already."

"Did my dad say how he found Benson?" Gabe asked. "Did he find someone else who knew Nadia?"

"Actually, you were pretty close last night when you suggested checking into medications," Antoine told him. "The night he found her body during Katrina, Rocky also found a medicine bottle with the name Jane Smith printed on the label as the recipient. The prescriber was from the same practice as Dr. Benson—his partner, Dr. Géraud Cousineau."

"Nadia used a fake name with her ob-gyn," Cicely said. "She was either ashamed that she was pregnant or scared of what would happen if someone found out. Like maybe the baby's father?"

"Poor Nadia," Molly said quietly. "She so wanted to believe the BS he was feeding her. She wanted a family."

Gabe sighed, afraid to ask his next question. More afraid of the answer. "What happened to Dr. Cousineau?"

"He's dead," Antoine said gently. "Shot himself."

Gabe swallowed. "Like my dad 'shot himself'?"

Antoine shrugged again. "Maybe. It happened a few weeks after Katrina. The hospitals and morgues were filled. MEs were working around the clock. If an autopsy was done, I don't imagine it was too thorough. Benson left the practice after Cousineau's death. He left the city, in fact, like so many people did. He eventually came back once he retired. He'd lived in the house where he died for less than a year."

Molly held up a finger. "Wait. April Frazier said that she gave Benson's name to Nadia. How did she end up with Cousineau?"

"He might not have had any appointments," Cicely said. "If she was in a hurry, they might have set her up with the other partner. Or she might have seen them both. It's often encouraged for pregnant women to have at least one appointment with all of the practice's doctors, in case her own isn't available for the birth."

"Okay," Molly said, frowning. "I guess I was reacting to the fact that Dr. Benson was murdered when he might not have even known Nadia. I guess it doesn't matter, but I'd like to know."

"What I'd like to know," Gabe pressed, "was how Benson's killer knew that my dad was looking for him. You said that Dad started calling him a month before his death, up until the day Benson died. But how did their killer know that they were talking? Dad was careful. They could have bugged Dad's phone, but then they would have known a lot more and sooner. Like where Xavier was."

"Yeah," Xavier said. "Why'd they wait six weeks after killing Rocky to come after me?"

Carlos frowned, very serious now. "I wondered the same thing. Seems like once they knew about X, they'd have come after him ASAP. Sorry, Mrs. M," he added when Cicely recoiled.

"Not your fault, Carlos," she assured him. "It's just hard to think that someone was stalking my son. Antoine, do you know why they picked Monday to come after him?"

Antoine tilted his hand back and forth. "I can guess. The documents I put through AI were not only fragmented, but they were also encrypted. I had to find the key. That made it more difficult and took a while. And I know what I'm doing."

"You said that whoever killed Rocky knew how to wipe his hard drive," Molly said.

Antoine shrugged. "It's a lot easier to destroy a drive than to put one back together. If Rocky's killer didn't have an IT guy as good as me, it could have taken them that long to sift through his hard drive and unencrypt everything. Six weeks seems like a long time, but it's possible it could have taken that long."

"What about how they knew my dad was searching for Benson?" Gabe insisted.

"I don't know yet," Antoine said.

"Paul Lott," Molly said thoughtfully. "It's the only thing that makes sense. He's the puzzle piece that we haven't known where to put, but now I think we do. I'm betting that somehow Lott knew Rocky's personal business. He knew about Xavier because Rocky set up a trust. He didn't know where Xavier lived, only that he had a UPS box in Baton Rouge. He was in contact with Mule the night that Rocky was killed. What if Paul Lott knew what Rocky was up to? What your dad was investigating?"

Gabe considered it. "I don't think that Dad would have told him. He didn't trust him completely. Not enough to give him Xavier's home address, anyway, or his personal cell number. Just Xavier's burner."

Molly grabbed his hand and held it. "I didn't say your father confided in him, Gabe."

Gabe frowned. "You think Lott was spying on my father?"

"I think we need to follow the money where Lott is concerned," Molly said. "If he knew that Rocky was giving Xavier an inheritance, he knew that Xavier was important. If nothing else, maybe he thought the same thing that you did initially—that your dad was Xavier's biological father. Maybe he figured he could blackmail your father. We need to know more about Mr. Lott."

Burke was nodding. "You're right, Molly. It's one of the loose ends that doesn't seem to fit anywhere else. Antoine? Can you get into Lott's bank records? See if there were any large deposits recently?"

Antoine was already tapping frenetically on his keyboard. "It might take a while, but I'm on it. That was all I had, by the way."

Burke rubbed his hands down his face wearily. "Then are we done?"

"No," Xavier said. "We were busy today, too. Nothing came of it—"

"So far," Carlos interrupted.

"So far," Xavier allowed. "We wanted to follow up on Madame Fluffy, Nadia's dog."

Molly sat up straighter. "You called vets?"

"We did," Xavier said, wincing a little because Burke was glowering.

"Without clearing it with me?" Burke thundered, then snapped his mouth closed, throwing a glance toward the bedroom where Chelsea and Harper were watching a movie. He exhaled through his nose, visibly trying to rein in his temper. "What did you do? And who is 'we'?"

"*We* included *me*," Cicely said sharply. "So, please watch your tone, Mr. Broussard."

Burke just shook his head, still angry. "What did you do, Xavier?" he asked more quietly.

"We got a list of veterinarians and called them," Xavier said nervously.

"We used Manny's phone," Carlos added, his chin lifted defiantly. "It's a burner, too, so no one can trace it to us."

"And we spoofed the number we called from, so the cops couldn't see a pattern," Manny said. "We'd used my phone to text with the guy posing as Paul Lott, so I didn't want that out there."

"We said we owned an Afghan hound," Xavier explained. "We said we'd gotten her as a puppy, but didn't know the breeder's name. Just the puppy's mama's name. Madame Fluffy."

Cicely's chin was also lifted. "We said that our Afghan had died recently of a hereditary condition and wanted to let the breeder know in case she'd bred that dog again—so that the other dog owners could be warned. We figured that if a vet recognized the dog's name, they'd know that its owner wasn't a breeder, but maybe they'd get back with us anyway. Breeders sell their older dogs sometimes. It was a decent story. Most of the vets said that they had no records of the dog or that they weren't around back then. But a few said they'd get back to us."

"We each made a few calls," Manny finished. "So that if anyone tried to connect the dots, the vets wouldn't have been able to agree on a single voice."

"It's what I would have done, Burke," Molly said softly, then turned to Cicely and the others. "But what happens when someone calls you back? You spoofed the number. When they call back, it'll go to someone else's phone."

"Only three people said they'd call us," Xavier said. "We gave two of them Molly's burner number . . ." He trailed off, wincing. "And we gave the third one Burke's burner number."

Molly smiled. "Exactly what I would have done." She gave Burke a pointed glance. "And what you would have done, too."

"Yeah, yeah," Burke grumbled. "Next time give me some warning. I could have given you fresh burners. But . . ." He rubbed the back of his neck. "It was good thinking. Thank you. And I'm sorry I shouted, Cicely."

"Apology accepted," Cicely said. "We called nearly every veterinarian in New Orleans and all the surrounding neighborhoods. I suppose all we have to do now is wait."

"And check Xavier's UPS box in Baton Rouge," Willa Mae said. "At one point, you, Burke, thought Lott or one of the others might have sent a booby-trapped package to that box, hoping to track Xavier. I think any investigation into what Paul Lott did or did not know has to include that box."

"You're right," Burke said. "I let that ball drop. I'll drive out to Baton Rouge tomorrow morning, first thing. Xavier, you said you had the key?"

Xavier started to get up. "Yeah. I can get it for you now."

Burke waved him to sit back down. "In the morning is soon enough. I'll open your box, but if there are any packages larger than the box holds, you might have to retrieve them personally or sign something that says I can. We'll see what's there first before I make any requests of the clerk who works there. Best to keep it low-key for now. Molly, can you recap?"

Molly scrolled back through the notes on her tablet. "Tyson Whit-ley, who killed Xavier's intruder, and George Haslet, a.k.a. Meth Guy, were both called from the same phone, both hours before Whitley killed a John Doe and Haslet was killed for his car. This was a separate number than the one Mule used to contact Tobin. Antoine is checking connections. Both doctors at Nadia's practice are dead. Paul Lott may have been spying on Rocky and might have given Mule a heads-up on Xavier's whereabouts. Antoine is checking."

"Antoine is busy," Antoine muttered.

"You love it," Molly said, and Antoine flashed her a smile. "The fe-male victim from this morning—who gave a fake name and posed as Nadia Hall's sister—has been identified by the ADA, but if it has been recorded somewhere, it's behind the same wall as Eckert's case files, which even André can't access. Which could mean that a high-profile person or persons are involved. Or the Feds," she added. "André said they were on the case, too. Also, Xavier et al. called New Orleans vet-erinarians seeking the owner of Madame Fluffy. And . . ." She paused dramatically. "Burke apologized for losing his temper."

Burke sneered, but it was followed by a rueful smile. "That is true. And tomorrow I go to Baton Rouge to check Xavier's box." He closed the recliner and stretched his arms toward the ceiling. "Time for bed. Molly, you're in with Chelsea and Harper in my room. It'll be a squeeze for all three of you in the bed, but I expect you won't want Harper that far out of your sight anyway."

"You expect correctly," Molly said, a shudder shaking her.

"Antoine? You staying or going?" Burke asked.

"Staying," Antoine said, not looking up from his laptops. "I'll be up most of the night. I'll crash on the couch if I need to catch a nap. Wouldn't be the first time."

"Gabe," Burke said, "I've got two inflatable mattresses that I can set up in my office. I snore, so if that bothers you, there's an extra twin bed in the room Xavier, Carlos, and Manny are sharing."

"I got dibs on the bottom bunk," Carlos said defensively.

Xavier rolled his eyes. "He'll break the damn ladder to the top bunk, Carlos. You're shorter. And younger. You should climb, not him."

Gabe laughed. "Thank you, Xavier, even though I think you just called me old. It's okay, Carlos. I won't steal your spot. Burke, I can sleep through snoring, but I'm too wired to sleep for a while. Molly and I just woke up a few hours ago." He rose and offered a hand to Cicely first, then Willa Mae, then to Molly. "Good night, everyone. Molly, coffee?"

She smiled up at him. "That sounds good."

"Antoine, you want some?" Gabe asked.

"Please." Antoine glanced up hopefully. "And anything you can cook. I'm starving."

"So am I," Carlos said.

"Me, too," Manny said.

Gabe laughed again. "I guess I'm cooking a midnight snack. Let me check what's in the fridge."

25

MOLLY HURRIED FROM the room she'd shared with her sister and niece, then breathed a sigh of relief to see Gabe at the stove with Harper standing beside him. She'd nearly had heart failure when she'd woken to find Harper gone.

But Harper was safe, solemnly hanging on Gabe's every word as he taught her to fry fish. Both Harper and Manny, in fact. Manny seemed to have found a calling, handling the pan of frying fish like a pro.

"Something smells good," Molly said, and all three of them whirled around to greet her.

"Gabe is showing me how to make fish for breakfast," Harper said, but still without a sign of her usual spark. This wasn't a huge surprise given the trauma of what had happened in their apartment, but Molly's heart still sank, nonetheless.

It was hard not to feel guilty, since she'd led the trouble to their door.

"Gabe and I caught it off the dock," Manny explained, then grimaced. "I've never cleaned my own fish before. It was . . . yeah. So much fun."

Molly forced a laugh for Harper's sake. "Oh, I've cleaned more than my fair share of fish."

Harper's eyes widened. "You have?"

"Oh yeah." Molly took the cup of coffee that Gabe passed to her, leaning up to plant a quick kiss on his mouth. "Your granddad took me fishing all the time. I miss those days so much." It was as woven into the memories of her father as putting down seeds in the spring. She thought about Gabe's suggestion that she volunteer in someone else's garden and promised herself that she would. When all this was over. Maybe she'd even take Harper. "But the fish I fried back then never smelled as good as this does."

"Secret ingredient," Gabe said soberly.

"Old Bay," Manny said with an eye roll.

Gabe laughed. "It was all Burke had in his kitchen and I didn't bring my spices."

It was good to see him so happy. The man truly was at home in a kitchen. She took a seat at the table and watched him show Manny and Harper how to prep for the sides. They were chopping chives and . . . other stuff she couldn't identify. Apparently for grits.

Her stomach growled. "Is it almost done?"

Harper looked over her shoulder. "Are you hungry, Aunt Molly?"

"Starving." She patted her knee, and Harper settled in. "How are you, munchkin? I wanted to spend all day with you yesterday, but things got busy."

"I know," Harper said in that too-grown-up way. "You promised you'd find who sent those men to hurt us. That's more important than watching some dumb old movies with me."

"Well, first of all, any time I spend with you is important and not dumb. Second of all, who made you the judge of old movies? I might have liked them."

Harper didn't smile. "Is there a third of all?"

"There is. I am trying to find the bad people and I don't know how long it will take."

"Do we have to stay here?" She grew visibly upset. "Forever?"

"Might not be so bad," Manny said lightly. "We've got internet, an Xbox, and this food is good."

"I didn't get to play Xbox last night," Harper pointed out, crossing her arms over her chest. "I had to go to bed, and you and Carlos got to play all night. I heard you."

"We weren't playing *all* night," Manny protested. "But I'm sorry we kept you awake."

"It's okay," Harper said with a slight lift of her shoulder. "I couldn't sleep anyway."

Molly shared a troubled glance with Gabe. *Note to self: make an appointment for Harper with her therapist ASAP.*

They'd all go, just as they'd done after Jake.

But before she could broach the topic of Harper's sleepless night, Manny saved the day.

"What about *Mario Kart*?" he asked. "Can you play that?"

"That's not on Xbox," Harper said, a pout beginning to form.

Manny wagged his finger. "This is true, but I brought my Switch, and it has *Mario Kart*. Play me after breakfast?"

Harper perked up. Not a smile, but not a listless frown. "I will smear you," she vowed.

Molly smiled at him over Harper's head. "Thank you," she mouthed, and Manny winked.

Harper turned back to her. "Is Lucien all right?"

"He is. I got a text from Val this morning saying that he should be getting out of the hospital in a day or two."

Harper sagged, relieved. "I was worried that he'd die. He was brave. He saved us."

"He was and he did," Molly agreed. "Maybe you can Skype with him later?"

"I will." Harper wriggled out of her lap. "But right now, I'm in charge of grating cheese for the grits."

"What have we here?" Burke asked from the back doorway. "Oh my, oh my. We are gonna feast this morning." He dropped a kiss on top of Harper's head, got himself some coffee, then plopped into a chair. "If I have to share my house, at least I'll eat the best food in New Orleans."

"Hear, hear," Molly said, lifting her cup. She leaned in to murmur to Burke, "You're not planning on going to Baton Rouge alone, are you?"

"I was."

"Well, you're not now."

"Bossy," Burke said mildly. "I thought you weren't supposed to leave town?"

Molly scowled. "They just say that. They can't keep me from driving a couple hours away. I'm not letting you go alone."

Gabe put some bacon on the table. "And where she goes, I go."

"You got ears like a bat," Burke grumbled.

Gabe grinned. "No, I just know Molly well enough by now to know she was negotiating to go with you."

"What are we negotiating?" Willa Mae asked as she joined them at the table. "What smells so good? Fish and grits? Now you're speaking my language."

"His French food's pretty darn good, too," Molly said loyally.

"That's because you're sweet on him," Willa Mae said with a smile.

"She is," Gabe agreed, serving the older woman a cup of coffee. "But it's still true."

One at a time, the house's occupants stumbled into the kitchen, Xavier annoyed that Manny didn't wake him to go fishing.

"You were sawin' z's, X," Manny claimed. "And I did try. You smacked me."

Xavier frowned in apology. "Sorry. I'll set my alarm tomorrow and get up with you."

"If we're still here tomorrow," Cicely said. "I'm hoping something breaks today. I'm grateful for this lovely place to hide, but I miss my own bed."

"I know," Burke said. "We're trying our best."

Cicely patted his hand. "And I'm truly grateful. Thank you."

That Harper was at the table was a good thing, Molly thought. She'd been craving normal conversation, and Harper's presence kept them from talking about the case.

But the respite was short-lived. After breakfast, Chelsea took Harper back to their room for another movie. *Time to get to work.*

Carlos and Xavier had made quick work of the dishes and Molly was afraid to drink any more coffee. She was wired enough. She and Gabe had stayed up late talking about his father and what he remembered about Paul Lott until they were both tired enough to sleep, but that meant that neither of them had slept much.

She wondered if Gabe had slept at all. He had to have risen before dawn to catch the fish. He looked tired. Or maybe it was everything weighing on his shoulders. After all, he'd killed a man little more than twenty-four hours before, and they still hadn't really talked about it. But now wasn't the time and here wasn't the place. She'd wait until they were alone for that.

"You talk to Patty this morning?" Molly asked him, choosing another pressing concern. Val had texted her updates, but she knew that Gabe had been worrying about his cousin. Hearing from her directly would be a good start at easing his mind.

"I did. She and Val are recuperating well, and Phin is still guarding them. Patty's been cooking for them all, and that makes her happy."

"One load off our mind," Molly murmured. "How about Harry Peterson? Has he regained consciousness?" The ME's assistant had paid dearly for helping Gabe and she knew that it was one more thing that weighed on him.

"Not yet," Burke said. "I talked to André this morning. They're waiting for Harry to wake up so that he can identify his attackers, but so far nothing. I'm hoping to find something in that damn box of Xavier's."

"You and me both," Antoine said. "I was online most of the night, and I'm still not into Paul Lott's bank accounts. I hope there's something useful in that box."

"Oh," Xavier said. "I'll go get the key."

But he and everyone else froze when Molly's burner buzzed. Remembering that the Houston folks had given her number to the veterinarians yesterday, she answered cautiously. "Hello?" she asked as Xavier made a show of crossing his fingers.

"Hi, this is Dr. Watts. I'm trying to reach Mr. Carlos Manuel."

Carlos Manuel? His last name was Hernandez. Then it clicked. Manny was short for Manuel. Smart, using a combination name that they'd easily remember.

"He's sitting here with me. Can I put you on speakerphone?" He agreed and she set the phone on the table where everyone was holding their breath. "Carlos, this is Dr. Watts."

"Hello, sir, and thank you for calling me back," Carlos said. "I'm hoping this means you remember Madame Fluffy."

"Oh, I do," the vet said. "Not often that a dog like her comes into my office. She was a stunner. I'm sorry to say that she passed away, though. She was twelve and that's rather old for an Afghan."

Molly's heart started to pound. *This could be it.* The break they'd been searching for. She prepared to take notes.

"I figured she'd have passed by now," Carlos said. "As we told your office manager yesterday, we'd really like to contact the breeder, just to let her know."

"Of course," the vet said. "But I don't think Madame Fluffy's owner was a breeder. She never mentioned it, anyway. It is possible the breeder wanted a litter out of Madame Fluffy, though. She was a magnificent animal. At any rate, I'm sure that Lucille would like to hear from you. She loved that dog so much. It was a gift from her husband, right after Katrina. The previous owner had to put the dog up for adoption when the flood destroyed her home. Lucille wanted to change the dog's name, but she'd only answer to Madame Fluffy, so she gave up trying."

"Lucille?" Carlos asked hopefully. "Do you remember her last name?"

"Of course. It's Ducote."

Ducote. Molly knew that name, but it couldn't be the person she was thinking of. It just couldn't be. But Burke's expression was grim, and he was googling as fast as she was. Antoine looked stunned as well.

"I haven't seen her for quite a while, come to think of it," the vet went on. "Tell her that I miss her and hope she's well."

"Thank you, sir. And thanks for calling me back." Brows raised in question, Carlos looked around the table, getting a grim nod from Burke before ending the call.

"Lucille Ducote," Xavier said slowly, looking from Molly to Antoine to Burke. "Why do you all look so freaked out?"

Molly stared at her phone's screen. "Lucille Ducote is dead. She shot herself in the head twelve years ago."

"Who was she, Molly?" Gabe asked quietly.

"The first wife of Lamont Ducote," Molly said. "And Lamont Ducote—"

"Is one of the ADAs of Orleans Parish," Burke finished.

Gabe stared, blinking in shock. "An ADA? As in one of the assistant district attorneys?"

Molly nodded, dread descending over her like a dark cloud. "This is really, really bad."

Bayou Gauche, Louisiana
FRIDAY, JULY 29, 8:45 A.M.

Gabe's brain was spinning. *Lamont Ducote.* An assistant district attorney of New Orleans.

The man who was supposed to be putting killers away.

He'd killed Nadia Hall.

Did he kill my father, too?

There was silence around the table, expressions ranging from shock to rage to confusion.

Gabe felt all of that, all at once. He didn't need to be a PI to know that if someone that high in the food chain was involved, it would be covered up. The alternative would be chaos in the entire New Orleans justice system.

The number of cases that might have been compromised was simply staggering to consider.

If Lamont Ducote was guilty, he'd be hard as hell to take down.

If Lamont Ducote was guilty, Gabe would do exactly that or go to his grave trying.

"An ADA?" Cicely finally asked. "Are you sure?"

"I'm sure that Lucille Ducote is dead," Molly said. "I'm sure that her husband is an ADA. As for her inheriting Madame Fluffy, I can't see why this veterinarian would lie. We'll check out his story, of course, but for now I'm assuming his word is good."

Cicely turned to Willa Mae. "This isn't the same ADA you talked to yesterday, is it?"

"No, that was ADA Cardozo," Willa Mae said. "I have to admit, I didn't see this coming."

Xavier had been standing, but now sat in his chair with a loud thump. "The ADA killed his mistress and gave his wife her hand-me-down dog? What kind of person does that?"

"The kind of person who has a mistress to start with," Willa Mae said.

"Especially the kind that kills said mistress," Cicely murmured.

"He wasn't an ADA back during Katrina," Burke said. "I'm not sure what he was doing back before Katrina, but we're sure as hell going to find out."

Cicely still looked shell-shocked. "Poor Rocky. I wonder if he knew?"

"I don't think so," Antoine said. "I haven't found anything suggesting that he did. But he knew something was off. Everything is en-crypted or coded or . . . simply not there. He's referenced another file, but I can't find it on his hard drive. It's possible it's been written over so that I can't get it back. I'll keep trying."

Gabe wasn't sure if what his father had known even mattered any-more. "If Ducote killed Nadia . . ." He swallowed and squared his shoulders. "Did he also kill my father? Could he have been the man in the hoodie?"

"It's possible," Molly said. "But we'll need more proof than a hand-me-down dog."

Burke pinched the bridge of his nose. "I have to tell André. Hope-fully he'll have some ideas."

Molly took Gabe's hand and held it tight. "But at least now we know *something*. Lamont Ducote's mistress got pregnant. He killed her and maybe killed her ob-gyn to cover the trail. At some point he may have even killed his own wife, because a whole lot of people are shooting themselves in the head."

"Wait," Xavier said quietly, and everyone turned to look at him. He'd borrowed Carlos's phone and now looked up from whatever he'd been staring at, his expression troubled. "I found his photo. He looks like the man I saw that night—or what I remember, anyway—except he doesn't have a scar. The man who killed Nadia *definitely* had a scar. And Ducote doesn't."

Gabe's stomach clenched. They'd been so close. *Back to the drawing board.*

"Let me see that." Carlos took his phone back and squinted at the photo, then pinched his screen to enlarge it. "He doesn't have one now. This photo is from earlier this year, but look at his cheek, X. Look closely."

Xavier leaned over, frowning as he stared. "There's a line on his face. But it's not the same scar. It was big and wide and . . . terrifying. I re-member the scar."

"Give me a minute," Antoine muttered, his fingers flying over his laptop keyboard. Then he smiled sharply before turning his screen so that Xavier could see. "What about this?"

Xavier flinched as if he'd been slapped. "Yeah. That's him."

Molly leaned forward to study a much younger Lamont Ducote—who bore a stark, noticeable scar that ran from his eye to his chin, bisecting his cheek. "He had the scar fixed," she murmured. "When was this photo taken?"

"Back in 2001," Antoine said. "He was a defense attorney back then."

"So that's him." Gabe's voice trembled, the reality dizzying. "I guess we just need to know if he killed my father, too, and if he killed Mule. And what role did Mule play in all of this?"

Molly sandwiched his hand between hers. "What did your father know and when did he know it? Did he have proof? And if he did, what was it and where did he hide it? Burke, let's talk to André first, then leave for Baton Rouge."

Burke had started to rise, when his cell phone began ringing. Sighing heavily, he lowered himself to the chair and answered. "Val? What's wrong?"

Molly stiffened because Burke's eyes were sliding closed, his shoulders slumping wearily. "You're going to call André, right?" He listened a moment longer, then nodded. "Call me if you get any more unexpected company." He ended the call and looked straight at Gabe. "Patty is fine. Val is fine. Both are unhurt with no new assaults. Phin's still with them."

Gabe's grip on her hand tightened. "Then what's wrong?" he asked hoarsely.

Burke's jaw tightened. "You had a mole in the Choux."

Gabe shook his head. "What? Who?"

"Donna Lee Green."

Gabe recoiled. "No. No way. I can't believe that. She's . . ." He tried to draw a breath, but his lungs felt so flat. "I trust her."

Burke looked down at his hands before looking up again, his expression full of remorse. "I'm sorry, Gabe, but she confessed. She heard what happened—what almost happened—to Patty and showed up at her house first thing, sobbing her eyes out. She saw Tobin's photo in the paper and knew she'd been 'used' for information. She felt guilty and couldn't 'live the lie' any longer."

"Who hired her?" Antoine demanded.

"She said it was Tobin," Burke said. "And Val said that the phone number in Donna Lee's call log matched Tobin's cell. Gabe, I'm so sorry, but she was reporting back to Tobin on your whereabouts. She told him that Molly came in to meet you at the Choux on Monday. You know, when you and Patty left with her."

"When someone followed us back here," Gabe murmured. *In an unmarked NOPD car.*

"What else did she tell them?" Antoine demanded.

Gabe felt Molly stiffen beside him, but she said nothing.

Still reeling, Gabe tilted her chin, forcing her to look at him. "What?"

She looked devastated. *For me*, he realized. And somehow that helped.

"The pathologist," she said quietly. "I've been worrying in my mind how 'they' found out about the private autopsy you had done. The only people that knew were here in this room, plus André and your cousin."

Gabe frowned, suddenly furious. He dropped Molly's hand like it was on fire. "You're saying Patty blabbed to 'them,' whoever 'they' are? That's ludicrous."

Molly snatched his hand back, sandwiching it between hers once again, holding fast when he tried to tug free. "No, she didn't blab to *them*. She told her parents, so they would know to leave town. To keep them safe. And if she told them while she was at the Choux . . ."

"Donna Lee could have heard her," Gabe said, his stomach feeling like lead. "Oh my God. Patty can't know. Not about Dr. McLain or Dusty Woodruff. She . . . My God. Patty dated Dusty in high school. They were friends. She'd never forgive herself."

"We'll do our best not to let her figure it out," Burke promised.

"Why did Donna Lee do it?" Gabe asked hoarsely. He hoped it was for a good reason. Two people had died because Donna Lee had told them things she'd had no right knowing.

Burke sighed. "Tobin had photos of her with another man. She didn't want her husband to know. Maybe she figured that Tobin was no longer a threat to her, since he'd been arrested. Whatever her motivation, her confession answers a number of questions."

Gabe lowered his head, trying not to lose it. But it was fucking hard not to do so.

This was betrayal. *Two people who helped me are dead because Donna Lee wanted to protect her marriage?* He wanted to scream.

"There's more," Burke said gently. "But this is better news. Donna Lee also had texts to Mule's number on her phone. She swears that she didn't know the name of anyone she was dealing with, but when Val pressed her for what she'd said to Mule, guess what she answered?"

Molly exhaled excitedly. "Something having to do with Lamont Ducote?"

"Right in one," Burke said. "She told Mule whenever Ducote came into the Choux."

Gabe's head jerked up. "What? He was in my place?"

"Donna Lee said that he was in your place several times," Burke confirmed. "Usually at lunch. Started up right after your father was killed, so I think he was keeping an eye on you. He came in once for dinner with his wife and another couple. He took a few texts that night before focusing on his fellow dinner guests."

"Who was the other couple?" Molly asked.

"Lyle Nelson and his wife, Lorraine."

Gabe frowned. "I don't know those names."

"Oh, I do," Burke said grimly.

"So do I," Antoine chimed in. "Nelson's a rich dude who dabbles in politics. He's part of one of the oldest krewes and has been for as long as I can remember. He's also a philanthropist and wants *everyone* to know it."

"Fancies himself a political kingmaker," Burke added. "If he's a donor, his beneficiary usually wins whatever election they're in."

Molly let go of Gabe's hand, her fingers tapping furiously on her phone's keyboard. "I wondered why this was happening now," she said triumphantly. "Katrina was over fifteen years ago. I wondered why, after all this time, he went after your father now."

"Because Dad went after him," Gabe said uncertainly. "He was running out of time."

Because he was sick and never told me.

Molly nodded. "True, but your father had tried to investigate this case many times before and all he got was either a reprimand or a threat that they'd fire him so that he'd lose his health insurance. I wondered, why now? It's because Ducote is planning a run for the Senate."

"State senate?" Cicely asked.

"Nope. He was aiming higher." Molly held her phone so that the rest of them could see her screen. Sure enough, there was the headline. *Ducote rumored to run for US Senate.*

Gabe's throat thickened. "He killed my father so that he could run for office?"

Molly sighed. "I'm sorry, Gabe. It looks like it. I mean, maybe he was alarmed that your father was investigating again, especially because Rocky had ramped up his efforts. Your dad had told them that the eyewitness had died in Katrina, but then he inadvertently outed Xavier as still alive when he asked Paul Lott to set up that trust. He was close to finding Dr. Benson. An allegation of murder would be a terrible scandal. It would destroy any political aspirations Ducote had."

Gabe rubbed his hands over his face. He was so damned tired. And every time he thought about someone forcing his father to take that drink of Grey Goose, someone drugging his father, someone putting a gun in his hand and pulling the trigger . . .

His eyes burned. *Dammit. You will not fall apart here.*

But he was going to. He could feel the sob forming in his chest and he couldn't breathe. Shoving back from the table, he lurched to his feet, ran out the back door, and stumbled down the stairs.

Just in time. He leaned against one of the pilings, bending at the waist because he couldn't hold his body upright another second longer. Grief and rage and fear . . . it all swirled like a hurricane, filling him. *Not fair. Not fair. Not fucking fair.*

The noise that came out of his mouth didn't even sound human. His legs folded beneath him and he fell on his ass and he didn't even care. He couldn't breathe, like an elephant was sitting on his chest.

Then he was enveloped in soft arms. Strong arms.

And the scent of oranges.

Molly. She didn't say a word, just held him, rocking him as he cried, raking her fingers through his hair, lightly scraping her nails over his scalp. He wound his arms around her, holding fast. Knowing that this was safety. He could cry in her arms, and she would never judge him.

And she would help him take his father's killer down. It was the one thought that circled in his brain, over and over. *We have to make him pay. We have to.*

He wasn't sure how long they sat on the ground. She never let him go and he clutched her like she was the last post standing in a storm.

Finally, he could breathe again. He shuddered out a final sob, dragging air back into his lungs. Then he sagged against her, confident that she wouldn't let him fall. She urged him down until his head lay in her lap. Her fingers never stopped stroking his hair, his face.

"Thank you," he whispered, unsurprised that his throat now ached.

"You're welcome," she whispered back.

"We should move," he said wearily.

"Nah. We're good here for a bit longer."

He frowned, trying to think. "But Baton Rouge."

"We'll get there. Don't you worry."

But he did worry. He did nothing *but* worry. "I don't want anyone else to die."

"Same goes. Except Ducote."

"Yeah," he agreed grimly. "He could die right now, and I wouldn't shed another tear."

She went quiet again, still stroking. His eyes were heavy and sore. "You're gonna put me right to sleep," he muttered.

"That's the plan. You didn't sleep at all last night, did you?"

"No. I kept thinking of . . . everything." He sighed. "I killed a man."

"I know," she murmured.

"I'd do it again, but . . . damn, Molly."

"I know," she said again.

He supposed that she did. "I'm so tired."

"Then sleep, Gabe. I won't leave you."

He yawned, her murmurs so comforting. "The ground is hard. You can't be comfortable."

"My ass has sat on far more uncomfortable surfaces," she said lightly. "But you can go to sleep in a real bed, if you want."

"Will you go with me?" he found himself asking.

She cupped his cheek. "Absolutely."

He started to get up, then slumped back down. "Everyone's in there." *They'll see. They'll know that I fell apart.*

"Yes. But nobody's going to say a word to you about . . . you know. Crying out here. I think we were all wondering when it would come."

He snorted a quiet, self-deprecating laugh. "Was there a betting pool?"

"No, not for that. But for us having sex? There sure was a pool for that."

He peeked up at her, wincing because his whole face felt like hamburger. "Who won?"

A little smile tilted her lips. "Cicely."

"You're lyin'."

She chuckled. "Still waters, you know? I would have thought it'd be Willa Mae."

"They can't know for sure. That was in the hotel." It was weird, talking about sex after he'd had the meltdown of his life. But it felt warmly normal at the same time.

"Val told Burke. She apparently heard us through the wall."

He grunted. "Gossips, all of them."

"She's just getting me back. I won the pool with her last boyfriend."

He gave his head a shake, sending pain exploding behind his eyes. "You guys."

"I know," she said soothingly. "We're reprobates. But you like us."

"You especially."

"I'm glad. You wanna sleep here or in a real bed? Your call, but I think your bones will thank you if you choose door number two."

Gabe rolled to his knees with another grunt. "My bones already hate me. I'd better take the real bed." He met her eyes. "You won't go to Baton Rouge without me?"

"And leave my partner behind? No way. I'll wait. Besides, Burke needs to talk to André before we do anything. This Ducote thing is gonna be nasty."

"It's gonna be covered up."

She shook her head. "I don't think so. We've got fifteen bodies. No, wait, sixteen. I forgot about Meth Guy."

"George Haslet," Gabe corrected.

She dipped her chin. "You're right. He deserves to be named. Anyway, there's been too many people killed—and many of the murders have been reported on by the media. People know. It's not going to be easy to cover up. Besides, we'll push until everyone who had their hand in this is named and punished. We owe your father that much."

He sighed. "I'm not paying Burke enough for this shit. I'm going to have to take out a second mortgage on my house."

"Don't you worry about that. Burke said that he'd cover what you couldn't."

Gabe blinked. "Is Burke a millionaire or something?"

"I don't know how much he's worth and it's not my business, but he's not poor. Look, your father was important to him." She hesitated for a brief moment. "Burke's father was an awful man. My dad and yours . . . they were like surrogate fathers to Burke. That means more than you know. So let's get some rest, take down that asshole Ducote, and figure out the money later."

He leaned in, pressing his forehead to hers. "Thank you."

"You're welcome." She scrambled to her feet and held out her hand. "Come on, big guy. There's a soft bed waiting for you."

He allowed himself to be led up the stairs and inside, sighing with relief when cool air hit his overheated face. And sighing with even more relief that the kitchen was deserted. He wasn't sure if he could have faced the others. But then another thought made his relief short-lived.

"What happens if he runs? Ducote?"

She shrugged. "Then we chase him. We chase him and we chase him and we make his life a living hell until he's in custody serving a life sentence. For now, we tell André and let him work whatever border control magic he can muster."

"Ducote could slip out on a boat. Lots of places he could escape without involving border patrol."

"True," she said as they walked past the living room, where everyone seemed to be assiduously minding their own business. "But right now, he doesn't know that we know who he is. He thinks he got away with what he did yesterday and all the other days. But Ducote is wrong, Gabe, because we *do* know who he is. We have the advantage and we're going to use it."

Bayou Gauche, Louisiana
FRIDAY, JULY 29, 9:10 A.M.

Xavier let out the breath he'd been holding as Gabe and Molly passed by. The chef had been so pale, his eyes red-rimmed. Xavier turned to the doorway, clueless as to how to help.

"He'll be all right," Burke said quietly. "Eventually."

Carlos sighed. "I keep thinking of Rocky as the victim, like on all the cop shows. I keep forgetting that Rocky was Gabe's father. This has to be killing him." He winced. "Sorry. Poor choice of words."

"We knew what you meant," Willa Mae said briskly. "And you're right. When I was practicing law, one of the hardest lines to walk was keeping the emotions of my clients out of the equation while remembering their humanity. It's not easy."

"I hope he gets some sleep," Manny murmured. "He was awake when I got up at six. I don't think he'd been to bed at all."

Xavier shoved his hands in his pockets. "What can we do while he's sleeping? I feel like we have to do something to move this along. For Gabe and Rocky and Nadia and all the others."

"We need to know everything about Ducote that we can find out," Burke said. "First and foremost, was he the guy in the hoodie? He might have killed Nadia Hall during Katrina—"

"He *did*," Xavier insisted. "I saw him."

Burke smiled kindly. "I know, and your eyewitness testimony will be critical when he's formally charged with that crime. But we'll make the case for Nadia stronger if we can show how all the recent killings were to cover up that original murder. Our energy now is best spent focusing on his current crimes, and that means proving that he murdered Mule—and the female victim he was disposing of in the bayou. Antoine, Mule's killer said something to Gabe."

Antoine didn't reply. He had headphones on and was staring at his laptop.

"Antoine," Burke said louder, and the other man's head jerked up.

Antoine removed the headphones. "Sorry. What'd I miss?"

"I was talking about determining if Ducote and the hoodie guy were the same. The guy said something yesterday when Molly was holding him at gunpoint."

"'And whose was it, boy?'" Antoine said, mimicking the man's deep voice. "I was just listening to it again."

Xavier had watched that video a few dozen times. "Gabe had just said that the man had killed his father's murderer, but that it wasn't his to do. The hoodie guy was mocking him."

Antoine nodded. "I thought the same. I found a video of Ducote giving a press conference a few months ago. Listen." He unplugged his headphones and turned up his laptop's volume.

Xavier closed his eyes, concentrating as Antoine played it. "They don't sound the same. Hoodie Guy's voice is deeper than Ducote's."

Antoine's smile was sharp. "Yeah, but he was faking it. Listen to the intonation, the way he says 'boy.'" He played the Ducote tape again.

On the video, a reporter asked Ducote if he thought he could get a conviction for the crime he was trying in court that day. "You can bet your britches, boy," he said with a charming smile that sent unpleasant shivers down Xavier's spine.

He shuddered, trying to shake it off. But it was hard. That man had been Nadia Hall's lover. *I saw him kill her. He's the man in my nightmares.*

"It's still not the same," Cicely said. "The guy yesterday had a deeper voice."

Antoine turned the laptop around so that they could see the screen. "Yes, but the sound print looks the same. The pattern of his vocal cadence is the same. As is his body size."

"How reliable are voiceprints?" Xavier asked.

Antoine tilted his hand side to side. "So-so."

"So, we can't prove it's Ducote," Burke said, "but we can't prove it's not, either."

"Basically," Antoine allowed.

"What about connections?" Xavier asked. "Molly's always talking about connections, right? Ducote connects to Nadia Hall through the dog. Ducote and Mule must connect through their jobs. ADAs and cops work together, right?"

"They do," Burke said. "But then again, Mule will connect to hundreds of other people through work, as will Ducote. For now, I'm assuming that Hoodie Guy is Lamont Ducote until we know better. Mule somehow knew that Ducote was at that exact spot on the water yesterday. They arrived at different times, but Mule couldn't have been following him. Molly and Gabe were following Mule and he went straight from his house to the bayou. He couldn't have used a tracking device on Ducote's car, because Ducote had stolen George Haslet's. Unless Mule knew which car he'd steal and that's unlikely."

"He could have a tracker in Ducote's phone," Manny suggested. "It's what I'd do."

"Possibly." Burke pulled his laptop from a case near his feet. "But I'm also thinking about the way the two spoke to each other. Their body language said that they were comfortable with each other—until Mule pulled his gun, and Ducote shot him."

Soon everyone had their laptops out except for Cicely and Willa Mae. Cicely looked over Xavier's shoulder and Willa Mae just knitted. But the older woman was listening keenly to their chatter, Xavier noticed. It would be a foolish person who underestimated Willa Mae Collins.

"Found it!" Antoine crowed.

"No fair," Carlos said with a frown. "You have three laptops."

"Don't pout," Burke said. "It's unbecoming. Antoine, what did you find?"

"They went to high school together." Again, Antoine turned his laptop for them to see. "I was thinking about when Gabe said that Patty and the mortician dated in high school, and that they'd remained friends. Ducote and Mule didn't date in high school, but they attended the same one and graduated the same year. Here's a post on Facebook—them at their twenty-fifth reunion. I don't think that Lamont was wealthy back when he was younger. That high school was in a poorer neighborhood, even before Katrina."

"Social media saves the day," Xavier muttered. "This is why I don't have a Facebook account."

Cicely patted his hand. "That's because I raised you smart. What about Paul Lott? How does he connect?"

Xavier had a thought. *What if* . . . He pulled up the one place online where he'd found the real Paul Lott's picture—in that local golf tournament. He searched the faces in the photo and . . .

"*Yes*. Paul Lott and Ducote golfed together. At least they're both in this picture." He showed them. "It's not a strong connection, but it's a start."

"It is," Burke agreed, staring at his own laptop screen. "They golfed together in a tournament for attorneys because both were attorneys. But their connection goes back further than this game. At the beginning of his career, Ducote was a defense attorney for a local firm. Guess who else worked there? Paul Lott."

Antoine's head was tilted as he squinted at his laptop. "Let me see that picture of Paul Lott again, Xavier. The one at the golf tournament."

Xavier took his laptop to where Antoine sat surrounded by his three computers. "Why?"

"Because . . . look at this guy here." Antoine enlarged a portion of the high school reunion photo. "Is that Lott?"

Carlos leaned over to compare the two pictures. "Looks like."

Xavier blinked. "The three of them went to high school together? That's wild."

"It is." Then Antoine frowned. "But it doesn't explain how Lott connects to Rocky. I mean, Lott was Rocky's personal attorney. When did Rocky start using Lott's services—and why? Rocky wouldn't have contacted a defense attorney to handle his personal finances. That doesn't make sense."

"Unless he thought he might need one," Willa Mae suggested. "If he was afraid that he was going to get into trouble for continuing to investigate Nadia Hall's death."

"I'm noting it," Burke said. "We'll ask Gabe when he wakes up. Knowing that Ducote, Lott, and Mule were connected as far back as high school is the most important thing. Antoine, can you search Rocky's old cases to see if he and Paul Lott ever met in court?"

Antoine nodded. "Will do."

Willa Mae set her knitting in her lap. "I have a question. Nadia Hall was living in a house that Ducote provided, right? Once Rocky knew her name and where exactly she'd lived—from the lady who still lives on her street—why didn't he look up the property record and figure out it was Ducote?"

"That's a very good question," Burke said slowly. "Antoine?"

Antoine frowned. "Because that house wasn't owned by Ducote. It was owned by a woman named Tanya Brown."

"Then Tanya Brown and Ducote have to connect somehow," Willa Mae said with conviction. "Again, assuming Ducote is Hoodie Guy, that means he knew George Haslet, the guy Ducote killed for his car. By extension, he also knows Tyson Whitley, because the same number called both men. Both men escaped justice after facing drug charges. I'm going to assume Ducote had something to do with that until we learn differently. What if Tanya Brown also was connected to Ducote in the same way?"

"Give me a minute," Antoine muttered, and they fell silent while he searched. A few minutes later he looked up triumphantly. "Got it. Tanya Brown's son was arrested for possession of heroin with intent to distribute, the year before Katrina. He was charged and took a plea deal. He served no time. Guess who his defense attorney was?"

"Lamont Ducote," Xavier said heavily. "They used their house to pay for the legal fees?"

Antoine nodded. "We'll need to verify it with Mrs. Brown, but so it would seem."

Willa Mae resumed her knitting. "Always good to dot every *i* and cross every *t*. It's these kinds of details that will allow the prosecutors to build a case. Since there's no body and no murder weapon, it's all going to rest on Xavier's eyewitness testimony and a convincing compilation of circumstantial evidence."

"True enough," Burke said. "Anybody else have a good question?"

"What about his wives?" Cicely asked. "Ducote has had three. Lucille, his first wife, died by suicide, or so the ME determined at the time. What about wife number two?"

"Got it!" Carlos called out, then covered his mouth when Manny socked him in the arm, shushing him. "Sorry," he whispered, then continued at a normal volume. "Francesca was wife number two. They were divorced. Here's the society page announcement of wife number three—Joelle. Wives number two and three look alike." He showed them his screen. "Gotta love the society pages. They have all the good dirt. Francesca got caught cheating and was divorced and *shunned*."

"Oh, the horror," Willa Mae deadpanned. "To be shunned."

Carlos chuckled. "I know, right?"

"You know who also looked like those two wives?" Burke asked, leaning in to look at Carlos's screen.

"Nadia Hall," Cicely said.

"You're right, Mom," Xavier said. Molly had shown them the photo she'd scanned into her phone while visiting Nadia's old friend. Xavier hadn't needed the reminder, though. He'd seen Nadia's face too often in his nightmares to forget.

"That's true, too," Burke said. "But I was thinking about the woman who posed as Nadia Hall's fake sister. Alicia Rollins, who is now dead—and whose body Ducote was dumping in the bayou. Looks like Ducote has a type."

"And a bad habit of murdering his mistresses," Manny added.

"True enough," Cicely said. "I wonder if wives number two and three would like to dish on Mr. Ducote?"

Burke grinned. "I think that's a wonderful idea. Wife number two might be more likely to give us the really good stuff, though. Antoine, can you look her up?"

"Just did. Sorry, boss. She's dead. Had an aneurysm a few years ago. Joelle is the only living wife at this point."

Burke sighed. "I guess we'll need to talk to wife number three, then. I think Molly should do it. She's less intimidating. She can also lay on the charm when she wants to."

"Ducote also tried to kill Molly yesterday morning," Xavier protested. "Either way, isn't that dangerous?"

"More dangerous if Ducote walks free," Burke said grimly. "I'll go with her."

"Are we telling André about this?" Antoine asked.

Burke hesitated. "He'll tell us not to visit her. He'll get to it, but with all the red tape and warrants and procedure, it could take a while. And what Gabe said when he was walking to the bedroom was right. Ducote is a flight risk. I'd prefer not to chase him if I don't have to. This is time-sensitive stuff."

"It's easier to ask forgiveness than permission," Carlos said wisely.

Burke smiled. "My thoughts exactly."

26

H EY, LAMONT?"

Lamont looked up from his office computer with a glare, discreetly closing the overnight police reports he'd been studying. No news was good news at this point. Ashley still hadn't been identified. "Yes, Jean-Pierre?" He tried not to say the man's name sardonically. Didn't seem like he'd managed it, though, because the other man's eyes narrowed slightly.

"Ashley didn't come into work again today. I was wondering if you've heard from her."

"I sure haven't," Lamont drawled. "Why would she be calling me?"

Jean-Pierre shrugged. "I figured if she was sick or something, she'd have your number in her favorites. I never got a chance to give her my personal cell phone number that first day."

Huh. He'd forgotten that Ashley had only been gone from his office for a day before her unfortunate end. "Well, she didn't call me. If she does, I'll be sure to let you know."

Jean-Pierre frowned. "Dammit. I hope this doesn't mean that I'll have to find a new assistant. Could she have just run off? Did she have a boyfriend or anything?"

Only me. "If she did, I didn't know about it. We weren't really that close." And once their relationship did come out, no one would blame him for lying. No one shouted the news of a secret mistress from the rafters, after all.

"Thank you." Disgruntled, Jean-Pierre muttered a goodbye to Carrie in the outer office before the door closed behind him.

"Sorry, sir." Carrie appeared in the doorway, her tablet in one hand. "I tried to get him to leave you alone, but he wouldn't listen."

"It's fine, Carrie. He can be a bit persistent. If he gives you trouble, report him to HR."

"Oh, he never gives me trouble. I was concerned that he was annoying you. I have your schedule for the day. Should I send it to your email?"

"That would be perfect. Do I still have that two thirty meeting with Mr. Proctor?" He'd better. It was an important part of his plan for Joelle.

"You do. His assistant called to confirm just a few minutes ago. Can I get you anything?"

"A coffee from that shop next door would be amazing, if you don't mind. I'm afraid I didn't get too much sleep last night."

"Of course I don't mind." She tilted her head, the picture of concern. "Is everything all right?"

"Oh, you know how it is. My wife is a little annoyed with me right now, and I was banished to the couch." That wasn't true, but it would be a nice setup for later. "We're having a few issues at the moment."

Carrie's eyes blinked wide. She was trying to look genuinely upset on his behalf, but he didn't miss the glitter of interest of the gossipy type. And maybe the slightest bit of interest of the lusty type. "Should I send her some flowers from you?"

He nodded. "That would be really nice. Again, if you don't mind."

"Not at all," she assured him. "I'll be back in a few with your coffee."

He waited until he heard the outer door close before getting up and checking that she was really gone. Carrie was the type to gossip his business to every willing ear. Which would ordinarily be an issue, but he planned to use her little flaw for his own purposes.

She was gone, and he firmly closed his office door before returning to his desk and dialing Cresswell.

The cop answered on the second ring. "Lamont. What's up?"

"Just checking to see if there's any news on Mule's killer."

Cresswell sighed. "Nothing new. We've checked all of Mule's cases, open and closed, for the past few years to see if the shooter's body size matches anyone he was investigating. So far, just about *everyone* matches the shooter's body type, so we got nothing there. We've been gathering Mule's cell phone records, checking voiceprints on the shooter, trying to dissect that video. You know, all the usual stuff."

Voiceprints on the shooter? *Shit. Why didn't I keep my big mouth shut?* Lamont cleared his throat to keep his voice steady. "You gettin' anything from that video?"

"Not yet. The guy's face simply isn't visible, and the tech guys haven't been able to clear it up. We're also checking connections to the five guys killed the other night—y'know, the guys breaking into that PI's apartment and the restaurant owner's place."

He'd expected this, but it still got his pulse racing. "I read about that."

"Yeah. They connected the two break-ins. The common denominator is Gabe Hebert, the guy that owns that restaurant in the Quarter. Le Petit Choux. The PI is his girlfriend, apparently. The other lady is his cousin and the co-owner of the restaurant. They must have expected trouble, because they had bodyguards stationed at both places. Of course, there's another common denominator." Cresswell paused dramatically but said no more.

"Which is?" Lamont asked, trying not to sound annoyed.

"Rocky Hebert, a retired cop. Did you know him?"

Be cool. Be cool. "I know *of* him. He died recently, didn't he?"

"Shot himself in the fool head, the asshole." Cresswell tsked. "He worked for me for a few years—right up till his retirement. Not a bad cop, most of the time. He had an alcohol problem, though. Supposedly got sober, but . . . boom. Ate his gun. Guess he wasn't enjoying his retirement overly much. His boy, Gabe, didn't believe his father killed himself."

"Does the family ever believe such a thing?"

"I expect not. But then, you'd know, wouldn't you?"

Lamont scowled. It wasn't often that someone brought up wife number one. Lucille had shot herself one night after getting wasted. Or at least that was how he'd staged the scene. Presto chango, he'd become a wealthy man.

"No family member should have to endure the suicide of a loved one," Lamont said quietly, hoping that Cresswell felt guilty. "It's a terrible tragedy for everyone. A terrible loss."

There was a beat of silence. "I apologize," Cresswell said stiffly. "That was unkind of me."

"It kind of was. I hope that Gabe Hebert is able to find some peace." *Eternal peace, that is.*

"I don't know. Nobody had seen him for a few days before they brought him in for questioning yesterday morning."

And if Lamont had known that, he could have taken care of him then and there. The lack of communication irritated him. "Where had he been before yesterday?" he asked.

"He'd taken leave from his restaurant. Said he needed 'time to process' his daddy's passin'." Cresswell's air quotes were audible.

"You don't believe him?"

"No. I think he believes that somebody killed his father. I think he's investigating."

No shit, Sherlock. He and Mule had known that since Monday. "Has he found anything?"

"Nothing so far. Or, leastways, nothing he's sharing. He got a private autopsy done on his father. Did you hear about the lady pathologist getting killed? Out in Baton Rouge?"

"I think so. Her lab was burned up, wasn't it? BRPD thought it was vandalism."

"That's what they said. But she was the pathologist who did Rocky's *secret* private autopsy."

Lamont knew all about it, of course. Killing the pathologist had been Mule's handiwork. But he hadn't been informed through official channels and that was . . . troubling. He'd have to find out why.

They can't suspect me.

Unless Mule told someone what he was up to, and he didn't think that was likely.

"What about the guy who was arrested for breaking into the PI's apartment? Is he talking?" Lamont hoped not. Depending on what Mule had told his bastard son, Tobin could destroy him.

"Not yet," Cresswell said. "But I expect that he will. So far, nobody knows how he connects to Mule, but we'll figure it out."

Lamont swallowed his sigh of relief. He'd have to make sure Tobin didn't talk, but that could wait. "What about the remains that were found near Mule's body?"

"The lady? All that was left on land was her head. Divers went in after the rest of her. Found her torso at the water's bottom, weighted down with a brick. It wasn't in terrible shape, but the gators had been snackin'. They found a finger, but it no longer had any usable prints. The rest appears to be digesting in a gator's belly."

"How . . . unpleasant." But just as he'd hoped. "Have they identified her?"

"Not yet. Look, I don't mind you callin', but I'm not telling you anything your office doesn't already know. You should talk to the ADA on the case."

Lamont frowned. "And who is that?" He'd planned to claim the case himself. No better way to steer the court proceedings the way he wanted them to go.

"It's that new guy from up north. You know, Cardozo."

Lamont's mouth fell open, then shock gave way to anger. "Cardozo? *Jean-Pierre Cardozo* is the prosecutor you're working with?" *That smarmy, New York City sonofabitch.*

"Well, yeah, that's him. I figured you knew." But there was a smugness in Cresswell's tone, a you're-out-of-the-loop glee that made Lamont's anger boil even hotter. "Maybe they're giving you a break. Lettin' you grieve. You know, since you and Mule were friends. You'd probably have to recuse yourself, anyway."

"That's true," he said, feigning acceptance. "I didn't think of it that way."

"Well, don't fret over it. You've got bigger fish to fry anyway, don't you? I saw you with Lyle Nelson a few nights ago. He's got deep pockets. Useful for someone considering a run for office."

Lamont didn't mind that people were gossiping about that. Publicity was always helpful for a nascent campaign. "Little birds have been squawking."

Cresswell chuckled. "You know how it goes in this town. Nobody keeps a secret for long."

Unless everyone who knows it is dead. "True, true. Listen, I'm gonna let you go. I have a meeting I have to get ready for and I know you're busy investigating Mule's death."

"Sure. I hope you weren't offended about me telling you to ask Cardozo for intel. If he's got his head up his ass and won't share, you come on back to me, now. Y'hear?"

"Absolutely," he promised, then hung up.

Cardozo *had* to know about Ashley, that she was the dead woman from yesterday morning. He would have been shown the photos, if not the remains themselves. *Yet he's come by two days in a row to check with me.*

"Or to check *on* me," he muttered aloud, rubbing his temples. This was like a game of whack-a-mole. No sooner had he taken care of one threat than another one popped up.

But nobody could connect Ashley's death to him. Not once Joelle was dead.

He snapped his fingers as a thought popped into his mind. *Silver paper.* He had to buy more presents and wrap them with silver paper so that no one—specifically James or the building's surveillance footage—could connect him to the boxes in yesterday's stolen car. And if anyone did make the connection, he'd say that he always used silver paper to wrap gifts for his wife. That she'd instructed the hit man she'd hired to wrap the boxes with Ashley's remains the same way.

To frame me. Yes, that was exactly the tale he'd spin.

Hell, it actually sounded like something that Joelle would do. She wasn't stupid, for sure. And she *had* been a woman scorned. Anyone mildly acquainted with her knew that she had a vindictive streak a mile wide. That she'd come up with such a plan wasn't out of the realm of possibility.

He'd get through the work on his agenda, then leave early for his two thirty meeting, because he was going to walk. It wasn't far, and he didn't want James to know where he was, in case his driver was questioned by the cops. The two thirty meeting was blocked for two hours but wouldn't last more than one. That would give him time to get the replacement gifts, more boxes, and more silver paper on his way home—where he'd set Joelle's "suicide" in motion.

Then he'd walk back to the office, clean up, and change clothes, after which an argumentative phone call between him and Joelle would happen to be overheard, establishing an alibi for the time of her death. Then he'd be ready for James to take him to his seven o'clock dinner meeting at the Monteleone.

He'd go directly home afterward, where he'd find his dearly departed wife's body—along with her guilt-ridden suicide note claiming responsibility for the death of Ashley Resnick.

He'd have to ride out the sex scandal of having had a mistress and a wife who'd murdered said mistress, but that was better than being charged with murder himself. And to avoid that, he needed to eliminate the one person who could still point a finger at him. The one person who'd seen him with Nadia. Who'd seen his scar. Once Xavier Morrow was gone, he was in the clear, once and for all.

Baton Rouge, Louisiana
FRIDAY, JULY 29, 2:30 P.M.

"Hey," Xavier murmured. "You okay?"

Gabe turned from staring out the back-seat window of Burke's Escalade to find the younger man studying him with a worried expression. "I'm okay. It's just that the last time I was in Baton Rouge, it was to consult with Dr. McLain about Dad's autopsy."

Xavier's expression changed from worried to pained. "Her death is not your fault. You know that, right?"

He smiled tightly. "Keep on saying that. I might eventually believe you."

In the front seat, Molly was driving, and Burke was giving her directions to the UPS store where Xavier had his mailbox. "Turn left at the next light."

Bringing Xavier with them had been a last-minute call on Burke's part. It had involved a lengthy, intense conversation among their group, weighing the pros and cons.

The major "con" was that Xavier would be leaving the safety of Burke's camp after having successfully hidden there for days.

The major "pro" was also a function of keeping Xavier safe. If they went to the box without him but found that they needed Xavier to retrieve the contents, they'd have to return with him later. If Ducote had someone watching the box, they'd report back to him that Burke and Molly had tried to collect its contents, which would give Ducote the heads-up that Xavier would be returning soon. He could have someone waiting to kill Xavier on the return trip.

Adding to the "pro" column was their ability to disguise Xavier so that his own mother didn't recognize him. Antoine had provided a pair of mirrored sunglasses and the wig of braids that he used when doing undercover work for Burke. Combined with Xavier's five-day scruff and a ball cap, he looked different enough that they'd finally agreed that having Xavier accompany them now when they had the element of surprise was better than having him go to Baton Rouge later when someone might be waiting for him.

Everyone had agreed except for Cicely Morrow, who'd left Burke's living room, lips pursed, tears coursing down her face.

So they'd all gotten into Burke's boat with heavy hearts. Nobody liked leaving Cicely when she was so upset, but Willa Mae had assured them that she'd take care of things.

Sure enough, Xavier had received a text from Cicely when they were halfway to Baton Rouge, telling him to be careful and that she loved him. That had lightened the tension a little bit.

Until they'd entered the city limits. Now Gabe was so tense that he wanted to run, to scream, to do anything but simply sit and wait.

Molly pulled into a parking space in front of the UPS store, and Burke turned so that he could see Gabe and Xavier in the back seat. "I'm going in first," Burke said, reminding them of their plan. "If there's something in the box itself, I'm coming straight back here and we'll leave. If the box is empty, I'll ask the clerk behind the counter if they're holding any bigger packages in the back. If he needs you to show ID, I'll come back to get you. Otherwise, you guys stay in the vehicle with your heads down. Got it?"

"Got it," Xavier said, but he was clearly nervous despite being adamant that they bring him along. "You have my keys, right?"

"I do," Burke confirmed. "You gave them to me before we left. Molly, keep the engine running and if anything looks suspicious—anything at all—you hightail it out of here. Leave me here. I'll be okay and I'll meet up with you later."

"Got it," Molly said. "Just get this over with, Burke, before we all explode from the stress."

Burke obeyed, getting out of the Escalade and entering the UPS store.

"This has to be over soon," Gabe muttered. He was so tired. He needed his life back. He needed to know that his father's killer would pay.

"Your mouth, God's ears," Xavier said quietly, his face obscured by his newfound braids.

"Molly, has Burke heard from André?" Gabe asked, even though he knew the answer, because he'd already asked several times.

"Not since Burke told him about our discovering Ducote through Nadia's dog," Molly said patiently, just as she had each time before.

"Sorry," he muttered. Burke had called André while Gabe had been sleeping. *After my breakdown.* Which was still humiliating. But no one had mentioned it, which he appreciated.

"Don't be," she said. "I've bugged Burke about it, too. So has Xavier."

Apparently, André had been hesitant to believe that Ducote was their killer but promised to make some "discreet inquiries." Whatever the hell that meant.

Then she sucked in a breath. "Burke took something out of the box. He's on his way back."

"I wonder what it is," Xavier whispered.

But no one answered him. They were all holding their breath until Burke got back into the Escalade, his mouth tight.

"An envelope for you, Xavier. There's something small in it, feels like hard plastic."

"Where is it?" Molly asked excitedly.

"In my pocket. I don't want to open it here. That guy at the counter was too damn curious. He started texting on his phone the minute I opened your box. Molly, drive us somewhere where we're out of sight."

Molly obeyed, driving to the other side of the street, then winding around to the back of another strip mall before parking.

"Give me a minute and we'll open it." Burke got out, opened the hatch of the SUV, and rummaged in the back. "Found it."

"Found what?" Gabe demanded, trying so hard to be patient.

"A faraday bag," Molly said as Burke slid back into the passenger seat.

"What's that?" Xavier asked.

Burke pulled on a pair of disposable gloves then held up a black pouch that looked like a case for eyeglasses. "This is a faraday bag. I think someone sent you a tracking device. A faraday bag blocks the GPS signals, so whoever sent it can't use it to find you, Xavier."

Gabe and Xavier leaned forward so that they could watch as Burke slit the envelope open with his pocketknife.

"Where do you even get one of those faraday bags?" Xavier asked.

Burke looked up briefly, smirking. "Amazon."

Xavier gave him a don't-fuck-with-me look. "Seriously?"

"Seriously," Molly confirmed. "We all carry them. Y'know, just in case."

Burke held up a small box, the size that might hold a ring. "The letter enclosed is signed 'P.L.' But it doesn't have Lott's letterhead on it. It says, 'Rocky wanted you to have this. Open it right away.'"

Xavier's voice trembled. "I probably would have taken it home to open it if I'd known it was here."

"Why didn't Lott put it on letterhead?" Gabe asked, then shook his head at himself. "He didn't want anything to connect him to Xavier's murder, assuming that was what would've happened next."

"Fuck," Xavier whispered. "I'm so glad I didn't come back here to check."

Molly was studying Burke. "You're disappointed. Why?"

Burke shrugged. "I was kind of hoping that Rocky had sent something to Xavier. Something that would explain all of this."

"But a letter from Rocky would have arrived before Paul Lott's letter with information about his inheritance," Molly said carefully.

Burke exhaled slowly. "I know. But there's still Gabe's mysterious aunt Gigi, who knew about John Alan Industries and who Rocky seemed to be confiding in. I'd hoped he'd given her something that could help us. I knew it was a long shot, but I'd still hoped."

As disappointed as Gabe was that the package wasn't from Gigi, at least he knew where his aunt was. Antoine had found that she'd used her credit card to buy souvenirs in Grand Cayman that morning and in Panama three days before that. They'd sent an urgent message to Gigi through the offices of any ship whose itinerary fit, but so far, they'd heard nothing.

Burke reached over his seat to give Xavier his keys. "This package does support our theory that Paul Lott didn't know where you actually live. It still doesn't explain how the intruder knew where to find you, though."

Xavier took the keys and bounced them in his hand. "So, we've got nothing new."

"Basically," Burke said glumly. "Next stop, Joelle Ducote?"

"Sounds right," Molly said. "After we take Xavier back to your camp."

But Gabe wasn't listening, unable to stop staring at the keys in Xavier's hand.

Or, more specifically, the key ring. "What is that on your key ring, Xavier?"

Xavier stopped bouncing the keys and held them up so that Gabe could see. "An angel. Your dad gave it to me about a month before he died. I wondered about it at the time, but when I heard that he had cancer, I realized that it was his way of saying goodbye."

"Can I see it?" Gabe asked, because he had seen the angel before. Or one just like it.

"Sure." Xavier handed him the keys, then made a pained face. "If you want the angel back, it's okay. It was your dad's, after all."

"No," Gabe said faintly. "He gave this to you. Besides, I've got one. Dad gave it to me, also a few weeks before he died. I'd forgotten about it." He ran his fingers over the ceramic angel, his heart in his throat. It was less than two inches tall, painted with an off-white glittery paint. "My mom made this. It was when she was in remission. She'd done some pottery in the past and wanted to do something fun. She made a few of these angels, intending to paint them, to make them into Christmas tree ornaments. But she never got the chance to paint them because she got sick again. She died not long after that. Dad had one of the angels painted for me. He must have done the same for you."

The knowledge of which warmed him but caused a sharp little spear of dismay at the same time. His father had considered Xavier to be a second son but had never felt safe enough to bring the two parts of his life together.

"It has an inscription on the bottom," Xavier said sadly. "'Reach for the stars, *mon ange.'*"

Startled, Gabe looked up to meet Xavier's gaze. "*Mon ange*? He called you *mon ange*?"

"Not recently. He called me *mon ange* when he was trying to settle me into the boat, the night he saved me—because I told him that my name was Angel. My birth mom called me that, too. I'd nearly forgotten until I saw what the angel said." Xavier's lips trembled up into the smallest of smiles. "It meant a lot that he remembered."

Gabe glanced at Molly, who'd leaned around her seat and was

watching him with a worried frown. Probably because his tension had just ratcheted through the damn roof. "What's wrong, Gabe?"

He swallowed. "My dad called me *mon ange* when I was little, too—because my name is Gabriel. But he stopped when I was thirteen. I told him it was a baby name. He didn't call me that again until the night he died. He sent me a text." He pulled out his phone, going to the text thread he'd shared with his father. "See? He sent it at a quarter to midnight, right before he was killed."

Hope you're having a good night, mon ange. Love you, son.

Molly sucked in a breath. "It has to mean something. Can I see that angel?"

Gabe handed it over and Molly turned on her cell phone's flashlight, shining it on the base. "There's a crack around the base, but it's been glued and covered with paint," she said, shaking it lightly. "Could he have put something in here? Burke, do you have your Swiss army knife?"

Xavier frowned. "What the hell? You're going to break my angel?"

"I'm going to open it up," Molly said, taking the knife Burke handed her. "I'll be careful."

"Please do. It's . . ." Xavier faltered. "It's the only thing I have to remember him by. We never even took a photo together. He said that it wasn't safe."

"I promise," she said. "Burke, hold my phone and shine the light on the angel?" She bent her head, her gaze fixed on what she was doing. She poked the blade's edge around the hairline crack, prodding it along the circle, over and over again until the crack completely broke and the base fell into the angel's body.

Actually, it was kind of hovering there, even though it was small enough to have fallen inside.

"Cotton," she said. "Rocky filled this thing with cotton. I wish I had tweezers."

"There's a pair inside the handle," Burke said. "Let me get them for you."

"No, I got it," Molly said, sliding the tweezers free. "Wow, this is a nice knife, Burke."

"Always need good tools," Burke muttered. "Hurry up."

"Be patient," she murmured, first grabbing the base with the tweezers and lifting it out, then digging out the cotton. "Oh," she breathed as she upended the angel over her palm.

Something small and black lay in her hand.

Gabe had to clear his throat to speak. "A thumb drive?"

"Yep." She looked up with a grin. "This is what Rocky wanted you to find, Gabe. I have my laptop. Let's see what's on this thing."

"It might not be safe," Burke cautioned.

She scoffed. "You want to wait an hour and a half to get Antoine to read it? My laptop's backed up to the cloud. I'll turn off my network connection, so no one can hack in. If there's a nasty virus on this thing, I can get a new laptop and recover my data later."

Burke nodded once. "Do it."

Quickly Molly pulled her laptop from her handbag. "Turning off the internet and . . ." She plugged the thumb drive into a USB drive. "One file," she said and clicked. Then frowned. "Well, fuck a duck." She looked up, her expression totally frustrated. "It says, 'Find Gabe at Le Petit Choux, *mon ange.*'"

"That's where my angel is," Gabe said, his head spinning. "In my desk drawer at the Choux." He ground his teeth. "At least I hope it's still there. With Donna Lee's betrayal, who knows?"

He still hadn't processed any of that. The woman whom he'd called his friend had been questioned and released, but André had promised that a trusted officer was watching her in case she tried to flee. They weren't sure what to charge her with just yet but were angling toward conspiracy. That meant the cops and the district attorney had to pull all the details together first, to show that a conspiracy existed. That all of these events connected together. He only hoped that Donna Lee would get her comeuppance. And he was petty enough to hope that her husband found out about her affair and left her, on top of whatever legal issues she now had.

Not now. He pushed thoughts of Donna Lee from his mind. They'd closed the Choux for the weekend, saying they'd had a pipe burst and needed to clean up. They'd lose a lot of money because it was a festival weekend, but they didn't want to risk the rest of their staff in the event that Ducote sent another thug to harass them.

Gabe would deal with her later. Right now, he couldn't take his eyes off Xavier's angel.

Had he been sitting on the evidence all this time? Right under his nose? *Goddammit, Dad, why'd you have to make this so hard?*

Burke buckled up. "Next stop, the Choux. And if Rocky were still alive, I'd kick his ass."

"You'd have to wait in line," Gabe grumbled. "What did he think he was doing? Some Dan Brown *Da Vinci Code* shit?"

"He was trying to protect you both," Molly said, her reproach crystal clear.

Gabe sighed. "I know. I know he didn't want anyone to find out about Xavier, and I know he was trying to keep me safe by keeping me in the dark."

"Still sucks," Xavier muttered as Molly gave him back his keys and the small angel's base.

Gabe nodded grimly. "It sure does."

The Garden District, New Orleans, Louisiana
FRIDAY, JULY 29, 4:45 P.M.

Lamont let himself into the house and placed the bag containing the flattened boxes, silver wrapping paper, and a few bronze sculptures on the foyer floor. The bronzes were freaking heavy. Not as heavy as Ashley's remains had been, but he doubted that James would be able to remember the difference.

He'd wrap the new gifts when he was finished with Joelle.

He found her in her bedroom, dressed in one of her fancy frocks. *Probably preparing for my big dinner party tonight. Shame that she won't be attending, after all.*

She sat at her vanity, staring at her reflection. But she wasn't seeing herself. Her gaze was unfocused, and her lips drooped sadly.

He might have felt sorry for her had she not hidden cameras in his study.

No, he still wouldn't have felt sorry for her. Joelle was an unpleasant person, and he hadn't realized how much he disliked her until he'd put a ring on her finger.

Stupid me.

But within a few hours, he wouldn't be burdened with her ever again.

He must have made a noise, because she jumped in her chair, pivoting to stare at him with wide eyes. "You scared me," she accused.

I'll do worse than that. "I thought I'd come home between meetings. We need to talk."

Her chin lifted. "If you still want a divorce, the answer is still no. You have no grounds."

He started to say that he didn't need grounds, but he wanted her compliant. "You could be right."

Her eyes narrowed warily. "What are you up to?"

"Nothing. I simply thought we should talk."

"Why are you so sweaty? You hate to be sweaty."

It was true. He was drenched in sweat. He'd nearly run from his two thirty meeting, and stopping to buy the gifts, boxes, and wrapping paper had taken valuable time. "I'm sweaty because it's hotter than hell outside. Come, let's have a drink and converse like civilized people."

She rose from the little chair and sauntered toward him, her hips swaying with every step.

Not gonna work, dear wife. That may have done the trick when she was seven years younger and he was a whole lot stupider, but not today. In fact, he had to fight not to laugh at her. She was ridiculous.

She ran her fingertips over the apology necklace he'd given her. "I might forgive you for another one of these."

He smiled then, because it was part of the act. "I might ask you to." *When hell freezes over.* He held out his hand and led her downstairs to the living room where they'd talked the night before. "I'll mix us some drinks and we can chat."

She curled up on the sofa, watching as he moved behind the bar. "Still not giving you a divorce."

He shot her a warning look. He couldn't come off as too conciliatory. She'd never fall for that. "We'll see."

She shrugged. "Suit yourself. But with the video in my possession, you'll be out on the street. I think I'll like being mistress of this household all by my lonesome."

He very nearly growled. There was no fucking way she was getting his house.

Calm down. She's not getting anything. You're killing her, remember?

Saying nothing, he mixed their martinis, adding to hers the last of the Rohypnol powder left over from Rocky's killing. He and Jackass had each kept a little of the powder. Funnily enough, Jackass had probably used the last of his share on Joelle the night he'd been waiting in the study.

Lamont added olives to his own drink, knowing that she wouldn't touch it. She hated olives. He handed her the drink and sat on the opposite end of the couch. "To civilized conversations," he said.

She snorted in a very unladylike way. "Whatever you say." She downed hers in three large gulps, just as he'd known she would. Then held her glass out for more. Just as he'd known she would.

She'd become a drunk in the years since their marriage. A mean, nasty drunk. But she wouldn't get mean or nasty today. In a minute or two, she'd be out cold.

He took her glass and went back to the bar, mixing her another drink, just to keep up the charade. She frowned, shaking her head.

"What'd you do?" she asked, having to carefully enunciate her words. "Lamont?"

His name sounded slurred. He simply sipped on his own drink, waiting behind the bar. He said nothing when she tried to stand.

"You bastard," she spat, then crumpled to the floor.

Leaving her there, he went to his study, turned on his computer, then opened the document he'd written the night before and printed it out. He then deleted the file and went into his settings and deleted the need for a password. That way if someone searched his hard drive and found remnants of the document, he could say that she could have used his computer at any time. There was nothing incriminating on this computer. Anything that was personally important he wrote longhand and left in his safe. Any communications were done over burner phones and he'd disposed of the ones he'd used with Jackass and Ashley.

Putting on gloves, he took the letter from the printer and reread it to make sure that he'd written it correctly.

Dear Lamont,

When I found out that you were having an affair with Ashley . . . I guess I just broke. I knew you weren't going to end it with her, even if you promised to. I knew the only way to get her out of our lives was to kill her. So I paid to have it done.

But it didn't make a difference. I realized last night that we were over. You don't love me anymore. I had her killed for nothing, and now that I'm thinking clearly, I'm finding that I can't live with what I did. She was just a kid. The same age I was when I was your dirty little secret.

I hope her family will forgive me. I would have done anything to keep you. That was my mistake.

*I'd wish you well, but I'm not that nice. I hope you're
miserable forever and never find another woman to hurt.
Goddamn your soul to hell. I guess I'll see you there.*

Taking the letter with him, he went to the garage to put it on the
passenger seat of her car before opening the driver's door. Leaving it
open, he went back to the living room, where she still lay on the carpet,
drew a deep breath, and hoisted her over his shoulder in a fireman's
carry.

"Damn, girl, you've gained weight," he muttered, then chuckled.
She'd hate him saying that more than she'd hate being murdered
by him.

Staggering slightly, he readjusted her and made his way into the
garage, where he shoved her into the driver's seat. Then he went back
into the house, took off his gloves, and filled the two boxes with heavy
sculptures.

He wrapped the presents and, making sure to get his fingerprints
on the silver paper, placed them in the same corner of the garage where
he'd told James to store the boxes the night he'd killed Ashley. James's
prints wouldn't be on these new boxes, but there wasn't anything he
could do about that now.

Then he tugged the gloves back on, put the keys into Joelle's limp
hand, shoved his foot between hers to hit the brake, and pushed the
button that started the car. She'd be dead in two or three hours. He'd
had the garage well sealed and insulated before marrying Joelle because some valuable paintings he'd had stored had been destroyed by
mold. So now his garage was as airtight as a structure could be.

Poor Joelle. She might not even last two hours.

Whistling, he shut the garage door behind him, cleaned their mar-
tini glasses and put them away, pocketed Joelle's cell phone from the
coffee table, and went back to work.

The Quarter, New Orleans, Louisiana
FRIDAY, JULY 29, 4:45 P.M.

"Did you find it?" Molly asked when Gabe and Burke returned to the Escalade.

They'd driven from the UPS store in Baton Rouge directly to the Choux so that Gabe could retrieve the angel his father had given him before he'd died. Xavier had ducked down when they'd returned to New Orleans, sitting on the back-seat floorboard so that he couldn't be seen.

Molly had wanted to take him back to Burke's place right away, but they'd all had a feeling of the clock ticking. They needed every piece of evidence they could gather, because Ducote was going to be a hard man to take down. Rocky had told Xavier that he'd leave Gabe information, and they were hoping against hope that Gabe's angel would yield it.

"I did," Gabe said, sounding subdued and anxious all at the same time. "It was in my drawer, right where I left it. It's just . . . the place was so quiet. We're normally packed this time on Friday night." He handed the angel to her. "It felt so wrong."

"You'll be able to open up again soon," Molly said, hoping it was true.

Trying to keep her hands from shaking, she pried the bottom from Gabe's angel. The base was inscribed: *Je t'aimerai toujours, mon ange.*

"What does it mean?" she asked.

Gabe cleared his throat. "'I will always love you, my angel.'"

"Oh," she whispered, letting out a breath as she shook another thumb drive into her hand. "Let's see what it says." Quickly she opened the drive on her laptop.

Then stared. "Motherfucker," she muttered.

"What?" Burke, Gabe, and Xavier all asked in unison.

"Only one document. It says, 'Call Aunt Gigi ASAP when you find this. I love you.'"

"What the hell?" Burke exploded. "Dammit, Rocky."

Expression weary, Gabe tried calling his aunt, but his call went straight to voice mail once again. "She's still got her phone turned off. I've left messages for her and I even called all of the cruise lines again, but I keep getting their voice mail. I don't know what else to do."

Burke exhaled heavily. "Now what?"

"We talk to Ducote's wife number three," Xavier said from behind the driver's seat.

"No," Molly said without even looking back. "You're going back to Burke's camp."

Burke checked his watch. "It'll take over two hours to get him to the camp and come back here. And that's after we get out of the city."

The Quarter was packed with SummerFest revelers. It had taken them over an hour to get to the Choux once they'd exited the interstate into New Orleans. Molly had nearly turned around, but Xavier had convinced her that they'd spend just as long trying to get out of the city as they would getting to the Choux. Everyone had been so hopeful that Gabe's angel would have the information Rocky had promised he'd leave them, so she'd kept going.

Molly wanted to sigh. That hadn't panned out very well. Rocky Hebert had been a little too careful. Although he had been spot-on when he'd hidden his phone's SIM card under the car floor mat. Still, it was hard not to be frustrated. If Joelle Ducote didn't pan out, they were back to brainstorming again.

At the rate they were going, they might be coming back tomorrow. If they showed up at her house too late, she might not answer the door.

"Just go to Ducote's house now," Xavier said.

"No!" Molly, Burke, and Gabe said together.

"Are you insane?" Gabe demanded. "He's the one who wants to kill us—you especially."

"He might not even be home," Xavier argued. "And all the other people who are trying to kill me are either dead or arrested."

Molly stared at Burke, who actually looked like he was listening to Xavier's arguments. "Burke?"

"He has a point," Burke said. "Let's find out if Ducote's even home. Hell, his wife might not be home, but we need to try to talk to her, to find out what she knows about her husband. If that clerk back at the UPS store was texting Ducote, he knows we're getting closer. He might run for it and then Xavier and Gabe will never be safe. They'll always be looking over their shoulders." He shrugged. "My gut's telling me that this is urgent. That we don't have that much more time."

Molly sighed. "I agree with Gabe that this is insane. But . . . what would be your plan?"

"You call Ducote's office. Find out if he's left yet. If he's still there, I'll drive us to Ducote's house. You can talk to Joelle and I'll stay and guard Xavier and Gabe, who will keep their heads down. If Ducote's not at the office, we'll go back to my camp and start again tomorrow."

"It's a good plan, Molly," Xavier said cajolingly.

"I promised your mother that you'd be safe," Molly said, hating the situation.

"You are keeping me safe," Xavier said, with the confidence of a twenty-two-year-old. "I'll stay hidden. Burke's windows are tinted and bulletproof."

"Bullet resistant," Burke corrected.

"Whatever," Xavier said. "Molly, the longer we sit here, the more of a target we are. Let's get moving."

Rolling her eyes, Molly searched for Ducote's office number online, then dialed. "They're probably closed. It's almost five now," she said, then blinked, surprised when someone answered.

"Hello, this is Mr. Ducote's office," a woman answered. "Can I help you?"

"May I speak to Mr. Ducote?" Molly asked.

"He's in a meeting," the woman said. "Can I take a message?"

"No, it's fine. I'll call back on Monday morning. Thank you." Molly ended the call and met Burke's gaze. "I don't like this."

"It'll be faster to get back to Burke's boat by going south to the Garden District where Ducote lives," Xavier said excitedly, "than it would be backtracking through the Quarter. We gotta go that way anyway."

"No, we don't gotta," Molly said. "There are lots of other ways to get to the boat launch."

"Molly." Gabe sounded exhausted. "Just drive. The faster we talk to Ducote's wife, the faster we can get Xavier back to safety."

"Let me drive," Burke said, opening his door. "You can go talk to Joelle and I can be ready to drive Xavier to safety if it gets dicey."

Feeling outnumbered, Molly switched places with Burke, hoping they weren't making a deadly mistake.

27

Tulane-Gravier, New Orleans, Louisiana
FRIDAY, JULY 29, 6:25 P.M.

THANK YOU FOR staying so late, Carrie," Lamont said. "I've got a big day in court Monday and I need to get these documents filed."

She smiled up at him, blatant interest in her eyes. "Of course. Anything you say, sir."

There was no way he was taking her on as a lover. He wouldn't even keep her as an assistant for too much longer. But he needed her for the next five minutes.

"Thank you," he said. Returning to his own office, he left the door open enough that she could hear everything that was about to be said.

Using his burner, he cued up the recording he'd cut and pasted together the night before. He'd practiced the dialogue, leaving just enough space between her rants for his own responses.

Using Joelle's cell phone, which he'd taken from the coffee table after putting her in the car, he called the phone on his desk. It was genius, really. He'd have a record of her calling from her own cell and the corresponding call length would show up on his call log as well. He'd put her phone back on the coffee table when he got home, before "discovering" her body in the garage.

His desk phone began to ring. *Showtime.* He answered it on speaker.

"Hello, Joelle," he said in a weary tone. "I don't have the time to argue with you right now. I have to get to a dinner meet—"

"I thought you loved me," recorded Joelle wailed.

"I did," he said. "Once. But I'm marrying Ashley."

"You can't do that!"

He noted movement through the opening of his office door. Carrie was listening. *Excellent.* "Watch me," he said to recorded Joelle.

"You can't do that!"

It had been a reuse of the same line, but he thought it worked well.

"What do you mean?" he asked warily.

"The whore is gone. Now we can get back to normal. We can work on our marriage. It'll be like it was at the beginning."

"Our marriage is over, Joelle. I'm filing for divorce."

"No. You will not divorce me. I won't let you. I will destroy you. Your reputation will be in tatters by the time I'm through with you."

He sighed heavily. "Joelle—"

"You'll wish you were dead by the time I'm through with you. You'll be sorry you ever crossed me."

"I need to go. We'll discuss this when I get home, like civilized people."

"Over my dead body," recorded Joelle spat.

He discreetly ended the call on Joelle's cell phone, staring into space until he heard movement in the office—Carrie scurrying back to her desk.

He pocketed Joelle's cell phone and packed up his desk with a smile—which he'd erased from his face by the time he walked by Carrie's desk. She was facing her computer, a set of headphones covering her ears.

He wanted to laugh but controlled the urge. She was trying to make it look like she hadn't heard a thing. It was really too perfect.

He touched her shoulder lightly, and she jumped a foot. "Mr. Ducote! You startled me."

"I'm so sorry, Carrie. I have to leave for my dinner meeting. I'll see you Monday morning. Don't forget to lock your station. The cleaners are coming through tonight."

"Of course, sir. I'll see you on Monday."

He left her staring after him.

Perfect.

The Garden District, New Orleans, Louisiana
FRIDAY, JULY 29, 6:40 P.M.

"Wow." From the front passenger seat of Burke's Escalade, Molly stared up at the stately Garden District home belonging to one Lamont Ducote. "It's even fancier than Mule's house."

Burke grunted. "He inherited the house and a lot of money from wife number one."

"After he killed her," Gabe muttered from behind her.

"Fucking asshole." Xavier's mutter came from the back floorboard.

"At least he doesn't have a gate," Burke said as he pulled up to the curb.

"And he's not home," Xavier added.

"Plan's the same?" Molly asked. "I try first, then if she's agreeable, Gabe will join me. Gabe, you're our videographer. Try to be discreet, but I want a record of everything if possible. Xavier, you stay in the SUV with Burke and *keep your head down*. Don't make me have to explain to your mother that you got hurt—or worse—on my watch."

"Yes, ma'am," Xavier promised. "I will. We might not have even needed wife number three if Gabe's aunt weren't still gallivanting all over the world."

"That's true, but it doesn't make this any safer. Okay, I'm off. I'm calling you now, Burke, so you can listen in on the convo." She dialed Burke's number and he crossed his fingers before hitting accept.

"Be careful," Gabe whispered fiercely. "Please."

She reached behind the seat to give his hand a squeeze. "I promise."

The Ducotes' lawn was impeccably manicured. Molly bet it took an entire team of gardeners to keep it this nice. She drew a breath when she got to the front door, tugging on her jacket to hide her holster. The gun in her holster belonged to Burke, because the cops had taken both of hers yesterday and hadn't given them back, citing their use in the killing of the men attempting to abduct Chelsea and Harper. She supposed she was lucky that they hadn't kept both her and Gabe, too.

Thank you, Willa Mae.

Bolstering herself, Molly knocked. And listened. She heard nothing. She pressed the doorbell and heard an ostentatious chime echoing through the house. But still nothing.

"Maybe she's in the backyard," she said for Burke's benefit. "Maybe they've got a pool."

She walked around the house, pausing when she came to the garage.

She could hear something here. An engine. She walked up to the side door to the garage and peered in. And her gut turned over.

"Burke, Gabe, you need to come. There's a car in the garage with the motor running and it looks like there's someone inside."

"Wait for us," Burke commanded tersely, then just before the SUV doors slammed she heard him remind Xavier to stay hidden. "Where?" he shouted as he rounded the house.

"In here." Ending her call with Burke, Molly shoved at the door with her shoulder, then winced. "Ouch, that really hurt. Gabe, you start recording. I'll call 911."

Gabe started the video then handed Molly his phone. "Hold this for a minute. Burke, together on three."

The two men slammed into the door once, twice, three times before the frame splintered. The three of them immediately started coughing at the exhaust fumes.

"This is 911. What is your emergency?" the operator asked.

Continuing to record her partners with Gabe's phone, Molly answered the operator on her own phone, giving her the address. "We have a woman in a garage with the car engine running. My partner is trying to get her out of the car and into fresh air. Please send an ambulance."

"It's on its way. Stay on the phone with me, please. What is your name?"

"Molly Sutton." Coughing, she recorded Burke and Gabe extricating the woman from the car. *Dammit.* It was Joelle Ducote. "I think the woman is the homeowner. We'll do CPR until the paramedics arrive."

Holding her breath, she continued filming as Burke carried the woman out of her garage, Gabe on his heels. Gabe took his phone and they followed Burke to the front lawn, where he laid Joelle down gently.

"There's no pulse," Burke said. "Goddammit." He shoved his phone at Molly. "Call André."

Molly muted her own phone and dialed André on Burke's. "It's Molly," she said as soon as he'd answered. "We're at the Ducotes' house."

"*You're where?*" André exploded. "Fucking hell, Molly. What are you thinking?"

"That we were too late," she snapped. "We found Joelle Ducote in her car in her garage with the motor running. We got her out, and I have 911 on the line. But I think she's dead. Can you get over here as fast as possible?"

"On my way."

André ended the call and Molly unmuted her phone. "We can't find a pulse," she said to the operator. "My partner has started chest compressions."

"Gabe, I need your help," Burke said through clenched teeth.

Once again Gabe handed his phone to Molly, then dropped to his knees on the other side of Joelle. "What do you want me to do?"

"I'm going to do mouth-to-mouth. I need you to continue chest compressions. You know how?"

Gabe nodded once. "I do."

Feeling helpless, Molly could only hold Gabe's phone, recording the two men trying to save Joelle's life.

Burke gripped the gemstone necklace that lay against Joelle's skin, gently pulling it over her head so that it didn't further impair her airflow.

Molly thought she recognized that necklace. A glance at her texts from Burke confirmed it. He'd sent her a photo of the woman who'd come into his office. "Burke, that's the same necklace that the woman who visited you wore. Or one identical to it."

Burke didn't spare it a glance. He started mouth-to-mouth, motioning Gabe to start the chest compressions.

"Hand-me-down dogs," Gabe said between shoves against Joelle Ducote's chest. "Hand-me-down necklaces, too?"

"Maybe." Then she put all thoughts out of her mind, concentrating on counting out loud so that Burke and Gabe could coordinate their efforts.

By the time the medics arrived four minutes later, both Burke and Gabe were sweaty and tired. The three of them stepped away from Joelle as the medics began to work.

Two NOPD officers arrived soon after, giving them the stink eye. "Aren't you the three who were there when Mule was shot?" one of them asked, then pointed at Molly and Gabe. "And you two when those three guys were shot Wednesday night?"

"I think you have a penchant for being in the wrong place at the wrong time," the other said, going for his cuffs. "Drop the phones and put your hands out."

"Get in the car," Burke said to Molly and Gabe.

"No," the first cop said. "You'll be getting in *our* car this time round." He grabbed the phone from Molly and twisted her arm behind her back, slapping one cuff on her wrist.

A car screeched to a halt behind them, a door slamming. "Cut the bullshit," André said loudly. "Remove the cuffs, Styles. Now." He gestured to Molly, Gabe, and Burke. "You three, come with me." He turned, frowning at first when he saw Xavier in the SUV. The young man had his phone out filming the encounter with the cops. "Who's—" André did a double take, his brows shooting up when he realized that the wig-wearing man was Xavier.

While Molly appreciated Xavier having their backs, she wanted to smack him. Did he have no sense of self-preservation whatsoever? "Get down," she mouthed. Xavier scowled, but complied. His phone, however, remained pressed against the SUV's window. Still filming.

"On second thought . . ." André gestured to a uniformed officer who'd just arrived on the scene. "I want you to escort these four into the city," he told the officer when he'd joined them.

Molly recognized the newcomer—whose name tag said McCauley—as one of André's trusted men. She'd seen him at the police station the day they'd been taken in for questioning after witnessing Mule's murder. He'd brought Gabe to the lobby after Assistant District Attorney Cardozo was finished talking to him. McCauley gave them a respectful nod before giving André his full attention.

"Where should I take them?" McCauley asked. "To the station?"

André seemed to consider it for a moment. "No. Get as close to the Monteleone Hotel as you can and wait for me there. I'll take their statements when I'm finished." Then he leaned over and whispered something in Burke's ear. "Go. Now."

The cop who'd started to cuff Molly began to sputter. "But—"

"Let them go," André snapped. "I will take their statements myself. Did you record everything, Gabe?"

"I did."

"Apparently, so did Xavier," Burke muttered.

André looked tired. "Send both videos to me as soon as you can."

"Can I have my phone back?" Molly asked the cop who'd taken it.

"Evidence," the cop snapped.

André's sigh said he was out of patience. "Officer Styles. Miss Sutton is not under arrest. She is a Good Samaritan. Give her the goddamn phone."

With a dirty look, the cop obeyed, slapping the phone into Molly's outstretched hand. It hurt, as did the wrist he'd cuffed with way too much relish, but she bit back the flinch, unwilling to let the asshole see it. "Thank you, sir," she said sweetly.

Gabe held the SUV's front passenger door open for Molly, then got in the back with Xavier, who'd finally stopped filming and was back down on the floorboard. They waited until Burke was behind the wheel and had closed his door before asking questions.

"What did he say?" Gabe asked.

"Why are we going to the Monteleone?" Molly asked.

"Is Joelle dead?" Xavier asked.

Burke pulled away from the curb. "We're going to the Monteleone because André said to. He told me that he'd meet us there and take our statements, that we could trust Officer McCauley, that he didn't want us going to the police station when he wasn't there to ensure our safety, and that we should keep our heads down. Yes, Xavier, she's dead."

"Fuck," Xavier muttered. "Another wife dead of 'suicide'?"

"If it ain't broke, don't fix it," Burke drawled sardonically and headed toward the Quarter. "There was a note on the passenger seat of her car. I snapped a photo of it, in case it gets 'misplaced.' She claimed to have killed 'Ashley' because Ashley and Ducote were having an affair but had second thoughts."

"The female victim yesterday morning?" Molly asked. "Could that have been Ashley?"

"Dunno," Burke said. "It'd make sense, though."

"Especially with the woman wearing the same necklace as Joelle," Gabe added.

"What are you talking about?" Xavier asked, and Molly told him about Joelle's necklace.

"Damn," he murmured. "This man is evil. How many mistresses has he killed? How many wives?"

"That's on André to find out," Burke said. "But it's on us to make sure that happens."

"I trust André," Molly said.

Burke nodded. "So do I. He's come through for us too many times for me not to."

"Why the Monteleone?" Gabe asked.

Burke shrugged, then hissed, rubbing his shoulder. "Don't know. I'm just doing what he said to do. Damn, my shoulder hurts. I'm getting too old to be breaking down doors."

"Me, too," Gabe said, rolling his shoulder with a grimace. "Think they'll charge us for breaking and entering into Ducote's garage?"

"I don't think so," Molly said, flexing her wrist. On top of not being able to talk to Joelle Ducote, the three of them had sustained injuries in the process. Everyone but Xavier, so she could be grateful for that, at least. "We have the whole thing documented, and we called 911." She'd ended the call to 911 when the ambulance had arrived and now googled *Monteleone Hotel* and *Lamont Ducote*. "Oh," she said after scanning one of the first articles to pop up. "There's a big political fundraiser tonight. Five hundred bucks a plate. Guess who's a guest speaker?"

"Lamont Ducote," Gabe said with a growl. "Motherfucker."

Molly sighed. "Yes and yes."

"Is André going to arrest him?" Xavier asked.

Molly looked over her shoulder. Officer McCauley was right behind them in an NOPD squad car. "I guess we're going to have to wait and see."

Hotel Monteleone, New Orleans, Louisiana
FRIDAY, JULY 29, 7:15 P.M.

"Lamont!"

Lamont turned to find Lyle Nelson approaching him, his wife on his arm. "Lyle. Lorraine. Thank you for coming out tonight."

"Our pleasure," Lorraine said with the kind of elegance he'd hoped Joelle would achieve but never had. "Where's your lovely wife tonight?"

"She said she was feeling poorly and said to offer her regrets."

"I'm so sorry to hear that," Lyle said with a momentary frown for Joelle, but then he was back to business. "I've got a few friends I'd like you to meet tonight. They're anxious to hear all about your campaign and your platform. Come along."

Lamont followed, letting it all sink in. *This is it.* This was the moment he was introduced as a potential candidate. Here, in the Monteleone, a city landmark. Where a jazz quartet played jauntily. Here, with the real money of Louisiana.

This is the first step toward what I've been working toward for years. Every case he'd taken, every scandal he'd made disappear. Every enemy he'd dispatched.

Even his marriage to wife number one had been carefully orchestrated. Especially wife number one. Lucille had been old money, her family practically New Orleans royalty. The day he'd married her had been the best day of his life.

Not because of Lucille, of course. She'd been older and far too stodgy for his personal tastes. But the connections the union had provided to him had set him on the path. He'd been employed at his father-in-law's prestigious firm. He'd done everything the old bastard had required, just short of wiping the old man's ass. *And I would have done that, too, if it'd meant progressing my career.* Luckily, it hadn't come to that, although it had been close.

Securing Lucille and her father's wealth and influence had been the first giant step. Not one ounce of it luck. He'd worked hard to catch Lucille's eye. He'd been a poor lawyer with a huge law school loan hanging over his head. She'd been his ticket to ride. He'd put up with a lot during those years.

And it was finally paying off.

Every step thereafter had been calculated toward achieving this goal. To hold the power of the US Senate in his hands. And later? Maybe even the White House.

Nelson's friends were easily charmed, and he walked away having secured their support.

"Nicely done," Nelson murmured. "Let's mingle some more before they start serving dinner."

"Lead on," Lamont said with a smile so big that it stretched his face.

Joelle would be dead by now, he had an alibi, and no one could connect him to any of the circus going on within the NOPD. Mule was being investigated, his legacy doomed.

Lamont, on the other hand, would come out of this—well, not smelling like a rose. There would be the scandal of his affair and Joelle's suicide following her murder-for-hire of Ashley, but he'd survive all that. He already had his black suit picked out. He'd be in mourning for a while, but he'd persist, and people all around would laud him for his commitment to the community in the face of tragedy.

Everything was gonna be all right.

"What's he doing here?" Lorraine said sharply.

Lamont turned around and—

No. Oh no, no no no. His gut went into free fall, his heart beating so loud that it was all he could hear.

It was André Holmes, that damn cop. And beside him . . . Jean-Pierre Cardozo.

Both wore suits. Both looked grim.

And both were coming his way.

Two officers followed them, checking out the room.

Oh my God.

They stopped in front of them, André giving a polite nod to Lorraine.

"What is the meaning of this?" Nelson demanded. "This is a private event. We have all the proper permits." He lowered his voice, leaning toward André and Jean-Pierre. "You're making a scene."

"Apologies," André said. "Mr. Ducote, we need you to come with us."

Lamont swallowed hard. "If you'll call my office on Monday morning, my assistant will be happy to give you an appointment."

Jean-Pierre rolled his eyes. Actually rolled his fucking eyes. "Don't make this any harder than it already is, Ducote. We know."

"What do you know?" Nelson asked in that quiet way that demanded respect.

André met Lamont's gaze. "We know *everything.* Do you really want me to spew it all out here? In front of all these people? Come with us peacefully, Ducote. It's your only option."

"I have no idea what they're talking about," Lamont said to Nelson, sounding outraged.

"Mule," Jean-Pierre said, then cocked one brow, the smug sonofabitch. "And Ashley."

Lamont couldn't breathe. People were staring. Some had their phones out, recording everything.

Nelson's rich friends were frowning and stepping back.

André took a step forward, putting him only two feet away. *Close enough to grab me.* "Mr. Ducote, please. I'll cuff you, but I don't think that's how you want to walk away from here tonight."

Jean-Pierre leaned in, his tone pitched low. "Joelle is dead, by the way. But I think you already knew that. We have so much to talk about. We have so much evidence to show you."

When he didn't move, André sighed and produced a pair of handcuffs. The room went wild. Flashes went off. Photographers were jockeying for position.

This can't be happening. I was so careful. This cannot be happening.

But it *was* happening. And he needed to get away.

In one motion, he drew his handgun from his pocket, stepped behind Lorraine Nelson, and put the gun to her head. Screams filled the air. He didn't know who was screaming and he didn't care. He only cared that they got out of his way.

Lorraine gasped and struggled, but he shoved the gun harder against her temple and pressed his free arm across her throat. "Don't fight me," he hissed, "and I won't hurt you."

She went limp, a whimper passing her lips.

Her husband made to grab for her, but Lamont took a giant step back, dragging the older woman with him. "Don't. If you want her to live, then don't." He raised his voice so that André and Jean-Pierre could hear. "Call off your dogs. My finger is on the trigger. I will kill her, right in front of you. I swear it."

André's jaw clenched and he waved the officers back. "Let's calm down now, Mr. Ducote. Put the gun down and let her go."

"No." Lamont dragged Nelson's wife back another step. "Get everyone out of my way." He wrenched left toward the stairwell and the old woman stumbled.

"She has a bad heart!" Nelson screamed.

"Then don't make me hurt her!" Lamont screamed back. Walking sideways, he kept an eye on André especially. The man had drawn his gun but was clearly afraid to fire. Which was kind of the point of having a hostage, so at least that part was working.

In André's other hand was a police radio and he was talking into it. Barking orders. Probably covering the exits.

I'm screwed. I'm so screwed.

But all he needed to do was get to the street. For once he was grateful for the damn festival. There were tons of people in the street. He could disappear. He could take another hostage. He could take dozens of hostages.

No. He would focus on disappearing. More hostages would just prolong this nightmare.

The crowd parted like the Red Sea and Lamont sucked in a lungful of air. It was so hot. He was dizzy from it. Sweat was pouring off his forehead, stinging his eyes. But he kept them open and fixed on the exit sign.

The cops were walking alongside him, clearing him a path, getting people to move out of the line of fire. If they tried to stop him, he would kill Lorraine. But then he'd have no shield.

This move rarely worked when criminals tried it, but it was the only option he had left. If they knew about Ashley and Joelle, he'd have no leverage in court.

He made it to the door. "Open it," he growled to Lorraine.

Hands trembling, she obeyed, and he dragged her through to the stairs. The two uniformed officers watched him as he descended, apparently waiting for André. The big cop seemed to fill the stairwell when he stepped through the door.

"Back off, Holmes!" Lamont shouted. "Do not test me."

André Holmes said nothing, simply descending the stairs one at a time, keeping pace with him. Not letting him out of his sight.

"I will kill her." Lamont's words echoed off the stairwell walls, and Lorraine let out a sob.

"I know you're capable of it," André said calmly. "But I don't intend to allow you to do it."

Lamont would kill them all, then. Every single one of them if he had to.

He'd descended the first flight of stairs and now stood on the landing. André was only four steps away.

Keeping his arm tight against Lorraine's throat, Lamont pointed the gun at André's chest and fired twice. The man collapsed, gasping as he rolled down the stairs.

Lamont shoved the gun against Lorraine's temple once again and dragged her down the remaining stairs and out the emergency door, setting off an alarm. Hot, moist air smacked him in the face, shocking after the cool A/C, but the humidity he usually hated was now the most amazing feeling ever.

Just another minute. I'm almost free.

28

IT'S TOO LOUD," Gabe complained from where they sat parked on Iberville Street down the street from the back entrance of the Monteleone. They were in a loading zone, but since they were being guarded by Officer McCauley—who stood next to Burke's SUV, hand on his holstered gun—Gabe figured they weren't likely to be towed.

Everyone was partying and there was music everywhere, loud enough to be heard through the closed windows of Burke's SUV. Normally Gabe loved the noise of the Quarter during a festival, but this was off the charts, especially since he'd been hiding out on the bayou where the only real noise was that of the birds.

"It's because of Satchmo," Molly said from the front seat, her gaze never pausing, looking for threats.

I know, Gabe wanted to snap, but bit it back. It wasn't Molly's fault that he was wound tighter than a damn drum. He could still see Joelle Ducote's lifeless body on the ground, her eyes staring up at the sky as he and Burke had done CPR.

He'd seen more dead bodies this week than he had in his whole life.

And his father had seen them so much more often for more than thirty-five years. *So suck it up, Hebert.*

He tried, drawing in a lungful of air and holding it for a few beats before letting it out.

"You okay?" Xavier muttered.

"No, not really. But I will be." But Xavier continued to look worried, so Gabe leaned in to whisper, "I'd never seen a dead body outside of a funeral home before this week."

Xavier nodded sadly. "I have. They were floating by my roof while I sat there waiting for your dad that night."

Gabe froze, his heart in his throat. "Oh, Xavier. I'm sorry."

Xavier shrugged, looking uncomfortable because Burke and Molly had turned in their seats to stare back at him. "It's fine. I had therapy. I think I'm gonna need a lot more after this." He grinned lopsidedly. "Maybe you and I can get a two-for-one discount."

Gabe had to smile, if for no other reason than to reward Xavier for trying to make him feel better. "You're on."

"Can you see anything?" Xavier asked Burke, effectively changing the subject. "Any sign of Ducote?"

Burke turned to face forward, then shook his head. "No. Only a few hotel staffers out back in the alley taking a smoking break. The ballroom on the second floor is where they're having the fundraiser." Then he tensed. "Sonofabitch."

The three of them turned in the direction that Burke was staring, and Gabe couldn't stop the growl that tore from his throat at the sight of the uniformed man walking along Iberville toward the alley behind the hotel. "Cresswell."

His father's old boss. The man who'd "accidentally" shown him his father's body, slumped over the kitchen table where he'd eaten family dinners for most of his life.

The man who believed his father would steal drugs from the evidence locker.

The man who may have even framed his father to look guilty.

Gabe wasn't aware that he'd opened his door to get out until Molly's sharp reprimand yanked him back.

"Not now, Gabe. You'll get your chance. For now, stay with us. We need to stay safe and where Officer McCauley can alibi us if something goes wrong."

Because André might be in the hotel, arresting Ducote. Or at least taking him in for questioning.

Exhaling hard, Gabe closed the door. "You're right. I'm sorry."

Xavier slid a finger under his wig to scratch his head. "I wonder what else André knows. It's got to be more than a hand-me-down dog if they're hauling Ducote in, even for questioning."

"Fuck," Molly muttered. "Stay calm, Gabe. Cresswell's coming this way."

Gabe had to shove his hands in his pockets to keep from balling them into fists. Probably not smart to punch a cop. Even one who deserved it like Cresswell.

And then . . . everything changed. Cresswell stopped walking, listening to the police radio in his hand. Then he turned on his heel and began walking back toward the rear of the hotel.

Officer McCauley was also listening to his radio and Burke opened his window in time for them to hear a deep voice say, "We have a hostage situation."

Gabe stiffened. That was André's voice.

"Cresswell, get to the back stairwell now," André continued.

McCauley drew his gun from his holster, giving Burke a mild glare. "You heard that?"

"We did," Burke said. "What's happening?"

"Just stay put," McCauley commanded. "Roll up your windows and keep your heads down."

Burke complied, but Molly rolled hers down enough that they could hear what was happening. Both Burke and Molly had tensed, both sliding their own weapons from their holsters.

Gabe had to remember to breathe. He put a hand on Xavier's shoulder, ready to push the young man out of the way should bullets begin to fly.

And then a screeching sound tore the air.

An emergency exit, Gabe guessed, then knew he was right a few seconds later when a man stumbled from the alley into the street, his arm around an older woman's throat.

And a gun to the woman's temple.

Lamont Ducote. Gabe felt a growl start in his chest, but he shoved it down. The bastard did indeed have a hostage. "What are we going to do?" he asked.

"We're going to stay here," Burke barked, his body coiled to move. As was Molly's. "It's Cresswell's job to stop him."

But Cresswell hadn't stopped him. Ducote was dragging the woman along the sidewalk and, by now, people were noticing the gun. Some ran away screaming. Others pressed closer, phones held high as they recorded the unfolding drama.

Assholes.

"Where's Cresswell?" Molly shouted over the noise coming through the car window, which was now mostly the screams of the passersby.

"I don't know," Burke shouted back. "But Ducote is coming this way."

And McCauley was approaching the man and his hostage, his service weapon drawn. "Let her go!" McCauley yelled.

Ducote's answer was to pull the gun from his hostage's head long enough to fire at McCauley. The officer dropped like a rock.

Xavier cried out in shock. Gabe felt frozen.

Outside the car, chaos erupted, the crowd pushing and shoving to escape the scene.

Then Burke was moving, rushing out of the SUV to drag McCauley behind it.

Molly cursed. "Where the fuck is NOPD? Where is André? Burke?" she called through Burke's open door. "What's McCauley's status?"

"He's dead," Burke said grimly. "He took a bullet to his temple. It doesn't look like anyone is coming for Ducote. Something bad must have gone down inside the hotel. If Ducote drags her into that crowd . . ."

They'd lose him. He'd get away.

We'll never be safe from him.

"He shot that cop," Xavier whispered hoarsely. "He *killed* that cop. Oh my God."

"I know." Gabe could feel panic skirting the edges of his mind and pushed it back. He'd known that Ducote was a killer. He'd seen him shoot Mule.

Ducote had killed so many others. Nadia. Joelle. The woman from the bayou the day before.

His breath hitched in his chest. *My father. He killed my father. I'm sorry, Dad. I'm so sorry.*

Sorry that it had happened. Sorry that he hadn't been able to stop it. Sorry that Ducote was still killing people.

But he couldn't deal with that now. Later. He'd fall apart later. He drew a breath and straightened his spine, disturbed by the realization that he was becoming too adept at compartmentalizing murder. He pushed back that worry as well.

Burke and Molly shared a quick look, then Molly jumped out of the SUV and followed Burke toward Ducote.

Okay, Gabe thought. *So we're doing this, then.*

"Stay here," he commanded Xavier, and, deliberately not looking at the body of the fallen officer, got out of the car to follow them. He wasn't sure what he was going to do, but all he could think was that he couldn't let Ducote hurt anyone else. He couldn't let Ducote kill anyone else. At the very least, he could direct the crowd away, giving Molly and Burke room to work.

Molly and Burke had split up, one going left of Ducote and the other going right. It looked like they planned to approach him from behind. But Ducote was still dragging the woman, whose face was streaked with helpless tears.

And then Xavier was at Gabe's side. *Goddammit.*

"What the hell are you doing out here?" Gabe demanded.

"Same thing you are," Xavier answered evenly.

Gabe grabbed Xavier's arm. "Xavier, go. Please."

Xavier gave him a look that didn't bode well. "No way in hell. We both go or we both stay. What are you planning to do?"

Gabe shook his head. "He's coming this way. If he gets into that crowd, he'll be gone. Or even more people will get hurt. Please, Xavier, go."

"Fine," Xavier said, but didn't move an inch.

"I swear to God you are as stubborn as my father," Gabe gritted out.

"So are you."

Ducote was close enough now that Gabe could see the fear in the hostage's eyes. Taking a deep breath, Gabe strode toward them, purposefully not looking for Molly or Burke.

If the two took Ducote down from behind, the old lady could be hurt in the process.

And that wasn't okay.

He hadn't been able to save Dr. McLain or Dusty Woodruff or even Joelle Ducote, but he'd be damned if this old lady got hurt today.

Gabe held up his hands, aware of Xavier behind him. *Run,* he wanted to yell to the younger man, but he didn't think it'd do any good.

"Mr. Ducote," Gabe said loudly.

Ducote's head had been swiveling back and forth as he frantically searched for a way out, but now he stopped hard, shock flickering in his eyes. The lady was grabbing at Ducote's forearm, trying to breathe.

He's going to kill her. Gabe knew it like he knew his own name.

Gabe took a few more steps forward, his focus narrowing on the man and his hostage. "Let her go, Ducote," he said. "She's not the one you want. I'm the one you want."

"No, *I'm* the one you want," Xavier said from beside him.

Gabe wanted to shove Xavier out of the way, out of danger. *He's been through enough already, dammit.*

Ducote looked from Gabe to Xavier. His eyes were wild, flicking one way then the other. Looking for a way out. "Who the hell is he?"

Xavier took off the wig and glasses. "I'm the five-year-old kid who saw you murder Nadia Hall. I'm the one you've been trying to kill all week. Let the lady go, and I'll go with you."

Something flickered in Ducote's eyes. Hope? Calculation? Then disbelief. "You lie."

The woman Ducote held whimpered, and Gabe realized that everyone around them had gone silent. He could still hear noise from the crowd farther down the block and there was a band playing jazz close by, but it was like the people around them were holding their breath.

"I'm not lying," Xavier insisted, and Gabe believed him.

Dear God. Xavier really was going to give himself up.

And then Gabe caught a glint of gold. The sun reflecting off of Molly's hair. She was mere feet behind Ducote, her gun positioned just as it had been the night they'd stopped Nicholas Tobin from hurting Chelsea and Harper.

Gabe knew exactly what she was planning to do.

"My father died protecting Xavier," Gabe said. "You're not getting him. But you can try to take me."

Ducote shook his head. "Your daddy didn't even fight. He was a damn coward."

Gabe felt the rage bubbling up from his gut. "Because you drugged him." He wanted to look at Xavier, to be sure that he was okay, but he didn't dare take his eyes off of Ducote. He needed Ducote to move the gun away from the woman's head, to point it at him. Then Molly could do her thing.

"Rocky Hebert was brave," Xavier said, his voice loud and clear. "The kind of man you'll *never* be."

And even without looking, Gabe could tell the young man held his head high.

"Hands where I can see them, Hebert," Ducote barked. "Or I will shoot your little friend and he can spend eternity with your father."

Gabe could see Burke now, standing just behind Molly. But he didn't see Cresswell or any other cops.

Where the hell is André?

It looked like this was up to them. Gabe needed the bastard to point his gun away from the old lady. *Point it at me.* "Go to hell, Ducote."

Ducote's face was red and dripping with sweat. "I'll take you with me."

Xavier took another step forward so that he was within touching distance of the woman, who was looking positively gray. She no longer clutched at Ducote's arm, now clutching at her heart instead. Something needed to happen fast, or she'd die from heart failure before Ducote could shoot her.

"Do it," Xavier said. "If you're such a big, bad guy, then do it. Or do you just hide behind other people who do the hard work for you?"

Ducote was gritting his teeth. "You fucking—"

And before Gabe could draw another breath, Ducote's arm swung, the gun moving from the woman's head to point at Xavier. Gabe shoved the young man out of the way and leapt forward, falling to his knees at the woman's feet as Ducote's gun swung away from Xavier and pointed at him. He closed his eyes, waiting for the shot.

But it never came. Instead, Ducote screamed, his gun clattering to the ground.

Gabe opened his eyes in time to catch the old woman as she slumped to the ground. Cradling her, he knee-walked her to safety, looking up just as Ducote went down—just like Tobin had, Molly's knee gouging the bastard's kidney.

Xavier rushed to Gabe's side, kneeling beside the woman and pressing his fingers to her throat. "I'm not getting a pulse," he said, then sucked in a breath. "Yeah, I am, but it's faint. Put her down, Gabe. We need to do CPR."

But Gabe barely heard him because Molly and Burke were still fighting with Ducote. Burke held the man down on the other side, but he wasn't giving up, thrashing and kicking his legs, desperate to escape.

"Cresswell!" Burke yelled. "Get your sorry ass over here and cuff him!"

Gabe heard Molly cry out in pain and watched as Ducote got his hand free. *No.* That fucker was not touching Molly. *Not today. Not ever.*

"Put her down, Gabe," Xavier said urgently. "She's dying."

Obeying, Gabe laid the woman on the pavement as gently as he could, then threw himself over Ducote's legs. From where he lay, he could see two cops running up to them, guns drawn. *Finally.*

"Get out of the way," one of them commanded. "Now."

Shuddering out a breath, Molly rolled to her feet and the officer started to take her place. A second later, Burke followed suit as the second cop took over for him. Gabe didn't move because Ducote was still kicking.

"Finally," Molly said, panting. "Where the fuck is Cress—"

The shot was a shock.

Gabe froze, not sure where it had come from. Then he lurched up, adding his own scream to that of the crowd. *"Molly!"*

And then he realized that Ducote wasn't fighting anymore.

Molly stood like a statue, staring down at the former ADA of New Orleans.

Who now had a huge hole in his head.

Gabe gaped, unable to form a single word.

"What the fuck?" Burke whispered.

"What did you do?" the officer yelled.

We didn't do anything, Gabe wanted to yell back. Then saw that the cop wasn't talking to Burke.

He was talking to Cresswell, who still had his gun pointed at Ducote's head. The man who'd been Gabe's father's boss didn't look shocked or grim.

He looked relieved.

"He was resisting arrest," Cresswell said calmly.

The two uniformed officers just stared at him.

A man in a suit ran up to them. "What the hell just happened here?"

It took Gabe a moment to recognize ADA Cardozo. Slowly Gabe rolled off the dead man's legs. He tried to stand, but his legs were like wet noodles.

Cardozo glared at Burke and Molly. "Why did you kill him?"

Burke opened his mouth, but before he could say a word, Molly stepped forward. "We didn't." She pointed to Cresswell. "He did."

The two cops rose, and Gabe had to swallow back the bile that rushed up to burn his throat. The officers were covered in blood and brains. Ducote's blood and brains.

Do not throw up. Do not *throw up.* He took a deep breath through his mouth, trying to settle his churning stomach.

"He did," one of the cops confirmed. "Cresswell shot him."

"He was resisting arrest," Cresswell repeated just as calmly as the first time. "He'd already shot and killed Officer McCauley."

Cardozo blanched. "What?"

"Ducote shot the officer that Captain Holmes assigned to guard us," Molly said, her voice shaking. "He shot him in the head. His body is on the sidewalk, behind our SUV."

"Cresswell knew that," Gabe realized. "He had to have been close enough to see McCauley go down, to hear Burke pronounce him dead. He's been close by all this time. And he did nothing."

Cardozo's lips thinned. "I see."

Cresswell merely lifted his chin and said nothing.

"Where's André?" Burke asked abruptly, looking around.

"He's coming," Cardozo said. "Mr. Ducote here shot him twice in the chest, but he had a vest on." He spun and stalked over to Cresswell. "We need to talk, Cresswell."

Cresswell holstered his gun and shrugged. "Fine. He was resisting arrest and officers were in danger."

Cardozo looked at the two cops. Both were shaking their heads.

"Where's Mrs. Nelson?" Cardozo asked, looking around.

And Gabe remembered the older woman. *Oh shit.*

He crawled over to where Xavier was still doing chest compressions. "Call 911," Gabe called over his shoulder.

"Oh no," Molly said as she and Burke rushed over to join them.

"What the—?" Cardozo started to ask. "Fuck. Get an ambulance for Mrs. Nelson."

"Can you do mouth-to-mouth?" Gabe asked Xavier, hearing one of the cops calling it in on his radio. "I wasn't trained for that, but I can do the compressions."

Which he'd already done once that evening.

"I can," Xavier said, putting the older woman's head into position, and Gabe remembered that the young man had worked as a lifeguard to put himself through college.

Molly began to count off and the three of them coordinated the CPR. Gabe lost track of time, barely aware of the older man who'd dropped to his knees beside them, wringing his hands as he watched.

"Lorraine," he called pitifully. "Lorraine, baby, don't leave me."

Her husband, Gabe realized, but couldn't remember the man's name. He only remembered that this was the man who was trying to make Ducote a senator.

Burke gently urged the husband out of the way. "Let them work, Mr. Nelson."

Finally, one of the cops crouched next to Gabe and put a hand on his shoulder. "You can stop. EMTs are here."

Gabe looked up to see two paramedics park bicycles on the street corner and rush up with their equipment. Exhausted, he fell back on his ass, unable to stand. He shuffled back a few feet, careful not to come too close to Ducote's body.

Or to Officer McCauley's. That loss would sink in soon. The man had died protecting them.

Gabe looked around, stunned and feeling . . . surreal. The crowd that had been pushing and screaming now gathered behind crime scene tape. When had the cops strung that?

Every single person had their phone out, or so it seemed. And he was too tired to even care.

He watched, detached, as one of the paramedics gave Mrs. Nelson an oxygen mask and, to his extreme relief, her chest was finally rising and falling on its own.

Gabe's gaze sought out the one person who mattered. Molly collapsed beside him, leaning her head on his shoulder. "Hey there," she murmured. "You okay?"

"I have no idea," he said truthfully.

"I know what you mean. I wonder if anyone would mind if we stay here for the next week."

"I didn't want to sleep on Burke's grass. I really don't want to sleep here."

"Then I guess we need to get out of here." Lifting her head, she first stared at McCauley's body, then, swallowing hard, turned and pointed to where Xavier stood, talking to one of the paramedics. "Xavier did good."

"He did," Gabe said, pride surfacing from his shock. "Just tuned out all of the drama to save that woman's life."

"You didn't do so bad yourself, throwing yourself over Ducote's legs like that. I didn't think I could hold him down much longer. You're a hero. You sure you don't want to be a PI?"

Gabe shuddered. "No. I'll leave the heroics to you from now on."

She smiled up at him. "You can be my hero."

Suddenly he could breathe again. "I will make you chocolate cake every damn day."

"Oh no. I'll go into a sugar coma. Once a week is fine."

A shadow fell across them and they turned to look over their shoulders. André stood there, hunched over like he was hurting. "You guys okay?" he asked.

"We're . . . here," Gabe answered. "I heard you got shot."

André shot a baleful glare toward Ducote's body. "Sonofabitch shot me twice. Hurts like a bitch. I think I've got a busted rib. Maybe two." Then he sighed, his next words tinged with guilt. "I think that's why he aimed higher at McCauley, to avoid his vest." His throat worked and he cleared his throat. "I've worked beside McCauley for years. He was a good man. A good cop." His broad shoulders sagged. "I'm going to have to tell his wife."

"I'm sorry," Gabe murmured. "It happened so fast. We couldn't stop it."

André's nod was solemn. "I know. I know you would've tried if you could." He took a step back, hands out. "I've got a lot to take care of. I'll take your statements in a little bit."

"There are enough videos that you really don't need to," Molly said. "I'm sure they're already online."

André shook his head, his expression pained. "We're already trending on Twitter. But I'll need all of your statements for my report. Can you stick around for another hour?"

Gabe didn't want to. He wanted to get out of the heat and take a nice cool shower. He wanted to hold Molly and never let her go.

But he nodded. "Of course."

"I'm going to have one of my guys take you into the hotel. I'll call a medic to check you over, just in case."

"What about Cresswell?" Molly asked frostily.

"I took his weapon and he's sitting in the back of one of the department SUVs. He has some explaining to do. A lot of explaining to do."

Molly looked around for the cops' vehicle, glaring when she saw it. "He didn't even try to subdue Ducote. He just shot him."

"I know. The two officers who followed Ducote out of the building said the same. They said once they got out on the street, you'd put your plan into action and they were afraid they'd hurt one of you, so they had to let it play out. Don't do that again, okay? I'm begging you."

"I'm done with my life of crime-fighting," Gabe declared, then looked at the woman lying on the ground. "Will she be okay?"

"She's alive," André said. "Thanks to you."

Gabe shook his head. "Thanks to Xavier. He's going to make a great doctor someday. Go on, do what you need to do. We'll wait for you inside the hotel." He forced himself to stand, swallowing his groan, then held his hand to Molly.

Together they stood, watching as Mr. Nelson thanked Xavier, shaking his hand over and over and finally embracing him, the older man's body shaking with sobs. Xavier hugged him, patting his back.

"His mama's gonna be so proud," Molly murmured.

"She really is," Gabe murmured back.

Mr. Nelson let Xavier go and their friend ambled over to them, his eyes bright with excitement and relief. "She's breathing on her own. I hope she's gonna be okay."

Molly hugged Xavier hard and he pressed his face into her shoulder. "You were amazing," she said fiercely.

"We couldn't save Officer McCauley or Joelle Ducote," Xavier said, his voice muffled against Molly's shoulder. "I didn't want to lose Mrs. Nelson, too."

"She's alive because of you." She let him go then poked him in the chest. "Don't ever do that again, taunting a killer to shoot you. For fuck's sake. You nearly gave *me* a heart attack."

"Gabe did the same thing."

"And I will deal with him later. Promise me. No more offering yourself."

"I promise." Xavier leaned his head back, staring up at the sky thankfully. "It's over. It's really over."

Gabe glanced over at Ducote's body, now surrounded with barriers so that the crowd couldn't take any more photos. "It really is. My dad would be proud." Taking Molly's hand, he put his other arm around Xavier's shoulders. "Come on. Let's get inside, away from all these cameras."

29

H EY, Y'ALL, ANYBODY home?" a familiar female voice called from the front porch.

Standing closest to the front of Gabe's house, Molly turned to the screen door, blocked out the very loud celebration going on behind her, and grinned. André stood on the front porch with Farrah and ADA Cardozo.

Glancing over her shoulder for Shoe—he was lying on his back next to the living room sofa, begging unashamedly for belly rubs from Harper—Molly opened the door. "Y'all are welcome, but fair warning— you may not fit."

It was true. Gabe's small house was filled to bursting with old friends and new, and Gabe was holding court in his own kitchen, his cousin Patty at his side. They'd all decided to put sadness for the victims aside for a day, to enjoy one another's company without the fear that had burdened them all week.

Xavier, Carlos, and Manny were on the back porch with Phin and Antoine, having beers and talking about football. Val, Cicely, and Willa

Mae sat on bar stools at the kitchen counter, each on their second glass of wine. Or third. Nobody was counting. Willa Mae had been asking all kinds of questions about roller derby and Val was telling stories that had the women howling with laughter.

It was so good to hear.

Lucien had been released from the hospital that morning and lay on the sofa, his feet in Chelsea's lap. Molly had been happy to see that the two were getting friendly. Lucien was a good man and Chelsea appeared ready to date again. That Harper already adored him was a huge plus.

Burke sat in Gabe's recliner, feet up, head back, eyes closed, and his hands folded on his stomach. It was his favorite pose. Joy sat in her wheelchair, smiling contentedly. The mostly empty hurricane glass in her hand might have had something to do with that. Patty had fixed it for her as soon as she'd rolled through the door, having remembered it was Joy's drink of choice from the night of Molly's birthday. But Molly thought that Joy had been most pleased with the ramp that had greeted her when she'd arrived. Molly had woken that morning in Gabe's bed, smelling coffee and hearing the sounds of a hammer and power saw.

He'd wanted to make sure that all of her friends felt welcome.

"Long time no see," she said to André and Cardozo, who'd taken their statements the night before. "And, Farrah, I'm always glad to see you. Come on in."

"Something smells good," Farrah said, giving Molly a hug as she entered.

"That's because it *is* good," Molly said. "Gabe and Patty have been cooking all day."

"Who's minding the Choux?" Farrah asked. "I heard that it's back open today."

Patty and Gabe had decided that with Ducote's threat neutralized, they'd reopen the restaurant. Keeping it closed on one of the busiest weekends of the year would only be hurting their waitstaff, who'd lose their tip income. They'd both kept their cell phones close by, but so far no one from the Choux had called them for advice or assistance. The lines to get in were even longer than normal, though, with Gabe's recent fame. The video of him standing up to Ducote had gone viral and the restaurant's social media was abuzz with those wanting a glimpse of the crime-fighting celebrity chef.

"The new assistant manager." Molly grimaced. "Luckily that Donna Lee bitch was training someone to cover for her on her days off. There's all kinds of food on the counter in the kitchen. Go and help yourselves."

"Oh, man." Cardozo looked annoyed. "If I'd known there'd be food, I wouldn't have eaten before I came."

"There's dessert," Molly said. "Gabe made his chocolate cake."

"Did you sneak a peek at the recipe?" Farrah asked.

"No need." Gabe made his way to the door, where he shook Cardozo's hand, gave André a man-hug, and wrapped his arms around Farrah for a legit hug. Then he gave André's fiancée a sealed envelope. "I wrote it down for you. Don't spread it around, okay?"

Farrah clutched the envelope to her bosom like it was diamonds. "Oh, I won't. But you don't have to do this."

Gabe teasingly reached for the envelope. "You can give it back."

"Oh, no," Farrah said. "I'm polite, not stupid." She folded the envelope and slid it down into her bra, laughing when Gabe yanked his hand back. "Safest place ever."

"Except from me," André said with an indulgent smile.

She leaned into her fiancé. "Except from you." She turned to Molly. "These two have come to talk to you guys. I came to meet the rest of your group. Introduce me."

So Molly did, bringing the guys from the backyard inside before introducing the three newcomers to everyone in the house. Gabe offered them beers and Farrah was immediately charmed by Willa Mae, as were they all.

"When André told me that you were representing Molly, Gabe, and

Xavier, I looked you up," she told the older woman. "You did some good work, ma'am. Helped a lot of people."

Willa Mae grew serious at the compliment. "You did, too. You gave Gabe, Molly, Chelsea, and Harper shelter when they needed it most. We won't be forgetting that."

Once introductions were done, André held up a hand. "We don't have a lot of time," he said when everyone had gathered round. "I figured you'd want some questions answered."

"And maybe you'd answer a few of ours," Cardozo added. "Quid pro quo, you know."

"You first," Burke said, his expression wary.

André shook his head with a chuckle. "Fine, fine. Good to know that some things never change. Okay, so . . . Cresswell was released." He held up his hand at the gasps of outrage. "He's been put on administrative leave."

"With pay?" Willa Mae asked with a scowl.

"Yes, ma'am," André said. "For now. We've had our eye on him for a while, so don't get upset just yet. You, of all people, know that these things take time."

"Didn't take you long to arrest Ducote," Antoine said, arms crossed over his chest.

"That's because we were already investigating him," Cardozo said. "*I* was already investigating him. I took this assignment primarily to go undercover at the DA's office. I've been working with the state justice department for the past three months, gathering intel on Ducote. We didn't know about any of this murder business, though. We were looking at him for possible extortion and bribes."

"He had a list in the safe in his home office," André added. "We found it last night. Over two dozen names of people he'd enabled to escape a criminal charge. Everything from murder to child—" He broke it off, looking over his shoulder to make sure Harper couldn't overhear. Luckily, Lucien had given her his headphones and she was playing a game on her tablet. "To the sexual assault of a child," André went on, lowering his voice. "Anyway, he'd been extorting favors from these people for years."

"Tyson Whitley," Molly said, "and George Haslet." The man who'd killed Xavier's intruder in the Houston hospital and the man whose car Ducote stole the morning he killed Mule. "He got their charges dropped?"

"Exactly," André said. "Two other names on that list were Cornell Eckert and LeRoy Hodges, the attorney who was representing him. The ME who did Rocky's autopsy was on the list, too. We picked up both the ME and the attorney and will question them. The FBI took over Eckert's case, as they'd been watching him for a while. They're hoping to close several cases with what they found when they searched his home."

"Hold on," Molly said, wanting to be clear. "You were investigating Ducote for abuse of power?"

"Yes," Cardozo said. "When Houston PD showed Whitley his name on Ducote's list—all the other names redacted, of course—he took a deal in exchange for admitting to being blackmailed into killing the man in the hospital. Ducote didn't tell him who the man was or why he needed to be killed, and Whitley didn't ask."

"What kind of deal?" Xavier asked tightly.

"Death penalty off the table," Cardozo said. "Whitley will serve time, though. No way around that."

"Is my son in danger from any of them?" Cicely asked.

"No, ma'am," André said. "Not as far as we know. We'll make sure you're kept up-to-date on everything that happens. Houston PD still wants to talk to Xavier, but I don't expect Willa Mae will let them badger him too much."

"Not while I live and breathe," Willa Mae declared.

"They were a little put off that you were his counsel," André said with a smile. "You've got a reputation."

Willa Mae lifted her wineglass. "Every bit of it earned."

"I will not disagree with that," André said respectfully. "So that was why Ducote was being investigated. When his assistant went missing, J.P. alerted us."

"Who's J.P.?" Carlos asked.

"That's me," Cardozo said. "Most folks call me J.P., because my name is Jean-Pierre. Ducote insisted on calling me by my full name and he always made it sound like it tasted bad in his mouth."

"The dead woman in the bayou was his assistant?" Burke asked.

Cardozo nodded. "Ashley Resnick. She was young and brash and . . ." He sighed. "Ducote was a charmer. He set his hook and reeled her in."

"She was responsible for her own actions," Val said with uncharacteristic venom.

Molly blinked, as did Burke.

Cardozo's gaze flew to Val, lingering for a moment before he nodded again. "You're quite right, Miss Sorensen. Ashley Resnick was responsible for her actions, and she paid dearly for her mistake. We don't know exactly why Ducote killed her. I imagine she caught wind of some part of his scheme. I don't think she was a lawbreaker, but she was very naive."

"CSU found traces of blood in the washroom off Ducote's office," André said. "We found a cleaver in the trunk of that stolen car. We believe he dismembered her right there in the washroom."

Antoine grimaced. "Goddammit, André."

André rolled his eyes. "For God's sake, Antoine. I had to ID the woman's head."

Antoine made a sick noise, wrinkling his nose. Gabe handed him another beer.

"It'll help," Gabe said, and Antoine guzzled the beer down, still grimacing.

"Ducote's driver came by the police station last night," André said.

"He was very shaken. He wanted no one to think that he'd been involved in Ducote's crimes. He was, in fact, able to fill in a lot of blanks. He said that he'd been Ducote's driver for twenty years. He remembered Nadia Hall and remembered taking Ducote by her house one night. Ducote didn't go in, but the driver said that Ducote seemed satisfied when he saw that the lights were on in the woman's house."

"He was checking up on his mistress," Molly murmured. "April Frazier, Nadia's best friend, said that her boyfriend was very controlling."

"Then that fits," André said. "The driver also said that the night before Ducote killed Mule, he left the office with two large boxes wrapped in silver paper. We found the boxes and the used paper in the trunk of the stolen car at Mule's murder scene. The paper had been wiped clean of prints, and Ducote had triple-bagged the victim's remains."

"He knew what he was doing," Molly said. "Probably saw enough criminals make mistakes and learned from them."

"I'm sure you're right," Cardozo said. "He had a really decent plan, but he didn't count on a few things. And that's where you guys come in. He'd planned to disassociate himself from Ashley's murder."

Burke's jaw tightened. "He blamed it on Joelle, his wife. We saw the note on the passenger seat when we were getting her out of her car yesterday."

"What was his 'decent plan'?" Xavier asked, using air quotes.

"He'd made a recording of him and his wife having an argument on his phone," Cardozo said. "Which, thankfully, was still in his pocket when he died—along with his wife's phone. Our tech guys were able to break into Ducote's cell. He'd used a program to create a clip of her voice, rearranging the things she said. Then, just before he left for the dinner, he used his wife's cell phone to call his desk phone."

"He played the recording," Molly guessed, "so it would sound like she was still alive?"

"Exactly," Cardozo said. "He knew that his assistant would be curious and made sure she could hear the whole thing. We think he planned to 'discover' his wife's body when he got home from the fund-raising dinner."

"But he'd have an alibi for the time of her death because the assistant heard Joelle alive before he went to the dinner," Burke said. "I have to admit, that is kind of a good plan."

"What time did he make the call?" Gabe asked.

Cardozo's lips curved into a satisfied smile. "Right about the same time you discovered Joelle Ducote's body in her car."

Carlos made his voice sound older and crotchety. "And I would have gotten away with it, too, if it weren't for you meddling kids."

André tried to hold back a grin but was unsuccessful. "Exactly. We might have been able to pin it all on him eventually, but you four showing up when you did was the nail in his coffin."

"It also didn't hurt that his new assistant was one of my people," Cardozo said. "When I heard that he wanted to reassign his assistant, I stepped up to take Ashley into my own office. I wanted to keep eyes on her because I suspected that she was involved in his schemes somehow, even if she was unaware. We made sure that Carrie was assigned to Ducote, and she played a very convincing gossip. Enough that he chose her for his alibi. When Ashley didn't show up to work Thursday morning, I knew something was wrong. She'd never missed a day, even though Ducote claimed she sometimes called in sick because of a hangover. And then . . . André showed me a photo of the remains."

"You knew her," Gabe said. "Why did you let me know that you knew her that day when you interrogated me?"

"Just in case you weren't who you appeared to be," Cardozo said. "I wanted to see what your reaction would be. André vouched for you, but I needed to know."

"And now you do?" Willa Mae asked sharply.

"Yes," Cardozo said. "Totally convinced. Otherwise, I wouldn't have let him go."

"Oh, I think you would have," Willa Mae said ominously.

"So now we have some questions," André said, segueing smoothly. "How did you know about Ducote's dog?"

"It was Gabe's idea," Xavier said. "I remembered Nadia Hall walking her dog when I was little. Before Katrina. Gabe wondered what happened to it because his dad hadn't seen a dog when he discovered Nadia's body that night."

Cardozo studied all of them with a confused frown. "What's this?"

Burke looked at André. "You didn't tell him?"

André shrugged. "I don't know it all myself."

So, Xavier told his story and the rest of them jumped in to add details as needed, including how they'd found evidence in Rocky's bank statements that had led them to Xavier. No one mentioned Xavier's gun and his shooting of the home intruder, but they laid out everything else.

Cardozo looked stunned by the end of it, André a bit less so because he'd gleaned bits and pieces along the way.

"That is an incredible story," Cardozo said. "I'm . . . wow. Impressed."

"As you should be," Burke said lightly. "We're damned good investigators."

"We found links between Ducote's wives and his mistresses," Molly added. "He gave Nadia a necklace and we found a photo of his first wife wearing either the same one or one identical to it. The same with Ashley and Joelle. The day Ashley visited Burke, she was wearing the same necklace that Joelle had on yesterday when we found her."

"That man was *bold*," André murmured.

"I'm surprised none of his wives or mistresses offed him first," Farrah said, disgusted.

"He may have killed Lucille, wife number one," Molly said. "She died just like Gabe's father did."

"We'll add that to our formal investigation," André promised.

"What about Mule?" Burke asked. "Have you connected him to any of Tobin's goings-on?"

"And Paul Lott," Gabe added. "He was my father's attorney, but we think he was part of his murder as well."

"You'd be right," André said. "We found Paul Lott's laptop in Tobin's house when we searched it. Took our tech guys a little while to break through his security. Paul Lott had planted a keystroke counter on Rocky's laptop and the Metairie sheriff's department found a tracker under Rocky's truck. We think Lott planted the tracker after Rocky asked him to set up a trust for Xavier."

Burke frowned, darting a glance at Antoine. "I specifically checked for a tracker on Rocky's truck. I didn't find anything."

"It was an older model," André told him. "The battery had given out at some point in the past six weeks since Rocky's death. The Metairie sheriff saw it when they put the truck up on a lift to check the undercarriage."

"That's how they knew my dad was looking for Dr. Benson," Gabe said quietly.

Molly slipped her hand into his, just to remind him that he wasn't alone. He squeezed lightly and turned to press a kiss to her temple. "I'm okay," he said.

"That's how he knew about me, too," Xavier said, quieting his tone as well.

It was easy for folks to forget that this was Gabe's father they were discussing so clinically. Molly would make sure they remembered that.

"But," André continued, "Rocky was too wily and secretive, so Lott didn't know where Xavier was."

"Not until I called him for help," Xavier muttered.

"Which was the right thing to do, given what you knew," Gabe said firmly. "Dad's priority was keeping you safe."

"And we will be grateful forever," Cicely said. "Your dad was a good man."

Gabe's smile was sad. "I know. But why did Lott do it?"

"Money," André said gently. "We found a deposit of fifty thousand dollars in Lott's bank account. We haven't traced it yet, but I expect it will have come from either Ducote or Mule. Payment was made the day before your dad was killed."

Gabe swallowed hard. "He killed my dad for money. When he died, did it hurt?"

"A lot," André replied, his tone grown cold. "We believe Tobin killed him and . . . well, Lott did not die painlessly."

"Good," Gabe murmured. "I'm glad. That might make me a monster, but I'm glad."

"Not a monster," Molly said softly. "Just human. Don't feel guilty about how you feel. André, why did Tobin kill him?"

"Lott had asked for more money. I guess they figured it was easier to kill him than to keep paying him."

"But how did Paul Lott know that Ducote and Mule wanted the information?" Molly pressed.

"Lott kept impeccable records," André said. "Back at the tenth anniversary of Katrina—when Rocky had tried to resurrect the case and told them he had an eyewitness—Lott was approached by Mule, who knew that Lott was willing to do shady deals. Lott agreed to keep an eye on Rocky. He never had anything to report until Rocky asked him to set up the trust for Xavier. At first Lott thought Xavier was Rocky's illegitimate son. But then he did a check on Xavier's full name and found that he was a survivor of Katrina. It was the Katrina link that sent Lott to Mule. That and the fact that he was facing bankruptcy. I don't know how Lott and Rocky met, though."

"Through one of the charities Dad volunteered at," Gabe offered. "I was still living at home at the time, so it was at least twenty years ago. Lott did some pro bono work with a few troubled teens that Dad worked with. You might want to take another look at those cases."

Cardozo groaned. "No more, please. We're going to be sorting through Ducote's mess for years to come."

Gabe shrugged. "Sorry."

"Not your fault," André said. "Your father trusted Lott and was betrayed."

"For money," Gabe said sadly, and for a moment no one spoke, everyone grieving with him.

Standing next to Val, Patty cleared her throat. "What about Donna Lee?" she asked, her voice trembling. She'd figured out that by telling her parents about the danger, she'd provided Donna Lee with the information that had led to two deaths, and as Gabe had predicted, she was devastated.

"We'll charge her," Cardozo promised. "We're not sure with what just yet. She knew that Tobin was an asshole because he was blackmailing her, but she says she didn't know that he was working for Mule or that Mule had been involved with Rocky Hebert's death."

"Do you want her to serve time?" Molly asked Gabe.

"I don't know," Gabe answered honestly. "I haven't had a chance to think about it."

"I don't know, either," Patty confessed. "But I do know that I have to do something for the two who died. I've known Dusty Woodruff for years. I know his wife. Gabe and I catered their wedding and the baby shower for her first child. I . . ." Her voice broke. "I have to do something for them."

Gabe put his free arm around his cousin's shoulders, which were now shaking with quiet sobs. "You didn't know, P. If you had, you would've turned Donna Lee in."

"We have counselors on staff who work with victims of crime," Cardozo said to Patty, breaking into Molly's thoughts. "You and Gabe certainly qualify. Let me know when you're ready and I'll send you the contact information."

Patty wiped the tears from her cheeks and nodded, sniffling. "I might take you up on that."

"We both should," Gabe said fiercely. "I still haven't processed Dad's death. He would have passed soon enough from the cancer, but those bastards stole what little time he had left."

"We assumed that Mule gave Tobin the order to attack Molly's and Patty's apartments," Burke said, taking the spotlight off the cousins, leaving them to whisper comfort to each other. "Is Tobin talking?"

"Not yet," André said. "But he will."

"He's Mule's son," Cardozo supplied. "Illegitimate son, so they didn't share a last name. Tobin was very loyal to Mule for a lot of years." He grimaced. "We'll be sorting through that mess for a very long time, too."

"And all of Mule's cases," André added wearily. "It's not going to be fun. Ducote and Mule had been giving each other legs up the ladder for decades. They'd been friends since high school."

"We know," Molly said. "We found photos of them at a reunion together, along with Paul Lott."

Cardozo blew out a breath. "We'll likely have quite a few more questions for you guys as we dig deeper."

"Always happy to help," Burke said dryly.

"And on that note, I have to get back to the precinct. The paperwork from this case is . . ." André shook his head. "I don't even want to think about it."

"I have to go, too," Cardozo said. "But if I could sneak a slice of that cake?"

"Give me two seconds," Gabe said and turned back to his kitchen.

Keeping his hands busy, Molly thought. She had some other ideas of how to distract him later. She'd have to watch the man closely to make sure he grieved and didn't hold it all inside as he'd been doing before breaking down at Burke's camp.

Only yesterday morning. Seemed like a lifetime ago already.

"I'd like to stay," Farrah said. "If that's okay."

"You are always welcome here," Gabe said over his shoulder. "Always."

"We were going to head into the Quarter for the festival," Molly said. It was the weekend of Satchmo SummerFest. "Our Houston friends wanted to go, and I've never been."

Farrah's smile brightened. "I can be your official guide. I have *never* missed a Satchmo. I know *all* the best places to listen to the music and get the best food. Second-best," she amended. "Best is at the Choux."

"Where you always have a table," Patty said warmly. "All of you."

Cicely smacked the countertop. "Then let's not waste any more time. I want to hear some jazz."

Molly walked André and Cardozo to the door. "I didn't want to ask about Officer McCauley in front of everyone, because Gabe and Xavier are still having a hard time with his death, too. How is his family?"

André's composure slipped, grief filling his eyes. "About as well as you'd expect. We'll be making sure they're taken care of, but thank you for asking."

Molly swallowed. "He was protecting us. He was a hero. His wife needs to know that."

"She will," André promised.

"Thank you," she said, then forced a smile, hoping to lighten André's burden. "Especially for not putting us in jail."

André winced. "Just try not to shoot any more people?" he asked hopefully.

Molly nodded. "I'll be happy if I never shoot another person ever again."

"That wasn't a promise," Cardozo said darkly.

Molly shrugged. "You want me to lie?"

André sighed. "No. Just . . . never mind. J.P., you ready to roll?"

"Yeah. Drop me off at the courthouse?" Cardozo asked as they went down the ramp that covered the stairs.

"You are one lucky girl," Joy observed from behind her when Molly turned from the screen door. "This whole mess could have ended up a helluva lot worse."

"I know." Molly looked to the kitchen where Gabe was putting food away. "But it ended up pretty damn well, I think."

Joy raised her hurricane glass, now completely empty. "Happy birthday."

Molly laughed. "I forgot all about my birthday. How about we get another piece of cake for the road?"

Joy put her chair into gear. "I like the way you think."

Mid-City, New Orleans, Louisiana
SUNDAY, JULY 31, 7:00 A.M.

"Gabe." Molly's sleepy voice roused him just enough to be annoyed. "*Gabe.*"

Her little elbow-shove to his stomach woke him up the rest of the way. "What?" he whined, too tired to care that he sounded Harper's age.

"Your phone. Is ringing. *Again.* Playing that song from the rat-chef movie."

"*Ratatouille?*"

"Whatever. Answer the phone, because that's the third time it's rung."

Reluctantly, he released her. He'd been holding her against him, and she'd been using his biceps as a pillow. She wouldn't stay here in his house forever, but Harper had cried when Chelsea and Molly had told her that they were going back to their apartment the night before. The child was afraid to return to the place where she'd hidden in the closet, terrified for her life.

Nobody blamed her.

So, they'd stayed, along with the Houston folks, who were leaving after breakfast. Gabe had no idea how long Molly's little family would need to stay, but to be honest, he was grateful for the company.

He'd actually been hoping for an early-morning round of sex before he got up to make breakfast for everyone. He might still be able to make that happen, especially since Molly was now wide-awake and glaring at him.

"You missed the call."

He blinked. "Oh, yeah. I forgot already."

"You're really not a morning person, are you?" she asked, amused, then reached over him to pluck his phone from the nightstand. Her eyes widened. "It was your aunt."

Gabe snatched the phone, his hands suddenly trembling. Sure enough, there was a notification on his screen. *Missed call: Gigi.* "What if she's not all right?"

"She's been on vacation," Molly said, using that tone that instantly soothed him. They were planning a trip to the stable later so that Harper and Chelsea could ride, and he'd thought he'd hear her use the voice on the horse. *Not on me.* But he was grateful for it, because his hands were shaking.

Swallowing, he dialed Gigi's number, sighing with relief when his aunt answered on the first ring.

"*Salut,* Gabriel."

"*Salut, Tante* Gigi. Are you all right?"

"Of course I'm all right," she said, switching to her heavily accented English. "Why wouldn't I be?"

He exhaled, feeling a weight roll off his shoulders. "I've had a bit of a week."

"As have I. I have been through the Panama Canal. You should do it sometime soon, *mon cher.* You work too hard."

"I'd love to hear all about it, but I need you to listen for a minute. I have someone with me. Can I put you on speaker?"

"Of course." When he'd done so, she barreled forward, as was her way. "I will ask you later about the 'someone' you have with you. But for now, tell me about your week. You sound stressed. I got a message from the ship this morning to call you. Are *you* all right?"

He laughed weakly. "I don't even know where to begin."

Molly tapped his arm. "You want me to start since you're still not awake yet?"

"Oh, I am sorry!" Gigi exclaimed. "I always forget about the time difference. It's already nearly lunchtime in Fort Lauderdale."

"It's only eight o'clock in Fort Lauderdale," Gabe grumbled.

"As I said—nearly lunchtime. And who is this someone?" Gigi asked slyly.

"My name is Molly Sutton. Gabe hired me to help find out who killed his father."

Gigi gasped. "*Mon Dieu.* What is this?"

"It's a very long story," Molly said, "but the short version is that Rocky was killed by a man who'd murdered a woman back during Katrina. Rocky discovered her body when he was searching for victims to evacuate from the flood. He'd been investigating her murder for years but picked up speed in the last few months. Because of his cancer."

Gigi sighed. "He wanted to tell you that he was sick, but he didn't know how. I told him that if he didn't tell you soon, I would tell you myself, but . . ." She was quiet for a long moment. "I thought he'd really killed himself. He was in so much pain. I should have known that he wouldn't do it in a way that would hurt you if you found him. I am so sorry, Gabriel."

"It's all right. I wasn't sure myself until I had a private autopsy done."

"That's part of the long story," Molly said. "We'll answer all your questions, but I need to zip to the end. We discovered the killer's identity and he's dead. But Rocky left some cryptic notes."

"Ah," Gigi said knowingly, but then hesitated. "Did you find . . . someone?"

"You mean Xavier?" Gabe asked. "I did find him. I also found that you're named as the president on one of Dad's businesses that he used to hide monthly payments to Xavier's mother."

She gasped again. "Oh no. Gabriel. What you must have thought!"

"I did, for a moment," Gabe confessed. "But I knew Dad would never cheat on Mom."

"Your mother knew everything, if that makes you feel better. She was very supportive of his efforts to help the Morrow family. Your father was a very good man."

"I know," Gabe said, just as he had the day before when Cicely Morrow had said the same thing. His father had been a very good man. *And hopefully now he can truly rest in peace.* "Let's get back to the angels. Dad gave both Xavier and me a little ceramic angel. We figured out that Xavier's had a thumb drive inside it."

"Oh? That sounds like a movie. What did it say?"

"That he should find me at Le Petit Choux."

"Is that how you met?"

"No," Gabe said. "Xavier was nearly murdered in his own home and came to find me."

Gigi gasped again. "Oh no. That poor child."

"He's twenty-two, *Tante* Gigi."

"And I am in my sixties now. I'm allowed to call all of you children. What happened next?"

"Lots of stuff, but once we found Xavier's angel had a thumb drive, we checked mine. It said to call you."

"Therefore, you did. I see many missed calls. I am so sorry, Gabriel."

"I was so worried."

"My poor boy. I had my phone turned off."

Gabe scowled. "I know."

"I cannot apologize for that. I forgot once and my phone bill was *astronomique.*"

Gabe rubbed his forehead. "What do you have for me, *Tante* Gigi?"

"I don't exactly know. I got a text from him the day before he died. It's a username for his cloud account. He said to send it to you when you contacted me and asked for information. I thought it was a letter and that he meant for you to wait until you were ready to read it. I shall send you a link as soon as we hang up."

Gabe blinked. "You know about cloud accounts?"

She made an irritated noise. "I'm old, not stupid."

"I never said you were," he said quickly. "You are one of the smartest women I know."

She harrumphed. "That's better. I will send you the link, and then I will cancel my flight to Montreal and rent a car and drive to New Orleans instead."

Oh boy. "Um, you don't have to do that, *Tante* Gigi."

"Of course I do. I must meet this Molly Sutton that you hired to 'investigate.'" She said the last word so slyly that his cheeks burned, and Molly grinned.

Gabe rolled his eyes. "I really did hire her to investigate. Things just . . . evolved."

"This is what I figured, as she is in your bed," Gigi said tartly.

"I can't wait to meet you, ma'am," Molly said cordially.

"The feeling is mutual. Now I must go. My party is about to disembark from this lovely ship. *Au revoir*, Gabriel. *Enchantée*, Molly." The call ended, leaving him reeling.

Molly looked up at him, still grinning. "She's a whirlwind, isn't she?"

"You have *no* idea." Suddenly panicked, he started to get out of bed. "I have to clean."

She grabbed his arm. "We'll all help," she said. "We'll put Xavier, Carlos, and Manny to work before they take off for Houston."

He nodded, his heart still racing. "You're right. She . . . I love her, but she is . . . exacting."

Molly's grin faltered. "Oh. Maybe we should get out of your hair, then."

He slid his arm around her and tugged her closer. "No way. She loves kids. We'll sic Harper on her if things go sideways. But they won't and there is no need for you to go. She will love you. I promise."

Molly nodded uncertainly, then pointed to his phone. "She said she'd send you a link."

"Oh, right. That woman makes my head spin sometimes." He went to his email and, sure enough, there was an email from Gigi, along with his father's username. "But there's no password."

They stared at each other for a long moment, then, in unison, said, "*Mon ange.*"

"But there also has to be a number in the password, right?" Gabe asked, but he already knew what it would be. "*Mon ange* plus my mother's birthday." Holding his breath, he tapped the phone's keyboard and shuddered out a breath when it worked. "Only one file, but it's huge."

They found out why once it had finally downloaded. The file contained pages of handwritten documents—scanned pages of a journal. "Picture files take up a lot of space," Molly said quietly. "Your dad had nice penmanship. These will be easy to read."

"I *knew* he'd bought a scanner. They must have stolen it when they killed him."

"I wonder what he did with the original journal?"

"I don't know. If he went to all the trouble to tell Aunt Gigi where to find the scanned copy, I'm betting he burned it or destroyed it somehow. I never checked his house for ashes."

"That may have been what Tobin was looking for when he destroyed your father's house."

"Maybe." But he didn't want to waste any more time wondering. He wanted to read his father's journal. "A lot of this is his search for Xavier," he murmured. There was page after page of dead ends and summaries of appointments with social workers that went nowhere. "He didn't leave any stones unturned, did he?"

"Oh." Molly's voice softened. "He found him through Xavier's birth mother's headstone. The one Cicely and her husband paid for."

"Cicely told us that," Gabe remembered. "Dad tracked them down with a canceled check."

"How many cemeteries did he search?"

Gabe counted as he turned pages. "Thirty-five. And it looks like he had to bribe someone at the final cemetery to give him the Morrows' information." He had to chuckle. "Here's a receipt that he wrote."

Molly snorted softly. "With 'bribe to slimy grave guy' as the notation. I wish I could have met him. He sounds wonderful."

Gabe's chest tightened. "I wish you could have met him, too. He would have loved you."

Molly pressed a kiss against his upper arm, then leaned her head against him as she pointed to his screen. "There's the note with Dr. Cousineau's name and the fake name Nadia Hall used."

"And a summary of his interview with Mrs. Royce, the neighbor we met." He froze. "Hell. We forgot to call her."

"I did yesterday morning," Molly said. "I called her and April Frazier to let them know what happened. Mrs. Royce drove home from her daughter's house in Huntsville yesterday and asked if she could come for breakfast to meet Xavier before he heads back to Houston. Xavier said yes, and I didn't think you'd mind. I told her to be here by nine."

They still had lots of time, then. "Of course I don't mind." He continued thumbing through his father's journal, swiping whenever Molly hummed that she was ready to move on. There was a sizable gap in the dates, and it made Gabe's chest hurt. "This was when my mom got sick. He wouldn't let anyone else care for her except for Gigi and sometimes Patty's parents. Rarely even me. He loved her so much."

"And now they're together again," she whispered.

He swallowed hard, some of the sadness easing from his chest. "They are. That may be the only good thing to come out of his death. Well, that and meeting you."

She smiled up at him. "I know what you meant."

He had to kiss her then but forced himself to look back at the journal before things got carried away. He wanted to read it and then not look at it again.

"Huh," Molly said, pointing at the page on his screen. "He suspected Cresswell of being involved after he threatened to fire him. I wonder if he has any evidence against him for some of the drugs that Burke believes that Cresswell stole."

Gabe swiped through the pages faster, satisfaction taking root where the sadness had been. "He did. Photos of Cresswell taking bribes, affidavits from witnesses . . . Oh my God. This is gold."

"André and Cardozo are gonna be so happy," Molly said, bouncing a little where she sat.

Then they got to the part where his father had found Dr. Benson. "'He won't talk to me,'" Gabe read, "'but I'm running out of time.'"

"He kept calling and calling Benson," Molly said. "And felt guilty for pestering the man, but he needed answers."

Gabe closed the file. "He believed Benson knew the name of Nadia's lover. He may have."

Molly sighed. "He went to Benson's house the week before he died, but Benson wasn't home. That's how Lott knew. He had the tracker on your dad's truck by then."

"So they killed Benson to keep him from telling my dad what he knew. I feel awful for the man, but also for my dad, y'know? Dad died knowing his search caused that man's death."

Molly shook her head fiercely. "No, he may have led the killers to Benson, but he was not responsible for Benson dying any more than you're responsible for any of this. He was trying to get to the truth. And he did."

"Yeah." Gabe cleared his throat. "He did. And then we did. Thank you, Molly."

"You're welcome." She sniffed the air. "Someone's awake and making coffee. Let's close the book on this for now, okay? Let's tell André about the journal, then go and socialize, and you can cook us a feast."

He smiled down at her, so grateful that she'd come into his life. "A feast?"

"With bacon. Which is a miracle that does not come from cute little pigs."

"I can do bacon. Let's go."

He slid from the bed, pulling on his clothes. Watching her do the same. Then he took her hand and together they made their way to the kitchen, where friendship—and coffee—waited.

EPILOGUE

The Quarter, New Orleans, Louisiana
SATURDAY, OCTOBER 8, 2:00 P.M.

GABE STOOD AND tapped his glass with a spoon. "Can I have your attention, please?"

The crowd filling the Choux immediately quieted, all eyes turning toward him, and Gabe couldn't contain his smile. They had a full house, and it was a very special day.

Molly was here, of course, with Burke, Antoine, Val, Lucien, and Joy. Even Phin had joined them, looking a little uncomfortable at the size of the group. Molly had promised Phin that he could leave the moment he needed to, but he was still here, an hour after the party had started.

Xavier, Cicely, Carlos, and Willa Mae were here—Xavier and Carlos having flown into New Orleans the night before. It was fall break for their universities, which was why they'd set the party today.

André, Farrah, and J. P. Cardozo were here, along with most of both André's and Farrah's extended families. And there were a lot of them. It made Gabe's heart happy.

Patty was here with her parents and Aunt Gigi. His cousin had been going to therapy religiously, as had Gabe. They still weren't completely over the events of the summer, but they were improving at managing their guilt over the innocent people who'd been hurt or killed. Fortunately, Harry Peterson, the ME's assistant, had recovered and was recently back at work. It turned out that Harry was caring for a younger brother and Nicholas Tobin had lured Harry home that day by telling him that his brother was hurt. Thankfully, both were now okay and here today.

And, also thankfully, the families of Dr. McLain and Dusty Woodruff didn't blame them. Gabe was grateful, but there were too many days when he still blamed himself. The therapist had assured him and Patty that forgiving themselves would come with time.

Nancy Royce was here, too. She and Xavier had met up over breakfast at Gabe's house before the Houston folks had left back in July. There hadn't been a dry eye in the house.

Chelsea and Harper were here, Harper looking adorable in her chef's jacket and hat. She was also still in therapy, and her smiles were coming more frequently these days. She, Molly, and Chelsea had moved out of his house a month after the night their home was invaded, having bought a house close to Gabe's. Chelsea had found a job, and Harper was a natural in the kitchen, even helping with today's feast.

And, speaking of helpers . . . "Manny, does everyone have a glass?"

"Yes, Chef," Manny said crisply, having found his niche after years of working jobs he didn't love. He'd had a line job at a factory before they'd laid him off. He'd been all too happy to quit his night job at the Houston convenience store. The man was a fantastic cook, and Gabe had taken him on as his apprentice. Manny now lived in a little hole-in-the-wall apartment in the Quarter.

"Thank you." Gabe drew a breath, bolstering himself because there was one person who was not with them. "I want to thank all of you for coming to help me celebrate what would have been my father's fifty-eighth birthday." He swallowed hard, trying to fight the rise of emotion, then giving up. "He would have loved seeing you all here. He would have hated that you were all here to honor him."

Patty and her parents choked on a laugh. "That's totally true," his aunt Viola called out.

"My dad was the best of men. He fought for the underdog and gave his life getting justice for Nadia Hall. I hate that Nadia suffered. I hate that my dad suffered. I hate that innocent people suffered. But those events have brought us together, and I believe, with all my heart, that Rocky Hebert would have been happy to see us together today." Gabe lifted his glass. "To Rocky Hebert."

"To Rocky," came the boisterous response.

Xavier lifted his hand. "I'm truly grateful to be here. I've been fortunate in my life to have had so many people to save me. Rocky on that night in Katrina, of course, but also my birth mother, who gave her life to save mine. Then there's my mom here"—he put his arm around Cicely's shoulders, stooping to kiss her cheek, which was already streaked with tears—"and my dad, who's not here to see this, but he'd have been so happy. And Carlos, who's been my brother since the day I punched his face in the first grade. But also all of you. When I needed help, you all . . . helped." His voice broke and he cleared it. "So I thank you . . . from the bottom of my heart."

Murmurs of *aw* rippled through the crowd and Gabe smiled through his own tears. He lifted his glass again. "To Xavier Morrow— my new brother, my father's second son."

Xavier shook his head, swiping his wet face with the back of his hand. "Dammit, Gabe." But he was smiling, too.

"I think that's enough emotion for now," Gabe said. "There's food and drinks, and I want everyone to have a good time." He waved at the zydeco band set up in the corner—old friends of his father's from the NOPD—and the air was filled with music.

Gabe turned to find Molly by his side. She brought his head down for a lusty kiss that drew catcalls and shouts of "Get a room!"

Feeling his cheeks heat, Gabe kissed her back. "How was that?" he asked.

She grinned up at him. "The kiss or your speech?"

"Both."

"A-plus. Now I have to get some of that cake before Chelsea and Joy eat it all." She started to pull away, but Gabe tugged her back.

"I can make you cake any day of the week. Stay with me."

She slid her arm around his waist. "You okay?" she asked, perceptive as always.

He hesitated. "I think so?"

She looked up at him, concern in those blue-green eyes he'd come to love. "What's on your mind?"

"I don't know. Everything is . . . good."

"Ah." She nodded knowingly. "'The other shoe' syndrome."

Gabe laughed. "The other Choux? Like my restaurant?"

She poked him lightly in the gut. "No, the s-h-o-e, and not your dog. I mean you're waiting for the other shoe to drop. And it might. Then again, it might not." She shrugged. "Either way, you're not alone."

As always, she knew exactly what to say, and it loosened the thing he'd needed to say. "Tobin was supposed to go on trial next week." But the bastard had just cut a deal. Twenty-five years in prison without the possibility of parole. He deserved life behind bars. He deserved death.

It was hard to be okay with that kind of a deal.

She sighed. "I thought you might be bothered by that. The way I look at it is that his testimony, along with your father's evidence and the murder of Ducote, put Cresswell away for life. And when Tobin gets out of prison, he'll be eligible for social security."

"It's not long enough."

"No, but he might not live that long anyway. He'll be meeting a lot of people inside those prison walls that he helped his daddy put there. And Cresswell? I don't give him much time at all."

Gabe frowned. "Is it bad that this makes me feel better?"

"Nope. Makes you human." She leaned up and pressed a kiss to his jaw. "Makes me love you."

He settled again, her words the balm he'd needed. "I love you, too."

The words were new. They'd exchanged them for the first time only a few weeks before. It had been a relief to say them out loud.

A clearing throat had them looking to where Willa Mae stood, her brows arched and a smug smile on her face. "I want an invitation to the wedding."

"Wedding?" Cicely all but squealed.

"Shh," Molly said. "Hush, y'all. He hasn't asked me yet."

"But he will," Willa Mae said with a hard nod.

Gabe was unable to hold back his grin. This was a happiness that he'd never expected to feel, and the anxiety he'd felt about Tobin's deal was already a bad memory. "If it happens"—he so wanted it to happen, but he was trying not to rush—"how about we record the askin' and the yessin' and send it over to you?"

"You'd better, young man," Willa Mae said, then surprised him with a hug that nearly crushed his ribs. "Thank you for closing your restaurant to give us this wonderful day."

"It's my pleasure," he said sincerely. "Maybe we'll make it a yearly thing."

Cicely looked over at Manny, who was lifting Harper so that she could reach the éclairs on the top tier of the pastry stand. "I'm so happy that he's found his place."

"Me, too," Gabe said. "He's really an excellent cook." And one day would make an excellent assistant manager. One who Gabe could trust.

"Ah, who have we here?" Aunt Gigi stopped next to the two Houston women. "We have not yet met. I am Gabriel's *tante* Gigi. I couldn't help but overhear something about a wedding?"

"I'm Willa Mae Collins, and this is Cicely Morrow," Willa Mae said.

Gigi bobbed her head. "The ladies from Houston. I've heard so much about you. What's this about a wedding?"

"We'll fill you in," Cicely promised.

And, just like that, the three became co-conspirators in his and

Molly's love life. The women walked away, discussing all kinds of wedding things.

"Sorry," he said to Molly with a wince, but she was grinning.

"For what? Promising to propose to me on video someday?"

He rolled his eyes. "We're going to have no peace at all. You know that, right?"

Molly bumped his hip with hers. "Peace is highly overrated. I'll take this life we've made any day of the week."

ACKNOWLEDGMENTS

The Starfish—Christine, Cheryl, Sheila, Brian, Susan, and Kathy—for all the plotting and the titles. Love you all.

Dominik Ciborowski for checking over all the French. *Merci beaucoup!*

David Comardelle for taking me on a virtual tour of the bayou. You made it all so very real. I can't wait to meet you and to take one of your swamp tours in person!

Marc Conterato for all things medical, both in this book and in our real lives.

Dominic Degeneffe for the information on chefs and restaurants.

Tina DeSalvo for sharing your love of New Orleans, your memories of Katrina, and for introducing me to your lovely family members. You're a treasure.

Caitlin Ellis for managing all the details so that I can write.

Andrew Grey for being my daily word count partner. The words simply flew from my brain, through my fingers, and onto the page.

Sarah Hafer and Beth Miller for all your edits.

JoCarol Jones for helping me find Xavier a neighborhood near Houston. And for all the hugs over our many years as friends.

Sonie Lasker for your knowledge of the martial arts. I'm so proud of you, Miss Harvard Grad. You make it look easy.

Jim Nettles for the information on restoring wiped hard drives. And for the Cookie Monster explanation that made so much sense.

Nancy Northcott for introducing me to Jim. ☺

Farrah Rochon for the New Orleans info. Hope you enjoy seeing your namesake again!

Margaret Taylor for all the fascinating tidbits about being a female police officer—especially one who is generously endowed like my heroine, Molly. I've been waiting to use the one about belt versus shoulder holster for eight long years, LOL.

Claire Zion, Robin Rue, and Jen Doyle for all your support. I miss you all!

As always, all mistakes are my own.